THE FIRST AMERICAN PUBLICATION OF
*THE SERPENT* by Jane Gaskell

One of the most astonishing fantasy novels of our
time—a work to rank with Tolkien's THE LORD
OF THE RINGS and Eddison's THE WORM
OUROBOUROS.

Set in the legendary beginnings of time, THE SER-
PENT tells the story of Cija, Princess of Atlantis,
who has been raised in complete seclusion, believing herself a goddess. Suddenly she is thrust into
the world on an incredible mission. She must
marry and slay the powerful general threatening
her kingdom—the strange, brutal half-human
Zerd, also known as The Serpent.

Crammed with lust, violence, intrigue, set against
the barbaric splendor of the world of sword and
sorcery, THE SERPENT is a gripping fantasy no
one will ever forget.

# THE SERPENT

## JANE GASKELL

PAPERBACK LIBRARY

New York

**PAPERBACK LIBRARY EDITION**

First Printing: *June, 1968*
Second Printing: *October, 1970*

**This Paperback Library Edition is published by arrangement
with Hodder and Stoughton Limited.**

*Paperback Library is a division of Coronet Communications, Inc. Its
trademark, consisting of the words "Paperback Library" accompanied
by an open book, is registered in the United States Patent Office.*
Coronet Communications, Inc., 315 Park Avenue South, New York, N.Y.
10010.

# CONTENTS

Foreword     7

PART ONE: THE HOSTAGE

    I    The Tower     11
   II    The Journey     43
  III    The High Tent     127
  IV    The Wilderness     179
   V    The Kitchen at H.Q.     211
  VI    The Bed in Southern City     290

PART TWO: THE BELOVED

  VII    The Palace     327
 VIII    Escape     384
   IX    The Possession     436

Epilogue     474
Bibliography     477

# FOREWORD

I've translated this as nearly as I can not only into the language of our country, but into the language of our day; for the Diarist herself used a great deal of then-colloquial slang, even in the earliest parts of her book, which leads us to suppose either that she picked it up from her mother's servants on the rare occasions that she met them, or that her nurses were not quite so abysmally strict as she came, in her adolescence, to believe. It will be noted how this style leaves her as her journey forces her out of childhood.

The almost unbelievable age of the Diary is indisputable. Also, most convincingly, its accounts of everyday life at the time of Atlantis almost exactly correspond with legend and the calculations of Atlantis experts. Quite a number of separate details in this book are now known as ancient myths. They are mainly ancient Celtic or South American myths—and Britain *is* believed to be a remnant of Atlantis, after it had grown ugly in the sight of Heaven and the princess who had found out the secrets of the Great Dikes helped to destroy it.

I can't go here into the proofs or otherwise that Atlantis and Mu did exist and that there was a time when the earth had no moon, (our previous satellite having circled nearer and nearer, pulled over millions of years by our greater gravity, and crashed on us), the conclusions of geologists, Gondwanaland, the evidence of flora and fauna, the dove-tailing legends of the ancient world, the world's languages, the patterned placing of the world's pyramids, the flocks of migratory birds which every year fly to the place where Atlantis is supposed to have lain, and circle round and round, searching for the land the Atlantis-believers tell us they know must be there because of the racial-memory instinct in all animals. Here I can give only a short, very incomplete, list of the myth-ingredients I've found relevant to this Diary. Students of this sort of thing will recognize them all anyway. Many of them I already knew; others turned up later and astonished me with their relevance.

7

Atzlan was the prehistoric birthplace of the Aztecs of America—the pride, *hybris*, of the Atlantes in Plato's account—The American Linapy tribe had an ancient song telling of the land of Rusuaki and how it was destroyed in a great fire and cloven by the Earth Snake, Zio, the scarlet-faced war-god of prehistoric Britain—The crocodile—demon Set of Egypt, always supposed to be a colony of Atlantis—The Aztec goddess Cioacatl "by whom sin came into the world" usually represented with a serpent near her—The whole story of Adam and Eve and the Garden—The sons of God saw the daughters of men that they were fair—There were giants in the earth in those days; and also, after that when the sons of God came in unto the daughters of men, and they bare children to them, the same became mighty men which were of old, men of renown—The rites of initiation into womanhood, for the South American jungle girls, which includes their promise that they will cherish the mortal men they must marry, and not resent them for their difference from the god to whom each girl was wed before her birth.

The puma dates from the Pleistocene, and the behaviour of Cija's "white puma" is perfectly credible. Even today the gaucho of the Argentine pampas calls the puma *amigo del cristiano*—The extra large snails of South America aroused interest in Colonel Fawcett—The huge birds used by the Northern army are obviously the prehistoric *Diatryma*, once prevalent in America, about seven feet tall.

Cija is pronounced Key-a. This slightly Celtic pronunciation gives the clue to the only other difficult names in the adventures.

Gagl—Gahl.

Ious—Yuse.

The main action of the book takes place in what is now South America.

# PART ONE

# THE HOSTAGE

# CHAPTER ONE

## THE TOWER

I can't see things so well from any other window.

The nearest mountain, a huge hazy turquoise-green thing, conical, terrible, is so near I can see the thickly-forested ridges and the blue precipices and the grey chasms. The mountain behind that, and separated from it by the sea, is less evenly shaped and on clear days looks as though it's going to lurch forward. It is fascinating but ominous. The third mountain, between and beyond them, is so distant that even on clear days I can't make out more than a vague pattern of changing shades, valleys and slopes, floating in the insubstantial horizon.

And beyond the horizon lie the Northern lands, where the terror-legends come from. My own nurses used to scare and horrify me with tales of how I would be given to the cruel barbarous animal-people there, if I were not good. The people there are animals, they are not descended from the gods as we are. There is no kindness, no mercy, pity or gentleness possible to their natures. They are avaricious and savage; at best they are callous, at their worst they are sadistic and no atrocity is beyond giving them pleasure. Physically they are brutish, graceless. So it is exciting to look out over the sea and mountains and know that they enclose me from the Northern lands, secure, safe in the benediction of our ancestors the gods, in our own prosperity and beauty.

And the sea is nearer to see from this window than any other in the tower. It would be gorgeous to watch it during storms except that then it is mostly hidden from me by the huge swift continuous sweeps of rain.

The tumbled stones lying round the ruined window-way were of a great heat when I first ventured to touch them.

One rocked, hesitated, plunged and fell into the abyss.

I leaned over as far as I dared and watched its awful drop. It left an unfamiliar space on the sill. That really was a day on which there was a *happening*. I was shaking all the time but I got up slowly, steadied myself, climbed on to the broad sill, and walked over the unsteady tumbled ancient stones on it until I had nearly come to the edge. I lowered myself with slow, slow care to stooping and then looked down for the first time on what is below.

It was wonderful; I felt like a poet and an explorer in one daring creamy skin.

I was so enthralled I almost forgot how dangerous my position was on the edge of the sill.

The first time was wonderful and the others have really been just as wonderful but also more conscious of the danger. There is a small round plateau down there. It is grassy in its centre and rocky round the edges and a little thin blue thing shone through it. And from my reading, I knew at once that I must be beholding a stream.

I gazed down at this new unguessed-of scene and all the time the corner of my eye was aware of a white glint. I craned round till my neck was horribly ricked and, my hands gripping violently at a bit of protruding wall, I saw a piece of a white stone building.

Unblinking, my eyes widened.

At least, I expect they did, they have to anyway for this type of happening, according to most of the prose I've read.

I hung, silently, gazing at new horizons.

The white building whose end I was seeing obviously began somewhere *quite* beyond my range of vision. I thought (just at first) it might be a bit of this tower but I didn't recognize it.

It's a stone terrace, open to the sun, behind a beautifully-worked stone balustrade which looks tiny from this distance, and behind is a flat-roofed hall into whose shady clean blue colonnades I can see for some way before it disappears into its own shadows.

It all looks so cool, and unattainable.

I wondered and wondered.

Was it part of my own tower? But no, I had explored it from corner to corner since babyhood. (I know far more about it even than they do.)

"It must be the end terrace of my mother's palace," I thought.

Then I twisted myself back till my whole weight rested on the hot board sill again. I clambered back over the uneasy stones and lowered myself into the secure little Passage beyond. I would ask my mother some questions next time.

So I did, and she evaded them and questioned me instead and I had to be very clever and evade *her* questions because I don't want anyone to find out about the Passage. But I am sure, by now, that that is the end of my mother's palace and that I have seen part of the outside World.

On the third day of every single week, every week might be permissible but *always* the *third* day, they put long revolting aprons over their trousers and scrub the floors. If they *think* I have been *particularly* bad, they make me help them and I have been helping them for months now with only one week off.

The whole point of my starting this diary is that I am utterly fed-up and I must work off my steam somehow and a good way to do it is to write it all down, *so I shall.*

Actually I wouldn't care if Glurbia got hold of it and read just what I think of her, and all the others but *particularly* Glurbia, but I am writing it in my private code and to keep it even more to myself I am keeping it in the Passage. At the rate of present *progress* (ha ha!) I may have to use this Diary as a safety valve for years and years and years but luckily it is a huge book made even bigger really by the fact that it has thin pages which are a nuisance to write on but gives me more pages. It is one of Glurbia's account-books which should have lasted her for the next five years but she's had to get another one because this one has disappeared. As far as she's concerned it has anyway. But she thinks she must have mislaid it because if I *had* taken it what *would* I have used it for? Well, we shall see.

I have made a place for it at the end of the Passage. Have hidden it, together with this sticky-tipped deep black scriber which I have attached to the lock of the book, together with the dear little key, by a long tape—have hidden it under some stones (which make it rather dusty but never mind).

And I have made a vow to be just as rambling and infantile as I feel like being because what else is a secret Diary for if not to be a recipient of *all* one's feelings?

Of *course, some* people can record *happenings* in their Diaries, if my books are to be believed, but *what* hope have *I* of *that?*

Their legs are thick and blue-white and when they pull up their trousers, nearly to the knee, so they can kneel easier, this is blatantly visible.

Not only are the legs repulsive but it almost makes me sick to have to look at them.

And poor little me, my own legs are of course longer and

13

slenderer and a much more aesthetic shape but it wasn't very nice to have to know that my legs were just as blue-white. Whenever the colour of the legs of the women in the books are mentioned they are "beautiful gold-brown legs." And I yearned for them. *But* I can't even get a little satisfaction like that, oh no. Glurbia caught me lying beside the fountain in the sun, with my trousers off.

"Cija!" the dear old lady gasped and went such a charming shade of magenta. "You *wicked,* wicked girl! Oh, you wicked—put your clothes back on at once. How dare you act in such a way? What would your mother say? You sinful, shameful girl!"

"I want to get brown," I said.

Mild enough. No need at all for all the nagging that went on solidly for weeks afterwards, and it's still always being mentioned.

Haven't breathed to Glurbia that I'd read of the women with brown legs. So she thought it was an original idea on my part—"original *sin.*" But if I reminded anyone of the existence of those books they'd be removed from the book-room.

At least, whenever I can, I sneak away to this window-niche at the end of the Passage.

And here, where the sun *pours* in past the mountains, I remove my clothes. I am now a beautiful creamy colour. Surfaces like my shins are a crisp gold like well-done fry. Places with a little almost-fold like where my breasts meet my armpits, or my tummy meets my groin, are pale gold. Veins still show blue though. From here, I can just hear the sound of their voices as they call, "Cija! Cija!" If they want me for some very annoying task, or if I am in a very daring mood, I just sit quiet and don't answer them.

They never search for me here.

I don't think they ever even knew of the entrance to the Passage behind the old wall-hangings.

They are very stupid.

The daily quarrel is over for today (unless it's a more-than-one-quarrel-day).

I had been here and ignored their squeals, "Cija, Cija, Cija," etc., etc., etc.

Then at meal-time, "Cija," said Glurbia, "where have you been?"

"Oh, nowhere."

"You are defiant and impudent," said Snedde. "Lately, Ci-

14

ja, you seem to be forgetting all the care and affection with which we have laboured to make you into a lovely and well-bred girl."

Not because I was *stricken* by remorse at the stark *truth* of Snedde's words but because it is rather a shame to upset the old imbecile, I quickly kissed her cheek. Snedde's moustache prickles. I withdrew myself from Snedde's answering embrace, trying wearily to stifle the distaste I *know* I am wicked and ungrateful to feel.

"Here is your bread," Rorla said, handing over a plate.

I took the plate, not even mentioning the charming cracks across it in which mould is growing. If I had mentioned it Rorla would be in for it from Glurbia for giving me the plate, because Rorla cracked it and is supposed to use it until the supplies come, including extra plates. I hope they come soon.

So then I asked as carelessly as possible, "When is my mother's next visit?"

"Your mother is coming tomorrow, so the floors must be polished."

"*Again?*"

"I don't like your tone," Glurbia said, using her cold voice.

"I wouldn't mind so much if the floors were dirty," I said reasonably. "But they are no less clean now than they will be when we've polished them."

"Your opinion as to cleanliness is not that of conscientious persons, Cija. And it's quite disgusting of you to moan whenever you have to set your hands to a little work. Other girls of your age have many more *hardships* to suffer."

In a couple of long cold sarcastic sentences she can make me hate her. In fact, I hate them all nearly all the time now.

All right, all right, so I'm selfish and lazy and never think of anyone but myself. (Incidentally, that's surely permissible when I'm the only interesting person about?) However, that seems to be *me* and I prefer it to changing to *them* so I shall stay selfish and lazy.

So just now I said, "Other girls of my age aren't treated the way I am—they meet people—" and then I stopped.

I know, really, that that one *is* going too far.

I suppose it is unkind, it is disobedient and immodest of me to talk in that way.

Only because I am so special (though not too special to scrub floors) am I allowed to reside in this finely-laid-out and comfortable castle, with a dozen women to look after me—if not actually at my beck and call. I am different from other

15

people, my blood is unique. I am treated with great care, have been since I was born, because I'm more than the equal of any piece of precious fragile porcelain.

But I shrugged my shoulders.

"What breaks my heart," I said bitterly, more to be disagreeable than because I think it true because I know a lot of it is my fault, "is that you all used to be so nice and talk to me and read to me and play with me before you suddenly started to scold me *all* the time!"

I turned my back on them and walked across to the fountain.

It hurts to know you've hurt someone as close to you as they are, but there's a sad sort of sour joy in hurting anyone.

I slipped my feet from my sandals and into the fresh cool spray.

"My darling child," Glurbia's sober voice said, and I don't think she was hurt and I don't think she was loving me, she was just *ticking me off* (they never, never, never, never do anything else), "what you fail to realize is that you have, in the last year, become intractable and moody and you can't bear to be told when you are wrong, even though you must know that you are."

"I'm sick and tired of being scolded," I remarked and began to splash my feet. "You treat me like a baby. I've been alive for seventeen years."

"You may have larger breasts and hips than you had a few years ago, but in other ways you are still a child and under our guard and guidance. You didn't resent our authority when you were eight, why should you now? And you will be under it for a long time come. You are not yet old enough for us to become your maids; we are your nurses and have every right to expect obedience and gratitude—at least respect."

I jumped up.

"That's what I can't bear!" I yelled as loud as I could. "That's the thing driving me mad! I'm to be stuck here with you how many years till I can see the World and new faces and become real? I'd like to commit suicide, *often,* I'm so bored and I only *feel* alive, my mind gets thrown back from its live sections because it has nothing but this all the time."

"Cija—"

"You tell me I'm precious, but what's the good in it for me?"

I snatched up my last piece of bread and honey, flung it angrily and wastefully into the fountain, and ran into the room

16

leaving them hurt and angry and offended and worried. By the time they had followed me I was here, inside my hidden Passage.

Hiccuping slightly, I walked through the cobwebbed darkness.

It makes me more angry, perhaps, than anything else does to realize that all the endless advice they're always giving me about running about during meals is quite correct.

It does give one hiccups.

The nurses bowed their heads down as far as they could, which was not very far because their rheumatism was bad again today, and my mother walked slowly between them.

She came to me, put out her hands, so that all her armlets and rings clanged together, and placed them on my shoulders.

"What a lovely dress, Cija darling. Who made it?"

"Cija made it herself," Glurbia said with pride.

"Indeed? You are teaching her well."

"They helped me a lot with it," I said sullenly. I didn't want to take all the responsibility for the dreadful thing.

"And has she been good since my last visit?"

"Quite good, Dictatress."

My mother smiled, the women filed past her, and the little courtyard was empty but for Cija and her parent who sat down beside the fountain, and of course but for the slaves who stood holding the Dictatress' train clear from the pavement.

"What sunny weather we are having."

"Yes, Mother."

It seemed to me my mother was preoccupied.

She was smiling vaguely round at the sky and the sunlit stone and the silky-looking sea far below the parapet, plucking with the fingers of one hand at the gigantic onyx ring on the hand which so maternally held mine.

I said one or two half-witted things, like—"I'm glad the extra plates have come" and "Snedde's turtle is rather frisky, it may be going to have eggs, don't you think?" and then I ventured. "Are you thinking of anything, Mother?"

The Dictatress turned, looked at me, and smiled less vaguely.

"I was thinking of some business which is worrying me in the world outside," she said. "But, see, Cija, I have a present for you."

"A present?" I echoed and the Dictatress clapped her hands. One of the slaves holding her train came forward and immediately another slave deftly took the vacated corner of the train.

"Bring Ooldra," said the Dictatress.

The slave's diaphanous trousers belled in the wind her speed created as she rushed out of sight.

"What is the present, Mother?" I inquired.

But the Dictatress had become vague again.

"The present is that which we should always enjoy lest we die tomorrow," she murmured.

"There is no need for you to quote things at me, Mother," I said crossly. "I get enough of that all the rest of the time."

"Poor Cija. And how fluffy your hair is, child. Has it just been washed? You should sleek it with that grease—you know—the brown grease—"

"I know the grease. It's brown and it also stinks."

"Well, have you no perfume with which to scent your head afterwards?"

"I am not allowed to use perfume—"

"Oh, Cija, quick, look up there, up there, dear—see those delicious little pink birds chasing each other across the roof?"

"How sweet. Mother, I'm not allowed to use perfume. Can't you speak to them about it?"

"Ah, here is Ooldra. Give me the package, Ooldra, the one for little Cija."

Half eager, half annoyed, I raised my eyes and met Ooldra's.

Ooldra smiled.

"Now here is the package, Cija." The Dictatress' square (not like mine) fingers plucked at the seal. "Look, Cija dear, a lovely necklace. Let me fit it round your neck."

"Oh," I breathed, at least I think I did.

Even the slaves bent forward to look.

There was a glitter of white stones and I felt their hard cold against my throat. I closed my eyes.

Someone screamed.

I opened my eyes, heard the necklace clatter to the pavement, saw the terror on the faces of the slaves, saw my mother snatch a lash from her wide belt and unmercifully beat a slave.

"My train! You have let my train slip and touch the ground!"

Realizing what had happened, I moaned with fear.

The other slave, holding both ends of the train, quivered as if there were a high wind.

"For the first time in two thousand years the Train of the Dictator has touched the ground!"

The sky had grown dark and it began to rain.

Great drops of rain hit my forehead.

The slave, appalled by the omen her accident had brought, did no more than wail in soft agony under the brutality of my Mother's whip.

The third slave stepped back and her bare foot crunched on my necklace.

Thunder spanned the sky in one leap.

It was too dark to see anything now, but even above the rain and thunder the whipping could be heard.

Ooldra laughed.


I folded into its seventeen intricate folds the dress Glurbia *insisted* on my making for myself and placed it neatly on my clothes-shelf.

The little room was dark. I'm never allowed candles after twilight.

I determinedly laid myself on my bed. "I will sleep now. I won't think of it any more.

"Oh, but it is terrible.

"It is terrible."

"It is terrible."

The phrase kept going on over and over in my head. I was tired, too tired to be, any longer, really terrified. I am still tired but somehow excited and my writing has gone all big and scrawly even though at every third sentence or so I start to try to control it.

The omen has occurred, it is the most terrible thing I could ever have known to happen, for the first time in two thousand years the Train of the Dictator has touched the ground.

A wind, gusting quite suddenly through the window, sucked the coverlet from my body.

I sat upright at once and stared and stared in superstitious suspicion at the window. I wonder if anything is safe any more.

Heavy raindrops spattered through.

I slid out of bed and went to fasten the shutters. But that would've made it so still and warm in the room.

I would be quite unable to sleep, yet anyway.

The room beyond is unfamiliar in darkness. No matter *what* shape any piece of furniture is, it looks exactly as if it had just gathered itself together to jump on you. They are all lawless at night and only sleep bars you from that nightliness.

The door behind the curtain doesn't creak, it is used so often now. This Passage has come to mean Security to me. A couple of months ago I realized that in a half-conscious way I had equated it with my own soul.

It is the first time I have been here at night.

It is almost utterly black—I am ruining my eyes and even so it is lucky I can make writing-signs almost by instinct of touch—and quite a strong draught was coming from this niche to meet me. I know the long fine cobwebs are swinging above me. The broken tiles were sharply cold under my bare soles. I came to the niche.

I think my life has changed today.

I am a new person. A catastrophe has occurred—I don't think a worse one could have—and in some ways I am more untouched than anyone else and in other ways matters have reached a crisis. Ah, I feel very relaxed, almost as if I were to be released soon, as if I were to be allowed to go from here and into the world that my mother inhabits. Anything may happen now. The catastrophe has occurred. It is perilous here at night. How the wind blows! Raindrops keep plopping on to my paper. I can't see anything but I am so very conscious of the abyss. A light—there's a light—I can see the fainter outer edges of it. If there were still such a thing as a Moon I might think it was that—but the Moon also fell thousands of years ago. I must see what causes the light.

I perched as near the edge of the sill as I dared to crawl on a windy night and peered sideways and I felt—I feel—what I don't know—the feeling is probably triumph.

I was actually seeing some of the life of the outside world.

On the terrace of the little building, I could just see several very brilliant little lights moving slowly, occasionally and disjointedly among each other, as though they were held by people who were pacing a little as they talked. Was this because of the omen this afternoon?

The wind was steady against me, with rain in it. I was still soaked but warm, and it was pushing me to the safety of the wall behind me and not pulling me away from it, so—terribly half-witted but I was so *curious*—I hung round even further and stared through the intense blackness to the little moving brilliant lights of the world.

Every pulse in my body discovered itself to me.

I'd never realized there are pulses even in my toes and my elbows—or was it blood throbbing through all my veins?

In spite of the rain and the wind and the thinness of my nightshift and night-trousers, the dark night isn't cold. I thought I could hang there for the whole night, if necessary, till I found out something more about the secret of the life behind the lights.

But after a while the lights gathered together and became quite stationary, and then, one by one, they passed sideways from my range of vision.

I feel awfully queer, I've just woken up and realized I've slept in the niche, and only just beyond the danger-point of the sill! I must have been half-witted with excitement last night.

But no fresh calamity has taken place, and now the sun is rising I might as well stay and watch it.

They never wake for hours yet.

I do like being alone and daring and full of complicity. It makes me very fond of myself.

There are bird-shapes sliding smoothly across the surface of the sky which seems to rise vertically from behind the nearest mountain. The morning is so very full of life, far more so than the sultriness of the daytime. There are small hairy serpents with heaps of legs meandering among the fallen stones. The spiders who live in the *mazes* of webs under the roof are scuttling about in them. Glurbia *would* hate to know how many cobwebs there are in the tower. I can see the eyes of the bigger spiders—they seem too intelligent and not cold enough to be the eyes of such things.

This morning is all blue.

The mist is sort of scented with dew and it is tenuous but blue, beyond and behind and above it the sky is pale blue, the valleys below are turquoise because of the young grass on their slopes which contend with the mists to let their brilliance be seen, the sea is the smooth colour of lavender, except for the line of a wave which every now and then appears and gathers the water to itself and rolls slowly in to the shore—a long thin slow wrinkle on all that lavender.

There's scent everywhere, coming up—from the glistening sand with its minute sun-gleaming-outlined pebbles on the shore at the mountain's foot—from the *drenched* grass growing out of the cliff of this tower-wall—from the sea, a small and yet virile breeze from the tiny milky curling of the young waves on the beach—from the flowers among the grass—from the recent rain lying everywhere—from the lichens which

21

enamel the unsymmetrical yellow and red chalk which comprise, and palisade, the cliff till it gets up here to my window-place.

Well!

There was a sound from below—the sound of a stone falling.

I turned in a panic to run back to my room, smoothing the grit and (as well as I could) the creases from my shift and trousers before it struck in on me the sound had been from below. I ran back to the edge and peered down.

The escarpment isn't particularly sheer—it was quite possible for me to see a person climbing up the slope towards my tower. I didn't believe it was really happening but the person climbed so steadily I, of course, had to believe it was real. At once I scrambled on to the sill-ledge.

The person was foreshortened.

I could see the top of a head, a black head encircled by a silver head-band, the tops of shoulders (too broad to be in proportion, they were the first thing that showed me I was watching someone deformed), a plain straight red cloak with silver shoulder-bosses—and that was about all I could see from here. She was climbing swiftly and with no difficulty whatsoever, but not carefully. The noise of stones falling, and metal-soled sandals against the stones, seemed to fill the valley. Of course, resonance is worst from metal.

"Be quieter, can't you?" I hissed.

Without hesitation—good sense of hearing and of direction, I noted—the head was turned up to me. The eyes narrowed in surprise.

"Hush, hush, hush!" I demanded before the stranger could speak. "You are sure to be heard! Stop kicking the stones!"

"Why must I be quite unheard?" she inquired in an exaggerated whisper.

"Someone may come to see what it is, and I will be seen and I'm not supposed to be here. And you aren't either," I stated, now having seen from her plain clothing and lack of jewellery that it *was* just another of my mother's palace women who are always coming to borrow things or deliver messages or lend things.

Now this woman, her head still upturned, her eyes still narrowed as if in disbelief, grinned at me and continued to climb quite silently and even more swiftly.

At a point as high as she could get she upturned her face to

22

me. I *do* wish I'd had a whip. She was grinning again, a peculiar bold *appraising* grin. I've never seen anyone with such a big body. As a matter of fact, she was practically a giantess! She leaned, lounged back against the biggest rock down there, folded her big arms, and raised one eyebrow.

I said "Er" which I wish I hadn't, it was undignified, and then I said, "Um—what do you think you're doing?"

"Well, to begin with I'm exploring this place." Her voice gave me a shock. It was very hard and alien. I wondered if she was of foreign extraction.

"Why have you come right here?"

"This tower is supposed to be haunted, you know. You're such a reassuring sight—and if you were a haunt you'd be a very reassuring haunt."

Stretching up a dark arm all sunlight on muscles and sinews, she could just reach to flip my feet. "Pretty little bare toes. Not even green talons." I wished they were talons, just then.

"But I didn't invite you—I only asked you to keep *quiet*."

"However, the sight of you did so *convince* me this is no abode of haunts, wild men or assassins, so——!"

I dislike women who think they're good at being funny when it really borders on impertinence, especially to pretend they've forgotten who *I* am.

"Well, I don't think you need stay any longer," I remarked very icily. "I am not used to speaking with serving-women, however eccentric, and you should be back in your quarters."

The other eyebrow this time was the one that went up. I've been practising but I can't do it so well.

"The two statements seem to be unrelated. And I should not be back in my quarters. They are very uncomfortable and I much prefer to explore this valley at dawn."

"I think that possibly it is my business to ask for your name," I then said evenly. "Your manner is presumptuous if not sacrilegious. When I know your name I shall have you reprimanded either by Glurbia *or* by my mother."

"Curiously enough, I still have no objection to telling you my name. Zerd." (Probably a false name, but still.) "Now are you adamant in carrying out your ghastly threat?"

I stared.

"Your behaviour is—is—You will most certainly be beheaded!"

"Oh, I don't know. I am useful to your mother. I presume you are Cija."

"If you *aren't* abysmally ignorant, if you *have* actually

23

heard my name, you should also know enough to refer to me decently as the goddess Cija."

"The goddess!—" The giantess grinned again. "Well, I do offer my congratulations."

Here it got most difficult for me. She knew she could be as insolent as she liked up to a point because like a dope I'd told her I didn't want anyone to know I'd been here—for the same reason we both knew I wouldn't lightly report her. (I'm scared *she* might tell she saw me here. Though unless she words it carefully it'll show she was where she shouldn't be, because except from close to I guess this window looks just like another bit of stony ruin in the wall, and she could never have seen me from a distance.) We looked at each other. I wanted to go back up the Passage, but it was for the *servant* to retire.

She still lounged—oh, yes, enjoying herself hugely—and regarded me in quite obvious amusement.

She was very hideous. I *hoped* she'd go before I had to call Glurbia to remove her. She had a very square angular face, sort of dark blue skin, an awful square big jaw, extremely thick and heavy black brows which were, however, astonishingly mobile, a full wide unpleasantly insolent mouth, heavy-lidded black self-confident eyes.

"Are you going or am I to call someone to remove you?" I demanded at last, after minutes of this mutual regard.

"Oh, you keep a particular force of strong men for throwing out unwelcome guests?" She sounded faintly interested.

How feebly funny.

"Are you going?"

"Don't sound so cross, sweetheart. I'm going. Tell your strong men they aren't to be dragged away from their sleep."

"Don't be a fool." I felt terribly relieved as I watched her turn, even though the actual retreat was not gratifying. I think she just suddenly decided to go because she'd got a bit bored, not because she realized she'd better.

Then she stopped for a moment. She turned back. I was scared she'd start saying something else so I walked stiffly back up the Passage, and then crawled back along the floor to sit here and write. The sun is quite hot now, I've been here a long time and the many-legged serpents are getting sleepy. Better go back to my room now.

My mother should have been far more worried by the fall of the Train than I've been—I'm merely shocked by a happening I thought impossible and which, for years, I've been taught would presage disaster should it ever by a remote impossible chance occur.

But when today, which is four days later, my mother again came to visit me and I composed my face into the suitable grave lines, I was really awfully surprised to find her expression and manner were as vague and placid as usual.

The Train was still carried carefully by the slaves.

As I sat down beside her and we exchanged the usual dutifully affectionate remarks, I had the awful sickening suspicion that my mother had deceitfully enjoined the slaves to silence and not told the country about the calamity, was pretending it hadn't occurred, and *that* was why she still wore the Train, and the slaves still carefully held it from the ground.

Today is white with heat. So unyielding a heat that the whole atmosphere of the day has been stark, sombre, melancholy.

The air is taut with thunder.

I want to cry. I won't. I can't let myself.

"Why are you looking worried, Cija?" the Dictatress said.

"I feel miserable. Every event that has ever taken place is pressing down on me. I don't know why."

"Adolescence, darling," commiserated the Dictatress.

My mother is always so sickeningly vague. She has no real sympathy in her, even deep down. Or perhaps there might be more understanding between us if we could talk together of the things that interest us. But I couldn't ever tell her of the things in my mind, she only always reiterated that I must try to conquer my secret self, I must be content to be a girl so special that I had to be kept away from everyone else; and she can't talk of her life in the outside world because I wouldn't understand.

"Have you—have you told the country about the Train?" I, tentatively, queried.

"Yes, darling."

"Are they all very worried?"

"Well, darling, you see—they are not very apprehensive because the disaster the dropping of the Train foretold has already occurred. It really happened a few hours after I left you."

I made an exclamation.

I was doubly astonished, because I hadn't really expected my mother ever to tell me any such news of the outer world. Politics, scandals—all that sort of thing is usually kept from me. I glean very little of it and when I ask about it I'm told I

25

need to know no more, it would not interest me.

I looked down at my sandals, sort of concentrating on them, and hoped that if I kept quiet she might forget I was never told anything.

However, my mother continued very readily, and apparently very much aware of to whom she was speaking.

"You see, Cija—I expect you will understand this because you have read a lot of this sort of thing, in your books—we are at the moment in rather an ignominious position. We are being occupied."

"Oh, yes," I murmured intelligently.

"That means, dear, that an enemy army has marched in and just, quite carelessly, decided to use us as a base."

"But didn't we fight them with our army?"

She frowned.

"It was impossible, dear."

"But our country has an army, hasn't it?"

"You would understand if you knew more about the general of the opposing army. Their general is—well, he is unbeatable, ruthless—"

"He?"

"He."

I laughed. "Oh, Mother!"

After a moment of hesitation, the Dictatress said, "Why are you laughing, dear?"

"You said 'he'!" (I don't usually point out people's little slips of the tongue unless I want to be disagreeable, but today I was nervous). "You were speaking of the general as though she were a man!"

"He is a man, dear," the Dictatress said, her tone stiffly determined.

"But men are extinct! Do you mean that there is one alive —a real man—an atavistic throwback or something!" Was wildly, wildly excited. Have also *always* wanted to see a brontosaurus, which Sneede told me are nearly as extinct as Men.

"Darling," said the Dictatress gravely, "for reasons of our own your nurses and I, purely in your own interests of course, have misled you as to the facts of existence in the world outside your tower. . . . As many men exist as women."

Well, I can't remember what I did or felt—possibly I just felt slightly ordinary for a minute or two.

"In fact, more," she said reflectively.

"Exactly the same as in my ancient books?"

I believe her. But I feel so queer. It is strange to have to realize something like this when people one trusts have taught one the opposite all one's life.

I am going to cry.

The Dictatress sighed and wiped my eyes with a corner of her undermantle.

"How sentimental even the best of us become when faced with a child's tears," she sighed self-tolerantly.

"I'm sorry," I gulped, raising my face at last from my mother's mantle.

"That's all right, darling. It *must* be rather a shock to find that men aren't extinct and that people don't come out of eggs but it really was for your own good."

"I hate that phrase."

"Yes, of course you do. Are you going to cry again?"

"I don't think so—Yes, I am going to."

"Well, dear, I'll talk to you at the same time," remarked the Dictatress as I again sobbed into her lap. "Don't worry, this crying of yours is quite a natural reaction. I suppose you realize I wouldn't have told you this if I weren't prepared to let you leave the tower."

"Yes, I realized that," I sobbed.

"You've always wanted that."

"Oh, yes."

The Dictatress caressed my head and continued to talk. "Yes, I have decided that it is necessary for the Warning to be disregarded. Your hair is dreadfully untidy, dear. It always is. You will have to be more careful with it when you begin to appear in public. That's right, laugh. You already know there was a Prophecy made at your birth that you must not come into contact with the world until you are of age. That is only part of it and now I shall tell you the whole truth about it. We had to make sure you would never meet a man until you had reached the age of maturity, when, according to the Prophecy, it would be safe at last for you to do so. Well, we decided that until you reached an age when you wouldn't be upset by the knowledge, you wouldn't even be told the truth about life Outside and you wouldn't be allowed to come into contact with anyone, even the priestesses, from the outer world—except for myself and Ooldra."

"And some of your women and slaves."

"Servants don't count."

"I met a sickeningly self-confident servant the other day."

"Mm? And I'll tell you why we decided that. You were always told that you weren't to meet other people because you must be brought up quietly—you were too high-born a child to be allowed to meet others of a lesser caste, even if they were not part of the real Outside—and therefore not enough to break the command of the Prophecy. You were resentful—Glurbia and Rorla and Snedde and the others don't realize how natural that is."

"And my specialness wasn't the real reason?" In spite of my wondering relief and joy at the turn events had taken, I felt rather humiliated that for so long they had deceived me into thinking myself so very far above every other girl in the country.

"Well, you are rather special, you see. That's what I'm telling you, Cija. You know that when you were born we, as usual, consulted the birth-auguries and a prohecy was made concerning you—that you would be one whom it would be hard to prevent from bringing disaster—that unless every precaution were taken, before maturity you would have fallen in love and by that love you would bring the fulfillment of an older prophecy, a prophecy known centuries ago."

"What was that one?"

"That the third in line of female dictators would throw our country into absolute degradation and ruin—let our country fall under stranger-rule—foreign rule." The Dictatress stared with eyes grown colourless, and as hardly absorbent as mirror, into the pool at her feet. "My mother was a very great dictatress; I succeeded her. I knew that your birth must never be made known; thought of the Prophecy would have driven the people mad and you would, in some way, have been destroyed. Because of the prophecies and because it would have ruined his reputation for it to be known that he had fathered a child, your father took you from me at your birth and would have killed you. The men he hired to drown you (like a kitten) were my men; they brought you back to me and ever since I have kept you in this tower. Your father thinks you dead."

"He doesn't suspect—"

"This tower has stood empty for thousands of years."

"Who is my father?"

"Your father, Cija, is a very incompetent High Priest who at the moment is making a nuisance of himself by attempting to stir the people up against me."

The Dictatress rose. Her sandals struck sharp notes from the pavement as she walked to the parapet, her fine draperies swung out on the simmering breeze.

She came to the parapet.

Her plump fingers gripped on the balustrade. She leaned against the palisade, looking out into the sunlight which was pulsing down behind the sea.

The sky was red.

My mother is a busy woman. She has other matters worrying her, out there in the world. My father is worrying her and the foreign general is trying to conquer us. There are men in the world—

"I have read that a man always loves the mother of his child," I said. "How is it that my father can wish to raise the people against you?"

"You have read legends and priests' myths," said the Dictatress. "Love is a thing which ebbs quickly when a man and a woman come to know each other. Personality is always petty, you see. We parted a very long time ago, and your father now no longer remembers me as someone with whom he shared infatuation. I would be impatient if he did. You will have to understand that reality of the world now that you are going into it, Cija. Those, and there are many of them, who cannot understand the harsh nobility of reality, call it sad that former lovers should be capable of mutual enmity later. Those people, whose ideals are weak and in themselves very sad, never taste happiness. Love your legends, Cija, not because they hold ideals you want to follow but because they are beautiful and unreal. They have a strange charm, but they are just off-key, not quite parallel with life."

Relentless, the sunset kept going. Just as if this were a normal evening.

"Then there isn't any such thing as a lasting love?"

"Oh, yes, of course there is. But it is rare—in fact, it is very rare. Few of the millions of lovers in the world ever know it. But marriage and the family are wonderful institutions—for the people; the leaders can form their own ideals. And there is such a thing as lasting, even deep, *affection*. That is what usually follows love. I am pleased by your intelligence, Cija. You have neither fainted nor had hysterics at the knowledge that nothing at all is as you have been told and believed all your years. I suppose the world always touched you so little that knowledge of the sexes in it mattered little to you anyway."

I didn't speak, then.

Attempted verbal amusement at her assumption that I am not terribly and terrifyingly excited might have resulted in hysterical laughing or crying.

I feel very queer—not mentally, as should have been ex-

29

pected; my mind is quite calm and keeps thinking quite intelligently about little almost irrelevant details; but physically I am weak and heavy and hot and cold and quite unconscious of my limbs and joints and rather afraid to move or stand up.

"Well," my mother said briskly, "you will need to know why you are being allowed to leave the tower quite definitely and for ever, and against all plans for you." My mother came away from the parapet. Her voice was brisk but her face was expressionless and her movements were slow.

Quite still because I couldn't trust my bones and my muscles, questioningly I watched my mother.

My mother's short body was dark, solid in front of the wide gold-stippled yellow sky. The loose fine gauzes with which she was covered hung listlessly, dark irregularities in the solid dark silhouette.

"I have decided whom you are going to marry."

"Marry?"

I stuttered.

"I have every faith in your integral intelligence. Moreover, you have a prophecy to overset. You must be firm and inflexible, Cija, and you will come through very well. I have decided on your future husband."

"But—but—" Hundreds of thoughts dashed through my mind. I wanted to choose my own husband, it would be no good saying that to my mother, this marriage is the only possible price of my freedom, as my mother said I must try to overset the prophecy, my mother had probably thought of a means. I said the only thing that was left to say, though I was aware it would sound pitiful and naïve. "Is he nice?"

"He is one of the most vile men who ever lived."

I plunged on to the next question. "Why does he want to marry me?"

"You have to make him want to marry you."

I said uncertainly, "Do you mean this?"

Five birds flew overhead. Their arched shadows slid across the white of the pavement.

I spluttered and managed to say, "Ugh!"

The water splashed down over my forehead and gurgled in my ears.

"You don't enjoy having your hair washed?" said Ooldra. (Presumably.)

Snedde poured another basin full of water, ice cold this time, over my head.

30

"Pardon?" I spluttered.

"You don't enjoy having your hair washed?"

"I only wish I could do it myself. I'm sure I could direct the water better so it didn't always get in my ears."

"I'll get ready the grease and the perfume," Ooldra remarked and moved over to the table.

"Am I going to be perfumed?"

"Apparently," Snedde grunted, sharply.

I didn't say any more. I didn't want a long quarrelsome argument with any of my nurses now I had just a few days left before leaving them.

My head was lifted at last and a large towel wrapped round it.

While I scrubbed I glanced covertly at Ooldra.

Ooldra, with long, young strides, so different from the walk of my nurse, came to me.

"Take off the towel," directed Ooldra, "and I'll rub the grease into your hair. Don't worry, it's perfumed this time."

I took off the towel and looked at the smooth scented mess of brown grease lying in each of Ooldra's palms.

Then I felt Ooldra's fingers massaging it into my scalp.

"I love your hands," I said.

"Brace yourself against their pull," said Ooldra.

"Raining outside," I said, allowing my eyes to peer sideways, at the open door.

"I'll shut the door," bustled Snedde.

"Oh, no, I like to look out at it," I pleaded.

Snedde hesitated a moment, and then left the door as it was and went back to the table.

"Are you afraid?" asked Ooldra.

"Me? Well. . . ." I said. "The fear is mixed with the excitement. I'm not really myself any more. I'm just a receptacle for strong emotions, but there are so many of them that few ever gain control. The only real strain is that it's rather hard to make myself confident I'll be able to kill him."

Ooldra laughed.

I was startled for a moment. Ooldra laughs so rarely. And when she does the sound is unfamiliar.

The rain gusted, wet, silvery, through the door and Snedde turned grimly and shut it out. Even during Cija's last days before going into the outer world, not *too* much indulgence of her whims.

I frowned.

It is that sort of little unnecessary observance of the house-

31

women's niggling enmity to the loveliness and genuineness of the elements that prevents me loving the old women as I should, even though soon we shall part, probably for ever. I knew quite well that a few drops of rain would have made it no more difficult than usual to scrub the stone floor tomorrow.

"Your mother will be here soon," said Ooldra.

I was sorry Ooldra had said that. I hadn't wanted the subject changed, I had wanted to ask Ooldra why she had laughed.

"I'm glad you'll be with me, Ooldra."

"Why?"

"You know so much about things. I can sense that, though I've never actually seen you outside of here."

"That is why your mother is sending me with you."

"Yes, I know. I'm glad."

"You can get up now. I've finished your hair."

Automatically I rose, my bell-shaped trousers swinging under my stiff short skirt.

"And now," said Ooldra, "here she is."

The door opened and the Dictatress came briskly in, followed by the slaves who always accompany her, two of them carrying the train.

"Pho, it's wet outside," the Dictatress announced, flinging off her high gloves and rain-riveleted cape. "All ready, Cija, my darling?" She sniffed. "Mmm, a fine perfume. Very musky. He'll like that. It's not too little-girl for him. Come on, Cija dear, find yourself a chair and sit down. You'll be saying good bye to your tower tonight."

*Tonight?*

"Yes. Snedde, fetch me a bowl of soup, hot soup, will you. I'm freezing. That odious rain. Things are happening quickly. That fiend works faster than any general of our army has ever had any need to. I suspect his king is hurrying him by messages, but still. You leave tonight, my dear."

"But I'm not ready—"

"Hasn't Glurbia packed your things as she was told to?"

"Yes, it's not that, I haven't composed my mind yet—"

"Nonsense, Cija. All our plans depend on you. You'll just have to take the necessary steps and compose your mind later. As a matter of fact, you'll have plenty of time to get yourself feeling ready. I don't expect you to manage to assassinate him the first night, you know. Make your own opportunity. You'll all be on the march for quite a number of months, you know. Thank you, Snedde."

"Oh, but, Mother," I wailed.

"Here," said the Dictatress, pushing a spoonful of hot soup at me.

I drank it, although I don't like using spoons which other people, even my mother, have used first.

The heat spread through me, till it had almost reached my cold toes.

"Feel more courage now?"

I nodded dumbly.

"Fine. Ooldra will be with you, you know. I'm sorry I haven't had more time to get you educated for life, because you're going to be a very important part of my planning. However . . . Just remember; you've been let out for one purpose, and one purpose only which is very important to you; all the other reasons for your freedom are mine and the country's—but *you* want to overset that prophecy. Well, you've got your chance. Snedde, take Cija's sandals off her feet and clean them."

Snedde, her eyes tearful, came and eased my sandals off my feet. Her touch was very gentle, and her face very sad. I realized that when I have gone these old women will have nothing left to live for. They have cared for me since my babyhood. I am going into the world but they are being left with nothing.

I put down a hand and touched Snedde's head.

Snedde looked up, her ridiculous nose blotchy as it always is when she cries.

"Slave," said the Dictatress, "call Glurbia and the others."

A slave sped out.

"Now, Cija," said the Dictatress, "no need to get upset and nervy. Everything will be attended to. Ooldra knows how to get you away safely once the thing's done. All you have to remember is that you've got to assassinate him somehow and the only way to do that is to get him alone. Quite probably you'll have to try rather hard to get him to marry you or whatever, but it's the only way to get him apart from his bodyguard. It won't be impossible. Be sweet to him. Flatter him, tell him you're my heir, and he'll belong to you."

"Isn't it a lot to ask a child to do, to seduce a seasoned lecher," Ooldra's voice had an odd stifled note, "when she's only just realized there's a sex rather different from hers?"

How sweet of Ooldra, I thought. She sounds worried, about me personally.

"If he's a seasoned lecher," the Dictatress said all brisk, "less effort for her. Cija, I suppose you do know that men are—not really at all like women?"

"I've read some of the books Glurbia didn't know are in the library," I said austerely.

"You know you're supposed to keep your hair washed? Your neck jewelled—don't look a pauper. Think of your body and men will have to, they'll catch the thought from you. Think of your waist while you're walking and you'll find your hips start a nice sway."

"He'll like that?"

"And you'll have it made," my mother said, rather crudely I thought. She started twirling a ruby on her finger with gusto.

"There you'll be, with him snoring and stupid," she said, skimming over the terribly difficult parts as if it were a row of asterisks. "Then—well, you have your knife. Keep that close to you, whatever you do. Only thus, by active positivism, can you overset the prophecy which says you will bring disaster to the country. Kill him—avenge your country's ruin which was brought about by his ruthless father and which I have spent decades in repairing. Kill him, our great threat. Kill him and break your birth-fate. Rid the world of his evil line."

"Dictatress?" said Glurbia.

"Ah, Glurbia. The others are with you? I'm relieving you of your charge. The army leaves tonight. Is her baggage ready?"

"Yes, Dictatress."

I looked uncomfortably at them. My eight nurses, all of them pale and trying to restrain their tears only from respect to the Dictatress. Even Glurbia looked as if she was about to weep. I remembered all the silly little things they have done for me. Their attempts to romp with me in my childhood; the many times I have hurt them; the affectionate stern sense of Glurbia. I felt a tear trickle down my own cheek, and was glad, because they would see it and think I was crying because I didn't want to leave them, where as I was crying merely because the whole occasion was so horribly melancholy.

"Someone fetch Cija's cloak," ordered the Dictatress.

Ooldra turned into the inner room to get the cloak.

"Now, Cija, say good-bye to your nurses. Don't cry too much, child."

There were dozens of little incredibly bright silver patches on the pavement and road. My eyes were dazzled by them. I was about to remark on them to my mother when the carriage dashed nearer to them. Almost above them I looked down and saw that they were puddles, nearly dry. When one approaches at an angle and sees the sun on them they look just like patches of inexplicable silver.

This carriage, in which me and my mother and Ooldra were being taken towards the enemy encampment outside the city walls, was a peculiar yet efficient contraption and I would have been quite astounded at it if I hadn't seen pictures of such things in my books. It jolted along at a great speed drawn by four horses—two brown, one a splotched grey, and one almost striped. The one which was almost striped kept throwing up its metal shod feet and trying to break the traces but when it found it couldn't it went on again with the others; then, after a little while, it tried again. There was a person on the little platform in front which is part of the carriage but not in it; the person kept shouting things out to the horses, especially to the horse which was almost striped. I suppose the person was a man. It is very bewildering to see men like this and have to behave as if they were ordinary normal people.

"Vicious creatures," remarked the Dictatress as the hybrid again tried to kick free of the traces.

A little while later, turning a corner, I looked back and saw we were being followed *and* being preceded, at some distance, by groups of them (men) all wearing the same clothes. Green and a sort of pink on their tunic edges. But they were hard to see; it was far easier to just look out the windows, which only showed the sides.

My gaze was now held by the buildings the carriage was passing. They weren't at all the sort of places I am used to seeing. When there was stone used in their composition, which was rarely, it was never marble. And so many exteriors all in rows—I have never seen any but one *inter*ior before, and that for my whole life. The newness of it all, the strangeness, the uncertainty and the responsibility of what I was going to, had made my whole being a fever.

I was noticing the crooked black nail which jutted out from the window-frame just beside my shoulder; the white fleck on one of Ooldra's fingernails; the intriguing texture of the nearly dry puddles we continually passed; but such things as the over-all palpitation of the dying sun, the palpitating fluctuating red wind, the grey architecture, the rows and rows of grey architecture, the disconnected people, the lights hanging from the balconies, the occasional tree, often rooted so far in to the centre of the roadway that the carriage could only just scrape between its trunk and the high side-paving—at these things I gazed earnestly to realize them, earnestly, but after a moment of blank inaction they whirled in to take their place in the whirling unstable elated fever which at the moment was myself. My head ached and I knew that I would be sick except for this incredible elation which was cold and high and yet palpitating and held me together even while it was the cause of my nausea.

Sunset and old rain—copper contended with grey, the blur grew, the streets were a soft queer colour. The houses were dark masses, the sky between them was soft, pinkly, yellowily, silverily pearly. Almost all the small spheres which hung from arches and balconies were lit. The carriage passed through arches: low black apertures, grey stone crumbling, fungus dripping from cracks, movement over the stones which if one looked definitely one would see as the movement not of dying sunlight but of small lank reptiles: the sort of stonework to which I am accustomed. There were squat buildings on these arches. Most of them looked deserted.

People walked across the pavements and disappeared into the half-lit doorways which threw reflections out at the road way. There were even a few other carriages; their wheels whirred and vibrated as they passed. Though it was hard to hear much over the roar of our own wheels and the marching men.

Few of the people stared as we passed; Ooldra has told me we were in a plain carriage and there have been so many carriages going to camp in the last few days.

The Dictatress, leaning back inside the carriage, looked thoughtfully up from her clasped fingertips.

"How do you like your city, Cija?"

I murmured something in a polite, small, unnatural voice.

The Dictatress nodded.

There were small satisfied upward-lines at the corners of her mouth.

She leaned back and looked pleasantly up at the ceiling.

"You're about to embark on a very thrilling life," the Dictatress said.

I turned and looked at her.

"I am very afraid," I said.

"You don't look afraid."

"I have no real emotion at the moment. But I have been afraid and I will be afraid again."

"Naturally. How strange all this is to you, and it is never a pleasant task to kill a man. But just remember what a monster he is."

36

I looked out of the window again. There was nothing to say. I already know all that, how vile a monster this man is. I know he is not only ruthless but cruel, that to conquer and gain power is his only objective and the only objective of the king he serves.

"It is a very luscious thought," remarked the Dictatress. "He will soon be quite dead."

"No son to govern the army in his place?"

"No, my dear, no. The only man who could possibly take over from him is his cousin, an ineffectual boy. That great country will be no longer be a power in the world when it has lost the General."

"The General."

"Contemptuous swine." The Dictatress' hands clenched. "He and his father between them have twice caused this city to be reduced to a pitiful barren place of ashes and weeds and creaking gibbets. Now he is so assured of our negligibility that he goes off to conquer another country far to the west, contemptuously leaving us at his back. He is leaving behind with us a sneeringly minute portion of his forces."

"Well, can't we send our own army at his rear as soon as he is gone?"

"How can we, my love? Apart from the fact that our army has not even yet recovered from the former ravages, he is taking with him hostages of whom you, my darling, are only one. There are sons and daughters and even wives of our most important individuals. In a way it was lucky for my plans that the other day he suddenly demanded my daughter as one of them. (I had previously merely been gently preparing the way, telling him of your existence, and thought he'd been seeming uninterested. It just shows you.) In all, he has taken about eight 'guests' as he calls them. The cur, the cur, the contemptuous sneering hybrid cur."

"Hybrid?"

"His mother was one of the huge black women of the north." She is really astonishingly eager. "I almost envy you," she then said with another sigh.

"It is such a responsibility," I excused myself. "I am sure I will not strike home deeply enough, or that I will strike at the wrong place."

"If you strike hard with the point into the side of his windpipe he'll die quite quickly and very certainly. There will be nothing to it which need distress you—glory in his unnatural blood—don't go trying to get him through the heart, you have to be experienced to get that right. The ribs are liable to deflect the blade—amateurs always think it's best through the heart but the side of the windpipe's easiest. You won't flinch, darling. And Ooldra'll get you away safely before his followers discover even that he's dead. Ooldra's very clever. Don't be afraid. Remember how much is at stake. Remember that when he is dead you will have rid the world of a monstrous brute. Nullified the prophecy that you will bring disaster to the land by failing to keep it from under foreign yoke."

I was darkened by determination.

I leaned forward, beside the window but unseeing.

The Dictatress leaned back, but her body was tense. Her short strong square-tipped fingers grasped at the pelt across her knees. Her jaw was not only square, it was taut.

Slowly the fact that Ooldra was not bent on the matter in hand became visible to both of us.

Ooldra's silence had made no impression on us, she so rarely speaks, but it now came to us that her mind and body were not bent to desperation and brooding resolve as ours were.

Ooldra lay back in the corner of the jolting carriage, one thin white arm raised to finger languidly the tassel hanging from the grip above her, her chin sunk almost to her chest.

"You are nearly asleep, Ooldra," I remarked.

Ooldra's eyes looked up, and that was all.

"We are passing the river now, my darling, look, look out there, there it is. A fine river, which my mother had diverted from its real course that it might water our city."

I looked out and saw the shining flattened bluish-silver dragon with floating scales of garbage, along whose unevenly cobbled western bank we were now moving. On the other side there was no bank, there was merely a sheer wall of rotting leaning houses rising from their foundations which must have been many yards under the water. Oh, it was beautiful. From the picturesque thin gables of some of the houses, of which storey hung out over storey and balcony retreated under balcony, depended little spheres. Their slim light gave here and there to the sight lopsided slittish windows, a few inches of precarious coping, a wooden cross intended presumably to hold together the rotting wall but which was itself rotting. It hinted at the bony height of a building squashed between two squat elaborate buildings, quite overloaded with dilapidated balconies and gables and railings and balustradings. The lit hints merged into the rest of the scene, which was totally dark. The river's surface, too, was hinted at by the reflectons of the spheres. Occasionally, as we watched, more lights would appear as they were lit from within the building. The face of the lighter would be seen for a few seconds beneath the sphere before stepping backwards into disappearance.

"Magical, this quarter of the city, isn't it?" the Dictatress chuckled.

"It's dreamlike," I said.

"Even in the daytime it's like that. Unreal."

"But aren't the people very uncomfortable living in those rotting leaning tenements?"

"They find the damp uncomfortable, but the river is their life. Look, down there—beside that sphere, quick before it is left behind us—you can catch a glimpse of their rows and rows of boats. They moor them at night. In the daytime —everything, everything from fishing to moving immense cargoes for warehouses."

This quarter of the city seemed to last for a long time.

My eyes grew incredibly tired as they fed on sloping roofs and winding narrow stone stairways leading up under pointed unsymmetrical broken archways to queerly carved roofed bridges, boarded warehouse windows, piles of empty fungus-grown barrels, and always rows of boats on the garbage-strewn, faintly rocking water surface—all of this in glimpses, nothing ever seen as a whole, slivers of silvery-yellow sphere-light picking out anything, beautiful or ugly, but all delicious. Now that I have written that it looks silly. Delicious in a grim way. My eyelids were hard to keep up, my eyes kept sliding sideways simply unable to focus on what I delighted in seeing.

"I'm so tired, Mother," I remembered murmuring.

I don't often call her Mother.

"Sit up and brace yourself. In a short while you'll be meeting some of your fellow-hostages not to mention the General—and his army. You'll be sleeping tonight in the camp."

"I don't want to leave you, Mother."

"Nonsense. You're tired, Cija."

"Yes."

"She's going into a perilous world," Ooldra said.

"What was that?" I asked.

"The driver yelling at those odious horses. Ooldra's right, you know. Yes. She's right." The Dictatress sighed heavily and twisted her body deep into the soft unresilient cushions. "The world is perilous."

"Oh, yes, I know that," I said. "There are diseases. And wild animals. And wars and all sorts of terrible things."

"No, most people are never really touched by those things —but the world is really perilous in far bigger ways."

"But it's all fore-ordained, isn't it? All foreseen and expected? Perils are never really unexpected," I said. "A good seer knows all that will happen and doesn't allow herself or those she serves to be taken by surprise."

Ooldra smiled her slow sidelong lilting smile. It looked even more enigmatic than usual in the glancing sphere-light from outside the carriage window.

"No, that's just the trouble—only too often the destiny of a nation for thousands of years to come is changed, by the action of one person, from that which was foreseen for it."

"Another thing, dear, you will find," said the Dictatress, "is that, in the world, just as you have gained self-confidence after a number of weeks doing the right things and never being contradicted by people or made to look a fool—suddenly it will all be shaken away and you will be small and frightened and hurt and unsure of yourself once more as someone ticks you off about something or as you commit an embarrassing solecism. It sounds little enough, just said like that. But it's really the worst part of life. Life means that sort of loss of self-confidence over and over again, consistent and never really expected, till you've reached the age of fifty at the very least."

"You will make your daughter nervous."

"Oh, no, I'm not nervous. Not—not—you know, not—conclusively. I'm terribly nervous because this is such a—such an incredible adventure, all of it, even though you have been preparing me for it for weeks now, but—well, shall I ever get any wonderful man to marry me when I have murdered my first husband?"

"Don't worry, darling, by murdering him at least you will be nullifying the prophecy and allowing yourself to live in the world instead of growing older monotonously in the tower —and to miss marriage is no hardship—I know—living with a man is fine for a while, you have a great time and think you'll do anything for each other—but it *inevitably* drags into dull affectionate dislike—or into actual dull loathing. For an intelligent person, the decision to get married is really the same as the decision of the person who is so annoyed that he will risk the horrors of guilt and execution so that he can have one three-minute orgy of satisfaction in killing the person who has so annoyed him. Many poor fools think it's their own faults that neither they nor their partner can go on living for ever, and bitterly reproach themselves and each other. So it's no harm to miss marriage."

"Your mother is a very intelligent woman," remarked Ooldra. Her voice is always expressionless.

"Thank you, Ooldra," nodded the Dictatress.

I looked from one to the other of them, as much as I could see of them in the dark inside of the rattling carriage.

"How will I be able to live in a world like this?" I entreated.

"Oh, it's not a question of instinct, Cija. It's a question of knowing the right rules. Most people only work those out for themselves after years of heart-breaking and back-breaking experience, but I'll give them to you to start off with now."

"Do tell me," I begged, feeling my voice a strain. I was feeling more and more nervous and unhappy.

"You must remember that it is very important never to believe more than one quarter of anything anyone says. Well—if they are someone you know well and whom you think trustworthy and honest you can permit yourself to believe as much as half. If their motive for telling lies isn't for some kind of ambition or gain, it is pride or the wish not to appear ridiculous. It is also extremely important to learn to tell satisfactory lies—be able to think up a good watertight lie on the spur of the moment. Tell lies as seldom as possible. You get a reputation for truth and then people will believe your lies too."

I was feeling sick now. The carriage was slowing.

Perhaps we were nearing our destination!

The pounding behind my breasts ricocheted from side to side, quite sickening.

Will I be able to stand alone?

Ooldra's eyes kept being lit as the carriage passed spheres more and more frequently. Every time Ooldra's eyes reappeared again from the darkness they were looking at a different part of the window.

Her eyes make me dizzy. Can't she stop looking around?

The Dictatress laid a heavy motherly steadying hand on my knee.

"The best advice *any* person about to embark on life—and that means everyone—can be given is to care very little about anything you witness or anything that is done to you, either physically or mentally. Maintain your own principles and ethics: they should be elastic but you should never violate them; and don't let anything hurt you. Don't trust anybody too much;

41

even when you love them greatly, keep in your mind a little reserve, the knowledge that they may not be trustworthy. Don't let yourself feel disloyal for holding this doubt; it needn't stop your love, it will probably heighten it, and you will be all the more happily surprised when you find that after all they are usually very trustworthy. Feel superior to everybody, but despise nobody, no matter what they are or do. Finally, remember that it is wise to be friendly to everyone until you have decided definitely whether enmity is the relationship you prefer with them. And to get people's friendship you must employ very careful tactics. Never, never let anybody know that you are 'cynical' as they call it: they will at once feel inferior before you, and that will make them hate you. Always pretend to be more innocent than you are—it is very useful to be among people who underestimate you.

"Pay no attention to anything I or Ooldra have told you if your intuition tells you otherwise. Your behaviour depends on the people you are with, and there are too many different kinds of people in the world for any rules to be kept when dealing with them."

"But the rules you have given me will generally be the right ones?"

"The rules we have given you will fail you with extreme rarity."

Well, I have managed to get them all down so that now I shan't forget them, and now it is time for bed.

# CHAPTER TWO

## THE JOURNEY

*Incredible* space. Devastating wideness.

I got down from the carriage expecting my attention to be drawn by the crowds of people, and the other carriages, and soldiers and everything but as I stepped down I glanced ahead and then couldn't pull the glance away.

There was a plain there, and it stretched away, away, till it disappeared up into the sky.

And it was covered, dotted with small red lights, close together, very very many.

The air moaned with the thrum of small black drums.

I started at the hand on my shoulder. It was not my mother's short heavy hand, it was the strange, alive, thrilling grip which is so completely Ooldra's. It is always hard not to start at the touch of Ooldra's hands.

"Come," Ooldra said.

We were moving in a long procession, along the wide paved top of the city wall. From it, the army encamped on the plain could easily be seen.

There were drummers everywhere.

"I'm frightened, I'm frightened," I kept saying.

"How surprising it would be if you weren't."

Well, I felt absolutely and totally bewildered too. There was all this noise and drumming and soldiers. Some of them were ours but the nearest ones were His—these, the Army's. They are of the brutish race, the race native to his world. They'd come to escort me the rest of the way to the camp. They don't wear such a pretty uniform as our soldiers—it's red with leather boots and the jacket has an odd sort of slanting cut and they have stiff caps with red cockades on. No one had forced them to polish their buttons when they were coming to meet me. There were crowds and crowds of people down below, on the city side of the wall. A queer collective noise came from their throats.

"What is that? What are they all saying?" I asked nervously.

"Various things," Ooldra said amusedly. "Some are talking to each other and some are calling out good wishes to you and some are cursing the foreigners."

All the time we were walking along and trying not to catch our toes in the cracks and little plants and things on the wall.

The soldiers ahead of me were not at all dignified, they were talking and joking with each other and laughing in hoarse voices. Men all have hoarse voices.

"Do the people know who I am?"

"Yes, they have been told," Ooldra said non-committally.

I would have liked to ask how my father has taken the sudden news that I am still alive, but at that moment the procession reached the edge of the wall.

The soldiers stopped and did various things with their spears at the orders of a careless-looking individual who was their leader. It was a kind of ceremony.

"I've never walked such a long way in a straight line before," I said. "The tower had no rooms as large as the top of this wall."

The eyes of the Dictatress followed me fondly for a while, but I know she is always quick to notice the mood of her people and she could not be unaware of the tension of the crowd.

She glanced over the crowd. Her glance was keen. She knows the crowd through and through, knows its moods and its impulses and is complete mistress of any situation involving it.

But she wanted to know how it was taking this situation.

Her ears, by long habit more attuned than mine to the voice of the crowd, were alert and intent as she walked along the wall to the Main Stairgate.

(Ooldra told me about this later.)

There were cheers for her. There were always those. They gave little hint as to the state of mind of the crowd, although sometimes if the cheers were unusually fervent it meant that the people were indignant over some move which had recently been made against her by one of her lesser political opponents. But she could also hear, could sense, the tension and the murmur of the crowd. Her stern mouth relaxed a little. The people were very excited. She saw the High Priest a small way distant. He was on the height of the platform beside the Priests' Stairgate. His attendant priests were chanting. He was pale.

"I'm afraid," I said.

I knew it was my father, they did not have to tell me.

Ooldra says I was white, whiter than my father. I trembled

44

and walked very uncertainly. I began to sway. I had lost my sense of balance.

"Hold her, Ooldra," whispered the Dictatress.

Ooldra's cool hand righted me.

"Cija," said the Dictatress. "My people, your people, are watching you. See that man in the white gown, standing before the others over there? He is your father, who thought he had killed you at birth. Do not falter in front of him."

I tried again to look at my father but his face melted before my gaze and the only things which were clear, which would stay put, were his eyes which were not looking at me but at the crowd. He seemed uninterested in my appearance but not in what emotion it had aroused in the people.

The spear ceremony stopped. The leader came towards me and bowed. He said something but it was not much good, the crowd were too loud for anything else to be heard. They had suddenly all started cheering. It was terribly loud, like a storm over the sea but much nearer, so that the air thrilled.

Suddenly I knew they were cheering me!

Now I *know* why my mother lives for the people. In the mass, they are something which can be as much a part of you as a building or a—well, I don't know, a sort of charge, a Thing with life. They were cheering me because the Dictatress had declared to them that I was her daughter and because I was going to the Enemy.

Ten more steps—the Dictatress publicly embraced the girl (me) whom she said was her daughter—the drums thrummed —the crowd stared and yelled and presumably disputed and then was, quite suddenly, almost hushed, as Ooldra and I and the enemy soldiers went down through the Stairgate.

I followed Ooldra down the black, basalt steps. That, funnily enough, was a moment of sheer panic. There was the human sound of marching soldiers behind and before us. But sound was flat enclosed between those walls.

There was a wind beyond the Stairgate, a wind pulsing coldly over the plain towards the camp.

And we went towards it too.

Well, it was the noises I noticed most, above the soldiers' marching, and after a few minutes I found them so interesting I nearly forgot to be afraid. The short raucous barks, so resonant, infrequent but, when they did come, dominating all the other noises of voice and metal and crackle spread all through the whole huge encampment, interested me most. I couldn't think what made them. The guards challenged us as a formality and our leader, I mean the leader of the soldiers escorting me, did something with his hand and we marched past. Once, when we passed a guard-officer he knew well he delayed us for ages while they talked together. There were tents and red fires everywhere, and in addition lots of men had torches. Almost all the men were eating by then, sitting round the fires, talking in their way (soldiers all talk mainly in growls and laughs), and turning meat to roast on the fires and cutting off bits to eat, and drinking. Nobody took much notice of us. Hostage after hostage must have been passed in that day. I passed the first birds in the shadows away from some fires, and I hardly noticed them because all the shapes everywhere were so odd with all those shadows round. Then some more were barking when we got to them, right close to me. I nearly jumped out of my skeleton when I saw them. Their necks were stretched out and their big narrow eyes were looking down at me. Yet in the dim red and black light they were less hideous than they are in ordinary daylight. Their general shape was monstrous, the flat body and the two strong legs with the eager inverted knees and the spurs and the spreading feet-claws, but we were past in a moment and it was only a horrible impression. The sound lasted longest, the barks, right from their horrible chests, vibrated and reverberated in my ears after they were left behind us. It's a bad sound from the distance but horrible when close. So their shape alarmed me but I did not see till the next morning all their scars, the knotty tendons, the vicious characteristics, the fearsome petulance, the feather-raising, the ugly, yellow-mottled, black feathers, the big, curved, dented, battle-grooved beaks.

Well, we got to this tent and our soldiers all did the thing with their hands and left us in front of it so I knew it was ours.

The leader started to smile at me but I suppose I looked utterly tired and afraid and unresponsive so he finished the smile on Ooldra.

"Well, this is it. This is yours," he said, as if congratulating us.

And it is a nice tent. It is dark blue with two gilded poles inside sort of keeping the roof up and it is much bigger than the soldiers' who, if they have tents, they are only big enough for a man to lie in and if he's tall his feet stick out. It is in two parts and there are two beds in one part for Ooldra and me and they are on the floor but very comfy and we can sit on them too and we have a clothes-chest each, all ready waiting for us when we came in (soldiers had taken them from the back of the carriage and brought them here while we were on the wall) and the other part is a sort of bed and kitchen place for the woman. Glurbia wantd to be her but I think my mother thought Ooldra and Glurbia might disagree over the way I was to behave and the woman, thank all the dear gods, is one of my mother's palace women whom I've never seen before and who obeys me the minute I suggest something.

And never argues.

Actually I hardly ever see her, her name is Tilia and she's rather bosomy.

"When is the evening meal?" Ooldra asked.

"Well, actually, whenever you like," the leader said, shuffling rather.

"You mean—?"

"The General," he said, discovering a formula, "thought you might like the privacy of dining in your own—um—private tents sooner than the strain and lack of privacy in the officers' dining mess."

"But surely he must intend condescending to meet his hostages some time?" Ooldra inquired.

He'd expected her to say that. You could watch him thinking what a nuisance it was dealing with the entry into the camp of hostages who were used to considering themselves important in their own little lands.

He repeated his formula but Ooldra interrupted him.

"When shall we meet him?"

"Well, naturally if you're keen—he'd be only too pleased—consider himself honoured—two such charming ladies —noblewomen, I mean—I mean, I could take you to him this evening—after he's eaten—"

"It would be suitable to meet him. Will you eat with us?"

"Be most grateful to. Thank you very much."

He accepted with alacrity, probably glad for any way of changing the subject. Also it was only polite for *someone* to take notice of us, our first night in camp.

So he went in and sat down and Tilia gave us a meal of roast flesh and white roots with a lot of very nice vegetables and spicy sauces but, though Ooldra seemed as usual and the leader was very enthusiastic and kept saying: "What a good cook you've got yourselves," I could hardly swallow anything. Chewing was a strain and I kept wishing I could go to bed and just sleep the whole business away.

It is bedtime now.

47

Ooldra had just poked her head through and told me to snuff my candle and get undressed.

All through the meal he told us things, being ingenuously courteous.

He kept starting to say the things to me, because I am the real hostage and the Dictatress' daughter, but my eyes presumably looked as lack-lustre as they felt and though I tried to look alive and interested at him it didn't seem to click with him what I was doing and he'd keep turning to Ooldra, and in the end he didn't bother me even with the beginnings of his sentences and talked exclusively to her.

He told us we could each have a bath tomorrow morning if we liked, and we said, "But aren't we all moving off tomorrow," and he said, "It is the slaves' business to pack up our tents in time, not ours to hurry for them," so Ooldra was glad because I think she likes being in water but I dislike the fuss and bother of bathing. Anyway I'd had one the previous night. But Ooldra says I must bath once a week at *least* as travelling gets one dusty and I have found it does.

Then he told us we each had a bird to ride on (though not our woman Tilia who would walk with the other servers and sometimes get a turn on a mule if she were lucky) and I said, "Everyone has mules and things in my country" (it was the first signs of the embarrassment I'm feeling about having been in the tower all my life. I keep pretending to people that I know all about life, as much as they do and that's why I find being with people a strain as it's a full-time pretence) and I'd forgotten that having no birds makes us sound rather backward to them as they're so used to birds.

So then he said, "Oh, birds are much better than the other things, they are large and strong and have been bred to carry soldiers on long campaigns and in battle."

"Aren't they very fierce?" I said.

"Yes, which is very useful, they won't carry anyone unless they know him. But they are amenable to discipline and totally loyal to their master. But don't worry, older and less fierce ones have been found for you and your companions."

"Companions?"

"The other—the other ladies and gentlemen from your country who have joined us."

"I see."

"Well, as we have all finished shall we go outside and look at them?"

48

It was very dark outside and I kept well behind the other two because I didn't want to bump into the birds but soon the leader and Ooldra stopped and so I came up beside them.

"Here they are," said the leader and I looked round to see them and suddenly I found that I was the one nearest to them and they were on the side of me I hadn't been looking at and one of them suddenly poked its head at my shoulder and I gave a squeal.

Well, the leader leapt to me as if I'd been being attacked and the groom sprang up and the bird put its head back again and I felt rather a fool.

I wanted to laugh it off but my laugher sounded tired and nervous and I think the leader was too prudent to laugh at me, and the groom was smoothing the bird as if he thought I'd upset it, and I began to feel slightly awful.

"This one is yours, I believe," said the leader to Ooldra.

Then he decided to point out mine to me and the groom rather grudgingly held up a torch for me to see by. My bird is very old and grey and has a nasty sidelong rheumy eye and I suppose he isn't mangy but his yellow splotches and greyness definitely make him look it.

His name is Sheg.

"Now my charge would feel it fitting to meet the General," Ooldra said.

"Of course," the leader said in an eager voice. I think he was forgetting the previous impression he'd made, and was anxious to sound conciliating.

So off we went, through the camp and fires and birds and pickets and everything.

I was getting really nervous now but at least I was in my best dress and trousers (except for my very best ones which are possible only for feasts unless one wants to look overdressed): my red, grey and gold striped one with full trousers and full sleeves, almost as diaphanous as a slave's. And I was wearing my hammered silver necklaces and the anklet and the blue shoes, not the ones with the mosaic soles, the ones that show every second toe, and on the big toe of my left foot I wore the ring with the white stone in it. Unfortunately the evening was only *just* a little bit too chilly not to have a cloak but I hoped it would be warm enough in the officers' mess for me to take it off and be revealed in all my glory. I hadn't taken the cloak off in the tent as it hadn't seemed very cosy to me, though warm enough with torches and a fire in the sort of earthen hole-stove in the kitchen part, so I hadn't been able to gauge my appearance's effect on the leader.

We arrived at it—not a tent, a large barn which at the General's arrival on the plain had become his officers' mess, probably whether the owner liked it or not.

We were passed in.

It was all torches and talking, etc., and something about it annoyed me, well, annoyed isn't the word, but something about all the lights and noises did something to me, and it wasn't somthing that made me like them but it stopped me being afraid.

People (men) kept calling out "Hello, Ious, you revolting scoundrel" and "Hi, Ious" and "Where've you been all evening, Ious? Oh, on hostages?" and "Stop for a drink, Ious? Why not? Oh, bad luck" and finally we got to the table in a big triangular corner, smoky with purple torch fumes, where a lot of men were dicing and drinking.

They drank from leather bottles and diced with ancient ivory enamel-marked dice.

At the time I didn't understand what they were doing—I still don't know *how* they play but know it is a game for money and is fascinating to the players because you never know who's going to win—and we and our leader stood waiting for a pause in the conversation which seemed pretty peculiar to me.

I can still quote most of it, though not the sound of it, the pauses, the sighs, the gulps, the wiping of the back of the hand across the mouth after drinking, the growls, the shouts of laughter, the rough good-humoured exercrations, the calm ill-humoured execrations.

"Gods curse your bones, Eng. Stop winning. You're collecting fortunes tonight."

"And one of them yours."

"It is not a humorous matter. The General won all last night and took one half my worldly wealth. Push the flagon over, Zerd."

"Staring poverty in the face, Clor?"

"You may laugh, you may laugh, were it not for the wine I'd leave your army. A debauched concern. Everyone gambles too much."

A page strolled into the corner and began to attend to some of the smokiest torches.

"These young sprigs have the softest position of us all, damn them," remarked Eng. "While the rest of the army, downwards from the Accoutrements Master, is breaking its neck so all'll be ready for morning, all these fellows do is wander round cosset-

50

ing torches—if they feel like leaving the cosseting at their mother's and sister's sides."

"And look at you, sitting at your ease, playing and drinking, in a warm bright barn," retorted the page.

"All our work is done. We've given the orders. Now we can relax while they get carried out. You should be here while the day's work is being planned. You'd have to scurry then. Gods' Hearts, Gods' Hearts," Clor started to moan, "My brain's still whirling round."

"Ha!" laughed the page, and continued his work.

"Impertinent little bastard. You're not backing out, Clor?"

"Lower the stakes."

"Hearts, man, you're not a beggar."

"Near enough. Near enough, near enough."

"He forgets all pride if he can get a brass coin for the begging," Isad said sadly.

Immediately with ecstatic yells they leapt for each other's throats. Eng continued to play, or rather to cast dice, Isad and Clor wrestled all over the table but Zerd looked up impatiently at our leader who was still standing behind his shoulder.

"The Lady to see you, General," Ious said, improvising a title for me.

He had obviously forgotten my name if he had ever heard it.

Zerd frowned, but glanced behind at us. For a frowning second his eyes rested on us. I started to feel sorry for the young leader whom we'd made bring us. But then Zerd's eyes looked at mine. All the time they'd all been playing I'd been thinking the General's name was familiar and when he looked up once, of course I knew. Before that, I found even his head and shoulders, bent forward over the table, intent on the game, familiar. only just at the last second stopped myself crying out, "But you're a serving woman!" before I remembered he is a man now.

His eyes are very bold (in an uninterested, slightly bored-contemptuous way) and black and cold, but when recognition leaps into them they—they leap at you, you feel as if you have been struck in the diaphragm.

"Sit down," he said, rather almost-cordial.

We did, at the same time trying to pretend we hadn't been nearly knocked flying by the threshing movements round the table of Clor and Isad, who were oblivious of all else.

Now I thought a strange thing occurred. As she seated herself Ooldra gazed very deep, I thought, into Zerd's eyes and I could have sworn that that very same recognition stabbed from his to hers. Oh, Gods, I thought, and for a moment I felt ill, they cannot be together—they cannot know each other—Oh, Gods, *no*, not Ooldra, I'm in her power here, she's the only person I know here and she's in control of me.

But of course it was my tired imagination. He turned his head casually away from her and she continued to look at him just as I myself was.

The General saw that our leader was still standing and nodded at him to sit also.

He pushed a leather bottle at me. After the way Ious had been treating Ooldra, I was glad of that.

But even though I was first to drink, I wasn't so pleased at the manner. It's difficult to drink from the neck of a big leather bottle and added to that the fact that all these foreigners had been drinking from it before me. I squinted down at the place round which I was expected to stretch my lips and was almost sick when I thought there was some saliva there but I valiantly drank because I knew I must not offend Him and as a matter of fact I now think it was only froth.

I found the bottle very heavy to hold up, but though there were mugs on a nearby table and it must have been obvious how difficult I found it he didn't offer me one. He just sat, tapping a dice in a rhythm on the table, uninterestedly watching me drinking and Eng casting left hand against right and Isad and Clor savagely and happily grunting and struggling round us all.

The drink was dreadfully hot, not in temperature but taste, like spice, only it wasn't spicy either—it hurt me in the throat and I coughed and coughed.

Zerd reached across and took the bottle from me and passed it to Ooldra. He patted me carelessly on the back. I felt an awful fool.

"I'm so sorry," I said, all sweet and confused. "How *silly* of me."

He accepted that.

I shrugged my cloak off my shoulders but he hardly glanced at me. I realized it was another mistake. I should have taken it off as I approached him, or as he first looked up, so he could have got the full effect, the line of the dress and the diaphanous trousers.

Clor fell on to the table. Isad dropped sprawling on him and kicked me (lightly—by accident) in the diaphragm, just where Zerd's eyes had previously struck me.

Zerd half-rose, reached over a long arm, pushed Isad a little in the stomach so that he fell back tumbling on the floor. He was more interested in his officers than in me. He neither apologized for Isad, ordered him to apologize, or introduced anyone to me. I began to feel rather desperate. His invitation to sit down and drink couldn't be meant to extend for the whole evening—for more than one drink. Ooldra had finished hers. Would Ious be allowed one? Yes, he was. Well, when Ious had finished we might not meet the General again for ages and ages, I didn't know *how* long.

"Oh, dear," I said, brushing the dust from Isad's boots off my dress.

Zerd frowned for Isad, and bent over to examine the damage. He looked only at that spot, not even first at my face. But I stuck out my chest and breathed heavily so that my breasts went up and down and sort of tried to waft my perfume over him. For the moment he peered at my dress I saw his face amazingly close to. His skin is very rough and it is— well, this sounds poetical, but I can't help it—if I said it was bluish-grey it would sound wrong—his skin is the colour of a thunder cloud. That, I presume, is from his mother's blood. He brushed the dust away—it was very loose and left not even a smudge, he probably despises me for my fuss—and I saw the roughness of his skin even closer. He is covered with large close-set scales ! ! ! Like a reptile. I was totally unnerved and repelled. My mother is right. He is not a man at all!

Well, this monster then noticed that Ious had gulped down his drink and Isad and Clor had also sat down again and were sorting out stakes so he said politely to me, "I am glad to have had the opportunity of meeting you again, Goddess."

We all rose.

I simpered.

"It was nice meeting you again. Yours is quite a familiar face among so *many* strangers."

He looked surprised. "Well, I hope you enjoy your stay with the army," he said. He even added another sentence. "Should you ever need anything, don't hesitate to ask anyone."

After two such sentences, great concessions to the polite way of treating a hostage, he bowed to me quite low but swiftly, bowed his head at Ooldra as she passed him, sat down again and resumed the game as we went away.

All day we ride with the baggage-train and the other hostages.

The birds are horrible, but one can manage one's own and the groom is usually there. He disapproves of me terribly but at

53

least gives help when I need it. He is usually called Blob. He is small and plump. He has a wobbly paunch, blue stubble on chin, lots of eyebrow, unkempt grizzled hair; and as a sideline to grooming, pretensions (practically unfounded) to pseudo-philosophizing. Liable to get huffy at slightest thing.

I like riding, in a way, except I still get frightfully stiff and on the first two days I was just a mass of pains and had to lie on my tummy when in bed and even Ooldra rubbing oil into my back didn't ease it.

I think she is used to riding already: anyway she and her bird seemed to get to know each other after the very first hour though neither shows affection. Blob admires her a lot.

Riding; feeling the wind and dust; seeing the endless columns, the marching regiments, their sandals and legs up to the calves coloured chalky with dust, the flat flat plain, the hugely broad winding river, which we march beside day after day, its colours, its rapids, the tiny mountains on its further bank, all the different uniforms; hearing the bark-bark-barking of birds, the shouts of riders, the yells of leaders, the rumbling of wagon wheels, the lowing of oxen—we carry all our own livestock with us and the oxen can carry baggage too—well, it's a huge life, a world, a world always on the move.

It rained today, for the first time. The endless lines of regiments slouched on through it, while it beat into their faces and hardly anyone could see anything. I enjoyed it for quite a while till it got rather too heavy and then I joined Ijleldla in her carriage. Most of the hostages prefer carriages to birds. The foreigners can't understand them and always offered birds first.

I don't like any of the other hostages.

Ijleldla is the worst but the friendliest to me. She insists on treating me as her bosom friend. She is the youngest hostage except for me but more sophisticated than I am. Actually it was nice in her carriage too today trundling through the mud all already rutted by the endless lines of men and birds and horses and wheels which had passed through it before us, and the rain flurrying through the windows and beating on the roof.

It is still raining now, beating on the tent ceiling above me.

I can even hear it pooling on the ground outside.

Hope it doesn't seep in over these rugs.

Ooldra is spending the evening with Ijleldla and probably some others, like Iren and Smahil, in Ijleldla's tent. They all like Ooldra; though she is so calm with everyone she looks so interesting and says such interesting things. They all think *me* very unsociable. Ijleldla tries to tease me out of it.

I dislike them all intensely.

At least, I *hate* the older ones. There is a horrid pompous old grey-bearded nobleman who is the uncle of one of my mother's head men, Ijleldla who is the daughter of another, a fat old woman of about forty who is someone very important's wife. Ijleldla has her brother with her, an eager earnest gallant puerile young dope called Onosander. I like the name, it's a shame his parents called him that because now I shall never hear it without thinking of him. Iren is thin and sophisticated and sarcastic, with what she and everybody but me thinks is a very strong personality. I hardly know Smahil, he is little and thin and pale, with almost white lank hair, but he is one of their set. He is somebody's adopted cousin. I am the seventh and last hostage.

There is a roar outside.

I ran to the tent flap and lifted it and peered out.

Rather funny.

The men are all rather miserable and grumbling-ish and they are sitting round in the pouring rain with blankets and things over their heads and have lit their cooking-fires in the shelter (?) of their tents. One of their tents, in the Blues, has somehow managed to catch alight. Is making a lovely blaze. All the Golds are dancing round it in joy. They hate the Blues and love it every time they do something stupid or have an accident, and of course the Blues are the same over them. They are the two regiments which hate each other so much they can never be set to work together at anything. While I watched, a fight started but several of their leaders rushed over and separated them, though they loathe each other as much as their men. It is called *esprit de corps*.

The rain isn't hurting anyone though Ijleldla was moaning and crying about the discomfort of it all day.

It's the approach of the hot season I'm not looking forward to.

Riding and marching all day under a broiling sun won't be much fun. And that's just about when we'll be leaving the river.

Today was warm.

The ground was practically dry again.

I was riding along getting wind in my nostrils and a tired seat and wishing I was safe and secure in my tower.

"Hello, Cija," said Ijleldla, leaning out from her carriage window. "We missed you last night, darling. Why didn't you come with Ooldra?"

"I had a splitting headache."

"You poor girl. Oh, come in and sit with me."

"I can't leave Sheg."

"Drat the animal. Why didn't you get a carriage like the rest of us? Riding all day is no pastime for a girl."

"I know, but I truly do like it better than a carriage, Ijleldla. A carriage gets musty."

"It does not."

"Well, it seems to, after you've been in it a long time."

We had half-snapped at each other, for no apparent reason. It's always like this. A long determined resentful battle on Ijleldla's part to get me to become sociable. I think she hardly realizes it's like that, but it is.

"Leave Sheg. Blob is just over there. He'll see to him for a while."

"I've still got my headache, Ijleldla. I'd sooner stay in the air."

"You talk as if my carriage is totally airless," Ijleldla said, laughing almost in spite of herself. "Oh, come on, Cija. I get awfully bored all alone," she pouted, beginning to look pathetic.

I don't mind being coaxed sometimes, but when it's all the time she makes me feel so churlish.

I made up my mind simply not to be browbeaten today.

"Oh, don't keep *on* so, Ijleldla," I laughed. "I feel energetic today. I *want* to ride." I spurred Sheg (hoping he'd obey me, luckily he decided to) and spurted ahead from her carriage. She can take that as she likes. Either she'll begin to respect my freedom, or she'll get all offended and sulky and tell the others about my bad manners.

I had ridden practically to the ranks and found myself among all sorts of unattractive oxen and hens and untidy herds of smelly goats driven by little boys who were almost naked but somehow didn't look so because of their unnaturally brown skins.

I meant to stay about quarter of an hour and then ride back and join Ooldra. It was so nice I stayed with that part of the line till noon.

Today as soon as I could I lost Ooldra and Blob and rode ahead. I have made friends with one of the little boys, who is called Ow by the others. The others know me too. They all chatter and tumble round all the time and the heat doesn't ever seem to make them tired or dizzy—it never seems to affect them a bit.

This afternoon one of the Accoutrements Officers found me.

He seemed worried and said, frequently bowing and politely calling me Goddess, that as I was the main hostage was I sure this was really the part where I wished to ride and I said, "Yes and please not to let all sorts of people come and disturb me, just go ahead as usual," and I think I finally got it into his thick head.

After the evening halt Ooldra said as calmly as usual, "Where have you been?" and I said "I went with the goats and oxen and everything in the animal part of the baggage-train," and she said "Why?" and I said "Because I like it and I don't like the other hostages."

"You are a fool," Ooldra stated.

That took me aback terribly. She is always calm and never glosses over what she means but usually she doesn't mean things like that.

"Why?" I said.

"You are cutting yourself off completely from them. To be with them in their particular communal life is most necessary to you. It is your only link with the life of the army officers—and Him—"

"We never see him. Now, really, Ooldra, he's always with his own commanders—at least I presume so, we *never* actually *see* him—"

"His officers will take notice of them soon. Ijleldla is a very pretty girl. From the life of the officers to the life including Him is a small step. You may despise them but it is folly to cut yourself off."

I had not previously thought of Ijleldla as pretty. Now I suppose she is.

I had not thought of it. It is difficult. She seems very popular with everyone but I thought that was only because they knew her.

So I said, "Oh, dear." I told Ooldra that possibly Ijleldla may not wish to have me back as a fulltime companion because I treated her rather roughly yesterday morning.

"Yesterday?" said Ooldra. "And you haven't seen her since? You must go round to her tent at once. I shall come with you, if you wish."

So of course I said I did wish.

I always feel better with Ooldra, she is my safety. Though I have asked her twice how she means to get me away when I have assassinated Him she says it is better for me not to know till the time, so I can rest simply on the knowledge that she will always be there. I feel so ashamed when I remember that night. How could I have been so ungrateful, so nervous-nervous and so treacherous as to doubt her?

We went to Ijleldla's tent and the whole lot of them were already there. I think they do gather there nearly every evening. There is not much room with them all there. Ijleldla was sitting on her brother Onosander's knee and Onosander on her clothes-chest. The fat motherly-bossy noble woman was hogging the soft bed. The head man's rotten old uncle was standing loudly and pompously holding forth about something with his thumbs hooked in his sash with its moth-eaten-looking sequins and his grey beard wagging. Smahil was sitting on the rugs pouring drinks into mugs for everybody and humming to himself. Iren, lolling all over him in a very undisciplined way quite unnoticed by the two elderly ones engrossed in their nattering, every now and then reached an affected languid hand over his shoulder and took his wrist and made him add more of one or another of the mixtures to one or another of the mugs. Ijleldla's lady usually stays in the kitchen with her woman.

In one moment, as we arrived and saw all this, Ijleldla looked up and saw us.

"My darling," she shrieked, leaping up off Onosander, neatly skipping over the noblewoman's knees and Smahil's ankles and arriving at the doorway and us, still with her arms held out. As she reached us she fervently embraced me. I was glad to find I, and not Ooldra, was the one who the "my darling" had been addressed to. I know they liked Ooldra's company and I knew it was possible Ijleldla had gone off me.

"I haven't seen you for *evenings!*"

Anyone would have thought an evening was a terribly long time-period. Well, they do go to bed much later than I do.

"Hello, Cija. Hello, Ooldra," said everyone in varying degrees of loudness and emotion, and Ijleldla seized me by the hand and dragged me to the clothes-chest. She pushed Onosander off it and sat on his knee on the floor instead, at my feet.

"Ooldra," said Moth-eaten Sequins, pompously insistent, "*you've* been to the Main Rotunda. What do *you* think of the extra domes?"

"Do you like exalitir in your drink, Cija?" asked Smahil.

"What's that?"

Iren squealed with laughter. "Oh, isn't she *sweet?*—*!*"

"It's the green stuff," Smahil said.

"I'll try some," I said. As usual I felt stiff and furious. Iren usually does that to me, sooner than later, in the evening.

"Here's your drink, everybody," Smahil said.

"I haven't seen you lately, Cija," the dear lady said. I think she rather disapproves of me. I think she thinks I'm too young to think I'm "too superior to mix with the other young people."

"Oh, Cija and I had a nasty silly quarrel the other day," shrilled Ijleldla. "That's why I was so *thrilled* when she appeared in the doorway just now. It means she's forgiven me."

I opened my mouth to speak (astonished) and she smiled at me with such warm fondness it almost looked deep, and reached over and popped a fruit in my mouth. "Well, Cija, how do you like your exalitir?" asked Moth-eaten Sequins with pompous condescension and kindliness, becoming for the instant more my uncle than the uncle of my mother's head noble.

"I haven't tried it yet," I said and hurriedly sipped it.

The next second everybody stopped all their chattering because I was coughing and coughing and coughing.

Ijleldla sprang to slap my back and Iren thoughtfully removed the mug from my hand just before it slipped.

"Ugh! Ugh, ugh!" I shivered as it went down inside me. "I'd have to be a salamander to drink that."

"She's very young. She's not used to alcohol," Ooldra said gently.

"I'm only a year older, and I was got used to it by having tiny quantities of it given to me since I was a little child," Ijleldla said, looking at me rather reproachfully this time.

"Her nurses were very strict," Ooldra remarked and thank my sweet cousins the gods that ended the matter.

Iren was giving a monologue and the others listened and laughed, even me to a certain extent.

I mean, you can't keep completely quiet and sour while other people are laughing with great enthusiasm around you.

Iren just talks and talks, with the completely self-assured assumption that she's holding everyone with her fascinating personality. And the funny thing is, everyone else seems to think so too.

She certainly has a repertoire of unusual mannerisms. Her speaking-voice is deep and husky, her hands flutter and sweep, her shoulders shrug and she has about five facial grimaces, each of which is quite expressive. But after half an hour with her, one knows all these tricks backwards *and* just when she'll make each one. After knowing her for a week her company seems terribly stale. And she never had any personality even in the first place. But apparently everyone else worships at its shrine. Onosander obviously adores her. I don't think he's in love with her, but she terribly impresses him and he tries to say witty things to impress *her* but she doesn't notice. One of Onosander's comments, anxiously oozing with what he hopes to be *his* personality, brought the next subject up.

"It was terribly funny," Iren said, using the adjective as a playground for her voice. The first two syllables were husky, the last a short squeal with a little break in it. She was on about a leather and silver-decorated wine jug, the feast-gift of one hold any. She was so upset. It had looked *so* beautiful, but the when we came to put wine in it we found it simply *couldn't* of her friends in my mother's city. "It *looked* so beautiful but wine simply leaked out from between the flaps. It was closely flapped all over you see, like a crocodile to look at."

"Like our host the General," commented Onosander: being Witty.

"Oh, he's *not* like a crocodile—" screeched Iren in excitement. "I mean the scales," put in Onosander, clearing himself. "He's absolutely divine," shrieked Iren over him. "His eyes are warm, not like a crocodile's—no, hot; they're hot *considering* black eyes, and he moves superbly. He's so big and—ooh, he makes me go all squoodgely inside."

"But why?" I said, managing to make myself heard. "He is not beautiful; he is not even pretty."

Onosander turned to me, smiling *at* me, and remarked, "Look, dear, perhaps it's time you realized the word for men is 'handsome'."

That was unpleasant. But I was saved being tittered at by Iren, who as usual noticed nothing *in* anybody's remarks but her own, and cried, "But in his case he's not even handsome, he's nothing like handsome, he's ugly, but—" her voice sank to a dramatic huskiness, "—he's *attractive.*"

"Magnetic," suggested Smahil, and began to mess about with more drinks.

"Yes, he's that," I admitted.

Iren whirled on me. "*You've* met him?"

"Twice," I said.

"*Twice!* My child! how? I've only seen him in the distance."

"He came to visit my mother." Well, that's true enough. He

was staying with her when he came climbing and to my window in the tower. "And then again I met him on the first evening we came here."

"You—well, you *are* honoured. He didn't deign to invite any of us to go and be greeted by him."

I kept quiet.

"Well, You must get us introduced to him."

"Oh, I can't."

"You must," Iren said, suddenly brisk.

I know it was only another facet of her pose but it annoyed me that she should try it on me.

"I can't," I repeated. "I'm *not* a freind of his. He's a malignant enemy of our country, a scourge to all true peace-loving patriots, he's a monster, even physically—are you giving the impression that you don't loathe him?"

Iren gave me a queer look, but saw that I was truly earnest in my refusal and she has sense because she at once ceased trying to cajole me or bully me and accepted her defeat but was off at once on another tack, teasing Onosander about his new cloak. At last Onosasder was happy.

Ooldra came over and said, "I'm going now, Cija."

"Oh, is it time to go?" I said eagerly.

"Not for you. You must stay. I'm going back. Noble Gagl will escort me back. The Lady Ronea is leaving too."

"You young people keep hours too late for me," she said, happily wagging a fat forefinger. She approved of me again because she was leaving me staying up late with the other young people. She loves all young people to be gay and naughty and innocuous and depressingly sub-normal.

At last we'd all taken our leaves of each other and out they'd gone.

To my surprise Iren and Ijleldla leaned back laughing helplessly.

"Oh, thank our gods they've gone. Ronea is so oppressingly motherly. And Noble Gagl's beard waggling up and down—*up* and *down*—"

I was astonished to find they don't like them either.

"I never caught his name before," I said. "To myself I've always been calling him Moth-eaten Sequins."

They shrieked and tossed with laughter at that, and collapsed on each other's necks.

It delighted them.

"This child's really something, you know," cried Ijleldla, embracing me. "Did you know she's the only one of us girls who

61

rides a bird, just like a boy? So strenuous. No wonder she usually goes to bed earlier than we do."

"Do have a drink," said Smahil. "You deserve it. You *deserve* it. No?"

"Thanks, no."

"And they're so horrible, those birds. Why, Cija, even my brother Onosander doesn't like them."

"How do you mean, Ijleldla," I said, " 'the only one of us girls'? There *are* only three of us, all together. Or are you counting Ronea as a girl?"

I thought they'd all laugh again but Iren looked at me and said "Haven't you seen the other carriages? Especially the neat enamelled one?"

"No, I haven't. What are you talking about?"

"Girls, Cija. Us girls, only not really."

She was so silly and so mysterious I began to feel impatient.

"Oh, what are you talking about?"

"I've seen the one in the enamelled carriage," Onosander eagerly told everyone. "She was leaning out of her window, from under its sunveil, and she was talking to one of his officers."

"What *is* all this?" But I had suddenly felt all cold.

"What's she like?"

"Ooh, glamorous. You'd be jealous if you saw her, Iren." "Indeed I would not." "Go on." "She has long jet-black hair and slanting jet-black eyes and a full pale mouth." "Is she dark-blue?" "Is she plated like a dragon?" "She's glamorous," Onosander repeated with that dogged note of self-conscious lascivious appreciation in his voice. "Well, what was she wearing?"

"Oh, sort of wispy white, with a ruby clenched between her breasts.

I went the two next nights, too, to Ijleldla's and to bed early last nght.

They seem to rather like me and for odd seconds of time I almost enjoy myself with them though I don't like them and now know I can't trust them—the Lady Ronea came up to me yesterday, *absolutely* disapproving of me as in a sort of way well she might, and said "Iren tells me you have been going round calling Noble Gagl *'Moth-eaten Sequins'*. Have you no respect for your elders? Such cheap adolescent wit at the expense of one who has—"

I hate Iren.

And since I heard of the women who belong to the

officers—and the Monster—what hope have I? I knew there
were camp-followers, women and wives of the men, but—

I have found my mother's eagerness and plans too headlong
in many ways when set into practice—it's obvious he won't
marry me. But otherwise the idea holds well. Get him alone, off
guard, if possible asleep—but will he look at me? He has her,
whoever she is, and she sounds—I mean, what's the good of me
trying?

One never sees him, but if I did find a way of forcing myself
on his notice—

I mean, there's a dreadful hitch my mother seems not to
have taken into consideration.

I'm not pretty.

I'm not even attractive.

Everybody, from Noble Gagl to a leader like Ious and Blob
the groom, gets fascinated straight away by Ooldra.

People seem to adore Iren's aura, women as well as men.

And everybody says Ijleldla's pretty and she's so popular.

But people just seem never to take notice of me, not much,
not in even the slightest *attracted* way.

Tonight I have a mirror in front of me.

But I've been looking and looking and can't seem to tell.

I shall list the apparent ingredients and see if we get far that
way.

I have a mouth, not a pale mouth like Onosander seemed to
think so terrific on that woman, but neither have the others.
Mine is wider than Ijleldla's, but not as wide as Iren's and my
lips are fuller than Iren's but not as full as Ijleldla's so that
doesn't prove a thing.

My eyes are grey, not black as they say Hers are, and Iren's
are a sort of muddy green which I wouldn't have thought at all
a good ingredient. Ijleldla's are blue. Ooldra's are a kind of
silver, bright clear grey, only you can't look into them very
well.

I have more chin than Ijleldla but less than Iren or Ooldra.

Ijleldla has fair hair, she has black hair, Ooldra's hair is a
light orange-gold, and Iren has dark brown. Mine is in between
them all, a sort of light brown, more fair in places than in
others.

Seemingly I have missed out all along the way.

If I had a little more mouth or a little less, or a straighter
nose or a wavier one than the one I have—

And perhaps I have no personality.

Nothing happened today. Tomorrow we leave the river.

Today we left the river. No more fish as presents to Ooldra from the spare-time anglers. The men all grumbled a bit in an apprehensive way but they all stocked with water skins to say nothing of all those in the baggage-wagons, and anyway it wasn't even a warm day.

From things I'm gathering, I think these troops—in fact almost the whole army—are all inexperienced. I don't understand it. I thought He was always making war. In fact, one knows he was, it's history to Ijleldla and her friends.

Tonight two rather young leaders, slightly drunk, I think, passed Ijleldla's tent as she looked out. They got waved to and invited in and everybody seemed to have a lot of fun. I was very shy with them because I know I am not pretty and nobody likes taking much notice of me. So when one of them sat on the bed with me and kept talking to me I felt very sorry for him because he so obviously thought he ought to talk to me and I answered in monosyllables to show him he didn't have to, poor man, as I'm not a conversationalist anyway.

Today Ow said I was pretty. He was running with the other goat boys and one of them called out (just being silly, little boys run round and round the whole time, never getting dizzy or thirsty, till they're in an ecstasy of silliness) "Give us a drink, Cija, I'm thirsty," and Ow cried, "Pretty Cija wouldn't give the likes of you a drink," and they started to hit each other in the flailing, purposely inept way small boys have. I know Ow likes me, but was he just good-humouredly mocking me when he said that? Is it an accepted fact I'm unattractive?

At least I don't have to scrub floors nowadays.

And when I think that I worried about having to leave the river because the hot season was just beginning!

The wagons, the columns have for two days been churning through slime in places as deep as the men's knees. The rain has never stopped and we are all shivering and soaked. Having left the river and the wooded strips, fuel is very hard to find. At night the army bivouacs on mud. What sticks one can find will not light, and the hostages are worse off than anyone, especially those of us who have no men-servants to forage for us. The food takes ages to cook even the slightest bit. In the day the lines, slouching and sullen, struggle slowly on through the heavy, deep, sucking mud and under the heavy driving rain. Everyone is in a foul temper. Nobody does anything to help the hostages. The officers ignore us.

My candle is guttering and I can hear the rain squelching outside and on the ceiling of the tent above me. The tent is covered with mud, even inside, though we scrubbed *most* of it off. Somebody had dropped it.

Today in the rain somebody came riding up beside me.

"Aren't you sick of all this?" the voice asked, muffled as all the voices are through the rain.

I thought it was Ooldra and said morosely, "Well, you'll have all the fun of visiting dear sweet Ijleldla's tent tonight, she's getting a worse cold," and the next thing I knew my hood had been pulled back so I had to turn round and look and it was Smahil.

"Leave my hood," I said crossly and tugged it forward in its place again.

"You really can't see much like that," he said.

"I don't have to. Besides, you got my hair all wet."

"Isn't that a pity? I'm sorry."

He obviously meant to talk to me but unless he had a set subject I was making it rather difficult for him and apparently he didn't have a set subject. He just rode his bird along beside mine. The two birds shied at each other, not satisfied with the rain they still had enough bad-temper to object to each other but we were silent and I stared straight ahead at the back of Sheg's ears and his wet draggled crest, which kept not being sure whether it was going to rise or not. Their vicious peevish ill-temper is never still but always fretful and you can't ever be sure it isn't going to develop this particular time into a real insane, ugly, berserk, powerful rage because sometimes it does. I've seen it with several.

"I can only see your nose and mouth under that hood," said Smahil.

"Does it matter?" I murmured.

"Pardon?"

"Does it matter?"

I mumbled it even the second time. For one thing, I didn't care whether he heard or not or just went on riding along or just went away, and for another thing I thought it might be a good thing if he ticked me off for not being more polite and then I could tick him off.

"Well, it is rather a nice face," he explained, reasonably, after a pause.

"So is my voice. You can put up with having only that. At least, until you go away."

There was another long rainy pause, and then Smahil said, "I wonder where we're making for?"

"We can bivouac anywhere, I suppose, as long as we arrive there at night."

"I didn't mean that . . . I meant, what country?"

I sat up and looked at him, tossing my head a little to get the hood back from my eyes. "It's to the East, isn't it?" was, I found, all I could say.

"Is it? We're traveling South."

"My mother said it was to the East. He is going to conquer it."

"Perhaps we've got to go South before we can go East. I know there will be mountains ahead of us. Quite soon. In about a fortnight's time we should see them."

"How do you know all this?"

"Somebody showed me a map. An officer I shared a drink with the other day."

"Didn't he tell you anything else . . . Smahil? I said, didn't he tell you anything else?"

"He said almost the whole army consists of inexperienced troops—men who've never been on a campaign before, much less in a battle. The officers are having trouble licking them into shape—only a few battalions have been with Him before —and apparently, added to that, it's a small army, compared to what we're going to."

Smahil looked at me. The raindrops ran down his hood, which he wears back on his head, and on to his fair almost white hair, making it lanker than ever. He was looking just as bewildered as I am sure I was.

"Have you told Ijleldla and the others?"

"They won't listen, they aren't interested in the army—and Onosander says he hopes they will all get killed and that's that—"

We found that we had stopped and looked ahead and saw another ox being slowly levered out of the mud. He began lowing through the rain, and the insistent sound, therefore muffled, sounded more brazen than usual. It covered the sullen, wet, gritted teeth cursing of the men.

Sheg barked and after that he'd evidently got into a barking mood because he went on and on. I myself felt like screaming,

I wanted to kill him and the ox and Ijleldla and the General and go back home and be safe. I hit Sheg over and over again with the flat of my hand but he wouldn't stop.

If Blob had been there, he would have been furious with me because it was just the thing to really upset the beast but queerly enough Sheg didn't seem to notice, just went on barking.

He had disturbed the other bird and they were both sidling and eyeing each other. I struck him hard on the head and his crest lifted right up, but otherwise he ignored me.

I thought the rain had become wetter and nearer and realized there were tears running one after another down my face.

Smahil reached out and tucked a lock of hair back under my hood.

"It's depressing, isn't it?" he said.

Ooldra's calm eyes and her smiling mouth which turns her calm eyes into a benediction put a centre into myself so that I am no longer afraid and no longer devoid of balance.

She was waiting for me when I reached the tent this evening.

"You are here early," I said.

"Cija, come in out of the rain."

I came to her.

"You are troubled, Cija," she said. "I have felt impatient with you lately." This in itself was a great admission; for when Ooldra is annoyed it so little disturbs her that it is a confidence for her to tell anyone of her emotions. "Now I have put forth my mind and discovered the core of your unrest."

"What?" I said.

"The company of Ijleldla and Iren troubles you. You think that, in surfaces, beside them yours is nothing. You do not know your own power. Cija, gain confidence. And I tell you, you will gain him."

I sat down and felt tired.

"Do you know this, Ooldra?"

"Yes." She smiled at me, as I looked at her. "Perhaps no one ever told you that it was I who read your birth-auguries? It was I who made the Prophecy at your birth."

"No, no, it doesn't surprise me, Ooldra. I don't remember anyone ever telling me. But I think I have always known it."

"You will always go with the hostages now? You know it is the only way."

I promised faithfully and humbly.

"So have confidence. Cija. It is only that which is needed to draw upwards all your own power and force."

"Can't you help to make him meet me? Can't you help me to get him?"

"I cannot do. I can only know. Now I shall sleep, for it hurts me to put forth my mind."

"Sleep, Ooldra. And you were present at my birth, Ooldra? Tell me how old you are?"

She smiled. "I am one of the Changeless kind. I do not know when I shall come to the end of my life-span. It may be to-morrow."

"I love you, Ooldra."

She had turned her face to the curtain and is asleep.

I can understand that she is one of that Kind. Her face and body are young but her eyes are not young. They are quite calm and I do not think they are expressionless but their colour is so clear and unreflecting a silver that it is hard to look into them to find the expression.

Her eyes could be terrible, but there is always a smile within the shape of her mouth to turn the calmness of her eyes to a benediction to me.


Today it was still very wet but in the morning the rain became so light it almost stopped. I think everyone began to feel happier. Then suddenly, when we'd been riding about an hour in fine almost pleasant drizzle, the sky and the whole scene got awfully dark and the sky started to rumble rather frighteningly and the rain just *poured* and *poured* and *poured* down, everyone and everything must have been wet through in the first instant, the birds squealed and reared. (They usually move with their heads down and backs bent and can go very fast that way.)

Sheg—it was very annoying of him to be so worried by the storm when usually nothing does more than make him ugly and peevish—reared up so suddenly I slid off his back and landed in the mud. Only the fact that the bird behind was also rearing stopped me being rather trampled on. I was riding with Ooldra but had to scramble quickly out of the way of other birds—claws look *very* big and heavy when you are down among them in a lot of sucking mud—and by the time I had managed to get out of danger I was quite lost. I couldn't see Ooldra, nor Sheg, nor even Blob, nor in fact anyone anywhere. I mean, the rain was coming down in torrents and one could hardly see the features of the nearest men. To make matters worse the birds were still bucking and squealing and the end of a frantic kick again sent me sprawling in the mud.

Avoiding claws—the ooze was too thick, I had to squirm rather than scramble—I managed to get to a place where I could struggle to my feet.

The whole army seemed to be rather in chaos.

There were a lot more carriages coming on. I hoped there might be someone I knew.

But they were different carriages from ours, bird-drawn instead of horse-drawn.

Then another flurry of riders came up and I was scared I really would be ground into the mud. I really didn't have any balance and one of my shoes was off and a frill half-off the bottom of my skirt was dragging around behind me. I was slipping and sliding everywhere. Just in time I grabbed hold of the back of the last carriage as it passed me and swung out of the way of the riders.

I was by this time quite confused and scared.

And the thunder was demoralizingly noisy.

I clung to the carriage which jolted along and kept throwing up most unsalubrious waves of mud which slurped all over me as often as not.

Then a lot more riders came up. Their birds were well disciplined, more fierce than vicious, and kicked only occasionally. One, a big black-looking one, its legs thickly spattered with mud, pulled up beside the window of my carriage.

The window was yanked open and she looked out.

It was her, I could tell because of the dead-black hair and the slanting black eye. (She was in profile to me.) There was the full pale mouth, a light dusky pink. It was painted, of course, but it is a very original idea. She has very long eyelashes.

She wasn't all in "wispy white" today but in red, bright glowing dry red, almost startling in the situation.

The figure on the bird pulled back his hood and said, "You O.K.?"

"It takes more than a storm to frighten me," she replied superbly, and laughed.

"Good," he said non-commitally. He reached out one large hand, pressed hers which was resting like a white crimson-tipped flower just wafted on to the window frame, and turned his roaring bird.

During this I'd been frantically trying to brush the mud off my face but it only smeared all over worse as far as I could feel. I was scraping my feet and legs against the back of the carriage to get the mud off, and I tore off the trailing frill of my skirt and yanked down the front of my dress to show more of my shoulders and breasts, only it went up again a bit because it is a new dress and the material hadn't loosened yet.

As he turned back past me I reached out and caught at his cloak.

I was unable to hold it for more than a second and I thought he wouldn't notice me but then one of his equerries said, "General, the Beauty's carriage-boy must have a message for you, he's trying to catch your attention," and the General said, "She doesn't have a carriage-boy," but stopped and turned back to me.

I looked at him but couldn't think what to say and impatiently he made his bird ride along beside me.

"What is it?" he asked through the storm.

"I—I'm lost," I said.

"Well, you don't belong here," he agreed. "What do you expect me to do about it? Whose are you?"

I looked at him more and he saw he was supposed to recognize me and did.

He laughed, damn him, and laughed again.

"I feel very sympathetic," he said. "And one of your sandals gone too. But from whom did you get that boy's jacket?"

"It is my dress. It got torn so I tore the bit right off and it is shorter than I meant. And my trousers are awfully muddy, they will probably never be able to be cleaned."

"Oh, dear. You fell off your bird?"

"It reared," I explained.

"Of course. Clor, Eng, escort the poor little Goddess back to her place in the lines."

I hate him.

"Oh, won't you come with me?" I begged him. "I should feel much safer with you. This awful big storm does so terrify me."

That is a much more sensible approach than hers, all the women in all the books I have read were beloved when they were scared and helpless.

"Well, well," he said. "I *do* find this pleasant. You weren't so sweet and polite the first time we met. I'd love to escort you back, Goddess, but I'm afraid I have a lot to attend to elsewhere just now. However, Clor and Eng will take you."

"Oh, I was a stupid girl, then," I tweeted. "And of course I don't mind if your duty calls you. Bye, bye—and I hope we see each other again soon."

He nodded and rode off.

70

Everything is grey and dry and it is the end of the month and I feel tired and bored and at the same time unequal to anything interesting even should it happen.

Which it won't.

Tonight in Ijleldla's tent, Ijleldla said when I got there, "Hello, darling, guess what has happened, we've all been asked to accompany some of the officers on a hunt, we're reaching a part of the plains where there are lots of forests and there are lots of all sorts of interesting animals in them and we've been asked to accompany—oh, this is Alurg, Leader, who brought the message; Leader, this is my friend the Goddess Cija, but we've all met before really, haven't we. Oh, I wish Iren would come so I can tell her—"

There was a Leader sitting on her bed, looking rather awkward and every now and then moving his long legs (in lovely shiny boots) uncomfortably and then stopping quickly as he remembered his drink was on the floor beside them and mustn't be upset.

He was the Leader who came with a friend some evenings ago and sat on this bed beside me and talked to me and I politely hadn't answered him to show he didn't need to.

He looked up at me and flushed a bit (perhaps I am an unpleasant memory) and mumbled "Howd'ydo" and then looked back at his boots again as if he did not expect me to answer.

But I decided to be more talkative today. Though this may be a selfish point of view, it is very boring taking care not to force yourself on people. I said, "Oh, that's nice. You're preparing for a good big hunt, are you?"

"Well, we have one whenever possible, we all get something every day (well, if we're lucky, I mean) but we thought the forests might be interesting—we thought you might like to join in—"

"How kind of you all to think of the hostages. But we don't know *how* to hunt, as a matter of fact, do we, Ijleldla?"

"It's only a matter of riding with us—I mean, you won't have to kill anything—"

"What fun!" said Ijleldla.

May He be one of the hunt?

Oh, He may, He may.

Of course, I didn't like to ask, though several times during the evening I thought of doing it.

Onosander came in and got told and boyishly whooped with glee and threw his hat in the air and couldn't catch it again.

While Ijleldla and the Leader Alurg dived to pick it up for him, Iren and Smahil came in.

"Oh, hello, everybody," said Iren. "You're all early," and then saw that the Leader was not, after all, someone she knew. Well, everybody got introduced and Ijleldla fluttered round pouring drinks for us all. The Leader settled down a bit again. He said he was enjoying himself and he promised not to tell his brother officers what good wine the hostages have as they'd descend on us like a horde of locusts and Ijleldla said, "We wouldn't mind a bit, we love company."

"The officers have been ignoring us a bit, have they not?" said Iren.

The Leader looked uncomfortable again and said, Well, it is delicacy, they'd never really wondered if we'd like a bit of their life, and Iren said, "The whole point was, wasn't it, they hadn't deigned to bother us, that *was* the point, wasn't it?" and the Leader looked more uncomfortable still.

"Well, now he has found out how good our wine can be you won't be lonely any more, girls," said Smahil, and he winked at me.

I don't know whether he was equating me with Iren and Ijleldla or not, but I felt angry at the thought.

I did not give him a friendly expression in return for his wink but merely looked at him; with a sort of half-frown I could feel gather on my face.

"I shall wear my yellow one with the silky trousers," Ijleldla said.

"My blue," Iren decided.

Ijleldla said, "It would be fun to have lots of officers here every night."

"Not too many, we'd all be sitting on each other's laps," Onosander pointed out.

"That might not be *too* bad," said the Leader.

"Oh, you are dreadful," Iren squeaked with laughter, the squeaky coy sort only the person who is making it thinks sounds natural.

Smahil leaned across the bed between me and the Leader and asked in a voice below the others, "Why are you scowling at me?"

I didn't realize I still had the frown on my face and said, "Oh, I'm not really, I mean there isn't any reason."

72

"Well, don't," he said. "It makes you look awfully bad-tempered."

The Leader had to squiggle away from me over Ijlelda's bed-covers when Smahil moved in between him and me. Now he jumped up and said to Ijleldla, "Oh, I'm sorry, Ladyness, I seem to have sat on a kind of package."

"Oh," cried Ijleldla, swooping at a little oval embroidered bag which had slipped from beneath the Leader off the bed, "I shouldn't have had it there, it's only my night-things."

"She wears pale pink night-things," Iren said.

"Oo!" said Ijleldla, trying to hit Iren on the head with the bag, "Don't tell everybody!"

"Transparent," added Smahil.

"How *dare* you?" Ijleldla giggled, scandalized. "How do *you* know?"

"Iren told me," said Smahil, getting up from beside me and dodging both Iren and Ijleldla.

"You mustn't discuss my night-things with people!" Ijleldla cried, turning on Iren and this time, after a tussle, managed to bring the bag down on her head.

It burst and a lot of transparent pale pink gushed out of it.

"How I'd like to see you in these!" chorted Onosander, picking up the trousers and dancing about with them.

Ijleldla made a laughing, agonized dash at him, found Iren had grabbed the shirt, dashed at her, chased them both round. Iren tossed the shift to Smahil, who got chased, and leaped over me and the Leader. Iren leaped over us too (she now had the trousers) and Ijleldla followed, wailing loudly. The Leader got rather trampled on.

"Oh, dear," he said to me, "perhaps your friend would prefer it if I left her tent now." He was rubbing a grubby patch on the glossy polish of his left boot where Ijleldla had inadvertently stepped on him.

"Oh, no, why should you think that?"

"Well—it seems to be rather an intimate incident—"

"It seems a shame for you to go now."

"Yes, but the starlight outside is very charming" (which sounded feeble to me, I must say) "—Perhaps you'd care to join me, a walk round for a while?"

"A *lovely* idea." I cried, jumping at it. Ooldra says the more officers in the army I get to know the better.

"Good," he said, looking quite pleased at my enthusiasm. "Is this your cloak, here, behind you, then?"

"Yes," I said and he put it round me and we stood up and went out.

It was dark and, of course, fresh but not really chilly outside. We walked quickly past the bird-pickets there and away from the tent till all the noise and laughter inside had died away.

"What a lot you hostages are," he said. "At least *you* look sane. Well, you *look* sane. Aren't they at all nervous? I mean, they're very young to be hostages."

"Nervous? We weren't aware there was anything to fear. Has He decided to eat us all for his breakfast in future?"

He laughed, rather doubtfully.

"Oh, no. No. But they're not exactly marching into a land of milk and honey and—"

"Go on."

"Well, it's going to be a pretty tough campaign in places, anyway it now seems as if it's going to be. The maps we were given seem to have been inaccurate, to say the least, in places—"

We edged round past some more pickets (we had to keep among the more populated parts, it's not allowed to walk among the tents at night, the men are supposed to sleep, it's everybody's duty to be tireless when on the march) and he recollected himself and said, "Of course, I'm not trying to alarm you in any way, everything will be just fine if we're careful—"

Well, I asked him a lot of questions about where we are going and why and at first he evaded the questions just so as not to go on about wars and everything but in the end he got rather worked up and I learnt quite a lot and this is what I learnt.

Their country is very enormous and powerful (and I believe this because even my mother said so) and it covers very nearly the whole North of our continent. And then there is quite a lot of lands that don't belong to anyone really except for a few odd tribes and then there is our country, on the West coast. All along the other coast apparently there are heaps and heaps of high dangerous mountains that no one has ever climbed to the seaside of because they are inhabited by lots of unsalubrious creatures. Then there are lots of plains and forests and rivers and things which is the part we're going through now and it is most enormous and will take a very long time and then there are some dreadful mountains stretched right across the continent in a great range from coast to coast. Behind it there is

74

another country, even bigger and more powerful than the Northern.

Well, the king of the Northern country needs as much of the *Eastern* coast as possible for trade and he has very little in his kingdom, big as it is, because of all the mountains along it which make it difficult for anyone to reach the shore or for ships to land there. And as for the Eastern coast outside his territories, that is impossible because of all the horrible tribes and the monsters and the jungles that cover the mountains there.

And we aren't much use, being on the *Western* coast, and not very interested in trade anyway and not having such a big country to look after.

So all that's left is the huge country South of the mountain range. It apparently has very good Eastern coasts, much more than it needs for itself, and the Northern Country sent some messengers on the long weary dangerous journey with many gifts, to ask the Southerners if it could trade with them or else use some of their more unused beaches for private trade.

And the Southerners, who apparently are very cruel and barbarous (even worse than the Northerners) and think themselves quite secure from any large force, behind their mountains, did something to the messengers, I couldn't gather quite what, but it was something adding insult to injury, like lopping off their limbs and then pickling them in front of their own eyes and then sending them back to their Northern king with the answer "No" and the messengers' own arms and/or legs, all pickled and nicely packed up, as return gifts.

Only about one third of the messengers managed to struggle back to their own kingdom. When their nation heard the message they had been given to carry back to their king, and saw the ghastly gifts, the whole Northern kingdom was absolutely furious at this answer to their peaceful overtures, and the mistreatment of their honourable emissaries. Also a bit alarmed. The messengers said they had seen signs of preparing for war in the Southern Emperor's capital—and who could the Southerners be planning to invade but them, none of the tribes and countries in between really warranted such preparations.

So the Northern King called many great councils and they all decided to send off their greatest General in command of as good an army as they could gather together and take the Southerners by surprise before all their plans were made, before they had time to make their own dreadful attack.

And the Northerners did not have a really big army since at

75

that time they were only just building up their territories and were attacking everyone in reach (us especially included). It took a lot of work to get up enough troops who've never before seen any action or hard campaigning (like it will be soon).

Now, I agree with what Smahil told me Onosander said—I hope they all kill each other and that'll be that.

"And now you are yawning," cried the Leader as I yawned. "I managed to get you away from that fair-haired fierce-looking youngster and then all we talk about is army business till it's time to return you to your chaperone! Next time you must tell about yourself, which will be a deal more pleasant and interesting."

In front of the tent he put his hands on my shoulders.

He leaned forward, but his eyes were questioning. I felt nervous but I was a bit surprised when at the last moment he kissed my face by the corner of my mouth. His own mouth was gentle but hard. I felt really odd being that close to someone of another sex.

He had put an idea in my head about Smahil. But as I went in to Ooldra, Iren and Smahil passed. Their arms were complicated around each other. She kept smooching her cheek against his as they mumbled, though he is not as tall as she is.

That's that. I am just an adjunct to their circle.

It is strange, here I am in this world—for a moving army is the world—and somewhere, somewhere in it there is also him. But we are apart, separated by rank and race, and he is never likely to meet me.

I *must* try *harder*.

I *must* try. Dignity, danger do not matter. Somehow, no not somehow, anyhow.

Ooldra says "Wait."

Ooldra is wrong.

Have just come back in, thrown off my cloak, Ooldra not in yet though it is terribly late. Gagl an endless talker. Should go to sleep but too cold and stiff so shall write. Have been out hours, went out immediately after deciding something must be done. Weary. Walked all round dark camp, among the large black tents and all the huge black frightening trees, was taken for one of the camp followers several times, one man (think he must have been a sentry) wouldn't be ignored, following me saying things. I was scared. He made a grab at me, I fell against a picket post, he reached behind me and grabbed me

76

back from knocking against the birds, and with the same movement pulled me up against him.

He said something about, Now then, wasn't I aware it was bed-time, and what was I doing, and I said, "Looking for the General's tent." But oh, I was scared. I have always hated people touching me too closely, and he was so near to me, and it wasn't that his breath was precisely bad, just hot and alien. He said again, "Now then, little girl, don't try to impress me, if you was bidden to the Tent you'd know where it was. And besides," he said, "I happen to know the Beauty's there to-night." "I do know," I said. "I'm just going there. Let me go." I wriggled a bit but his grip harshened and hurt. "Now, now," he said. "You don't want the Beauty to scratch out your most useful parts. Stay here and do your stuff." He yanked me down on the ground. I thought of screaming and screamed but my head had got entangled in the folds his cloak had taken at his movement, and the sound wasn't successful. I was too confused anyway to scream well. I thought then, as his other hand reached me, he'd fumble about in my bodice which is what happened to Mirianya the Beautiful Martyr in that book but he must have been a very forthright sort of man because he immediately pulled up my skirt. I brought up my knee and jabbed him in the stomach. He let go, cursed, and grabbed for me again but I scrambled up and ran. One of the bird-pickets heard and chased me a short way but I lost myself and him in the trees. For a while I heard both the picket and first sentry shouting behind me but got back here safely, except for scratches on legs from undergrowth, which of course can never be much cleared where we strike camp. Very late. Shall do better tomorrow night. Ooldra coming back now, yawning, which is a very unusually expressive gesture from her.

I love watching the Beauty brushing her hair.

Her hair is very thick. It is more than that. Now that I come to think of it, it is a peculiar texture. It is obstinate, tenacious as to its own shapes and not those its owner wishes it to take. The brush, held by her steady hand, does not falter in its rhythm, but the whorls of strong glistening black hair cling to the brush's bristles, attempt to foul them like strong waves hanging against the oars of a boat, and spring back into foam-shaped twists when the brush has forced through.

She prefers to brush her own hair. I think she loves it; it is recognizable even to me as an element; to her it must be a sensuous materialization of her own personality, which certainly is what she loves most deeply in all the world. I stand behind her and am allowed only to pour oil upon the hair when she is satisfied that she has brushed it to its full tameness for the night. Sometimes she likes me to braid it; at other times she is disturbed if I so much as touch it. Twice, when I have touched it without her expecting it, she came out of the trance the brushing induces in her and turned on me with a sort of snarl. For it is a trance which her own hair induces in her; and it is the hair which does it, more than the regular movement of the brushing. When her hair is loosened completely at night it is like a cloud of some black, static, ominous wind. Its own natural scent is powerful, and it is not fine or soft to touch, but very coarse.

But tonight I am in the chamber alone, for she has gone early to his tent.

The minute I was left alone in this one I leapt all over the Beauty's bed, and mine, and swung from the cross-bar, and did cartwheels all round the walls.

I used to be very good at cartwheels when I was in the tower, but I hadn't done one for months. There is such a space here! It is really three tents with their interior walls looped back to make one. Oh, beautiful big tent, in which I am quite alone without the crippling fear of Ooldra's imminent entrance! I have rifled the Beauty's sparkling chiselled-crystal chest of unguents, and wiped her dusky pink on my mouth, not as much as she uses but enough to make me quite different from usual, but I dared not use any of her exquisite scents for she would be sure to recognize any of them on me. There is only one lamp in the whole tent, here, beside my bed, but the shadows are so gentle on the silken textures of everything here that I feel made happy by them, much less frightened. The bottles and boxes on her table sparkle at me. They are like jewels, each facet of their surfaces has become larger as if trying to reach out of their darkness towards my light, and the movement of the lamp flame causes them to seem glowingly to expand and contract.

It was silly of me.

Of course I should have known.

Ijleldla had kept so quiet whenever the General was mentioned. Even a moment's thought would have shown she was at the edge of a big crush on him.

How she found out where his Tent is, and where he rides, when I have been trying for a couple of months, I do not

78

know; but I suppose she used some quite simple expedient, such as asking someone, which I had always been too full of guilt-complex ever to think of.

Anyway, one day when I was riding with Ow and the animals, Ijleldla on a horse sidled up.

"Hello, Cija. A lovely sunny day."

"Oh, yes, it might be, if one could see it between all these leaves. What are you doing on a horse?"

"Riding it," Ijleldla said in an airy way, but with an unnecessary simper. She was so obviously looking natural, that I felt suspicious.

"I always thought you preferred a coach." At this moment Iren's carriage bowled up to us, scattering the geese, with Onosander and Smahil riding beside it. I thought Ijleldla looked annoyed. But she greeted them prettily, and said, "I told you there was no need for you to come. I was only passing the time of day with Cija."

"No, it's nicer now we're all together," stated Iren. "It's quite fun, actually, here with all these animals and things, isn't it? Perhaps we could come here oftener."

I hardly had time to reflect anxiously on this. Ijleldla gave a loud and ear-shattering scream, and careered wildly away from us.

"Her horse is bolting with her!" cried Onosander and he and Smahil galloped in pursuit.

I had seen, I was sure, Ijleldla kick her heels into the sides of her horse and yank its rein sideways. The scream had diverted one's attention, but it had seemed to me *quite* an uncalled-for scream. Leaving Iren, squeaking questions and futilely fluttering in her unwieldy carriage, I followed more coolly after the two boys.

(We all went slower than we'd have liked, of course, because of all the roots and leaves and creepers, etc., everywhere in the way, and the animals will shy at all the insects about. Most of them are harmless. But they are so big and make such a whirring noise as they hover on the thick green air with their wings going so fast in order to keep them motionless that they are only a sort of glinting invisibility. Actually it was much worse beside the river, with all those gnats and mosquitoes and clouds of midges and things.)

Now I come to the part I do not understand.

The long hairy leaves of the creepers bent to quiver on my face—my neck—Smahil and Onosander seemed to draw far ahead but I was being pushed back and held back—I grew

79

afraid as Sheg stumbled on roots which seemed to thrust themselves suddenly before his feet which were usually so magically alert—I lost all sight and sound of the two ahead, there were only Sheg and I and the millions of trees and the warning, quivering, incessant touches of the leaves—there were no familiar sounds, no lowing, no tortured screeching of wheels. I began to think I had been separated from the train.

"Sheg!" I cried. "Sheg! Turn back, you have lost us!"

I do not understand how I came to fear so.

I am not usually imaginative—or I do not usually believe in my imaginativeness.

But the forest itself did not seem unfriendly to me. It was warning me—in this ridiculous, fearful waking dream I had—it was trying to push me back, even the touches on my face were attempting to turn me, the whole unfamiliarly quiet forest was frantic with a need to *warn* me; not to threaten me. "Sheg!" I said, and I began to believe the forest. "Sheg, turn back! You—you have lost us! We are on the wrong track!"

And all the time I knew that we were not lost, that we had merely drawn ahead of the baggage-train for a few yards, and that if I kept still I would know what the forest knew. But something else in me, though not myself, was desperate *not* to know; and Sheg went on, his ears flattened with a strange quiet fury every time a root deterred him. He stumbled and kept on and I clung with both hands to the horn of my saddle and the long leaves came faster, faster, more desperate on my face and neck—and they fell back as the sunlight burst like a clarion call full upon myself and Sheg, and see, we were in a clearing and Ijleldla was speaking with the General.

That was the first thing I saw, though funnily enough Onosander and Smahil were between them and me and should have been the first things to meet my eyes.

But he wore a great cloak—a heavy sheepskin cloak but of no normal sheepskin: it was the pelt of a golden beast, a ram of gold, and the sun struck blinding stars from it that hung dazzling in its substance. His chest was bare—and, oh, my unknown Cousin, my own God, the sun struck sparks also from the scales of his chest and arms. Except in strong light one can mistake him for a man, but now he stood, clearly seen, a monster—and, my God, he was *beautiful!* I found him beautiful, in his arrogance and his evil, shining like a mighty dragon that fears nothing! It was only the illusion of a moment but oh, my Cousin, I should not have felt like that. And it seemed so real!

There were other men about—Clor, Eng the second-in-command, others of the highest captains. They had apparently stopped here, apart from the main train, for a short conference of some sort—over on the edge of the space, slaves and servants were preparing a meal. The space was full of people, but Ijleldla and I would have been the only women had it not been for the Beauty. The Beauty sat a white bird at the far end of the space and watched us all.

I got Sheg in between Onosander and Smahil.

"What is all this, for heaven's sake?" I demanded.

"Dear Cija, always irritable. Ijleldla just ran smack into the General, who grabbed her bridle for her and stopped her. That's all."

"What are they saying?"

"Nothing much, it's only just happened, Ijleldla is apologizing and the General being polite—but if you shut up we can hear more clearly."

Ijleldla was gazing up into the General's eyes in a nauseating coy way, which I recognized with half shock and half amusement as the expression I had assumed to attract him on the occasions I had met him. Ijleldla's obviously came from the heart. But even as Smahil and I stopped talking the General nodded to Ijleldla in his cursory way and turned from her. It was a dismissal.

I understood the desperation she was feeling—but would never have had the courage to do what she did: she ran to him, put her hand on his arm and looked up into his face with a look so openly languishing that I felt embarrassed for her.

"Thank you again," was all she could think of to say. "I should have more control of my animal."

Over by the edge of the forest the Beauty's imperious brows twitched together.

I know now that Ijleldla would have got away with it had she attracted him, but he was bored, perhaps, or already cloyed. "Excuse me, lady," he said impatiently, "your horse ran straight at me. Be satisfied with that."

Ijleldla's hand fell.

None of us would have understood his sentence if Ijleldla had not made it so obvious that it must all have been a subterfuge; but Onosander started forward in fury.

"Do you insult my sister?" he cried.

The General stopped again and turned to look him over.

"Well?" Onosander shouted. "We understand your filthy jibe, don't think it will be tolerated." I pressed Sheg a little further forward. Onosander's handsome gallant young face was lilac and his adam's apple bobbed convulsively and righteously among the corded veins standing out on his neck. He clenched his fists and strode close enough to the General to look him in the face. I shared his fury, for the General's insult had been unforgivably in the worst of taste. Without even giving the General an invitation to apologize or retract, Onosander cried, "You filthy reptile!" and hit him across the face.

He waited for a moment, but the General did nothing. We had all known he would do nothing, for Onosander was a hostage and a younger smaller man and it would have been foully dishonourable to attack him. Then Onosander gave a little contemptuous laugh and strode away.

The General was looking amused.

"Jaleth," he said casually, "take this lord away and give him six lash strokes."

Jaleth made a sign. Two men came forward and seized Onosander.

His face had fallen from disdainful pride and conscious courage to amazement and horror, but even as they dragged him to a tree and competently bound him, face towards it, I could not believe anything except that the General was bluffing, and would release him if Onosander apologized or begged for mercy. But the General said nothing, and one man lifted a huge plaited whip—an instrument of pain, stiff with lines of serrated metal like no whip I have ever seen before—and brought it down whistling on Onosander's back.

Ijleldla whimpered. She was too shocked to scream yet.

The cruel metal points tore immediately through Onosander's jerkin, and down it, making in the cloth a long wide-topped gash with red edges. As the whip lifted again we saw Onosander's back, pale flesh gouted with oozing swelling crimson. That had only been the first stroke. Onosander sagged pitiably from his bound wrists. There had been two screams just then: one was Ijleldla's and the other Onosander's.

I hesitated a moment as the second stroke came down. But Smahil had not even leant forward on his bird; his lips were tight but that was all. I was the only other one. I ran to the man with the whip and caught his hand, clinging to the wrist, as it came down. Even so I couldn't deflect the blow. The thin points fell sideways across Onosander's shoulders, each point drank new blood. I was close to Onosander now, and saw the ripped flesh, the patterns the points had made on the edges of the rips, the little torn hanging strips of skin, the blood swelling

82

over big bruises already dark green. It was all shaking: Onosander was sobbing. I felt rather sick.

The whipman glared at me but I still had his wrist and he was not sure what he was supposed to do to me. The General came up and stood a few moments with his thumbs in his belt, like a big kindly uncle examining me, rather quizzically because I had done something unprecedented.

"Is this how Northerners treat their honourably given hostages?" I panted.

He didn't bother to answer. He never speaks unless he feels like it; he prefers to watch people speaking to him. That it discomposes them is only incidental, though I don't suppose it displeases him.

"Loose Onosander," I said, nearly crying now and afraid that I would disgrace myself before him by it.

He smiled at me, a slow friendly smile, the first time I'd seen an expression like that on his face, and at the same time his hand made a sign to the whipman who proceeded again. I got hold of the General's arm with both hands and tried to shake it. I found that I *was* crying now. I cried out "Stop it, please, please, oh, Onosander"—I couldn't think of a constructive sentence but it would have made no difference, even to me my words sounded indistinguishable from my sobs. At this moment I saw Smahil dismount quickly and come over to me but I only remembered that afterwards, at the time it made no impression. I did realize, however, that the General was laughing. He stopped my hand easily as it seized at the dagger in his belt and at the sensation of his fingers on my wrist I stopped crying. My head was aching badly, the sun was broiling down. They had stopped whipping Onosander, who could now be heard sobbing quite loudly. I did not know whether they had stopped whipping him because of the disturbance or because he'd now had his six strokes. The General's harsh fingers were still round my wrist. He must know, I thought, that I hate him. But it had all been so involuntary and confused that I could not even remember if, when I had seized at his dagger, I had meant to kill him.

At this second the Beauty spoke.

"Well, what a hostage this is," she remarked interestedly. "Absolutely charming. I wish I'd seen her before this. I could have had her as a personal maid all this time instead of that insipid plump slave."

"A good idea," the General said politely to her, and led me over. She looked down at me appraisingly. She seemed to approve. I don't know why, I had been crying very hard and unbecomingly and my nose was running, I can't have looked very prepossessing. Perhaps, on second thoughts, that is why.

"What is her name?" she asked the General. "Do you know?"

"I've forgotten her name," he said. It didn't occur to either of them to ask me. "But she is the most important of them—she is the bastard of the Dictatress and her High Priest."

"All the better," she said.

They stopped looking at me and I realized I was supposed to move behind her. I was hers from now on. But I had to have Sheg—I was shaking with unexpected triumph and excitement—and I ran over to get him. She gave me a look of surprise as I left her but didn't say anything. Smahil followed me. As I mounted Sheg he said, "So now you're a personal slave to a General's jumped-up Northern mistress." "In this community it's higher than any of us have been before," I stated. He looked satirical but I was wildly excited at my good fortune—there was no longer any chance of seducing the General. But I was going to be near him the whole time, my chances of assassination would be *legion*—I pictured Ooldra's face as I told her—the years of waiting, for they seemed years, were over—and I glanced coldly at Smahil, whom I had begun to despise for not coming to Onosander's rescue, and prepared to ride back to the Beauty.

"Well," said Smahil, "—I suppose we shan't see each other again for some time."

"Probably not," I said vaguely and spurred after the Beauty, who was already riding away, together with all the others who'd been in the clearing. I had to swerve to avoid Ijleldla, who was lying huddled on the ground whimpering and wheezing hysterically. Over at the tree two soldiers were unbinding Onosander. He stumbled away from them dazedly. I didn't want to talk to him. The Beauty was disappearing among the trees. As I caught up with her I realized that Smahil had been saying good-bye, and I had been both rude and careless; I was sorry, but it did not matter much because now I was no longer a hostage, one of those downtrodden parasites ignored by everyone important. I was a member of the General's entourage.

At first, it didn't work out as well as I'd expected. I had thought I would be allowed to have Ooldra with me, but the Beauty said she couldn't be bothered with a troop of women in her tent, two was plenty. "Ooldra isn't a troop," I said. "She's *my* maid." "Maids don't have maids," said the Beauty, frowning. "Stop jabbering and braid my hair." I think that, when she remembers about it, she gets a kick out of knowing that she has the daughter of a country's Dictatress for her maid.

Ooldra was funny about it, too. She seemed almost annoyed when I told her about my luck.

"But, Ooldra, now my chances are innumerable! It's the best thing that could have happened—we didn't dream of it because it would have seemed so impossible. You told me to get near to him."

"Getting near to him is a different thing from being actually in his entourage."

"But—Ooldra—you don't mind? You want me to stay—I know it's—"

"Very well then, tell her you need me with you."

But as I've said, that didn't work out. And really, I'm glad. I feel unimaginably free without Ooldra all the time. I never thought her absence could have made such a difference.

I have seen the hostages once again. Yesterday, as I rode on an errand for the Beauty, I passed them. Iren leaned out of her carriage and pulled at my sleeve. I had to chatter with her for a few minutes. She, at least, seems very envious and impressed by my advancement. It is nice to be openly envied and deferred to by her, when I remember how she was always queen of our little society and took it for granted that she completely overawed me. From the corner of my eyes I saw Ijleldla, stiff and pale, eyeing me as if she hated me. Smahil nodded but made no further move than I did. He does not appear to think of my change as an "advancement". Onosander was not with them, and at that time neither was Ooldra.

But I have more important things to think of.

For one thing, life now is very gay and full of laughter and music and luxury. I am already accepted as one of the belles of the army. I now have a dozen young leaders like Alurg around me, and several higher serving-men, though I admit no one pays me more attention than any of the other girls about gets. The food is wonderful and Sheg has just had to make his mind up to get used to a new groom, someone or other who must be far more self-effacing than Blob, since I can't even recall having noticed him. The Beauty is very fond of music, or possibly noise; there is always someone with an instrument near her, usually one as discordant and twangy as possible, like a ghirza or one of those little drums worn slung from the neck. I claim

85

ours is the safest part of the whole army to ride in, for it is certainly the noisiest. (Apparently the meeting we came upon that day in the clearing was *because* of the clearing. For it *was* a clearing—there were recent axe marks on some of the bordering trees, and old stumps in the grass. We are in a part of the jungle thickly inhabited by people of some sort, not inclined to be friendly to intruders or so the legends say, but our noise and numbers and weapons are confidently expected to keep them from attacking. Anyway, it's a funny feeling that we're being watched from every side as we move.)

And there's another thing to think of.

He has no idea I hate him—I have spoken with him twice since that day, he comes to this tent sometimes in the evenings and speaks pleasantly with the Beauty and her companions and eats fruits and listens to the boy with the ghirz—and he is amused with me for that day. Last night he put his hand under my chin. "Do you still hate me, Goddess?" he asked while she laughed. Though she never does so, she likes him to call me Goddess, it reminds her that she owns something considered important. "Why, no," I stuttered vehemently, blushing hotly. It was of course the best thing I could have done, though it would not have been except for his stupidity and conceit. So he laughed and they went out together. He looked a look at me, though carelessly, as he left. I am afraid of that one. I shall kill him, soon.

And today we reached the riverfalls.

We should have heard them far in the distance for many days, their thunderous plurality of every single drop, roaring and yet tintinnabulating, becoming less of a roaring echo and more of an echoing roar every day—but our own noise covered that and only yesterday evening did I first hear their unmistakable sound. And it was loud then.

Today we marched beside the lurching river, half faded by strong sunlight and half in gurgling mauve shadow from the high right bank, but all rushing and sweeping and hurling and throthing around sharp rocks. As we went on the bank became unsteady. Immense masses of green stuff drooped to the water; and the whirling spray spurling over the rocks sucked powerfully at the vegetation masses and beat incessantly, tearing through their heavy fronds. How many seconds of how many minutes of how many days of how many years of how many decades of how *many* centuries had this river beaten its drops through the vegetation masses on its banks, I wondered. And

86

the weight of the drops in the hanging fronds had pulled the roots cracking an inch a year through the rock of the bank. There were big splits, and cracks. As we passed, each man's step loosened more stones for the danger of the man behind; and several men, up and down the line, and some animals, were lost in the green and mauve and spurling cream torrent below before their nearest companions could catch at them.

Now the sound we had been hearing resolved into vision. As we turned with the bend of the river through the jungle trees we thought at first that we were seeing an uncanny wind in the great arching pale growths before us; but at the instantaneous shift in our focuses we saw they were not growths but curving sheets of pale-green water hurling from awesome heights and leaping again to that height in a continuous yellow-white mist which because of its great speed appeared always to be the same, and quivering but rooted.

"Death of the Serpent," breathed the Beauty, which was to her a blasphemy signifying slightly alarmed admiration.

It was at this instant, when most of us in the van were staring at the falls, that the bolas came at us. Almost half of the soldiers before me were killed before I had realized what the heavy whirr was; but it was a covey of bolas, and the stones on the ends of the thongs had been whirled round the heads of our assailants and let fly so that each one was accurate. Someone, probably Clor who was near me, knocked me from Sheg to the ground; I thought in furious bitterness, "Has he turned against us now in this time of need?"—then realized he had only just saved me from a bolas which skirred over me and knocked the boy with the ghirza off his bird and toppling, his body slowly arching—at least it appeared slow to me at that time—and his neck already broken, down into the raging water below.

Down among Sheg's dangerously hesitant feet, I met the eyes of the Beauty. She had not been pushed but thrown from her bird. It was dead. We scrambled away together among the claws to the side, immediately above the river. She was laughing a little, silently, from pleasure in the excitement. "This is like that day, ages ago, of the storm in the mud," I said. She nodded, her eyes alight, before I remembered that she could not get my full meaning. But the general chaos was the same. Or worse. Our men were sending javelins into the trees in the direction from which the bolas had come, but now more were killed, and from a different direction. The Beauty and I crouched on the unsteady rock above that awful water. She was laughing aloud now, her crystal head-circle had been lost in the scramble and her black hair was whorling across her face and shoulders. I had never imagined her scurrying and crawling over the ground between moving claws, but her dignity wasn't lost. It was intrinsic. "Lady," I said, wondering at her, "your white gown is all rent and fouled." Quiet, slave," she said. "Must you be maid enough to worry about your work even at a time like this?"

Two men pitched past us into the water and we edged along to a cleared place. As we did so we felt the stone rock under us. The Beauty lurched to the side but caught her balance again a I grabbed frantically to steady her ankle. She turned back on me a moment, snarling at the interference as she does when I unexpectedly touch her hair, and we crawled onwards, one behind the other, keeping scrupulously to the centre of the rock so it could not sway too much to either side. As we reached the next rock, that one pitched behind us into the river. It had been balancing on a single up-thrust knife-edge of packed earth.

"Stand up," the Beauty ordered, "and see what is happening."

"It's all confusion, all of it confusion—men knocked off their birds and horses by bolas—some dying on the ground—ah!" "What is it?" she said sharply. "Sheg—my bird is trampling on a man—oh, God, I feel sick. Pity me, Lady. Let me down, don't make me stand any longer." "On your feet, fool. Where is he? What is happening with him?" I stared before I realized she meant the General. I shook off her hand at that moment. For a while she seemed corrupted, because even the parts of her which were inmost had been given over to his use. "He is alive," I said, as expressionlessly as I could. "There is only blood on his shoulder where a bolas' stone that was jagged got him. It is shining, very thick blood," I added, half reproaching her. But she only said, "Yes, his blood is like that . . . Is he fighting mightily?"

I was about to reply that his javelin throwing was no worse than anyone else's, when suddenly our opponents appeared, rushing out of the trees and whirling their bolas as they came.

They whirled their bolas about their heads so that one could hardly tell which was the shining of their scales and which the half-visible swing of their weapons, and as they hurled them they shrieked. Long hair streamed behind them. Their shrieks were ululating and their eyes glared pallid yellow, like angry mucus.

"They are scaled," I said in horror. I added weakly, "Perhaps some of his kindred?"

"The Fouls!" she cried without hesitation. And leaped up and ran.

She raced to the head of the promontory, straight towards the falls, where on the bank the vegetation was thickest. As I raced after her I was foolhardy enough to look back. The foul creatures were all in among our men now. They were few in comparison, but had not only the advantage of surprise but the swifter weapon from a distance—for they could throw before a sword could reach, and a javelin is no good at all to throw in a crowd, being so long—and they seemed to be everywhere. I did not know the Fouls lived in these forests. My feet pelted on after her towards the falls, and I heard my own terrified dry-weeping as I ran.

Into the shelter of the thickest trees above the falls had been pushed the oxen, geese, and hostages.

The Beauty reached there first, passing within the haze of water drops which hung in all the air there around the head of the falls. I thought she would gain refuge among the trees, but her plan had changed. She seized his sword from Smahil.

"No, Lady," he said through the roar of the riverfalls. "Take Onosander's, he has no use for it anyway." He took his own back from her.

"Onosander?" she repeated, puzzled. Smahil pointed at one of the carriages.

Now I passed within the moist haze, and cried, "Smahil! Onosander has no use for his sword—Is Onosander dead?"

Smahil glanced at me as if he saw me every day. "Onosander's lying in his carriage," he said, "as he has been for over a week now, a chronic invalid."

"*Oh*—was the whipping that bad?"

"His sister insists it was."

"Lady," I cried, as the Beauty reappeared with a sword, "you aren't going to fight! You must stay here." I didn't think she'd heard me and I left Smahil and ran to her. "Don't importune your kind precious mistress," Smahil said dryly. "But perhaps you mind if she kills herself." Then I came to my senses. It didn't matter to me if she died. In fact, she'd be more useful out of the way. I was her servant for only one reason. And Smahil was right, she was one of our enemies, and one of those with power and position among her kind. A minute before, I had been thinking of the fight as between "our" men and the Fouls: but they were all aliens, enemies. In this case, at least, Smahil could not be called a coward though he did not fight. I stood back.

But the Beauty did not mean to fight, merely to stand guard with a sword.

"Get a weapon, silly little deity," she commanded me fretfully. She did not want me dead.

I looked round. I did not want her to see the one I always carry sheathed on my neck-chain, under my clothes.

Smahil handed me the dagger from his belt. I took it as silently as it was offered, and held it in my hand. I looked around me for Ijleldla, Iren, and eagerly for Ooldra, but saw only Noble Gagl and the Lady Ronea staring from the window of a carriage. Ow and the other boys stood in a tight group among the animals. We looked recognition at each other but could not bring ourselves to wave or call out. Then I felt a gladness as if I had come home; another carriage door opened, and Ooldra stepped out towards me.

"Ooldra!" I cried.

She reached me gravely. "Cija," she said. "Are you rejecting at last your ideals, your mother and your country?"

"Ooldra," I whispered, taken aback, "what are you reproaching me for? Ooldra! You must know *I* have done nothing."

She glanced at the Beauty and lowered her voice below the water-roar. "Yes, Cija, and it grieves me that you should say it! You, the strongest hope your mother had!"

"Ooldra, don't talk in riddles! I beseech you, what have I done? I swear to you I love my mother—but you know that, how should I need to swear to you on—"

"Nothing. You have done nothing. Even now the Northerners are winning. While the battle lasts, change your mind, deny your repudiation, seize loyalty again and kill the Monster whle there is yet time!"

"But, Ooldra," I cried, amazed, "what are you saying? I can't run into that inferno and simply kill him!"

"You were nearer before and rejected your chance. No one would have noticed in the confusion. You must run in again —"

"No, I won't. I'm not going to. I can't, Ooldra!—you must see—the Fouls—"

"You must," she said, catching my arm in her strong hand. "You will come to no harm—Cija, listen to me, I tell you I know you will come to—"

Suddenly I stopped struggling as I felt Ooldra's fingers prised one by one but swiftly and inexorably from my arm. Smahil held her hand. Their eyes met in mutual surprise.

"Lord Smahil, loose me," she said quietly but so that he realized, if he had forgotten, that it was an impertinence to touch her so.

But Smahil remarked, in a very courteous tone but without apology, "Lady Ooldra, you seemed to be pushing the Goddess in the direction of the battle. No matter what your argument with each other, surely it should be left till another time——" As he spoke, neither Ooldra nor I smiled, which might have been easing for him since he had chosen a light tone. I was weeping inside myself. Did Ooldra think me false for not seizing such a chance to kill Him? For her to despise me——. But the thought of rushing into that chaos filled me with a sick panic. I could not tell myself that neither would the Fouls mark me down nor one of His side see me and testify later against me—the Beauty here would see, for one—and did Ooldra, even Ooldra, think it possible to reach back to civilization again, alone, through this forest? Oh, my mother, I must fail your strongest hope! For if my body *will not* believe myself and Ooldra, I *shall* falter and perish!

The battle was swaying nearer to us. I heard screams from the carriages behind me. The Fouls, from the start, had been herding the Northerners to the bank.

The General was fighting with a sword in one hand and a javelin held shortened to stab with in the other. I turned to Ooldra and her gaze left Smahil's for mine. Hers was compulsive. I longed to be worthy of her. I wanted to nod but I couldn't. However, her eyes must have sensed my yearning. She reached across Smahil and pushed me with great force so that when I had stopped skidding and had stumbled back to balance I was beside Him. There was a Foul on his back and another one at his throat. Both were screaming vilely with excitement and triumph. I hesitated another moment, but my hope that they would kill him for me went as first one, then the other on his back, were hurled to the ground gurgling and tossing about in agony at his stabs. I ran in, Smahil's dagger raised for His throat. I filled my mind with Ooldra's eyes for my only confidence. As I ran, He turned and saw me with surprise. There were Fouls about us but they had almost all lost their bolas and their teeth and claws were no match for the soldiers' swords. "In another minute they will win. It will all be over," I thought desperately. "I am here, I must kill him *now,*" I went for his throat. His arm caught me. I thought, "He is holding me from him." But he was not. His arm turned me and as I lifted the dagger back I saw Smahil race in amongst the fighting and round to push me away. In a moment the chance was lost, He and I were separated. "Loose me, Smahil," I sobbed. "What have you done?" "Come to your sense, Cija," I heard his anxious voice. He seemed to have been saying it, sharply so that I should hear, over and over. The fighting-sound receded but another took its place. "You have brought me beyond the trees," I said. "Hush," Smahil said. "You can't go back just yet. Do you want her to thrust you into your death again? You were lucky the General caught you. Gods, Cija, now I know why you left for that woman's service! Ooldra is half-mad. Why does she hate you?"

I could not tell him the real reason for Ooldra's forcing me into the danger. We lay and panted in the long grass. We were hidden beneath the tanglings of several low bushes. Beside us the river flowed deep, and smooth as wimpled blue glass; immediately below us it poured over the cliff frothing and spuming, roaring reverberating beating on itself, white ever-moving-always a roaring wall.

I turned and saw Smahil's face a few inches from me but rainbow-shaded through the water-mist we were lying in and which the sun struck on.

"Over there," I said, pitching my tone beneath the tone of the falls, "they are killing the Fouls that are left. They have won. Shall we go back now?"

"Wait," he said, "till all is clear. You must ride with the Beauty as usual and try not to pass Ooldra."

I suppose he did not ask again about Ooldra from delicacy. We lay side by side, quite still, in the mist, watching the scene far down the bank. Their actions seemed unreal, since we could hear no sound of theirs though from the slaughtering going on there should have been lots. The animals were re-ordering in the column. Little figures were running about in the orange sunlight, their tiny shadows being tugged wherever they went.

Smahil's hand was still about my wrist in the grass. Our fingers, our fingernails, every blade of grass was beaded with round silver drops. They hung on Smahil's skin, sliding very slowly, following each plane of his face, and hung from the tips of his eyelashes. Infinitesimal drops hummed in the rainbow air about us.

A little insect came flying, dipping drunkenly, its wings

waterlogged. We watched its unhappy movements. It lurched into my hair. It was so flimsy. Smahil fished it out. I caught at his raised arm. "Smahil, you are wounded!"

"What a melodramatic way of putting it! Now I feel a hero because I was lucky enough to be scratched with one of our own side's swords." He paused, on saying "our own side", but decided it was pointless to explain as we both knew what he meant.

"But you are hurt!" I insisted. "Here, even if it is not deep it must be bound up. Let me tear your shirt." He was wearing a loose fine white shirt. I put both hands to it and tugged it in opposite directions but it and the air were soggy. "Gods," he said. "Do I have to help you tear my own bandage? How fearsomely strong you are!" He tore a length for me and lay back to let me bind his arm. "It was very brave of you," I said, "to run in because you thought me in danger. With so much going on it was as easy to be cut down by a friend as a Foul."

"Thought you in danger!" he sneered a little. "You were in danger. There were two Fouls behind you and thank heavens several sword-waving Northerners missed you, by a hair's breadth! And the General couldn't have held you safe for ever. What do you think she pushed you into? A dainty little flower garden?"

I tied a knot with dignity.

"I only mentioned your bravery, and that because I thought you a coward. It was your place to run in to save Onosander that day."

"I didn't see that it was anyone's place. It wasn't doing him any harm."

"Wasn't—But then, I knew you never really liked Onasander. Are you jealous of him because of his robust handsomeness and—" I was about to say "tallness"—"gallantry?"

"He asked for that whipping. He insulted and struck the General in front of his men, then stood in front of him to give him the conventional chance to strike him back—he and everyone there knew he was perfectly safe, for the General wouldn't strike a hostage and a whipper-snapper into the bargain. And then he walked away with a careful contemptuous laugh, as if the General were a coward to stand there after being treated like that. For a start, the General had to let his men see how such behaviour was rewarded! For another thing—Onasander deserved it. I never expected you to take watching a whipping so hardly."

93

"I saved him something!"

"They let him tumble away after five strokes, if that's what you mean."

"Come on, Smahil. The affair's over. They're moving."

The clear silver beads quivered all together on his eyelashes as he turned to me.

"It was you used the word affair," he mumbled. I started to ask him what he meant, then realized he was closer to me than ever before. The water beads fell as he lowered his gaze to my mouth. He pulled me towards him across the blades of grass so wet that they and we seemed swimming in a stream. At the same time he pushed my head back so that I found I was lying looking up into close foliage and his wet lips were on my mouth. My fingers clutched but slid in the ripped folds of his shirt, but his body within them, heavy on my breasts, was warm though it was smooth with water. The incessant roar of the falls became rhythmic in my ears as his mouth opened mine. Our youth called us, called us closer than is possible. I had not realized being young could be so intense, not since my childhood and the intense sun-drenched days of joy and exploration and hate in the tower. It was not to the point whether Smahil cared for me or I for him. We lay, mouth fused to mouth, shoulder on shoulder, chest to breast, till quite suddenly I half-thought "This is going on too long. It's no longer new, it's time we went down or they'll move without us." I pulled away and turned my head. In the darkness of the low foliage Smahil gave me a surprised glance but of course neither of us spoke.

We stood up, went down the bank, blinking in the sudden hard sunlight.

I went to my place in the line beside the Beauty, and mounted Sheg. His claws were bloody and I loathed him.

Smahil went past Ooldra silently to his place. She stared after him. She was staring not at his bandage but at a tiny brand mark on his back, where the ripped shirt left it bare.

That evening the General came to the tent.

The Beauty cried out at the sight of him. His back was bound across and across, which showed under his cloak. The Foul must have scratched nearly all the skin off, and good luck to it, though it had not gone deep. Not satisfactorily deep, anyway. He was rather pale and could not make any movement except stiffly—which shows that it was bad, for he would have hidden that too if he could—but no pain showed on his face, though he smiled only twice and was grim or sullen all the time he was with us. The girls tried to turn their chatter, as always, to please him. The new ghirza boy, mindful of his fine brand-new position and its million chances, played his liveliest but did not get so much as a pat on the head. Lounging on the piles of scented cushions with his head in the Beauty's resilient lap (she kept saying "You shouldn't have come, you should rest, you must ride all day tomorrow," but I suppose he felt like resting that night on a softer mattress), he lifted his winecup to me for a moment, his eyes above the rim holding mine.

I stared back questioningly because I knew my question might be answered.

"Were you hurt?" he said.

They never use my name, even when they are being pleasant. They treat me always as a slave.

"No."

He raised his brows. They are very mobile, I can remember a time when that astounded me. "No? But you ran in among the fighters," he said. "I happen to be asking you about it."

"A woman pushed her," the Beauty said as I hesitated. "It was the woman you called your maid," she added, turning to me. "Now you must be glad that I did not allow you her here."

"She did not mean me harm," I defended Ooldra.

"Then she was lucky that none occurred," the General remarked. "What was this reason of hers?" I waited as the little winegirl saw that his cup was empty and scurried to pour it full again. My mind worked in a trap.

"Well?" said the General from the Beauty's lap as the winegirl went again and still I hesitated. He was now amused. He saw that I was uncomfortable and now it was certain that he would not let me go till I had given an answer.

Now the little winegirl spoke unexpectedly. She blushed hotly and stuttered. It was harder for her because the ghirza boy, who twanged his instrument softer when we spoke, did not do so for her. "Lord," she said. "My brother was with the goat herds and saw it. The woman who pushed cried out, 'There is a Foul on my Lord's back! Go save him with your knife, for he is hard-pressed!' "

I looked keenly at her. I already knew that Ow had a sister among the winegirls, and had guessed which was her, but that she should know when to lie for me was pretty helpful.

The General leaned back. He, also, looked surprised and almost disappointed at the turn the answer had taken when it actually came. "So Ooldra cared much for me this afternoon," he said. "I would not have thought it like her. Nevertheless she gave the edge of the job to you. Fill the Goddess' cup," he called, settling the matter (for he saw that my cup, which I had clutched and gulped at nervously, was empty) and a plump winegirl ran to me, for Ow's sister was still trembling from having spoken to the General.

It astonished me that he knew Ooldra's name. But I was not likely to get any explanation, and I went to other thoughts. In this entourage, one must expect only the possible and learn to change one's mind quickly and without regrets.

"Fill the Goddess' cup."

It is like a nickname now. Everyone calls me goddess, all the little slop-pages and the heathen babies carried on the backs of the camp-followers who know me. Is the blood in my very veins, my divinity to be mocked by the races born of the earth and natural to this world? No, not mocked—admitted but treated as nothing, but respected because neither understood nor thought of. At times I feel the anger of my God, not against me but against them. But I am helpless and, my Cousin, for the time being, ignored. What do we matter to Him?

He continued to talk with the Beauty for a while, and their voices were lower and private. But once he winced as if in sharp agony, before he could stop himself, and I don't suppose it was because of her stroking hand.

Finally the Beauty told us all to go. The groups stopped chattering a moment, rose and hurried out with their various paraphernalia. We had camped early this evening. The red sunlight still lay within the threshold. The nearest trees were black, but the foliages behind the sun were still feathery with its reflection, and held in their green golden all the colours that the sun gives an evening—pink and blue and peculiar violets. Beyond the doorway I stopped the little winegirl who had spoken. As I had thought, he had seen merely that I did not wish to answer for myself nor to blame Ooldra, and she did not discovered something that did neither. She was very shy and I soon let her hurry away, though I would have liked to talk further. I dropped the flap and went back in. The Beauty had doused the lamps, so that all the tent seemed as velvet a black as the cushions I knew they were lying on. But I know my way by now and walked without pause towards my own end. "They are all gone?" said the Beauty's voice. I didn't bother to answer the obvious. As I walked across the floor, treading the cushions left lying all about, my foot was caught in something hard. I tried to step it clear, then realized I was held. Iren and Smahil used to laugh about how keen the Beauty must be in order not to mind being chafed and crushed against him, but his skin is hypnotic and patterned-smooth and lithe as the touch of the snake Glurbia once caught in the tower, except that was cold and he is warm.

"Was the imperious Divinity frightened by the battle to-day?" the voice asked, laughing softly. Here was a chance to tease me. I kept my foot still.

"It's a few less people messing round in the world," I said.

He laughed, at me; my foot was released but tingled. I went on through the dark to my bed and dropped the flap across it so that I was alone in my own tent. As they murmured in the next room my knife jerked on my neck-chain.

I saw Ooldra the other day. She asked me what I meant by it; there are rumours that she had pushed me into the fighting to hurt me. I said surely that was better than anyone knowing it was to hurt the General, and she became very cold and hardly moved or spoke, like quiet ice. Then I said I had nothing to do with the rumours, and I had heard one that she did it to save the General because she feared very much for him. At that she became colder still and it was impossible to ask her why the General had mentioned her so by name. I left her because I can't leave my place for too long.

I hate riding Sheg. He is horrible.

The forest has begun to have a queer pervasive smell.

Not the usual smell, which is a compound—the odour of flowers living, dying and dead; and fruits living, dying and rotten; leaves and insects and bark and ferns and undergrowth and animals and water and sunlight on those things and shadow on those things—it is a smell which all these have taken alike. The other day when I pressed my face to a tree trunk to force to my senses for a while the clean pungent smell of bark—it would not come!

I smelt only the new universal smell.

One longs to smell something different. Everybody remarks on it. It is not that the new smell is what one would ordinarily describe as unpleasant—it is a puerile smell, strong only in quantity, not in pungency. Rather like rubber or stale water. Everyone's nostrils are burning from longing for anything else.

There are many theories but none seem sensible. Even the animals seem to find it oppressing, and I find we are all going more quietly.

I think the officers are worried about the men. There have been no real signs of strain so far, but they are after all raw troops.

Ious says there is danger from Fouls (or other tribes, maybe) too.

Ow's sister is really rather sweet. Whether she has chosen me to have a hero-worshipping crush on him I don't know; but she follows me about and looks long wondering looks at me from her wide eyes, and hangs trustingly on my silliest sentences. It is lovely. But she is a nice companion too. We giggle at the same things and have already evolved some private jokes—and it's not just imitation, for often she starts first; she is wild and shy, but not uncouth, for her life in the entourage has sophisticated her a little.

Her name is Narra. She is older than Ow, about eleven or twelve years old, and little and slim. She is very sweet and one day will be lovely.

The strange deadness of every other smell continues. Each step has become cautious.

Every here and there fire-embers glowed sluggish scarlet, if scarlet can be sluggish, in the rich camp-darkness, unaware of the stars. I pushed head and shoulders out of the cavern of the tent, then stood. I moved between the tents. No sentry challenged me. Even in the night I am familiar enough to be recognizable and my presence respected.

I wandered without a purpose. I longed for Ooldra, and half hoped that she would hear my longing and come to me; but it seems that wherever she was she slept, deep. I passed between the hoarse shadows of the birds and my confidence made their breathing no more irregular than as if I had not been there. Mostly the pickets can not even have been aware of my presence, for I wore my black cloak about my night-things. The tents slept.

Two bird pickets squatted before their line of charges. One of them had some round fruits—they must have been sneaked from the cookhouse. But he and his companion were not allowed to eat in peace. The end bird, hearing the munching, would not be quiet till it had been given some. It shuffled and thrust its beak against the man's shoulder and wimpered coaxingly. When it had been given some, to keep it quiet, the next bird knew it had been given something and was jealous, and made a fuss till it had a bite too. This stirred the bird beside it, and so on, till the other end had been reached. The men laughed and settled back to the fruits which were left. And yet I was quiet enough to observe all this unobserved.

So I was surprised when someone behind me said "Busy?"

I turned. "Not particularly," I said as composedly as I could. But my heart was beating to hurting-pace. He wore the gold sheepskin but in the starlight it too was heavy starlight, gold pale to silver. "Of course," I said, "I had forgotten your habit of wandering alone at sleeping-time."

"I never knew of yours."

"Only tonight, I could not sleep."

I must have started perceptibly when he spoke first: it probably pleased him but he didn't mention it, nor my confusion when I saw him. But a wish for him was something I had aimlessly formulated, when he spoke. I breathed thanks to Ooldra. Or perhaps my Cousin. I wished only that I could keep that note of defiance out of my voice nowadays when I spoke to him.

But he seemed to think it quite in order. "You know," he said, and he flicked a lazy finger under my chin, "I don't think you've forgiven me yet for that day of the whipping."

There was a subtle difference in his tone, it was not quite his usual tone. There was a caressing whimsical note in it—but smooth, too smooth.

"Of course, my Lord," I said. "Though it upset me a little."

"It was not like you, little hostage goddess, to run in to save someone pain, and in such a rage. Do you know, you even seized my dagger? Would you have forced yourself to threaten me with it?"

"I—I don't know," I said, afraid. "I have forgotten."

But he laughed. "You surprised me that day," he said. "I had not thought you could surprise me."

How spineless he must think me. Well, it's all the better. But why harp on that day, I thought impatiently, Why not talk of now? "My Lord," I said, "how beautiful your cloak is."

We were amongst the trees at the edge of the camp now, and as we went under their foliage the pelt ceased to shine. Startled, I felt his fingers on my wrist lead my own finger to the soft long-haired pelt. "Yes," he said. "Feel it, it is the finest sheepskin in the world."

"There is a sort of grittiness amongst the softness," I said.

"That is the gold."

"Was he a magic golden ram?"

99

He laughed loudly, one of the long uncomplicated shouts of laughter only men do not restrain. "How awed would you be if it was, little goddess?" he then said in his smooth teasing tone.

In the darkness I twisted my face into my hate for him. "Oh, my Lord," I said, "it seems you mock me, but truly how should I know whether there are golden rams or not?"

"I thought that the women of your country believe in anything."

"Anything?"

"Things they cannot see, the work of witches, divinity in their own bodies—"

It had had to come. "There is in our nation's veins the legacy of the gods who favoured our women in the ancient days," I stated furiously. "And each of my house are related more closely to the gods—"

"Do you call your race a nation?" he asked, amused. He had not bothered to listen to the rest.

"You are pleased to be contemptuous, my Lord."

"Is patriotism your only emotion?"

". . . My Lord?"

"I mention anything touching your country and you become quite unlike yourself. Come, you are usually sweeter than this." His hand was in my hair, caressing the side of my face, sliding against my neck, across down my shoulder, and back again. It was all I could do to keep from jerking away. "Why, what soft hair this is! Far softer than my magic tribute cloak. For your golden ramskin was the gift to me of a chieftain. In the Northern wildlands they use sheep-pelts to dredge the gold from the streams. In the end, the skin itself makes a costly cloak."

"It must be very heavy though."

"No trouble to me." For a short space his voice had lost the artificial wooing note and had taken on a note of almost self-consciously casual pride. I preferred that to the other. One's reason tells one that the smooth voice should make one feel insulted, because it holds one in so little respect that it is switched on glibly whenever it suits his purpose; but one's senses tell one just the opposite, they tell one what he wants it to tell one, that I am warm and desirable and admired by him.

Nevertheless, it was the wooing note it was my duty to bring on myself.

"How strong you must be," I gooed.

I wouldn't have been surprised to hear him say modestly, "Yes, I am," but instead he cuffed me lightly. "Your friend

Ijleldla is more subtle. How impressionable were your women when they succumbed to the gods—or don't you inherit your divine ancestors' manner of flattery?"

"You speak of sacred things very flippantly," I said, "which is displeasing to the gods. I hope you do not speak of your own gods so."

"I have no gods," he said. Just like that—. Casually. In passing. Oh, I believed it, one had only to hear the way he said it. I wondered if it would not be best to try stabbing him here, quickly, in the darkness, and rid the world right away of his impiety.

We were walking further into the forest. I felt him run a finger up my spine, pulling at my waistband to see if it was tight. I fumbled for my knife.

"Funny," he remarked once. "But the smell seems to be getting stronger now."

"Is it?" I was getting my knife free. "It's been with us for so long I've been forgetting it and now everything seems normal."

"Well, it doesn't." He put out a hand to stop me. Suddenly I did realize something—that he was serious, we were now no longer progressing, he to a love-tryst and I to a murder but together, to an unknown danger. I kept my mother's knife tight in my hand. "Why don't we turn back?" I whispered.

"Don't be foolish, goddess. Don't you wish to find out?"

"But it may be very dangerous—it is your duty to your army to conserve your life."

"Yes, I see. Go back then."

"You must come with me."

"Then, if you would be afraid alone, keep on, but be silent."

However, he did not rebuke me when I whispered, "What do you think it is?"

"I am never a man of theories. But yours?"

"Ooldra says it is a decaying in the etheric life of the forest." I said Ooldra's name carefully and clearly so that he could not mistake it, but he gave no reaction. His arm pointed ahead—I saw the movement from the gleam of the metal arm-ornaments—and as I looked, dizzy with nervousness, I felt him soundlessly chuckling beside me.

At first I could not see anything important, and then I realized that ahead of us, on the ground, on the trees, on top of each other in mounds, like turtles, were dozens of huge snails—still but revolting-looking, all queasy together.

I could not laugh. Even as it was, the whole thing was too surprising.

101

"I never knew snails had a smell," I said.

"They were never before big enough for it to be noticeable."

*"Aren't* they big! But we would have seen huge snail tracks all over everything—"

"They're hibernating. Now—"

"I'm tired. Take me back." And indeed, my knees were trembling too much for the rest of the night's work.

Today our line of march led past the sleeping-place of the giant snails. I knew that Zerd must have changed our route since last night only for that, to let the troops see what lay at the crux of everyone's recent days of fear. Indeed, everyone was tremendously relieved and very gay about it; it was amazing to hear the forest, which had been so silent from our fear, now ring all at once with yells and guffaws. The racket seemed extraordinary. The birds in the trees and big insects which had become used to our presence whirred away terrified; our birds caught the fever and in some parts of the line became unmanageable, one turning on his rider and rending him so that an officer had to order the man speared quickly to put an end to his pain. As for the bird, it was soon calmed and given to another man who'd lately lost a mount. This incident occurred in the Golds, at which the Blues were mightily pleased.

Soon the men began to run up to the mounds and pillars of snails—for that is what the trees looked like, pillars of snails, the creatures were layered and stuck so closely to them—and began to kick them derisively, while the poor creatures awoke inside their bashed shells, sizzling and hissing. This was not from their mouths, which somehow made it pathetic, for it was from their whole flesh as it died. The men yelled with laughter and fell smashing on the shells with their weapons. It had become a kind of carnage. The row was terrific. I was sure the officers would stop them but the ranks were not greatly broken, and I think they thought such an outburst was more good for the men, than bad for discipline, after the days of solid fear.

"The crux of the matter is," Smahil said, coming up beside me, "that we're going to meet harder things and the men must have confidence. Such raw troops must be a continuous strain of anxiety to the leaders of the army."

I hadn't met Smahil since the day of the riverfalls and my glance was awkward as it sort of flickered towards his.

"Why, what things could be harder?" I asked lightly.

How did he look at me? His manners are not all they could be, he did not look at me the same as always but with a difference, a kind of possessive knowledge. It only just misses being offensive.

"Plenty could," he said absently, for we both knew my remark was stupid. "Tighten your hold on Sheg's reins," he added. "He looks too excited."

"That may anger him," I wailed. "I hate him. I can never trust him, never know him."

"Blob would say that's because you aren't a good rider."

"I am a very good rider!"

"All right, but Blob says you aren't. He also says he saw you last night, with our mighty host the General, going into the forest." Smahil looked sideways at me while he steadied his own bird's movements.

"Now, is a brute of a fool who was once my groom to pretend he is a spy on me?"

"Are you cross, Cija?"

I looked at him scornfully, then saw he was grinning at me. I scowled. "Oh, shut up. There's nothing funny about it—am I to keep quiet and sweet at that sort of fool informing on me?"

"Of course, he has a nerve. He's never liked you. But he knew what he was talking about. He didn't make it up out of spite."

"He could have imagined it."

"Did he?"

I was taken aback by such a direct question from someone who had no right to ask it. My habit of falsehood is by now so deeply engrained in me that I was about to deny it when I remembered my mother's warning me that lies are the depths of folly if they are easily proved. "No," I said ill-temperedly, "he didn't imagine it but you weren't to know he couldn't have. I was wandering because I couldn't sleep and the Northern General was walking about, too—I could hardly have refused to accompany him when he talked."

"Into the forest?"

"We were attracted by the smell, and found the snails. That's why he led us past them today."

"A perverted smell to be attracted by. Never mind. But why weren't you more careful about being seen?"

"Because I didn't think anyone would be spying," I snapped. "Why are you questioning me like this—do you think you have a right to control all my movements because you kissed me the other day? All right, then, if you want to know, he tried to kiss me but I more or less stopped him."

Smahil had been going to say something else, but at that his eyes danced. "You more or less stopped him?"

"The snails helped. We came to them suddenly."

"Oh. Well, I wanted to warn you that Blob has let all the hostages know, and you're not being approved of by Noble Gagl, and Her Ladyness, fat Ronea. Well?"

"But—oh, I don't care about them, they're no longer any part my days, but—it's disgustingly impertinent of Blob! Well, thanks for the warning. I didn't need it, as it isn't likely to happen again."

Smahil's eyes suddenly danced again, he can never resist taking up any likelihood intrinsic in a conventional remark. "No?"

As I looked at, and then irresistibly into, the grey of his eyes my hands on Sheg's rein trembled. I remembered how the youth of our bodies had called Smahil and I together and impossibly close, above the riverfalls pounding and pounding, and how it had not mattered whether we cared for each other as long as our bodies could be young together. I struck the snarling Sheg and spurred him, angrily champing big, wet mangy jaws and shaking himself, away from Smahil.

Tonight, in the tent with the Beauty, the General's subsidiary interest has been Lisia, a tall, bold, jelly-fleshed slave who would be wanton if she were interesting. He touched her hand as she poured his wine, and gave her his purposely intensified glance at times throughout the evening. But I understood why he chose the Beauty for his journey; she is always the most exciting, never loses her vitality. The lines of her body, her deep, hard breasts, her plump sinuous arms, hard stomach, black living hair, long muscular legs are dedicated to sensuality; she is a hard unrefined animal femininity, and if I were a man I would desire her greatly. She lays stretched behind him on the fur cushions, mistress of the tent but his slave when he is in it. That is, of course, really one of her professional skills; she does not really think of herself as his slave. She is *his* mistress too, if no more than that.

Narra and I giggled and talked together in a corner, in the shade of the tent-hangings, but I was uneasy and troubled. The lack of reverence felt by these people, even friends like Narra, towards the gods who impregnated our ancient ancestresses had begun to oppress me; I saw they think of our gods only as stupid lechering beings which must have women, instead of as bright unutterably holy spirits who had chosen our race to be blessed above all others. And as always with impiety, it was vaguely catching. I had begun to feel wretched and less firmly secure.

This night the wind howled outside the camp as if it hated it, and Narra and I heard the screaming of it at our walls, and knew how desolate the pickets must feel, and how out in the night the fires would be only red moaning smoke.

But inside the tent the General and his minions were merry; the wind set the tassels from the roof-hangings swinging slowly above their heads, and the wine rippled in the gold cups; but the sheltered lamps burned steady enough, and everyone laughed and sang to the boy's ghirza. Some of the commanders were here tonight, and among them Clor and Eng were already very drunk. Clor had a girl half-lolling across his lap; some time before he had pushed up her skirt to fondle her, but now he had lost interest and bawled a song out of tune. The girl had fallen asleep, I think; her legs twitched every now and then and the gold embroidery on her trousers glinted in the lamplight.

Otherwise everything was quite decorous. The Beauty was a good hostess and there was plenty to eat and drink and listen to. Two commanders had small drums, which they played well for amateurs, and which sounded better anyway matched with the ghirza: Isad had a horn which he blew in everyone's ear. They all roared loud drinking-songs. I thought at times I had caught which was the General's voice: it is deep and resonant but not really in tune.

Once too many cups were empty all at once; I had to leave the dim corner and go to help. Isad hooted in my ear and was offended when I did not jump. "Alarm, alarm," he yelled which is the army's warning cry. I meant to look startled when I realized it would please him, then decided not to bother and gave him a cold, blank look as I filled someone else's cup. He pushed the horn at my arm and glared. "Who do you think you are, unsociable little bitch. Eh?" He made me spill some of the wine, and the man whose cup it was looked up at me and laughed and slapped me on the behind as I turned away. The General ignored me; he had seen me but he was kissing Lisia so I was spared that laughter.

When I got back to Narra she twisted her neck sideways to peer up into my face.

"Why do you look so serious, Cija? Your lips are quite together."

"Those louts!" I said, rubbing my seat.

"Oh, I know you are not used to it, but they mean no harm. And many of them don't know you are a princess—"

"Well, they should. And I'm not a princess. I've told you often enough but you don't understand."

Her eyes got big and desperate to be worthy.

"I'm sorry, Cija. I know you're really a—a descendant of your gods—"

"Of your gods, too, stupid. Everyone's gods."

"Yes, Cija." She nodded violently. But she doesn't understand, she thinks each country has its own gods.

I hugged my knees.

"Oh, the wind."

"Are you frightened, Cija?"

"Of course I'm not. But don't you feel depressed?"

"Only now you are."

The heavy, swinging tassels made big obscene shadows across the tent. Somebody spilt a jugful of wine. Without warning Eng started up and vomited, his eyes swivelling apologetically to the Beauty. The General grinned but the Beauty raised her brows. "Narra," she called, and the little girl ran out for a pail and rag.

"Surely it's getting time they all went home," I thought. "Surely they'll notice the party's helping itself to run to an end?"

Narra ran back in, but she ran straight to the General. "Immense One, Immense One!" she shrieked.

As he glanced at her to speak, several sentries ran in, paused at the doorway, but darted up to the General.

"We're surrounded!" "General, we're done for!" "It's the forest tribes, Immense one!" they jabbered. The General stood up, swung his scarlet cloak back from his sword and strode out with them. The girls looked apprehensive. The Commanders followed, drawing back their swords. Eng stumbled and Clor was last. The Beauty did not move except to raise herself on one elbow, her eyes narrowed so that she could concentrate on hearing better.

All I could hear just then was Narra's gasping as she crawled to me and clutched my skirt. But I had known the wind was right.

The forest race had surrounded our camp thick on every side. Our scouts had brought us no warning: they had been captured and silenced out in the jungle depths. In this terrain the Northerners are really no kind of a match for the forest race.

The Chieftain, who spoke to us himself in the jungle dusk

with his fierce-eyed men behind him, was an immensely tall man, dressed in skins. At first one thought he was wearing no ornaments, and that did not matter because his fierce presence was enough to proclaim him a king. Then one saw that he wore many ornaments, armlets and broaches and strap-bosses, of unobtrusive metal the colour of his dun skin garments, which only occasionally caught the light. He wore two necklaces of heavy enamel pieces, hanging in the folds of his tunic.

There are innumerable forest men, as many as the trees of the forest figuratively speaking, impossible to gauge and all incredibly skilled. We are prisoners.

"Why did you come to my land?"

"We have not come to your land, Forest Chief," replied the General. "We are passing through it."

"And you disturb our life and slay our animals for yourselves and fill our world with noise and tracks and forbidden intrusion, you have given no tribute, no toll for the passage of the forests."

There was now a kind of immediate parley. It was short, but even so the forest men got bored with listening and threw spears at our men. Their aim is very good. This was when Narra and I, who had crept out to listen, now scuttled back into the Beauty's tent to report as much as we'd found out to her. It was no use. We are utterly surrounded by rows on rows of men who are as at home in the forest as fish in the ocean. We have no chance from fight or flight. The General was being courteous, which is a sufficient sign. The Chieftain will if possible be conciliated.

This morning after breakfast Narra and I slipped round trying to glean bits of excitement or information. We didn't expect much of either, and more of the first. Information is very difficult to get in a camp, though rumours are a different matter. Of course there was no question at all of moving off this morning. The forest men have been camped in a circle all round us during the night, very careless and noisy. Our men have a sort of holiday; they are taking advantage of a rest from being always on the move by doing their mending, visiting friends in other regiments, or even polishing their harness. But mainly they are just lying round in various states of harmless pleasant coma. Naturally, the officers don't like them to be doing nothing and would think up jobs to occupy their time except that all the officers are very flurried by the new situation and are going round shaking their heads nonchalantly but nervily at each other and strengthening the pickets and then going and countermanding their orders and halving the pickets again so that the forest men don't get suspicious.

Meanwhile groups of the forest men have come into the camp in the later morning and wander round looking curiously at everything and speaking of it to each other.

There have been no nasty incidents, except for a Northern soldier who objected to a forest man looking at his canteen-pack and knocked him down. The forest man set up a great yell, which brought his companions running, and knocked our man down. The others leaped on him but some leaders, apparently, of both sides put a stop to it. The forest leaders were very careless about it and seemed hardly to mind whether there was a fight in our camp or not, but our leaders resolutely and anxiously pushed the matter.

"There is a likely-looking tent," Narra said.

"Um."

We both knelt down and experimentally put our ears to the flap (which was closed).

"Just a lot of talking, nothing clear," Narra said in disappointment.

At this moment the flap was suddenly drawn back and we tumbled in. As my head flew towards the ground my eyes passed the metal-bound leather boots I knew belonged to the forest Chieftain, and I heard the General laughing fit to burst himself. Narra's foot somehow got in my mouth for a moment and a few instants later I felt another impact. The slave who had drawn the flap through which we had fallen, had immediately gone across to draw the opposite flap—we had arrived at the end of the meeting as everyone decided to leave the tent—and two other people had fallen in on top of Narra and me.

"Get your damn little slippers off my neck," Smahil's voice said, and my feet were rudely shoved away from their present position. For a moment we all tumbled together, calling each other surprised names, like a nest of otter puppies. Then we separated ourselves but rose to glare as one at the laughter of the Northern General.

"My hostages," he explained, introducing us to the Chieftain.

The Chieftain bowed shortly but gravely, concealing any impatience he felt.

Narra's skinny chest swelled with pride.

Then He, the Chieftain and the followers of both filed out

and we were left to regard each other. The person with Smahil was Ijleldla.

"So Zerd does not take you into his confidence, Cija. You have to eavesdrop," she said, smiling hate at me.

I realized at once how things had twisted in her mind.

"Nor you, Ijleldla," I chuckled. I was as offensive as I could be, treating her with candid friendly amusement, as if I didn't notice her hate which must have been maddening for her.

"He has no cause to take *me* into his confidence," she spat at me. "But you, our innocent young friend the Goddess, who goes into forests with His Mightiness—"

"My, my, our jealousy is making you gullible, Ijleldla. Did the fact that you were scared they were true make you believe all Blob's nasty insinuations?"

"Who told you of those?" Her big blue eyes smouldered from me sideways to Smahil. "Another thing. Miss Turncoat, Iren won't like the way you're throwing yourself nowadays at Smahil."

"How stupid of me to be unaware that Iren owns Smahil."

Ijleldla choked with rage.

"Smah—Smahil, tell her to guard her tongue with us—"

Smahil was smiling his special enigmatic smile at us both and opened his mouth to speak when his eyes shifted to Narra. Instantly his expression changed. "Ijleldla, you've made the child cry." "Well, I like that!" exclaimed Ijleldla, excusably astonished. Smahil put his arm round Narra's shoulders and jerked his head at me and we left Ijleldla.

Smahil's tent is smaller than the other hostages' I'd seen. His manservant was out and Smahil sat Narra down in a pile of quashy cushions and dried her tears. She continued to gulp but accepted a mug of milk. "You mustn't let Ijleldla frighten you," he crooned, waving me to a seat on the rugs while he concentrated on Narra.

"I can't bear to hear Cija loathed so," said Narra, her treble now husky from crying.

Smahil raised his brows at me.

"Who is this little girl?" he asked. "She seems to worship you more than your own kind do."

"Don't you worship me, Smahil?"

"Don't come the Divine stuff with me. Your Cousin is one of our Grand-uncles, so that's enough to make me feel your equal in divinity."

"It shouldn't. It's common knowledge you're an adopted son, in any case. Narra—"

109

"I must go," Narra said. She had finished the milk and of course was perfectly happy again. "She'll be needing me."

We hugged briefly and she ran out, almost too shy even to dip her head to Smahil.

Smahil leaned against the tent's centre post and folded his arms. He was smiling at me. When he smiles like that, his mouth closed, his lips make a kind of raised weal of smugness above his chin.

"Why, Cija, did you mock Iren's claim to 'ownership' of me instead of denying with maidenly indignation the indictment that you were 'throwing yourself' at me?"

"I was too angry to defend, I wanted to attack." I stood up but Smahil didn't move at all. "Aren't you letting me past?" I reminded him of his position with a flicker of irritation.

He laughed.

"Come on, throw yourself at me." And he held out his arms to me.

I stood a moment, then shook my head.

"No."

"What's the matter with you?"

"If you kiss me now, today, Smahil, you'll kiss me every time we're alone together for a minute in the future, and I'll have no right to stop you."

He left the tent pole, strode to me, lifted my head—I didn't want him to, he is stronger than I am—so that my eyes had to stare up the few inches into his. The little spikes whirled round and round his pupils and from his pupils my own face stared back twice at me.

"And what would be wrong with that?"

"We don't love each other, Smahil."

"Gods—" he was disgusted. "By your Cousin, Cija, I didn't think you were that sort of whiner. No, we don't—but surely you've realized we *do* feel right with each other, as with no one else, no matter how attractive they are. Has your body ever throbbed to anyone else's just as it does with mine? Has it? How can it have?"

"I don't know, no one else has ever kissed me," I said as primly as I could.

He let go of me in surprise.

"But the General?" he said.

"Your manners are really amazing!" I said furiously. "What do you really think I am?"

My roles are sometimes difficult to separate at the right times, but I didn't tell him I have been trying for months to get

110

the General interested in kissing me.

My mind was vaguely wondering what I could say next when I found Smahil's lips on my mouth, my head tipped back and his hard fingers gripping my neck.

The curve he had forced on my back was a strain unless I leant back even further. That meant panic. There was nothing behind me. I tried to struggle. But though he is light and young, he is so much stronger, useless for me to try. I could not speak against the determined pressure of his mouth. The only relief I cou d get for my back was to unstiffen, to yield to the strength of Smahil's arms, and I was allowed to fall gently back, back, back on to the rugs. As soon as I was safe from my fear of falling I kicked upwards. I was feeling the desperate youth we share, but I had given him my reason for not wanting him to kiss me now. It was an important reason. I do not want to belong to Smahil.

His grip did not loosen, it shifted. He savaged my neck. He had determined to bring me, literally, to my senses, and he is quite right. No one could be less repulsive to me. If he were anyone else, if his breath or his teeth or the roughness of his skin or the taste of his tongue or his weight or his age repelled me, I should have had every right to struggle but Smahil might be my own self, everything about him is pleasing to me but I *shall not* become someone he can always kiss in a corner, someone who is being absurd and coy if she ever refuses a kiss, she has given so many before.

I threshed and turned. Smahil's muscles angered me. I bit his arm. He was angry now too at my stubbornness. He continued to use his body to excite me but it was I who won. I never ceased to struggle.

I was fighting for my individuality.

Everything would have been different if Smahil had loved me.

There was an unexpected third grip on my shoulders and someone hauled me up and administered a sharp slap stinging across the side of my face.

The Noble Gagl's eyelids quivered with distaste as he looked at me.

"Stand up," he said. "This is a dirty thing to come in and find. I was expecting to come in to talk with Lord Smahil, and I find you at your work here. Go back to the community you have adopted, and leave us in peace."

"You'd better pull your dress together," Iren added. She was the one who had accompanied Gagl in. From the grim twist of

111

her expression I gathered that no matter how little the Noble had expected to find this, she had brought him here hoping for something milder of the kind. Ijleldla had prattled to some purpose for once.

I looked down and found my dress torn and one breast nearly bare. I think I would have cried if it had been quite bare before them, it would have seemed the last straw. I bit my lip and held the cloth together.

Smahil—I had torn his clothes too—looked contemptuously at Iren.

"How could you—this little hussy—" she panted at him.

"Go on, get out," he said.

He pulled his cloak from a screen-hook and put it round my shoulders, while the other two stood glaring at me.

"I meant you, you know," he said, turning to them and raising his brows.

"Smahil—" Iren began sharply.

It was stupid of her to start sharpness with him. She should have known that with the other familiarities he had allowed her he had been pleasing himself, not her. Now he said in a silky tone which chilled me, "Are you staying longer in my tent?"

Iren looked at him, deeply amazed, offended and puzzled.

But Noble Gagl turned to leave. Iren was deserted, she had to follow him. Her long face was dead white with a spot of red on either cheek. It was the first time I have seen someone's face go like that, though I've often read of it, and it is most venomous-looking.

At the door-flap the Noble turned.

"Are you not sending the trollop with us?" he asked, his eyes popping with annoyed incredulity as he saw that I had not moved.

I knew Smahil would not be able to resist it.

"Yes, you can take Iren with my compliments," he replied casually.

I thought he had brought everything down to a safer but more mundane level, just by giving in to his usual weakness for any kind of word-play, and I breathed a sigh of relief but almost of disappointment, too, for in a way a real row full of real hate could have been satisfying. So my contempt rose when I found Iren had taken that as a spiteful declaration of war from him.

"You dare to speak so of me when *she* is beside you—"

"You must apologize to the lady," Noble Gagl cried.

I thought Smahil would turn to me and apologize for something, but he controlled himself.

He walked to the door-flap, making them retreat before him, and lifted it. Noble Gagl bent instinctively to pass through it, and remained like that, staring Smahil in the face with his apoplectic eyes glaring. He felt very righteously furious and looked very silly.

"You send us away and keep this—this slut with you!" added the old noble. "Your lady foster-mother would have something to say if she knew!"

"I doubt it," Smahil said dryly. "Come on, not gone yet?"

Noble Gagl's lips drew down in a grimace of repugnance as if Smahil and I were deliberately a smell of rottenness. He bent himself out. Iren, about to follow him, snatched at my dress and tore it open again. She spat in my face. Her face was contorted; she was pretending to spit on me as a decent hostage spitting on a treacherous wanton, but it was an excuse to force her loathing on me. I felt nauseated at the poison of her face. My knees trembled. I must appear a coward, for I sank against Smahil's shoulder and did not even say anything to Iren.

"Your General shall hear of this morning," Iren gloated over me. Smahil slapped her face and she bent her neck like a snake about to strike and slowly left the tent.

Trembling, I weakly pushed away Smahil's arms and wiped Iren's hate from my face.

"I'm sorry this had to happen," Smahil actually said.

"So am I. I'm glad you're sorry."

"Have this wine. Go on. I haven't touched the top with my mouth, it's a new bottle-skin. You should have told me it is the wrong time of the month."

So that was what he thought must be the cause of my resistance. I don't know why, but I always feel insulted when the supposition is wrongly applied to me, as if it were something people should think beyond me, though when it is true I accept their sympathy as my due. Now I remembered that from a man it really is an insult at any time, as men should pretend not to know of these things. No, men should not know of them in any case, there should be no reason for them to pretend.

"Once and for all, Smahil," I said wearily, and the wine warming my throat only made me feel more disgusted with everything, "you are nothing to do with me and never will be." Then I felt that was unfair, for he had just lost the friendship of the other hostages—what they were already making me think of as the "good hostages"—but then again, it was not my fault.

I stood up and went over to the flap. My knees were still trembling.

"You're afraid of what she'll tell the General."

I shook my head in a final way to show him it wasn't that. "No, Smahil, I'm not." I went out.

A little way further on, I saw the General on his great black bird and speaking with Iren. As I stumbled up to them, Iren turned away and passed me, giving me a fully significant glance of hot malicious triumph. I could hardly have been luckier. As I stumbled blindly towards him, I saw that he was even unaccompanied.

I tottered, and felt his stirruped foot come out to steady me. I had hoped for his hand, but that would come later anyway.

I swayed against him, hoping the bird wouldn't kick, but it was too well-trained for that. For a moment of panic I thought he wouldn't speak, but then his voice said, "Are you all right?"

I immediately moaned. "Poor Cija," he observed, "you are ill." And at last he stretched down an arm and mounted me before him. I shuddered against him, burying my head on his shoulder. He put a hand on mine to soothe me. I had not quite bargained for that hand. It had seemed all right in theory, but its reality was heavy and deliberate and far from soothing. He has very masculine hands.

"My lord," I murmured, "you cannot carry me thus to your companions."

"For the time being I'll have none but you," he answered. "And you needn't trouble, the tangle of these damned plants is too thick here for even the nearest tents to see us. Drink this." He put the familiar leather bottle to my lips and I schooled myself to drink without flinching. It was an old bottle, very stained and repulsive, which hung from his studded belt. "I hope never again to have such troublesome hostages. The forest big noise won't return till dusk for my answer, and I could not bear the flutterings and arguments of my commanders, but even here I find I cannot be undisturbed. Better?"

I realized he meant me and nodded.

"But I'm still trembling." I was, too. I wondered if I should invite him to touch my knees and feel how they trembled, then decided it might be unwise. But it seemed an awful waste of good genuine authentic trembling.

"Your thin friend told me some quite fascinating rigmarole,

114

from what I could gather of it. But you don't seem as happy as she pictured you to me."

"I'm not!" I jerked my head from his shoulder and sat up. His eyes went down to my bitten neck, my badly torn bodice and my scratched arms holding it together. Unfortunately none of the scratches were bleeding, though some had begun to sting.

His heavy mobile brows rose slightly. "Am I to understand the young gentleman attacked you—and you *weren't* willing?"

My rage and shame made me gulp a little before I could sweeten my plaintive expression again and go on. Each hour this morning had deepened my humiliation to degradation. They are not sentences I should have to listen to, and if only I could be myself and not the creature of my roles they would not be spoken to me.

"No," I said, "Smahil did nothing. All this—" I raised my arms a little to display their scratches more dramatically and realized I was still wearing Smahil's cloak. That was a mistake, when I had walked out stating that I would never have anything else to do with him, but Narra could take it back—"All this was done to me by Iren."

I began to cry, which was a very good touch and came more or less naturally, I was so wrought up.

"Iren? Your thin friend?"

"Yes—the girl who told you the rigmarole," I had to interrupt my sobbing to say crossly.

"Don't cry," he said soothingly but rather automatically. That's the trouble with a man like that, who's already known so many women that feminine tears are no longer touching. "Here, take this broach and stab your dress together. Why did she do it?"

"She hates me," I snuffled.

"Couldn't you have retaliated? You let her come to me so very neat and tidy."

I looked suspiciously up at him, but by "you let her come" he didn't mean what I meant. "It was so sudden," I said. I wept again and chattered my teeth. Nothing was so important as being allowed to stay with him. As I fastened my dress with the pin of his huge copper and malachite broach, more like a dagger than a broach, I let the edges fall back enough to let him see a glimpse of my white flesh—my pale tan left me long ago—curving firmly up and out, and hoped he was looking.

As soon as I'd finished pinning, I found a large slab of bread and meat being pushed at me. I took it, more to defend my face from it than because I wanted it, and began manoeuvering my jaw round it.

I ate as slowly as I could.

He ate too—the food had been in a pouch slung by the bottle—I had thought generals could afford richer food—and stared ahead at the stupid trees.

"What a magnificent bird yours is," I said, anything to keep his attention.

"Thoroughbred. Yours isn't?"

"Isn't magnificent, you mean? It certainly isn't thoroughbred," I took advantage of his polite reply to jabber on. "My bird is called Sheg; he's *loathsome*." I became more heated as I remembered how loathsome Sheg is. "He's old, and mangy: with a very ill-temper—I can't control him—he often frightens me. I'm sure he dislikes me and what could I do if he ever decides to run amock?—and once I saw him trampling a man."

"He must have been excited."

"That's not the *point*, it's not an excuse—" I stopped as I felt my brows drawing down and realized my face must look ugly with annoyance. I quickly sweetened it again and blessed the tearstains on my cheeks. I glanced at him a second. I thought his eyes on me were intent. Hurriedly I sweetened my expression still further, pouting a little to explain my recent frown, and drew a deep breath which made the rents in the thin stuff over my breasts quiver interestingly. "What a heavenly smell the forest has acquired here," I observed.

"It's nothing but the usual smell of everything, including our men and beasts."

"Uh?"

"Don't be startled. I only mean that the snail smell has been left behind us, and everything it's been covering is now normal again. No new wonderful scent has suddenly appeared."

"Oh." I hadn't been noticing anything abnormal about the snail smell for some days past. I remembered how I had first seen the snails, and blushed.

He ran a finger down the parting of my hair.

"How much hair have you? It's like a silk cloud."

"It goes fluffy when I've just washed it."

"I hope my wife will have such hair."

"Wife? Do you feel you need a companion, my lord?"

He looked at me, then grinned. "Someone a little more rarely-bred than my present, official Companion, yes, possibly. Are you all right now, floss-hair? Slide down, unfortunately

116

our meal is over and I had other things to attend to."

I darted away from him, dismissed, my cheeks burning. "I attained nothing," I thought. "Nothing but some absent-minded, rather insultingly-worded kindness."

But this evening a man came to the Beauty's tent with a young black thoroughbred bird. "With the compliments of His Mightiness," he said. "I'll call her to receive it," I said. "No, it's for you," he said.

Before dusk, it began to rain.

Nevertheless, there was an inordinate amount of bustle in our part of the static camp and at every spare minute I ran to the flap to watch.

The Beauty kept calling me back. She had a headache, and had decided to have no one in her tent that night, but to go to bed and relax. She is very careful about this, loosening her whole body, pore by pore she says, upwards from the feet. She explained it all to me once. But she wouldn't let me go. She wanted the candles moved, her pillows changed for flatter ones, her forehead bathed, not in that water, stupid child, water that fern has been crushed in to ease her ache, some wine put by the bed and did I *have* to wear that absurd colour of magenta?

It's not that she's fussy, but she gets nervous when she goes to bed early because it's strange to her, and as for the magenta she likes to have her household looking well. I explained that it was a shawl I had borrowed from one of the camp-followers, a groom's wife who is a friend of mine, in order to wrap round my bodice and hide some tears in my dress which I hadn't had time to mend.

She told me to take a silver-sewn green stole of hers instead (which I have always coveted) and never to let her see the magenta thing again, and at last sent me away.

I paused now that I had my freedom. I daren't stand at the lifted flap, looking out, or the Beauty would excusably complain of the draught and I had no one to go out with for Narra had had to spend all the afternoon in the cookhouse and was still there.

I decided to go and see my new bird properly.

I was tremendously excited about this. I had already sold Sheg to an officer for quite a good price. I had thought it wiser not to tell Beauty of my present, considering who it came from, for it was an important present. She was almost sure never to notice that my mount had changed.

117

I went across to where it was picketed. The groom, a zealous man, had erected a light awning and all I had to do was wrap a cloak round me and dash from the Beauty's tent to the bird-picket tent. On the way someone stopped me.

"Smahil!"

"I was coming for my cloak back."

"Of course—I was going to send Narra—"

"I came in time, then. You're wearing it."

"No, this is mine, they're very alike . . . If you wait here, only a second, I'll go and get yours. It was a shame for you to have come for it."

"Why do you think I absent-mindedly let you walk out with it?"

To this development I found no answer. I simply frowned anxiously and ran back for his cloak. I found he was beside me, simulating my pace. I had to say something.

"You're making things very complicated."

"There's nothing more simple."

"It's not simple."

"What a glamourous wrap you're wearing."

But we were already at the tent before the conversation could develop. "Wait here, Smahil, she's in there trying to sleep."

I tiptoed through. The candles flamed a slim dusky yellow, the Beauty appeared asleep, her arm, sinous as a silent cobra, out-flung lustrous from the bedclothes among the unconfined cataract of black hair.

I emerged again into the oustide world with its twilight atmosphere composed of continuous wet movement, and handed Smahil his cloak.

"Thank you."

I started for the pickets again without speaking a word, but Smahil fell into stride beside me. His fair head, uncovered, swam faintly glimmerng through the sibilant silver darkness.

"You are really preposterous, Cija," his voice murmured amiably. "Dashing briskly about, anything rather than be alone with me."

I didn't answer.

"After all, just name what you're so afraid of."

"You flatter yourself. I'm going specifically to see my bird."

"Ridiculous, you loathe him."

"If you insist on coming too, I suppose I can't stop you," I said unwelcomingly, and turned along the line under the awning.

118

Smahil stood and stared at the great, fierce, glossy, blue-black, rare-bred creature which confronted him. Sheg was nowhere to be seen, and the groom talked as if this were mine.

How come I have resisted showing him off now we were here?

"His name's Umsarunza. He's a young male, his father belongs to the Northern King. I call him Ums for short, it's a baby-talk name but irresistible since it really is his first syllable. He lost that eye in a fight over a female, but he's already been in several battles and never hurt."

"Where did you get him?" Smahil said, slowly.

"The General gave him to me."

"And I'm the only person who's ever kissed you?"

"What do you mean, Smahil?"

"You know what I mean. Very well, stay faithful to the lover to whom it's more expedient to stay faithful. But it's a shame you're a liar."

He turned and walked out.

I had had enough of Smahil. I snarled, "All right, now you've decided on a conclusion I hope you'll stay jumped to it," but I didn't turn immediately back to my bird.

The glimmer of the fair head moved gradually to invisibility in the heavy wet gloaming.

About fifteen minutes later there was a commotion of shouts, jingling and barks. I ran out to watch as the General and the forest Chieftain rode past. They were followed by Zerd's commanders and a line of forest men. The forest men walked, holding their spears like staffs, and they were picked men, all tall enough not to look dwarfed by our commanders on their birds. They were the Chieftain's bodyguards; the forest races are mainly small. The Chieftain rode a smallish, shaggy, ungroomed grey bird which had wise but frightening dark silver eyes.

Zerd saw me and swung his hand in greeting.

"Mount your new bird and come with us."

He must be in a good temper. Breathlessly I ran in and made them saddle Ums. I mounted him cautiously. It was the first time. But he was quite still for me. Beautifully trained. I touched on his rein and at once he turned and carried me out to the cavalcade. His whole body was throbbing with black life. I rode to the head and joined Him.

He didn't speak, which disappointed me.

We rode through the camp, among the fires sizzling to their

death in the rain, under the fleshy canopy of the foliage.

We rode into the dark forest.

I wanted to ask where we were going but dared not. Instead I studied the rider beside me. We must be going to some great parley, for I had never before seen him in such clothes. Over his shoulders and chest was a strapwork of leather, each strap buckled where it crossed another, the buckles being red gold set with polished agate. A gold band about his brow held the flow of his hair which hangs heavy all in one curve like a black mane, and set in the band, at the centre of his brow, was a polished agate. The straps were studded with bosses of red gold, and jagged spikes of unpolished raw agate, and were covered over their leather with a tracery of coloured enamel. At his belt hung the bossed sheaths of his longsword, his dagger, a ceremonial dagger, and two oblong mirrors hung there too, thick to avoid cracking and silver-edged to avoid cutting. He wore on the arm nearest to me a long, heavy wrought-gold armlet, with chips of ivory and crystal set into it. It enclosed the whole forearm and a flap extended down over the back of the hand. This, though magnificent to see, makes the wrist less supple to use swiftly. It is a compliment, a formal assurance to a doubtful friend that though ceremonial daggers are worn they will not be used. But I noticed Zerd wore his on his left arm.

The nocturnal forest rustled, whispered, crept.

Small scurryings fringed the passage of our birds' claws; the creepers overhead made swift unnatural sounds and when I thought of snakes my flesh crept, as it does not in the daytime; green and pallid yellow half-moons of eyes stared at us from different directions and then vanished.

Once there came a muffled exclamation from behind us, and one of the men cast his spear. A shrill scream split the forest, something wheeled away over my head and for a moment I caught a glimpse of a completely unearthly narrow head, a voraciously open mouth with jaws serrated to form sharp rudimentary teeth, and eyes blinking in sudden terror. Then it was gone.

"One of the reptile birds, rare nowadays," Zerd remarked to me.

"When one sees them," I said, shuddering, "one understands that they are not of this world."

"Not of this world?"

Even in the darkness I could sense the quizzical jut towards me of his long cleft chin, the nearly impatient amusement of his eyes.

"Their spores of life drifted from another planet."

He threw back his head and laughed in the jungle darkness.

My hands clenched on Umsarunza's reins. "You find me contemptible, my lord?" I thought with almost cordial venom.

"Where are we going?" I asked presently, since the silence between us had been broken.

"To the Hall of our friend there, he's invited me to a feast to let his council and people hear my assurances as to my peaceful intentions. Your new bird, is he restive?"

"My hand clenched involuntarily a moment ago on his rein. The darkness is intense, it frightens me a little. I knew you were going somewhere special, or you would not be wearing *mirrors.*"

He looked aside at me. I think he was smiling. "You're a more wholesome child than you'd care to believe. Mirrors are a dandyish ornament, true, and the fops brought them in to see if their hair were always clear of tangles and lice. But while I'm combing my hair—which is only courteous to my host—I can see what happens behind me. Or, if leapt on unexpectedly, I can always flash the light with my mirror and blind my enemy a moment. Disdain no kind of help, floss-hair."

"Your life you lead is very strange, sir. We do not need to think of every means of hurting our companions."

He ignored me for a space now and I wondered if I had gone too far. But I think I see now that he cannot be bothered always with what he thinks my vehement nationalism, and he cannot often be bothering even to be amused. He spoke with the Chieftain, and I could not hear what they said but it does not matter, it sounded only casual conversation.

Later he said to me, "You haven't thanked me for your magnificent black bird."

I was grateful for his renewed attention. I thanked him profusely for the new brute, told him of my disposal of Sheg and several other details. I ended girlishly, "The others are so jealous."

"The other hostages? They're lucky they're all still with us."

"Why should they be glad of that? They hate you Northerners and their position with you."

"You mean they'd have preferred being with our friends the Foresters?"

"What—but why? No, of course not, but it doesn't have any connection—"

"No? Ridiculous little hostage, if things had gone as they began I should have had to pretend the old man with the fancy sash was my uncle and give him as a token of my intentions to the Forest Chief, who maybe would have asked for a pretty young female too, my sister's daughter Ijleldla perhaps —ostensibly as a companion for his own daughter of whom he's very fond—"

"But—we're honourably given hostages—you can't break your contract with the Dictatress like that—"

"Why, do any of you poor children march with us each day under the delusion that you'll ever see your homes again?" His humour was tickled at the thought. "Surely not. Once hostages are far away—their lives are no longer worth keeping as surety of their country's behaviour, because the country's well behind us—they're only a drag on the army they're travelling with. When conditions get bad they get thrown aside—or used—in one way or another—"

"Then—but" I checked myself, though I was horrified. I remembered things. I thought perhaps Smahil did know, and possibly Noble Gagl and the Lady Ronea, that they would never return. "Did the Dictatress know this—that you planned this teachery—to keep her from attacking you until you were well away, and yet never to let us return?"

"Your mother is a laughable commander, but I think she has at least sense enough to know she'll never see you again. She let you out so your father's reputation could be thrown as much in doubt as possible by your appearance—no one could prove you were his daughter, but the fact that she claimed you were was enough to lose him the confidence of many of the people (who thought him holy) and reinstated her as the country's undisputed leader."

"She let me out for another reason too," I thought. "Yes, me at least she hoped to see again." Nevertheless his casual statements had shaken me. I said merely, "I'm surprised you wasted a good bird like this, even temporarily, on someone you expect to get rid of pretty soon."

He laughed.

"Don't apologize, I am as ungenerous as you thought you were pretending me to be. Umsarunza is an investment. I don't intend to get rid of you. We might even find you a Northern husband."

I caught my breath. It was all beginning to fit together . . .

"So you need no longer be nervous, floss-hair." He reached out one heavily, metallically ornamented arm, and mussed my hair. His voice had lowered to the almost irresistible caressing note. "Let's talk about something pleasant. Tell me about your-self—"

"There's nothing to tell—"

"Oh, come. You are a very interesting person. Tell me of your country—I know very little about it, though my wife has been there in peacetime—"

"Wife!"

"Yes, why, didn't you know? Surely you've heard that I'm the son-in-law of the Northern King?"

I was stunned to silence for some moments. Then, forcing my lips into movement again (and surprised to find it was still possible) I said, "No, I didn't know."

I remembered now, rumours of long ago, my nurses think-ing I could not hear, gossiping of the foreign army commander currying favour with the Northern Ruler's daughter, and thereby gaining the position of High General. At that time I had thought the foreign commander a woman.

The blue, light smoke kept coming between me and what I was looking at, except when there was a hole in the roof over the direction I gazed and then the rain coming through the roof made holes in the smoke and dispersed its existence.

The Forest man beside me poured me more wine. He was a young, handsome man. His name was Falicq. He had told me. He poured me so much wine I might have thought he was trying to weaken my commonsense for some reason but he talked too enthusiastically and ingenuously for me to suspect any such thing. He sat beside me and talked. He hardly looked at me. My head nodded, I wasn't sure whether I was nodding at his conversation—I gathered vaguely it was about grain-stooks at the moment—or from drowsiness.

The blue odorous smoke kept eddying between me and Zerd and I couldn't see him where he sat with the Chieftain's daughter. They sat on one of the wooden settles grouped everywhere about the long rambling hall. This smoke was not so heavy as the purple fumes from the Northerners' torches and camp-fires. I should be able to see him through this smoke, but perhaps my eyes were sleepy.

Oh, shut up, I'm not really interested in grain-stooks.

The settles on which the best people sit are covered with rather smelly goatskins. The goatskins cannot have been prop-erly cured. The smell of the eucalyptus logs they are burning is nicer. There are bright blue flames in the fires. The seats of

123

the more unimportant people are innumerable, I mean the settles they're sitting on, and lots of them are placed under the
parts of the roof where the rain comes in. The rain goes drip
drip. It goes gurgle splutter splash plish plink. It is falling
through the roof and from the leaves on to the ears of the
Forest men sitting on the settles. And there are other people
too—*everywhere*—it really is too much—one of them is offering me a huge plateful of roast rodent-hams. But I shake my
head. I'm not hungry any more. I was hungry when we arrived
here, ages ago, after coming through the suddenly turned-on
downpour of rain over the swinging bridge woven of grass
ropes, swing-sway-swinging over the river all milky in the fierce
light as it frothed over the rocks. We had to leave our mounts
behind us, they couldn't cross the bridge to this noisy secret hall
of the Forest owners. I hope our birds are safe with the Forest
people we left them with. I was afraid the bridge would not hold
even our weight together with that of the beating rain. I was
very hungry, but not now, no longer hungry. We have been
here ages.

"Falicq," I said, sitting up and grasping his arm, "why are
the rafters up there all black?"

"From the smoke," he said, looking round at me, interrupted.

"Centuries of smoke . . . ? Oh, but, Falicq, the smoke is
blue, why has it made the rafters black? They should be blue?"

He shrugged uselessly and, pouring me more wine, went on
talking. Now I was sitting up, I seemed to understand him better.

"Oh, Falicq, I'm sorry," I said, "I thought you were talking
about grain-stooks, I didn't realize it was fish-hooks."

He looked at me in surprise.

I drank and sat back and nodded at him to go on.

But I found that sitting up had also widened my eyes a little.
I looked across at Zerd and the Chieftain's daughter. They were
absorbed in each other.

She was pretty, but not beautiful. She had soft fuzzy eyebrows but long ashes. I couldn't see the colour of her eyes,
which baffled me somewhat, for I can never feel I know a person until I know the colour of their eyes. Perhaps she had
those eyes that nobody *can* tell the colour of, because they're
always changing. (I was right, she has.) She has rather a plump
chin. She looks very sweet and gentle. She wore soft rose pink.
My green and silver is much more exciting, I thought. I had
worked out a gay comment on it for Zerd, who was sure to

recognize it once in the light of the hall, but he has not looked at me all evening.

He is married.

I thought he was going to marry me.

I wonder if he minds all those little pink pigs nosing round his feet in the greasy floor-reeds. He doesn't seem to notice them.

Now they are bringing in dancing-girls. Falicq swivels round to watch them. They are wearing very little and they jerk their large tummies into rather nauseating movements. Their flimsy little jackets jerk, too, at each movement and sometimes they jerk up enough to show their nipples. The smoke parts around them, it embraces them. They dance on ignoring its embraces. The lights are behind them and the smooth shadows wriggle on their bodies. There is no music but the men are clapping hands and stamping feet to the exotic, erotic, jerking rhythm. He does not look at them either. He and the rose pink girl continue to absorb each other.

What a commotion there was after we first entered here, such a time ago!

The Forest men, all of them, shook their fists and spears and insisted on tribute from us in return for their forbearance and tolerance in believing our intentions peaceful and not killing us outright. Many animals and lots of our sharp metals for each four days that we spent in the forests. It was impossible to say them nay. Only their kindred, they howled, are allowed to traverse the forests without paying. They got quite excited.

That girl has a stupid mouth, why should she catch so much of his attention?

I got up and went over to them.

His voice was the familiar artificial voice which makes me weak in the veins at the backs of my knees. "Now tell me all about yourself," he said. His arm was stretched along the top of the settle behind her. "Oh, there isn't much to tell . . ." she faltered, gazing adoringly up at him.

I walked away again among the nosing small forest pigs.

Neither of them had noticed me.

How could I ever forget the re-entry into camp late the following afternoon?

The troops stared, the black drums beat. Clor, of course, was still drunk from the leave-feast. He lolled across his bird's crupper. There was the business of farewell to the escort. The girl wept as she embraced her father, then smiled tremulously

125

as he rode away. She couldn't keep the smile off her face for long at a time, the afternoon sky was paling to the faint green horizon. The sun was pink as through a mist; its pink rays struck on the girl's dress. Her favourite colour is pink. The rich smell of cooking spiced the whole camp.

The Beauty's white bird was soon before us.

On it she glowed like a jewel. She wore blue, blue with a depth to it like the sea I used to watch from my high tower. her black hair streamed over her shoulders. Her big white breasts tautened the low-cut blue of her bodice, her full pale mouth pouting as she fixed her gaze on him.

"How late you are!" she complained. "Come to the tent at once, I've prepared as good a rest for you as I can. After your journey you must eat and drink. Did everything go well with the treemen or whatever they are?"

She rode to him and drew her white fingertips caressing down the side of his face. One corner of his mouth quirked sardonically. He stilled the hand by taking it in his but was otherwise unresponsive as she continued. "You are tired? Did they demand tribute?"

"A lot," he said.

The little girl was watching them unblinking, her face as pink as her dress. The Beauty rode beside him, leaning on him, her hands possessively in his hair. The commanders had gone to their own parts of the camp; the soldiers had left us. Only we, the nucleus of the group, continued towards the tent. From it the noise of the usual mirth and music floated out. We reached the doorway. The Beauty, from Zerd's side, signalled me impatiently to lift the flap. Hesitating, I obeyed. The Beauty, magnifcent as a sapphire, swayed fondly and sensuously towards Zerd for him to lift her from her bird: he took the pink princess's hand in his, and helped her carefully down. The Beauty, sitting still ignored on her bird, seemed to notice her for the first time. The brows twitched a little; she asked, "Zerd, who is this?"

"This, my dear," he replied over his shoulder, "is the Forest Chieftain's daughter Lara, my wife."

# CHAPTER THREE

## THE HIGH TENT

No one mentioned to Lara that she is not, strictly speaking, any legitimate wife of Zerd's; no one mentioned that he already has a wife, a King's daughter, waiting behind him in the great Northern kingdom. None of the commanders thought it necessary; none of the entourage dared to, even at their cattiest; the Beauty did not; I did not.

The Beauty, pale all over, and as pale as someone ill, observed that doubtless now he would have to pay no tribute after all; and after that kept silent to him. He did not go at night to her tent any more, but the new queen of the camp objected to her flamboyant presence and complained that the late junketing in the nearby tent disturbed her rest. So he cast the Beauty aside as if she had become nothing but lumber, no longer useful nor interesting, and she became one of the camp followers: a leader's woman. She was not even allowed in the entourage; the sight of her offended Lara. Lara must have known perfectly well what had passed between her husband and the Beauty at one time, but now that she had come it was all over, so that she could be satisfied. She saw well and truly to that.

She hangs always on Zerd; he defers lovingly to her in everything and we march through the forests unmolested and without paying tribute to the new kinsman of our General.

They cannot, her father particularly, have been less than horrified at her decision to wed this particular new alien; but her father can deny her nothing she really wants, and she certainly really wanted this.

Now that I have seen how quickly he can work when he wants to, I doubt if he was ever more than mildly interested in me.

The Beauty, now utterly disgraced, unseen and hardly heard of, could have no use for a horde of maids and servants; she wanted one maid, but her new lord already had a woman-servant whom he would not get rid of because she had nursed him, so I wondered if I would be given back to the hotages and the care of Ooldra. I thought I would have liked to see Ooldra often again, instead of every now and then, but the new wife wanted a full following to boast of and lord it over and she chose me as her personal maid, even though I had been the Beauty's, when she found out from me that I am a high-born hostage. I was asking her if I could go back to my previous position. I took care not to mention my divinity, though; I could not have borne to be mocked by her.

So every night now, when I would have been tending the wild, thick, black flowing hair of the Beauty while she cursed me or laughed with me, I braid the thin, neatly waved, glossy, light-brown plaits of the bride. The princess, is how we must all address her. Then Zerd comes in, as a dutiful husband should, when she is ready, all daintily tucked in the pink bed, and I bob my head to him and run out while he tells her that the ancients needed a moon in the sky but he needs none, having her. Or some such thing.

I sleep uncomfortably with Narra and the other winegirls now.

She has redecorated the tent.

It is now all pale pink, except for the ceiling-hangings, which are rose pink. The brilliant cushions are all re-covered; the table now holds pink pots of gentle flower fragrances; I miss most the smell of musk which used always to be exotically strong in the tent.

She never curses me nor shouts at me, but twice when I have done something she didn't like she has beaten me on the back with whatever she has handy, a thing the Beauty never did.

But generally she is as gentle as she looks, being very insistent only upon the fullest possible formal respect being paid her.

She can be very illogical and haughtily unjust.

There is no one in authority to whom a slave ever has the right to complain.

"But he is already married!" I finished.

"It makes little difference," Ooldra said contemptuously. "His wife he married only because being the son-in-law of the king would ensure him the power he wanted in the army."

"But he didn't need to do that to get it—he is one of the epoch-making generals of the North on his own merit—"

"He had to make sure he was given the scope for being so. Advancement is difficult for an alien in that hidebound hier-

128

archy, even though his father was great. As I was saying, he married only to get advancement. In this case he's saved himself a lot of trouble in the forests. While he's in them, and she's within call of her people, he will of course bow to her every whim, cross her in nothing, and act generally like a loving worm."

"But the Beauty—he cast her off with a couple of sentences after the pink bride complained of her proximity. I was there when it happened! What disgrace to put upon her like that, in the eyes of the whole army *she* is now quite suddenly *nothing*! The humiliation of it—after all that they have been through together—does his callousness stem from his blood? Is his blood cold—is he totally a man-reptile?"

"I know this, Cija. He is one of Us—for he is not a mortal."

"Then it was not a god who found his ancestress fair, but a demon, in the shape of a crocodile or a serpent. It may be his strange blood—a coldness of emotion—he scares me because the quality of extreme callousness is allied with concentration on ruthlessness."

"It could give him a satisfaction," Ooldra said. "With various exceptions of individuals or circumstances, animals are joyful or grieve when something pleasant or unpleasant happens; a human being's enjoyment of, for instance, a meeting with his beloved—is heightened by outside and very abstract factors—say, for how long a time they have been parted from each other. Higher beings depend almost entirely for their joy or grief upon the abstract factors—time, space, the emotion of others. Joys and griefs which are purely physical—such as food, hunger—matter not really at all to them. A sudden sharp violet seen beside a sudden soft purple can be to them what intense physical sexual ecstasy is to a human—and I don't mean they're 'sublimating' it."

I stared at her before the doubt in my mind resolved itself to me.

That was all intensely interesting—but how much she hates Zerd! The malice glittered in her silver eyes as she brought out this measured information against him. "Surely, Ooldra, you don't really think he is a higher being whose joys—who is a kind of super-sadist? But it's impossible—he's as earthly, almost as animal, as anyone could be. He's almost wholesome from that point of view. He even jeers at the supernatural."

She sighed.

"Yes, for someone so intelligent he is so animal that, knowing he is not a man, there is only one explanation."

"What?"

"Life is perilous."

"Oh, yes, you've told me all that before . . ."

"No, that is peril of the world; there is a larger perilousness, a desperation which is the cause and the goal of all things—not in life, but in Life." The second time she said the word there was a dreadful stir in her voice. "It is true, Cija, irrevocably true that it is possible for a being—a human being or a greater creature too, to lose his soul."

I had forgotten how big the sky is outside the forest. It is quite amazing.

However, there is not a very far-flung low horizon. This is because while we were in the forest the mountains were getting nearer and nearer and now, when at last we have seen them for the first time, they are already large and near. The sun beats down upon their white crags.

Already the sun is a penance.

The jungle is only a week behind us, and already the General's deference to his princess is noticeably a little less.

The sun, which we were so glad to see uncluttered by the moist, confused, jungle shadows, is terrible and we long for the protections of those same shadows. The men march all day slouched nearly double under the merciless weight of packs and arms, their sweat dripping off them, flies buzzing black all over them, crawling thick in their sweat. They have given up brushing them away, they only settle again immediately. The cavalry regiments are a little better off, they pile their kit on their saddles, strap it securely, and feel free to brush away the flies without losing too much strength and patience.

The inexperienced troops grumble terribly; the comparatively few brigades of veterans have had to be split up from their comrades and distributed among the rest of the army to keep its spirits up. This was done to a certain extent at the very outset, but not to such a degree as the General advised, and the changing-around at this late date is causing more trouble among the men resentful at being parted from old friends and regiments.

The river is barely worthy of the name. It is narrow and muddy and mainly stagnant, humming with hovering fogs of insects. The places where more or less pure water runs are few and far between. Water is rationed out carefully but the young troops will not believe it when they are told they must force themselves to drink as little as possible. As soon as they begin

130

to sweat they gulp down their water, and then feel very ill—with nothing in their bottles to console them later. They receive little sympathy from their officers or from the veterans.

The ground is arid and sandy with no shade for miles and miles on end. At night, wrapped in their blankets, the men nearly go mad from the ceaseless attacks of huge hairy fleas which live in the sand. Some men and animals have caught fever from the insect-clouds over the bad reaches of the river.

My mistress complains dreadfully of the insects which find their way into her tent. I spend all my spare time trying to swat them with an ineffectual little bat she proudly plaited for the purpose. It is absurd work, as no matter how many are killed there are always more. I would do anything in the world for a bath.

Early this morning I hung around till she had finished her bath. Then I ran to prevent the slave taking away the tub of used water. "Princess, let me use the tub," I pleaded. She turned with raised brows. She does this if one speaks without being spoken to first. "I will certainly not have a slave using my private bath," she said.

"Madam, I would not contaminate it quite as much as a slave would. I'm dying for a bath, so I must remind you I happen to be an honourably given hostage—"

"You never cease reminding me." I have only told her three times, but I held my tongue now and she said, dismissing the slave with a nod, "Dry me."

I threw aside her pink towel.

"Madam, while drying you I might touch you with part of the towel which had previously just touched my hand. I dare not." I ran out at once after the slave who was carrying the tub and said, "I'll take that."

"I was going to use it," she said. "My skin is so dry—"

"You can have it after me," I said, looking as commanding and aristocratic as I could, and the woman handed the heavy thing over with a look of reluctant fright.

I dragged the tub to a tiny space to which the backs of the tents round it were turned. I set it down carefully, undressed quickly and furtively as possible, and stepped into the lukewrm scented only-once-used water. The touch of water on my parched travel-dusty body was ecstasy.

I had meant to step in and out immediately, risking no discovery but it was impossible. I twisted in the tub, made the water lilt over my aching back, dipped my face in it, lifted it in

131

my cupped hands and trickled it over my head and felt it wet the greasy strands of my hair and finally reach between them to my scalp, which seemed to have been burning these days.

I even reached the ticklish parts I leave till last, the navel and between the toes and the soles of the feet I have to go careful with.

I knew that several people had come into the little space. The sound of splashing, I realized, had been bound to arouse attention. I paused, and looked up.

There were several troopers, staring in dangerous susprise, as much at me as at the water. A few of them I recognized vaguely by sight; the only person there I knew was Smahil.

"Smahil, send these men away," I said nervously.

"Having a happy lickle barf, miss?" one of them asked politely.

I looked a frantic order at Smahil, who looked expression-less but casual, just as anyone would who hardly recognized me.

The biggest man wandered over to me. The others followed him.

"Now, miss," he said. "Jump out. We won't harm you if you get out, if we have to make you we might get rough, not on purpose of course."

"But I'm naked," I explained.

Several of them laughed, one spat, but the big man said, "Yes, we knew that already, miss. Come on, out with you."

I hesitated and one of his immense hands clamped round my upper arm, not brutally but like a vice even though I was slippery.

Smahil, who had been lounging watching, now said, "All right, fellows. That's enough."

They turned their belligerent eyes on him. I was already terrified.

"She's one of the General's fancy ladies," he said.

We were soon alone in the space.

"You'd better get out before anyone else comes," he said.

"You needn't stay."

"You need someone to stay in case someone else does come," he told me coldly.

"Well, turn your back."

"Why are you so prudish? This won't be the first time you've been seen bare by a man."

I caught up my neck-chain with the knife on it from beside

the shallow tub, and hurled it at him. He stumbled back. "Why—why—" he stammered.

"Stop your endless holier-than-thou-scoffing," I choked.

He came closer again, picked up the chain and knife, and put them down on the pile of clothes beside me. "All right, Cija. I'll turn my back."

I got up, tied up my hair in two seconds and shook the drops off my legs. By that time, from the heat of the sun, I was no more than slightly damp. I slipped into my clothes and stalked silently away past Smahil to the opening between the tents.

He hesitated, but decided to speak even if the sound of his voice offended me.

"You're always being annoyed with me, Cija."

"Yes."

But that seemed unfair. I stopped for a moment, though hardly glancing at him. "You're always annoyed with me," I pointed out. I walked in but this had given him his usual confidence and he stopped me, his hands on my shoulders.

"You're so damn touchy," he said.

"You'd better go and have that bath if you want it so much."

"I don't, I bathe in the river, such as it is. I'm not supposed to, the parts with water in have been reserved for the General and his staff—and, of course, your rival. But sometimes the guards are slack, and I slightly resemble one of the staff secretaries. Why on earth were you bathing in the open, anyway?"

I told him briefly, attempting to shake off his hands which he didn't budge.

"I wanted a bath but she's in a bad temper because since leaving the forests he twice has missed his nightly visit to her so she refused me a bath. I don't usally like all the bother but in this weather it is a joy. So I took her tub from the slave—"

"She'll be furious," Smahil said, his mouth twitching sideways. His instinct was laughter, not sympathy, it is a little thing but shows what sort of person he is.

"She is. I refused to tend her and I was rather impertinent. And I called her Madam because I am a hostage, and as the General's wife she is no longer technically a princess. I am perfectly entitled to behave so, but all the same I am liable to a beating for it, I suppose."

"She doesn't beat you?"

"Occasionally, but so far never hard. But there is a weal on my shoulder where she hit me with something sharp."

"The bitch."

Smahil looked very indignant for a moment. Note, his instinct was of execration against the princess, still not sympathy for me.

"And now," I said, "thanks to you, it'll be all round camp that I'm the General's plaything."

"It saved you."

"You could have saved me by exercising your authority as a lord. You were only being malicious. Don't you realize—if she hears it I shall be flayed alive!"

"How madly gay. Nonsense, even if it did reach her ears I suppose he would protect you. I'm not pretending he's kind, if it had happened in the forest he'd have let her torture you but now that her wishes are no longer so important he'd save you—"

"For a rainy day? You're a fool, Smahil, and a stupid one at that. Your mind is just too ready to jump at things."

"All right, Cija. I get it now. You want to appear virtuous, for several very practical reasons. But it's no use trying to convince me. Your black monster Umsarunza is enough. The fastidiousness you display with me is well done—I was foolishly taken in by it for quite a while—you even hate (to lead the conversation from sex for a minute) to drink from someone else's cup—but you can bathe in someone else's bath water—"

"You are a squalid little brute," I said with loathing. This is the tent, so you can leave me. You're too nauseating to have to deal with in this heat."

"So this is the tent." He regarded its shell-pink exterior with interest. Then he took my arm and led me firmly inside. I whispered frantically. "No, you damned idiot, she's already in a rage—"

Inexorably he yanked me in, and stood looking round at the pink ceiling, pink walls, pink rugs, pink cushions, and pink hangings. She sat at one end, wrapped in a long pink towel, with a fat sweating slave doing her toenails while another a fan to keep off as many mosquitoes as possible. "Come in at once," she screamed, catching sight of me. "Where do you think you had a right to march off to?" Then, seeing Smahil, she heistated in surprise.

Smahil loosened my arm and made an impeccable bow. "Princess," he said, "with my compliments, your slave returns to the Womb."

134

Pushing me forward, he swiftly bowed himself out leaving the princess as pink as her surroundings.

When the dutiful husband came to her tent in the evening, there was a bandage across my back. She held out her hand to him, gazing up at him from the pillow with her big, soft, changeable eyes, twisting her head and pulling in her chin in order to simper lovingly at him.

He strode eagerly over to her. It is astonishing the way his face can take on an honest ingenuous eager look. On the way I gave my usual servile bob and started to scurry out. His hand caught my shoulder, he stopped, and from the corner of my eye I saw the simper on her face fade.

"Here, what is this, floss-hair," he said, taking the bandage between finger and thumb. It pulled a little from my wound and I could not help giving an involuntary whimper, which I stifled immediately. I was very much aware of her presence.

"I whipped her," came the soft, suddenly cold, little voice from the bed.

His mouth pulled into a grin. "What a shame, she dislikes whippings. But the pain looks bad. What did she do to deserve that, my love?"

"I'm glad you ask that," she said, raising herself on an elbow. "She has been a wickedly naughty girl. She is insubordinate, insulting and insolent. Today she refused to tend me and ran out, after insulting me, before I could stop her. Later she returned with a man."

"Returned *here?*"

"He brought her back and left her here. But he insulted me too—"

"He did, too?"

"I—I won't repeat what he said. But she will be in pain for days and the marks may never go." She relaxed, after telling him all this. "Now you may go," she said without looking at me.

He sat me down on the bed, pulled off my bandage and looked at my back.

"Yes, the child will be in pain for some days. But you flatter yourself, my love, your gentle arm is not as strong as you believe. The marks will heal well—unless they fester much." He went across to her table and came back with an amber pot.

"Zerd, what are you doing?" she said, watching him in suspicious frustration. "Zerd, I won't have her old bandage lying almost by my face—"

135

He reached behind him, tossed the bandage away on to the rugs, and began to rub thick, cool, fragrant unguent from the amber pot into my back. I sat upright, willing myself not to flinch, though the unguent moving under the ruthless movement of his strange fingers into my sore back burned like fire or the teeth of a wild beast.

"It will sting a little," he said, "but it means that they will heal cleanly."

"Thank you," I murmured through teeth tight clenched.

He bound a new bandage crosswise across my back, and told me to go, I nodded, rose weakly, and stumbled out.

She hates me now. She'll never stop.

The plain does not improve on acquaintance. The ground is treacherous. Men and animals stumble in sudden pot-holes. Often the animals break their legs. There are also bogs, black and deep and stinking, to which the sun's broiling makes no whittle of difference. A picket fell in the other night; his cries awakened the tents. I have never before heard such terror laid stark in a human voice. Purple-flaring torches were rushed out to light his rescuers, but he had wandered too far before realizing what he was in, and then in a panic had gone the wrong way, and no one could find ground near enough to grip on in order to tug him out. Finally the rescue was effected with ropes thrown to lasso him. All the time, out in the dark, the man was sinking and sinking with nothing beneath him but miles of cold stinking suckingness, nothing above him to grip on. His cries were terrible. When he was finally safe, and everyone stood round holding their noses, it was seen by the fleer of the torches that he was covered with a thick layer of tiny wriggling white worms. They feed on the corruption in the bog. How many lonely terror-impregnated bones have they eaten the marrow from?

The men march fearfully and swiftly, frantic to leave the plains which they say are cursed by the ancient alien spirits which fell with the Moon when the Moon fell thousands of years ago and left the sky alone with the white stars.

The heat is terrible. My back is slowly healing. I long for cool water to soak my bandages in, but it is impossible.

Every day men fall aside from the line of march, gasping for breath, so dry they can hardly sweat.

Many get sun-stroke, but that is because they will remove

136

their stiff helmet-caps. The old soldiers keep theirs on even when the hair seems to be roasting on their scalps.

I could stand the heat if it were not for the flies. They are incessant. Some of them are poisonous, they are all maddening.

Nothing affects Ums, his powerful legs carry him onwards steadily, swiftly and easily. He is beginning to surprise me by signs of affection. He is not what one could call an *affectionate* brute, but he is intelligent and seems to anticipate almost everything I do. He snarls and kicks at just about everyone who tries to touch him; only with me is he gentle.

In spite of the sun so savage above the snow on the mountains, the water is mainly stagnant, perhaps years old. Maddened by their small water ration, the men frequently risk drinking the stagnant stuff. Recently three men died. Before they were buried a movement was noted in their corpses. At first it was thought they must still be alive; but it was ascertained that they were definitely dead. Their bodies were cut open, and an immense torpid pale worm was found in each man's entrails. The seeds of these worms are obviously in the stagnant water, and strict orders have been issued that no more of it is to be drunk.

I dare not think what the days would be like if I still had Sheg.

And, from that, comes doubts which I am contemptible to feel.

But it seems senseless to kill a man for such small hate as I feel for him. I hate him, but when I look at the hate in Ooldra's face I feel ashamed. My hate is small and lukewarm. She hates him, she waits patiently for the day of his death. She does not bring to her hate the vehemence my mother and I could summon at times, she might almost be listless, but she waits quietly and with certainty. A hate like that is deadly, and not at all human. It brings a chill to me.

I have thought of inviting Ooldra to do it for me, for she would certainly do it joyfully and with no mistake, but I must break my birth-prophecy.

I have decided that Smahil is ill.

He has been stung by some kind of insect. The place has

swelled up and gone all bluish-black. When I touch it, he has to groan. I thought at first it was only a bruise. Blob (who is now Smahil's groom as well as Ooldra's) came to me this evening. We greeted each other ungraciously. "The lord's ill," he said. "You're to come." "What lord?" I said. "My master," he said. "If you mean Noble Gagl," I said, "I'm not coming because I couldn't be less interested."

He grunted as if my own statement had borne out his opinion of me and so he instead of me was on top of the conversation.

"It's young Smahil," he said, "and he wants you."

The tone in which he brought out the last part of the sentence is indescribable.

Well, I went with him, though I thought it was another of Smahil's cheating-tricks to get me, and Smahil was lying in his tent which I was astonished to find looked very familiar to me though I had only been there once before. However, that time was intense so must have impressed itself on my eyeballs. Anyway, he was lying on top of his bed and looking pale.

"O.K.," I said, noting that Blob left me and went out again as if prearranged, "I'm here."

"Cija," he said, turning a heavy head to me over the pillow, "Could you do something for me?"

There was only a little torch flickering in the room but though I couldn't get much of his face he was lying rather still.

"What's the matter?" I said suspiciously.

"Couldn't you try and get me some water?" he continued, turning restlessly.

"Everyone wants that."

"*Anyhow*—just try—you're the only one who can help. It would be no good asking anyone else for water—but you could steal some—*she* must get a generous ration—"

"She does, but there's fat hope, I must say, of me getting any—and if I could, why should I give it to you?"

"*Please*," he said weakly.

"You're pretending to be ill," I said. Cautious.

"Yes, on my chest," he muttered.

Thinking I'd call his bluff, I went determinedly across to him and was bold enough to open his shirt. But on the pale narrow chest whose smooth male muscles I remembered so well, with its flat wine-dark male nipples, there was a bluish-black shock. The light flickered ugly over it. "*A bruise*," I said. I touched it and he yelped and shocked me worse, and then he caught his lip

138

fiercely in his teeth and scowled at me because I'd heard him yelp.

"What is it?" I said. "It's not a bruise."

"I know that, fool. Look, can't you get me some water? Please." His voice trailed away. I bent over him in anxiety but the light was too bad and too uncertain.

"What bit you?" I said.

"Yes, I think it's a bite. Looks like a snake. Can't be."

"You're finding it difficult to talk? Let me put a few more cushions under your head."

His fingers slid against my arm, caught my wrist. His skin was hot and harsh.

"The water?" he said. "Look, girl, *any* way, can't you . . .?"

"You're sick," I decided intelligently.

"Not very—if it weren't so hot—"

"I'll try for some water," I said and ran to the doorflap.

He stopped tossing for a moment. "Wonderful," he breathed. And then, "I knew you would."

That was laughable. I stopped feeling quite so sorry for him. "Don't try to bribe me to good deeds with insincere compliments on my character—" I said.

"Cija," he called as I was on the threshold.

"Well?"

"Will you nurse me? Blob can't—no one will—"

"Don't worry."

I hung around, seized a water-skin as soon as I could, whipped it behind a cushion and continued my tasks. As soon as she let me go I dashed out, hiding the skin in the folds of my skirt, past the General who turned to stare rather at me. Head down, I pelted with the stolen goods to Smahil's tent.

He was breathing heavily when I went in; the torch had nearly guttered and so far as I could see he hadn't moved at all since I'd been in half an hour ago. I leaned closer; his breathing really was stentorious. At first I thought he was unconscious; then he stirred and said, "What—time to march already?"

"Hush, it's still night-time."

"Not Cija?"

"You sound incredulous."

"I thought you weren't going to come any more—"

I was unscrewing the leather top and now set it to his lips. He gasped and his eyes squinted down and widened. His mouth

139

took an immediate greedy sucking grip round the bottle-neck and he gulp-gulp-gulped until I stopped him.

He reached feebly but angrily for the bottle and I hit his hand away.

"Stupid, you can't have all now. Besides, you'd be sick. Couldn't come earlier, she wouldn't let me go. She was upset because I was late in."

"My fault."

"Don't worry. I wonder if coolness would help that bite? Is it burning?"

"No, it's only tight. Don't waste water on it. How I'd love some on my forehead, though."

"I don't think I'd better—have you any water still in your mouth?"

"Yes, I'm swilling it round."

"Spit it out on this bandage, it'll be cool on your forehead. Cooler than this air—if you call it air—"

I pressed the cooled moistened wad of stuff on his brow, his cheeks, his chin, the dusty arch of his throat, and by then the virtue had gone out it it; but his breathing lightened and I left him for a moment to light two more torches. By the new brightness I saw that his eyelids had been lowered and his mouth smoothed with an expression of relief, but the splodge of poisonous colour had spread, like ink on porous paper, to either side and up to the base of his throat.

I did not go to my own bed that night.

I sat scribbling the first part of the above entry on some paper I found—I stuck it into this Diary later—and Smahil lay beside me breathing. At times the breathing sounded painful, but he was asleep. I had to wave away endless swarms of flies, but at least that and the scribbling kept me awake. I was desperately weary. Every tendon wept feebly, pleading for sleep which I wouldn't grant. I had a hard day of riding and another evening of anxiety ahead of me so I should have slept while I could but I was new to nursing and was afraid to sleep in case anything happened. Once, when Smahil started to snore and I thought he was deeply enough asleep for me to risk it, I held one of the torches close over him and peered fearfully at the place. It had not spread much further, but the texture of the skin it coloured was very tight-stretched and shiny.

I thought, "The best thing to do is to cut it and let out the poison," but there was no lump just the flat discoloured skin. I dare not do it, I was afraid of piercing some important artery or nerve. I know nothing about anatomy, but I do know my mother told me to strike at the throat to kill. Amateur hacking at the base of Smahil's throat wasn't going to improve things.

Twice I ran out to find Blob.

The first time he was surly and baleful, said he'd help look after Smahil when I couldn't but no more, he had his own life between working hours, didn't he, no he didn't know where a surgeon was. I was sure he did know where one could be found if he only troubled to think. But I didn't stay to argue. I was terrified something else would happen to the wound while I was away.

The second time I ran to Blob he was sitting slumped, nasally snoring. I didn't dare wake him and ran, almost distracted, back to Smahil.

As daylight seeped in, the black blot looked uglier and uglier to my nervous exhausted eyes, though it had not grown any bigger.

At dawn Smahil woke and blinked up at me in surprise.

"Cija?" he said.

"I stayed all night," I explained.

"Silly, your eyelids are swollen. Didn't you get *any* sleep?"

"A little. I was too worried to sleep except when I had to but it can't have been more than a few minutes each time."

"Worried? About me?"

"About your wound. Now don't worry too, it's not bad—"

He didn't squint down to look at it, I suppose he remembered well enough what it had been like and didn't exactly feel like gloating over it. I didn't tell him it had spread.

"You'll drop off Ums asleep today—"

"No, I can relax in the saddle, I'm used to riding by now . . . Smahil, do you know where there's a surgeon?"

"The army must have them. No, I don't know where—I don't need a surgeon—"

"The poison must be got out. It might—spread—" I said with difficulty.

"Then I'd be black all over!" He laughed at my look of scared revulsion. "Why, Cija, I'd be just like your friend the General then!"

"I can't tend you all the time—I mean, I *must* get *some* sleep—can't I get Ooldra to nurse you?"

"Ooldra? I don't want poison in my food as well as in my chest."

"You've got Ooldra all wrong," I protested in distress. "She's good, and kind, and gentle. She hates only the enemy, whom

141

she hates as all from my mother's country should."

"You haven't asked how I am."

"You're as well as can be expected, I presume. You're weak. How can you ride today? Would Ijleldla or Iren let you share a carriage?"

"I'd sooner not—their carriages are so sticky—even they are riding nowadays—"

"I'll get some wagon-driver to take you and put an awning over you for shade. I'll have to ride with you and see you get your food, and this water—"

He put his dry hand on mine as I rose.

"You're a cheap little so-and-so, Cija," he said, "but you're nice to have around."

"If I'd been your cheap little so-and-so," I said, "you wouldn't have been calling me priggish names."

I went out, leaving him grinning feebly, to my surprise, for I was angry and expected him to be.

I went to the stuffy little sleeping-tent of the winegirls. But Narra was already outside and immediately we saw each other she pounced on me.

"Where have you been? You didn't appear all night. I was worried about you."

"I was with the lord Smahil—"

"Oh. " She blushed and shut herself up.

"—He's ill," I said. I sank sitting on to the ground, and she put her arms round me when she saw how exhausted I was. "Narra, there's some horrible poison in a bite he must have had—do you know where there's a surgeon?"

"Yes, I'll go and get him." She ran off.

I went in, lay down among the other girls, and was soon as asleep as they were.

I was awakened by uncertain movement outside the tent. I stumbled up the flap at the same moment as Narra lifted it and peered in. "Oh, here you are," she said. She caught my arm and guided me maternally to the hillock outside where a man in civilian clothes was sitting. He didn't rise as I approached, which angered me. "Are you a doctor?" I said.

"I'm a surgeon."

"I am a lady, one of the hostages." He didn't even bow his head. "One of my friends is ill—there's a big purplish patch on his chest, near his throat—"

"Take me there and I can see for myself."

142

We set out, me first, then the surgeon and Narra with her skirts clinging to her skinny little legs in the growing heat of the morning. I love that child.

Smahil looked up as we entered, but he didn't say anything. Only his eyes moved, his head must have seemed too heavy. His eyes had become slow and bleary and the recognition in them wasn't quick. He didn't seem interested. He had begun to sweat profusely, his skin was no longer grittily dry, and the flies which I hadn't been there to brush away were crawling all over his helpless body, in and out of his shirt, apparently drinking his sweat.

"Stay outside, Narra," I said, but when I next turned I found her still beside me.

Meanwhile I watched as the surgeon bent over Smahil. He brushed away the flies—they were too bold and too glutted to wave away—and we saw the wound. The alien colour had spred again.

"Whew," said the surgeon. "You should have called me a whole day and night ago—nearly thirty hours ago the creature bit him."

"I didn't know till yesterday evening—and no one would find you for me. Is he all right?"

"Of course he's not all right," the surgeon said irritably. He stood staring down at the torso which seemed divorced from Smahil's pain-tired face.

"I mean—will he die?"

"If only he hadn't been bitten just there. On an arm or a leg—but one can't amputate a chest or a neck."

"Then he'll die?" I clutched Narra's hand. "But, by my Cousin's Knuckle-bones, you're not to let a man just die like that. Get the poison out somehow."

I stared at him and he stared back as haughtily. "I'll remind you, madam, I'm an army surgeon but this man is not a soldier. He's a foreign lord and there's no compulsion on me to cure him—"

"To save his life!"

I flung out and dashed to the officers' quarters. There was already activity, slaves and grooms getting ready for the day's march, even packing up the tents of the earliest risers among the officers. I thought anxiously of the water-bottle in Smahil's tent. I must make sure no slave found it. The first officer whom I knew was Clor, one of the General's subordinate commanders. I ran up to him so suddenly that he choked on the bread

143

and cheese he was just swallowing, and had to spit it out before he could swallow it again. "Oh, so it's you!" he said. "Well, holy winegirl?"

"Clor—my lord, I mean—one of my fellow hostages is very ill—the surgeon won't tend him because he's not a soldier—"

"Get another surgeon, there must be one somewhere about."

"If I had the same trouble with them all, Smahil may be dead by the time they're willing. Can't you use your authority?"

"But I'm having breakfast. Oh, all right, but it had better not be too far."

We marched to Smahil's tent. I couldn't run, as the commander followed behind me, grumbling and chewing his bread and cheese.

When we got to the tent, only a three minutes' walk, the surgeon had just come out, with Narra pleading and tugging at his arm but being ignored. He saluted as he passed Clor.

"Get in there and cure that man," Clor said.

The surgeon gulped, said "Yes, sir," and darted back in. We all stood round him while he began to lance the centre of the discoloration. Clor chewing and spitting rind into the corners. "This will be a long and ticklish operation," the surgeon said over his shoulder. No one spoke, and the surgeon said, "Yes, sir," and continued his work. The lancet edged along strongly and delicately just beneath the surface of the skin, in all directions from the centre puncture. Smahil began to gain consciousness; his face twisted, he groaned. He tossed and the surgeon said, "Damn" and other things very swifty and nervily. I went over and held Smahil's hand tight. I bent down and murmured in his ear, "Smahil, the doctor's taking out the poison. It must hurt but if you move it'll be dangerous. Dig your nails in my hand or something. Don't move. It'll all be over as soon as he's finished."

"Idiot," Smahil said with difficulty.

Thick, greenish-black pus began to ooze in driblets from the central puncture as the surgeon's fingers over the skin stroked towards it.

"Narra," I said in exasperation to prevent myself being sick, "*will* you go out as I told you?"

"I'm holding his other hand, though, Cija," she said. She looked pale but was gazing at the rugs.

Clor chewed stolidly, watching the surgeon.

I had to keep brushing away flies from the place. They were attracted by the pus and the surgeon cursed luridly in a soft

144

unending sentence without many verbs.

"Less foul language before a superior," said Clor who swears like a demon himself.

More stroking, more lancet.

It was certainly taking a long time.

When the lancet came to the curve up from chest to throat it could not bend, it could go no farther. "You see?" the surgeon said with grim triumph. "You should have called me yesterday."

"Stroke the poison down," Clor said.

"I can't, sir."

Clor stopped chewing and stared at the surgeon and the surgeon gulped again and started stroking, cursing faster and softer than ever.

I wondered why the pain in my hand had gone and realized Smahil's gouging nails had at last numbed my palm.

"Nothing's moving," Narra said.

"You see, sir?" the surgeon said. "The way isn't open. It's no good."

"I told you to do it and you'll obey," Clor repeated, unfairly.

"But if I puncture it again and go up his throat, I'll kill him outright," the surgeon protested frantically.

"Will he die anyway?"

"Probably, sir."

"Then try it. Control your damned hand, don't go so deep."

The ears of the surgeon's bent head reddened angrily. He made another tiny incision, in Smahil's taut throat. Smahil breathed through his mouth, his eyes closed. He seemed quite calm except for the quivering in his arm as he directed all his pain into the hand that gripped on mine. The lancet drove slowly up under the ugly skin. It stopped; it was drawn out backwards. The surgeon stroked downwards, and the thick poison bubbled out of the hole.

The surgeon brushed away more flies, wiping his sweating hand on the seat of his trousers, wiped away the poison on a piece of linen, did more stroking, wiped away more poison.

"The patch has shrunk a little," Narra whispered.

Smahil's eyelids quivered.

"It'll never all come at this rate," I said.

There was the sound of bustle near outside. The surgeon continued stroking. A slave put his head in the tent, and backed out again with an apology.

"We'll be moving off soon, sir," the surgeon said to Clor.

"Is he all right now?" Clor asked, hesitating.

"If the poison is regularly stroked out, and the hole is kept open."

"Isn't there any quicker way?"

"Only if someone puts their lips to it and sucks it all out," the surgeon snapped. "Sir."

Clor looked at me.

"You wanted him saved. Might as well get it done."

The surgeon, folding up his things, looked at me and grinned.

"All right," I said. Without giving myself time to flinch I bent down, set my lips to the hole and began to suck. I heard Narra gasp.

"Don't swallow any," Clor said.

I heard the doctor go out. I brought up my head, spat, sucked again, spat. When I looked down Smahil's skin was nearly all white again, or rather pink, and sore-looking. I set my lips to the next hole.

After what seemed a long time the blue was gone. I stood up, feeling dizzy. Smahil was unconscious. Clor steadied me. There was a hideous taste in my mouth, and I was terrified I had swallowed some. "Have some cheese," he said. I shook my head. I thought I wanted to be sick. He looked closely at me, shook his head, and again shook the cheese in front of me. I took it and felt better. "Narra's gone?" I said.

"She went out to arrange things with a wagoner. Well, you've won."

I smiled up at him but he looked serious, which seemed strange on Clor's face which is usually placid or bluff. He slapped me on the shoulder. "All right now?" he said. "I've got to go. He'll do."

The theft of the water was discovered but suspicion didn't fall on me. I was obviously as dusty and thirsty as everyone else.

I gave the bottle to Smahil, who hid it in the straw on which he lies jolting under a rough awning. He finished it the first day, proving how much he'd needed it, and I was glad I hadn't had more than a sip or two to mobilize my parched tongue, though he'd offered me some whenever I rode up to see how he was doing. He didn't even ask for any more for two days, aware that he'd already caused me trouble by pleading for water, and had to make do with the ordinary water ration, not half enough to do him any good. He has fever; most of his water goes not on drinking but on cooling his bandage and forehead. He spends a lot of the time unconscious or semi-conscious, and the rest of the time tossing. His hands, always wet with sweat, will clench and unclench, spasmodically, over and over again till I want to scream.

The boredom must be almost worse than the jolting, the heat and the pain. I ride beside him to talk to him whenever I can nip away from the entourage, though lately I've had to curtail the visits to quite an extent because she was furious when I kept not being in my place.

He likes to have someone beside him, to talk to, but the only person who talks to him, the wagoner's mate, sometimes talks incessantly about nothing, certain he's "taking Smahil's mind off it," in reality driving him to screaming-point.

Sometimes it is wearing simply to watch Smahil. His hands, brow and mouth twitch, even his cheeks under their sweat seem drawn merely by incessant muzzy pain. Today I said, "I wish I could bear some of your pain, it would be easier in a way for both of us then."

He said, "Think what the world would be like if that were possible. Acquaintances you met in the street would say, 'Got a cold today' when you greeted them with 'How are you?' And instead of replying, 'Oh, I'm so sorry' it would be expected of you to say politely 'Oh, let me take some of it for you.'"

"But," I said sensibly, "perhaps people would have the sense not to make that an accepted convention when it would be so inconvenient to them?"

Smahil replied, "You are too idealistic, you don't know the world."

I was quite taken aback as I thought I already knew everything about the world.

Blob, who said he would tend Smahil when I could not, has utterly gone back on his word. He does nothing, and the wagoner does as much as he can without anyone ever asking him to. I've reproached Blob and he glared at me, said he hated the army, had contempt for trollops, and refused to foul himself by tending their lemans, surely tending the leman's bird was enough for anyone, wasn't it, and if not, so what?

"But you promised," "I'm busy, go to hell."

It's a good thing my mother taught me never to really trust anyone.

I must get more water for Smahil, he must have it.

Last night I tried to get water but there was no chance. Blob was hanging round the tent in the early evening and later I could not get in anyway because Lara and Zerd were in there.

Tonight I shall try as hard as I can, all today I have to watch Smahil lying feverish, tossing on the soiled straw, his hands clenching, his dry mouth twisted. His skin is peeling, the lips seem to be composed of hanging shreds. When I changed his bandage I found the place from which the poison was drained has come up in large blisters which I keep picking so they shall stay flat. They look quite ordinary healthy blisters; I suppose it is all right.

This morning in those dreary hours when I always used to think all the healthy world must sleep, I woke myself almost forcibly, crawled among the sleeping winegirls with my head nodding like a wounded bear's, and out through the white ashes of countless fires guarded by sentries in their last defeat by sleep—to the tent.

I skirted the late-placed guards before it, and crawled silently under the wall in the place steadily frayed by Narra and I in the days when it was the Beauty's tent.

Everything inside was dark.

I crept to the table where I know the water is kept.

Now I swear I made no sound whatsoever, not one that a mouse could have heard—for my feet know how to take the floor lightly and swiftly but ball first, testing the ground for potential sound, then the toes, and at last the heel while the ball of the other foot is already testing for the next step. But he has the senses of a lynx, I have often thought that.

"Ah," said a voice, bland and terrifyingly loud in a darkness where all one's instinct was to whisper, if one must speak. His hand, I would know the touch of it anywhere, closed round my waist.

A light was struck.

She had lit it, leaning over in her bed, smiling at me. She was wearing her frothy night-shift and trousers, white decorated with pink and blue flowers, rather dishevelled now as her things always are in the morning. Zerd, holding me, wore nothing. My glance flickered at him and away. I should have known better, but I am afraid I was embarrassed. I wondered if men all look like that, when they'e naked.

"We thought we'd be honoured by a visit from you some time tonight," he said.

"How could you know?"

"Didn't your amiable accomplice tell you we caught him last night?"

"I have no accomplice."

"A short, large-bellied man, creeping in here for water last night, as you do tonight, and when we caught him he blurted that he was doing it for you, otherwise you threatened him with awful threats."

"I know who the man is, Immense One, Blob, a groom. But I never sent him to do anything for me. He wanted the water for himself, and blamed me when you caught him. He hates me."

"Interesting, though squalid, to find out what petty hates go on among our servants," commented Lara.

The General answered me, grinning with his mouth closed. "Yet you come for water. You're a thief whether or not you have an accomplice."

"I need the water for my friend who has fever."

"Who?"

"The lord Smahil."

"Then let him die, if he can't manage without being a receiver of stolen water. I told you, hostages are useless."

"I won't let him die."

"Sick men who are not even soldiers are a drag on a campaign. If the maps can be believed—and they should be, where patches of civilization are concerned—we should be reaching a town in the foothills in a week's time. Since we aren't going to pillage it, it should be a safe harbour. Leave him there."

"I won't. I presume there'll be a lot of water there. He can last till then."

"On stolen water?"

"He'll manage somehow, thank you, Your Mightiness. I'll take no more of your water."

"Good."

He loosened my wrist and turned back to the bed, ignoring me, to show that I could go.

"I'm glad you've shown me in time how untrustworthy you are," said Lara.

I turned. "Princess, you've shown me you despise me—"

"Yes, I do." "—Surely you no longer want me as your slave? Can't I go back to my own rank of hostage?"

"I shall do nothing to please you. You are my winegirl, from now on, no longer my personal maid. It is no fit punishment for all your deceit."

149

"He called this a town?" I said as Narra and I, in the baggage-train, rode side by side up the street.

The street was narrow and stinking, littered with refuse. The central drain was uncovered, and more like a sewer than a drain. Furtive faces watched us from windows and doorways like rat-holes. The tramp of the army echoed like endless roars from gigantic lions. At first, reaching a town by a pure river at which everyone had first slaked their thirst, the men had sung marching-songs. But now they did not sing. The march-echo was bad enough.

"But it is a town, Cija, a big town. That's why a whole regiment is taking up cantonments near the palace instead of us all being camped outside the walls—and that's why there is a palace anyway, with the town's governor living in it, where the General and his staff and household can be lodged. This isn't just a village, Cija."

"But the squalor!"

As I spoke, a ball of muck, which the feet of the men before us had been idly kicking along, one after another, now bowled against Um's claws. He shied indignantly.

"Ums has got worse, Cija, he was so well-trained when you got him. Now that he knows you, he obeys no one else and shies when he wants to. And to get back to what we were saying, this is obviously a prosperous town!"

"Hold your nose, we're coming to a bad part!" I called back to Smahil in the wagon behind us. "Prosperous!" I snorted to Narra.

"I've seen really poor towns," Narra said, "and in those the streets are as clean as a lady's rug. Every twig and nail and scrap of paper is picked up and polished and straightened, and made some use of. Old men crouch on street corners with two nails for sale; boxes can be made from old chips of wood."

However, the higher parts of the town near the palace improved quite a bit.

Later Zerd reined in beside me for a moment.

"Glad of civilization again?"

"Civilization! The lower parts are slums, and these streets are avenues, with trees all along them!"

"Different from your mother's slagheap, eh?"

"Who made it a slagheap?" I muttered under my breath.

"Your friend nicely buried?"

"He's in that wagon."

150

"Dead?"

"No, better."

He sat upright in surprise and his hand tightened on the rein so that his bird curvetted. "Whose water have you been getting at to steal now? By the World's First Quiet Midnight, the water ration wouldn't have tided over a man with fever. When you left that night I was certain you'd reach here mourning him."

"Commander Clor has sent a boy each morning with a half-full water-skin."

"*Clor?*"

"Yes."

"But he's not in his dotage yet."

"Well, he seems to be capable of kindness."

"Come, I thought we were friends."

"I dare not hope so, Your Mightiness, after the other night."

He glanced at me sideways under the black bar of his brows. The brows rose. "She's been treating you like a winegirl, I suppose, since she demoted you to one? Been beaten again?"

"Not quite, my lord."

"I see."

I looked ahead. From the corner of my eye I saw him beside me. He rubbed two fingers across his long chin, eyeing me steadily all the time. "I don't think you should remain either a winegirl or a hostage," he remarked at last.

"I haven't much choice, my lord."

"Come to my room tomorrow night."

I looked up. He smiled. One corner of his mouth went up. He knew, of course, I would accept. Suddenly I felt happier than ever before. I forgot everything, forgot Smahil, forgot Narra, forgot the strangeness of the streets, forgot the marching troops, forgot the agonies of the plain-journey, forgot the weary months.

"Your wife will expect you," I said.

"She is not my wife," the General said, "and she can wait."

Suddenly I laughed and flung my arms wide. The General laughed, threw back his beautiful head on the strong arch of his throat and laughed, and the troops looked round curiously at us as we spurred our birds.

The regiment with us made camp in and about the courtyard of the town-governor's palace. Officers found billets in the houses nearby, but strict orders were given that the native

151

civilians were to be treated with courtesy if not respect, and that any man found committing rape, manslaughter or anything approaching it, or plundering would be hanged high in the courtyard before everybody.

The Golds, one of the smartest regiments, should have been chosen, but that would have been disaster, the non-existent Moon alone knew how many fights would have broken out in the Blues and the Golds if the latter had been chosen. So the men in the town are the 19th foot, with whom I was unfamiliar. There is a large percentage of old campaigners in this regiment.

When, to a certain extent, living off the land—for the town is having to feed us—it being, at the same time, land we wish more or less to conciliate, old campaigners are, apart from anything else, more economical. It's astonishing how, whenever possible, the men prefer a bedstead of any sort to their sleeping-bags, even if it's only a few planks under their palliasse. The raw soldiers are inclined to chop up any wooden boxes they can find, for bedsteads, only to find they were valuable. And young soldiers never believe that very little hay is needed inside a sleeping-bag. They will stuff themselves in like field-mice, waking up later cramped and chilled instead of warmed.

But veterans have more nerve.

Unpacking the tents for the courtyard, it was discovered that one of the poles was broken. They went to the Accoutrements Master but there was already a long queue and that side of the army is always anguish to deal with, you have to prove in triplicate that you really need a new tent-pole, and when at last you're told to come back for it at noon tomorrow exactly, everyone's on the march again anyway. So three men went down to the encampment outside the town where everyone was dashing about settling in. They marched up to an empty tent, all nicely set up, and two of them measured the pole while the other took an official-looking little black notebook from his tunic-pocket and busily scribbled in it. They then removed the pole, left the tent to collapse behind them, and marched back with it to their own camp. Nobody accosted them; they looked exactly as if they knew what they were doing (which they did) and as if they knew that they had been ordered to do it by thirteen commanders in person (which they didn't).

Their officer, when he found out about it, kept his mouth shut. He now had the requisite number of poles, that was all he cared about.

We were only told of this later, with many guffaws. Meanwhile we were being rather flurriedly welcomed in the palace hall.

The hall is more an inner courtyard. It must usually be very quiet but for the plashings of the fountain. It is partially unroofed. Curiously enough, by coincidence in this elegant hall there is a tree growing, just as trees grew in the foresters' hall. But this is a rarely-bred, exquisite deformity of a tree, bearing many different fruits all together. It is small and slender, just as this hall is polite and airy and a hundred times lighter than the hall in the forest. There is a beautiful marble staircase leading up to the upper floor.

The town-governor and his household were lined up to greet us. They wore their stiffest clothes and bowed deep and creakily as we entered. They must have been astonished at our rough, careless, boisterous entry. We also wore our best clothes, but they are mostly stained and badly-creased, and the commanders yelled any remark they made as if it were a battle-command, and pushed each other into the fountain, while the grooms ran in with birds to be told where the stables were. The General, after bowing courteously, cut short a long-prepared speech from the governor and introduced his wife and his principal commanders. The governor and his little lot bowed decorously to each person as he was named, but began to blink nervously as Isad and Clor were indicated. It is difficult to bow to someone who is pushing someone else into a fountain and completely ignoring you. Lara and the staff secretaries wandered round looking at the bright wall-panels. The winegirls stood chattering and glancing around, clustered together. The governor, quite bewildered by so many people taking no notice of him, grew purple in the face. He is a big thickset man with a bull neck and protuberant greenish eyes. He is about fifty, and exudes a feeling of aggressive masculinity. I don't know why, he is the sort of man who makes me shudder a little.

"Now we should like to see our rooms," Zerd said.

The governor led him over to the staircase—the more menial of us followed closely, the rest trailed behind or simply didn't bother—and the governor stood aside to let his guests precede him. I ran up, two steps at a time, and only when I was at the top did I realize that everyone else was still at the bottom.

They all stood quiet, with upturned faces, then gasped.

"What's the matter?" I said, feeling appallingly self-conscious alone at the top there. "I'm sorry, I thought we were

153

supposed to come up here—" and I began to descend again, feeling the blushes rising up my throat and scorching my cheeks.

"How do you do it?" "Where did you learn?" said several voices.

"Learn what?" I asked, most embarrassed.

"She *ran* up, *two* at a *time*," said someone.

I was now at the bottom and a crowd of winegirls ran forward cheering me, and Isad came up, dripping wet, hooting on his pet horn. Lara looked sour.

"Do it again, do it again!" cried the winegirls to me.

"What is it?" I said.

"You're so fast, could you do it again just as fast?"

"Of course, my country is full of stairs. Our houses are often four-storeyed—aren't yours?"

"No," Zerd said. "We don't have stairs in the North. Do it again, Cija, it's fascinating to watch."

So I ran up and down the stairs for them twice more, and they cheered me and chanted compliments, and at last all trooped up after me. The governor, who had been waiting impatiently by the stair-rail, heaved a sigh of relief.

Later I stood in the corridor above, leaning on the balustrade and looking down into the courtyard. The governor, having shown the last commander into his room, came out, closed the door and leaned against it. He saw me and at once he came across and chucked me under the chin.

"All deserted, pretty little girl?"

"Yes, sir." I moved my chin. He is one of those men who stand far too close, stooping to stare in one's face as they talk. His breath is bad.

"There is a bond between us, my pretty, isn't there, since both of us are native to stairs!" He laughed laboriously and I laughed too, wishing he'd go to hell. I was more astounded than anything else when, after that brief, preliminary conversation, he shoved his hand down my neckline and grabbed hold of one of my breasts.

Please, sir, this is hardly—" I began when I felt the strength and roughness in his large, blunt, hairy hand. He was, of course, quite ignoring my protest. He stared ahead, breathing fast, his hand in my dress. I was wondering how to deal with this—to kick him would have pushed him backwards, without his letting go, and probably I would be hurt—whether to spit in his face or bite his wrist, when one of the doors behind us opened and shut again as someone came out.

154

"Excuse me, this is rather ungentlemanly conduct, isn't it?" said Zerd, coming at the right moment just like a hero in a book.

The governor swung quickly round, became puce, put his chin up and stared haughtily at Zerd. He became aware that his arm was still hidden up to the elbow, drew it carefully out, stood looking sheepish, glared.

He walked away.

Zerd laughed but I felt sick, as if I had been *used* for something horrid and had become horrid by helping.

Zerd leaned on the balustrade beside me and looked down at the fountain. Then he glanced aside at me.

"Don't look so sick," he said. "He didn't hurt you."

"I feel defiled," I said.

"Women always say that," he said, eyeing me ironically, "if anything happens to which they haven't given *their* permission. Apart from the fact that it's a very melodramatic word, it's very conceited of them to think of themselves as so pure and heavenly that a man can defile them by touching them."

"You're wrong, you're wrong," I said, hiding my tears. "He could wash every day with scented soap, he'd still be filthy and pollute anything he touched in that hard-breathing *using* way."

"Here, lean against me and be cleansed," he said. I leant against him and folded in his arms I was cleansed, but he was still laughing at me.

"My room," he said, his chin brushing my hair as he spoke, "is that one there. Remember it for tomorrow?"

"Yes, my lord."

He lifted my face and I found that we were smiling into each other's eyes. It is a queer sensation, I have never done it before, it is like drowning must be. "I wish it were tonight—or today," he added. "How is your room?"

"A big attic to share with the other girls, but quite pleasant. Everything is lovely here. I've never seen such magnificence!"

"You've seen nothing. The Northern King's hall is paved with gold pieces—not just ordinary gold, mark you, but gold coins laid all together, to make it more valuable!"

"Ooh!"

"But, of course, this isn't too bad, particularly after the plain."

"Why aren't we plundering it?" I asked curiously. "Surely it's unlike you to restrain your army unnecessarily—and this town is an outpost of the Southern Empire, against which you're marching."

"Because any news of our pillaging this place would spread like wildfire to the other towns and villages in the mountains we have to cross, and we'd meet with resistance we don't want yet. Besides, it might even spread to the City beyond the mountains, and then we'd be done for. A lot of good all our plans would have been."

"Why?"

"Is it possible you don't know everything?"

"You're mocking me."

"And you always hate that, don't you? All right, floss-hair. You didn't know we are going to act as the Southerners' allies before we conquer them?"

"How? Against whom?"

"Atlan."

"Atlan? What a beautiful word. When you said it I felt a singing here."

"You don't know what Atlan is?"

"No, tell me."

"In the East lies a continent called Atlan. It used to be the most potent power in the world but as its priests and scientists grew more and more skilled and noble, its sovereigns grew less and less warlike. Until at last they foreswore war and the management of their colonies, and enclosed themselves in an era of utter peace, and there is no trade, no communication between them and any of the other continents, and has been none for centuries."

"Utter peace? Has no one ever tried to conquer such a great land?"

"Before it enfolded itself from the world, the scientists threw a wall right around the continent, and though it is invisible neither beast nor bird nor man can penetrate it."

"What is it?" I said in awe.

"Make no mistake, it's not magic, it's science. They withdrew all air from the area of the barrier. Atlan is surrounded by a mile-wide vacuum, holding nothing. One can go to it, watch little birds circling around in the air above the sea—if they get a wing too far over into the vacuum—they hurtle. There's nothing there to hold them. Nothing to breathe. No army, no ships, can get within a mile of those shores."

"Fish?"

"Yes, but what army is going to swim underwater for a mile?"

"Then what—?"

"Our Northern scientists have long desired to find a way of

piercing the barrier, our kings have long desired to conquer and own Atlan. They have all died with that closest desire unfulfilled—until the lifetime of this generation. In the North we have discovered how to inject atmosphere into a vacuum. We shall do this to Atlan's monstrous vacuum—sail up to it, make it air again, sail through it, land on the forbidden selfish shores—"

"But the Atlanteans, even if they have no soldiers, must be dangerous to invaders—their scientists must have great powers—"

"That is why we need an army larger than any one country can give, particularly our Northern army with its raw troops which I've had to drag through so much."

"Then?"

"We shall inform the Southerners of our discovery—though without revealing to them the formula—and promise them half of Atlan and everything we find there if they help us to gain it—With their army and ours combined we'll take Atlan by surprise, conquer it before it can build up any resistance—then we'll take back our promises to the Southerners and possess all Atlan and the Southern Empire, too."

"I had no inkling of any of this—"

"From whom did you get your information?"

"From a leader."

"Leaders don't know everything."

"No, I see that . . . I must sit down a minute, I'm bemused."

We sat down side by side on a stair.

"I would kiss you," he said, "but if you're the Cija I guess, you'd struggle because there's someone down there in the courtyard?"

"They're not watching."

"They might. They oughtn't to get too bad an opinion of me, they've already been present when the governor—"

The someone being honoured by our attention was an old bent man with a large white moustache. We watched him tidying up the courtyard which looked as if it had been struck by a hurricane. "Look, there's even evidence of the birds brought in here," Zerd said. "What careless fellows our grooms are."

"Oh!" I sat bolt upright. "Talking of grooms—Your Mightiness, might I ask a favour of you?"

The two fingers caressed his long dark chin. "You might," he said, the black, black-browed eyes considering me.

"Blob, the man who informed untruthfully against me—can I have him punished?"

157

"Of course, my darling. Clor! Clor!" he shouted. "Eng! Isad! Gods curse them, there's no one about. Wait here. I feel like some action. I'll see to it."

He went quickly but carefully down the stairs, strode out through the courtyard, making the old man scuttle out of his way, and presently I too got up and wandered down to examine the wall-panels.

Someone came in and I turned.

"Smahil!"

"Hello," said Smahil nonchalantly but with an ill-concealed smirk.

"You're walking!"

"Narra got me up. Had you forgotten all about me?"

"I was with someone—I've been busy—"

"So I presumed," he replied equably. "A nice hall, this, isn't it?"

"Very. But did you know that the hall of the Northern King is paved with real gold coins?"

"Rot."

"It's not rot."

"Who told you that?"

"The General."

He took that amiably too. "He was teasing you. No one could have gold coins on a floor. Gold is so soft that after about two people had walked across it it would all be blurred and indistinguishable as coins so what would be the good of them anyway?"

"Oh."

"Yes."

"You're very amiable about the General's relationship with me suddenly."

"You've stopped denying it."

"You never believed my denials."

"Well, there you are, then."

"How are you feeling? You look different, somehow."

"Thinner and whiter, yes. I feel O.K., except my knees are a bit shaky."

"You look different from what you were before you got bitten."

"I'm more resigned to everything, perhaps?" Smahil suggested flippantly.

"I don't know. You look calmer and yet wilder—like a —like a forest man."

"Shall I put a large snail-shell on my head, with an edging of

158

gilt added to each whorl to smarten the whole thing up, like I saw a man in the forest wearing?"

"Did you? What a delightfully simple idea for a hat—if you live in an area infested by large snails—"

Smahil touched my arm. I twisted round, and saw the General enter, two soldiers behind him. The General stopped on the threshold. His eyes went from me to Smahil, and the cold look descended over his face. "My Cousin," I thought, "is Smahil's mere presence to ruin everything again?"

But I believe I flattered myself. The General might not have been pleased, but I am only a winegirl, nothing to be possessive about.

He came forward. "Your prisoner will be brought here soon, lady."

I gurgled with laughter, intent on removing the cold look. "Oh, Mightiness, lovely to be called Lady!"

He came to stand beside me, and in doing so glanced indifferently at Smahil. Smahil caught his eye and bowed.

"My friend, the lord Smahil, who was ill," I said. "You haven't met him before, I believe?"

"No, we haven't," Smahil said politely. The General said nothing. I had expected him to ask after Smahil's health.

"He is, as you can see, up and about again after all my care," I explained archly. Smahil glanced at me with surprised distaste.

Another soldier escorted in Blob.

They halted in front of us. The soldiers saluted. Blob looked paunchy and sullen. He stared boldly at the soldiers, but his eyes fell before Zerd's. His gaze crept away, sideways like a crab. He saw me and looked realization and hate at me. I looked back, disdainfully.

"What a pity your nose isn't longer," whispered Smahil beside me, "to look down."

"Your name?" said Zerd.

"Blob, Mightiness."

"And your excuse for existence?"

"Beg pardon, sir?"

"What is your job?"

"Oh. I—I groom birds. The gentleman's there, and the young—woman's—at one time," he added, pointing at me. I stopped myself recoiling, though I felt almost as if I were being accused.

"The young lady was recently the victim of an ill-judged lie on your part," Zerd said, obviously beginning to enjoy himself

159

as he heard himself becoming more improbably pedantic.

Blob's brows crept into an unbroken line of blue-black resentment.

"You falsely claimed that she had sent you to my wife the princess Lara's tent in order illicitly to obtain water. Goddess, you asseverate that this is the man who falsely claimed . . . ?"

It surprised me for a moment to be called Goddess. I had almost forgotten that I am. "Yes, Your Mightiness, this is the man."

"Then," said Zerd, running out of pomposity and relinquishing his responsibility, "what punishment do you wish him to receive?"

"Seven strokes of the lash," I said, enjoying myself.

"Jaleth, seven strokes of the lash for this man. Take him out."

Blob turned on me a look of burning venom which heightened my exultation, but unexpectedly he said nothing. I knew that he had already been whipped, some days before, for entering the tent. Well, I'm no longer the little darling who gets hysterical at the thought of a whipping—not for someone like Blob. He was taken out.

A civilian servant came running in. "My master the governor begs you to honour his private table with your presence and that of your wife." "I thank you," said Zerd. "Accept the governor's offer for us." The servant ran out. "Dinner time already," said Smahil. "I'd better find my tent again. See you later, Cija." He sauntered away. The courtyard by now was dim with violet dusk which had been coming through the doorway and the open roof and steadily intensifying. The designs on the walls could hardly be made out. The fountain plashed and liquidly twittered in the sudden stillness; only distant sounds, barks and shouts, could be heard from the camp outside. "Till tomorrow night, my lord," I said. He seized me by the shoulders, pulled me in under the rustling violet branches of the multi-fruit tree, and kissed me hard and for the first time. A wave of perfume seemed to sweep round me; I could not tell which of the many fruits if any were predominating in it. I closed my eyes, I thought I swam, that other kiss beside the riverfalls had been nothing to this for this was the riverfalls too, his lips pulsed like the riverfalls in which I drowned, in a drowning clashed through with—well, I can't describe it any more. I'm getting lost and precious, but when he released me and I opened my eyes I was surprised to find myself still standing on my feet. "Till tomorrow night," he said.

160

After some difficulty I managed to find Ooldra's tent. It was strange how familiar it was.

"Cija!"

"It's me, Ooldra!"

She looked at me in astonishment, then recollected herself, got up and embraced me.

"Dear Ooldra, it's happened! It's happened at last! I'm certainly going to his room tomorrow night!"

"Cija!" She held me from her, staring at me.

"Ooldra, you've actually forgotten yourself enough to stare at me! You'd given up hope, hadn't you? So had I!"

"You have your knife?"

"Be sure."

"The throat, Cija—strike at the throat."

"I will. And you'll arrange our getaway? Tomorrow's not too soon for you?"

"I'll arrange everything," she said rather grimly.

"Well, this will be my second-last evening meal in the Northern army! Don't you feel wonderful, Ooldra? What are you giving me to eat?"

It was a lovely meal. Fresh meat, water—somehow, after the plain, nobody looks upon wine as a delicacy beside water—vegetables with a spiced sauce, all served by the beaming Tilia. Before she left she brought in the fruit-bowl.

By this time I was drowsy.

"Here, sit up and take this fruit," Ooldra said, smiling at me. I took the fruit from her hand, smiled back at her, and bit into the soft, dreamy, wholesome-perfumed, juicy flesh. Then as I reached the stone a long wriggling maggot, livid and blotched with green, raced rearing at my mouth in blind panic as I penetrated its long home. I screamed, threw the fruit from me. Ooldra was genuinely horrified.

"Have you seen it, Ooldra?"

"How could it be, Cija, what are you talking of?" she cried. Her face twisted; she raised the hand with which she had given me the fruit, her palm still smeared from the delicious pulp. Then swiftly she shrugged and her mouth again held the old smile which tells me that her inscrutable silver eyes hold a benediction for me. "Come, sweetling," she said, "no nervousness from us now. Everything will be all right."

"Have you seen it, Ooldra?"

"For years I have known you will compass his death."

I crept into her arms and she rocked me to sleep.

But in the night I came back to the winegirls' room in the palace and have written crouched in my alcove-corner ever since, with one candle, because I cannot sleep.

Tomorrow night.

Tonight.

All this day we have all been free to come and go just as we please. I washed my hair this morning and while it was drying slept up here in the big, daylit, empty attic in order to take the bruise-blue shadows from under my eyes and to relax my nerves.

I have polished my nails, blacked my lashes—they are already black but it thickens them—put scent in the parting of my hair, behind my ears, in my armpits, and between my breasts. I had a bath before I dressed; I put scent in the water, and splashed cold water on my breasts to tauten them. I shaved my armpits, which is difficult when there is no one who can help; I wondered about the hair between my thighs, but it would be so difficult and for all I know men may like it? I've plucked my eyebrows, burnished my hair till it shines, and piled it on my head, skewered with malachite-headed pins. I'm dressed, in my very best clothes, which I have never before worn; my mother gave them to me for just such an occasion. Now I sit and wait and write to calm myself, and occasionally put out a leg to admire its long pearliness and the straightness of the shin beneath the glimmering stuff looped in by black ribbon at the ankle. I hate looking at women with legs forcibly sloped by the width of their hips. Though, now I come to think of it, the fatter a woman's hips and seat the more feminine she looks. The most popular camp-followers are those.

Gods, why should I worry? Does it matter whether he likes me? In a few hours' time he'll be dead, and I'll creep out as any pretty winegirl might from his room and I'll meet Ooldra—and tomorrow I'll be far away, with Him dead, the world saved from his menace and my country revenged and my birth-prophecy nullified—

But Gods, I want to please him. I want him to think me beautiful though he is evil and my enemy; and I cannot please him, I shall be inadequate and innocent.

Is it stupid of me to have dressed like this? Should I go to him in the same clothes I wore yesterday? Will he laugh at me when I go to him?

He will not know I am virgin, he will think me experienced. Will he be sudden, will he be cruel? Ooldra thought him a

162

sadist; my Cousin, give me endurance.

Those relentlessly strong scaled hands will soon be plucking galvanically at the air, that firm mouth open, loose and desperate, his dark eyes glazing—or looking up with astonishment and final realization at me, his hostage-plaything.

The little knife hangs round my neck in an enamelled scabbard shaped like a fish. It looks like an ornament. I have sharpened the blade, it is thin as a razor, and the point is barbed.

When I close my eyes and place myself in the dark-blood throbbing enfoldedness beneath my eyelids I feel again all that fear, that desire, that terror (a different thing from the fear), that revulsion and that determination all of which I felt that night and thought agonizing, but which now is a release, absurd to find such emotion a release, absurd in any other situation. And one thinks, One day, there can be another situation, another situation in which, maybe, I will let myself feel the emotion I dare not feel now and for which I substitute that night's emotion—and it will be a release, what I dare not feel now will be a release in the situation which one day will be on me. Things can always get worse.

Never trust—never trust. And that, at a time like this, at the threshold of the kind of life I shall from now on think of as life, is one of the most comforting things I can think of. Like bread and milk when I was sick as a child. A talisman of comfort if not of cure. Never trust. Be beyond trust, be above it.

There is no one and no thing. To know that already, is to be guarded from the ardent wrenching griefs of the world.

One develops a mind with two compartments, and the dividing screen is pale and transparent and very fragile; in one compartment is me, turbid, dark, moiling with shrill grief and bitterness and despair but passionate, despair passionate; in the other compartment is I, very new, unknown to me before; regarding the larger compartment through the screen with pity and a determination to keep the screen intact. And so I coldly and clinically watch myself, guarding myself from harm, deliberately thinking about my grief instead of feeling it. It is an effort, but it is beginning to get easier. I have not cried since it happened.

At the appointed hour I dropped scent into my sandals and put them on. I went out from the large, empty, mattress-strewn room of my innocence just before the other winegirls were due to return. Feeling for the first time that particular crescendo of fear-desire-terror-revulsion-determination which then was an-

163

guish but now is release, I crept through the long corridors.

The governor's palace was dark by now in its upper reaches. Occasionally the twisted brass pillars were gleam-lit by flambeaux behind glass screens. The flames bit uselessly at the glass, tearing nothing from it but darts of scintillant tiny colours. A large dark animal of strange shape loped the width of the passage before me; it did not trouble to turn its head to me so I could not even see the colour of its eyes. I passed the shadows where I knew it was. I wondered what sort of pets the governor kept. As I went on through the passages, up and down short stairways—but I had memorized the way well—I had the feeling that I was in a vast building breathing night-intrigue, pullulating with lovers. There were dark couples, a couple but one shape, in the niches; the whispering in the air could have been the draperies stirred by a draught along the corridors, but it was not. A girl passed one of the alcoves: she had bare feet which at each step met their pale serene reflections in the polished floor. The crystal beads on her anklets and trousers were made each a little rainbow by the light behind her. I said "Good evening" because from the shadow-blanked oval of her face her eyes had met mine. A man whom I had not suspected was in the folds of a great door-curtain reached out and caught her. Just two arms and she turned away past me without a word; there were the sounds of sharp panting immediately. I ran on. Even the light staccato of my soles on the marble embarrassed me; I took off my sandals and held them by their ribbon-thongs as I went onwards.

When I came to the door I simply stood in front of it.

What did one do?

Knock on it and wait for him to open it and say "Come in"?

It seems absurd, I thought. The whole situation is absurd. Come on.

I tried the door, found it unlocked, and went in, knocking as I pushed it to show that I was here.

The room was empty.

At once my heart, which I had not realized was beating hard, calmed and become more regular. I realized that my shoulders were hunched and a tightness in my arm muscles stilled as if I had meant to stab him as soon as we met. At the same time, a kind of aching intensity numbing my groins melted.

I looked round. I was conscious that soon I would be anxious and puzzled but meanwhile I was feeling sublimely relieved.

I went to the immense shallow-bowl shaped bed, an amazement of intricately wrought and sprung metal, which hung from the ceiling by a delicate-looking chain, and sat down on it because my knees were weak. It rocked slightly. There was a girl in it.

She had been watching my entrance and my movements with inscrutable pale eyes which now met mine.

Her expression was so non-committal that in the first seconds all my own mind noted about her was the shapes her hair took as it spread all around her on the pillows, and the pattern of the enamel tracery on her big earrings and the necklace as it rose and fell on the pulse of her brown throat and disappeared down under the bedclothes. Only when I thought "I wonder if she is wearing anything below the necklace or if she is naked under the bedclothes!" did I realize how inexplicable her presence seemed.

I was about to ask her mildly if she had the right room (though feeling rather awkward before that calm unwinking, unquestioning, upward-glowing observation) when the lips parted. "Get out," she said.

I drew back in astonishment.

The eyes had disconcerted me because they seemed incapable of thought or emotion and now she said this.

"But no," I said, "I have come here for His Mightiness."

For a moment she continued the yet-unaltered gaze. Then she sat upright with a shrill scream and grasped my hair by its beautiful chignon. The work of hours tumbled down in an instant between her steel-arched fingers. Immediately she altered her grip and hauled me toward her. She had already slapped me once with her other hand when I first thought of retaliating. That's the trouble, I'm always so slow in these encounters. Bemused. Anyway, I reached out (the pain in my head was excruciating where she was still wrenching at my hair) and I spread my hand fingers-wide at the base of her throat and pushed. She gulped and became flushed and screamed something filthy at me. I didn't catch it but I knew it was filthy because all that kind of word seem to be composed mainly of the same letter. We rolled over each other, scratching and clawing to grasp and yet defend. The bed swayed and swung from its delicate, strong spring-chain, though this was not the kind of movement it had been designed for. I caught at her necklace and tugged and it broke. Instead of subsiding, the flush on her face deepened. Her face snarled, her mouth was a mute square. Neither of us made any sound except for involuntary grunts and gasps. I jabbed her in her naked stomach with my knee, and she spat in my face. I was so astonished by this trick that I stared for about ten seconds and missed the next chance, for I could easily have caught at her near throat which she had hitherto been trying to protect. She drew back and we rolled over with each other again. She had very long crimson-painted nails but they were too brittle and broke as soon as she tried to claw me. This was lucky as the stroke ended across my eye. When she was on top her teeth caught the lamplight and glittered in the mute square. It became a regular occurrence. I wondered when I was on top if my teeth glittered and if she were noticing and hating it. I wondered if she were wondering if when she was on top her teeth caught the light and glittered and if I were noticing . . .

When Zerd came in he had to pull us apart otherwise we wouldn't have noticed him. Naturally, that mattered to him.

It was the texture of the hand on my arm that brought me to my senses. He was laughing. I let go of my companion. She sat up, stared at him, and immediately the inscrutable look became her face again. You couldn't see beyond it, it was her face. However, it looked less awe-inspiring now that she was less deliberately deshabille. He and she stared at each other. He looked quizzical now, and both eyebrows were raised. I had time to examine her properly for the first time.

She was small and brown-skinned. I'm not tall but she was the sort of graceful, womanly, self-possessed little thing that makes me feel gawky. She had originally been dressed in an ornate thick jacket and long tight sleeves and a high neck but which left one breast startlingly bare. Her stomach and loins were bare but she wore long opaque trousers ruffled and frilled with different materials and with shirred ribbons looped across them. The hair between her thighs was twined with little purple flowers and leaves. At the moment, however, all this provocativeness was rather spoiled, or rather its deliberation was, by the fact that the ribbons and frills already trailed, one sleeve was ripped, her face-paint was grotesquely smeared and her jewellery broken.

Zerd's hand went over to it and picked up one of the ostentatious semi-precious beads which were lying scattered about all over the bed-rugs. He examined it idly and smiled at us. He seemed quite content to go on swinging the bead by its broken thread and looking at us in a pleasantly diverted way without inquisitiveness for ever, but finally he said to the girl "Who are you?"

"Yle," she said. At least that is the nearest I can get to spelling it. Suddenly, as though speech from him had released hers, she sat up straight and pointed at me. "I am my lord's bed-girl; we Southerners are hospitable, let it never be said that we are not. Holy Eggs, what are we, barbarians? And I came to my lord for his joy tonight, and was this other girl hitherto unknown to me and probably unknown to many to take my place? She is a common slut for I have never even seen her about before and she comes to you, my lord, having obviously decked herself in hope to please you and when she finds that there be one before her she—"

Zerd wandered away in the middle of this. He selected a handful of fruit from the pedestalled bowl in the floor-centre, poured one drink, for himself, came back, sat on the bed and looked polite attention with his eyes at her over his fruit as he bit and chewed, felt the bed's sway, looked at it with interest, saw how it depended, swung it experimentally at first and then in increasing fast arcs. Yle broke off her monologue, not because of any interruption, but because she could no longer stand the unnerving swing of the bed and the sensation that she was being paid no attention. At the last wildest and biggest swing she stopped speaking, offended, at the same time making an involuntary grab for safety at my shoulder. Zerd stopped swinging the bed, looked up as he noted her sudden silence and waited civilly. When she didn't reply he seemed to gather his thoughts together and then picked up another gold-striped bead and swung it by its thread-tail, watching its pendulum-swing with his head on one side. "Yes. Well. You see—er—Yle? Yle, I regret to have to refuse the governor's kind hospitality but I prefer to use one of my own bed-girls."

I thought how unwontedly courteous he was being until I realized that he had finished.

He continued dangling the bead and eventually we both realized that she was to leave. She got up, the ribbons trailing behind unnoticed. The expressionless eyes went to me, then went back so that the whole expressionless face was turned to him. I knew now that the inscrutability was not something on the sublime side, not something worthy of a kind of awe; it was an almost subhuman lack of mental elasticity, of union between the emotions and the features.

"My lord," she said, "the governor will not take this kindly."

He looked up, hardly interested. Only the keenness of his glance, uninterested though its expression was, showed us that he knew perfectly well that the governor would not be offended if he had any sense.

"Your wife," she said, "it would be all right if she were to spend this night with you, but you cannot put me aside for this sluttish amateur."

He yawned (not affectedly, it was a natural action, he had been feeling bored ever since his entry) and looked up and said, "Cija, show this lady out."

I got up, went over to the door, swung aside the heavy draperies before it, opened it.

We glanced at each other's eyes as she went out past me. Since I had won, I was glad to see how she hated me. I shut the door.

"You have only to complain of her to the governor and she'll be dealt with," I remarked.

"Um," said Zerd, swinging the bed and spitting out pips on to the floor.

He was not in a conversational mood and was still gently bored.

I realized I had presumed.

I stood by the door, irresolute.

I had wiped my face of the blood and spittle but I realized I was no longer the appetizing sight I had been when I entered. I was modest. I was diffident. He didn't seem interested any more. This continued for some minutes, agonizingly uncertain for me, me standing by the door and Zerd lounging on the bed, absent-mindedly spitting out pips on the floor and scraping the floor with his foot each time the bed swayed. He had achieved a kind of rotating rhythm.

"Aren't you coming over here?" he said.

I started. I had almost got to believing he'd forgotten me.

I went over to him and he reached out and caught my wrist and pulled me down beside him.

He looked sideways at me.

"Dear me." He smiled and spat out another pip.

"What's wrong?" I said coldly and defensively.

"No, don't both to wash your face or anything," he said as if I had suggested it. He finished the fruits after a while, offering me none, tossed off his wine, got up to refill his goblet, jerked an unused one at me.

"No, thanks," I said.

He looked surprised. "Oh, you must." He poured one for me, came back to the bed through the big dim room. The lamp

168

was burning low. He seemed bigger and darker as he caught an aura of the gathering dusk in the room. Silhouettes were now fuzzy. The big shadows of the draperies and tables in the corners would have terrified me, I thought, had I been alone. Soon I would be, and I would run out then as if the shadows would pursue me. I could imagine myself doing it so vividly that my muscles contracted and it was a shock when I saw him still alive and drinking beside me. In the dying light his eyes looked aside to me fleering like the eyes of a demon. Which he was. But this would be a casual coupling, I thought, with sudden hope; there seemed little passion in him tonight, he was merely passing the time for want of something better—or perhaps someone better.

When his two hard lips came onto my mouth I was not so sure.

The alien hands slipped over my shoulders, unfastened my bodice by pulling at the hooks—I felt them give—and, without the lips moving from mine, made me naked. I closed my eyes. But he held me away from him. "Not bad at all," he said. His face was by now in shadow—the lamp was guttering—but I could hear the grin for it was in his voice too. He unclasped his belt so that his shirt, which it had held at the waist, was open. It was pulled off and thrown aside. So was his metal surfaced loin-guard, and he kicked off his groin-high boots. With each succeeding movement the light became murkier and my unreasoning insane dread increased in spite of myself. Each of the little diamond-shaped scales in the texture of his skin seemed jerking and sliding in the last flickering red dimness of the lamp that had once been a smoky gold. His eyes fleered at me, his body fleered at me. His immense straight shoulders with their hard-as-stone bas-relief muscles, his high, wide male chest, the living sculptured column of the rib-cage and waist, the narrow hips, leonine, the long, straight male legs wider, both together at the muscular curve of the thighs than at the hips but less wide there than the chest was, the shock of hair, black as on his head, the myriad sliding shadows and lights—were all larger than in life now, naked, imminent, black and red.

He is the demon. He is the conqueror. He is the render, the destroyer, the faithless. He plans to destroy the world, attack the secret continent with the beautiful name and make its rivers—if it has rivers—run as red as his snake-skin in the lamplight, make its plains—if it has plans—lie as scarlet as his dragon-skin in the dusk. He plans to destroy and filthy Atlan, to turn against his allies who helped him break her, to straddle the world. He is the Enemy.

At the second kiss we were form against form. The snake's tongue moved in my mouth. The fish scabbard tensed against my neck, his fingers brushed it sideways.

I was drowning again, but this time not in water, in darkness and it was scarlet.

There was a click. A voice suddenly screeched, "Oh you—"

There she stood, trembling with rage.

"My, my," I said, "you're wearing green."

Her next sentence was postponed by surprise. When it came: "You breast-cursed manikin, what right have you—? My husband! With my own husband! This passes all bounds! You reach high indeed, behind my back! Get out! Go on, I said get out, get out! You shall be whipped for this because I trusted you. And now—!"

All the old clichés, brought out in shrill pink-faced sincerity. I would have run from the room, forgetting I was bare, but his hand stayed me by my wrist. He had not even risen.

"Lara," he said, "I'll spend my nights as I wish." She stayed staring, so he said, "I mean that sometimes I enjoy change. We'll discuss it in the morning perhaps."

She said in a wondering whisper, *"Are you dismissing me?"*

He nodded lightly.

Her face was distorted. Even her nose quivered. I said, "Isn't it rather bold to come uninvited to your lord's bedchamber?"

"For such a sweet little honey-speaker to men as you are, your tongue and more than your tongue can be very sharp with a rival," he said to me. He was amused. He was enjoying the presence of both of us.

"Someone told me what I might find here," she said. Her anger had frozen by now. In the shadow only her hand moved. It clenched, rose a little, fell a little. I realized what it was doing. It was savouring the feel of the whip tomorrow.

"Yes, I know who told you," I said. "This teaches one not to get acquainted with foreign bed-girls—or if one does so, to do so in a friendly way."

I took my clothes from the bed and began to put them on. She watched in satisfaction, he looked annoyed and made a move to stop me.

"No," I said. "I shouldn't stop me if I were you." I said it quite quietly. Suddenly I commanded all the attention in the room. I felt myself grow upon it. I pitched my voice softly, though my tone was clear-edged. "I have been used often enough by you. Take that as you wish, madam, it is true of him. I have been frustrated too often. I loathe you, monster, as much as anything has ever been loathed." His face became mocking. He didn't believe me. He poured some wine for himself. Suddenly his grin became incredibly twisted. I realized his face had slid before my tears. "You think I am a despicable little foreign-court-slut, honey-tongued and vicious." The tears scalded down my cheeks. "I hate you," I cried. My own voice sounded strange in my ears, not the cry of feminine rage it would normally have been but a cry as full of truth and desolation as if I had known what that night would bring me. "I hate you." I sobbed and ran from the room. My knees felt not as running flesh and bone but as running liquid, and my sobs filled the night. My head was light, it was at a different perspective to my body. The shadows swung away across the marble and hangings and were replaced by the new ones. A strange creature ran across the stairs and then down them before me. As we neared the courtyard and the starlight pushing a silver air-veil down through its open roof the thing's shadow stretched up, up the steps to catch my feet as itself fled away down before me. My ears were ringing, "The truth!" "The truth!" "The truth!" in clarion echoes swinging far and back again. In the courtyard a score of dark shapes similar to the one before me detached themselves from the shadows around the sleeping multi-fruit tree and the alive white-blue splashing fountain and darted away, scattering the perfume dreaming heavily on the air and pulsing it in waves against me. In panic I ran out, my muscles contracting and dilating as I had known they would, for I believed the shadows pursued me. My third eye saw a stream of them, behind me, all the shadows I had passed, the hanging shadows, the corner shadows, the marble shadows, the long shadows of the steps. But he was still up there, alive and drinking. Indestructible, the strongest nightmare. I dashed across the outer courtyard, full of shadows and starlight covering the paving, so that by the time I reached the gate I had skeins and tangles of shadow and starlight all clinging and tangled round my feet and ankles. Ooldra! Ooldra! ("The truth!" "The truth!") I must find Ooldra and I would be safe. "Ooldra!" I cried for her arms, the tears were warm on my cheeks for her warmth. "Ooldra."

I stumbled into the familiar blue tent which meant home now that I was no longer a child in the tower.

She shrank away from me. Slowly she shrank from me,

holding out her hands palm outwards as if to ward me off. Gestures meant a lot to Ooldra. She made signs with her fingers and I stood there.

"You do not vanish. You are stronger now than I," she whispered. "I did not think you could be. What do you want to say?"

I did not even give my lost lamb's cry of "Ooldra!" I knew now that something had happened which would not be put right by crying to Ooldra.

"What have you done, Ooldra?"

"If you do not yet know," she cried, "I can get rid of you—" and she threw a powder on the fire and made signs through the smoke. I stood there. Her eyes began to glitter their silver.

"I'm alive, Ooldra," I said.

"Is that all? So it is simply that the soldiers missed you. Never mind, they'll be here again soon."

"I haven't killed Him, Ooldra. He, too, is alive."

She came crouching close to me, looking in my eyes.

"Why, Cija, did you not kill him?" she asked softly.

"No reason. Just, I didn't kill him."

"You have bungled."

"His wife came in."

Her stance and appearance changed. "Then, my sweetling, this is nothing. There is tomorrow night."

"I can't try again. I told him I hate him."

"A thing any girl could do, balked of her night."

"I said it. It was the truth. He knew that. When I ran out he didn't follow me. That is significance enough."

"Everything can be retrieved, child," she said. Her eagerness was too tense. "You must try again. Offer yourself, no pride matters."

"It can't be retrieved, Ooldra dear. Why are these soldiers you mentioned coming?"

"I told them you had gone to His room, but that I had found your dagger missing from its usual place and I feared for him."

"And they've gone to his room? And they'll knock, and he'll answer and they'll find he's not a corpse after all."

"So, my child," she said, sitting down again, "they'll return here and find you."

"Not much use to you, Ooldra."

"Yes, I have proof anyway that you meant to kill him. Your knife is obviously new-sharpened. Apart from that, witnesses saw you sharpening it just before going to Him. The guard-captain will say he saw anything I ask him to have seen. Blob also would have said anything for me, but you made him worthless as a witness by bringing an accusation against him so that his evidence would be construed as malice. But the guard-captain—And it will be obvious to everyone that the entry of Lara was well-timed enough to prevent a murder."

I thought again of the Southern girl Yle who had been the cause of Lara's entry. She was another witness. She was well-acquainted enough with everything on me—she had noted the fish about my neck. She wouldn't hesitate to say so.

"Your continued existence isn't worth a surmise," Ooldra said, pouring herself some water with one of those hands whose vibrancy I have so often loved. "If I can't have both your death and his, at least I'll have yours."

"Why do you want me dead, Ooldra?"

"Why will I have you dead? Your father never loved your mother," she said, smiling into the surface of the water. "They shared an infatuation once, when he was a boy. He has been mine for all the years since. We have had several children. When your mother is dead and he is Dictator I shall be First Lady of the whole country. I hate your mother, I have hated her all the years of your life, only less than I have hated you. I have moved well for this end and waited long. Now one of the deaths I coveted has slipped through my long-long-long-patient fingers but it was not yours."

"Why did you want Zerd dead? If it was not from love for me, to see my birth-fate annulled, what was it? Do you love my mother's country so much that you wish to avenge his depredations of it?"

"The 'Dictatress's country'! Pah! What He did to it was well done!"

There were sounds of marching outside.

I wanted to clutch her arm, for she was still Ooldra.

"Not long to live," she said in a dreadful hiss, then waited amused to see my reaction.

I kept my face under control, which was not hard, I feeling as numb already as the soldiers could soon make me.

Then swiftly, breaking the link with her eyes, I turned and dashed from the tent.

I doubled back round it as soon as I was out, dodged the marching phalanx, ran head down between the numberless dark tents and the fires throwing their sparks and thrusting their smoke at heaven.

Blob's short bulk stayed me. I cried out in new terror when I saw his face.

173

"Now, now, missy," he said, "what's to do? Is this the night she would set the guard on you?"

"You know?" I said. "Blob! Blob!" I clutched at him. "Can you save me? We are not friends but you would not see me murdered?"

"A swift knife is less pain than seven lash-strokes, missy."

"It is more irrevocable, Blob!"

"Now," he said, "she told me I'm ineligible as a witness now. I'll not get any witness-pay. So you die but I get no profit. There's hate between me and you, but I'll not stand by profit-less and see you killed unjustly and borne false witness against by avaricious false witnesses I'm not one of." He whispered. "This way now."

We scrambled past endless guy-ropes.

"Where are you taking me, Blob?"

"Just trust me, and shut your little gob. To get that bird of yours. You don't want a fine creature like that to leave with the army tomorrow dawn and you not on its back, do you? Well, then."

Blob went in to get Ums because his fellow-groom must not be able to say later that he had seen me.

Ums is not Sheg. There was no snarling and whining and coughing. He came quietly out with Blob who is good at birds, his great slanting red eye only glaring.

When he saw me his neck unstiffened and the half-raised crest went down. I went to him and talked to him and he turned his neck and thrust his beak between my arm and my left side as if it were symbolism of trust.

The little shadow now joining us is Narra.

"Narra!" I said. At Ums' side we embraced. We ran together and irresistibly embraced without having meant to. I held her tight to me. I realized with glad surprise that she was straining me as tight to herself. The crooks at her elbows were as sharply angled as her little arms were bony.

"Stupid brat, why don't you run away again? What are you doing here?"

"I've been up late till now, Cija, the lord Smahil asked me to take water to his tent and then he made me stay and drink to be with him and sing my Northern peasant lullaby to him. I hope he's not getting worse again, so soon after being better. He was ever so fretful. I did wish you were there, we always used to nurse him together."

"And you're still up late. Go up to the girls' room in the palace."

"You're in trouble, or you wouldn't be stealing your Ums with *him*."

She irritated me. "Go on up, Narra, or I'll be cross."

"You'd better hurry and/or shut up," whispered Blob heavily. "Those soldiers'll be after us here soon, and the regiments'll be getting ready to move before dawn. We ought to be out of camp as soon as possible."

"Cija—" She pronounced it Ceee-yah, drawing the whisper out in half-wonder-half-realization. The skinny fingers fastened painfully on my arm.

"Shut up, don't listen to him, darling," I said frantically. "He's only waffling."

"You're leaving, you're in trouble! I'll never see you again! Oh, Cija, Cija, don't leave me. By All the Gods you mustn't leave, I'll never see you again, don't leave me—!" And she said it all in the darkness, only her hands clutching at me, the little-girl's voice whispering, muffling her fast sobs. "Cija. Take me with you. Oh, take me with you." She whispered very low, afraid of embarrassing me, but saying it out of despair. "I love you." She couldn't control her frightened sobs now. "Take me with you, I promise not to be a nuisance, I can cook, you know I can, you've tasted it, I can sew—"

I heard marching.

It might have been the slaves coming to pack up the tents ready for leaving, it might have been any soldiers, it might have been the guard of Ooldra's latest dupe. Narra's sobs were hysterical now. I pushed my hand over her mouth. I thought of leaving her in the entourage now that she had known friendship and could know loneliness after it. I pulled her sideways to the ground behind a tent, throwing myself on top of her. Blob jerked Ums with us.

The marching passed.

Peeping, I saw the captain of the guard, looking significantly grim, a sword unsheathed in each hand. His men were orderly behind him.

Blob pulled me out, shoved me up on Ums. I'm a tolerable bare-back rider and Ums'll take any sign from me, but that wasn't the point. "Another bird for Narra!" I said.

"I can't," he said.

"We'll need one! It'll be miles alone through the mountains, take weeks maybe. And one for yourself."

"I'll get some mules later. Come on."

He put a hand on Ums' neck to guide him by, as there was no rein, but Ums jerked the hand off.

175

"He doesn't like to be touched," I said. "You go ahead and I'll make him follow."

Grumbling, Blob showed us the way and Narra pattered on behind. A narrow stony way that was presently a rocky ledge led swiftly aside out of the camp and out of the town too. Remembering that I had once been told Blob rated me a poor rider, I made Ums go as fast down that ledge as Blob could lead, and presently he had to drop behind us, panting and wearing. I had no fear for Ums' footing and balance, he's as sure and swift and wily as a thoroughbred forest bird can be.

At the foot of the ledge Blob had to take the lead again. The stones and rocks were difficult to negotiate in the dark, and some of them were dangerous. Blob got himself cut by unexpected points, and once a boulder lop-balanced on another toppled. Narra yelped and gave one wail and won savage, whispered curses from the groom and I was afraid her foot had been crushed. But apparently she had not been seriously hurt, only hurt, and she limped on after us till I recollected myself and had the sense to give her Ums.

There were pools soon, as well as patches of grass, between the boulders; we splashed into them and emerged dripping. The water weeds tangled and left leafy souvenirs in our sandals.

When the sky was still black, but in the blackness before the dawn, we looked back as the first of the thousands of tiny lights approached uneven along the cliff road above us.

"It's them," I moaned.

"Ah, shut up," said Blob, "wasn't the army leaving at this time?"

There was soon the harsh sound I knew so well, the stirring aggregate sound of the moving army.

"You were too late," I said, "to get those mules."

Up above us, endlessly, passed the torches, the curses of men and leaders and riders, the clop and the clip of hooves, endless marching boots, rolling rocks, kicking boots, rumble of wheels, crick and crack of whips, creak of carts, barks of birds, neighs and snorts of horses, coughs of mules, resonance of metal. Still the army passed above us while we crouched down at the cliff-foot, among the boulders, and the little wind that skirls always before the dawn fled skirling after the darkness, and the darkness melted away leaving the stars till last. Big, big white stars; and you could see the smoke of the paling torches snaking up between them. It was still dark, not yet grey but less violently black. You could not make out the separate sight of

176

these things above you, but you knew they were there. Up there He went, Zerd, the beautiful Enemy. Up there, went the playing entourage, the pink princess, the winegirls, the pages, the grooms. There went Zerd's faithful commanders. There went the hostages' carriages. There went Ooldra, unless she had already embarked on the long-planned magic of her miraculous escape. There went the men, all the regiments I knew, all the trundling dusty life I had grown into for months and which had grown into me, the only life I had ever known outside childhood's tower.

I crouched with my head in Ums' feathers, and found them moist.

A stone rolled and jerked over the cliff and fell into the abyss. A stone into an abyss was ending what it had begun. It hit another near us; there was a furious startled bark from Ums before I silenced him.

In the chrome torchlight I saw the figure of a man standing at the cliff-edge while my life passed dark behind him. "Is anybody down there?" he called. No one answered him. Even at that distance I saw his head turn as he looked to see how far his place in the line had already travelled beyond him. But he had heard a bird down there. He waited. He must be a leader. "Is anybody down there?" he yelled again, louder but more uncertain. No answer. I breathed into the wetness of Ums' feathers. The torch wavered; the man ran on, without us.

"Well," I said, "you're stuck now with a long, hard journey over lonely moutains, Narra."

It was still not quite dawn.

The gliller of water, in the pools, beneath the silhouettes of the water weed leaves, the glicker of the huge liquid stars in the sky, the glitter of the torches glittering away into receding distance, the flicker of the wind on all the star-faded grass....

Blob said we must get mules from the palace. "Come back," he said, "just to the outer courtyard. A matter of a half-mile, and you're safe now the army's no longer in occupation."

We went back with him.

It was nice for Blob, the governor was in the courtyard just as we got there.

"Oh, hello, governor, sir," swaggered Blob. "Good to find you right here. I brought her, as I said I would."

The governor looked at me. He smiled.

"You'll have your reward," he said to Blob.

"Excuse me, but there's a bird I managed to get away as

well," Blob said. "I'd be satisfied with him."

The governor looked Ums over.

"I'm sure you would," he said. "But he's far too valuable a beast for you. You shall have gold and a peaceful, healthy working-life in my fields."

He raped me in the morning. He did not sleep after it. He even let me keep my knife. He had no fear, or perhaps it didn't occur to him I should dare to use it on him. In any case he was justified. Never have eyes been so wide. He never sleeps with me. As soon as he's finished with me he sends me away. I fought, I have never fought so hard. He held my hands. I screamed at the pain. It was a hard first entry. His eyes stared away above my head, he jerked and panted and forced. I lay beneath him, as he used me and yet swore at my difficulty, in the last extremity of horror and degradation. He drew away afterwards, dribbling, and sent me away. I ran stumbling down the passage. I felt I must bathe immediately, but I could never bathe him from me. I was in pain. I thought it would ease it to write it here but it has not.

# CHAPTER FOUR

## THE WILDERNESS

Two days now since the army left.

Narra and I sleep together in a tiny room in the eaves. We don't fit into the life of the other servants of the palace—except that we take our meals with them. Otherwise, we are apart from that peculiar life the upper servants, the decorative servants, share in any big institution, a life subservient to, but otherwise just as idle and pleasant as, the life their owners lead.

I have passed Yle several times. She looked inscrutable at me, and I wondered if there was surprise and triumph, at my presence here after the going of the Northern army, behind the features.

The strange animals I saw my second night here, which live usually jabbering about the tree and the fountain, are a small tribe of hybrids or half-human freaks. They must have been captured, perhaps generations ago, from somewhere in the surrounding mountains and have been tamed as pets or servants. I suppose they are mainly pets, but they are used to prune the lawns and trees, as grass and leaves and all that stuff is their diet, so they are allowed to feed on it on condition they take only what should be taken. They are called not by names but by numbers. In their own way they each have a limited kind of individual personality. 3 is a perky little thing, male I *think,* with a cock's comb on its head. 7 is definitely female. She is taller and strangely beautiful and almost humanly attractive. She is the especial pet of the governor, in fact her status and mine are about equal, and she is luckier because presumably she dislikes it less. They call her too by a number. She doesn't know she is a number, she knows the sound is *hers* and presumably thinks she has a name just as all humans and dogs do. She comes to it blithely, unaware she is considered only as a brute. Of course it wouldn't mean anything to her even if she could be told, but it doesn't seem fair.

It has now dawned on me that Yle does not feel gloating triumph about my captivity, but envy and respect for the honour I have been shown.

Yet I am not, except in the one sense, at all a mistress.

The tiny room Narra and I share is nothing. I am not allowed to speak to him, it makes him impatient and he only grunts. I am allowed no privileges.

Twice I have begged him to excuse me when he called for me, because it was my monthly period. He replied that that made no difference to him. So, of course, twice my subterfuge was revealed. But in that case I'm not looking forward to the time when it will be true.

Deadening myself, repeating to myself that I live the daily life of a slug, *in* corruption and degradation, I can look no higher and am not subjected to fits of racking bitterness or violent grief which is nobler but hurts too much.

I am allowed out in the town in his litter, guarded and watched of course by the litter bearers. No chance of escape, and I wouldn't anyway without Narra.

It is fresh air, of course, but very boring; just a provincial little mountain town with a couple of squalid streets debouching on brown hill-slopes—if you don't count the palace lanes which are more like avenues but *only* for private traffic. Apart from that, it is depressing to see the poverty there as opposed to the fairness of the palace. The beggars may not sell bent nails and scraps of paper as the ones Narra told me about, but they lie in the gutters with the flies and crawling-insects thick on their sores, their arm-stumps or their blind eyes festering, too weak or their senses too atrophied even to lift their alms-bowls as we pass.

The money Yle buys a new comb with would keep a family like that in food for a half-year—for most of them are starving.

Today I took the litter of my own volition. As it passed through the courtyard I saw Ums being groomed in his stable; he lifted his head frantically at the sight of me, kicking over the man with him, but I was gone before I could see him more.

I had taken a bag of coins from the governor's coffer, which is not well guarded and from which most of the girls are allowed to take for anything they need, and whenever we passed a beggar I threw a handful of the coins. We were late returning and he had been calling for me for a half-hour.

I went up the stairs to him as he roared over the banister.

"Where have you been, you Northern little slut?"

"I went into the town."

"Why were you so a really nasty word late?"

I told him. I was not as splendidly defiant about it as I would have wanted to be. The morning had gone less well than I'd expected; in fact, as is always the case with good deeds, it had got out of hand. The litter had been followed by hordes of yelling, unclean creatures with neither respect nor gratitude, even attempting to leap into the litter and tug the gold from my hand. When the litter bearers tried to restrain them they retaliated, and one of the bearers had nearly been knifed. When I tossed money to the poor wretches lying blind and sore in the gutters the others leapt upon it and tore it from their bowls before they could even realize what they had been given.

"You *what?*" he bellowed. "What have you done?" (This was rhetorical now.) "The town'll be overflowing with gold now, prices will be sky-high, diseased vegetables will sell for eighty-nine times the price they did and still be diseased, don't kid yourself, there'll be a glut, how the \*\*\* are we going to trade with any other community?"

In the bedroom he continued to grumble. "Blasted little Northerner, making a muck of everything."

"Shut up!" I screamed, tasting the reckless joy of losing all caution. I added, "The Northerners are coming as allies of the Southerners, anyway."

He laughed a little, making his torso waggle helplessly on top of him.

"Allies!" he said. "Allies that have to be damn careful of their manners in case we stop calling them the pretty name. Allies we can do anything with—didn't we send back their messengers pickled in their own brine, and now they march on us in peace and not in war? Didn't you notice how lily-livered your titchy little army was when it was here? Make no mistake, every Northern soldier hates every Southern soldier as much as every Southern soldier hates every Northern soldier. A lot of hate, eh? But there'll be no war till we see which one of us gets Atlan! I have a hunch who it'll be," he said.

Incidentally, I should like to know why good deeds almost invarably go wrong.

It may be that when we just stay idle and go on in the same old selfish way the evil genius of the World leaves us alone because we are not troubling it. An act of positive good arouses

181

the evil to fight and subdue and disencourage.

It could be, that if we were to continue doing the good—after all, why should we be put off? We have a perfect right to do good if we want to, haven't we?—the evil would fall away behind us and be able no longer either to disencourage or to hinder.

The air is getting stickier. My experience of the plains has made me value water in every way, and I go daily to the fountain-room. The Southern fountain-room is a wonderful idea.

There are plain, white-tiled rooms—the richer ones are not tiles but marble—floor, walls, ceiling. In it is a ceaselessly-gushing fountain in a large circular basin set into the centre of the floor. That's all.

It is the epitome of attractiveness and utter cleanliness. It combines the uses of latrine, bath, wash-basin, drinking-tap and interior decoration. It is lovely to run one hot and lie in it beneath the fountain's motion.

O my beloved Cousin, here I wish you were within me.

Here I need your self for mine.

I have not seem Ums close to for some time and this morning it was a shock to see him. I see with new impact the great head, much more than a foot long, with the strong beak compressed on the sides, the curved natural hook at the beak-end proving that this was first and foremost the monstrous bird-of-prey. His one eye gleamed red and the scars on the other side of his head seemed as hatefully raised and fresh as they must have been the day they were made.

He had just kicked over a groom and been prevented from savaging him. The Southern grooms are of course awkward, not only because they are not used to dealing with such an animal but because they hold him in some awe. Big birds are unknown in the South where only horses, mules and donkeys are used for riding. Nevertheless, once Ums would never have turned on any groom, no matter how awkward. How often Narra has said to me. "A demon has grown into Ums since you came to own him."

The governor wanted to ride him, but as soon as his foot was in the stirrup Ums careered away, knocking him to the ground, and when the groom at the rein tried to restrain him—well, I've already explained what happened to him.

I saw this as I passed through the courtyard. I ran to Ums' head and pulled him back from the unfortunate groom. He gentled at once and rubbed his head in my oxter.

182

"See what the Northern girl can do with the fiend," whispered the grooms in awe.

The governor finished brushing the yard dust from his hateful behind and came over to me.

"Can you always gentle this brute?" he asked me.

I nodded.

"Always?"

"Yes, yes."

"Well, walk him or ride him twice a day till he's used to the idea you're around. Get him manageable. Start this evening."

"This evening?"

"I shan't be needing you in the bedroom. I've had you, all of you, from now on you're the bird-girl. Ha ha. This evening I'll take your little friend, the one with big eyes."

I was at a loss for a moment till I realized he meant Narra.

I cried out, "No, no, you have me—she's only a baby, she's only eleven years old—"

I realized that telling him that had been a mistake. There was no hope now.

But catching at his sleeve, I pleaded with him. "Leave her, spare her, she at least—"

He picked his nose as he answered, regarding his trophy on the end of one finger, ignored me. I suppose he thought this was a gesture of hauteur.

"I've told you my wish, and my wishes are decisions. Back to the stables; everybody."

So I spent the evening in the loneliest kind of horror and despair.

Dusk fell as I rode Ums. I could have escaped now, but not without Narra. Perhaps he had thought of that. I was so strung-up I could have wept and dithered but I was just as useless as I rode about rigid-muscled and gazing into my dreadful thoughts.

I saw the little girl's hysterical fear—her horror—her revulsion—her slenderness. I knew it all, and I would do anything to spare her. And she is littler than I am—she is only a baby. It's trampling on a new flower with a deliberately filthy boot—

"So little," I thought. "It may harm her—he'll rip up her, for she's such a slight child."

I caressed Ums' head.

When I led Ums through the well-known corridors they were already rustling with their night-life. I was scared. Had the idea arrived too late? The rainbows were struck from the glass screens, the shadows hung and brooded or shuffled giggling. You could tell the adolescents: they giggled very breathily and "he-he-he"-ishly, obviously for the benefit of their companions. I suppose I was like that months ago. I was afraid Ums would attract too much attention but there was no fear of that. They are so expert at being unnoticeable that they can no longer notice. And I kept him in the shadowiest ways. He was a great stalking black shape behind me, his great red eye glowing out at me as he followed me unquestioningly through this strange place.

The door was locked, which was merely a matter of luck, sometimes it wasn't, nobody would have dreamed of going in anyway. But it was maddening today. I thought my heart would erupt. I knelt down and fiddled with my knife blade in the keyhole while Ums stood behind me. The barb on the knife-end was a miracle—the lock turned. I burst in, knife-point forward, dragging the huge bird behind me. I breathed a sigh of relief. The governor was leaning forward, not yet dishevelled, on the pile of cushions; he had turned to gape at the unique disturbance. Narra, in the most pitiful attitude of defence, cowered behind him.

"Cija!"

She leapt up and dashed to me, catching my hand. Hers trembled, trembled.

"What are you doing, little Northern slut?" the governor asked, rising and coming towards me after a brief glance at the still thing behind me. The big hands clutched meaningly at air; soon they would be at my throat. I had reached my climax of annoying him.

I stood aside, swiftly.

I wondered if Ums would understand the word. It was a crazy gamble altogether. All crazy. How could he know the word and understand it? The big, coarse, hairy hands grabbed—

"Kill," I said.

The bird whipped round at the big man, curved preying-beak driving straight at his chest, into it, a choked scream of offended surprise from the autocrat, a spurt of blood, spatter, the hooked beak driving in again, again too, the great claw coming up, spread on the human chest, hacked human flesh, subsiding.

The killer turned, came to me, nuzzled his great head against me. He knew he had understood.

I threw my arms about him. "Ums," I murmured, babytalk-

184

ing. "Diddums." It was a good way to show I cared. Without shame, with rapture. I threw my arms about the affectionately twisting neck as we shared our relief, our release, our blood-triumph. I shared the hammering of the great bird-heart within the bird-ribs beneath the black blood-spattered feathers.

I turned aside to see the foe made negligible and the joy of Narra—and stopped. The child lay beside the man, covered with blood, her dress hanging off her in a long tatter. A moment of total instant knowledge—rejection of it just as subconscious and instant—moment of blank bewilderment—I dropped to my knees beside her. She could never live again. The terrible first darting stroke of the hooked beak had glanced across the child's breast as it went to the governor's, torn and hooked into the child's flesh, touched the heart now laid bare. It must have stopped immediately. I gathered her up and, weeping, laid her upon the bird's back.

Fourth day in the brown mountains. The trail of the army I am following is nearly two weeks old. But I'm in no danger of getting lost.

A bleakness, a strange lassitude.

And in some rather terrible way I have grown closer to the bird. It is not just the solitude about us, always the mountains' solitude, netting us together; it is another link, a deeper link, and I almost fear it is Narra's death.

And why not? Why no closeness with a noble animal, my only companion, who slew to save both me and the child? I defy anything to say we should stay apart. True, it was no strange thing, no innovation for the bird to kill.

There ought to be a revulsion from a brute being which has killed human beings—and a child I loved. But I told him to kill.

He only obeyed.

*She* died instantly and painlessly. She was expecting the stroke no more than I was, she was expecting freedom and a joyousness of long friendship. It was a happy death. She died in joy that I had rescued her from terror and turned her hopelessness.

Soon I shall have told myself that she died looking at such and such an object in the room, and thinking such or such happy thoughts. Then I shall have convinced myself that that is all that matters, and I too shall be quite content and comfortable.

Ums and I have finished the last of the fruits I gathered

from the multi-fruit tree in the courtyard, from which the freaks scattered gibbering when I came. I have long washed the last of the blood from my clothes and his feathers, into the cold, green mountain streams. There is less heat as we penetrate higher on the indelible trail of thousands of wheels, hooves, claws and feet. Life is far simpler, for the stunted trees and bushes on the slopes, beaten over generations by the wind into grotesque positions, bear plenty of large fruit. I could have left more on Narra's grave: I wonder if those I left will become trees of the fruits I left, or if each fruit from that tree can become another tree of many fruits. Or if the rotting fruit will be snatched by wind or creatures, the seeds fall on ground less fertile than the child's grave.

I shall never know what those fruits become, for though every day as we penetrate deeper and higher into the mountains so that we can stand and look out over endless miles behind us, the governor's palace and town a huddled toy among the foot-hills, the plain a shimmering, arid cruelty far below the reaches of our clean air, the forest a green haze further back—and beyond that—beyond that, somewhere, my mother's land—we turn our backs upon that, every day it is a day farther behind us.

Never return to the palace whose corridors we traversed in nightmare, a little, blood-covered, broken body swaying at every stride of the killer which bore it, the loose-hanging head upturned, with the tangled hair, hanging from one side, the thin blood-stippled legs hanging from the ragged dress on the other—and I, weeping, weeping when I saw the unclosed stare of the child's eyes, terrified as I led the big, black bird past shadows I knew could be our ruin if they turned too quickly or glanced with too much interest. Never return to the strainingly-dug lonely grave nobody else would recognize, outside the town limits.

For there's no backward pull that way.

As far as I can remember now my mother, she was a woman who would find only bitterness in my return without His head to my credit. And Ooldra returns that way even now. No backward pull, no backward pull.

I must go on, following the harsh-stamped trail. I must go on. I must go on, no backward pull, says the rhythm, the wild melody inherent in the bird's stride, the black bird's loping, stalking, mile-devouring stride.

Ums sometimes catches small animals or birds, but though he appears content with them I can't make fire and also find it hard to pluck or skin them.

Every now and then we pass hill-villages, wretched peaceful huddles with conical turfed roofs and spreads of parti-coloured crops.

The peasants, usually surly, indeed so taciturn as not even to express the surprise they feel at the appearance of Ums, occasionally greet me as we pass.

I have been warned that these are puma-infested mountains.

Mountain-weather, it's begun to rain.

After two days of rain the little gullies are no longer gullies but the rocky channels of rushing, gurgling, obstreperous streams.

The little crops are beaten and drenched but they are of grains anciently mountain-bred and are not spoilt. They have obviously suffered more from the desultory ravages made upon them by the army before me. I suppose it was quashed wherever possible; the despoilers may even have been executed; but on the whole I think the Northern army can get away with some living off the country here. Amiability is at such a low ebb between the Northerns and Southerns that it can scarcely be worsened—and we do, I mean the Northerners do, to some extent hold the whip hand because we know how to un-vacuum vacuums.

The few peasants we pass wear straw rain-cloaks, and wooden pattens strapped on their bare feet.

This is a wicked night. Even the starlight seems to shy away from the shadows as if it were afraid of them, as if it were as afraid of them as I am. The shadows lie, menacing and hideously black, everywhere beneath the rain. I can hear what seem to be chuckles, triumphant, goblinish, from the queer, sparse undergrowth at my sides. But it may only be the crepitation of rain falling on and past and on the leaves and stalks.

I shiver against Ums' great warm body as I write this. Again I thank my Cousin that I have been able to teach myself to write in the darkness. It is a great comfort, it is something for my mind to cling to.

Ums, roosting, his mighty legs folded under him, is a warmth and a presence, and he would wake if I called his name, but meanwhile I am cold and lonely. And yet not alone, for there are presences hanging in the rain-mist. I shiver for, though at night Ums spreads a large rudimentary wing over me like a half-shelter, half-blanket, my clothes are the thin shimmery things I have worn since the night I went to His bed. Or rather, they are still thin but no longer shimmery. I put round my shoulders the big sacking bag I filched in the courtyard to hold the fruits in and it is thank my own God large enough to sit on too, otherwise I'd already have pneumonia from the drenched ground. At the time, when I took it, I was troubled by its size for my needs, and tried swiftly to find a smaller one, but was unable to.

Now, as I scribble frantically, putting down anything to keep my thoughts on paper and not in rain, the crepitation in the undergrowth seems to grow thicker and thicker and rise and become unintelligible whispers beating about my head and choking my ears and my God help me if I should ever come to understand them. . . .

When I woke, unaware that I had been asleep, for the lulling effect of the whispers had been quite insidious, I saw that an immense animal was sitting watching me.

Ums was asleep; I was in the same position, my book had slipped on the ground and its tape-attached scriber had spilled farther out, almost within the shadow of the animal's body. It was a cat-like animal.

It had stopped raining. Even so, I could scarcely have made the animal out had it not been that it shone as if luminous.

If the animal had stood up it would have been as tall as a standing bird.

It did not occur to me to wake Ums. Indeed, it was only days later that it occurred to me to wonder why Ums had not immediately sensed the animal's presence and woken of his own accord.

We remained perfectly still, the unfamiliar and I, gazing gaze into gaze. The huge eyes sparkled like liquid. The long, lean body moved only to breathing-rhythm. I realized that its breathing-rhythm and mine matched exactly. The talons of the paws which could have broken a bear were sheathed and still. I presently fell under the illusion that the paws had grown out of the ground, the animal rising from above them, and I broke my gaze into the liquid gaze. We were so still and calm, I saw the soft hairiness of the lean, breathing flanks, the wide, flesh-coloured nostrils, the black and white ears, the black spot in the centre line of the white upper-lip. I cannot remember any fear. Finally the animal rose, unfolding itself, its gaze still fixed upon me, stretched itself so that it seemed an incredible length, shook its head and quarters a little, and paced towards me.

My gaze was again fixed into its, and as soon as it had fully caught all my concentration it turned its head and drew my gaze round until in order not to break the link my head also had to turn. In this way it directed my gaze until I found I was looking back the way we had come.

It now pulled me in this direction, still by the medium of our linked gazes, and I rose to follow it.

As I rose I must have jogged Ums, who immediately lifted his head. When his eye rested on the animal his crest rose and he came upright with a hoarse bellow. He stretched his neck forward almost at a right angle from his body and raced on the animal. When they met, the hideous black monster and the bright animal, the animal's sparkling gaze at last left mine and he looked straight at the charger. There was nothing other than a sparkling calmness in the eyes. The beak feinted at the immense breast. There was the most terrible menace in the bird's movements. Ums was between me and the animal which turned its gaze again to mine, fixed it, turned it, turned it down the track up which Ums and I had travelled. Ums reached a paroxysm of fury. His beak darted like black lightning. At the instant the animal turned, rose on its hind legs, towered foreshortened against the stars, and brought one immense paw down on Ums' back.

Ums collapsed, fell to the ground.

I ran to him. There was no blood, nothing torn or broken—the paw's talons had still been sheathed—but when he struggled repeatedly and furiously to rise he couldn't. I looked up. The animal still stood there, in the track, on all fours again and looking at me. It turned its head down the track. I fell on my knees beside Ums and raised his head. The animal lifted its head, uttered a most weird and unearthly scream, finally severed our gazes and padded away down the track without looking back.

With difficulty I helped Ums to his feet. The spell had been broken: I now realized that we had both been in frightful danger and that Ums had probably saved me from being lured to the animal's lair where I would have met certain death.

Ums did not seem seriously hurt, but he limped angrily.

I now wondered what I had been thinking of to forget all sense of danger before Ums took a hand in the scene. I was terrified the puma would return and as soon as Ums was up I led him up the track and aside to where I knew there was a village.

At the first house I came to I knocked frantically, looking back over my shoulder. When a large, sleepy, peasant woman answered it, I cried, "May I have shelter? A big puma—just attacked my bird—"

She looked apprehensively behind me but seeing no puma she turned to me in astonishment.

"It may return," I panted. "Please—oh, please—"

She tugged me inside, called her son.

"Turg! Turg! Come and attend to this animal! It's wounded, been wounded, by a puma, one of them big Northern birds—"

"What, have that army returned, then?" said a bullet-headed youth, tumbling into the room.

"No, this be a little girl, as cold and wet and scared—Go on, get out to the bird."

She shoved me to the fire, stoked it up, at once began undressing me and wrapped a warm goatskin round me. As she prepared a hot pottage over the fire she talked. A younger boy, about my age, sidled in the door from the other room.

"Will my Turg find your bird sore wounded?"

"I hope not—I don't think so, the puma only brought its paw with the claws in down on his back."

"That could break a bear's back—the pumas in our mountains are bigger than most—the puma didn't know its full strength it could have used—and you're not hurt at all?"

"It didn't touch me, only my bird. It gave a horrible scream and went away."

"A scream? Pumas don't make any noise," interposed the boy.

"They do at times," said the woman. "I've heard tell of it, once in two lifetimes a villager hears a puma scream. They do it only when they're wounded, and not always then—Did you not hurt it?"

"Not at all—Ums would have, but was hurt instead, and I have no more than a dagger—It did not seem wounded, it was very large, and white."

"I've never heard of an albino puma," said the boy.

"There are none," the woman said. "It was the moonlight tricking you."

"Funny, I could have sworn it was white."

"Here," said the woman, and put the spoon in my mouth.

The pottage was hot, steamy, savoury. I ate in delight.

The woman squatted in front of the fire, watching the drying of my rather soiled and ragged diaphanous dress and trousers.

There was no other light in the room but the glowing and leaping of the fire. The shadows were black and peaked but friendly. The boy crept closer. He was slender with large lustrous eyes and tangled greasy black ringlets falling to his shoulders. He wore shapeless patched trousers under a voluminous sash with several pockets in it. His tawny-skinned smooth torso was bare except for a short, open-fronted fur jacket. It was impossible to tell the original colours of any of their clothes. Obviously there would be no fountain-rooms in this patch of Southernland. The bare arms were dark on one side, light the other, and the dividing line between the dark and the light flickering, flickering, as the firelight flickered, flickered. At last the boy put out a hand and touched the now-tawdrily sparkling things on the hearth. The woman slapped his arm and said, "Mind your own business, Lel."

The bullet-headed young man came in.

"I've fixed the bird in the outhouse. He limps, not badly, but no good for long distances at a time," he said. He came to the fire and warmed his hands, ignoring the boy until he leaned in front of him to put a fallen brand back. Then he said, "Out the way, will you, Lel, got up to do no work," and faced squarely to me. "Now, missy, we'd like to know who you are riding a Northern bird and coming here at night."

"I was kept hostage by the Northerners. I escaped."

The woman filled my bowl again and twitched the goatskin closer round me, clucking.

"That's all very well," insisted bullet-head. "Where are you going and what are you doing?"

"She's staying with us," said the woman, "till her bird's better."

I and the woman sleep in the first room, Lel and Turg in the other. I help with the cooking, learning at the same time, and in the fields at reaping. Ums will pull a cart if I am at his head, and in the spring he will pull a plough.

A strange thing, there is no scar, no mark, but Ums' leg will not heal. The big puma he saved me from—and I shall always think of it as white—must have injured some nerve at Ums' spine or shoulder. I cannot venture on really long distances.

And what would I be going to?

Life in an army alien and unfriendly to me, with no place for me in it? Futile trying again to kill its General—who now knows my hate for him. If I escape the vengeance of the guards Ooldra primed with information against me, what life would I find crushed between the quarrels of lands all alien to me?

And there's no lure the other way. My mother's disappointment, Ooldra's hate ... No backward pull, no forward pull.

My long loose tunic is warmer than the diaphanies, which are folded away on top of the only cupboard in the house. Though sometimes I am embarrased by remembering there are no trousers under my dress, the hem is far too long for it to matter and anyway the whole thing is very modest, just a straight line from neck to shin. If I were a voluptuous slinker with breasts like lovely melons, big pointy ones, and a really big seat under a really small waist, the folds of my loose tunic might reveal just enough shapes to be becoming when I walked or sat, but though so many months of riding have broadened my seat I don't think it is really volupuous, and though my waist is small so are my breasts, which are more melon-shaped than gourd-shaped if anything but not really anything. Unfortunately.

We don't often see other members of the community but when we do the other girls look at me spitefully and call out "Think you're high-and-mighty, skinny miss-nose-in-the-air!" "Think you're posh, don't you?" "Think you're too good for us!" "Yah wipe your long nose!" and even if I walk with modestly downcast eyes they call out. This is because I wear sandals, and everyone else has bare feet.

When they first started throwing things at me I was so surprised I didn't think to kick back or anything, I just stood like a pathetic dope saying, "Stop it! Please stop it!" and they kept saying it after me. "Sto-o-p itt, sto-o-p itt." I think they were trying to mimic my accent. And the funny thing is they all do have rather low-class accents, but I wasn't thinking about that at any time, I'm so used to hearing those accents in the army, I don't look down on them or anything, in fact some of them are rather endearing, like the non-commissioned leader in the Blues, who was not at all an endearing man but deeply admirable. I was simply eager to be friends with the people who will from now on be my neighbours. But they seem to resent me rather a lot.

Lel and Turg defend me, because I am the girl of their household. But sometimes they aren't there. Last week I was caught by a crowd of girls. The sinking feeling one gets when one is totally surrounded and herded into a corner behind a street deserted by passers-by who might intervene and save one—!

They walked round and round me, making the most genuinely sickening remarks, in drawling malignant sneers made as offensive as possible, pulling my hair, occasionally pushing me over in order to teach me, they said, not to walk so straight as if I thought I was better than they were. They mimicked my accent and grammar and finally, in an ecstasy of realizing that I was at their mercy, they all set on me at once, kicked me and rubbed black muck-mud from the gutter into my face, mouth, nostrils, hair, and down the neck of my tunic. Then they left me, taking my sandals.

It's not the pain I mind quite as much as the crippling feeling that everyone hates one.

This was the first time I have come into contact with the passionate, brutal, envious hate the lower feel for the upper classes.

I have always before this believed in the widespread legend—I won't say myth, because some of it is true—legend of the honest, worthy, deserving poor. They certainly know how to victimize those who have by birth what they envy.

For the next few days I was more or less complaisant about the loss of my sandals.

I would have been trying in any case to get along without them, and when the boys noted with surprise that I was barefoot I said I'd left them off on purpose. But when I developed blisters and callouses and big sores, which opened each day though I partially closed them with ointment each night, Lel came into the firelit first room where his mother was mulling some bedtime wine on the hob and I was settling into the hay and goatskins in my corner.

Lel came quietly over to me. He was holding the household boa round his neck. This is the snake which lives in the rafters of the house and kills the vermin and big lice up there in the thatch. Ours is not a very large one, about five feet, unvenomous snakes can sometimes reach thirty feet long. Lel sat down on my bed (if you can call it that) and we both caressed the snake which slid looping around our necks and shoulders.

"Cija," Lel said, "—your feet be in a rotten state."

"They'll get better."

"But they won't. Feet don't stop getting sores till they've already healed and your sores won't heal if you keep getting them open."

"*Must* you talk about 'my sores' like that?" I said.

193

Lel looked earnest and let the boa slide round and round his chest under his small fur jacket. "Where've your sandals gone, Cija?"

"I don't actually know where they are," I said honestly.

"Someone took them?"

"Why, Lel?"

"Has someone took them?" he persisted.

"Well, yes."

"Who?"

"Some girls last week in the village. I don't know their names."

"Let Cija get to sleep," his mother said from the hob. "Put the snake in its place. Tuck yourselves up in there."

So I drank the hot wine and turned over and went to sleep with the sound of the occasional, stealthy, lengthy rustling up above me.

The next evening as I was leaning to drink at the well before the evening meal Turg came up and tossed the sandals down beside me, slapping my behind to draw my attention.

I picked them up, exclaiming.

They were in quite good condition. Only one thong was missing; someone had replaced another with a twist of straw.

"How did you get them, Turg?"

"Lel told me," was all he said.

Now, when I go into the village, I get dirtier looks than ever. It is probably because they feel I have an unfair advantage in owning Turg and Lel.

I'm trying to slouch slightly the way they all do, and blur my vowels and leave my words unfinished, but I'm not very good. I don't look or sound authentic, just all the more different from them. They seem to believe I have manufactured this whole difference my whole life long simply in order to set myself above them, whereas in reality I would do anything to be like them. I must fit into my new life. But apparently, even setting aside the way I speak, my difference stamps me at once to their acute eyes. The way I walk, the way I hold my head are objectionable to their sensibilities.

I'm teaching Lel to ride a bird.

Ums doesn't mind, and it's fun for Lel and me.

I don't know yet whether he's a good rider—at the moment he's only just getting so that he can stay on. Of course Ums is

194

not a good bird to learn on, but then Sheg was worse.

You have to be very good indeed to ride a bird at all well. The saddle is bucket-shaped and the under-strap under the bird's belly joins the crupper to the two neck-straps—this can't exactly all slide off backwards because the under-strap holds it, but the whole thing has to be kept forward by the balance of the rider. (In addition, one has to be far more at one with one's bird than with a horse. The neck and head rise immediately before one's own, one's knees press in front of the shoulder and you can't jab any old way with your knees like I'm told you can with a horse because a bird, even a huge one, is more feathers than flesh and bone. Besides, not many birds take kindly to it. Any bird is always liable to run amok without warning. You have to be at one with your bird: any gentle pressure means what you want it to mean. There must be almost telepathic communion. One thing, most birds already have very hard mouths: you can yank as furiously on the bridle as you like.) Most people spend their time staying on and call it riding.

Sheg was utterly unmanageable. It's a prodigy I ever stayed on him, considering he was the first thing I'd ever been on the back of. No wonder Blob called me a poor rider. If he'd had to ride Sheg he wouldn't have been so damn ready.

Lel and I spend a lot of time together.

Turg isn't always rough, but at times something about Lel's personality seems to irritate him in the extreme. And when Turg's irritated it's the same thing as saying he's aroused to a bull-frenzy.

Since I've been here he's even taken the butt-end of an axe to beat him with, but Lel, who is tremendously wiry for all his slenderness, ripped the belt of Turg's trousers with an upward slash of the knife he's not supposed to carry, dodged and ran away.

So we went riding together, or rather in turns.

I am determined to make a success of the only life left open to me.

In time everyone will become used to me, and I to them. The life is warm, could be always cosy, and above all is secure.

Where else could I go now?

I could move to another village but are the people and the youth in one Southern mountain-village likely to be any different from in another?

Where else would I find a woman willing to let me stay with her indefinitely—something this one is welcoming the thought of—?

Ums looks at the Southernmost peaks which were always ahead of us and all his fierce soul is in his eyes.

I am getting good at curdling goat's milk cheese.


I have so many nightmares.

Almost every morning I wake sweating, and sometimes I am afraid to go to bed because I know my dreams will be horrible.

The whisper-dreams are worst, for I seem to hear the voice of Ooldra, whispering, whispering, clogging my ears with whispers.

I wake and cry, for I loved Ooldra.


The other day when I took Ums to meet Lel (who is becoming a real rider) in the fields I was first to arrive. I waited for Lel, and waited. Finally I saw a small beautiful woman, not like any peasant coming towards me. She wore full trousers, and a short full skirt with a ribboned bodice, and in places the clothes gleamed as the sun caught them. She smiled shyly but michievously at me as she came forward.

When she was quite near I saw the raggedness of the beautiful clothes, suddenly everything clicked into place, and I recognized her as Lel.

"Lel!"

He ran forward.

"Do you like me? You're not angry?"

"No, I don't mind you taking them—But you looked beautiful! I didn't realize it was you. I wondered who the lovely stranger was!"

He blushed, then smiled—then caught my arm.

"Cija, will you promise me something? Never tell anyone—they—they only laugh at me."

I thought he was only imagining it, how could anyone laugh at a boy for dressing in girl's clothes when he could look so beautiful in them, but I promised.

Now we often change clothes when we are out together.

I don't feel *right* in boy's clothes the way Lel does in girl's, but it is certainly easier to ride in them.


Last night there was a festival. The villages were celebrating the gathering-in of all the year's harvest. There was dancing and music all over the mountain sides, tumultuous peasant danc-

196

ing, whirling and stamping, to the twanging of ghirzas and the blowing of horns and the pound-pound-pounding of drums. Everybody danced, and stamped, and shouted and clapped. There was a fabulous amount of wine. When it was dark the women caught glow-worms and put them in their hair. Everybody got drunk. I was new to the steps, and retired from the dancing early. Lel and I sat side by side on a dark bank watched the bobbing lights of the dancers.

"Strange how Ums' leg doesn't heal," Lel said.

"The puma," I said. "It *meant* to make Ums incapable."

"How could it, pumas can't think."

Lel was usually unanswerable.

"You're usually unanswerable, Lel," I said. "Not that I want to answer you—do you know what unanswerable means? —but it doesn't really matter. . . ."

"You're gabbling, Cija, you must be sleepy," he smiled.

We drew back as a drunken man blundered past us. He lurched into some bushes and we put our arms about each other.

"This is strange," I said. "Ordinarily we'd have been in bed hours ago, after talking and playing with the snake—it has such a familiar skin to touch—Last night I dreamed about the person the snake reminds me of. I'd gone to sleep with a fly buzz-zz-ing round the room and I dreamt of an enormous black fly which buzzed and buzzed and grew slowly but steadily until it—it filled half the world and all the people in the world were crammed, living their lives and taking for granted as part of life its fearsome shadow, while still over the centuries it slowly grew. It filled three quarters of the world—and its shadow filled the other quarter. Still it grew, over the centuries . . . and I woke up."

"That was a nightmare," said Lel, kissing me on the cheek.

What beautifully soft skin he had.

"What beautifully soft skin you have, Lel."

The dancers outlined like constellations by their captive glow-worms in the dark swung nearer and back. They clapped, and stamped.

Lel's eyes filled with tears.

"You must not tell anyone," he whispered.

"Why not?"

"They don't laugh—they say I am filthy, that I am a monster to want these things, and I must curb my vile instincts. Nobody knows I am still like this, that I haven't changed since they found me out three years ago—"

"Lel—"

"Don't hate me now you know what other people think, Cija."

"I love you, Lel."

"I want to be a girl—I have always wanted to be a girl—when I cry at night Turg calls me a filth, and kicks me—but I am a girl inside, I do what girls do, I had to learn to throw things and carry things the way a boy does because the others thought me queer. My voice hasn't broken even yet. I have always been miserable, and I will always be different from the others," he whispered. "You know what I think, Cija? I am a girl gone wrong—you can warm frog's eggs when they are about to become female frogs and suddenly they all get born as male frogs—Couldn't something have happened to me?"

"Don't cry, Lel. Please don't have this dreadful feeling of grief and difference from the others."

He wept silently. I tried to hold him to me but he was afraid of touching me.

"I don't hate you, Lel—I am not disgusted—it changes nothing—you could have told me right at the beginning what the others always thought about it—"

I had suddenly a glimpse of what Lel's life had been. He had lived as many years as I, he might have been me but for an accident of birth—or what seems an accident in this world—and yet all the years of his life had been spent in the passionate despairing grief, the lonely forced untruthfulness, the doubts and corroding shame which I have only just met. When he was a baby, when I was running round the tower and gurgling happily at new toys and ribbons, he was just beginning to realize that he was in the wrong body, that he must at all costs not appear *different*, or he would be loathed as he instinctively loathed his body. He must learn that he was caught and trapped in hopelessness, in despair which was physical, that while his very soul rebelled he must not.

Suddenly he unstiffened. He let me hold him in my arms, and while the darkness deepened and the faint-lit dancers whirled and the ghirzas throbbed and the older peasants drank we were breast to breast, knowing together the utterness of a grief which was always new and always rebelling and always hopeless.

I knew what these people were like.

I knew the hatred I had incurred merely because I spoke differently.

198

In one village I have seen them stoning a cripple—they would feel righteous if they tore Lel apart, limbs from body, for his difference from the herd is sexual and therefore evil as well as vile.

I was aware the dancers had stopped and were drifting aside from each other. There seemed to be men on horseback—where they had appeared from I don't know. They were questioning the peasants. There was a lot of noise, everybody talking at once.

Lel and I looked up, letting each other go. There was something in the air. With one accord we stood up and plunged into the crowd.

Lel's mother caught my arm.

"Cija—"

"What is it? What is it all about?"

"They are looking for you!"

"For *me?*"

"Men from the town—on horseback—they say you killed the governor—"

"They have traced me here," I said.

"Yes."

We stared into each other's eyes. Her mouth had dropped open.

"I did," I said, "I did kill him. My bird helped me. Please don't be sorry you took me in. He had—he had—he made me sleep with him against my will. He used me—"

Her face changed. She put out a hand and touched my shoulder.

"Quick, out of the crowd," she said. "You be a good girl, not like my daughter who went off with the man she done it with. In the Northern army when it passed—a small man with red hair—I complained, I up and complained to the officer, 'It's not right,' I said, 'your army, Northerners, our allies now or no it's not right, have him executed,' but when they would have made an example of him they didn't because she'd decided to stay with him."

She pulled her hand across her eyes.

"I've disowned her anyway," she said. "There, in there with you. Don't stir till I come and let you out."

I was alone on a pile of dirty straw in a tiny slope-roofed cupboard at the back of the outhouse. Ums was moving about in the larger part. As soon as he sensed me he came to where I was, lowered his head, staring at me and nudging me.

199

It had warmed my heart, even in my panic, to hear of the army's familiar treatment of its men and allies.

I realized now why she had been so ready to have a girl in the house. I had filled the place of the lost daughter.

Lel scrambled into the outhouse.

"Where are you?" he whispered. "Be you all right?"

"Over here. Lel, go away, you'll bring them in on me—and take Ums away somewhere, he'll give the whole show away—hide him in the hills."

"Right," Lel whispered. "Cija, take these first. Get into them. This is a time it's necessary. They won't be expecting it, it may put them off a moment or two—"

Blindly I grabbed the bundle from him. He led Ums, who is used to the idea of him as a friend, away over the protesting straw. They blackened the dark doorway for a moment, and were gone.

There were sounds of hooves and clamouring voices coming up the slope in the distance now. Steadily they grew nearer.

I peered at the bundle Lel had thrust on me. I fingered it. In a moment I was feverishly pulling my tunic over my head, tearing at it in cursing panic as it caught in my hair, pulling on the tights, the shirt, not bothering to do it up, only the jerkin left now, I yanked it on over the shirt while I pushed my feet into the straw to stir it up round my discarded tunic.

Were the sounds going past—?

No.

Well, they wouldn't have omitted my benefactress's outhouse—My heart nearly stopped as they all entered.

My eyes were by now used to the gloom and I could recognize separate figures.

There were several of the older girls, my benefactress drooping as if with fatigue and apprehension, Turg looking bull-necked with a big stick in his hand, three large men standing very upright and commanding and looking round, by the movement of their silhouetted heads, with an air of authority.

"No one here," said one of them in a town voice.

"I'm sure she'd hide here," insisted one of the girls, and the rest shrilled around, reiterating that this was the surest place I'd come.

"No sign," said another of the pursuers, after a lot of trampling about and poking had gone on.

They all turned to go out. I felt the relief flow from the woman's figure.

"Wait—!" cried the flattest-faced girl. "What be that?
200

*There's* a little cubby-hole—!" and she ran at me, stooping and pointing.

I kept very still, not even breathing, but as they all stooped and peered the glimmer of my face must have met them.

"There!" yelled someone and there was a sudden cacophony of shrieks and whoops. Turg with the stick ran forward.

I rose, shaking myself of the clinging straw, and sauntered out. There was a falling aside, a stilling of the clamour. It was dark, but they could all see my long legs, the short jerkin. I went forward between them. "Be you a'wanting me?" I said. "I were having a snooze before going out to the hens."

It was as phoney as it could be but it wasn't what they'd been expecting, so they did not at first notice the false ring. I had strolled nearly to the door when the biggest girl, probing noticed my tunic in the straw and gave a piercing scream as full as I hope never to hear again of the lynching-lust they had worked up in themselves. "It's her, it's her!" she screamed. I bent nearly double, charged the man before me, butted my head in his stomach, leapt over him and out through the doorway.

I tore down the slope as hard as I could pelt.

At the bend of the track I doubled back, raced up the slope again, to the house. The madness drew me as surely as if it were physical and had an irrevocable grip on me.

The madness had driven a spike into my breastbone and tugged on it. I could not leave my Diary.

This is probably the most stupid thing I have ever done in all my not particularly brilliant life. For a book, pages between two covers, I stayed behind when I could have won to freedom. I ran up the track. I jumped over the threshold—my veins were hammering through my skin, I knew this compulsion was suicide but the Diary is by now my inmost friend, it is almost a sense—and to be severed would have been impossible pain. I jumped across the floor, caught my foot in a hollow in the earth, fell on my straw, sent most of it flying, pulled my Diary from the heart of the straw, clutched it to me and leapt again to the doorway.

The jerk had loosened a sandal thong which I had no time to do up. My braids had come down and now even in darkness there was no hope of being mistaken for a boy.

They burst yelling through the door.

I sprang for the rafters, felt the slip of my fingers against the harsh wood, strained unbearably, did an awkward rather unintentional back somersault with a swing of my legs and found myself in the rustling rafters. The familiar snake slithered past me and in an instant its slithering sound and touch were translated into slithering vision.

Below, Turg's stick now bore a spitting burden of flames.

I didn't bother about where he had got this—somewhere outside—as I saw him raise it and the faces around him all turned upwards to follow its illumining with an eager gleam of simultaneous eyes.

The shadows swung away over the rafters. I and the snake made for the still inviolate blackness of the corner. A single footslip between the wooden beams and I'd have been hurtling.

Several voices cried that something had moved up there!

"It was the snake," said the woman who owns the house. Her voice quavered.

"That's right, you can see it," said someone in a disappointed voice.

Huddled in the corner, clutching my Diary, the snake wreathing about me and through my hair, my left sandal steadily falling to bits as the joggled straw thong frayed.

"You be up there, bain't you?" cried Turg.

I dared hardly to breathe.

"You be up there, traitor-girl, hospitality-thief, bain't you?" yelled Turg.

Someone threw a burning coal dropped from the brand, hissing and laughing and licking their fingers as it left them. It hit me on one shin. I managed to restrain my groan but though the coal was out as soon as it landed, the cloth of my tights was alight. Everybody must have heard the flurry I made as I beat it out.

Turg now swung his brand in artistic arcs. He knew he had me trapped and that he commanded everyone's breathless attention. No one was likely to look away no matter how long he took just now. He played with my suspense. I had time to consider the death a governor's murderer gets—slow flaying from the feet up.

At that moment I remembered my knife.

I drew out the chain from the neck of my shirt, pulled the knife from its sheath and stood up, crouching. Each foot balanced on a thin wooden rafter and the snake still wreathed heavy about me.

The light swung ever nearer like a slow menacing pendulum.

The knife slit busily deep through the turf roof-thatch.

The next arc would be two feet from me—unless Turg decided to end it all and flash straight to the corner.

202

The turf was lumpily parting.

The next arc would be one foot from me—unless Turg was tired now of the game, so near its ending.

I stooped for my Diary, clasped it to me, reached for the supplementary rafters above me, found it was no good with one hand, stowed the Diary precariously in the chest of my jerkin (hoping the belt wouldn't give way) as the arc swung at me and passed me. I seized the upper rafters, leapt up, bursting through the roof, throwing off the snake, and my nostrils and my face met the air of the free night. I heard my left sandal fall, clattering, fall down behind me.

Emerging all into the starry air, I sped over the roof. I went as quickly as possible for reasons of flight but would have had to anyway, as at each step I nearly went through. The roof was soon a ruin behind me.

I leapt down as soon as I could.

The ground was a terrifying way away, and it was a tree branch I leapt for. The big Diary in my jerkin nearly fell; I saved it, nearly overbalancing, and drew back into the foliage as a sudden uproar in the hut showed that they'd discovered I was gone.

Pouring out from the doorway in full cry—I couldn't know whether they had noticed the tumbling cut roof or not—they streamed past the bole of my protector the tree. Up about my ears the sweet leaves rustled, living, fresh scented silk against living, fresh scented silk. The breezes blew down the back of my neck.

When the human hunters had passed, I shinned down.

Limping one-sandalled across the little hills, I was well away by morning. Between these mountains and the snow mountains of the Southern capital the plain lay wide to welcome me in among her copses and marshes, rivers and streams, trees and woods. I am now within reason impossible to trace.

To be safely away seemed at first a miracle, although by the law of averages I supposed luck must sometimes be good.

Dawn arrived in the world as I arrived in the plain.

The grass was damp and in it my hurrying footsteps squelched; the trees ahead were a black, tangled witchery against the nakedly cloudless, yellow sky.

I can hardly weep for the loss of Ums. The bird was beginning to have a strange hold over me, body and soul, which is apparent to me now that I have lost him. I was grief-stricken by Narra's death, but, I now realize, hardly appalled. His hideous rush at the bright animal I later called a puma should have opened my eyes. It only cast a greater pall over them. I thought he was nobly defending me from the bright animal's insidious night-attack. *Was* he! He would have done anything to get his beak deep in the bright breast. But at least he succeeded in sending it away. The animal's cry of pain as I stayed with Ums I shall never forget.

There is plenty of water to drink—springs and streams. Ice-cold, they go, rippling, wimpling, the streams flowing with each liquid layer laving the liquid-loved, liquid-shaped pebbles, the falls eternal shiny white comets.

I eat well.

White roots, wild fruit, many of them quite large, mushrooms, eggs—probably reptiles' eggs as I always find them on the ground. I pierce them at either end and put my lips to one hole and suck the raw stuff through. Very nourishing. Makes me feel strong. Not unattractive, either.

The shining puma wanted me to go North.

Why?

I would have run into the town's searchmen if I'd gone back that way.

Or I would if I'd been alone.

But the puma ain't with me now.

What am I supposed to do?

North, or South?

If I go forward I shall find my life hard and maybe short.

I can't go back the exact way I came, I mean I can't, and if I go off at a tangent Northwards—there are higher mountains I could endeavour.

Behind me, to the distant right of me.

I see mountains whose far points are crystal with ice and shot through with the sharp crucifying rose of the sunlight. A snowy delicacy, a tranquillity, lies over these mountains. Their extreme aloof innocence, their milky far fragility which because of its very austerity is not fragile—these mountains will lie for ever for me beyond the snow of the valleys and the foot hills, unattainable because across a space of many hundred miles their unassailable virginity can still be felt. No, even if it is the easier way, and it does not look to be, I can not go by mountains. Has a human foot ever touched that chill, white, remote, indifferent beauty? I think that truthfully the answer is no, and that mine can never do it.

They were his best clothes that Lel has had to let me keep. The tights, covering me from toe to waist, are of well-fitting navy cloth. The shirt is white with long full sleeves and slant-peaked collar and cuffs which are now beginning to lose their starch. The jerkin is a leather thing, reaching below my hips, it's composed of two squares of leather sewn together with the top left free for the head to go through, the bottom of course unsewn, and two holes left for the arms.

In addition, I have one sandal, which I wear though it means limping. The sandalless foot of the tights is already getting full of holes.

At night the nightmares converge upon me. There is no obstruction on the plain. They rush whispering at me. I hear the whispers when I wake now too. I hear them with my ears in the loneliness. They are beginning to take on their actual reality.

Before me swell the flanks of purple moor, on and on to the jagged Southernmost horizon. I climb from the cup of the valley, and I stand on the brink and watch the ferocious desolation of these plains roll unhurriedly before me. They have no understanding, no pity for the human. Nothing on them will obstruct the whispers. I bring my gaze lower, see every blade of grass, every stone, patch of scrub close to. Every step. You cross a landscape step by step.

I cannot be following the way the army took. They would never have embroiled themselves in the fen-country I'm crossing now. It is growing dusk and I am totally alone. I have sat down to rest here for there is a disturbance in the grey light ahead of me and I fear that the tall—pillar of greyness—that I seem to see at the centre of the disturbance is moving.

Approaching slow over the fen, cautious, having to *know* but terrified of seeing, I came to the thicker greyness on the small island-patch. It was a tower which had been built there and long since rotted half away—a single pile of masonry, architecture unbelievably ancient, perhaps dating from the era before the moon fell, purposeless now. I did not like to look too closely, for the bleakness of the rotted walls and fallen archways horrified me as if aeons-long loneliness had accumulated there like a disease. The disturbance I had seen was a nation, a cloud, of bats all about it, in the evening, and the bats wheeling out of the windows drew with them in the wind of their wheeling the long grey cobwebs draping the windows' inner sides.

I hurried past at a safe distance, my breathing shallow so as not to inhale any of the lonely ages.

I am at the mercy of the demoniac night.

The fungi hang in great dripping blankets from the boughs, and when the breeze takes them they shuffle or whisper, in an urgent way. I think that they are shapes stalking me, stealthy, occasionally moving, and the whispers are almost intelligible words now, it is an effort not to hear them. I must not, I must not hear the words of the whispers. All my Gods, and the Creator of Gods and men, the Father of all, the High Deep God, *help me*.

But what is this sweetness falling through the trees? It is just the coming of day, and day is terrible for it presages the coming of night.

The purple flanks of the purple moors are flattening to bronze, and they no longer roll, they climb upwards to the rim of the world once more. The plain sweeps day by day to its end. The winds hurtle and howl across it, hurtling and howling Northwards. I have come to the beginnings of the winds, I watch them believe they dominate the cruel plains, but I know their endings, I know how the wideness of the plain-land defeats them simply by its existence, too contemptuous even to use an effort, and the winds are dispersed over the plains I come from, and are unnoticeable.

Every day I must braid my hair anew, and wind it round my head because of the winds.

The winds are my friends against the whispers. In the normal moanings and groanings and gurnings and squealings of the boisterous winds, all meaning nothing in the long run, the whispers cannot be heard.

There is no trace of the army's great passing before me, though I know they must have reached the rim at about this place. It must have been quite a time ago. I have not kept count of the days.

I saw the tracks of two horses in the ground which was becoming muddy. There was a slither with them which might or might not have been the trail of wagon wheels. I followed the hoof-pocks in the mud for some miles. I went as fast as I could, for they were very recent, though just how recent I haven't the skill to tell, and later I was rewarded by the sight of a wagon trundling ahead of me. It was growing evening by then, the air was smoky, the sun was not visible except by its rays which were broken by the atmosphere, turned here and there at peculiar angles, and magnified into red and orange lights floating in blues. I ran and shouted, but for some time I could manage only to keep the blessed sight always on the horizon.

At last, tired out, the reds and oranges submitting to the blues and merging into them, afraid of losing the only hope of companionship I'd had for wild weeks, I stood quite still and gave all my lungs to bawling at the precious, little, receding haze.

It disappeared into the evening as I shouted. I sat down where I was in the mud, and wept bitterly. I was also panting painfully. Presently I heard creaking and jingling and just as the shades of night fell finally over all the colours of day the wagon materialized beside me. But it was night; having been left to the ruthlessness of night on the plains, whose every trick and treachery I knew so well, I no longer trusted. I remained sitting. The wagon, like a wholesome messenger from the day, floundered in the night passing me: and as the wagoner called I realized that I had *not* been abandoned and leapt to my feet.

"Where be you? Who called out?" the wagoner was shouting. His voice was becoming increasingly hopeless of receiving an answer.

"Here," I cried. "Here."

I ran forward, desperate not to be lost again, and my hand met the unfamiliar nose of something that backed. The nose snorted.

Horse, I thought. I've never met Horse.

"Here," I said again.

A groping hand caught eventually at my collar. "In the wagon with you," said the voice.

Half hauled, I obeyed thankfully.

On the way back the wagoner asked questions over his shoulder. Not many questions, just How long had I been lost? and Was my village near here? I was already in love with the burr of his voice. I answered weakly from my new pile of straw that I was making for the city ahead and had no means so had travelled on foot across the Wide Plain.

The wagoner's cottage was a pink light which grew out of the night, became larger, threw off its surrounding haze, and became yellow.

He whoa'd the horses.

I climbed from the creaking wagon and tottered into the house by the door he indicated for me. He introduced me to his wife as a poor youngster been lost in the plains, and went away to stow his wagon and the horses and unload the peat he'd got today.

He was back surprisingly soon. In the light he was a short grizzled man. The wife was large and fat and a dozen children, babies, hens and a goat tumbled round the floor, in the yellow light, apparently all inextricably mixed. I never saw one of them separate, a baby without another baby, or a child without a hen, or the goat without a baby.

The wife terrified me.

As soon as I got in she began to scold me, called me names, hustled me into a corner and stood over me so that I was hemmed in. Only when she pushed brutal slabs of ham into my mouth did I realize that she had not been standing merely scolding but had been cutting them while she scolded: also, that she was mothering me.

"You shouldn't have been out on those plains, no means or not," said the husband from where he sat devouring ham and by the look of it, two babies who had climbed on to his knees and were poking their snot-nosed faces at his face.

I couldn't have found the breath to answer over the row of clucking and crying and squealing and quarrelling there was in the room, but I wasn't given the chance anyway.

"No, you shouldn't," the wife immediately scowled at me. "They're not safe for us, not safe at all. What do you think you are? Mightn't you've been sucked in the marshes, drowned in the streams, lost in the woods or eaten by the reptiles? You could've been lost in there for ever, and never got out again, and then where would you've been, and you with obviously no more sense than your age. Did you not see the murderess on the plain? You lads have no more sense than hair on your beards. There, you wicked brat, up if you must." She hefted a squawling baby up where it lay astride her hip and stopped squawling as it pulled on her breast. She watched it and stopped talking. The husband took advantage of the momentary lull. He saw I had finished my ham, stuck a roasting potato on the point of his knife, pulled it from the cauldron, and tossed it to me. He spun the knife, letting it leave his hand completely, and catching it by the hilt again. I am not generally neat at catching. While I grovelled for the piece amongst the straw on the floor, he said, "You'll need to cut that hair, too, lad. How long were you in the wild for it to grow like that?"

I had almost forgotten that I am a boy now.

I felt my braids and said—"Oh, well, in the village I come from we wear our hair like this."

"Well, if you're for seeking your fortune in the city you'll not be wanting to wear it so any more," he said. "Are you unhungered? We can do it now, before sleep."

He stood up, and, stampeded, I went over to him. He was expert with the knife. I was heart-broken as I saw the shining hair slide to the ground. It has never before been cut since my childhood. He spun the knife again, caught it, grinned and said, "For all your time in the wild you're not needing a shave yet, milk-tooth." He slapped me on the shoulder and said, "O.K., buck, bed now." He whistled and immediately the children, babies, hens and goat scampered scrambling to the sides of the room and the light was extinguished.

In the morning after the noisy breakfast the wagoner said he'd drive me into the city and leave me there, he going the same way himself to sell his peat. I thanked him and the woman said I must have boots, for one sandal was worse than two bare feet. "My husband can spare a pair," she said unequivocally while he winked at me.

"No matter how many pairs he can spare I'm not taking his," I said. "I'll earn myself a pair in the city. And one sandal is better than none, for this way there are holes in only one foot of my tights." I was learning how to wedge in speech in this household.

"Holes in your feet! No wonder, all that way," said the wife. "You with no more sense than to start on your journey when the army was already across, and though they're Northerners they'd have taken you if you'd worked your keep, they'll use anything and everything, and no more sense than to walk to the plains when the army was already across and the murderess loose."

"Murderess?"

"They've been asking for her this side already, galloped fast to tell all in the city to watch for her when she crossed. No good searching for her on those endless plains, and it's my

209

belief she's the sense to know it and will stay in them."

"Ready, buck?" said the man and I swung up into his wagon with the peat and straw.

He made strange clucks and flapped the reins and as the horses moved the woman threw something clattering into the wagon and ran back to the house.

"She's thrown in the boots, and a hood," I said.

"Keep them."

"But I can't take—"

"Keep them," said the wagoner and clucked to his horses.

I picked up the boots, and tried them on. They were soft leather from the uppers to the ankles and the soles were grooved wood. They fitted so well, the wagoner being a small man, that I hadn't the stamina to refuse them. The hood was good dark cloth, with a long peaked tail dangling from the crown of the head. The whole thing was very grubby but with it on even in daylight my face was practically hidden, and I put my fingers in the dust on it and wiped them across my cheeks and forehead and the bridge of my nose.

The land, though as unbuilt-on as ever, was soon obviously tilled and cultivated, and then divided itself into roadways with rutted lanes leading off them. Later hedges appeared, and ditches, then houses, straggling hamlets, workers in the fields, passers-by, villages. It was a frosty morning, there was rime on everyone's hair. I shivered in my shirt sleeves and drew the straw up around me. The sun still shone but the cloudless blue sky grew harder and the air bleaker as we rose into the hills around the Southern Capital.

# CHAPTER FIVE

## THE KITCHEN AT H.Q.

When the early evening of the City clamped down on the steep narrow streets, lights sprang out of the icicled windows and threw their reflections flat on the snow. I lost count of how many reflections our horses trampled through, how many times our wheels changed the patterns in the snow. And all the time even the latest patterns left by feet and horses and wheels were ceaselessly obliterated, silently but thickly powdered over. The snow smudged the outlines of the roofs overhanging the streets. The streets wound and wound, and the corners were hairpin bends. The traffic was not heavy on this snowy evening but what there was, including us, dashed round corners with gay yellings and whipcracks which were very likely to bring down all the roof-snow and icicles on oneself or some innocent passer-by. Gay confident yells and whip-cracks, yes, but no lessening in speed: the idea being that the noise warned anyone coming round the corner from the opposite direction. Of course, *they* would be doing the very same thing. We didn't see any collisions. I suppose everyone grows expert.

One of the reasons we were going so fast was that I was cold.

I was huddled in the straw among the peat. The kind wagoner had bought a long woollen scarf from a street-seller. I wound it round me as well as I could, but it was a poor substitute for a cloak. I didn't dream of telling him, but the wool was very poor quality, I could put my finger through it without the slightest effort. Indeed, it is wrong to say I was uncomfortable because of the cold. I was now numb, and felt nothing. I could only bless Lel's leather jerkin; without it I'd have been frozen stiff. The flakes fell on my shoulders and hood and knees and did not melt. The snow did not fall off, either, even when I bobbed my head to avoid hanging inn-signs. It seemed to be sticky or worse still, to have a tenacity of its own. Only when, every ten minutes, I blew upwards, did the snow on my nose melt.

I had an idea I wouldn't find it so cold if I had a cloak and were moving about instead of having been sitting for hours in the same place. Snow is less cold to the atmosphere than the dry, uncompromising, arid cold which can spike even at your eyeballs and the marrows of your knuckle-bones. There were children playing in these streets; they were little bundles of leather, furs and wool; but their hands were bare and they took up the snow in them and laughed and poured it all over each other.

There was no wind; only the fluctuating, falling, flickering of the white snow; and up in the navy sky above the rooftops one could hardly tell which were stars and which were snowflakes.

As the mossy-textured streets became bluer, the window reflections redder, the sky darker and the stars more silver, the doors opened brief golden oblongs in the walls, shivering the icicles, and parents called the noisy bundles of leather, furs and wool in to meals and my teeth watered and I saw mirages of food and fires in the blue streets and the horses hurried ever onwards.

"What part of the town do you think to set me down in, master?" I asked.

"Peat merchant's."

"Oh?"

"You'll be warmed there—given a meal along of me. Free, not like any inn. Not much money, have you?"

"No, none."

"Well then." He yelled as we rounded the corner, then continued in the silence of the muffled streets, then said, "Besides, he might be the man to give you that job you've been looking for."

I thought of myself, apprenticed to a peat merchant. Not a *particularly* pretty thought. It just didn't seem me. But I need food and a roof—I need a warm place to sleep in. I have given up hope of nullifying the prophecy and more than already done. So I have nullified it in effect by trying to do so and going away. I can never go back, never go back, so I shall never be near enough to hurt my mother's land.

A particularly raucous burst of sound heralded the approach round the corner of more evening travellers—but these were on foot. Three men in blue slant-cut tunics with groin-high boots and rough, hessian-hooded cloaks were lurching along, each roaring a separate drinking-song. It was so long since I had seen one that at first I didn't recognize the uniform of the

212

Blues, Northern Army. One man seized the nearsider's bridle and the others, babbling at us and each other, gripped the side of the wagon and tried to get in. "We wanna ride," was all I could make out, from the biggest, and that was sifted through a stiff wet moustache. It was a lovely moustache. One of those really long ones, bristly and red and ferocious and picturesque. But they were very drunk. The man at the horse's head was useless; we didn't have to do a thing to get him out the way, the horse simply shook its head and didn't stop. I hit at the hands gripping on the cart-sides, and they dropped away. It warmed me up a little. As we careered around the next corner, I looked back and there were the three ruffians, one in the gutter and two sprawled on the snow in the middle of the road, shaking wavering fists and calling querulous curses at us.

"By the Belly of the First Woman, for which we must all be thankful, but them Northerners should be shut up if they're to be quartered in our city at all, allies or no," cried the wagoner, himself roused to swearing.

I kept quiet.

How could I tell him that my heart had been warmed a hundred times more than my body by the meeting with those Blues?

In a minute cul-de-sac, so roughly cobbled that the wagon jolted wildly even over all that snow, we caracoled (rather awkwardly and unbeautifully) to a stop before a house.

This house had three lopsided upper storeys, mounting in tiers so that each overhung the street more loweringly than the one below. As the upper storeys of the house opposite also did this, there was the merest silver of navy sky, twinkling stars and flickering snowflakes to be seen if one looked upwards. The door was a leaning green door with a kind of blue radiance on it reflected from the snow. One mounted to it by three little steps, hollowed in the middle by countless generations of step-climbers, and the snow was packed so close on them and so polished by all the recent passage over it that it was slippery as ice and you had to cling to the knocker. There was a window beside the door, divided into countless little panes. An orange light glowed through, but one could not see in, the thick glass was so wimpled. An arrangement of icicles hung, very decorative indeed, from the eaves; they must have been dripping a lot of water at the instant the ice came. The wagoner banged the knocker (it was shaped like a little man warming his hands at a fire) and behind us the horses poorrurrr'd and snorted plumes into the air.

I was so extremely cold that after the door had been knocked on, the boundaries of my mind and body faded. I swam in blue cold, light-headed, dizzy I suppose from my eventual descent from the perpetual wagon-jolt, and was only aware after they were over of the steps inside the house coming to the other side of the door. As soon as it was opened. I fell inside like an unthinking nail drawn straight to the magnet of warmth.

Inside the door there was a hot red passage.

I leaned against the wall while my wagoner and the peat merchant, holding a torch, greeted each other and I think I was introduced.

Minutes later, just as I had begun to thaw and to realize that the passage was by no means *hot* except by contrast with outside, and that the redness was only the colour of the clay forming the walls, I was pushed into a room, with an order to get some life into my veins, and the two men went out again to unload the peat.

The room was really hot.

An immense fire roared in an even more immense fireplace, like a soot-backed cavern, at one end of the room. This was the first time for nearly a year, ever since I left the tower of my childhood, that I have seen a fireplace. At first, faced with such irresponsible and incessant movements, my eyes ached. I thought the whole room was leaping with the flames.

On fur mats in front of the fire sat a woman and a girl of about ten.

The woman lifted her eyebrows and stared a question at me.

Going shyly forward, and taking off my hood, I said, "I've been brought by the wagoner—the merchant said I could get warm."

I spoke in the vowel-blur of the Southern peasants I had heard so constantly in the last months, as I'd remembered just in time that I was supposed to be the wagoner's assistant.

"Fine assistant you are," the woman said at once. She had finely plucked eyebrows and a lot of face-paint, and she spoke in a metallic voice with genteel clipped vowels. "Well, sit down," she added. "Do you want something to eat?"

It was an ungracious question, but I couldn't refuse. "I'll mull you some wine," she said. She set a pitcher on the hob and meanwhile gave me big wheaten biscuits to crunch with chocolate-slabs. I hadn't tasted chocolate since, as a child, small squares had been given to me as "sweets".

The little girl sat up on her heels and watched the mulling

214

wine. They both remained quite quiet, but they hadn't been speaking when I came in, so I didn't feel I had interrupted anything and simply looked at them both.

The little girl had a stupid low forehead, wide brown eyes, sweetly innocent enough to be irritating, and a loose rosebud mouth. She wore her brown hair in braids as mine used to be. She didn't wear the loose shapeless smock which in all my previous experience even high-born children wear till they are a certain age. Her dress was a long green woollen one, lined with fur, and with an embroidered belt. Under that she wore tight green leggings and leather laced shoes. The woman wore a dress and trousers of pink wool brilliant with little sequins, both boots with forked toes, a bead anklet and lots and lots of necklaces of painted wooden beads decorated with metal filigree. Their clothes surprised me at first, but I learnt later that the merchant sells not only peat but faggots of wood as well, and in fact calls himself a "fire-merchant". These are wares tremendously in demand in the wintry Southern Capital, and though he doesn't live in a good part of town his wife and daughter can have practically anything they want.

The woman would have disliked me if I'd been a girl. I'd braced myself instinctively when I saw her face, infallibly recognizing her type. If I'd been an older man she'd have roused herself.

I was glad that I am something as uninteresting as a young boy. Quite a young boy, for my voice obviously hasn't broken yet. For the first time I felt it lucky that my breasts are small, small enough to be unnoticed under a loose leather jerkin, and my hips and seat have got small again after my recent Long Walk.

As the wine hissed on the hob I glanced aside.

Over the fireplace, so placed that in that light I hadn't noticed it before, was a mirror.

The ferocious desolation of the plain had purged me, spirit from body. I was all thought and consciousness, observation, analysis and emotion. I had forgotten that there is an outside of me as well as an inside. Importunate mirror. I saw again the narrow curve-in from the forehead at the top of my nose, the smallness of my mouth which is inclined to look prim, the tiny pimples on my forehead which first came with that *eruption* of pimples in early adolescence and never since disappeared as the others—after agonizing years—did. Little things which stand out only to me, who knows them so well. Things I always have and always will dislike and find alien about my own appearance. For I have an appearance again. That importunate mirror. I am back in civilization.

I slept in the cellar among the faggots. It wasn't as bad as it sounds. I was given a blanket to lie on and two blankets and a rug to put over me. *And* a cushion under my head. Naturally, there wasn't even a candle—anything of that sort might have sent all the fuel up in disastrously premature flames. But it wasn't really cold and though it was dark I wasn't alone. The wagoner *snored* beside me.

During an early breakfast I was hired.

This was thanks to the wagoner's kind efforts. He pretended that he had known me for a long time, and would personally vouch for my honesty and efficiency.

"O.K., sonny, you're hired," said the merchant.

I knew that after that I must work very well and hard, it would be disgusting to let him down.

When the wagoner had been bade good-bye and had left for his home again, I was given a short warm woollen cloak and a pair of mittens and sent out with a tall boy who had just arrived. My job would be to deliver faggots to the merchant's patrons, taking it to the addresses of people who had already ordered it. The tall boy, who also does this, would take me round with him the next days to familiarize me with the streets.

His name is Jode, he has red hair in nearly as uncouth a crop as mine, and the woman was as a matter of course bright and coy with him. He is nineteen, a year older than I am and about five years older than I am pretending to be.

We went out together into the snowy streets, I slithering and sliding in panic under my load of faggots because Jode had gaily pushed me, and I was glad that my jerkin reached to below the joining of my thighs. It sums Jode up to say that he is the sort of boy who makes jeering remarks about the smallness of the other boys' genitals.

He chose to treat me like a country bumpkin, and I let him say what he liked. I thought he'd be safest while being patronizing. He pointed out all sorts of innocuous little places of interest, using traditional guide language.

"That's a well at which a god once drank in the childhood of the world."

I know something about architecture and could not resist saying, "A second childhood, maybe? It's no more than a couple of centuries old."

He stared. "All right, expert, want to deny the priests to

216

their very faces? Up them steps sharp, this old lady likes service. Right . . . That there's the barracks the stinking Northern army is mainly cantoned in."

"Don't let nobody hear you call them stinking."

"Rot." He swaggered. "Blank blanking rot. No need to be blank scared. Anybody what heard me would be so pleased and agreeable to what I'm saying they'd give me a kiss on the arse instead of a clip on the ear. Except one of them fellows, of course. They have to watch public relations."

He nodded at a group of horsemen now clappering down the narrow street. They were cantering, probably for show, and any pedestrians had to dash for the walls and be quick-witted about it. The horsemen gave no warning except the muffled sound of hooves on the snow and the lesser sound of accoutrements jingling. The horses, even at a glance from someone like me who is unfamiliar with horses, were quite different from the wagoner's animals. These were lean and fierce and elegant, terribly beautiful compared with the Northern national steed, with flaring pink nostrils, hard lean quarters, deep in the girth and long in the shoulder, short backs and prominent withers. The harness was red leather with heavy silk tassels falling from the neck-straps and the stirrups. The riders, even though they were cantering, sat very straight with the dagged reins gathered in one hand and the other hand resting lightly on the hip. Nearly all our cavalry slouch in the saddle. These riders wore spotless white leather uniforms, so you could tell at once they were only parade-ground soldiers. They wore smart, wide-topped, elbow-high gauntlets and you could hardly see their disdainful faces under the shadowing brims of their high cylindrical helmets. They were armed with beautifully hilted, unsheathed, silver knives, and there was another knife in the sheath attached to the neck-strap of each man's horse. This magnificent sight passed at once in a spume of snow.

As Jode and I trudged on with our loads, his eyes were ridding themselves of a dazed glazed look and I knew mine were as well. We had just seen soldiers pass and we were both boys.

As the day went on our loads lightened.

Some of the customers were bad-tempered and seemed to expect the impossible in the way of service. One woman, I should really call her a lady because she lived in one of the more suburban quarters, who was quite hale and hearty enough to run her own errands, called out from her steps as we delivered the faggots and asked us to go to the nearest vendor and get some sewing silks for her. Jode sent me and as soon as

217

I was back she tweeted, "Oh, I *am* sorry"—looking synthetic languishment at me as if her sweetness could make up for anything—"I forgot to send you for some needles at the same time." I smiled back like a dazzled young lad, it seemed only polite as she was so certain I *was* a dazzled young lad, and once more ran off. Later Jode told me that it would be bearable occasionally, but she always takes advantage of the delivery boys in this way and never tips them—never tips them money, that is, only a silly smile.

But other customers were kind. One gave me a hot new bun, which when the door was closed Jode promptly annexed.

For the noon meal we went back to the merchant's and were given sandwiches and mulled wine in the kitchen. Then we set out with a new load.

The air stung on our bare faces. Our breath became intricately wreathing blue veils before us.

I was sure I should never learn which winding street was which. As I got tireder and colder, Jode became more boisterous. It was already dark, the Southern City's early evening, when we had at last only a few deliveries left. I had been walking all day in strange surroundings and wanted only to get back to the evening meal, whereas as his load lightened Jode became more playful. He stooped and gathered up snow and made balls of it and threw it at me and the passers-by. Some of it trickled down my neck, turned to water, ran down my spine and chilled me and made my shirt soggy. I begged him to stop but this pleased him and he kept on, perhaps wanting to see how ridiculous I could look when I got angry about something. The winding streets continued. I felt lost. I could place no dependence on Jode; if he took it into his head to desert me and let me find my own way back, he would. I thought how different he would have treated me if I had been a girl. He would have thought me attractive and special in my azure dress and trousers, with my face clean and my hair long and well brushed. I could have found him attractive. He has high cheekbones and was beginning to look unshaven. I like young men with long unshaven chins. The lights appeared in the windows and on the snow. Lights in windows always make me feel shut-out.

One could no longer see the mountain-sides which lower over this City in the clift.

"Night comes early in this City because of all the dirt in the atmosphere," Jode explained, reverting to guide language. "The darkness is attracted to it and sticks on to it."

"You oughtn't to be proud of that."

"You shut up, youngster, we City folk are proud of what we want to be proud of."

On the street corner was a girl tending a cauldron full of bubbles and smell. It was a high cauldron, its rim too high for any of all the dogs around to benefit. In this City, as in no other I've ever seen or heard of, dogs are allowed to roam about the streets and they make an awful mess everywhere.

"That looks savoury, sweetling," Jode remarked.

The girl looked up, pausing in her stirring with the great wooden spoon. "It is, but it has to be paid for," she said.

"Is that so?" said Jode, making a swipe at the spoon which he grabbed from the cauldron and licked empty. The girl ran round him giving little cries of distress, and Jode winked at me over the spoon.

The girl hit at his arm and defensively seized the spoon.

"All right, all right, you can have it," he said, grinning. "Don't get so excited. I don't mind. It's empty now, anyway."

"You ought to be ashamed," she said coquettishly.

"What've I got to be ashamed of, eh?" Jode cried, pretending high astonishment.

"What a one you are," she said, plunging the spoon in the cauldron again.

Jode and I came nearer and he rested his faggots on the snow and kicked aside some dogs and seated himself on the cauldron edge.

"Here, what about giving my mate some of that?" he asked.

"I don't want none," I said uneasily.

"Rot. It's good, isn't it, sweetling?"

"Not without paying for it."

"All right, all right. You ought to be friendly though." He leaned towards me and behind his hand whispered loud enough for her to hear but with sincere relish, "Proper little googler, 'nt she?"

I did not think so. She was not half as stunning as I can be when I'm clean and in feminine clothes. She had a large face, a curly mouth moistly pushed into an ostentatious pout, small brown eyes and bright pink cheeks. You could see her riot of chestnut curls under her hood, and her tightly-belted cloak showed the outlines of big, firm, shapeless breasts, a flattish waist and big hips. Even through her clothes you could see the shaking of her breasts and buttocks as she took up some utensils and ingredients from the cupboard beside her, and vigorously grated more vegetables and spices into the simmering cauldron. The snow all round it was running in little streams which could not affect the main coldness.

"What you putting in?" asked Jode, friendly.

"Hen livers, onions, radishes, salt, pepper, spices, honey, pig's bacon, sheep's tripe, garlic, carrots, yams, cactus, cauliflower, cheese, grass, cabbage, vinegar," she recited. "And what's it to you?"

"Well, *your* bacon don't look too bad, for one thing," cried Jode, gallantly.

"My, you aren't half rude," she squealed, giggling and blushing.

"That's better. Now, ain'cha gonna be real friendly?"

"Depends what you mean," she wiggled coyly.

"Well, for a start, just to prove it, give my mate some like I asked at first."

"I don't want it," I said.

"He don't want it," she said.

"Well, he's gonna have it," said Jode, masterful.

"Oh, is he?" chanted the girl. "You can drag a goat to water, but you can't make him drink."

"Ho?" roared Jode, and before I or the girl he was impressing realized what was happening, he'd grabbed two great handfuls of stew and daubed them steaming and lumpy on my face and jerkin, on Lel's last present to me.

"Why you bastard," I shrilled and launched myself at him, feeling instinctively for my knife.

He threw me off, scowling at my anger, forgetting to laugh.

"Yah, scared of a kid!" cried the stew-girl, adding her mite to incite the pretender to her admiration.

Once again Jode rushed at me and this time I went sprawling, staining the snow with lumps and gravy. The dogs sniffed at me. Humiliated, I waved my arms and yelled a blood-curdling yell at them. They scattered, dirty tails between legs or wagging placatingly, trotting away feeling unwanted but not as scared as I'd have like them to be. I rose.

"No need to frighten all the little doggies," sneered Jode, "even if you can't frighten me."

"You bully!" I said.

"Who yer kidding?" said Jode. "I haven't hurt you, and wouldn't. Stick to the dogs, they're more your size."

At this I am afraid I was so furious that I seized the spoon and hurled it at him. It hit him on the bridge of the nose. He came and stood over me, arms akimbo.

"Now, look here, wetmouth, don't tempt me, don't tempt me." he said.

"Where did you read that?"

He aimed a cupped fist at my ear.

I ducked and ran.

Perhaps I thought Jode would chase me. Perhaps I had an inkling of how comparatively badly I had behaved, and was both fleeing from the scene and expecting to be chased as I deserved, not as was likely. I was alone in strange streets before I realized how far or how near I had gone.

I tried to trace my way back, misjudged a turning, was alone.

As every night in the Southern Capital, snow began to fall.

I wandered.

I saw a great cloud in the night sky. It floated. An *immense* eye. I shuddered, then told myself it was senseless to believe that the eye came to look at me. If a cloud *could* be an eye (ha ha) it could watch the whole city, not just me.

I suppose I looked lost.

A man walking up the street over the blue and white snow and the faint orange reflections looked curiously at me. Soon, two strangers walking towards each other and soon to pass in a city street, we were coming stares together. I thought our stares would sound a clash, they were so firmly fixed into each other, would sound a clash when we passed. Slowly I realized I found something familiar about his face. I tried names to it, but it was not a face with a name. Whom did I know whose name I had never known? He was not in a uniform . . . As we approached each other, the distance of stinging air between us lessening, I began to shiver. I had last seen him in Lel's village, he had been coming through the doorway, our startled eyes had then met, just before I swung myself up into the rafters.

. . .

I had been in these clothes then.

He was one of the three men who had come to look for the governor's murderess, and then had come on her trail to the Southern Capital.

He had seen me before, and in these very clothes.

Had he recognized me? Why was he staring at me? Was he just puzzled by a familiarity in my face and clothes? But he must have fixed them in his mind. Does he believe at last that he has come to the end of his quest?

There was a side-street on my right just before we met. I was very curious to hear the clash our stares would make, but I turned and went up the side-street.

Perhaps I had turned too abruptly, but in any case he must, with a low-man's efficiency, by then have recognized me.

He followed me.

A babble of song and talk from further up the street, also the hanging, black, wrought-iron sign and the splashes of bright light-gold on the snow indicated an inn.

I raced for the inn, at the same time taking care to control the knock-kneed way all women run.

If I were fast enough he couldn't know where I'd disappeared. I was glad, as before I had been distressed, that it is impossible to trace any one person's tracks through snow so track-covered as this.

I dived through the old stone archway and dodged through the tiny zigzag passage before the inn's open doorway. Such passages are the taprooms' only protection from the cold outside. I sat down quickly at a table between the door and a window, and slumped into my chair as if I had been in it for ages. There were only two windows to the noisy, smoke-wreathed room, one each side of the door on to the street-passage, and two of the only four lamps in the room glowed on the broad inside sills of these windows. I sat with the smokiest light behind me, and my features must have been very dark to make out at all. At the table there were also two Northern soldiers who ignored me. They were leaders, a little drunk. They leaned across me and talked to each other. They screened me a little. The pursuer entered and looked around. My heart was hammering. He stood in the doorway, turning his head from side to side, which is what he always seems to be doing because of me. He attracted the attention of the busy tap-server, who hurried over on his way to another customer.

"Wine, sir?"

"All right. A jug." He sat down almost opposite me and looked round.

My heart, still hammering, leapt. This almost made me sick. He wasn't certain whether I'd come here—he'd been too far behind me to be certain.

I slumped, my head on my chest, my hood almost covering my face, and snored a little, my legs stretched out in front of me. In spite of the darkness I knew I was in, I half-closed my eyes.

When my man got his wine, he asked the fellow questions. I was near enough to hear most of it.

"Has a young lad run in here?"

"A great number, sir. Lots of young Northern officers—them that overflowed the barracks is mostly quartered round here."

"No, no, I mean just now."

"At this very moment, sir, and will be for some time if the talk be correct—"

"I mean has a young lad only just run in here?"

"Oh, I wouldn't know, sir, I'm that busy. It's very likely, though."

The law-man snorted and, a gesture dismissing the server, gulped his wine. I had not moved but as my attention at least eased from the dialogue and withdrew back to my own body, I found that the whole of me was tremble-tremble-trembling inside my clothes and my careful slumped position. I tried to calm myself but my nerves would not obey my will—even when I had convinced my mind that I was quite calm and cool. It would have been better if I had just continued sitting, and not noticed my own trembling condition. Though I'm pretty sure I didn't move, my concentration on myself must have given me a rigidity unsuitable to the sleeper I was being, and when I realized that the law-man's eyes had again wandered to me, my eyes flew wide open and I gulped. But he had already recognized me. The taproom was clotted with noise but the only sound I heard, and clear and loud, was the scraping of his stool as he pushed it back ready to rise. My right shoulder gave an involuntary twitch as I thought of what in another ten seconds would be unforgivable reality, his hand heavy on my shoulder, soldiers and servers looking, myself publicly arrested and the sentence—flaying alive for murder—that tiny nerve-movement brought Movement into my being again and I was conscious of no thought, only Movement, as I tipped over the lamp behind me, heard its crash past the table and the tinkling discordancy as its glass broke and the quiet crepitation of the little glass splinters on the stone-flagged floor in the darkness. The sudden smoke bellied about me but I held the coughing in my throat as I made for the door. The tiny zigzag passage was kind and cool and my wooden soles made only a slight sound. I was out in the blue snow before the pounding pursuit came pounding behind me. On the inn-wall at my back I felt a metal pipe for drainage and I shinned badly up it as the law-man and a couple of helpful leaders emerged. I was some way up the pipe when my leg-grip slipped and I fell again. I've always been so inexpert at that sort of thing. Luckily I didn't fall far before I stopped myself, but I'd dislodged such a lot of snow from the pipe that I was sure they'd notice, in fact some fell on the law-man's head, not just one of the helpful leaders but the law-man himself, and I was just about to slide down and give myself up when they all three disappeared down the side-street, as fast as they could go so as to catch me in time.

So I hauled myself up and here I am on a dark, snowy roof on a cold, dark, snowy night, huddled against a snow-packed chimney-top. My leg is hurting where I slipped coming up the pipe: I pulled down my tights for a closer look and it is badly grazed but not bleeding much. I patted some nice clean snow on to it which stung a lot but eased the ache, and pulled my tights up again and here I am—and I'm so *cold*. My heart is still pounding. I cling here against the chimney stack and if I look down I can see passers-by in the street below, foreshortened, all the tops of heads and feet below that. I am quite high up here, and nothing shields me from the white, light flakes which whirl here and there on the cold airs. It must be deep night. Men keep leaving the inn below me, I hear their talking loud in the cold silence and some of them sing and I look down to see their lanterns golden on the snow around the doorway. They are friendly sounds to have so near but they are all leaving, group by group they leave and there must be very few left in the inn. I have chilblains. There is now a light even closer to me but it is a menace. A light in the gable window which overlooks my part of the roof, and I dare not climb round on the narrow gutter to get past it.

I had not realized I had made any noise shuffling in the snow to get comfortable until the very instant the window was thrown open and the arm had shot competently out. It grasped my collar. "Ow!" I said. It was the first time for hours that I'd spoken and I started coughing. "Now you can't fool you're a cat," said the voice the arm presumably belonged to. I turned round at last in spite of the firm collar-grip. The arm belonged to a woman leaning out of the window. She was a youngish Southern woman, with hair in red curls half of which had come loose, and a very loosely tied dressing-gown.

"Come on, up you get," she said.

Her other hand caught my shoulder in a no-nonsense grip. Before I had time to collect my thoughts or muscles I had been dragged over the sill and into the lit room.

I half-stumbled, then stood rubbing my leg while she shut the window behind me and bolted it.

It was a small room, yellow and unstable as the light of the two candles lurched it about. It was very untidy and rather cosy and along the furthest darkest wall was the bed with a man on it, watching me, leaning on one elbow. The shadows there only just allowed him an outline. There were discarded clothes all over the floor; in these few seconds as she bolted the little window behind me, I noticed among the mess on the floor a great length of creased bright purple cloth, which I presumed was her dress, a sandal with untied long satin ribbons seemingly spilling everywhere, and a brilliant scarlet cloak with a metal shoulder-broach with which the sandal's ribbons had tangled—I was sure I recognized that cloak and broach: I had seen it before, yes, my army-days—so she'd been sleeping with a Northern soldier. I looked again across at the shadow and recognized him.

She came from behind me, pulling her loose dressing-gown top tighter into its sash.

"So you wanted to do a little thieving, huh?" She pushed at me. "Good thing for the inn it was this bit o' roof you chose, eh? Not talking. And a bit young for this game. But the small ones are the best for it. It doesn't surprise me, not a bit." She pushed at me again, roughly, while she talked and I had to look at her.

She was redheaded over natural Southern dark brown. She was a sturdy young woman, perhaps for a few more years the way she went stockily out-in-out could seem attractive to Southern inn-frequenters or Northern troopers, but surely he had seen too much better than her for her to have attracted him. Beside the brief vivid memory of the Beauty, the first time I had thought of her for what seemed years, this woman seemed actually plain. But perhaps no one else had been handy tonight and he had not bothered to look further. Suddenly I realized a fact quite new to me. I realized that most women in the world are used by most men in the world. Just used. That is all they want them for, and though it is nicer for them to be beautiful it does not matter for one night. I had thought the governor an unusual monster.

Seeing Zerd again, all the old choking hate rose in my throat, added to new hate for the beastliness I had once let him hold me to cleanse me from.

As I saw him again the choking hate rose in my throat, and I coughed and coughed. They both waited with an odd unintentional politeness for me to finish. Zerd, he was wearing a long, loose, black officer's shirt, had swung lazily out of the bed as if

225

he might as well. But he made no move to dress. It was at least a wonderfully warm room, even I was beginning to thaw physically. I half-expected him to thump me helpfully on the back, but I had forgotten I am no longer Cija.

My coughing-fit at last under control, my bent-over swaying back and forth subsiding, the woman again pushed me. (It was hard, but I didn't totter.)

"Nasty little thief-boy," she said. "I don't know what the Capital's coming to."

"Crammed full of thieves and beggars," agreed Zerd.

His voice was again, after all these months, in my real consciousness. It was still the same, just the same, deep and resonant, lazy, holding unfathomable powers. The months might not have been.

"I'm a country girl, you can't rile me about the Southern City. Nowadays you daren't walk down a street with anything in your outer pocket. You'll find it offered to you (or someone else, if you're unlucky) for sale at the other end."

I was standing sullenly. My hair had flopped over my eyes and I had not shaken it back. Through it I was examining the door straight before me. One dash across the room, my hand straight to the handle—and it *might* not be locked.

"We're taking *you*," she said, "straight down to the inn-room. You're one little brat who won't get away with it. You'll be given up to the law and you won't enjoy it."

I started for the door like lightning, one moment I was perfectly still, the next a perfect snake-movement, and before she had time to realize it my hand was on the handle—it was not locked! I had been right about these old inn-rooms—all the inside-keys probably lost or melted down centuries ago! I turned the handle but before I could pull on it his hard arm about my stomach pulled me back. I gripped on that metal handle as I had gripped on nothing in my life before. My feet slid and scraped backwards across the floor-boards, but still I had not quite let go. There was a roaring in my ears. I could not hear him laughing, though I knew he must be. With my last mite of strength I twisted on the handle. The door opened—and I fell headfirst through it, flat out banging my chin on the floor outside it. It was the only way I could get through the door. And that was not through any burst of strength on my part, but because of a galvanic bound I gave which he couldn't have expected. The next instant he'd hauled me up with the same one arm.

But not before I'd realized that out there on the landing I'd fallen full-length at someone's feet—I had seen only the feet before Zerd hauled me back, two small, dainty, pearly feet in sandals, two slim, elegant, pearly-tawny ankles in diaphanous, half-transparent trousers. Behind them, more in the background, was another pair of feet, booted.

Zerd's hard arm turned me.

I realized he had not been laughing at all. He was hard and still. I wanted to see his face. I was so near him that to look up into his face I had to tip my head right back, but I risked it. I met his shadowy eyes. I thought he was gazing narrowly at me and had a sudden fear which was at once banished by all the reassuring factors about me. No possible recognition—the light was bad, I was in boy's clothes, with a mop of cropped hair half of which was in my eyes, I was still shivering with cold, covered with dirt and some blood, and he had not seen me for a half-year.

"Well, well!" said a tinkling and refined, but young and peculiarly delightful, voice. "Fancy finding you like this, Jaleril."

The door was still open. At the voice Zerd's arm had slackened. Nursing my painful jaw, I turned.

The little lady sparkled forward and put one arm about me.

"My dear! Jaleril! So you come at last! And here's your tooth."

What wonders had been done to those old glitter-clothes! They had been lovingly washed, ironed of all their creases, cleaned of all their difficult stains, and the torn sleeves had been mended and covered by blue velvet bows, which I could just see under the fur cloak. I took the tooth from the small fur-gloved hand which must have thoughtfully picked it from the floor. I hadn't realized I'd lost a tooth but it explained the pain in my jaw.

"What's all this?" demanded my captor, the woman in the dressing-gown, and:

"Who is this?" a man demanded of Lel. He was a tall, aristocratic-looking man with exquisite clothes and an angry, nervous face. I presumed he was the pair of boots I had seen behind Lel's feet.

"This?" Lel tinkled refinedly. "Why, this is Jaleril, a friend of mine."

"Oh, is it?" the man said ill-humouredly.

And before I knew what it was all about, the man was challenging me to a duel over Lel. Lel, little brat, looked rather pleased and I could have slapped her—I mean him. But I had

227

to admit that his quick wits in claiming me as a lover come to a rendezvous had just saved me from the obvious fate of a thief and I tried to stand straighter and put my shoulders back in order to seem a worthier lover.

"I'm sorry," the woman in the dressing-gown said to me. "Just finding you on the roof I thought you must be a thief—I forgot you might have been coming to an assignation. Forgive me." It was an untidy but sincere apology.

I bowed and smiled at her, and looked at Zerd, but he obviously had no opinion of Lel's or my own quality, lovers or thieves it was all the same, Lel so fluttery and refined and myself so young and tousled, and he had gone back into the bedroom and was pulling on his trousers.

I would have loved to find out everything, why Lel was here, and how he got here, and why he was with an obviously smitten Southern aristocrat, and whether the aristocrat knew he wasn't really a girl, but there was no time for anything, already a dagger was being handed to me and the aristocrat was asking Zerd if he would stand by to preside and see a fair fight.

"Just as you wish, Commander," Zerd said accommodatingly.

So my opponent was a commander of the Southern army, and already known to Zerd. Help.

"But look here," I said quickly, "I'm not a City man. What are the rules of this dagger duel?"

The Southern commander stared at me. "Puppy!" he said.

"I'm not afraid," I added, indignant at his contempt. "Is it to the death or first blood?"

"I can't fight a man who doesn't know the rules," said the Southern commander disgustedly.

"Tell them to me, then."

"Rubbish. And win a fight against someone who's only just learnt the rules? But you can tell he's a poor specimen," he added to Lel.

"How dare you call him that?" Lel said spiritedly. "He's my brother."

I thought of my lack of resemblance to Turg, and smiled.

The commander stared at me again. "Why didn't you tell me?" he asked.

"I'm not one to dodge a fight, it's a coward's way," I said smugly. What a stroke of genius on Lel's part to claim me now as a brother! My mind ranged quickly back over the recent conversation. No, it was not really practical—

"Why does your *brother* have to climb in illicitly to meet

you instead of coming ordinarily in at the door?" the Southern commander inquired.

"It might have been locked," I said nervously, "at this time of night." While he glared at me I remembered that Lel when asked who I was had introduced me as Jaleril, a friend. Not such a stroke of genius. But I think that though the commander also remembered this he was willing to let it go. In any case he would ensure that Lel was his alone from now on. Only as he turned away he said puzzledly to Lel, "And, anyway, how did he know it was to this inn you'd be coming? Surely you didn't mean to come here even before I met you and brought you?"

"Oh, yes," Lel said, lifting innocent eyes to his.

We all trooped down the winding wooden staircase—it felt strange to be inside the inn after all this time outside it—we were going to the inn-room for a meal. Apparently Lel and the Southern commander whose name by the way is Iro had only just arrived at this inn and had gone upstairs to put their things in their room and now wanted a meal. Zerd and his lady friend had been invited too and I tagged along because I had nowhere else to go and I knew at least Lel wanted me.

I was dead scared of going out to face the streets and the law again.

The staircase was very long and steep, each flight at an angle from the previous one, with doors opening off each landing. There were no windows in all its length but there were torches stuck in sockets at some of the balustrade corners. Even so it was very dark. Some of the torches flamed and flared, but most of them fleered and flickered, and the whole staircase-length was acrid with smoke.

Iro led the way: he seemed to know this inn well, perhaps he often brought pretty travellers here, though I shouldn't think it was too often, by the special way he'd been looking at Lel; then went Lel, pattering daintily, one slender hand on his shoulder. Next trod the Southern woman; she was very awed at being asked to share a supper-party with a commander and a general, it was quite a different matter and far more flattering than being told to take one of them to her bed: she was tasting high life and so had pulled her dressing-gown round her right up to her throat and had put on both sandals. I was last, trailing behind Zerd. By the torchlight I could see our line as it turned down flights below me; but when it was dark I walked carefully and once I stumbled and Zerd's hand came up to steady me. Now after a whole half-year the touch once more of his skin on my bare hand unnerved me. I trembled in every vein. I prayed that he would not recognize me by my unrest at his touch as he had not by my appearance.

We came into the inn-room by an inside door.

It was now a different room; bigger, and barer, for almost everyone had left. There were only a few regulars in corners, two drunks snoring—they were Northern soldiers but you could hardly tell if Zerd even noticed them, outstanding though their uniforms were—the tap-servers sitting about, a well-earned rest, and there were also one or two late-night customers, street-cleaners, a watchman and the stew-girl. I hardly expected her still to recognize me. But, just in case, I sat behind Lel with my face averted.

A relaxed server advanced and asked for our order.

"We want a full meal," Iro said. "I'll have a good Southern stew with plenty of vegetables. And wine."

"And for me," Lel said. No *please*. Lel was not disdainful but had quickly and naturally become so prettily haughty to the servant-class that I hardly realized it had ever been different.

The Southern woman gave a copious order, including oysters, and Zerd said he'd have a famous Southern stew.

Iro raised his brows at me, looking irritated at my presence there at all with them, and I ordered before he could change his mind. At least I'd get a good meal and perhaps a talk with Lel before I had to ask my way back to the peat merchant's.

"A stew," I said, leaning back to order the server, "and mull me some wine."

"Very good, sir," said the server. Iro snorted.

"And grate nuts in it," I added, before the server hurried away.

"In the stew or the wine?" Zerd said.

"I meant in the wine," I answered, surprised he'd spoken to me, "but I don't mind if I get it in the stew."

"As I hear, your Southern stews will take anything," Zerd said politely to Iro.

"Yes, they can be weird and wonderful concoctions."

"They're a magnificent tradition," I said airily, adding my mite.

"Not what you said when your mate gave you the dollop this afternoon," said a giggly voice. To my horror I found that the stew-girl had come across and was leaning over my shoulder.

"Clear off," I growled, "this is a private party."

She looked round at my companions. Even the Southern

woman was a higher class than she was. "My, we are mixing in circles," she said. She still hung and giggled over my shoulder.

"Introduce your friend," lazily said Zerd, who seemed to be taking more interest in me than I thought I deserved. I was not very keen on the rather callow youth I seemed to be creating, but at least it was better to be a very young boy trying to seem manly than a completely unnaturally feminine personality wearing a jerkin and tights.

"My friend the stew-girl," I said.

She giggled enthusiastically.

"Well, well," Zerd drawled. "Pleased to meet you."

Our food arrived but she still hovered. As I ate I silently cursed her and Zerd spoke to her.

"You have a regular pitch, I suppose?"

"Yes, oh, yes, on the street."

"Could you be induced to leave it?"

"Leave it, sir?"

"My wife is already tremendously fond of Southern stews and would love to own a private cook so that she could have them all the time." He ran the two long fingers over the long blue chin in the musing gesture I know so well. "I can't ask you to leave your practice," he said to the girl who didn't say a word because she was staring open-mouthed, only half-assimilating his sentences. "You?"

There was a pause before I jumped.

"Me?"

"Yes, you. Since your friends cook stews, I presume you can?"

"Of course," I said defiantly.

Again the two fingers. "And have you something you can't leave?"

I resented his desire, casual though it was, to please Lara whom I so dislike but I said, "I can take over tomorrow." I didn't add that elaborate stews are *not* solely a Southern prerogative and that I have helped my nurse Glurbia to make them time after time in my own despised country.

"Right. After this meal you can come with me to my billet."

I ate thoughtfully for the rest of that meal. I now had a job connected with the Northern army, probably the only place in this City where I could avoid the eye and arm of the Southern Law, but I might be in even daily contact with Him. I pulled my hood even lower and spooned my stew.

It was a long meal; one by one the other customers left or fell asleep by the embers. The servers made no attempt to dislodge them and disappeared behind the counter; this was obviously usual procedure. Even the stew-girl left at last, after giggling vainly at me. I'm not half so exciting as Jode.

At last Zerd went out to see to his bird and Iro, being the host, went with him. But I could tell he was reluctant to leave Lel and me together and was induced to do so only by the fact that the Southern woman was also with us.

But she, like him, was convinced I had come that evening to a prearranged assignation with Lel. As soon as Iro and Zerd were gone she beamed at us, said heartily that she really must get some sleep and so would leave me with my pretty companion.

As soon as we were alone Lel and I lay back in our high-backed settle and laughed and laughed.

"Oh, Lel, Lel! But how lucky for me you arrived and said what you did! How clever of you to see I was in trouble—"

"It was easy enough to guess you'd been somehow mistaken for a thief, Cija."

"*Too* many questions! Why are you here? How did you get here? Why are you with Iro? Does he know—?"

"Do you like your clothes, Cija? I did them up nice, didn't I?"

"I wouldn't have recognized them."

"They were always so pretty. It was unbearable after you left. Hard and dull and nobody liked me, but it seemed twice as bad as before you came. So I did up the lovely clothes you left me and ran away."

"Lel! All that way! That long, hard journey—"

He laughed. "You did it!"

"But you're so small—"

"Poor Cija, you did it all on foot. I came fast and easy, on Ums."

"On Ums! But he couldn't travel when I—"

"Three days after you left he was well again. He seemed awfully glad and eager—I think he knew we were following you."

"It's strange," I said. "Turg said he'd never be able to do long distances again."

"The night after you left a white puma was seen on the slope, at least the child who saw it said it was white but no one believed her—"

"—So the Puma was kind," I said. "It didn't want to incapacitate Ums for ever. It only wanted to stop me going South—but we're out of its purview now—"

"So I arrived here. I'd always wanted to see the Capital. But before I'd taken in the look of the first great streets two men up and arrested me as the murderess. They said they'd been warned she'd arrive on a big black Northern bird."

"Lel!"

"You didn't ought to worry, Cija, as you see I'm safe now."

"For all that, I seem to have done better in your clothes than you did in mine."

"No, I've done better in yours—for even before I'd time to be terrified up rode this gentleman on the white horse and said, 'What's all this?' They all bowed to him and said, 'We've caught the murderess, sir,' and he said, 'Nonsense, you can tell just from using your tiny eyes she's no murderess'—and that was that. Oh, you can see the nobles here are above the law, Cija. They let me go, just like that. And Iro brought me here with him."

"How thankful I am!"

"And he's lovely, too, don't you think?"

"You're not keen on him, Lel?" I said anxiously. "Because he may be angry when he finds out tonight—"

"I have to risk it," Lel said, but seriously, and I thought of the decision it must have been to ride out alone from the only known life, and the high courage which had disguised helpless loneliness and fear in refurbished tawdry-gauzy rags and a cloak and gloves of rare furs caught in a home-made trap. I get sentimental at times.

"So the future must rest until the end of this already very long night?"

"Meanwhile come and see Ums, Cija. He'll be so happy with you again."

"I don't want to see him, Lel," I said. "Please keep him. I don't want him—nor to see him—"

"Never again?"

"Never . . . He had a strange hold on me once. We seemed to identify ourselves with each other far, far more than is usual with mount and rider . . . It may have been all right for him, but I was—"

Lel put his arms round me maternally and, terribly wearied, I closed my eyes and rested my head on his small furry shoulder.

I started up but Lel was imperturbable as Zerd entered.

Out in the cold streets I ran with my hand on Zerd's bridle. It was the same black thoroughbred bird and its stride

devoured those white Southern streets at such a swift, ungainly, jogging devouring that almost at once I was finding it
an effort to control my panting. After all, I'd had a long day
and it was now hours past midnight. I drew the sharp air convulsively into my lungs which soon were sore. The light flakes
tickled my throat and whirled from every direction at my eyes.
The bird's long, black, warty legs were very near and my hand
on the bridle was an unaesthetic mauve with orange spots.

"You pant beside me like a grampus," said the drawling
resonance.

"I'm—not—panting," I gasped.

"You're out of condition," he informed me and laughed. He
lifted me by my collar and arm and I was before him on the
bird. I shuddered.

"I can run. This is not fitting, master."

He ignored me and one arm held me while the other attended to the dagged reins.

Now our speed was more visual and less organic, and I
recovered my breath (though it was painful trying to keep the
operation silent and dignified) and could look ahead and see
the silent snow flattening the ground before us and rushing
towards us to one flat white expanse, and could look to the side
and see the silent gables and mullions and snow-thick arches
rushing past us, and could look above me and see the dark im-
passive face, the jaw and the shoulder and the glimmering
cloak-broach with a pin like a dagger and the steady forward
gaze of the shadowed black eyes, and could look behind and
see the swift ungainly bird-track disappearing down the winding streets rushing away from us just as soon as all the other
tracks on them were flattened by the silent falling white to one
flat white expanse.

In at a snowy-heavy metal gateway and off, the bird led
away by a wide-awake Northern groom who'd been in the
stable with a warm lantern and a smell of wine and cheese.
And birds. Up snow-silent stone steps and into a house. And
Lara still awake. She swung out in her night-things to meet
him.

"I thought you weren't coming back tonight."

"But I found the stewer you've been so feverish for."

She didn't recognize me but she looked suddenly intense
when told what I was, and waved me to a room which I went
into and found full of the legs of sleeping forms but where I
eventually found a place on the vast blanket- and sleep-cov-
ered mattress which paves it. Before I shut the door I saw her

and Zerd ascending the stairs. The bright saffron gold of the lantern he held was behind her and I saw her clearly. I knew then why she was so anxious for one particular food, she is pregnant.

This morning I awoke and found that the room was a room full of still-asleep or just-awakening pageboys, about a dozen of us in one room. I've found a small storeroom, have put some blankets in it and appropriated it since I'm the Official Stewer.

It's a pleasant, large, Southern house, at the moment housing Zerd and his staff and household. I passed Clor and Isad on the stairs this afternoon but had no fears. If even Zerd and Lara don't recognize me, why should anyone else? For she visited me in broad daylight today and informed me as to my duties. It's board, lodging and Northern protection for jam. All I have to do is make a big stew for the household every evening. I made the first one today and from what the serving-pages tell me it was well received. I have only to go to the kitchen, choose my ingredients from the store of the cook who is a friendly man, put them in an immense pot, mix them, boil them, and leave them to simmer. There are plenty of little pages already willing to stir for me. The place is swarming with pages, and commanders and grooms and soldiers with messages—but I haven't seen Zerd at all.

This morning I forced myself to go and give notice to the peat merchant. I didn't expect him to make any difficulty over *that*—he didn't need me at all, only took me in the first place to oblige the wagoner, but I couldn't just let him down without any explanation, simply *because* the wagoner had been at such pains to recommend me. And I was scared of going there, in case Jode had reported my absence and the law already identified me with the "boy" pursued yesterday. But for the wagoner's sake I'd despise myself if I didn't . . .

So I asked the cook how to get to the peat merchant's house and set off.

It was late morning, the sun was warm and the shadows tepid, the snow full of tracks and the streets of bustle. I began to feel better, alive and real and safe, an indistinguishable *one* in such a multitude. Without even having tried to memorize them, I found the streets already familiar. "I recognize *this* street," I kept thinking, "oh, so *it* turns off from *that* street." They were all beginning to piece together. It is no longer a nightmare but a town.

There were dogs and children, street-sellers, stewers—I saw my stew-girl and we waved to each other—marketing women, all in wools and furs and leathers. Down one street I glimpsed the tail end of a marching line of Northern 13th Foot, and later two of our commanders on badly behaving birds and three Southern commanders on wonderful white horses went past, the commanders all very friendly with each other.

When I came to the inn I was astounded by its morning life.

It seemed to have as much outside as in: there were maids shaking mattresses and dusters out of upper windows, and emptying slop-pails; the gutters of this City are always unattractive, muck lying on the snow, till the street-cleaners come along to cart it away. They get it up with long spades, the spoons of which are equipped also with prongs. As fast as the gutters are cleared they are messed again, though I have seen tidier people take the trouble to bury it in the snow, which keeps it unseen and odourless till Summer. I was glad that at least this inn—and, thank gods, the house we're billeted in —are equipped with fountain-rooms, running hot and cold. At the inn doors there were sellers, chaffering with the servers and guests; there were grooms bringing up to the door horses from the stables; and guests issuing out for a morning walk.

Among these I saw Lel and Iro; Lel hung on his arm and they were smiling at each other. Iro saw me and scowled; Lel saw me and waved and beamed radiantly so I knew everything had turned out all right.

Iro must be androgynous, or bi-sexual, I've heard it's quite common (as it were) among the nobles of this Southern Capital.

What a charming family picture I saw when I arrived at the peat merchant's house.

In the room with the big fireplace it was the time of the noon-meal. The merchant and his wife, with the child on her knee, Jode looking untidy and handsome, morosely eating and hardly looking at the maid-servant, and there was a stranger, an old priest eating with them, who struck me at first as a dear old man.

The merchant stood up and then decided not to come round the table to me.

"Well, lad! You found your way back?"

"Yes, sir."

"Just in time for the noon-feed," sniffed the maid who thought me too young.

"We've been worrying about you. A country boy in our

236

great City for the first time—" the merchant said awkwardly and gravely.

I wondered what Jode had told them, whether they knew I had dashed away after a fight. Well, that wasn't quite a fair word, it had been more than an argument but far less than a fight and being young and nervous I'd made rather a fool of myself. But how did they think I'd got lost?

"I got lost," I murmured.

"Have you been lost all morning too then?" asked the maid, half-shocked to sympathy and half-suspecting me of truancy, and "Did you find a warm doorway to sleep in?" asked the good merchant. The wife and child were ignoring me, eating together, and Jode glanced up at me with a sullen supercilious look.

"Yes, thank you," I said to the merchant. "Master, I'll stay with you if you're wanting me, but this morning I was offered a fine job—"

"Well," the merchant looked almost relieved (I was already proving a nuisance as an employee) but pulled at his lip.

"In the Northern army!" I said.

"Well," cried the merchant, deciding, and clapped me on the shoulder. "I'll not say no to that! What lad wouldn't like a job in an army? Page, is it? I'm sure it's all my friend the wagoner could hope for you!"

"Thank you," I said.

"Well." The merchant cleared his throat and pushed a pie across to me. "Eat while you're here."

"Are you a thirsty child?" My eyes met the priest's as he asked the question and their grey was the grey of the sea I watched from my childhood in the tower, so profound that it seemed I floated when I merely gazed. I forgot to nod, but he lifted the jug and poured wine for me since the maid had made no movement to serve me.

I took the cup and gulped at the warm, harsh liquid's refreshing mellowness and the priest with his foot scraped a stool near him up to the table. I sat down and as he turned back to his food I looked at him. He was in pale, clean, grey leather which was so gentle and clear to look at that the ache behind my eyes vanished.

"How you stare at the holy man," the maid said. "Can't he visit a reverent family without being stared out of countenance?"

"Holy men are made to be attended to, one way or another way," the priest said.

237

He turned and smiled and I smiled back up at him like a child gently and trustingly enraptured because someone is being kind to it. At first I thought his smile was as honest and friendly and undemanding and satisfying as simple things, as bread and warmth, as the kindliness of rest after a day's work close to the earth, and then I saw the radiance behind that and for a moment felt that every shape in his face was singing; and so it was, but one couldn't be attuned to hear it all the time. The priest has a completely simple face, a broad, flat, almost ape-like, peasant face, nothing complicated about it; and yet its radiant wisdom seems to understand all the storms and twists which can possibly afflict the minds of the complicated.

A pet dog came to the table and the little girl wriggled around on her mother's lap to give it food. The maidservant made a fuss of it, the merchant snapped his fingers at it. Jode tossed me a fruit.

"Get your trap round that, kid," he said. "You might as well get as much of your pay for yesterday as possible, since you're not getting any more."

For the agreement had been my board and lodging for my work. Also, I'd missed yesterday's evening meal.

I grinned in relief at him because he'd shown he morosely bore me no ill-humour, but he hardly looked up to see. I was glad I was leaving. In no time at all I'd have got a crush on Jode.

Later when I left the priest said he was going that way himself so would accompany me to the billet.

Out in the bright bustling snows I was not at all shy alone with him, but nevertheless did not know what to say.

He didn't leave a pause. He examined me with a sideways but candid glance. His wisdom took me all in, all that there was for a wise unsupernatural human being to see or deduce: my age, my intelligence, my breeding, my emotion, my love and my shyness now, and I wonder whether he saw me as a boy or as a girl.

"A place in the army is a fine thing for a boy with ambition," he remarked.

But *I* wanted nothing. Once my whole aim, the aim of my life's purpose out in the World, had been to kill Him. Now I am too many thousand miles from my home to bring it harm. Even the *thought* of murder is too exhausting, too great a responsibility. Besides, Ooldra is no longer here to get me safely away afterwards. In those other days her ready presence

238

gave me illusions which at least comforted and wrapped me secure.

"I have no ambition," I said. "I lost it all..."

"No one ever loses their Ambition. They may transfer it to a different, perhaps smaller, thing."

What do I want?

Promotion in my comfortable new billet? No, the easier the job the better, and as little contact with my superiors as possible, please.

"The word ambition is an illusion."

"Oh, as to that," his smile deepened, "every word is an illusion but Illusion; but if you are going deep you must go deeper where one reminds oneself that *words* are not even a scratch on the ultimate Rock at the bottom of our life."

*"Our* life—"

We swung past men running with heavy baskets swaying through the crowd. The crowd treated the priest with respect, but for all that one needs athleticism or strength to avoid being knocked over in these streets. The priest is a strong peasant figure, maybe sixty, maybe seventy, with a young man's skin, fresh and rosy-tanned, except that it is wrinkled deeply at the eye-corners, with deep bags under the narrow sea eyes, deep wrinkles at the mouth corners and down from the nostrils of the big bulbous-twisted nose. It is the nose of a self-willed horse. His head is an urchin's head, with large right-angle ears. His hair is an old man's.

His expression is sly, quizzical, humourous, loving, deceitful, kindly. illiterate, wise, forgiving, sympathetic, malicious. It is an expression which could pursue a lifelong vendetta. Seeing him, you would say, "That man would murder his mother and looks so capable of it that he has probably done so," or "That man would cherish the dying and tend the diseased with his own hands." When he smiles you see him spending his life doing nothing but playing with the children in his parish streets. His face contains everything. He knows life and chose the priest's vestments. He may have been in them since boyhood. I dare guess nothing about him; he may have broken all the rules of the temple, but I would say that he has broken none of them.

"Then what can we form in our life?" I begged.

"What have you heard?"

"They tell me, good deeds."

"Thought," he corrected. "Thought balances itself and so

realizes it includes love. Thought is life, and life is death, but thought is not death. Death is life, and life is thought."

"They don't know that here," I cried, gazing up into his face, dodging a seller and skipping to keep up with him.

"They approach nearest to knowing it in the Land Beyond the Rain Gusts."

His urchin's lined face bent forward in the humble way of priests, his hands meekly folded in his sleeves, his smile and his upward glance gave him a look of slyness. He stopped a barrow and the man gave him an orange fruit for nothing. He handed it to me and smiled the smile while I peeled it enthusiastically. The sky was blue, the great mountain cream at the end of every street, the snow blue and the air fresh.

"Shall I find you often at the merchant's house?" I asked him.

"I'm not going there again."

"Oh. Why?"

"They are attending to holy men in this city, not in the one way but in the other way. I shall disappear."

"Where to?"

"They know that in the Land Beyond the Rain Gusts. I shall remain hidden for a while."

"Why are they attending to you? Who?"

"The Superlativity, the Religion-Emperor of the South, in the palace-city the other side of that mountain. It has finally been decreed that it is sacrilege to worship any but him. We who bother to do so are to be executed."

I'll keep quiet about my own Cousin, I thought. Then:

"But the Northerners here? They have their own gods."

"They won't be popular," he cheerfully remarked. "But I suppose *they* will have the sense and courtesy to pay lip-service.

We parted at the iron gateway.

Only in the afternoon did I realize that I had not asked where to find him and, perhaps for my sake, he had not told me without my asking.

This is a big house, kept well warm and always full of life. There are innumerable, narrow, crooked flights of stairs splitting it all the way up into two parts, the part of the house where the servers and the cooks and the pages and the grooms come and go, and the part of the house where the commanders and the General and their ladies and their entertainers and their visitors from the Southern army come and go. All these stairs are a little sudden to me after my last several months, but the Northerners must be now be as used to them as if born to them.

There is a big walled garden, with an orchard of fruit trees, at the moment snow-logged, and the kitchen window overlooks it. The kitchen is an immense room, stone-flagged and lined with tables, fires, turning spits, greasy little boys, onions and herbs hanging voluminously from the beams, bubbling cauldrons, fat pussies and doggies, several darling, very fluffy, tiny kittens, a page's tortoise whose back gets used for grating cheeses and spices when the grater isn't handy, a continuous hum of sputtering fat and quarrelling and arguing voices and the smells of roasting, baking and spices over all.

Today, sitting on the table while a willing page scraped potatoes for me, I asked the head cook what the Land Beyond the Rain Gusts is?

"It's a phrase, means Nowhere. For where don't you get the rain? Like in Mu, the continent at the world's foot, they've got a regular moon-madness. Always swearing by the moon, the folk down there. They think people go to it when dead. At first it was a symbol of going *from* the earth—but now they take it literally and it sounds very silly that anyone should believe anyone can go anywhere non-existent."

"That's right," said the General's taster, who was lounging on the table. "Now, are you going to make that sea-food thing you gave us last night? It was a rare good 'un. Well received, too—they'd all like you to give it them again tonight. They liked it, especially the Princess."

"Lara," I said, "can lump it. I'm sick of sea-food already. Today we'll have a mixture of different eggs, leeks, sharks' roe and rum. I wonder what it'll be like? The sharks' roe is a concession to the sea, that should do them. Can you go and find a seller with some sharks' roe for me? You might as well be some use—after all, just tasting everything before our masters eat it, every night, can't be very hard work for you. And you never even pay for your keep by finding any poison in it. Not in mine, anyway."

The cook snorted and chased me round the table with a ladle in his hairy hand, and we bumped into a page entering just then and knocked out of his hands a collection of ants and beetles he'd been bringing to me because he thought I'd like to use them as seasoning.

The pages have got to bringing me things like that: small snakes to fry, magnolia leaves.

The taster is a Southerner, a cheerful man who loves the stews, but Zerd's camp never before boasted a taster and the fact that one has been employed is a sign in itself that everyone is perfectly well aware of the unrest seething below the surface of Southerners' and Northerners' genial relations with each other.

Now that my sleep is becoming less of a luxury to me it is less intense and my mind has more time—to dream. My dreams were once a rich and satisfying second life to me, indeed in the tower they seemed at times the only rich part of life. It is terrible as well as bitter to what they have given way. Now I am afraid to sleep. I sit up late with my Diary and a lamp (forbidden in a storeroom) beside my heap of fur and woollen blankets.

Ooldra's voice seems at times to choke my ears.

Today I saw Zerd. We passed on the stairs, I going up with a basket of peacocks' brains, he coming down with a gaggle of Southern commanders and some of his own following. (I looked for Iro, but he was not among them.) I don't think he even saw me. His scarlet cloak whirled and touched my arm as he passed down.

The city is full of demonstrations, parades and military inspections. The allied armies are fast preparing for the vast attack on Atlan. There are many executions of priests of the old faith. I stay indoors. The headquarters of the Northern army is no stronghold in the midst of a risingly hostile population, but walls, stairs, warmth, irrelevant servers' bustle, and a roof all give an illusion of charming security.

This is a cruel hard city, hidden away behind the mountains and doing what it wills. From our windows overlooking the streets we see the clean grey priests led away to execution. The Southern troops who lead them are mainly callous, and dig at them with their spear butts. Some are grave but they carry out their duty. Perhaps they don't care much either—most of them. The priests are usually quiet and walk erect. Sometimes they are captured several together, apparently from one hiding place, and they are driven to execution like patient droves to market, not spoken to except with herders' cries. But one man yesterday was driven screaming because they beat him when he wept.

It is all being done discreetly, the beasts, because they are loth to arouse the townspeople by the murder of any particular favourites. But the knowledge has leaked out, and the townspeople are equal beasts. They deprecate it, and tut-tut it and tch-tch it, and some of them hold heated discussions in the market places and come to the decision that it is a disgraceful business, and some of them even revile the soldiers when they happen to be present at the dragging-out of a priest from a hiding place, and then they go off and do their shopping. There has been no organized revolt, though surely they must all realize that if they *all* rise they can't *all* be beheaded, and they could stamp out the evil.

"Who is this Superlativity, Religion-Emperor?" I asked the cook.

"Some Southern affair among the high-ups," he remarked indifferently. "It's a Southern thing, nothing to do with us."

"Who is this Superlativity?" I asked our Southern taster.

"Now, don't you go meddling in such knowledges," he answered. Poor simple soul, he looked quite uneasy for once and quickly started scraping a bowl.

I asked a young officer who came with a message and had come to visit the kitchen and sit on a table swinging his legs while he munched fresh biscuits.

"Who is this Superlativity?"

"Oh, he's some Southern big-noise, lives in a luxurious marble village, other side of the big mountain, he's been the official Southern god for years but now he's passed a law that adherents to any of the other gods are sinning blasphemers—"

"Surely the people don't believe in him?"

"Well, they've got to, haven't they? This jam is very good. They've never been a religious city, anyway."

I don't know whether they have yet captured my priest, perhaps he is still safe, more probably not.

Today I had a visitor come into the kitchen to see me. I was given half-envious, half-amused, half-admiring glances—well, one-third-envious, etc.—because my voice hasn't really broken yet and here I was with such a daintily grand visitor. Lel has new clothes, beautiful and softly stiff with newness, blue, with a short swaying skirt over very modestly full trousers thickly embroidered in gold.

We embraced, Lel chattering all the time.

"I knew you'd be here, Jaleril, how comfortably we both find ourselves! And when be you coming to visit me?"

"Whenever you like."

"Well, I'm ready now."

"So am I."

I was only cutting up eels, an unnerving task, that way they have of jumping about even when they're dead, muscular reflexes, I suppose, still it's gruesome and I willingly left it to one of the bloodthirsty little brats around.

Lel and I ran out together.

In the courtyard a great black bird was stalking, back and forth, waiting. He stood out from the other birds and horses, like a big, black, thoroughbred demon, they are all dangerous but he has tasted the murder of man and can never be quite leashed again. We walked across the courtyard, between the grooms, horses and birds. There was a lot of smell, and also noise. Barks, snarls, shouts, the shrill neighings of awakening fury. The horses don't stay still near birds, the air is always full of imminent fights. The species don't mix well together. But they respect each other—it is nothing like the relationship of cattle and horses when corralled together. If anything, it would be the birds to feel contempt.

He sensed my presence the instant my gaze was on him, and turned his huge head.

The narrow eye glowed fierce red.

With a bellow he turned and raced straight at me. In the wind created by his own lolloping swiftness his black feathers streamed, big, curved, coarse feathers. The claws lifted and struck outspread clanging on the stone courtyard paving, lifted again. Other birds and mares and stallions threw up their heads and passaged out of his way, grooms tumbled from his path, neatly somersaulting in their haste.

He bore down straight on me, the single eye gleaming on me alone. His rudimentary wings were raised and flapping, rasping the air. It was a sort of lolloping scamper, but terrifying in a creature of such size, hideousness and strength. Insane fear seized me. I was such a puny creature: my head was as high as the hook on his beak. He stopped still within a foot of me. I stood petrified but the cruel head bowed and he thrust it into my oxter, nuzzling me, making a kind of low moaning boom, which seems to be his usual bark, thrust low and gentled.

I caressed him, as I used to. One couldn't stand there attempting to ignore him.

Besides, I was afraid. My heart unevenly hammered. He was

so immense, so powerful. And I could not reject this love. It is too concentrated. It would not turn, but it would include fierce rages. But when I loved him we became part of each other. Please help me not to love him again.

"Up you get, Lel."

"Oh, you must ride him, Cija."

And I saw that I must. I patted him, put my foot in the deep stirrup, threw my leg over him.

Lel got up behind me and kept his arms round my waist. As she mounted I saw that she—he—wore soft leather spats over her slippers, to save the ankles being chafed by the stirrups. The leather was covered by a gold tracery. He also wore delicate metal spurs, not the screw-in type but chained over the slippers, they were long spurs with a roundel of sun-ray points spiking out from the end.

"Surely you don't need to use those very often on Ums?" I remarked.

"No, never," Lel said with heartfelt sincerity.

It is about two months since I was in the saddle and seems longer. Oh, unless you count that night when the General hoisted me sleepy up before him and kept me cradled by his arm. But now the reins were in my hands, again. Lel behind directed me as to the way, which streets to use, and I was again in command, feeling the swaying speed between my legs, the awareness of the slightest pressure of my knees, the forward-jerking neck, the knowledge of my hands, the wind in my face.

This was a quarter of the Capital I'd never seen before. The barracks are in the city but the palaces are in a large block of their own. There were marble steps and pillars, snowy gardens glimpsed over walls, turrets and domes, huge adzed doors.

"And this is ours," Lel said.

Ums didn't like being left with the grooms again but Lel fluttered me through the door into a large circular hall with a fountain, painted wall-panels and grand staircase. The general design and materials used were much richer, and there were no tree and open roof, but in lay-out it was the same type of hall as the Governor's, which had been so familiar, and I shivered at the memory of the time before I met Lel.

"Is Iro out, Lel?"

"Yes, today."

We both understood the situation.

Lel showed me over the whole part of the palace owned by Iro. We had a wonderful afternoon. We talked and talked, and laughed, and confided in each other. Lel says he is deliriously

245

happy with Iro, and with his circle of friends and acquaint-ances. In the village he had always believed himself a monster, perhaps even unique, certainly born with an irrevocable inner *rottenness*. Now he found a society where he is accepted as normal, and, besides, loved jealously and tenderly.

It is certainly a terrific place to live.

The living-hall is walled in glass behind which, on every side, are giant aquariums. In these wave water-weeds and swim fishes. Tiny brilliant fish darting in swarms like animat-ed jewelled bubbles; large, somnolent, silvery fish; black eels; fantastic little sea-horses; turtles with world-weary grins, cor-uscated shells, and flapping flippers; sea-snails and a couple of fascinating rapacious octopi which are kept separate from the others and fed each day on less valuable creatures. All this one can see as one sits in the room used to receive visitors. It is al-ways bathed in a subaqueous green-blue light, which dims one's features as one sits on the carpets or couches covered in the fur of snow-leopards.

Lel clapped his hands near the door and called, and a little boy of the golden-skinned race came and brought us a tray of fruits and wine, and a small roast chicken each, which we held in our fingers and nibbled daintily.

The bedroom is hung in silks, striped diagonally across with stripes of thick fur, thin gold thread, and different colours of silk. The floor is covered with furs, some with their snarling heads still on, and tumbled piles and piles of fur and silk cushions. In every corner there is a great marble pedestalled jar of brilliant fragrant flowers. They must grow somewhere in an indoors garden.

The bed depends from the ceiling so that it sways at any touch, and is shaped like a metal chariot (its wheels only just not touching the floor) drawn by a team of metal horses which prance nearly across the room. They are beautifully made but I said I thought it rather a florid idea in interior decoration. Lel said he didn't know those words, though he is learning lots from Iro's friends, but he thought I was absolutely wrong if I thought they weren't grand.

The ceiling is a smooth flat sheet of highly polished silver which reflects everything that happens below. Gosh.

Lel has come up in the world.

A return to this book after an absence of some time. My days have been fuller, my sleep deeper.

I have paid quite a few visits to Lel. This was after I had

paid a second visit and Iro'd come home earlier and discovered us together. Luckily we were discovered in the living-hall, with pails of water and waterweed over our arms, feeding the fish. We were giggling and joking very childishly, and splashing each other (and Iro's carpets) now and then. Keeping up the fiction that I am Lel's brother, we greeted Iro with respectful delight. Several of his noble friends were with him too, and we all spent a very enjoyable evening together in the big greenish room, sitting on the floor, eating small birds and talking, and one of the friends became pleasantly drunk, not because he'd had heaps to drink but because the atmosphere was right, and he climbed up the feeding-steps and dived into one of the tanks—splashing us hugely—and swam about underwater until one of the octopi showed signs of determined pursuit.

After having been so publicly accepted (or if not accepted, not knocked-back), I decided it would be ridiculous not to visit my relative again whenever I wished to, so I do. Of course, I didn't have Iro's invitation, but that was only a technicality.

I know perfectly well Iro can't believe I'm Lel's brother, but he is now used to me and my behaviour with Lel, and I think he may have decided I am a childhood friend of Lel's, who lied about our relationship to make sure of turning away Iro's wrath on that night of incriminating circumstances.

Lel is treated like a beloved toy. Iro is a nice person in private life. I find him rather unapproachable, but that is only to be expected. I can see him being a competent efficient Southern commander.

It is a society I should feel horribly inferior in if I were a girl.

They can never mention women except to add a contemptuous comment on them as breeding-machines only, who try to glorify their squalid function with the nauseating myths of mother-love and sexual allurement. Of course I'm getting to think that way myself. I've met few women I've ever really approved of, and the sight of Lara illogical, cruel, imperiously and coyly pregnant all over our billet is quite nauseating. But I remember that their attitude is born of malice and jealousy, even though the majority of them are unlike Lel, don't want to be women or if they do don't know it.

And after all, and this applies both to me and them, women never do *like* their own sex in general.

I think now that Iro, with an accurate and unerring eye of long practice, was sure as soon as he saw Lel that he was a boy.

But as I am a boy I come in for a good deal of attention. I

already received several flattering proposals I reject with the look of amiable innocent candid youth which I've decided on and which luckily never seems to give offence.

Anyway, in this society, where everyone seems to come out with shrill squeals and giggles and wears face-paint and/or unsuitable clothes, I can afford to relax and be utterly and completely myself. In the kitchen, life, though enjoyable, is one continuous strain and I have to concentrate on being an urchin because it is no use trying to be masculine.

We saw fighting in the street. They fought in the streets yesterday—the Northerners and these Southerners. We watched them from the windows. Finally Lara herself came to find out what was holding up the serving and found us all peering out. She pushed herself to the front of us, also peered out, and gave a shocked gasp, her hand to her breast. She turned round, pivoting from her hips, an alluring trick she has learned from watching her husband's mistress. Waving an imperious airy hand, she sent a page for the General. I remember how, when technically innocent myself, I thought when I first knew Lara that a sweet little untouched girl like that was really just right as a wife for someone like him.

Soon several of our very highest military gentlemen reeled out and replaced us at the little windows. It is the first time I have seen the General in the kitchen—the first time for nearly a month that I have seen him at all. Like the others, he was rather drunk. I kept out of sight. For a few moments we servants, with Lara and several other ladies who had begun to drift out of the inner room, watched the nobles at the windows. There were he, the commanders, and some high-ups from the Accoutrements side of things, also a number of important Southerners, commanders, subsidiary generals and civilian aristocrats. They leaned on each other, flung arms about each other, hiccuped, guffawed, and finally decided with curses that members of their separate Southern and Northern troops were fighting out there.

Belatedly they buckled on sword-belts and hastened lurching out.

Once more all we servants surged to the windows, but had to make way again for the ladies. They clustered gazing out, teetering on their high-soled feast-sandals, gasping and exclaiming and presently the gentlemen returned, having routed their various disturbers of the peace, and were lauded and twittered over. I wondered how much the ladies had seen; if they

248

had noticed that big Blues sergeant lying on the pink snow with his head bashed open and the man doubled up groaning by the gates.

The gentlemen seated themselves on the kitchen table and called for wine.

I had to help. I couldn't just stand by while the others served, but I picked a sleepy Southerner as far away from him as possible, and went to him. But Zerd, who had an arm round Lara's shoulders, gave a great yell at me.

"Hey! Master Stew-boy, that's good red wine you have there, bring it over here instead of this muck!" And he kicked away the helpful taster with white wine.

I pushed my way towards him.

He bowed at me, thereby dragging down Lara by the heavy arm still over her neck. She'd had a lot to drink too, her cheeks were immovably flushed and her eyes sparkled at me over the rim of her mug.

"Ha, my protégé." He took time off to drink. "Where did I drag you out of? . . . Well, d'y'enjoy yourself more among the steaming greasy carcasses here—" he nodded round at the dismembered cattle always turning on our spits "—than among the steaming greasy carcasses I rescued you from in that brothel-quarter?" Lara giggled and threw her arms round his neck and he drank deep again.

So that *was* what he had thought of Lel. I felt myself harden into ice but I was boiling within that. I walked away from him with my flagon but before I'd taken a few steps into the moiling noise the hand pulled me back—I knew from its hard grip on my shirt whose it was.

"More wine, sir?" I said evenly.

"You didn't answer me," he observed.

"Yes," chimed in Isad who'd been noisily listening beside him, "he must know if you're happy here."

"Perfectly, thank you, my lord."

"And you don't miss your pretty friends?" tinkled Lara with such an insulting, condescending leer, adding her own mite to what she'd deduced from her husband's remarks, that I couldn't trust myself to speak and merely stared at her. From the table beside us a man in the uniform of a Southern commander suddenly pitched forward and lay sprawled snoring at her feet; it was Iro, but she didn't even blink at him. "All right, kiddy, fill my cup," she said, holding it out before me.

"In your condition, is quite so much wise, madam?"

I took care to sound solicitous.

She went white, but flushed-white as it were, and glared at me with increasing venom.

The General flung back his throat, dark against his white open jacket and laughed and laughed against the separate cacophony of the others until when he opened his eyes again and looked at me his eyes were bright with tears and he was wheezily squeaking, husky with laughter. He looked very drunk and happy, his mouth wide open and his savage teeth gleaming. Even taking into account his drunkenness and Lara's gorgeous venomous look, I didn't see why he found things quite so amusing.

"I've had only one other underling who ever treated my family with such insolence," he remarked.

I stepped over Iro.

"Wine sir?" I said to Clor. I went between the servers and guests, they were now roaring a drinking-song, and all the time I saw that Blues sergeant, he'd once fixed my sandal-heel for me when it broke, lying on the pink snow with his head bashed open.

It's not the first time we've heard of fighting between the allied troops, but only the first time we've seen it.

I suppose I've subconsciously been waiting some time for this to happen.

—And now it has.

I had gone to visit at Lel's house—well, I mean Iro's—and it was evening, a dinner-party. We all sat round a long table, and even I was wearing my best clothes. Oh, yes, I have best clothes now. A fine shirred shirt the taster gave me because he could no longer let the waist out far enough, a closely-woven woollen jerkin, scarlet, which the cook's daughter made for me at the same time as she was making one for her father—an unexpected gift, that, which touched me—and a pair of old gold slippers which Lel offered me because he'd got tired of them. My tights are the same ones, but so neatly darned by the cook's daughter that they're as good as new if I sponged down every now and then. And with a peacock's feather (from one of the more exquisite meals prepared in our kitchen) in my cap I looked very fine indeed.

I suppose I don't stack up against all the nobles' jewels and furs and lace, but they don't mind, they all like me, they respect me and yet pet me far more than they ever dare to pet Lel when Iro's around.

But for looking fine the nobles in the army are the grandest,
250

each one of them is covered in medals. Rows and rows of them, a gleaming, scintillating, sparkling, glowing, chinking display, and when you look at them closer you see each one is different, all lovely, different shapes and designs.

Of course not one of them means a thing. In the Southern army they are terribly keen on medals, you get one every time you run a message or get a scratch. A Lavender Heart for a wound—and if you get the wound in battle it's an *Amethyst* Heart.

Well, here we all were sitting round looking fine and eating elegantly; and talking a great deal of polite intellectual conversation. It always sounds very deep, and sometimes even controversial; but really we are all so used to it and adept at it we could do it in our sleep and probably do.

Suddenly the door opened much more quickly than usual and instead of a server the little golden boy came in.

He ran in up to Iro and bowed on one knee.

"Please, lord, a Northern army lord to see you—"

"Oh, gods," frowned Iro. "Business at this hour of day."

I felt like reminding him that probably the *Northern* officer had been working hard all day and was certainly not finished yet, but I kept my trap shut.

"Don't invite him to eat with us, Iro, unless he's obviously a gentleman," advised one of the friends. "He's liable to be appallingly uncouth, or even plebeian, they frequently raise their officers right from the ranks."

"Show him in," Iro said to the golden-skinned boy, who ran out.

"Surely it's worse to be uncouth than to be plebeian."

"Don't you find," interposed a fashionable young artist from further up the table, "that in spite of their admittedly rather unsavoury ideas on life, the *real* lower classes are the best part of the nation? The upper classes, present company excepted, of course, are so frequently insipid and, of course, the conventional middle-class is too sickening for words."

"Of course, the barbarian communities don't really have any of this class mutual-loathing business," said Iro from between mouthfuls. "There are captains and warriors and women, and that's about all." Lel looked deliciously snooty.

"I like the *real* lower classes, the city lower classes," I said. "The vagabonds and street sellers. But the majority of the working classes are unnecessary. They make slums and are stupid—and vulgar in a horrid refined way." I was going on to speak of the peasants, but Nasir, a sentimental the-working-

251

classes-are-the-salt-of-the-earth noble who would have been horrified if he'd ever met any working-classes in their native habitat and not graciously receiving from him, but who could get very indignant and nasty-tempered with people like me (even though technically, I am a servant) broke in—

"Oh, they *are* necessary. They are the backbone of the nation. If there weren't any labourers to lay bricks and plough fields where would all the so-called necessary architects and scientists be?"

"If everyone were intellectual," retorted a hard light voice which here sounded unusually masculine but which I couldn't trace, "they could invent instruments to do all that work at the moment done by unintelligent and usually downright lazy yahoos being paid by the City—and our taxes!"

I was just thinking that this was the most flippantly serious reply that could have been brought out at Nasir's cliché when I saw who the speaker was. A young, thin Northern leader had just entered in a draught of cold air, there were snowflakes on his shoulders, and he was followed by a very junior subaltern, grinningly staggering under a burden of army crates.

Although he looked taller and older in his boots and smart, untidy crimson and gold leader's uniform and with a white scar across his forehead and nose I recognized him at once.

Smahil.

"Smahil!"

But it was not my voice which had said it. Iro had greeted him with a sound of relief, apparently this was someone else in the Northern lot he already knew.

"Dump 'em there," said Smahil to the very junior subaltern who grinningly dumped the crates on the feasting-dais.

Smahil strode up to Iro and saluted rather haphazardly.

"I've got some stuff of yours here. Be a help if you take it off my hands, none of it's any use to us."

"Right," Iro said. "How'd you get it?"

"One of my chaps brought 'em to me, said he found 'em. I didn't inquire into it."

Iro frowned severely. "Well," he said, "yes, I can take them. As you see we're engaged at the moment. Are you free to join us?"

"Sure thing," Smahil said, sitting down at the end of the table. "I'm not on duty again till tomorrow morning. Thanks."

"Set a place for the two Northern lords," Iro said to the little golden boy, and the subaltern flushed and seated himself beside Smahil. Smahil fished about in his tunic breast-pocket and brought out a pad and sticky-tipped scriber. "Would you just sign for 'em, please, sir."

"Of course," Iro said and gave his signature with a flourish. "By the way, what are they?"

"Medals," said Smahil and grinned disarmingly into the sudden silence. "I suppose really I ought to scoot now but I've more sense of hunger than of shame and your charming invitation—"

"Medals!" said Iro. "Gods' Marrow Bones, what a responsibility! And I suppose your fellows have already looted more than half of them?"

"Well, yes, sir, and that's why I had to come to you. I couldn't get rid of them to anyone of lower rank, they always asked what they were. No one would accept the responsibility of handling half-empty crates of medals."

"Gods' Marrow Bones," blasphemed Iro again.

"Cheer up, sir. Nobody could suspect *you* of pinching medals. Well, I mean, for one thing, where would you fit another one on?" And he stared with earnest well-meaningness at Iro's sparkling torso. The child brought a crystal tray, placed a full flagon between Smahil and the subaltern, and piled fruit and flesh on to their plates. Smahil reached across the still-serving child's arm for the flagon and began to glub-glub it deliciously frothing into his goblet.

I watched him in the blue-green twilight of the room. It was ages since I'd seen him. He is harder and more irresponsible. He was always the sort of person it is impossible to twist round your little finger, but now merely from *looking* at him let alone having contact with him you feel he is a personality but a dangerous one, you never know what he's going to do next, he is living intensely all the time but can never normally be depended on for sympathy or kindness, which is all the more unfair as he *can* be depended on for understanding. I'm not building this concept simply on a little incident between the Southerners and Northerners who are hostile allies anyway, that has nothing to do with it, I formed this opinion from watching his face.

"Well, Smahil hound," cried Nasir, who can be hearty, "how are you getting on these days?"

"All right," Smahil said, letting the subaltern have the flagon.

"How do you like my room?" Iro asked. "As you see it's recently been redecorated."

"Is it significant," Smahil inquired, "that your aristocracy al-

253

ways share their palaces with so much animal life?"

There could easily have been a duel here, it's happened before now between Southern and Northern officers as between their men, but there was only a nasty look from everyone and then Nasir asked, "And how's the beautiful Terez?"

"Oh, she's all right," said Smahil. "Would've sent you her love, if she'd known I was coming here."

"No, thank you," grimaced Nasir though he looked more gratified and less malicious than usual when speaking of a female. "She's more likely to have thrown her heaviest bracelets at me. For such a gorgeous she's got the most hellish temper—"

"Clever, too," said the young artist. "For a woman of the golden-skinned race, with amber eyes and golden hair, she's very clever to gild her nails and always wear golden and gold. They say she paints even her areolas golden. But of course I wouldn't know."

Smahil smiled but didn't vouchsafe anything. I studied him. It hadn't occurred to me he'd have a mistress—and apparently a famous one.

His leader's uniform was carelessly put on but brilliantly designed—he's in the 18th Foot. For the first time in that rich colourful company I felt poorly dressed and was conscious of the darns in my tights. That wasn't because of his uniform so much as because of the way he wore it—he'd moulded its brilliance, cut and untidiness to his own personality and it had a spectacular look, individual and yet a great deal more contemptuous than defiant. He is no longer what I had once come to think of as "my Smahil". I'd known he never had been, but now he could thoroughly unnerve me. At that moment, as I sat there looking at him, his eyes came up and met mine.

His gaze lingered a little, but I don't think there was recognition in it. It went down me to my ox-hide belt and the bottom of my woolly jerkin (my darned legs were hidden below the table) and up again. I suppose he thought I was out of place in that company and wondered why they hadn't at once given me silks like their own, but he hardly glanced at me again through the rest of the meal.

Finally I rose.

"Time I was going, anyway," I murmured.

There was a small polite but sincere clamour, Iro stood up and nodded at me and sat down again, and Lel jumped up and

254

cried, "I'll see you to the gate, Jaleril." I saw Smahil glance at me in surprise at my treatment.

Lel rustled out with me into the courtyard—as we went out Lel was busy putting on a fur cape because of the cold outside and I was a little conscious of my tights.

"Must you really go now, Cija darling?"

"Afraid so."

As we walked across the courtyard to the gateway, Ums broke free from a groom and pranced over. I caressed him nervously. At a sign from Lel three grooms ran forward and forced him away again. His eye was murderous and he lashed out with beak and claws but I looked away. Lel stood on tiptoe and kissed me on the cheek.

"Bye for today, Cija."

I looked anxiously at the window of the exit-hall, half expecting to see Iro there glowering at us, but instead I saw Smahil with the subaltern, who must also be just leaving. Smahil's eyes were on the furious black bird and there was a look of wonder in them. Then they came back to me—and I saw in them something I have never before seen in anyone's eyes because of me: real Joy.

As I could not sleep last night, and so wrote in bed the account of how suddenly I met Smahil, I cannot sleep tonight. I toss and twist; I've got out and up and gone twice to the fountain-room, to splash cold water on my forehead which keeps seeming too warm and dry.

I was out of the gate almost as soon as I saw Smahil that evening—and all through the streets on my way home here every time I heard footsteps behind me on the snow my heart thundered in my throat. I'd forbid myself to turn round but after a few minutes of intense self control I'd steal a glance behind while my heart beat a crescendo of nearly-bursting—and then fell dead as it was always someone else.

Why did I leave so quickly? He can't even have known which way I left that courtyard. Why didn't I hang round outside the gate until I heard him coming out?

I was leaving the billet early this morning on one of my daily shopping expeditions. Oh, how beautiful the snow is in the early morning, after a fall in the night. The snow is so lovely when flat, white, like new, crisp, unmarked paper—or when there are just a few blue footprints, not overlapping with even one set of others. There were me, the cook, the taster, and a couple of half-grown pages. Our feet crunched on the new snow. And up came Smahil, all brilliant in the white, cool, sweet morning, and took off his shako to me so that his fair lank hair fell over his forehead.

"Good morning—er—Jaleril. I hoped to find you. I've a message for you from the dinner the other night."

"The one at Lord Iro's house, my lord?"

"Of course," he bowed.

How polite he was being.

I let the others go on towards the market place while behind them I fell naturally into step with Smahil.

"How nice of you to bring me the message yourself, sir."

"Well, as I was passing... I thought—"

"Of course. Still, it was very kind of you."

We had now reached some stalls and the still morning was enlivened by smells and chaffering, though not much compared to what there would be later in the morning.

"Hey, Jal," called one of the pages, turning round to me, "what about these cloves?"

"All right, get them," I said.

"These shrimps don't half look nice, lad," remarked the taster, eagerly rubbing his tummy.

"All right," I gave my permission. "You can get them, to taste tonight!"

Smahil, walking neatly along with the toes of his boots turned out and his hands clasped behind his back, gave me an inquisitive sideways glance.

I let them choose all the shopping this morning so they turned away from me and left me with my companion. Demurely he strolled with me between the stalls.

"I am the stewer for the Northern headquarters," I explained.

"I see." Again he bowed gravely.

"I choose the ingredients—and simmer them up later in the day..."

"Of course."

"It's quite an exalted position—really..."

"Rot."

"It's not rot."

At this familiar exchange we both burst out laughing and in our laughing admitted we both knew I am Cija.

"I thought you were dead, for months I've thought you were dead—"

"Smahil—"

"Then I saw Ums, and I knew it *must* be you. But how different you look—"

"I'm the stewer—"

"—For the General."

"But *he* doesn't know me. He hasn't recognized me."

"Dear me, is it possible?"

"Yes, it is."

We scowled at each other. I realized with a leap of the heart that with me Smahil does not even dream of retaining his new intrinsically sophisticated self—for him I mean our old relationship, effortless and bad-tempered as passionate late childhood—and with another, different, sort of leap of the heart I realized that my legs are visible right up to the top, and in tight tights, not a lady's full trousers. Thank my own Cousin my legs are as I would wish them to be were I an embryo choosing my body—long, slim, shapely, strong.

"I *know* he hasn't recognized me because when he engaged me as a stewer, if he'd done so purely to get me into his purview again he'd have engaged me *before* the duel was suggested, in case I got killed."

"He might not have cared if you'd got damaged—after all, his wife's pregnant so they must be friendly. Sorry. Anyway, what about telling me the whole story?"

So I told him, leaning against a wall in the market-place, long after the others had returned to the billet and kitchen, while the market morning bustle grew around us ignoring us. I left out nothing, from Blob's treachery to the present time. This morning Smahil's whole behaviour was a melting exception to the rule I deduced from his expression that other evening. When I told him of the governor he looked actually distraught. The tears which welled up into my eyes were not because of my defilement (I have long ago forced the bitterness from that because bitter memories only poison) but because of his tenderness now which floated me up and melted me into itself.

I have not been able to expunge the corroding wrenching bitterness from Narra's death, but I have tried to forget it as much as possible. I was surprised and ashamed at how well I have succeeded—when I was telling the story to Smahil I nearly left out Narra's death altogether! I stopped crying, for they had been gentle tears of something deeper than happiness. I told him of the mountains, but the puma I glossed over because I believe Smahil would find my surmises about its super-

257

natural quality ridiculous. I told him of the village, but I kept Lel's secret and talked of him as a girl who had become my friend and so followed me when I had to cross the plains. I told him of the crossing of the plains, of the wagoner, the merchant, the inn, the General. Of my life now.

"I don't want anything at all nowadays," I said. "I live now moment by moment."

"You've become a philosopher," he said glibly.

I remembered the priest and I said, "I don't think so. I've lost something, not gained. I'm deadened now, sometimes I realize it. I'm no spirit or mind any more, only body and emotion." I could have told him that any mind in me is kept going only by exercising it in writing this Diary, but I want to keep this existence private from everything and everyone. "I live moment by moment my comfort, fun, anger. Perhaps I have gained in one thing—I'm often quite reckless."

"You never were devastatingly cautious."

"But now I'm reckless for the savour of the moment—" I told him about my encounter with Lara in the kitchen. In the cold light of day even to me it sounded rather vicious. "I think I have a nasty streak where Lara is concerned," I said: one of those sentences which begin in compunction and end smugly.

"Stupid streak. One of these fine days you'll find your delightful little creamy skin hanging off you in decorative patterns."

He put a hand on my cheek, the first time he has touched me since our meeting, and drew it slowly down my face, slipped it under my jaw, down my neck and into my shirt under the straight leather jerkin. His hand sliding over my shoulder made me, also, aware of how soft my skin is and what creamy curves it covers. In the crowd of jostling, ignoring marketers I met the gaze of a keen-eyed pedlar in grey rags. I shrugged my shoulder at Smahil's hand.

"But I have lost all my purpose in life," I said, bringing back the conversation.

He smiled down the few inches at me. The smile entered from his eyes to mine and pounded through my veins. He lifted his hand to trace my chin with one finger. "Yes, you always seemed very full of some purpose or other. It was probably your own quality of youth. You're only settling down now into normal life."

"It's not yet a year ago, Smahil."

"Yes. But you're a woman now." He smiled again, lightly and tenderly. "Though a very skinny, young, boyish one."

I knew he meant what the governor has done to me, and that though with almost a killing rage he deplores it, he also thinks my reluctance for himself must have vanished.

I touched his hand, almost pleadingly. "Smahil, I never was—That was the first night I was going to spend with Zerd. And I ran out because Lara came in—I was afraid of and hated everything and the way I was going—I knew the Northern army held nothing for me and I wanted to get myself and Narra away. So Blob—"

"You could have come to me."

"You don't understand—"

"I understand that you're far too independent. But that's *you*. You have got what you call a spirit, and that's what is so independent; whereas I can only grope—"

He was smiling and though at first it gave me a shock to hear Smahil talking like that I realized he doesn't mean that he is groping after a spirit but that he seems to spend his time groping after mine—and will till he gets it . .

Last night was terrible. I slept, yes, but I lived again and again and again the worst nightmare of all, which has also in *my* life been actual experience—the monster you cannot kill, the demon with whom you fight only for him to rise again and again, resurgent, inconquerable, despair; and yet you must keep on fighting or be destroyed.

And the whispering of Ooldra's voice wrapped it all about.

But I have stopped fighting.

Even the fate of the continent with the beautiful name behind the airless ocean, even the thought of the fate of That leaves me feeble and powerless.

How can *I* do anything?

When I was a self-important little girl with a knife hanging from round my neck I thought I could change the fates of the world. Now I use the knife to slice onions.

Although it was noon, Smahil would not let me leave the other day without promising I would meet him again in the market this morning. I was a little frightened at his determination. But I said, "Yes," because our conversation had seemed so tiny. We had not even touched on the things I really wanted to ask.

Today he had borrowed two spare birds from a friend in the cavalry. We rode out of the City—he knows the way—and spread our saddles on the snowy river-bank and we sat on them and talked, undisturbed by the jostling and noise of the market. There's a big waterfall out there, frozen hard, the Southern children toboggan down it. Their cries, thin in the cold air, were merely a background as we sat on the saddles and talked. The two birds beside us peacefully searched in the snow for what shoots they could find.

"What's been happening all this year to you, Smahil?"

He grinned at me as if he were my big brother.

"I'm in our hated Northern conquerors' captors' army now."

"Well, if they offered you a post you could hardly refuse it."

"You don't get the point, revolting little fire-eater. I like them. I don't mind them."

"My mother's country—The country you grew up in—"

"Yes, but that's behind us. Thank the good gods our relatives. And there's no turning back."

To hear him echo my own thoughts so off-key was queer. "Smahil, you have no emotions—"

"Haven't I?" He lay back on an elbow and grinned up at me. Though he is not much taller than I, and is thin, he is a man. We can sit side by side, our elbows, our knees opposite, and yet though at first glance we are the same size, he is bigger, in every way he is *bigger*. He dabbled his fingers in the snow while his eyes didn't waver from my face. It is his insistent teasing moods which unsettle me most. "Now we can see how small that country was."

*"Our* country—"

"You pertinacious patriot. Wasn't it a little country? Now, wasn't it? Didn't it have scrubby countryside and a rickety Capital? Didn't it have teeming slums and—"

"I saw none of those things," I interrupted (truthfully).

"—and a poor army?" He was looking mocking now.

"It was *He* who did that—"

"Your mother was an enthusiastic Incompetent and the High Priest could be called corrupt if even at the beginning he'd had any religion, but he has only a craving for power—"

"Tell me what has happened ever since that night I left your army," I said firmly and settled down to listen. I remembered that night when the Northern army passed above me, the marching troops, the cavalry, the birds, the wagons, the carriages, the baggage-train, the beautiful enemy and his faithful commanders, his household, the pink princess, the hostages but not Ooldra who had apparently by then already embarked on her miraculous escape—

"It was only several mornings afterwards that I discovered

260

for certain you weren't with us. On that very first morning I expected you or at least Narra to come to me, but neither of you appeared. On the third day I became angry. What if I'd had a relapse? You couldn't have cared less, could you? No, I suppose even if you had been with us you wouldn't have. I inquired round and about, and Ijleldla and one or two winegirls and pages whom apparently you'd made friends with also came to *me* with inquiries about you—and then we heard of Ooldra's . . ." He paused.

"Ooldra's disappearance," I prompted.

"Oh, so you *have* heard about that, have you? You don't seem very upset. Yes, Ooldra's disappearance. So I believed there was nothing for it but that you (and probably the little girl) were dead." He pulled at his lip. "I *did* consider, at one time, the possibility that you'd stayed behind somewhere in that hot little town—but I couldn't see why you should want to. As a matter of fact, I considered everything. I was very keen for a while on one idea that the General had you locked away in his tent and wasn't showing you to anyone, not even Lara. Naturally. That was while I still had fever. Well . . . I suppose I then realized after a few weeks that even such a charming ingenious idea as that was impracticable, and I stopped mooching round the General's tent every evening and morning at unexpected points in the hope of glimpsing you. As far as I was concerned you've been quite dead for months."

He pulled at his lip again.

"So what happened?"

"So we crossed the mountains, ravaging a little as we went, and skirted the plains. That was when the General casually decided he was tired of carrying useless hostages with him and we might as well do something for our living."

"But *hostages*—"

"Oh, use your nut, darling. I should have thought you'd have realized by now that hostages aren't sacred. Your Zerd, sorry, His Mightiness Immense One the General, can do what he feels like. Your mother won't make war on him, how can she, and if she did do you think it would matter? And her only real chance is gone, that was when we were still within several hundred miles of her, I do mean our, country. But he took hostages to ensure the Dictatress' behaviour, not his."

"It's terrible."

"So the Noble Gagl was offered a job which curiously enough he was perfectly content to take. He's now a pedantic but respected staff secretary. Her ladyness Ronea refused

261

affrontedly to accept any post so she dropped off on the way and now she's in a little town bordering the plains. Gods only know what she's found to do there. I became an officer, and a damn good one I am. Ijleldla and Iren were allowed to choose which officers they'd like to belong to. They made a great outcry and wailed publicly for days. You should have seen them when the willing officers were lined up before them. I've never seen two girls enjoy themselves more. They looked everyone over in minute detail and with expressions of shrinking modesty, and eventually chose the two handsomest, saying to them, 'You will be sympathetic and gentle with a poor girl in such a predicament, won't you?' Oh, it was charming. Only Iren was slightly upset. She had chosen me first and I turned her down, I said I wouldn't have missed this for worlds but I'm here only as an observer, Well, who can blame me? At that time I'd just set eyes on Terez."

"Terez? Your golden girl?"

"Golden woman."

"Oh. And—and is Onosander an officer, too, now?"

"My dear girl. My dear Cija. *Can* you see Onosander being any kind of an officer?"

"Well, he is a bit of a sonk. But what—"

"He's a groom."

"But isn't he scared of the birds?"

"He grooms the commander Isad's mistress's pet rodent."

I leant back, half off the saddle, feeling the snow cold beneath my shoulder blades.

"Oh, Smahil."

"Oh, darling."

"And here we all are in the Southern Capital, all working for the cruel Northerners, and liable to be assassinated any minute by the cruel Southerners who hate their allies the cruel Northerners."

"Yes, here we all are. Yours is the most charming situation. A girl dressed in boy's clothes, probably your friend Lel's who is—"

I sat up straight.

"I *never* said I'm wearing Lel's clothes! Lel is a—"

"A boy."

"I didn't tell you that!"

"It's as obvious as the silly little nose on your face isn't. Do you think I don't know Iro's society? Do you think I think that they'd tolerate any girl among them, even one as pretty as your friend Lel?"

262

"Oh, Smahil, I really wish you didn't know."

"Why?" he said simply.

"For one thing, it was Lel's secret, not mine."

"You can trust me with it now that you know I know it," he said reassuringly. "Haven't you trusted me with the knowledge that you're the wanted murderess—and with the tale of your shameful deflowerment—which, knowing you, you must think appallingly shameful?"

I didn't say that I trusted him with secrets concerning me, but that I know he is intrinsically irresponsible and lacking in any sympathy.

"How amazed I was to find you there that night," he said. He stared into my eyes. "Why the hell didn't you wait round the gate for me afterwards? I had to go back the next day to find out where you were billeted. And I walked in in the middle of a row between Iro and his superior on the Accoutrements side, over the missing medals."

"Oh, Smahil. Poor Iro. Couldn't you have made your men give back the ones they looted?"

"Why should I? It makes them feel fine to have several dozen lovely Southern medals each. One of my men is now a fully-fledged Southern general."

"You should have stopped him."

"Why, when I'm one too?" He opened his tunic breast-pocket and brought out several shiny, semi-precious Southern rosettes.

My nightmares are getting worse again.

I have not seen Smahil for several days. He wanted to make an appointment for every available morning but his sweep-ingness scares me. I know what he intends for me and the more often I meet him the less resistance I shall be able to gather round what he kindly allows me to term my spirit.

Lara must be quite a few months gone now. She wears shapeless richly embroidered and beribboned sacks, over her full, shapeless, richly embroidered and beribboned trousers. She looks vile.

Well, re my last entry, to be fair it wouldn't matter how vile she looks, someone who loved her would think she looks vile but sweet, but she *will* be so unfair and unreasonable and illogical and imperious and ill-tempered and unjust.

Last night I woke after a nightmareless night and woke weeping because I thought the twisted crumpled blankets were Smahil's arms about me and he wasn't holding me tight and lovingly enough.

I gave them edible fungi and ox-tail tonight.

Tonight I gave them that sea-food thing they once liked so much. I long to be anywhere but here. This is a terrible city, stark and sadistic and unclean, full of the clash of allies' arms and the screams of tortured priests. I have seen old aristocrats visiting our General with stiff miserable little girls I thought were their daughters until I was told they were their wives, and have nothing but death to look forward to—for though they are so young and their husbands old enough, one would think, to die soon and release them, at their husband's funeral they are taken by force by the mourners who bury them beside the husband in the grave—with the difference that they are alive.

No wonder the governor was ready to take Narra.

But I was sick when I was told about that—had to lock myself in the fountain-room and was ill.

I *hate* these Southerners.

They are not even clean people, in spite of their fountain-rooms and street-cleaners. I have found that in the market I have to be careful to buy natural food—some of the farmers send in produce which they have reared in double-quick time to get themselves double-money; only they do it by using artificial fertilisers, made with chemicals. (For they are clever with chemicals in this land, only they haven't been quite clever enough to find out the formula of the vacuum-injection which is the Northerners' only real whip-hand over them.) Onions from those farms are like wood; the carrots bright red in the market but tasteless on the palate; everything is tasteless or bad; and rarely fresh, because they are mixed with chemicals to preserve them for an indefinite period, fresh in appearance and stale as a preserved corpse inside; and worse still, we know the stuff they use is poison because when some cattle recently drank some by accident, they died in agony. That's what, on those vegetables and fruits, we get tiny driblets of all the time. We get less at a time so we're being killed more slowly—but being killed we are, if we pay money for that muck. But what gets me about these Southerners is that they *know* all this—the story about the cattle has been circulated in the Capital for months together with many similar stories—and yet no move has been made to ban the use of these chemicals and one is always buying the wrong vegetables because in the market they are not even segregated from the wholesome food.

I wish I were anywhere but here.

Preparing all those oysters and sharks' roes and crabs and shell-fish I wished until I could have dissolved in tears of the most passionate wistfulness, wished that I were swimming through cool, green water like the pool in my childhood tower where I learned to swim, going nowhere, coming from nowhere, returning nowhere—simply Limpidity, no responsibilities, no horrors, no apprehensions.

O God, Oh Cousin, I wish it a million million times more in this cold, cruel City than I did in the heat of the army-journey before we reached the mountains.

If only I could do something to help.

Smahil came today. He came into the kitchen, and marched straight across to me. The others looked interested, he took me aside.

"Good morning, Cija."

"S-Smahil."

"Well, well. Why the stammer?"

"I didn't. I simply greeted—"

"Can it be you're surprised to find me coming here? Surely not. After all, for several days now you haven't been to the market—though I've ridden through every day in the hope of seeing you."

"Sit down," I said politely.

He looked round for a chair but had to seat himself on a table.

"We can't talk here, Cija."

"Why not? And don't call me Cija. You'd better stick to Jaleril—for that's what I am nowadays. I'm thankful Lel chose an elegant name to bestow on me—since his spur-of-the-moment whim has had to stick. It's not a village name."

"I expect he had a favourite doll called that. From his earliest days he seems to have been an ingrained snob."

I stared at him with hostility. "Have you come for any real reason?"

"I wanted to. To ask you to ride out to the River bank."

"I'm busy."

"Yes, frantically so. As a matter of fact you'd actually *like* the damn bank—it's got ever so pretty, little buds breaking

265

through the snow. The trees are like some of your best effects—points of pink sweets breaking through small globular clouds of cream."

It was at my jerkin he stared, hopefully.

"Do you mean to say this City isn't perennially snow-logged?"

"I'm assured it gets quite hot and rustic in Summer."

"How do you know the river is so lovely now? Have you already been there with Terez?"

He stared at me and then gave a whoop and threw his shako in the air. "You're not *jealous*, Cija?"

"No, I'm not," coolly I assured him. "I just wondered why you knew, you wouldn't have a parade there, the snow would get in the men's boots. Oh, look, several pages are running over. They think we must be having a good time. Come on."

We grinned at each other, he grabbed my wrist and we went out.

Outside the kitchen he pulled me through another door into the little armoury there.

The daggers and sabres hung round the walls flashed past in a silvery arc as he forced my head back. I clung to him. I felt that Smahil was everything in the world. He was not just a man, the man whose arms were holding me so close that this throbbing life seemed my only new life, I was conscious in every pore that he was Smahil, the thin, strong aggravating friend of mine whose irrelevance to life has always frightened me a little because he lives his irrelevance so strongly and it makes me feel that all life is irrelevant. No purpose—except for Smahil's heart to beat like that against mine, triumphantly, as he kisses me at last and I can only cling to him.

Suddenly Smahil laughed and, still holding me tightly, moved a little nearer the wall, as someone came in.

I turned just before a second's thought convinced me I'd better keep my face hidden—and my startled gaze met the General's gaze.

Now I would swear he'd been looking amused just as I turned—but when our eyes met a cold look which was strangely familiar descended over his face. His eyes went from mine up to Smahil's. He gravely strode to the end wall, took down a sabre, automatically running his thumb along its edge, and went out nodding briefly to Smahil as he passed us.

The dark door-curtain's folds fell into place again behind him; his straight scarlet cloak had seemed to fill the room, I could still almost see the stride of his sandals on the wooden boards. I turned to Smahil.

"How can you laugh!"

I didn't shrill it out: I'm becoming more of a boy; I'm not unreasonable; I wasn't angry with him; but I was surprised that he could laugh. "He'll think that you're a homosexual now; and me too!"

"Cija, that's why I'm laughing. And you look so insulted and troubled. How many disguises will you pile on top of this one until you stop worrying about the reputations of your identities? What is Jaleril going to disguise himself as—and find himself becoming? Try a tree or something next time. When you become involved it's less troubling."

"At least think of yourself—it could jeopardize your career."

"And I *do* so want to become a famous *and* a respected commander at the end of my life. Zerd doesn't care a damn, he'll forget it today—or has already. Do cheer up and think of the worse things he can still do. He can see your pretty friend Lel and outrank Iro—or, for that matter, me with Terez—or he can see Ums and of course recognize him at once, after all wasn't he a present from him?"

I disengaged myself and, avoiding his eyes, stared ahead at his chin.

"Smahil, if you're so afraid of losing Terez, you'd better go back to her."

I felt the still force of his eyes, but I did not meet them; I dropped my gaze still lower to the brilliant leather and straps of his short jacket.

"But you were coming to the River bank with me."

"I didn't even *say* I would," I said, virtue coming through my depression. "I didn't *mention* it, let alone promise. You must admit that."

"And you'd hate to break your word, wouldn't you?"

He turned to go. I stood there, still not raising my eyes. But the brilliant leather hesitated. I looked up. He kissed me. It is the first time he has ever kissed me tenderly. I ran my finger down the white scar on his forehead and nose.

"What foray did you get that in?"

"Terez threw a knife at me once," he said shortly, and left.

Though I have not seen the River out in the country all beautiful again (and in the City it is a slow-flowing collection of floating filth hemmed between thick brick walls with unbeautiful brick bridges), I can see Spring coming to the City.

The orchard beyond the kitchen window is throwing off its snow, which was beautiful but of which, because of its uniformity we were beginning to tire and even to take for granted, and is suddenly showing unexpected radiance in colour and beauty of leaf. There are little sprinklings of starry buds everywhere one looks in the city, and the rich men's gardens are becoming exciting. To be true, there were weeks of horrid slush; and then, suddenly, there were showers of soft silvery rain which washed it all away through the gutters. Now the whole City is full of the gurgling and tinkling and rushing of gutters and drains, it fills one's ears everywhere, and after the long snow-months sounds like singing.

The sun shines all day now.

There are little birds all over the place, flying and cooing and settling.

Lel came to beg me to take Ums. Since he has seen me and knows I am in the City he has become unmanageable, will obey no commands and is dangerously surly. I refused, for Smahil's words ring in my ears, and what if Zerd were to see Ums *with me?*

Besides, Ums' effect on me when we are together is also quite dangerous.

Some of the leaves are like little fingers.

I am glad they were not pointing at the body; it was the foliage further along under which the body lay staring until someone threw a cloak over it. A little girl, very pretty, about fourteen years old, who had jumped from the window there. Her ancient husband had begun to show signs of illness.

Great excitement. Our Princess herself entered the kitchen to tell us that a great banquet must be prepared for the third night next week.

"General Harmgard himself will be here," she said.

"Oh. Him they call Hammerfist?" raggedly chorused the scullions, wide-eyed.

Like the fool she is, she had to reprove them for disrespect. "General Harmgard," she repeated. "The great Southern general. He's been quelling tribal rebellions"—she had it all off pat—"beyond the Superlativity's temple-palace the other side of the Mountain. Now that he's returned and is here in the

268

simultaneous swift arcs so that she moved her lithe, clear skill in a blur more than the sparkling blur of her gauzes through which you saw the quivering of her breasts but not enough to tell what was their shape or whether, indeed, she does gild her areolas. The circle of mirror set in her naval flashed a light across the ceiling and faces of the feasters, but *she* was movement.

I was ashamed to go to Smahil.

Why did he play with me when, of all the new-cantoned Northern army, it was he who had won Terez for his mistress?

Did he want me so much because I had said "No" when we were children together a year ago—or rather, when I was a child and we were together?

Why must he have what he had marked any whim on—and must I be ashamed because she and I existed together and he knew both of us?

I filled the goblet held unseeing up by a noble with a beard busy kissing a lady. When he felt the weight of the goblet in his hand and knew it had been filled for him he brought it round and tipped it over her face. He laughed a lot but she meant her screams as it poured sticky down her face and into her taut-necked dress.

I bumped against a page who was hauling a commander from under a bench.

"He's early, isn't he?" I said conversationally as I sliced a ham.

"The man beside him stunned him with the edge of his plate," the page said wildly. He was quite young.

The ham was so highly spiced I had to blink my eyelids at it.

"A sad accident," I said.

"He did it on purpose: I saw him," said the page. "Because he wouldn't pass him the salt. It's dreadful that such things should happen at a diplomatic banquet, and it's only started too. It hasn't been going more than two hours or so."

"When you've been in the business as long as I have," I said cynically, "you'll think nothing of serving a drunk king with one hand and holding a vomiting general's forehead with the other."

I sneezed into the ham.

When the dancing came to an end for a while, Terez and the other girls sank on to low stools on the dais, and some boys stood up and began to sing. They had peculiarly sweet voices, but it was the dancing which one now realized had held the feasters relatively spell-bound. The din now became deafening, and one could only tell the boys were still singing because they were still opening and shutting their mouths. I began to get into the swing of things as I went to and fro between the tables. Actually I like serving in a crowd, even in the first days of my indignant servility to Zerd's mistresses in his tent after the day's march I liked it, the dodging and swaying with trays and flagons one must not spill, the pride in each catastrophe skilfully averted—one's competence gets a fine rhythm. In its way it *is* like dancing, with continual small rewards—a catastrophe averted, a smile from an attractive noble looking specially at one's eyes. I keep forgetting that men smile at me under the illusion I'm a boy, but the effect and intention's the same anyway. The ladies smile, too. It wasn't at all a bad party, just crowded and noisy, I'd been boasting to the page, it was really innocuous. I kept looking about for Lel and Iro, but they weren't in this part of the room, and the other half was separated from mine by an impassable press of nobles and officers trying to pull the dancers down from their stools on the dais.

I didn't like that, for it reminded me again of Terez's existence and I felt so inferior I could there and then have committed suicide and screamed.

But now I began to feel rather tired, even though I had been among the last servers to come in, when the thing was already going strong. I decided there were enough others to carry on while I had a quarter-hour's rest. I sat down on a bench, beside two richly-dressed young women; there was a space where I could sit down because their officers had gone off to join in pulling down the dancers. The two women had tired of all the rich eating. They were gossiping and picking their teeth with little carved ivory picks, which had been laid beside every plate. That was all very well for them; but I was hungry as well as thirsty. I called across to the Hammerfist's taster, standing over at the long table.

"Hey, Gobbler, is this elk any good?"

When the tasters swung round at me, ours smiling and the stranger glaring, the Hammerfist did too. Also beyond them Zerd heard, which I had not meant, and looked at me.

"It's very good, the toothy opposite of poison," our taster demeaned himself by declaring.

"Use your own taster or pay for stealing the uses of another man's," Zerd yelled at me.

I picked up the haunch of elk beside me and turned my back of them and the banqueting cacophony and began to gnaw into

274

this. It was tender and juisy-roasted and the gravy quickly gravitated to my chin. I used both hands.

"What things are coming to," said the thinner of the two ladies beside me. "When a server can be seen eating his employers' food instead of serving it, and not obtain a reprimand."

"But since," the plumper said, "it is so, here's a flagon to go with it."

And she pushed to me the flagon she'd tired of.

I put out my hand for it but she kept hers on its handle. I knew what she wanted—she wouldn't let go until I looked up and met her eyes and saw how pretty she was. I was used to ladies trying hopefully to flirt with me, and sometimes felt bad that I must always seem obtuse and chilly and knock back their warmth. I wanted the wine so I looked up and at her eyes. She had her head on one side and was not half so pretty as most of the women I see nowadays; but her look was so confident of her sweetness and popularity that I felt my lips stretch into a grudging smile, just as in the old days.

It hadn't occurred to me these could be Ijleldla and Iren. For one thing, they were so bejewelled and bedizened. Not that they hadn't always dressed as richly as they could, but now it seemed they had far more means to do so.

Encouraged, she slid along the bench further towards me without altering one jot in pose or in her sweet friendly smile.

Thank my Cousin, I remarked to myself, these are the very last old-time acquaintances to meet again. There are none left—and thank my Cousin for that, not one of them but seems to cause trouble or make a nuisance.

"It's a good banquet, isn't it?" she said.

"That's a brilliant opening."

"I beg your pardon?" She raised her *darling* little brows. I could have hit her, she knows so well that everybody loves her, and the worst of it is I suppose it's still as true that everybody does. But she's become even more artificial: her puzzlement at my reply would have been genuine except that automatically, from habit, she immediately transmuted it into pose. I wonder if she ever feels any crying-out, any lack, anything but numbness from her atrophying emotions. Still, she's a nice little person, and I'm intolerably priggish.

"Yes. It isn't bad," I said politely. "Do you come here often?"

She giggled. "Silly boy. How shy you sound. Here, come and sit with us."

She was already as near as she could get, but I did a sort of shift on the bench and actually stayed where I was. She took possession again of the flagon and poured prettily into a goblet for me.

"A toast to our noble army," I said.

"A toast to our noble army," they followed suit. I got an obscure satisfaction from that, though I wouldn't have been surprised to find they've both forgotten our land's very existence.

"What's your name?" Ijleldla asked in her confiding way, which is now so automatic that it no longer disguises any boldness.

"Jaleril," I confided back.

"Oh, how pretty!" She clapped her hands. "Isn't it pretty, Iren?"

"Very," Iren said coldly. She knew that I was set as Ijleldla's prize, by the law of finding's keepings, and she resented being used as a girlish companion to chaperone the situation until I was fast hooked.

But just now there was a buzz and a rustle through the whole hall. We turned to see everyone turning; Terez and the others again stood up on the dais. The boys who had been singing sat sulkily down in a cross-legged line. There was scattered applause, but very desultory: perhaps it was merely from some of the boys' lovers who happened to be present. Then there were shouts of acclaim at the dancers, their names were called, but the predominating cry was, "Terez!" "Terez!"

A man with a flute and one with a pipe hung with bells took their places among the ghirza-strummers. The drummers went away to a brazier; the skin of the big, crimson-inlaid, metal drum had to be warmed again because its tension was slackening.

Terez and the others bowed and smiled at their acclaim with a skinkling of beads shrill enough to be heard, Terez tugged one of the tassels off her jacket and threw it into the crowd. The tiny thing twisted scintillating in the air and fell, grabbed at by a dozen hands and was caught by a young officer in the uniform of the 18th Foot. As he turned to bow, waving it at Terez, I saw he was Smahil. They smiled at each other; the bells jangled together as the piper lifted his pipe, the ghirza-strumming became more integrated, the dance was beginning.

We were joined by a very handsome Golds leader who sat down between Ijleldla and Iren.

I could not tell which of them he owned, or perhaps he was

276

a friend of their owners', for he treated them both with equal gay charm, and completely accepted my presence although we weren't introduced and every time Ijleldla giggled she had to sway towards me so that her dainty brow nearly touched my shoulder. Her curls kept tickling my chin. I didn't mind until I was scratched by one of her agate pins.

"I wonder why that yellow girl gets all the attention?" Iren said, looking weary and toying with a necklace as she watched the dancing.

"Her name's Terez," said the Golds leader.

"Oh, of course, you *would* know!" sparkled Ijleldla, with upcast eyes, as if that was a very daring proof of the leader's incorrigible masculinity.

"She's superb," I said raptly, ignoring Ijleldla's hand hovering towards me under the table-top.

Ijleldla wasn't sure whether to be archly piqued while feeling archly piqued, or archly piqued while feeling piqued. She hit me with her silver perfume-stick.

"Now you just *tell* me what you see in her!"

"All those sexy gyrations," winked the leader.

"One has to adore her," I said bitterly. "It's fashionable. Look at every man in this hall."

They looked round.

"The Hammerfist isn't even drunk," Ijleldla said. "There isn't much excuse for his table manners, is there? And look how he stares at the yellow girl. Oh, look! Just look. I do declare he's about to get up and go across and pull her down—"

I am afraid it was quite obvious. The Hammerfist was rather a bluff sort of person, and for a few seconds those who could tear their eyes from Terez watched the fate of the party hang in the balance as he got up, a greasy breast-bone still in one fist, and took the first of the few steps from the long-table to the dais.

Zerd lounged back in his chair. Perhaps he didn't *care* what happened?

The commanders of both sides looked apprehensive. Lara frowned at the bad-mannered old boor, though she obviously hadn't yet grasped the full implications of the situation. There were a lot of people in the hall who did, to go by the look of them. They glared fascinated at the Hammerfist as swiftly through their minds rocketed the pictures of the Hammerfist in a second's time pulling down Terez, a very different matter from the purposeless play-acting of the officers with the dancing-girls between dances—the insult to a famous entertainer and to the Northern General's hospitality, the remonstrance necessary on the lady's behalf from the General, the certain remonstrances of any number of adoring leaders a little drunk and only too ready to seize on the growing rift, boiling with resentment, between the allies . . .

The lean priest Kaselm saved the situation.

With a dry look about he said, "Will the Superlativity find the ladies of his Capital wearing such scanty garments to entertain him when he comes here?" And at the clearness of his voice everyone suddenly realized how quiet the hall had become.

That did it. The Hammerfist sat down again almost before he had got up. The noise flowed back again. The contretemps need not have been noticed or understood by the bulk of the banqueters. But the priest Kaselm smiled and yet looked bigger and blacker and leaner than before.

"A small reminder," said the Golds leader with us, "of how powerful the new Southern religious-regime is, and how even their army fears its disapproval."

"How could he have been sexed up," said Iren virtuously, "by *that* brazen jiggler?"

"No accounting for men's tastes," Ijleldla sighed. She pouted at myself and the leader, seizing as usual on any old pretext to remind people that men and women are ever so different.

"Remember that pale-faced prunes-and-prisms girl with us on the journey—so pallid and prissy though she straddled a bird all day like a tomboy—but Smahil quite liked her. The General himself played at liking her."

"The sly, quiet ones are always the best," the leader clichéd, hearty. "Piss-faced by day and fierce as f...by night. Eh, mate?" He jabbed me in the inside of the thigh, which was still sore minutes after.

"Now Smahil has a thing about that yellow girl. They're never out of each other's little pockets—"

"Have you seen Smahil lately?" asked Iren.

"Not me, not likely!" Ijleldla tossed her hair so it flicked my face. "But I do hear he's always about with the yellow hussy, like I say. He buys her jewels and they go to parties together and sort of coagulate all over each other."

"She *has* got a figure—" Iren said doubtfully.

"*But*—"

"So *obvious*—"

"And I hear she's got a delightful temper—"

278

The leader groaned at me in conventional despair, and together, behind Ijleldla's and Iren's backs but so that they could see us, we toasted Terez.

After a while the guests got tired of not being waited on (most of the servers had somehow got to doing what I was) and started serving each other themselves.

It was amusing to see ladies in flowing draperies and nobles and officers in jewels and gleaming uniforms passing about between the tables with trays and flagons. Some of the nearest pages got kicked back to duty, but not many; someone tapped my shoulder.

"Wine, sir?"

I turned to see an officer bowing beside me with a proffered flagon. "No thanks," I waved him away. "But my companions might be grateful for a little service."

He stared at them and shuddered.

"Gods, no! How can you sit beside them? I'm scooting before I'm noticed!"

"Your dancing-girl may be thirsty," I reminded him. I put my hand on his arm as he went. "Congratulations," I said with the beam of the loving sister I've sincerely decided to be. "She's beautiful."

But he scowled and stalked away, his long legs in their pale leather thigh-boots lurching a very little.

Presently, at the long table, just before everybody got too drunk to appreciate it, the *tour de force* of the evening was borne in on a narrow wooden platter the length of the table itself. Numerous liveried scullions staggered under it as if it were a monstrous millipede and they its red and sweating legs. It was one of those rare swamp-lizards, a young dinosaur, crouched as if to spring and with its magnificent tail tapering full of good fat out behind it. Its belly and stumpy bent legs rested on a mass of hot vegetables and spices. The smell of its passage filled the whole room as the bearers carried it among all the other tables to the long one. There was a lot of shouting; my teeth watered; people reached up and grabbed fist-large vegetables as the procession passed them.

It was placed on the long-table; and all the gentlemen there fell upon it and began to carve it up. There was rivalry for the best innards, and presently most of the gentlemen were all but in it. A golden slave brought a huge crystal flagon to the General: he bowed to the Hammerfist, to whom the slave presented the flagon. The Hammerfist held out his goblet to be filled, and, scrambling on to the table and standing there balanced on the vegetables, he flung his arms wide in a gesture that splattered most of the wine from his goblet and bellowed:

"Drink to the Divine Downfall of Atlan!"

There was almost silence in the hall except for the ring of his bellow against the high rafters, and the gurgling, grunting and cursing of two men rolling, fighting for the heart at his feet in the gravied belly of the corpse.

Then there was a shout that shook the company as they made it, men and women rose and raised their cups and cried, "The Divine Downfall of Atlan!" They howled it in a fervour of loyalty and enthusiasm to their cause and their hosts. I had never heard anything so ugly. They were like wild beasts, bejewelled and emblazoned, tearing down with their drunken opened mouths in their eager, dedicated, drunken faces over their gravy-splashed, wine-stained uniforms, tearing down all that was left divine in the world for no other reason than that it is divine, for they can know nothing of what they will find behind the airless sea, whether it will be rich or worth their trouble, and they call their tearing-down divine. The company cried out its great toast again and again, the glasses splintered and the tapestries gusted from the walls in the howling hall. Zerd lay back, his dark face less aloof than I have ever seen it, on it a fierce abandonment to the toast. He drank with long slow deliberate-spaced gulps, as though it were the savoury blood of Atlanteans there in his goblet. The Hammerfist on the table screamed like a madman and there was froth on his lips. It may only have been from the wine, I don't know. There was a crash as one of the iron candelabra dashed from the roof-beams to the table below. There were screams from those around it, but I doubt if most of the company even noticed it. A woman had been crushed under it; some of the men with her hauled it up long enough for her to be dragged from beneath it. She lay whimpering on the table and presently died. The shout continued and continued: wine-cups were filled again and again. It had all been so unexpected that I was still staring fascinated at the suddenness of this exultant mob-mania ("The Divine Downfall of Atlan!" "The Divine Downfall!") after the innocuous tenor of a diplomatic banquet at which people worried about the bluff intentions of the Hammerfist for a dancer, when two men hurled past me and lay on the floor and lay there shrilly laughing and screaming. "The Divine Downfall!" as they writhed. At first I thought they were fighting, then I realized and looked away. I tried to make my way to the exit. I was thrust aside again and again by fighting and loving couples and still the insane shout swelled and bellowed. Did they feel such hate? Was such immensity of hate ready in their breasts for the divinity of anything? Many were merely in a state of hysteria, all drunk, but the hate must have been there. I felt that the hate-heavy air was choking me. I fought my way, I began to beat at the backs and faces of those who would not let me through. I too, was becoming infected by the infesting hysteria. Suddenly I was near the long-table. I was just in sight of the exit, but I saw the long-table. Both soaked and un-recognizable in gravy, one of the men in the corpse was stab-bing a knife again and again into the neck of his quivering brown opponent. A spurt of blood fountained up: the victor was quick enough to get his mouth in it before it ebbed, it was a red drinking-fountain. He shook his wet head and laughed. "The Divine Downfall!" The hall was swiftly breeding a miasma not only of insane passion but of something worse which struck with insane terror. The hall will have to be burnt later, I thought wildly, it has held all this. Then I realized that all this had been in the breasts of the calmly feasting pleasant guests, the hall had held all this, just the same, before it had dreamed of being shown. Zerd lolled half-across the gravy and blood-pooled table. Two ladies lay on him, grasped in his arms, hanging on him as they tongued him. Nearly dead, I dashed to the door. As I passed the table, I met the gaze of what seemed the only other pair of sane eyes in the hell.

The big black priest Kaselm sat smiling a dry wry smile, but not with his eyes, and picked at his meat with his silver skewers.


It is a month since I wrote my last entry a week after "The Night of the Dinosaur". My hand travels across the page but feels no kinship with it or with anything.

Everything has become quite strangely hollow, there is a flat taste in everyone's mouths.

The cook killed himself with one of his carving-knives, no one knows why. It may have been because he had prepared and cooked (so lovingly) the dish which some simple people have taken as the symbol of that night.

Lara has had a miscarriage.

Several people aren't seen about at headquarters any more, they were crushed or fatally injured in the press.

There has been from the very first bitter enmity between the Northern troops and the troops the Hammerfist brought into the Capital—that night. The streets seem more battle-grounds

281

for the Northern and Southern ranks, than anything else, market-places, thoroughfares, parade grounds for allies.

I have seen Smahil once or twice, never alone.

Sometimes the Hammerfist with members of his train comes to visit here with the General.

The sun shines all day. Much of the snow on the top of the guardian-mountain of this City is melting.

The river runs more turbulent through the brick channel in the city. Small boys fish from its walls.

No one ever mentions the Night of the Dinosaur.

For all the mention it gets it is as if it had never happened.


"It's going to be a delightful campaign," Smahil said moodily.

He was sprawled in a kitchen chair, staring at the flagged floor, his thumbs hooked in the loops of his belt.

I was at the big sink, scouring pots. The water had boiled not long ago, but the grease wouldn't go, merely shimmied from one place to another. My hands were swollen and red, and there was a tidemark of crumbs of grease round my wrists though I had carefully bathed only last night.

We were nearly alone in the kitchen; there were pages and scullions down the other end, but the kitchen is always quiet nowadays.

Smahil swung his leg and scuffed at the flagstones.

"A charming campaign."

"Did it ever promise to be anything else?"

"Yes, it did," he said. "But now we'll never *get* to the mysterious Continent—we'll have all been killed first."

"Dear, dear."

"Picture us marching, all day, and all day and every day each army is weakened by its allies' sniping."

"I couldn't care less," I said. I began to hum. The water swilled round my fingers. The grease would never move, once a fact is clear it is easy to be resigned to it. "I'm not coming. I don't want to see the Continent fouled by your army—and I don't want to be picked off by a greedy-aiming spearsman from the other army—"

"So you'll stay in a deserted kitchen—"

"And why not? At least I'll be its sovereign. At the moment I'm nothing, no longer the god of even the youngest pages. I have to fill in with jobs like this because since Lara's miscarriage she no longer has stews every night, in fact she no longer even likes them much at all. It couldn't be duller than it is now—everyone is as depressed as you, Smahil dear, the new cook lives steeped in melancholy, perhaps he thinks his predecessor's—a bad omen—"

I went on stolidly scouring as I spoke. I had been tremendously fond of the cook, but all my tears have been shed, probably for many a year to come. I feel a curious lightness.

He sneered, "A real little kitchen-sloven you've become, haven't you? All right, stay in your greasy backwater."

"While you march gallantly away, soldier. What have you become?"

"What do you mean?"

"It's hard to tell."

An impasse, we each continued our occupations, he scowling at the floor, myself swilling at the many pots.

"Why I came to see you, I don't know," he said after quarter of an hour.

After a further five minutes I looked aside at him. I caught his eye. How intensely he can regard me.

He did not turn. He did not blink. Reflected in his wide grey-blue gaze which dazzled me was the window behind me. The whites of his eyes, glossy and tinged with blue, for moments mesmerized me. A wind fluctuated hard against the     panes. In Smahil's eyes I saw the sky grey. I went to the window. Endless lines of glass beads, slipping through fingers unseen in the sky, above and bigger than the clouds—were the lines descending or ascending, or motionless?

"Winter not gone yet."

The little clatter at the other end of the kitchen seemed so remote. The work of scullions by the door-tables, the pages casting dice on the bagstones with the spit-boy at the fire. Here all was quite sombre and desolate.

I began to sing again as I scrubbed, a dreary ballad full of falling cadences in the minor key. I am most at home in dreariness.

Smahil put his arms on the table, his head on them. The beads continued to click from outside against the panes, splishing, spreading down in sluicing channels.

And at this moment, which seemed to sum up the end of most things, there was a row outside. A harsh, unsteady noise, shouting. Some clashes.

A stone smashed through the window.

I was still bewildered as it bounded into the biggest pot, rico-

283

cheted on the grease I'd been trying so long to remove, and bounded up again. It hit Smahil a glancing blow on his cheek-bone.

There was shouting at the other end of the kitchen. Then the far door opened. A number of soldiers reeled in, our fellows, awkwardly carrying some wounded.

Smahil, bleeding, strode up to them.

"What are you doing here, hogs? This is the General's head-quarters."

"We know that, sir." A tattered sergeant touched his shako-peak. "Beg pardon, sir it's all we could do. There's everal of our poor boys hurt, sir, and more than half of us \gain is them Southern bastards out in the street."

Smahil didn't waste time with silly questions like, "They at-tacked you, did they?" He was already strapping on his sword belt when the General himself and several other commanders walked in.

Everybody straightened up and saluted in astonishment, and a wounded man who'd just been propped against the wall lurched down again.

"Something doing out there, boys?" inquired the General and they guffawed. "Yussir, if you please, sir," said the wounded trooper. "Them Southern bastards again, sir." The sergeant frowned but the General clapped the trooper on the shoulder. "Officer," he said, and Smahil who had relaxed came to attention again.

"Sir."

"Take a few of these men and scatter those Southerners."

"Yessir."

Smahil went out, with the sergeant and unwounded troopers again.

The General came unhurriedly over to the sink and leaned out of the window, while his commanders crowded behind him. I flattened myself beside the pots.

There was a lot of noise outside the street. It was a nar-row street, but Smahil seemed to be having difficulty in dispelling the larger rabble.

"The trouble is, they're mounted," observed Clor.

"That they should dare to come right to our doorstep, though," deplored another.

"Drunk, must be," said Isad.

"Perhaps," Zerd said indifferently. His scarlet shoulder brushed me as he drew himself in from the window. "Here, sink boy, run down to the courtyard and get my bird."

"Zerd, you're not going out," protested Clor, but I was already running out.

The ground was wet. But it had stopped raining at last.

By the time I'd gasped to the General's groom to saddle up, the General himself was in the stable and helped to hitch the girths. The other commanders trampled about on the straw. Suddenly the courtyard gate burst wide open and a horde of yelling Southerners surged in. There were still a few Northerners alive too. The General and I were opposite each other and for a moment our eyes met over the bird. Then he had swung into his saddle. His big hand was held down to me as his bird swung into the mêlée.

"Here, child, close at my side."

I ran, keeping at his stirrup, as the yelling scum in their green Southern uniforms closed at at the stable.

The other commanders were now mounted and followed, but there were mounted Southerners as well as foot-scum. The General swung and slashed with his big, whistling, blue sword. Blood splashed over my jerkin. The hot smell began to clear my confusion. At first I had concentrated only on keeping at least one side of myself protected by the bird. Now I noticed that footsoldiers and riders alike were aiming cuts at me, and I drew my sharp carving-knife from my belt-sling and began to thrust with it, keeping it up to defend my face. The courtyard was soon a shambles, a carnage. We were amazingly outnumbered by the green uniforms. I kept wonderering how they dared to keep this going so long. They must by now have recognized their most important opponents—but they seemed even to be attempting to strike the General. They might be afraid of surrendering, but surely they knew that sooner or later reinforcements would arrive, and whether the reinforcements were Northern or Southern these insurgents would be court-martialled and whipped. If they kept on much longer they'd be hanged. Perhaps they knew it was already too late and wanted to wreak as much havoc with us as they could while they could—but that was absurd. It looked almost as if this had been a deliberate project.

I cut at a man who was attempting to pull the General from his saddle, and found to my surprise that the man lay dead on the cobbles at my feet.

The General glanced down at me, smiled.

"There is blood all over my soft boots," I complained.

An arm caught at me.

"Out of this, Cija. This is going on too long. I'm going for

285

reinforcements. I'll lead 'em back but you can't be here any longer."

Smahil had got a bird from somewhere. I set my foot on his and clambered up, putting my arms round his waist, while he leaned forward to fight off an attacker who had taken advantage of the bird's momentary immobility.

At once we were away, scattering the others, towards the gate. But at the gate there was resistance. I had already seen, from the corner of my eye, other Northerners try to get away here and fail. It was incredible! Yet other Southerners had arrived and they too were fighting us!

"What the bloody hell do you people think you're bloody well playing at?" bawled Smahil as he parried with his sword the spear of a hawk-eager young mounted Southern leader.

"Your guess is as good as mine, friend," the Southern leader answered with an expert thrust. "I only receive the orders, but I'm making hay while the sun shines."

"Who gave the order?" Smahil inquired politely, but they were separated in the middle of the encounter. Next I realized only when Smahil hauled me back that someone had tried to drag me down. All the shouts and lurching were getting me confused again. The bird barked hysterically and dashed sideways as something landed with a wet smack on its head.

"Someone's brain," said Smahil.

At last we were out of the courtyard. The cacophony jerkily faded. We careered down the narrow street, shying at bodies. I clung to Smahil.

"I killed a man," I said.

"Felicitations, kiddy." He was managing the bird well, it was only just not bolting.

"Are you going right to the Northern barracks?" I asked.

"Well, I'm not going to the Southern, nearer though it be. Someone may well already have done that, and a bloody lot of good it was." He yanked viciously on the bridle.

Big drops of rain began to fall again.

We crossed the river by a bricked bridge, and lolloped over a small hill where the rain splashed in the foliage. The Northern Barracks is some way out from this loop of the City.

"Perhaps by the time we come back the General'll be killed."

"Nonsense, they'd take blasted good care just to capture him. And you're not coming back." He sniggered. "I'm not certain that I am."

Smahil pulled at the bird's head and slumped forward suddenly. We lurched past the barracks-sentries, Smahil giving the password in a weak whisper, and demanded to see the commanding officer on urgent business from the General.

The commander came out in less then five minutes, his staff anxiously behind him.

"Cursed Southern allies—attacked headquarters—the General beseiged in courtyard—" Smahil gasped out.

"Reinforcements, quickly," the commander rapped out, and as his orders were obeyed he looked keenly at Smahil. Smahil was slumped in the saddle, there was blood oozing from the gash on his cheekbone though already there was a murky green and bright yellow bruise there, as though paints had carelessly been allowed to run together, and his face was covered with blood where he'd wiped his hand across it. There was also some on his uniform where I'd been pressed against him.

"Get a surgeon to this man," ordered the commander.

"Oh, no sir—please—I don't warrant that," said Smahil feebly. "I'd like to go back to the defence of the General—only my bird seems to be wounded—"

The commander looked at the splash of brains on its head, at its wild eyes and hysterical demeanour and the twist of its mouth which Smahil had unmercifully wrenched.

"Where's your billet?"

"My companion will see me there. There's a surgeon quartered there too, sir, anyway, sir."

"I'm glad you've given in, you're in no state—" the commander remarked hurriedly, obviously relieved. "And as for that, there's no need, all that's under control. All right, I suppose you can get there."

"He didn't even offer me a change of mount," Smahil said as we trotted back up the road, the reinforcements already a galloping flurry in the distance.

The trees were like fountains on the hill now, but Smahil made a detour over it.

"All this is doing down my neck."

"Never mind, there's a spring at the top."

"You aren't thirsty, in this?"

"No, but I'm sick of looking like a rusty beetle. The resemblance has served its turn."

Preparatory to washing, he took off his leather tunic-coat, laid it across the pommel. Under it he wore a black linen shirt, open at his chest which is smooth and tanned.

The path to the crown of the little hill was steep and thickly wooded. Already half squashed by the rain, berries and the dungballs of little animals squished and loose stones rattled under the bird's claws.

Abruptly we emerged into a curved space, a cup in the hill's summit, the grass short as though used regularly for grazing, surrounded by the trees. To one side was a gravelly incline, overhung by a small chalky cliff. Little grasses and flowers quivered from its interstices under the rain. The underside of the overhang was glaucous with thick wet moss, and a spring gushed from it.

Smahil dismounted.

I slid down and landed in Smahil's outstretched arms. They closed around me and I felt their muscular sinewy *hardness*. Instead of waiting till he released me I tried nervously to wriggle away but I was helpless. He laughed and held me closer, and I wished I'd let well alone. We were so close that I felt the laugh in his chest. I realized that his heart was thumping. He slid one hand up, under my jerkin. His fingers were warm, sliding over my thin shirt, they slid round my waist and their firm touch trembled for a moment in the fold where my shirt buttoned. For a second I felt the actual texture of his fingers, the horny rein- and sword-callouses on his fine officer's hand, scorching on my bareness.

I had been lulled in spite of myself, now I jerked away.

I stared at him. My body was weak and palpitating, as if I had been running very hard.

I saw nothing but his eyes, intent, gleaming through the rain.

"You're very moral." He slurred his words.

"Leave me alone."

He grasped me, in a brief wrestling moment he had ripped off my jerkin. The great drops fell on me but his arms scorched as they pulled me against him. He was panting, his hard arms trembled about me he was in such a hurry to have my mouth, then all his mouth scorched into mine. His tongue felt much bigger. He kissed violently.

I writhed but my arms were pinioned.

Without removing his mouth he was groping for the opening of my shirt. His hand ripped up it like a paper-knife, I felt the buttons give and then the rain was fast and cold on my breasts which he grasped in his fists, though they didn't really quite fit.

His mouth lifted for a moment. His breath was coming faster and faster.

I tried to scream but heard myself sob. My throat felt tight.

Smahil grasped me even tighter and dragged me over to the little cliff's overhang. Here he threw me on the slope and leaped upon me, pressing against me. The gravel bit with innumerable little teeth at my back. Smahil's hands were one each side of my shoulders, caging me, his mouth on my throat, my mouth, my breast. His vitality seemed electric to my body. An indescribable scorching languor lapped me.

In the green shadow his face approached, a feverish blur, his eyes and the white scar glaring from the blood. My nostrils flared to the smell of blood and the primeval muskiness of his armpits.

I kicked up desperately with my whole body and we fell under the spring. It poured heavy on my breasts. I cried out at the heaviness and the pain of the gravel cutting, grinding under my back. A kind of growling seemed to pervade the world as I scrambled to my feet, slithering on the incline, and ran for the open. The rain tore the tatters of my shirt from my shoulders. It was quite dark: I realized the tintinnabulating growling was thunder.

Smahil followed me and threw me again to the wet ground. Here it was soft, it seemed paradise to my back. His body was incredibly hard and close, I turned my head from his mouth.

"Cija," he pleaded, his voice a hoarse sigh.

My arms went around his shoulders, I clung to him. The reaction of my body in the brief escape had been astounding. I had felt weak and trembling, my legs fluid, as if I were only half here, as if a limb had been forced from me. His fingers tore at my belt, at his own. Now I knew my terror was irrevocable, but there was nothing in the world I could do except cling to him.

The thunder and thunderous rain shook the hill, he crushed me beneath him.

At the last instant he forced back my head in order to look at me.

His eyes were not fixed, staring glassily into space as the governor's had been; Smahil's eyes sought mine, and his were vivid with life, triumphant, tender, mocking.

# CHAPTER SIX

## THE BED IN SOUTHERN CITY

Smahil lifted me on to the saddle and solicitously bundled his wet coat round me. He mounted and, cradling me before him, rode down the steep path.

His arms were very tender. We had not spoken a word. I wondered if he were embarrassed. I felt drowsy and innocent. I had one hand on his black lapel, and felt rocked like a child. I knew that I am at least as safe with Smahil as no other woman can ever be.

I looked up at him.

His face, which he had cleansed, seemed to hold an intense gravity. His lips were closed, his flaxen hair, darkened by the teeming rain, was plastered in thick lank strips to his head. He peered down at me. The bulkiness of the coat had slipped a little. He tucked it round me again, his muscles hard and warm through the sodden shirt. I was held closer as he kissed my hair again and again.

"You belong to me at last."

The bird's claws rang no longer on the stony path of the hill, but on the roadway.

"This is not the way to H.Q.," I roused myself presently to murmur.

He laughed contentedly.

"I shall always be sure of you while you are such a child."

We turned down an alley with high, grimy brick walls. At first I accepted the rebuke, thinking this was a short cut I didn't know of, but when we came to turnings he consistently took the wrong one. We began to meet people, scurrying along through the puddles with their cloaks held over their heads, and I was glad that the leather wrapped me, for what shreds of my shirt remained clung transparently to my flesh.

"Where are you going, Smahil?" "Home," he replied, his lips against my hair.

Presently a row of high, narrow, grey-gabled houses rose out

of the rain. We clattered into a courtyard, about a quarter of
the size of the one at headquarters. It was quite deserted, but
birds and horses could be glimpsed in the boxes which lined it.
Ours picked its way splay-clawed across the puddled cobbles,
big splashing puddles in which were droppings, manure, a lot
of straw and fruit peels and cores. Smahil carried me to the
ground and led the bird into a stall. I stood shivering in the
dry, straw-filled gloom while he unsaddled.

"But, Smahil, this bird isn't even yours."

He rubbed it down perfunctorily.

"I'll send the inn-woman's son back with it when the rain's
over. Well, come into the house."

We emerged into the rain and then into a gloomy passage,
paved and walled with cracked, grubby white tiles. The effect
was both antiseptic and squalid, and I was grateful for Smahil's
presence. At regular intervals there were windows, without
shutters, which admitted both the chill, fluctuating, grey light
and spatterings of rain. There were pools on the tiles before
them.

At the end of the passage was a wooden staircase.

Smahil took my hand and led me up it, it wound into real
darkness and some of the treads were rickety. The whole contraption creaked and rattled mournfully at our use.

There were doors opening off from its side, darker oblongs
in the darkness, one would have to be familiar with them to see
them without peering, and Smahil opened one of these. To step
easily from the stair to the narrow wooden doorstep required
skill, particularly as the doorstep was rounded, but almost at
once I found myself in a reasonably large room. Smahil shut
the door behind us.

"Well?"

He faced me, his thumbs in his belt.

"I *should* be glad of a towel and—a change of clothes?
—before I go home—"

"You are home."

... "But, Smahil—"

"You are home."

He pushed me gently into a chair, and began to pull off my
boots. He removed my shirt, and put his arms round me to un-
do my belt.

"No ..."

Rain rattled against some window I could not see, perhaps
behind one of the wall hangings. Smahil laughed softly. My
belt fell, but there were his arms instead. He ripped off my

291

soaked tights, tearing them. My skin appeared lavender in the dimness of the room. I shivered.

With a large, coarse towel he scrubbed a warmth glowing into me.

"Cija, my Cija—"

He lifted me, caressing me, and carried me over to a kind of broad cupboard door which he opened with his foot. There were several around the room. Inside the cupboard was a wide, soft bed covered with a pelt of some kind on which he laid me. He shut the door and we were alone in the cupboard bed, its privacy freshened by a breeze bearing raindrops through the little window in the wall-side. Smahil flung aside his shirt, belt and trousers and gripped me violently against him.

Three other young officers share this room with Smahil. I met them when they came off duty that evening. I was wearing some clothes which Smahil happened to have here, a plunge-necked jacket shimmering with gold threads and buttoning with gold dragons, a stiff, short, gold skirt over transparent trousers.

"I'm sure Terez would prefer your other mistresses not to wear them."

"Nonsense, you look so beautiful! Oh, Gods, how tired I am of gold in gold, eternally conscious in every fibre of nothing but its own hard flamboyance, like the mythical coin-floor of the Northern king—You point the difference—You have always pointed every difference. Damn you, Cija, you *are* mine now."

I reminded him that he is harbouring the murderess.

"You are never going back to that monster's headquarters," he said.

"You're very melodramatic—"

"Because you're no longer the child whose body drives me insane, from whom I want never to be separated, and who behaves as if I were an interesting rock she passed one day and thought about never again except when it made her—because I know something about our Mighty General which it would be more than my life's worth even to think of too often—because I know if he ever remembered his hostage Cija he'd have her at once—"

"Do you think I—" I cried.

"Yes, I do think you—" he mimicked. He kissed me hungrily. He is never particularly gentle. He really dislikes me, I'm sure.

292

I see little of the other three who are usually on duty and with whom generally we do not even eat. Even when they bring home girls they only disappear with them into their shut-beds. I have seen such beds in the houses of the wealthier peasants, they obviate the need for a separate bedroom, but these are carved, and wide. The young leaders are quite ordinary young men, not even particularly pleasant, though perhaps I'd see a nicer side of their personalities if they thought me more than Smahil's strumpet. Occasionally it happens that one of them is off duty while Smahil is away, though mostly I am alone all day; the army is working its officers and men hard. And when they are off duty, it's unusual for them to do anything but stay in their billet. But once when I was playing chess with Anad—I *thought* he was playing very off-handedly—he suddenly seized my hand as I was making a move, and dragged me across the board; the men clattered to the floor and rolled. "All right, little Queen," he said wittily. He gripped me as I lay on the board and kissed me.

"Anad!" I said angrily. "Stop this at once!" and I hit the side of his head as hard as I could with the flat of my hand. I was surprised when I didn't hear his ears ring. Before anything else could develop, Smahil walked in, stripping off his cloak. He saw the situation, bounded at Anad and buffeted him back and forwards across the head. Anad stood for it at first, then decided he wouldn't, and with a roar kicked Smahil's feet from the floor. They rolled over together cursing curses unfit for a lady's ears. I threw a bowl of water over them, withered flowers and all; Smahil rose and marched me off to bed, and nothing untoward has happened since. Besides, I think they all realize by now that I am a very nice girl, which I am when nothing's bothering me.

Smahil hires the inn-woman to bring up meals, she is an indifferent cook and will sniff haughtily at me. Also, the things are usually cold after being brought up all those stairs, and the cutlery and plates are dirty.

Sometimes nowadays he takes me out to a nearby tavern. We sit in an alcove sticky and smelly with lamp-smoke, and Smahil keeps up a sneering patter with me and glares at any man who looks at me. These visits are only possible since he bought me some clothes. "These are rather squalid outings," I remark calmly one day, more in sympathy than in rancour. Immediately he snarls sneeringly at me. "Regretting the days of your kitchen-sloven innocence, sliming yourself in grease to prevent our beloved fighting monster, getting food-poisoning?

293

Or some such thing. "Talking of food-poisoning—" I said hotly one day.

"It's all I can afford on my pay," he pointed out. "Aren't you being a little demanding, doxy darling, considering that I now have to feed two mouths—and buy you clothes to make you presentable." He always likes to mention the fact I belong to him, he seems full of resentment for the time when I kept holding him at arm's length or forcibly rejecting him. Apparently we were not such good friends as I thought in those days. "You should have kept the clothes Terez threw at you," he finished, then pushed his plate across the table and kissed me. He can never stop touching and kissing me nowadays, and it is true, Smahil and I call fiercely to each other, flesh to flesh, bone to bone, youth to fierce youth.

Wanted by the law, no longer with a place in the Northern headquarters, I am offered a home and protection which I must take: Smahil is not the good gay playmate I had once got into the habit of thinking him, but it is true, we are violently young together, his lithe hardness makes me tremble and it is the one stable thing I have to cling to in a rather squalid little world of loneliness, chilly dreariness, cold, dirt and the corroding tongue of someone who resents the hold I have over his body and the long time for which I denied him even that hold. Physically he seems to have a core of fire.

Terez came uninvited to see him one evening. I was sitting alone, listlessly staring into the empty fireplace, empty that is except for cobwebs. I have nothing to read, I can't remember reading properly since the days I raided the library of my tower; books used to be passed backwards and forwards between the hostages and the young leaders and waiting-girls of the Beauty's household, but they were all either coquetishly pornographic, or endless lovesick poetry.

Sometimes I sew on buttons and cobble tears in Smahil's shirts, though I loathe sewing, but that doesn't take up much time—and I can't be writing in my Diary all the time. And I'm rather nervous of walking alone about these streets.

So there I was, pouting at nothing, when the door opened and in walked this superb vision in gold.

She had been magnificent in the headquarters' kitchen, now she was overpowering. She stood in the middle of the room, stared at me, and said abruptly: "Do you know—the lord Smahil? A fair gentleman, is he in the house?"

My mind ranged quickly over the three uncouth young officers. Which did she guess I belonged to?

I rose, smiled and said, "He'll be in soon. Do sit down. Would you like some kind of refreshment while you're waiting?"

She looked surprised, but sank into a rickety chair and loosened her flimsy wrap.

"It's a nice day outside," I remarked.

"Yes. The sun is shining," she vouchsafed, slightly off balance.

She stretched out her legs in front of her, tapped on the chair arm, completely ignored me.

Now I was wearing her own transparent trousers, the only women's trousers in the place, incompetent as they were. And over that one of Smahil's black officer's-shirts, which are long enough to serve the gentlemen as nightshirts when not tucked in their breeches. I found the gold jacket and skirt too bright and stiff. Curiously enough, the combination made quite a smart effect if you didn't look too closely at the skirt: so I felt perfectly at my ease with her, and was sitting relaxed when Smahil came in.

She immediately jumped to her feet. I went on filing my nails.

Terez embraced him, her bell-shaped skirt swinging up behind her as the front was flattened against him. She really has a terrific body, at the same time rounder and more muscular than mine. She was not wearing very high-soled shoes, presumably because it was him she was coming to see, and so she was only about half an inch taller than him, a few inches taller than me.

"I'm not dancing this evening so I thought I'd give you a treat," she said, expertly winding herself about him that she was kissing the back of his neck before I could see how she'd managed it. "This odious army business, we have not met each other for so long."

He caressed her so boldly that I was shocked.

But he had still not disillusioned her about her new status as his ex-official-mistress. Perhaps he really meant not to forgo the pleasures she could bring now she was here, but in any case it was obvious it was not her but myself that he was in a hurry to get jealous.

"I'll go and get you both some refreshment before I go for my walk," I promised with cordial grace, and made for the door.

"Ah, don't bother," she sighed disdainfully, meaning "I want none of the fruits of this household's kitchen." As I went she turned to look at me and she saw my trousers. Her eyes widened.

"I like the gold tracery on your ankles," she said expressionlessly.

"Do you?" I smiled my nicest delighted-smile and closed the door on them. I felt so happy for some reason as I went down the stairs.

Avoiding too many streets, I crossed the bridge and wandered in the countryside. The trees were mainly in blossom and the air loud with song and insects. I took off my sandals and felt the grasses between my toes. Everywhere were flowers dancing with their shadows. Breezes chased ripplings of light and shadow across the meadows. I heard the maa'aa'aaing of goats and the tinkle of bells. The goatherd greeted me from the distance and when I reached him we sat down together on the bank of a blue and white stream, gurgling with stones, and ate black bread and goats' cheese. As if it was very important we discussed the seasoning of cheeses, comparing our opinions. I felt like a girl in the mountains with the peasants again. It is so long since I have been a real girl, able to toss my hair on my shoulders and smile innocently as I watch a man's eyes come shyly to my breasts, then away, then again, exploring, wondering. Perhaps they would have married me to Turg if the lawmen had not come, and I should not have minded. I am of godly blood, but events have pitch-forked me far from my natural niche and meadow air is the sweetest and yet the tangiest. I felt a nostalgia for Lel, whom I remembered I have not visited for so long, but there is nothing left of the wild timid brat in the little town lady with the flow of refined chatter and the nest of sophisticated vicious patrons. The goatherd and I leaned back on the bank and chewed long grasses, making their feathery tips twist in the air far out from our teeth. He was a boy my age, heavily built, his arms and legs and torso shining bronze, his greenish eyes startling pale and live in his bronze face, his grin a flash of teeth which looked clean against his face, his feet chalky with stale dust and dirt; he wore peasant boy's clothes, a goatskin jacket, a sash full of pockets, tools and knives, a pair of full, faded, blue, ragged knee-pants.

As dusk closed in the crickets came out. They went kreeepkreeep. Kreeep-kreeep. Kreeep-kreeep.

The boy took a pipe from his sash and blew into it. The maa'aa'aa'ing increased around us from all directions and what sounded all distances. The boy bounded to his feet, held down a hand for me. His was large, the horniest and most calloused whose fingers have ever caged mine, yet if ever a hand could have a respectful expression this was it.

I nodded and smiled through the twilight, and walked towards the city. The breeze made the grass a silky sea-edge about my ankles. I felt young and supple and feminine through and through, the whole universe loved and was at one with my ankles. My dress, the breeze being against me, followed the movements of my legs. I looked down and realized my dress, simple and attractive as it was, was Smahil's shirt; I shrugged. Moths flowed on the air in and out among the pin-prick stars, the sky was still china blue. The gurgle and gush of the stream down beside me in its stony bed mingled with the bells and bleating as the goats gathered. There was a smell of onions and cheese superimposed on the heady scent of meadow twilight; the boy loomed up beside me, his eyes shining on me from the bronze.

I faced him in the breeze.

"What be your name?" he asked.

"Cija."

"Keeya." His voice was hoarse as it hushed to handle the name. "I'll remember," he said simply.

I ran on into the dusk which gathered like a swift sigh from a vast purple mouth half enfolding the world. All the scents in the meadow sharpened. My sandals swung against my side; from my trousers as much as from my slim, delicate mould the peasant boy must have thought me a fine city girl.       –

Suddenly a hill reared up above me. A stony track, deep on either side with drifts of wildflowers among the trees' roots, led up to its crown, dim in this light but I could see its wooded shape. Was it?—My shoulders bowed and my body ached.

The mountain conical guardian of the City rose hugely black beyond the conical shadow of the hill.

I climbed the stairs slowly and entered immediately after knocking. I hadn't expected to find Terez still there.

The light in the room seemed exactly the same as when I'd left: the seven dusty sunbeams seemed hardly redder. I'd been away little more than an hour.

Terez was squatting mainly naked on the edge of the open cupboard bed. Her hair was dishevelled, her lips swollen and her eyes glinted topaz from under languid violet-stained lids. But in sharp contrast to her physical satisfaction was the bitchiness she forced out upon me.

She glared at me with the greedy topazes as I walked to the middle of the room and again kicked off my sandals. Her head

297

swung to follow me without a stare-flicker.

It was now I saw Smahil. He was laying back behind her in the bed-gloom, sinewy-naked, munching an apple. His face was chiselled and remote, the face of the audience at some primitive, savage blood-sport. For the first time I could expect no help from him.

And it was true. I did feel a stir of jealousy. Do I look like that when Smahil has finished with me? How intricate and yet passionate their love must have been, here in my familiar lonely room, in the hour I was gone. Of course she is a practised mistress in the art, which to me is only a new willy-nilly experience, something which happens to me.

"Slut!"

She hissed.

Suddenly I wanted to laugh. I knew that I am this particular courtesan's superior in wit, in whatever else I might be her inferior. "You look so much more yourself, madam, as you are." And, just as I had smiled at her earlier, I gave my very nicest, most genuine, candid chuckle.

She leaped up, her claws shimmering. For a moment I didn't even mind inciting her to draw blood. Gods know, I am used enough to fighting women, it has been consistently forced upon me. But, as she plunged on to me, I remembered again that she is my superior in size and strength and certainly in experience. I remembered again her hell-cat reputation. Oh, Cousin, *damn* Smahil and his looker's-on desire to see me at last forced into displaying some strong emotion-action for *him*. *Damn* his cruel, self-ridden, looker's-on, masturbating hate for me—the curse, swift as it had to be, was like a gush of venom in my brain.

I was under her and she unremittingly heavy as any lover, without hesitation, the first thing, her nails straight for my eyes, I shall be torn and blinded and the pain—

I spat in her face and twisted, burying my face in the rug. This strained my neck almost to breaking point. The nails dug themselves into my scalp and pain stung through my eyes and ears. She was wrenching at my hair. My hand groped convulsively for something to hang on to, my only chance was to keep my face away from her, and my fingers felt something long and smooth. For a moment they didn't think to inquire what it was; then—a thong! The ribbon thong of my sandal! I clutched on it, drew the sandal in towards me, got a frenzied grip on it, turned and bashed it into her eye as the nails tore down my cheek. *"Oh you-filthy-littlesoandso,"* she screamed all

298

in one gasp. It was so piercing that I was assailed by acute nausea. I tensed all my muscles ready for the next onslaught but she had got up and was clutching her eye. "Oh, oh, you've driven it right through my head," she moaned and staggered, calling me a string of the filthiest names I've ever heard, though filthy was the adjective she put for me in front of every one of them.

A few months ago I'd have been stricken with apprehension and compunction, but now I stood there, disregarding the hot blood steaming down my face and neck, a fierce alert triumph burning in the place of pity.

She had removed her cupped hand now and was blinking and grimacing. Suddenly she lurched to the chair her clothes lay on and flung them at me.

"Take them, take them all then, lice-spawn!"

As they sparkled to my feet she came at me with the last garment in her hand, the jacket stiff with raised gold thread, and seizing me before I realized what she was about she was grinding it into my back. It was far worse than any fistful of gravel could be and I had to bite my lip to prevent myself screaming. I was strongly held, there was nothing I could do but endure this merciless vengeance.

I thought it would last for eternity and when she stopped my nerves were still writhing exactly as though the torture were still continuing.

"Remember that for the rest of your life as you sleep sore in your fair boy's arms," she shispered.

I heard her dress and wrap rustle as she pulled them on and ran down the stairs and up the alley.

Weeping, I pulled back the hanging and looked down. An amber glowing beetle in the brick alley, scurrying along after the expression of a hate like a pus-filled sore always ready in her for this or that excuse, she seemed to me the most hideous thing in the world, I stooped and gathered up the shimmering skirt and blood-streaked jacket, holding them gingerly for I loathed their touch, and dropped them through the window. Behind her a group of gutter urchins without even looking up to see whence they had come fell on them dragging them from one another like animals and finally made off, some with the skirt, others with the jacket.

I turned slowly into the room again. I had not the strength to keep the hanging held up; I let it fall, shutting me in with the dreary, dank lack of light, and Smahil from whom I knew without testing it there would be no warmth, no compassion.

I felt like a very old woman. I was tired, I wanted to sleep, and sleep, and sleep. To sleep; nevermore to aspire to anything, to accept with my numbed mind my degradation, the humiliation of all my divinity and the rare high hopes I had been fashioned and born for; to accept with my numbed senses the pain which lapped me and which I was too utterly eternally exhausted to try to soothe alone.

"Your creamy back will hold those marks to your dying day," Smahil's voice said. "She rubbed till her arm fell with the fatigue of it."

From a long way I dragged my voice, "I have been whipped before."

"But I have no unguents for you." His voice was smooth and gloating... "You see, I can't afford it—"

"Smahil, how could you?" I asked slowly. I only wanted to know this. "You are not cruel for the sake of cruelty. Why did you let her...? She knows you let her."

"I wanted to see you suffer." His voice was quicker, nearer now, but I couldn't see him. Perhaps my eyes were closed, perhaps my weariness had blanked my sight after all. "You never show emotion, you're always like an icicle, aloof, untouchable, untouched no matter what is done to you—You live, you breathe, you worry, but you don't reach out to other people, you keep your passion for the Reptile—"

His arms slid on my lacerated back, he was covering me with kisses. The sound of his panting roused me.

"Oh, my back," I moaned.

He threw me into the bed where the stuffed bear's head still attached to the pelt glared at me in the murk.

I moaned and wept as he caressed me. Even the touch of the linen sheet beneath me was agony. I was too weak with pain and despair even to plead with him. But now my sight was no longer numb. I kept my eyes open.

Even...

He was not even gentle.

"You are good like this," he mumbled. "Terez is a clever fire—consuming me for itself—you are always mine, you cling to me as if I were a rock in Chaos, you cling to me—you'd cling to the marrow in my bones—I can feel even that moving towards the rhythm of your heart—poor little child—my Cija—poor little weeping child—"

I was nearly unconscious but I felt his tears on my mouth as I relaxed my always-pleading convulsive grip—

I lay for a long time in pain and darkness. Most of the time I could not keep even my vague instincts in a straight enough line for a thought, let alone enough thoughts in a line for an idea—it was all pain, degradation, despair, no one to turn to —That was it; No one to turn to, I have no friends, no one can help, no one can be kind to me—

It is not the pain that makes me ill, I thought; it is that I have no friend, no one who can help—

I was roused by Smahil, he was rubbing unguent with firm fingers into my wounds. I cried out, moaned and shuddered; he held me gently. I began to hear; he was whispering, frantically he whispered as he rubbed into my back the unguent which first was fire, and then was soothing. "You'll be all right, Cija. I got this from the cavalry commander in exchange for my next three months' pay. It's all in arrears anyway. It's tremendously good, you won't be scarred, you will be healed and oh, so comfortable, you'll see. You'll be well, I'll make you happy, Cija. You mustn't cry, it's making you well again. If only I got to it in time..."

The hysteria is long over, it was not as bad as it seemed, there seems to be hope when the sun shines, there *is* hope—and preparations for the Atlan campaign go forward so slowly. There is something at work in the temple-palace beyond the mountain, something which wants in my opinion only to get from somebody high in the Northern army the secret of the scientific formula which is capable of filling with air the immense Vacuum; Smahil told me what Terez let him know, the reason for the infamous Southern attack on Northern headquarters.

The purpose, obvious enough to anyone who reflects for a moment if they already know as I do of the vital-formula (very few even of the Northern side know of it, I'm not sure even Smahil does)—the purpose of that attack was that someone big wants to capture the General himself. Even if he doesn't know the exact formula, he's important enough for those who do to give up the secret in order to get him released. And according to Terez who has access to the highest table-talk, the Hammerfist instituted the attack, on the official grounds that immorality and impurity are too rife among the Northern controllers. He has not even kept out of it; the supreme insult to us, their allies, the Superlativity has presented Hammerfist with a medal of rock-crystal veined with gold for conspicuous gallantry and foresight in "leading" an assault on impiety not to say treachery to the prevailing, pervading hospitable and holy religion of the Southern land of the most holy . . . etc. It is a weariness.

There is of course bloodshed everywhere in the streets. Our men are bitterly furious.

Everyone knows for which actual action the Hammerfist is being rewarded.

The officers no longer bother even to separate the forces, but instead join in when they come upon a mélée, which is incessantly.

That too seems a weariness.

No more parades, or inspections, but broken heads, fury everywhere; no safety anywhere in stepping out of doors, and above all the bitter certainty that once we, the inferior force, are made to hand over our secret we shall be neglibile, kicked aside, treated with contempt and worse, despised and also enslaved . . .

And as an accompaniment the mountain is rumbling to life, twice a week it is heard grumbling in the clouds and it belches out horrid little puffs of flame and smoke . . .

My back no longer hurts me, nevertheless I think I shall carry those scars to my death. They are very deep.

Smahil would not hold the mirrors to show me my back, but one day while I was alone I managed to arrange it for myself. My back must have been in ribbons . . . The scars are now clean and silver, raised weals which will presently fade and fine down . . . And when I am old, if I ever do live till then, they will shrink and draw my skin with them in crumpling wrinkles.

The brand I love to feel on Smahil's back will be nothing to that. "How did you get it?" I asked him once. He was quite surprised. "I never knew it was a brand. Are you sure you're not making a mistake?" "Yes, it's very tiny but it's a brand mark, a rusty black oval—" "I don't know, no one has ever branded me, I must have had it always . . ."

That is absurd, but I don't think it matters . . .

I don't think anything really matters . . .

The whispers have found my new dwelling-place.

That, too, is another of the things from which I feel secure only in Smahil's arms. This place is so lonely all day, so dank and dreary that sometimes I have to get up and stride from corner to corner, back and forth, biting my lip to prevent myself screaming; or I fall upon the bed in a passion of weeping for which I can find no real reason. I play endless games with myself. I redecorated the room as I would if I had unlimited riches and resources, but how futile it is, if I had them I should not keep this room. But if I *had* to—But no. It is too pointless.

Smahil has forbidden me to go out, even to the river bank in the country, and I confess I have no inclination to go out either—not with the city in such a state of ferocious turmoil. He has forbidden me even to visit Lel. He forbids a damn sight too much, but as I pointed out I intend to obey him from my own sense.

Sometimes I go out of the room and down the stairs, along the sleazy passage and back again. I even find myself playing the game of walking on every third tile only; a game much more interesting in the hot tower which prisoned my genuine, happier though even lonelier childhood, for then there were great floors stretching far out ahead and to every side, squared with red and black marble. I would step only on the red, never on the black. Alas, I am sure it was the black that followed me with the red into the outside world. The horror I feel when my foot slips to the second instead of the third cracked tile is familiar. But the nervousness with which I scurry into the shadows or back to the staircase when anyone enters—that nervousness is so real, so far removed from make-believe, that it clutches at the pit of my throat and my hand leaves a moist print on the rail. But they are only other officers who live here. Sometimes I have to pass them on the stairs: they are always preoccupied and in a hurry. Northern officers are particularly harassed these days—not only by the danger of their position in the Capital at all, and by the growing insubordination of the troops who want only to harm as many of their allies as possible, but also by the fact that whereas the formula-greedy, power-confident Southerners are letting the campaign preparations go hang, our officers are desperately trying to get the whole business under way and the two armies mobilized; it perhaps would be disastrous, perhaps is our only chance.

It cannot be the normal life of cantoned military. For one tiny instance, we hardly every get Smahil's or the others' friends in for supper or brief calls—and when they do come they are terribly for-tomorrow-we-die-jovial with sudden unexplained silences.

"Miss me?" Smahil says like the imitation of a conventional newly-wed, as he returns in the evening (later and later), flings his tunic at the table, his belt at the chair and looks gloatingly at me and at his hands before bringing us all together by a master's right.

"It is lonely all day. I am—I mean—Sometimes I feel a brooding presence—"

"Well, no presence with any gumption is going to brood in a dump like this—"

"My breasts are sore, don't crush them too hard—They've been getting sorer for days," I said quickly.

He stepped back and gazed narrowly at me. "Has it occurred to you that perhaps you're pregnant?"

"Yes . . ." I couldn't tell if he was pleased at the possibility. Of course, it would be an excuse for him to rejoice more than ever in his complete ownership, and of course it would be madness to bring a child into the world now. "I have none of the other symptoms. I'm lucky to have had that time with the Beauty's household. The gossip taught me in a few weeks all the knowledge that another girl's upbringing would have given her by right, and which I might have missed so acutely—"

"You can sound appallingly *vulgar* at times," he triumphantly interrupted as he carried me to the bed.

"I'm glad I'm not having your child, Smahil," I murmured, all languid and innocent, a simple remark.

"Why?"

His sudden defencelessness did amaze me.

"A child—I don't want a baby, not *now*," I explained.

His eyes questioned, "Later?" My arms went round his neck. "Oh, Smahil," I murmured. He was pleased. I realized that I hardly ever vouchsafe any gesture, let alone any of affection. Of course, how often can I feel like it?

"Your breasts are growing," he said. His tone in the darkness was strange—was it with a kind of wonder? I could not see his face. His hands were warm. "They are high and firm and yet with such an unfathomable softness." He whispered. "I have made you a woman."

I was thinking as I lay there with him that I am indeed physically richer now. Though even in the past they have been only women who called me plain. Now I have a rich rare appearance, a translucent skin, sparkling eyes which really reflect any sky of grey, azure or aquamarine, a full almost scarlet mouth, and hair, like stiff honey, springing, waving, heavy from my scalp. And my body too—always vivid with youth and now with a kind of lusciousness, foreign to me and which I regard shyly, blooming over my slenderness—

Outside in the room there was the scrape of boots coming off. Anad or one of the others had entered, a yawn, the bang of a shutting bed-door.

304

From the other side, below in the street a scuffling on alley cobbles, cursing, the familiar almost nightly clash of steel on steel.

A lantern was lit in the alley as the sky became pitch black. Perhaps further away there was the flare and glow of the volcano.

Smahil's face hung poised above mine, a strained, pale, golden visitation, long, pallid eyelids and glinting eyes drained of colour by the night.

"Smahil . . ."

But afterwards a sort of fierceness pervaded him.

"You even breathe like a goddess. You tempt me at times to believe you a goddess, a small goddess. But you are really so ordinary. I must remind myself you are—this—remote, tender warmth—only because you have been reared from your conception to think of yourself as everything. That is what makes you care so little in the long run about what happens. In ordinary circumstances you would have had few hobbies and not been particularly clever."

Abruptly he pulled up the bed-covers enough to show me, as in a warm, dark tunnel, our bodies still twisted together. They seemed to float contorted in a golden aureole of light, a lascivious unreality . . .

"That is the only reality. Remember it, my own Cija. I love you," he whispered, "I love you more than any other woman in the world."

I could not make the mistake of believing he really loves me as I know the word.

He loves every pore of my body, every one of my movements, the scent of me, the taste of me, my every eyelash: but it is not the love I want. When other people love, they love also the soul, the mind; but not Smahil, or not Smahil with me.

So he regarded me.

"I wonder why," he said. "You're by no means the most beautiful woman I've known."

I fell asleep, clinging to this person Smahil, pressing my head to his chest, to his heart-beat, to hide my ears from the intangible.

I am still shaken by compulsive shudders as I write this. Tonight I had fallen asleep in the chair. I was awakened by a noise of loud talking around me. Smahil, Anad and Dani were in the room. Dani is another of the officers. The room was very cold, so that I shivered, and dark so I knew I had slept a long

305

time. However, Smahil was now lighting the lamp.

"What is all this noise for?" I asked, sitting up.

"You were asleep and Anad came in and sat quietly opposite you, reading orders till the light failed, so as not to waken you, like the good little boy he is," replied Smahil briskly. "But he must have been dreaming too, for just as we came up the stairs we were brought rushing by his yell, and he says he saw the door open, he looked up thinking it was us, and a huge, gusty woman walked into the room and seized you by the arm—"

"I didn't say she was huge—I can't remember whether she was tall or short, she just seemed—*big*—" Anad was rubbing his eyes but was still too impressed by his dream to be shamefaced.

"And as he yelled out she disappeared. Then the door opened again and it really was us this time. Bursting in and finding nothing but a—"

I yawned and stretched my arms above my head. In a sudden silence I realized they were all staring at me, I myself finally looked up at my arms, from which the sleeve-folds had fallen. There on my flesh were the bruise-prints of four fingers and a thumb of more than usual size.

As I crawled with Smahil into our cupboard bed it seemed to smell more unpleasant than any shut place need when it has an open window.

"A *big* woman with gleaming eyes, but she did not look at me. If she had, I would have been unable to make a move, much less yell," Anad mumbled, no longer interrupted. "Gleaming silver eyes. I am glad for Cija's sake she was asleep . . ."

We received orders to be completely ready within a few days, to leave the Capital. Zerd was tenting the army outside. He officially claimed that the life in the City was being too much for the whole army, troops and officers, and that he was putting it outside under tentage in order to get it under control. "More likely because you're scared we'll murder you all," jeered the Southerners, stoning and pelting with filth the lines evacuating through the streets.

It was a savagely hot day, and the crowd's temper as savage.

Yapping dogs biting at calves of legs, gutter brats and even middle-class children with stones, women howling out their wrongs interrupted the order of the marching lines. The beggars rose up, forgot the weakening diseases they claim incurable, and belaboured the soldiers with their crutches; decent trades-people poured slop on them and reviled them from their windows. The men, grumbling, limping, pretending to ignore everything, were kept forcibly in line by officers channelling their fury into discipline. Some of the Southerners also had split heads or were limping because of stones, but they didn't desist, though in the narrower streets it was hard for a missile always to get its intended mark.

It had taken me nearly half an hour to accompany this evacuation only for the length of three streets.

The sun broiled down, every temper was shocking, the streets seemed to burst with temper, and the thrumming of each regiment's small black drums instead of keeping upright our dignity only served to madden.

"This is impossible!" I cried furiously to the trooper beside me. I was not even with Smahil. "I don't mind them stoning you, but any minute they're liable to get me too if they're not careful!" Sometimes, afraid of being swept to the back of the crowd, I clung to the uniformed arm; it was patchy with sweat.

Glancing at his officer in case he was noticing, my trooper thrust his scabbard point viciously into the stomach of a sturdy gutterboy contesting his way. As the scabbard was worn very thin the steel came through, and the boy somersaulted aside with a shriek and then picked up a steaming fistful of manure, relic of the passage of our own baggage-train, and threw it. It caught my jacket at which I dabbed ineffectually and finally took off and threw away. A group of girls stopped stoning in order to pounce on it; then looked at me reproachfully. I clung again to the trooper's arm as we struck a bad patch. The marching could no longer follow even every second rhythm-beat of the drums. The trooper irritably shook my arm away.

"I need room," he yelled, making it a kind of battle-cry, as this time he had to raise his scabbarded sword and use it like a club on the roaring townspeople.

I kicked the shins of a man who looked so angry that I darted into the ranks and sought a (somewhat jostled) protection among the most crowded troops, pushed in on each other's lines by the narrowness of the street—made even narrower by its walls of rabble.

"Here, you oughtn't be here," stated a new neighbour, squinting at me.

"I know," I said feelingly.

"I tell you what you ought to do," he told me in snatches.

307

"You ought to find an empty house, there's plenty of billets suddenly empty right now, and stay there till we've all gone past."

I found to my surprise that my presence had been noted by all the men around me, and another trooper now said to me, "No, I tell you what you ought to do. You ought to stay here in the City the night, and go in to the camp tomorrow when we're all set up. They'll mistake you for one of themselves then, they'll all be flowing in, to bother the commission our Blue Scales has set up to deal with all their nasty little complaints: damage, rapes, begging your pardon, girlie, murders of providers, etc. My advice, miss."

"Yes, thank you," I gasped, knocked to one side by some sudden surge.

"Here," he said kindly and I found he had rescued my bundle for me. "O.K. now, miss?"

"Oh! Thanks," and I struggled to the side once more.

Even at the back of the crowd I found movement against the main stream impossible.

I was about to give up (I was in the mood to call it despairing rather than resigning myself) when I lifted my head and recognized some buildings we were approaching.

All this, four winding streets of it, had been unnecessary! Just like our Administrative Section, some incompetent staff-officer had mapped the path of our evacuation and we had taken a lovely wide detour, now passing again the barracks and inn. I could easily find my way to my own late billet from here. Forcing my way to the front through the cursing troops, into and through a corner of the baggage-train, skirting five Southern girls each with a presumably premature baby (for we haven't been here that long) besieging a soldier, past a group of civilians trying to pull a lowing ox out of place, I was presently once more in the familiar small, cobbled courtyard, completely deserted, not even the horses and birds looked out from the stalls. They had all gone.

I went along the passage and up the stairs, quietly, though I knew the inn-woman had probably gone to join in the excitement.

The room was a furnace but when I heard steps on the stairs I thought I'd better hide as someone else had had my idea.

I slipped into the shut-bed which had been mine and Smahil's, taking care not to leave my bundle behind. This was just as well; for sure enough, it was the door of this very room

308

which opened and there was quite a noise as about half a dozen people came in.

I recognized the voice of a man very high up on the Accoutrements Side, a man known to be a scientist.

"The birds seem to have flown."

I was positively stifling in the shut-bed. Up through its window came the sound of the still passing army, and from the other side these voices.

"But this is the young leader's billet, sir."

"We appear to be too late."

"Well, now we're here it's as good a place as any to wait till that scum below have passed."

I clutched my bundle and nodded at the stuffed head attached to the pelt. Yes. I know that voice.

What is our beloved General doing here?

"Look, here are some of his lady-friend's things still lying about. It's possible she'll return for them, then I can give her the message."

How maddening, how unfair. I haven't left anything about, they're being encouraged to stay by a few beads and the discarded waist-ribbon left by Dani's last girl-friend. He didn't like her well enough to collect them for when he might see her next.

So here I am, I thought, imprisoned by the presence of —And who's that new voice?

"I'm glad you're at last considering me. The streets are torture." (How can she have reached the stage of demanding his consideration for her welfare?) "Oh, how is it, how is it we accept such real *monsters* as our allies?"

"Don't worry, I have my plans." He sounded amused.

"All leading up to—" one of the scientists began smugly, and then I nearly jumped in my bed. What business had they mentioning *that* in front of her, the High General's wife though she is? For they went on to speak grimly, yet too casually, of the Formula which is their only hold over the Southerners. Once the secret of *that* is out—and I have it! I heard it! Not even here shall I write it down, I fear it might burn the paper, and I have told myself to forget it, but then at night I find myself repeating it in my head over and over. Then my tongue shrinks back and I am afraid I may have spoken it out loud.

"Do you suppose there's any food in this place?" one of them suggested after a pause.

"Yes, Gods' Fingerjoints, we could do with a little meat or wine or both, now that I come to think of it."

"Perhaps in the kitchen . . . ?"

"That'll be at the bottom of the stairs."

They went out and I heard them making the staircase clatter; Zerd and the scientists—the action-commanders weren't here, I'd not heard their voices, they must be out presiding over the evacuation. I moved cautiously but then was warned by a sigh and a creak that one person had been left in the room and was leaning against my very door. I heard the rustle of a settling dress. It was a very fed-up sigh now in private. Why would a woman begin to scold Zerd? She was unsure of him, to say the least, and I could guess that her life must be a continuous ill-tasting search for ways to hold him.

Oh, this warring, this lust for dominance, even she has it. And he, it's his whole vile life, possession, penetration, air flooding with a hiss of sudden turbulence, moiling with all its bacteria and currents the great nothingness, the wall of passive protection to peace—swords, blood, torture, grief brought for its own sake to the only shores one might have considered safe, the last stronghold in the world of the *purely* Divinely-descended race . . .

Abruptly as she leant on it the bed-door, which had not been fastened, swung. She turned. We stared into each other's faces.

Now a funny thing happened. It could so easily have happened at any time in the last few months, but now was just the time it was most unlikely. But it was as her late stew-boy she recognized me. The little hostage-slave Cija doesn't seem to have taken up much space in the most people's lives—except of course in that hostage's who is now an officer and spent his time in greed for all of her. But now in the shadows of the bed perhaps I did still resemble Jaleril. I was wearing a low-class Southern teenager's leggings, all we could afford, instead of a lady's full trousers, and my plain, short, cotton dress was hanging outside my belt, like a shirt, because of the heat. My hair, in one thick braid, must have been behind my head and out of sight in the shadows. Anyway, this delightful princess gave one sharp stare and then as the door opened to admit the General balancing two plates of meat and rather wrinkled fruits and a wine-jug, she disarranged her hair and bodice and ran to him sobbing.

"Oh, Zerd, Zerd, my Zerd—avenge me—as soon as you left me alone that door opened and the boy who'd been there all

310

the time came out and started to assault me—"

He didn't say anything but set down the plates and jug on the table as she flung herself sobbing and crowing for hysterical breath against him.

Her face was blotchy and she had worked herself so ingeniously into real tears which revealed with their devastating damp just how much paint she laid on her skin. For the first time I was shaken by pity. Not compassion—but pity for her *efforts*.

He strode to the cupboard and looked in at me. At another time I might have laughed.

"See—he was—"

"Our stew-boy, yes." Suddenly this big, genial, half-human man in his black and scarlet highest-General's uniform turned and spat into the cleft between his wife's breasts in her self-disarranged *décollatage*.

She fell back, silent except for her panting, her eyes fixed with a look of horror on his face. He was still genial but he looked her once down and up with contempt.

As there was no alternative except to skulk like a fool, I gathered my bundle and walked into the room.

The General's hand heavy on my shoulder turned me and he smiled without pleasantness, at my braid, at my chest, at every line of me.

"Our stew-boy, yes, but I don't think there was an assault."

This was an intensely personal incident now, for as I tipped back my head to stare into the eyes they were as intent as mine. He knew me. My hands, my body were clammy. It seemed an irrelevant interruption as the poor wife, believing the room filled with her humiliation and tragedy, bowed her head and crawled to his side.

"Forgive me, Zerd—I made a mistake . . . "

"The other gentlemen are in the kitchen," he said coldly and she ran from the room.

The General sat on the floor and leaned against the door. He balanced a plate on his upraised knee.

She only wanted to make you jealous and protective, I wanted to say, but found that my mouth wouldn't speak. I also found that I had backed against the table and was facing him in a ridiculous position like a beast at bay. I lifted my head and willing my hands at least not to shake, I began to drink from the jug, a reason for having come to the table.

"So you've been here all the time?"

"It *is* my billet."

"And that of several young leaders—I'm sorry I won't be able to send the leader Smahil any greeting via you."

His eyes widened on my fingers trembling, gripping the table edge.

"But you did hear the Formula, didn't you?"

"I am afraid so."

"But this is very unwonted humility. You've changed, floss-hair."

"Well, there are two compartments in my mind now," I said wryly.

"What a pity this all is. Isn't it? But I'm afraid I can't let anyone loose on the world, as you might say, with such a secret on the tip of their—charming—tongue."

He was drawling, slurring his words with an air of disregarding them, letting them come as they would, as he watched with the straight-browed, glowing, black gaze every movement I made, every expression. I tried to still all emotion. I didn't even notice the effect of cool courage which resulted.

"Everyone has to die, General. I'm sure you won't torture me unnecessarily."

"Dear me, what a life of tenterhooks you must have been living to be able to put on so readily such resignation. You don't cling to life? I know camp-following can be rather dreary, but you seemed to enjoy yourself sometimes with the pots."

"You watched me?"

He bowed courteously over his meat. "But could you doubt it?"

"You guessed I was not a boy?"

"When you ran into my arms the first night, in the inn, it was deliciously obvious you were not a boy. Then of course there was very little difficulty in recognizing my most interesting hostage, in fact now I come to think of it, I can't remember ever having had any quite as interesting, though many more accommodating. It amused me to watch you after that."

I inclined my head.

"How nice to have been able to lighten some of your hours of duty."

"Hm . . . So you ask nothing more and will presently be put out like a light?"

I remained silent, analysing his mockery, and presently he ran two fingers across his chin while above his gaze never shifted. "As a matter of fact I am really loth to waste this . . . Doesn't it seem, even to yourself, that you have outgrown your little fair playmate?"

My mind turned in. It is true. I have sloughed the need for girlish, kittenish, desperate, adroit lying every different moment, and with it the genuine adolescent whose mother let her out of the tower. I have outgrown Smahil.

"You are asking me to sleep with you."

"I am asking you to be my mistress, a securer position, involving regular sleeping-habits——"

"But then when you tired of me the danger would be as before."

He raised the brows.

"The temporary reprieve doesn't seem to you worth it? Your death, as you remarked, is unlikely to be unnecessarily painful, you don't want merely to postpone it? You are perhaps overmodest as well as certainly uncomplimentary. Perhaps by the time I tire of you the conquest of the Continent will already have been accomplished and your danger-potential nullified."

Nullified . . . Always that word following me, pseudo-urgent.

There was only one temptation, but I knew it wasn't in me to assassinate *anyone* in cold blood. I could make up my mind wonderfully, but I would put it off till tomorrow, till tomorrow, till an even better opportunity. He must know that too, and/or be determined never to let me near him with a dagger, otherwise he'd not be willing to take me on after the accusation Ooldra must have made before she left for home. So I'd never get the chance anyway.

"Yes, General, I do believe it isn't worth it. You had better execute me after lunch."

"You mean it." He peered at me. "What calm determination. Am I, on mature reflection, so unattractive to you? Is it still because I am the enemy of your country?"

"Of every country, I think. Apart from that you are usually quite pleasant, except of course——"

"My skin? I am, naturally, quite inferior to the human army I lead. But women never previously seem to have taken exception to that."

His naïvety thrilled me.

Is it possible he has always been a little sensitive about his difference, inherited from his father's predilection for the big, black women of the sub-human Northern ribes?

313

"Come, hostage."

I shook my head. I felt nothing. I knew only that I could not let this power-poison touch me.

"You will be placed under close arrest." He did not look at me again, but still leaning against the door transferred his complete attention to the meal.

It was ugly, really, but when I saw again the hard, hot sky which is that blue because of its depth, and smelt the unattractive, real, big bird smell of the bird the General had mounted, I knew I wanted to *live*. The—potency—of this world we have been born into clamours more *in* our veins than our blood does, though sometimes I have thought *it is* our blood. But this has nothing to do with courage, though a lot to do with determination. Zerd dismissed the scientists on to the various places where they'd presently be needed. Lara went with one, not looking at us. "Here, up," Zerd said.

I mounted reasonably well and swiftly without touching his proffered hand.

When up behind him I had to hold on in order not to be dashed into the crowd because of the bird's gait. However, I crooked into his belt only one finger, though it soon ached.

"We're going to the camp where you'll be guarded for the short time till your execution," he said conversationally.

He chuckled, really as if helluva amused, and with the reins in one hand he half-turned back to me and without urgency removed from round his neck the black kerchief worn in hot weather and in whose folds had been caught most of his sweat. This he now stuffed into my mouth before I realized what was intended. Then he took both my hands in his and turned to the front again so that my arms were round his waist.

"In case you decide to shout the dread secret out to these ladies and gentlemen, though it's doubtful that even the nearness of death could make you feel such kindness for the Southerners, and it's also doubtful that any of them'd hear over their own vociferation," he explained. "But then, it really is quite an important formula."

I tried to spit the pungent cloth out of my mouth, but he had tucked it in with the dexterous hand probably of experience. I was exposed to full view and as I was again dressed as myself I felt remarkably embarrassed. I kept my eyes lowered, afraid of meeting some recognizable gaze.

The way he had pulled my arms meant that I was stretched close against him. Because of the heat, the scarlet cloak had been looped to one side and I felt through his black shirt the smoothly-scaled ripple of the muscles of the mighty bas-relief back. The sway of the bird was enough to ensure that my own breasts had just sufficient maddening freedom to quiver or be thrust against these muscles, so that I was as shamed as someone can be whose main consciousness is centred on approaching severance from life itself. The only reason I was glad he was wearing only a shirt, no jerkin even, was that it was poor protection if anybody happened to throw something very pointed at him. But we were among the Golds, and the streets were wider, and somehow it didn't happen.

I kept my hands lax in his. I hoped he might slacken his attention. Then maybe I'd be able to get at least one arm free. But even when he raised a hand to wave a brief greeting to another commander, he kept my fingers barred in his and my arm was raised to make the wave too.

It would probably be beheading. They were good with their swords, some of the guards, swift and sure. It was only the imminent, quickly nearer, unknown I had to fear, not the pain. Yet in the confusion and business of getting under tentage on a hot day after demonstrations from a hostile public—might they entrust me to an inferior executioner, someone badly practised? Or might even the best man's sword slip? Everyone makes a few mistakes in a lifetime, but what is a mistake for a craftsman who in annoyance and pride promises himself, "Better next time", can mean agony for the particular victim who happens to catch the mistake. Yes, as I bared my neck ready I would be shaking with fear, panic of butchery as well as of the unknown. And if I shook I'd be a bad mark . . .

I am terrified. Oh, if only he gives me another chance, if only he asks me again before the moment . . .

But you know, with luck, your immediate reflex would be to say "No". Better to suffer a little physical pain . . .

Every minute, every jogging moment, every second, O God, Oh Cousin, every sharp second is bringing it nearer.

We are still riding through the Golds and the shouting crowd but the roar is only the roar in my ears. It's all broken up into sharp stabs of colour and each a second of the time—the only Time allotted to me. How hot the sun is. How hard these cruel hands round mine, the rippling of this against my breasts, which I am beginning in my panic to feel physically chafed, ceaselessly . . .

Suddenly I had a thought which seemed to me so dazzlingly, brilliantly simple that I knew why neither he nor I had foreseen it. With a fatuous joy I kicked hard with both feet simul-

315

taneously at the bird's sides. I heard its bark and it started sidling. I had time to kick it once more, so that it reared nervously because it couldn't dash forward owing to the thickness of the crowd before it. The General with a shout gave both hands, still holding mine, to the reins. I wrenched mine free and jumped.

My hands caught the stone of the bridge I had seen above us.

It seemed unbearably rough and gritty.

I heaved myself up but I'm not acrobatic and my thudding heart and my panting almost split me in two. Sweat had started out on my forehead and my fingers were sliding before they'd groped the few inches up to the balustrade-edge.

Would the desperation of my need give me unusual strength?

That thought did it. I slipped and, with a gurgle behind my stuffed mouth, clutching frantically at nothing—I fell—

I landed on something harsh and prickly but soft enough to break my fall. This was a big, jolting straw-cart on to whose immense high-piled load I had fallen.

As I looked up in amazement at the fatal grey-stone bridge-thoroughfare spanning the road, I saw Zerd on foot race on to it. How quickly he must have seen my jump, leaped from his bird and up the steps on to the bridge as he saw me clambering on to it. But he was in quite the wrong place, wasn't he? I saw him shoulder his way through the townspeople crammed on the bridge to watch the army's passing, and his dark face turning swiftly and concentratedly here and there. Even in this while I was busily removing the black linen sweat-rag from my mouth. The pungent taste it left seemed bitterer when struck by air than when the thing itself had been there. I shook my head with my mouth hanging open, to dry out the taste, and looked down about me at the carts and the Golds marching, ahead. At this moment I heard a shout. Zerd was leaning over the parapet. He had seen me. The great General turned and disappeared into the crowd up there. The cart lurched on.

Well, what to do now?

Breathlessly safe, but for how long?

He knew this cart now, and wouldn't I be abler on my feet dodging through this multitude?

I scrambled across the hay to its edge. The load was very high. The closely-packed heads beneath seemed very far away, the invisible ground therefore even farther.

Nevertheless, I half-scrambled, half-slid down the precarious swaying load and vehicle. I now discovered my hands had been hurt by the bridge, there was a lot of skin off them and a lot of blood on them. I hurt them even more now, but it was one of those times when you don't feel pain except as just another urgent sensation.

At the bottom of my journey I found myself grasped by numbers of the Golds who had laughingly watched. They should not have so much as *glanced* out of line, particularly they who are so jealous of their reputation against the other regiments', but there was so much need for action during the marching today that those who hadn't been stoned were treating the whole thing as a holiday. Almost complete anarchy reigned everywhere.

I hardly heard the laughing, lewd shouts of welcome I received, I hardly felt the many rough grasps and breaths.

The glare of heat on my uncovered head was making me feel, as I dashed between the marchers, that I was getting ringing head-blows. My eyes and ears were confused, my panting was drying my tongue till it swelled, and to run was a real bodily effort. I was not thinking at all now. This is proved by the fact that only at the end of the chase did I put my hand up to my throat and think, "Oh, so this sore ache is my tight collar and not the beheading blade!"

The threat pursued me. What a threat—big, scarlet, black, muscular, tall, important! My heart thudded.

Well. I ran through the soldiery, the soldiery marching through thrown stones and verbal and physical filth.

I sensed the pursuit.

Except as I turned corners I never saw the General. I was too busy looking ahead, but I heard behind me the pounding of his swift, steady running-strokes, the respectful murmurs of the men as they crowded together to let him pass, and as I passed soldiers who took no notice of me I saw them turn to stare at his approach. Before they could realize that there was not merely a pursuer but a pursued, I was ahead again.

A soldier presumably intent on approbation or even promotion started to chase me, but was soon behind the General.

I blundered into another part of the baggage-train.

"Cija!"

The word was repeated twice before it became a name, and again before it made sense to me. I stumbled aside, one step, and saw a little boy grinning anxiously at me.

Ow, the goat-boy, Narra's brother.

317

"You be in a hurry, Lady Cija."

As if I'd never been away. Had he, in his little goat-herd world, even noticed my long absence—and his sister's?

"Ow, I'm running away from someone who's *furious* to punish me—" His urchin's eyes glittered. "—Ow, for Gods' sakes drive your goats across the street, behind me—"

I lurched on, my whole being a prayer.

The goats surged across the street, I could hear their numberless, disharmonious separate bleatings, their acrid stink burdened the air.

As I turned the next corner I glanced back.

Away at the entrance to the street the baggage-train was blocked by the goats. Drovers were cursing. The curses became frantic and still the animals milled aimlessly, effectively. Among them, not in the least dignified, flailing his arms and lashing out with his boots, was the big black and scarlet threat.

So now I had a head-start.

I doubled through a long tavern room. It was crammed with good Southern gentlemen who had come in to refresh themselves during their hard day's work, and who'd stayed till now incapable, poor dears, of throwing a single stone. I knocked against several who hit their neighbours, either because they blamed the knock on them or because they aimed for me and missed. As I nipped out of the back window I saw the General caught in the fighting, moiling room. At first exasperated, temper still in his face from the goat-incident, he tried to shoulder his way through the drunken turmoil but soon had to defend himself from fists eager for any mark. He shoved men aside and struck down others, impatiently, but was caught and had to fight in earnest. That would keep him going for some time. I clambered over the sill and for an instant between the fighters in the length of the room he looked up and saw me.

I felt the same stab in the diaphragm that I have had several times from him.

I found myself in the tavern's back yard, a tiny square almost all taken up with a vast, peak-topped dung-hill.

I skirted this but found the paling-fence behind it impossible to climb. I tried again and again, but it was just too tall, the paling had pointed tops, and my foot slipped even when I could get it between them. I hurt my feet, wrenching them desperately out when they got jammed, I had no time to ease them out properly, and my hands were full of long nasty splinters. It was one of those ventures when every movement slips and ends wrong, my chin descended heavily on the points of

318

the palings as my feet and hands slipped, and I bit my tongue, and my chin hurt so sore and was covered in blood, and I think I wailed. I turned frantically to find another means of getting out of the yard.

There was a door into the kitchen, full of fires and movement but perhaps no one would stop me, but meanwhile a figure had appeared at the window. Landing a last blow on someone behind him, he swung out. I hid behind the dung-heap. I had wasted my precious hard-won breathing space on that wretched paling fence.

I was sobbing, silently I think, and my gullet where I felt the blade was cold.

He didn't speak, but strode round towards me, his boots and sleeves catching dung. We circled once and then by changing his direction unexpectedly he had me. The black eyes glittered grimly down on me. The mouth smiled. I bit his hand, my teeth grated so that I thought I had struck bone, so savage was my determination, but I could not even puncture those scales.

"I carry my own armour-plating with me, you see."

His voice hurt me.

"Reptile!"

His expression, beneath its surface of grim triumph, was unfathomable.

He was so inescapable in that tiny squalid space, I nearly despaired.

As his other hand came to me; fingers flexing to frighten me and impress me with my helplessness which Gods knew weighed on me already as heavy as the pattern going through marqueterie, I seized the pitchfork sticking in the hill behind me and lunged it at his face. I longed to see blood gush from his face by an action of mine, that thick, dark blood. He let go my wrist, seized the fork. This was like a game of chess, he knew I would be away again but I had checked him, he had to admit to the efficacy of that sharp threat.

He cursed me, angry now, and I fled.

I made for the kitchen door, but he was between me and that and there was no room to pass him even if I were adroit enough. The window to the long room was behind him too.

I sprang up on the yielding soggy hill, and before I could sink in it I leaped for the nearby shed-roof. It wasn't high.

I ran along the top of this, hoisted myself on to the inn-roof. He threw the clattering pitchfork, missed, and was up after me. He had the speed of some horrible, nimble, big animal, a panther or, yes, a crocodile. I had to flee so fast that there was no time to choose a route and soon I was splashing in the roof-gutters. These were at a sloping angle and my panic heightened. I held out my arms to balance myself as though tightrope-walking. He came on. He was laughing now, stalking me slowly, steadily—certainly. I leaped for the next roof, landed sprawled on my knees in its gutter. Tried to climb up the roof-slope, but a tile fell and me nearly with it.

There were just I and the General, more an animal, more a brilliant kind of brute able to lead the higher species because of his instinct for savagery and his form of love for prey, now up in a little roof-top world of grey and blue tiles, dormer windows, clouds, the roofs of narrow, easily-leapt, back streets where not even a dog yapped below, streets deserted for the procession—a scrambling, slanting grey world with this one live black and scarlet focal point, a laughing animal, striding over the street-spaces I leapt wildly, and I the prey.

The air itself struck sparks from the hot tiles till the grey and gold neutralized each other, swimming in tension.

The blast from a chimney under which some big kitchen-fire had suddenly been lit nearly sent me flying.

A panic scream wailed till far away on the heat's tension, it was mine. I was crying. He laughed and came on. Our speeds were about equal, he was gaining but imperceptibly, but whereas mine was maintained by wild leaps and clutches and sprawls, leaps up-again, accompanied by a frantic sobbing, torn clothes, bitten lips and bloodied hands, his was easy and competent. He was stalking me surely. His big head was thrown back, and his gaze on me, noting every humiliating effort, his mouth open, his laughing coming out never-ending, real mirth, harsh, ferocious, ringing.

Big clouds gathered above the heat haze.

The desolation grumbled.

The dusty tiles were pitted with moist roundels.

A great crocodile went thundering round the sky and back again. The heat haze trembled, split. Water came pouring down. I clung with both arms round a chimney-stack as my only defence against being washed away down the roof-slope. For a moment even he was hidden by the mass or rain. The gutters gurgled.

Still he approached, he was very near. It was as if there had been no change.

I screamed because he is a demon.

I flung wide a half-open window and somehow got through

it—a tiny attic window. The attic was evidently that of an upper middle-class home, judging by the lumber of outdated glitter-sewn ball-dresses and trousers, curl-toed slippers, curtains, a pile of tarnished silver plate two generations old, a big chair with ripped upholstery. I dodged over all this musty richness, through a door there, and locked it behind me.

I blessed its key which I had so miraculously found in the lock, and tiptoed down the carpeted stairs.

This was some near-noble's town home, as I guessed from the furnishings and rooms I glimpsed, but deserted as far as I could make out. In the upper storeys there had been the brief pounding of the General's boots on the door he'd found locked after he followed me through the window, but though I had waited appalled, quieting even my breathing, no one had come.

Now I did hear a sound, down below. The General had entered below.

The tradesmen's entrance must have been open. And there was no mistaking the sound of that stride—so sure, so untroubled, so inescapable, so aware of its inescapability.

I dashed aside through another door banging it behind me, there was no key in this one. But thank Gods the room was empty. Yes, the house was quite deserted, everyone must have gone off like loyal patriots to the allies-baiting.

I ran across this room to the farther door which opened on another staircase.

"Cija!"

The empty rooms reverberated.

I ran as silently as possible but soon had to sacrifice quietness to speed. He was on my trail.

"Come, little hostage, don't you find the game is tedious when it has no more point?"

I searched the lock of every door I passed, but there were no more keys. My clothes dried a little. I could hear the rain-flurry on the dark-silvered windows. Up the top of a narrow, dark staircase, the first without a carpeting, on which I'd found myself suddenly as I ran from a light airy room littered with a child's toys, I heard a moaning.

Startled, I was still for a moment, listening fearfully, till I was reminded of the pursuit by the click of a door just below me.

No help for it, so up the stairs and into that moaning room.

As I entered that dark, ill-smelling, shut-up room an old woman sitting by the bed rose up.

321

"What are you?" she said.

I strode to the window and opened it.

She shrieked.

"What will Zerd think?" I thought.

"And this will benefit your patient," I said. The fresh air swirled into the room, forced into eddies against the sick-room atmosphere. I leaned out, into the pouring rain. The ground was very far below. Before I could make sure of the means I saw of climbing down, the General entered.

He came over and his hand turned me.

"Shouldn't jump if I were you," he said. It was a wolfish tone, resonant with complete victory. And that death awaited me behind it.

The heap on the bed stirred.

She sat up.

I shuddered as I saw the eyes fixed on him, staring out from that discoloured face. It took me back to the heat, the terror, the smells of that time when I nursed Smahil all discoloured with blue poison—and in the weeks since I had last seen this woman, the poison must have spread across her whole body.

The fever-bright eyes glared on him, a wasted blotchy blue arm was raised.

She got out of bed, drew closer to him. Her white shift was dark with bitter sweat. I turned my eyes from the blue blotching of her breasts, whose swell had once been so proud and white.

She gripped him, pressing against him.

"Do you want me now, Zerd? Great General? Does my skin at last match yours which tired of mine? Let me lay it against yours. If only the poison would spread back to whence it came and prove deadly now augmented with mine, for Gods know I hate you deadly enough. You, who have allowed me a few days more to live, hidden away like a cancer in my father's house, till swollen blue with your derision—"

The harsh whisper which he had left for her voice continued and continued.

I didn't wait for it, I didn't wait to look at his fascinated, amused, proud, inhuman *man*-formed face—I was out of the window and my hands soon on the wall-creeper out there. The rain tried to tear it and me apart, but when it eventually won and ripped my hand from the stem I was near enough to the ground for it not to matter.

Now I knew another secret of the General's—the secret even Smahil had not dared do more than hint at.

And she was the woman whom I had last seen hanging, panting, near-nude, like a drowning woman on Zerd on the Night of the Dinosaur.

I was on the brick river-wharf.
The river boiled under the rain.

Crouched in a little boat among rows of empty others, jamming myself under its plank-bench, soon myself impregnated with the smell of sodden wood, I saw him through the rain-sheets, emerged from the house, scanning the street, the windows, the roofs, the river.

He turned away, walking across the brick bridge, a silhouette in the drumming, leaden air. He did not even shrug, his rather leonine profile containing every possible expression and each negating the others, but there was a definite expression to his shoulders as he disappeared in the maze of rainy brick alleys the other side of the bridge.

The abandoned rainfall slashed at the river.
I climbed from my little boat on to a bigger one, hid among the baled goods unseen by the rain-weary watch before the crew boarded her, and was miles up-river and at their destination before, a night and day later, they discovered me.

PART TWO

THE BELOVED

# CHAPTER SEVEN

## THE PALACE

As I write this I lean my book on a thick, quashy, purple cushion. As I wriggle with the satisfaction of what I write, my bed on the end of its chain from the ceiling sways and springs, responding to my every emotion, the most aimless of my kicks at this superfluity of coloured cushions. It is a very different bed from that cupboard I've been incarcerated in for the last weeks.

The morning sunlight was pale and fluttered on the waves. It struck sharp directly through my thin clothes which had seemed so much too heavy a day ago. With the sharpness of a knife it divided the deck, pale strips between the clear-cut shadows of moving men, shadows diagonal across the vertical lines of the deck-planks. Because of the ship's gentle heave and roll on the waves, the slanting of these actually-vertical lines gave the illusion that they were sliding apart from one another in independent motion, and presently the ship would disintegrate and we would all, captain, crew, cargo and stowaway, be ourselves rolling in the blue water, but it did not seem to matter at all.

I leaned back at my ease among the crates. I watched the crew swabbing the deck, and later preparations for landing.

White birds made dozens of tiny arches over the ship. They alighted in rows on the bulwarks; and the crew, big bronzed men in red sashes and very little else except for metal jewelery and knives, threw to them meat-scraps I wouldn't have disdained.

One bird alighted on a crate up-ended beside me. It peered down at me with a pearly pink eye. It was so far the only being on this ship which had discovered me.

In spite of my emptiness, stiffness and chilliness I was more contented than I could ever remember and, as I looked around at water, sky, wind and sunlight, I kept realizing that there was a fond, perhaps faintly foolish smile on my face.

I knew I should be discovered when we landed and unloaded: if I were a boy I should have been kicked, bullied, perhaps made to work for the passage I'd taken; but when I behaved like a charming little lady I should be off in a few minutes.

Then, what should I do in an unknown port? It might be difficult, I was quite alone and a stranger, and my bundle of humble but useful belongings had been the only thing I'd lost in my flight from the General.

But I had a feeling I should begin a new life in this new place. Helped by this core of balance I had this morning discovered born in me—acceptance, confidence, ableness to deal with whatever life would send and which I should accept—a balance somehow fostered by the sunlight, the wind, the creak of boards, the crack of a sail against the mast, the slap of spray on the gunwales and of water swilling in the bilge. This was complete freedom. A continuance of life in a *new* world miles even from memories of everything before.

I have never felt as though inexperience were a part of me which would soon be overlaid with "the wonder of Experience": I felt as if inexperience were a thing, a thing like a pall, hanging over me and clouding my intrinsic Experience and its truth; and soon that pall would be twisted away and there I would stand, at last, myself.

This was the first time I'd been on a ship—well, this didn't deserve the name; this was a river-trader. I was enjoying myself and very proud that I was evidently one of those things, "a good sailor". Actually I had felt a little queasy when she moved off last night, so it was a good thing I'd nothing in my stomach. But this morning I was hungry and had remained in the same position for hours under a chill wind, and I'd never felt so healthy. Every smell was a delight: I had smelt this river for the last half-dozen months or so, but never had it smelt like this, so wide, so salt, so *free*. There was the smell of tar and galley-smells which made me vividly hungry.

It was hard, among the piled crates, to catch many glimpses of the shore, but I don't think I'd have seen much more from any position on deck. The river was tremendously wide here. The shores were far, hazy lines, here suggesting plains by their flat grey-green haze. There were other boats though, yammering before the wind, down-river over the whorls and swelling, swaying, green currents and the blue, sunlit, wind-whipped waves.

There was almost always a sail, near or far, faded orange or

328

striped, patched and bellying, rakish-slanted or stolidly rectangular, even on my limited horizon.

The hoarse shouts of the crews, cross-wind from each other, and the froth and leap of the waters all spoke with one virile voice: it was Summer, the river was bounding away from the brick City and bearing me heart-bounding on it.

When the sun was high there was much tacking of sails by men scrambling in what rigging there was, and some of the crates farthest from where I lay began to be shifted, with grunting.

I braced myself for the rapidly approaching climax of my lovely illicit passage; pushed the salt-stiff hair back from my eyes and tried moving what parts of me I could.

Presently I heard bustle of a different sort, far more voices than the crew possessed, a different sound to the splash, and though we still lurched and rocked I could tell we had nearly stopped because of the slackening of the wind on my eyeballs—the rest of my face and body was by now too numb with continuous wind to feel it at all. There was the creaking of ropes and the men began singing, all together, some song in a foreign language with few words and those few much-repeated in a slow beat-beating rhythm. I peeped out.

Yes, we had berthed and were unloading.

All I could see of shore was that it was a high-sided stone wharf, equipped with great metal rings for the ships' ropes, and that it rose in stone steps which were covered with the most active crowd I'd ever seen. I could see no buildings behind them, but perhaps if I strained my neck—

Long before I was in the right frame of mind, the crates hiding me were yanked aside.

There was a split instant while I was still not-seen, and then—

"We-e-ell," said a gravelly voice and I was looking straight ahead at a pair of wide salt-rimed boots.

This was an abrupt change from the endless crates which had been my companions, and there was yet another moment suspended before I raised my head and met the eyes of the captain himself who had been assisting in unloading. You could tell he was the captain, Gods know, not by the quality of his clothes but because he was wearing several.

He stood looking down at me with one fist on his hip, thumb hooked in weapon-belt, the other hand pulling at his lip.

"Found something, Shaj?"

"My oath, yes," said the captain.

The other speaker came forward. He was not the mate as I had expected, but a visitor just fresh from shore, a tall, lean man in a black robe, caught in folds to one side by a plain gold belt. As the newcomer's eyes rested on me I was sure I had met that gaze somewhere before (always memories, after all, catching up with you, but it was not an unpleasant memory).

"Just wanting, sir, to show you the prize of our cargo," said the captain, "and . . . "

"If you stand back I'll have room to stand up," I said.

"And I'm not sure that you haven't found the prize," said the newcomer.

The captain automatically stepped back and I got shakily to my feet. My ankles were for a moment too stiff to hold me up, and I put a hand to the crates behind me to support me. Before I touched them the newcomer had placed an arm round me and held me the moment I needed.

"She's not part of my cargo, you know," the captain apologized. "She's a stowaway."

"Evidently."

"Yeah."

I was the apex of the triangle. They considered me while I considered them, the circulation returning to my legs and my mind like a frog's tongue leaping for a fly a quarter-inch out of reach—where had I met this man before, and if we had met before did he recognize me? It was impossible to tell from his eyes, candid though their consideration seemed.

The captain wore in his right ear a red jewel which glinted in the sunlight and hypnotized me a little. He couldn't wear anything in his other ear, you could see under his coarse hair and half-healed scar where it had been. That must have been quite a recent fight. It was much warmer in the sun when we were not on the move.

"Excuse me, sir," I said to the tall man. "I've a feeling we've met before, but I can't put a name to your face."

"More or less what I was about to ask you," said the captain. "Usual questions with stowaways. Who are you?"

"I can't pay you for the journey I've had," I said. "I'd better make that clear at the outset. But I've had only a night and three-quarters of a day, and they were cramped and cold—and no food."

"Ho. And have you reached your destination, or aren't you satisfied with the time of your discovery?"

"I'm quite happy here, thank you."

330

*"Good."*

He continued to pull at his lip, red-brown in his beard, then turned to the other and burst out, "Damnedest things, stowaways. Rare and you never can tell with them. It is true you've met her someplace, sir?"

"It's possible she's seen me."

"Of course. You don't remember noticing her? Probably seen you in one of your processions. Do you want her?" said the captain on a kind of open-handed appeal. "There's nothing I can do with a young lady, what with people unwilling to take her on the market because they'd be afraid she's been stolen, and she's obviously one, for all her lack of *means* . . . " I was longing for him to bow and apologize for my uncomfortable journey but going that far did not occur to him.

"What would *I* do with her?" said the tall man, amused, but with a strange inflexion in his voice.

The captain looked as though he'd committed a social solecism but didn't think it would be taken too badly. "Ah, you should know that better'n me," he said. "There's always the vaults for secrets . . . "

"Why did you leave the Capital?" the man asked me.

I was startled. At first I thought he must have recognized me after all and remembered seeing me in the City, then I realized it was obvious where I'd come from by the number of days I'd said my voyage had lasted.

"I was fed up there," I said.

"And what about your poor parents?" cried the captain virtuously. "They might pay to get you back?" he suggested.

"I've none."

"No guardian?"

I thought briefly of the General, my legal guardian, in whose care my mother placed me. "No guardian."

I looked round me. "What is this place," I asked.

The captain began with hoarse pride to recite the full name of his ship, foreign and full of ceremoniously-guttural words, but I said, "No, I mean the name of this town."

"Thought you said you meant to come here?" stared the captain.

"No, I didn't."

"This is the Superlativity's Temple-town," said the tall man.

At that I recognized him as the Priest Kaselm. Now I was not so sure that he could possibly recognize me, he'd hardly noticed me and I'd been a boy then. Why had his face suggested a pleasant memory? Gods know, it had been a terrible

331

occasion, neither had I thought at the time that his keen shrewd gaze had struck me as at all likeable.

"I need lodging and food and I've no money," I said. "Can you tell me an inn that needs a girl?"

"Several, but not your sort," interpolated the captain chuckling.

"No," said the Priest.

I was taken aback by such a flat denial. "I've no right to ask, but can't you advise me?"

"Come with me."

Without giving myself time to catch my breath at his abrupt decision, I followed him—I had to, he was already on the gangplank. He was my only hope at the moment, and this morning I had made myself a motto I meant to keep like a rule—"All or nothing; you can expect to obtain nothing without demand or risk."

I have already lived long enough in the Outside to know that I have led a far more adventurous life since I left the tower of my childhood than most people ever do. And when I was little I thought that everyone in the World lived lives of incredible interest! So they do, compared to my early life—but fate is making up to me for that now. I felt very confident as behind the Priest Kaselm I threaded my way through the crowd up the wharf-steps. I will go on making my way through adventures.

So far I have come out of most of them reasonably well, though I am neither strong, athletic, very knowledgeable nor devastatingly beautiful. Even when the worst comes to the worst, somehow one eventually does find some reserve of power, of *acceptance* therefore resurgence, which enables one to emerge after all worthwhile. So I thought now—for though I knew that there are in the World kinds of *the worst* from which no one can ever recover, I sensed through all my youth and health and resilience, in my toes to the tips of my fingers to my breast-tips to the ends of my hair, and all young and real and *mine,* that I should always withstand diseases and maiming.

The Priest did not turn to see whether I still followed—now I came to think of it, he had not even turned after he first said, "Come with me" to see whether I followed at all. Indeed it was rather difficult through a crowd of this turbulence.

Presently doubts began to creep through me, but so exalted was I this morning that they did not bother me at all.

"Escape"—that was actually the story of my life.

Only once had I met tragedy face to stark face, and it had

332

not marked me. In deeper moments I wondered if it should have marked me, and knew myself lacking, but for the fact that it had not I blamed the big terrible bird, and from it too I had now separated myself. I! I was learning, really learning at last, the intoxication of the reality of self.

Suppose the Priest is taking me to the lair of the Superlativity, suppose he remembers having seen me as a Northern army-server, and wishes to sacrifice me on the altar of his masters' hate for their allies? No matter what he means, it is what my fate means that will be.

A white wall leaned before us without warning—the Priest took a bold black key from his belt and unlocked a rotting wooden gate in the wall. This gate he locked again after I'd followed him through it.

We were in a green garden, and so thick was the wall that the garden was also quiet.

Still without a word the Priest led me across the springy sward, past a bed of pink plants, under another arched gate, along a cold, blue-white, stone passage unlit, through a nail-studded black door and into a small rather bare room where he signalled me to seat myself—I asked first for a fountain-room, he directed me farther up the passage, I came back to the room and seated myself on a stool opposite him.

"Well?" I said composedly. It seemed I had lost even that persistent habit of feeling my heart beat hard and irregular every so often in the nerve-racking life I lead.

The Priest leaned forward, elbows on knees, hands in opposite sleeves, conversational mouth pushed a little forward.

"Are you here as a spy for the Northern General Zerd?"

"No."

"Then . . . ?"

"I should like sanctuary from him." I paused. "You remember having seen me—in his—household?"

"On the occasion of a very interesting entertainment he provided."

"I am a hostage whose—privileges he abused. I fled from the army during the confusion of its being placed under tentage—you've heard of that?—and beg sanctuary."

"How do I know you are not a spy?"

"Send me anywhere if you will not keep me here. I did not mean to come here." I thought of liquidation by these people of the priests of the older sect. "I wanted merely to leave the Capital. And if you decide to let me stay I will work at anything; you can place me under any surveillance."

"You say you were a hostage. From what land?"

"The land north of the forests, north of the plains, north of your mountains—the land south of the Northern Kingdom—"

"The land of a female dictator?"

"I am her daughter."

He leaned forward, rocking the stool, black eyes intent and mouth pushed into a silent whistle.

"You would have to prove that."

"I can see no need to prove it. I can only insist that I am a hostage and not a spy. Besides, I can't see how I could prove it."

"The Dictatress has had reputed liaison with only one man —The High Priest there."

My spine became just a little colder and this time I did not answer.

"What is your name?" Kaselm asked.

"Do you know what it should be if I am telling the truth?"

"Yes."

"And what will happen to me if I give the right answer?"

He smiled for the first time since I'd met him that morning, but it wasn't a reassuring smile, the amusement was too cold, too self-shared. "Now you say *if* instead of *when*—and your hesitation is most eloquent. Well, Cija, come with me to the Superlativity."

That gentleman admitted me almost at once. There was hardly any time to wait with the dry-smiling Kaselm outside the August Apartments. The messenger returned almost immediately to admit us, and I could not tell from Kaselm's behaviour whether I were to prove myself to an order of death. After all, a High Priest's daughter in a town where a priest's chastity and austerity was his point of honour—

The Superlativity lives in four rooms farther up the same blue-white stone passage. They are larger rooms than Kaslem's, but as austere.

He himself came forward to greet us. A gaunt man, with sunken cheeks and large-pupiled obviously short-sighted eyes, he was surprisingly not much taller than myself. He wore a scrupulously neat, belted, black robe, skirts fluttering round him like a brisk dowager's, and his gaze was all for me. We all three seated ourselves. The whole conversation took place in the presence of a black-robed young man who was writing over a desk before a window. The window overlooked the pleasant sward-stretch.

"You—forgive me, we must be sure—*call yourself* the

334

daughter of the High Priest of the land south of the Northern Kingdom?" eagerly asked the Superlativity.

"Yes," I said, not too vehemently.

"And your name—?"

"Cija."

"Your father sent you—a goddess, descended from parents each descended from parents descended on both side from the gods—as a hostage with the Northern hordes?"

"There were reasons . . . You know a lot about the tiny country divided from you by so many dangerous lands."

I had risked that. To my surprise he was almost apologetic.

"Please do not think this catechism presumptuous. You understand we cannot indulge outselves in mistakes. However, we shall soon learn if you are indeed the goddess Cija; I know much of that land from my own High Priest Kaselm's personal experience of it during his years of travel—ah, yes, there can be little communication between us but your father is in his country working for the same ends as we in ours—the Pious Rape of the Introvert Soil of Atlan—"

"Why did your father send you with the Northerners?" Kaselm asked.

So they revered my father—I must risk the possibility that they were pretending esteem for him in order to lead me on. The Superlativity, in the manner of great little men, seemed intense but transparent enough.

"There was a prophecy at my birth—" I said.

I had to tell them even of my assassination-task, but it only aroused the Superlativity's sympathy. He patted me on the shoulder with his solid, papery-covered hand—a hand rather like my mother's, but severely innocent of rings.

"That is all over, Goddess. In your sincere *efforts* to dispose of the monster, you have in effect nullified the prophecy. You are too far from your beloved country ever to bring it to harm. A noble sacrifice, self-imposed banishment. Noble efforts against odds too great for a young girl alone even if fired with divine blood."

But he was immediately brisk again; you had the impression that his emotions were in rigidly separated cupboards, just like his papers in the care of that industrious young black-robe over there, cupboards which he could open and shut with an automatic, perfect sense of what was appropriate to each moment of each occasion. It is an unattractive chilling fact, of which adjectives applied to himself he constitutionally can have no inkling, that he is utterly sincere in these Emotions as far as

335

they go. It is not that by discipline he keeps them in their place and forbids them to affect his work of administration: he is simply what his own type call a model human being. He lacks some kind of core—but I can't call such a lack a drawback, seeing that it has left him free to build up his own clear-cut empire.

He would shed tears with a man apprehensive of execution, then with quivering distaste order the execution. I should guess he never does anything with cold disinterest—he *feels* the emotion appropriate to each action.

Anyway, I convinced him of my identity.

Apparently, my birth-prophecy was a hush-hush bit of knowledge which even Kaselm (who seems to be a man of resource) had difficulty getting hold of. My own knowledge of it, combined with several other matters I mentioned, was conclusive.

My mother was not mentioned at all.

I took care not to mention her. If they hold my father in such esteem, they must hate her, his rival for rulership.

I longed to ask what my father is like, but dared not betray such ignorance.

As I was led away to the apartments and slaves which were to be mine, I wondered how much Kaselm knew that he'd not told the Superlativity, and if he'd even tell him now. He had been the colleague of my father, who wants me dead—had apparently discussed me with my father, since he knew my name and the prophecy—and yet seemingly did not know my father's hate for me? He has not even asked me why I was in boy's clothes when he first saw me.

No, the Priest Kaselm is playing a game of his own. It is almost certainly a very deep one. I must watch myself when I am with him—It will do me no good to watch *him* when I am with him, his bland, lean, black-a-vised face will tell me nothing.

I received my biggest surprise of the day when I came to my own apartments.

They are tremendously luxurious.

They are in the Court attached to the Temple—a Court at the moment chock-full of the Southern nobility most of whom seem to have deserted the Capital as soon as the Northern army marched in. This was because they didn't want to be in the midst of the trouble—and trouble they knew there'd be. The exacerbation of the allies was planned well ahead on the part of the South.

336

This court has also been the home of Southern nobility for longer than it has been the home of the Southern religion-emperor.

The result is that the Court, while paying *very elaborate* lip-service to the religion, continues in its own sweet way. It seems to me most corrupt. The Superlativity keeps to his own bare suite in the Temple and can't know much of his subjects' *life*, only of their elaborate attention to ceremony, ritual and his theories. But the Court is full of black-robes, scurrying here and there on religious and/or administrative business. I think some of them are too unworldly, or too sure of their way, to see beyond the Court's surface; others are power-seekers, toadies to Court as much as to Temple.

And one great lady has already said outright to me, "A fastidious noblewoman must always prefer her lover to be a priest. Ordinary men are all very well for common women: but a priest's manhood is superior because it is never stunted by the wearing of breeches."

It is so nice to be priggish in my Diary about the corruptness of this Court; then to go down and enjoy being made a fuss of by all the corrupt noblemen and some of the corrupt noble-women.

It is so nice to be Goddess again; but I am not quite certain about this. Their words have the correct reverence, but the tones and behaviour and glances and actions of all the men seem to show that they think of me only as a very young (and very desirable) girl. It is not that they don't believe I've divine blood: just that they don't know how much that ought to mean.

Another nice thing is that though I am the fashion because I am new here, I think the way they treat me as desirable is sincere. This is the kind of civilized society to which I am afraid I am just suited. Not stupid children, nor envious peasants, nor uncouth young officers on their worst, most informal be-haviour before what they called a strumpet—This is a Court of polished sex-addicts, the majority young, some jaded, all with time on their hands, genuinely thrilled by anything new, unresentful of the Chase which they find all-absorbing. They all know how to make themselves pleasant, they have won-derful manners and know almost exactly when to use them, though the fashion at the moment is for mock-boorish stand-ing-off-ceremony.

The pretty women are divided in their behaviour towards

me. A percentage, those who were till now the accepted "goddesses" or were chasing noblemen now devoted to me—these ladies are very jealous and do anything to throw a spoke in my wheel. Of this the noblemen are all aware. It all makes for more fun for everyone.

Other women, equally pretty, have found that they genuinely like me. We make good companions for each other and have already had lots of very happy times. They know that in a few months, more or less, my brilliant meteor will have settled and I shall be ranged with them when another extra-fabulous newcomer arrives. But when a meteor has settled, the other stars rise once more.

I am having such a really lovely time mainly because I gather I have a new sort of appeal. I found it out almost by accident but it is now obvious.

I am not very witty, I can't indulge in hours of brilliant back chat and I sometimes take seriously things which turn out to be sophisticated and long-established witticisms. This amuses people who have lots of mounting hysteria at my expense. I never resent it, I am not even embarrassed by it, because it is done openly and with fondness.

I am sincere, usually tell the truth because I have an ineradicable idea that people want to hear the truth in answer to their questions, also I am shy. None of the other ladies have these qualities, but are richly endowed with their opposites: it is the way they have been brought up.

I am also obviously virtuous; bets are being laid on to whom I shall give in first. I am not supposed to know about them.

I am virtuous, not because no one attracts me: almost everyone does. That's the trouble; they have almost the same appeal. It would seem so wasteful to take one kind, gay, tender, handsome, irresponsible, protective young lover when I could have had any one of nearly a hundred others.

At times, yes, I wake and find my body lonely for the love Smahil taught it to be so used to; in the night I wake blindly and reach out to absence. I find no shoulder for my head, no throat for my brief sleepy mouth, no hands for my breasts as though they were sleepy doves which might fly away, no Smahil to mutter his dreams. The bed becomes a vast abyss, acres wide, and I am tiny and lost in it.

At times, yes, I yearn till occasionally I smile with surprise to find tears in my eyes from the very intensity of my yearning, for a lover who would look after me, never demand too much of me, and not spend his time finding jealous fault with me; but no, really, it is too much to ask me to do, take a whole new lover, another human being. I have never needed people and don't have to start now. Of course I am not lonely.

There is also a large minority, a leavening of respectable nobles and their women, old or elderly or even young, who look on my set and therefore myself as nothing more than—well, I won't use the word. They certainly never would.

These people whisk their skirts away from me when I pass.

It is all rather unjust, I am neither really in one camp nor in the other, but the camp that provides most fun likes it just so.


Everybody wears fabulous clothes, including myself.

Almost all the clothes at Court have been at least partially designed by their owners. Original ideas, no matter how bizarre, count at the moment far more than elegance.

Every morning everybody takes a long walk in The Cloisters (they are vastly long-pillared arcades surrounding gardens open to the sky) in order to exchange gossip and compare their clothes with everyone else's. A ridiculous custom has grown up of waving your arms in the strangest gesticulations at whoever you're speaking to. You place your arms in any one of the hundreds of possible variations: you hold them there for about twenty seconds, then change to another position. You can hold your arms out at different angles, place one on your hip and the other on your head—anything at all strange, in fact. All this while you talk and laugh quite naturally. After fifteen or twenty minutes with one companion, you leave each other by some mutual timing-instinct and move on to the next friend, acquaintance or enemy. You can do the rounds of The Cloisters singly, in pairs, or in threes. Any larger group is infra dig till you get to about ten, which is again permissible. All these rules, crazy gestures, etc., are only for The Cloisters. Anywhere else in the Court you behave normally (more or less).

Clothes take almost any pattern but there are male and female motifs.

Women's dress revolves almost all round the *veil*: this floats from the head, the shoulders, the top of a peaked head-dress, or even from one wrist. If it is a long veil, its end is held by the little attendant page almost everyone has. I have a conventionally delicious, rather insolent nobleman, very chubby and with marvellous red curls, five years old. I wish I could have had Ow. A secondary motif in the ladies' clothing is the elaborate matching of the trousers to the dress. This has always been the basis of peasants' clothes, which of course are made, trousers and dress, from the same piece of woven cloth—Now at this Court the nobility have adopted and embellished it.

The central motif of the men's dress is the codpiece. There are some adorable ones, on which much thought and fond care have obviously been lavished: some stick out inches, most are ingenious shapes, such as a big shell or a huge fruit drenched in appropriate scent.

It is a lovely Court—most of its life revolving about the bedrooms, the gardens, the staircases, banqueting halls and of course the Cloisters.

There are flowers everywhere, trained up the walls if they can't be present any other way, or blossoming creepers encircling the pillars. These incredibly tall, incredibly slender, silvery blue pillars rise everywhere, ostensibly holding the rafters, or flanking the staircases which recede into watery blue distance in stately convolutions, up and down. Fountains spring over balustrades of peculiarly high, slender, narrow marble staircases rearing like steep hills in and out of the lines of pillars and the complicated rafters of the Court, sometimes in the open air for no reason.

(I am told these fountains are turned off in winter so only their statues remain, decorative jewelled, metal figures and abstract shapes without the yards-high jets springing from their orifices.)

Every here and there in the Court, from a base of flowers and fountains rises a vastly tall, glass screen. The water spreads itself upon this, fanwise against it, or jets from its very top and drops swiftly, a tempestuous, artificial waterfall.

The rafters of the Court halls are very mazy. White and turquoise birds perch on them or fly cooing amongst them. There are droppings everywhere, one has to get used to them, even on one's favourite dress, even on the banqueting table.

There are lots of organized games, and almost everyone can play a musical instrument or sing. There are songs of which everyone knows the words and which are sung all the time till they are loved to death and the next song becomes the fashion. Every song harps on love and presents it in a lyrically physical way which promises all joy but ignores the existence of any spirit. They are a form of art, for the words if heard or read without their music are puerile in content and punk as writing, and the music if heard without the words is empty rhythm; together they lend an emotional depth to each other, their meaning *and* their quality, and also to love, life . . .

I persuade myself, almost, that life here is not an unreal dream, that it can last and last without cloying me, without wakening any ambition in me, without dissolving into war.

I am very happy.

Occasionally the Court receives news of the Northern army's manoeuvres.

I have pieced together what has evidently been happening.

Zerd drilled his troops unmercifully for nearly a week outside the Capital, to harden them for marching, but the Southerners said it was because he wanted to regain harsh discipline. One dark night he marched them on about ten miles—towards the Southern coast but also towards this temple-town of the Superlativity. He is now immobile again, a focus of conjecture to everyone—does he intend to visit the Superlativity? Does he (horrors!) intend to make the Atlan campaign himself, dispensing after all with the troublesome allies, and to overcome the Southern fleet on the coast and sail complete with secret of formula intact?

Meanwhile he just sits tight there, under tentage again, drilling all day (now, according to reports, with a more practised air as if merely to keep boredom at bay) on the plain beside the river I sailed down at the beginning of Summer, a maddening mystery to everyone.

I bet he's enjoying himself in his grim, competent, contemptuous, vivid way.

I escaped today from a picnic. There were so many rustly billowy skirts, so much back-chat, so much fuss about where to sit—perfectly delightful mossy hollows were impossible because everyone's skirts were too wide to fit in—and I do like compliments, but not when they are couched in difficult metaphors that you have to be awfully quick at answering. It's not fair, it's easy enough to make a compliment but horrible to have to answer right away and in the same metaphor, and it gives you absolutely no time to gloat over actually getting the compliment, and if you just blush and look away you are laying yourself open to being sniggered at.

I found that the grounds stretch right down to the river—and beyond too, only I couldn't find a bridge.

They get quite wild, untended, and bordering the river there is a part of the orchard where, as I ventured into it, I thought "I shouldn't think anyone has been here for ages."

The trees, five different kinds of fruit-trees, had been planted wide apart but now are tangled together. The undergrowth is thick, not not alarming—that gentle country kind of undergrowth, furry seed-balls, tickling-headed grasses, docks near any nettles, pleasant with bees. I wandered amongst it, my head bent, watching the tiny insects scurrying and passing each other on perpendicular stems. The foliages were tangled together by loops of flowering creeper, and in Spring the mass of blossom in this old-orchard must be tremendous, but now the trees were dotted rather sparsely with little wrinkled fruits, the kind that come from trees whose inspiration is just about over so I was breathing in all the scents but watching the undergrowth and picking occasional spiders off my frills—when I banged into a foot.

At first I thought it was a bough or creeper my head had struck, and tried to brush it away without raising my eyes—but it swung rather nastily.

I stood there, among the pretty flowers, looking up at the row of men. Six men, and a small boy, in peasants' and artisans' clothes, and all in varying stages of decomposition, one of the men nearly quite rotted away. But the latest could only have been strung up yesterday or this morning at the earliest—the cheeks and lips still pink and fresh-smooth, the skin almost pulsing with life, a beard, I'd've sworn it, pushing itself through. I stood there watching them, one of a society which had been in this part of the orchard for some time—the men and boy dancing a little on every breeze, the bees communicating with them, a couple of spiders friendly in a web depending from one foot to another, the web lissome and elastic when necessary, a few buzzing blueblottles crawling in and out of clothing folds—of course the nearly decomposed gentleman was nearly alive again with flies, whirring, scintillating, gregarious chips of fur-legged lapis-lazuli. There was a sweetish stale smell—of course each must have had his own separate smell according to his age but all together—oh, no, really, it's not a think to stay calm about. I stood there far too long, several seconds, so every detail was stamped indelibly into my brain as I turned to dash away, blundering through grasses and tangles, splashing through a stream hidden under fronds, insects spattering from what I touched like specks of spray—

The nightmares have caught me by the throat again. They have found me in my new happy existence—I think the sight in the orchard laid me open to them.

342

I hear vague knockings at night as I start awake in bed, which is soon clammy with my own sweat—they seem to advance, retreat, advance as if anxious to break through- -not the wall, they're not against the wall, they're always just above my head and the tempo quickens, I'm sure they'll break through one night, *one* night soon, and then—? And yet as soon as I'm not hearing them I doubt if I have, memories of the nightmare, I tell myself, and everyone has nightmares.

I think the time has come for me to face it—at least the question: Is something trying to get at me? Oh, God, at least let me keep the question-mark, not—not Something is . . .

God, Cija, face it, write it down, put it on your page, can a nightmare break through into waking life and *that* into- -into vivid supra-life, something reaching to destroy, something out there intent on me, drawing ever nearer, reaching its concentration out to *me* all the time from the other side- -nearer and nearer, no longer whispers as in the City, here in the kind laughing Court that leaves me quite alone at night while I lie sweating and rigid, small and unknowledgeable, and terrified and utterly alone, while it draws steadily nearer night by night, knocking, not stealthily but calmly, little groups of knocks on the wall separating it from reality—quite ready to flow through—reaching all ready and eager to reach for *me*—its long goal—and it may *be* tonight.

The talk at the evening feast was all of the Northern army's approach.

"Pouf, what can the Dragon-General do even if he does come here? With his straggling little army of fretful novices—"

"Rest assured, he'll not even reach here."

"Well, I couldn't be sorrier. I'd like at least to see him before it's all over. He's said to be devastating."

"Couldn't we all arrange an excursion and go and watch while our Temple Guard do their slaughtering? You might see him quite close to."

Forialk peeled some nuts for me and teased me to open my mouth so he could feed me. He is the one with a conceited line of blond beard emphasizing his jaw-line—which, I must admit, is a good one, young and strong and clear-cut and arrogant. Would he keep me safe tonight, when eventually even this late-feast reached its finale and I had to go up and—fear—? In his arms, would anything intangible be able to grip me?

343

I explored his dark-blue gaze. Deep down there was more potential kindness than I'd expected. The pupils widened and I could not look away—I realized that, with a stab of triumph, the boy had misinterpreted my intentness.

(Why I think of him as a boy I don't know, he's several years older than I am.)

Suddenly in our own private quietness at that noisy table, he turned my hand over and ran his finger down the back of it.

I smiled indulgently even while the tingle went through me.

How many young men have used my hand so? A favourite trick among the officers who frequented the Beauty's tent—

Couldn't I really find someone better?

And yet—tonight—I would want to run sobbing pleading after him, as soon as I clicked my door shut on myself alone tonight—

I took my hand from his, careful not to snatch it.

"I'm not hungry tonight, Forialk. Are you?"

His eyes widened on mine, he shook his head.

"Let's walk, outside."

I rose and walked away from the table. I didn't bother to turn to see him following me. As we went between the tables to the courtyard, questions and those eternal conundrums were laughed at us, but no one was seriously interested. They are all so used to my unassailable virtue—they are quite sure it will crack one day but it never seems likely at the moment. However, as we got nearer the courtyard entrance something in Forialk's eager, taut, smug-cornered smile must have awakened suspicion—the young noble Ecir caught the velvet swing of Forialk's sleeve and said quietly, "Where are you taking the Goddess?"

Forialk disengaged his sleeve, smiling his provocative smile.

Ecir started to his feet.

"Goddess—" he offered his arm, his eyes pleading.

He had realized the imminence of urgency.

I glanced from one to the other, while we were watched with covert interest by those near, openly by those farther up the table.

While there was still time to choose, which did I prefer of these two who had presented themselves out of a hundred tonight for my need?

As I glanced from Forialk's impatient arrogance (he was tapping his foot and his eyes on me were hot) to Ecir's speaking glance, I realized that Ecir is in love with me. His lips were

344

trembling, he was pouring a message to me through his eyes. At a word from me Forialk would be dealt with—But they both knew it was for me to choose. I hesitated no longer after I pictured the involvement of giving myself to someone who would tell me he adores me and would later tell me that gave him rights where I am concerned, who would most probably become wild at times and other times glower at me from corners—I placed my fingers again on Forialk's sleeve and we went out together without looking again at Ecir.

In the courtyard the tall fountains were striped with starlight. There was cooing from innumberable hidden sleepy birds.

I knew Forialk was looking at me but I kept my profile clear.

This courtyard was not deserted, there were figures in the colonades, lovers mostly, but there a group of pages talking with spasmodic horseplay in torchlight, and now and then a sedate or scurrying black-robe, and there the priest Kaselm, for his stride at its most casual is easily recognized from anyone else's.

The next courtyard was nearly empty, and silent but for fountains and birds, and a breeze in the creepers.

Forialk turned me to face him when I was about to walk on.

"Whoa, what's the hurry?"

"I thought we came out for a walk."

I was being not only disencouraging but rather obvious. My usual idea is not to show that I know what they want of me in starlit courtyards—it saves embarrassment at times. This evening I couldn't care less. It was enough to make his eyes flicker uncertainly before mine and he walked mechanically a few steps before recollecting himself and again turning me to him.

His hands were firm on my shoulders, as I stared straight ahead at his shapely lips they parted and his large teeth caught the starlight.

He looked down at me for a moment, then gave a strange tender little laugh in his throat and pressed me to him, his hands strong against my shoulder-blades. I had to hang on to the points of his big starched collar in order not to lose my balance.

I didn't return his kiss but I was complaisant till I realized the character of the kiss. It was a passionate kiss, greedy but not hungry, not respectful enough considering that I am the little goddess Cija, most sought-after noblewoman of the Court and just about the one with the best blood, and he knew this is the first time I've been kissed since arriving at Court. He's tried once or twice before, himself.

I stood there under his kiss, my mind now working separately, while he worried at my mouth like a young bear at feeding-time.

This man would make a rotten lover. Well, for my purpose anyway. He'd be generous and gay and ardent. But he'd pooh-pooh any ideas that he had to stay with me all of every night. He'd be bound to be off dicing and drinking in places where a lady couldn't follow and wouldn't be wanted if she did. And it would be even harder to change from him than from someone like Ecir who's in love with me—once he had me he'd take care to keep me because I'm the prize of the Court. There'd be annoying ugly scenes, maybe duels.

At least it wasn't a phoney-maudlin kiss, he wasn't insulting me by pretending to be in love with me. But it was time it was ended—I was finding it difficult to breathe, anyway.

I stepped back and twisted from his grasp when he wasn't expecting me to.

Now that he'd kissed me his gaze burned into mine so that I shivered.

"Please, Forialk," I said, "let's walk on."

It was as if he hadn't bothered to hear my words, he reached for me again.

"Or even go back," I added.

"I thought this was what you wanted."

My gaze dropped. I had indeed led him on. If I denied it, he'd believe me because of my reputation, he'd think he'd made a mistake. Still . . . It was better not to be frank, and he was no good, I must discard him even at the risk of a night of horror on my own.

"I'm sorry, Forialk. It's not what I wanted. Will you take me on to look at the gardens—or back, if you're not interested in the gardens—?"

I looked at him almost humbly.

He took a deep breath of the darkness. Suddenly he gripped my hands in his and led me over to a bench half-covered in a seclusion of tangled creepers. We sat facing the whites of each other's eyes, which was just about all we could see there, our knees nearly touching.

"Now that I've got you here I'm certainly not taking you back in. Look—You're acting strangely this night, Cija . . . " He tried the name on his palate. Of course it's not the first time he's used it, but now he was giving it an intimate flavour. "You're like a disconnected doll—You don't seem to care about anything much, yet something's worrying you. Give. What's up?"

His voice became unbelievably gentle.

"Tell me . . . ?"

I felt the wry twist of my mouth. I thought of telling Forialk that I have nightmares, that I am neurotic enough to think them so bad I was prepared to take a lover to keep me company during them, that his kiss had convinced me he was no good . . .

"Cija?"

Pause.

"You are worried about something, aren't you?"

I had hesitated too long now for a denial.

"Yes, I am, but it's nothing—only I'm a little depressed."

"Let me fix it?" There was a pause of a couple of heart-beats before he added hurriedly, "Let me try?" Then his mouth was down on mine again, his tongue was ruthless, the closed firmness of his embrace invincible. It was a very—not exactly ungentle, but an exacting way of comforting—But curiously enough, I did find it comforting. It was so real.

Swimmingly I raised my eyelids and his eyes glinted down at me, probably slightly crossed because of the close range, but so unnerving as to be endearing.

When he comes up for air, I promised myself vaguely, I'll entrust myself to him, I'll tell my loneliness and fears and he'll say I'm sweet and be kind and carry me up that big, chilly, creeper-grown staircase until it winds under the rafters and comes to his living-quarters.

Forialk's head was yanked back by a tense-knuckled hand. immediately recognized the big topaz ring.

Forialk turned with a curse, saw his assailant, released me and stood up. He wasn't allowed more than a second before Ecir knocked him down again with a crack that shivered the creepers even before Forialk crashed into them. Forialk started up, immediately furious, and there were some fierce blows with both boys swaying on the balls of their feet. I watched for a minute but neither even looked at me. I couldn't be sure which would win, they were evenly matched. I couldn't even be sure which I wanted to win. I backed away, found myself in the shadows of the colonnade, someone steadying with my shoulders.

"Take it easy, they probably won't kill each other."

347

"Holy Kaselm! I'm quite calm, I assure you. But aren't you going to stop them?"

"I'm not going to inconvenience myself so, Goddess—Unless, of course, your wish is to be my command?" He bowed in the gloom.

I pushed my hair out of my eyes. "Oh, no, by all means don't bother—" I seated myself on the plinth of a pillar. The sound of blows continued out in the starlight but I wasn't watching. What is going to become of me tonight? I was busy wondering, and it wasn't pleasant for me.

"You were having trouble?" In spite of his tone, I felt the question too familiar to be courteous. "I'm sorry I didn't know as I was passing. I assure you it would then have been myself who would have interfered." He set a foot on the plinth beside me, rested a hand on his upraised knee, his chin in the palm of the hand. In the starlight shiftingly magnified by the fountains, I saw the wide absent-minded meditation of the black eyes. The worldly black robe, caught in folds to one side of the belt, fell away from the priest's long lean thigh, long, hard, flat muscles and sinews tautening the black tights.

"You are trembling, Goddess?" But he wasn't looking at me, nor at the fight.

"I am cold, Holy Kaselm."

"That's too bad. You are wearing a velvet wrap and it's a Summer evening."

"I—I am afraid, Holy Kaselm." He waited, and I turned to him and let it come in a rush before I could be sorry and control myself. "Lately I have been having terrible nightmares, really terrible ones, I am afraid of being alone at night, I have no one to turn to, I cannot sleep with my friends among the noblewomen—"

"They are usually accompanied by harsher comrades?"

I bowed my head.

"They—sleep lightly for companions, Holy Kaselm."

"You do well to blush for them, Goddess. So you wish for a safe place of sleep, with an unfrightened companion close by? Your personal maid is unobtainable?"

"At night, I would not like to claim her away from—for the sake of night-fears—"

"And yet they are really bad?"

I whispered bleakly, "Yes."

I added, "I couldn't be calling her all the time. I need another presence—something to keep them away—"

"Them?"

"I hear knockings . . . " I began to cry. I gulped myself to a stop, shuddered, staring quietly ahead again.

"If you agree, Goddess, I shall offer you the sanctity of the priestly Corridors until you feel yourself safe again from these night-terrors. This means that you would sleep in my cell. I would be a few feet away, readily within call. I would know as soon as you were in distress."

I turned my head to stare at him.

"I can only say Thank you, Holy Kaselm. I—I would be tremendously grateful, it sounds a solution, a security. I have been—May I ask you one thing? Do you believe in ghosts?"

"I don't, Goddess."

"My maid does. It's one of the reasons she'd be no good—"

"I know how terrible dreams can be. I have seen sane men crazy from them—"

A splash recalled us to the fight. Ecir sprawled in the basin of a heavy fountain.

Forialk lurched towards me, bowed when he saw the priest Kaselm. "Your slave, Holy . . . Cija . . . " He presented an arm. There was a bloody contusion on his forehead, his dishevelled hair falling stickily across it, one velvet sleeve hanging in tatters. His mouth was open, he blinked at me from between swollen lids.

"How many teeth have you lost?"

Forialk glanced at the priest, unsure how to take this.

"None, Holy Kaselm—I think."

"I'm going with the priest, Forialk. He has offered me—sanctuary—"

"What are you talking about?"

"I have been having uncomfortable nights. I shall feel better, I am sure, in the holy quiet of the Corridors."

I half-put out my hand, for an instant touched the split lip which so recently had been whole hard on mine. The priest was already walking away. "Have someone see to you, my lord . . . "

He woke into life again as I began to follow the priest.

"Cija—Goddess—You can't go, not with him, that priest is known—"

A fragmentary protest meant nothing to me. I followed Holy Kaselm over the pillars' shadows. My mind and body were already vague, longing for the rest with the confidence which, if strong enough, was all that was needed to defeat the fear.

A single candle hazed the small bare room. I was already in the priest's black shirt, too large for me, between the rough linen sheets, when he returned with a flask of wine and two exquisitely wrought goblets, obviously Temple property and so not to be looked upon as luxury. His shadow wavered over wall and ceiling, surged into the impenetrable, stagnant shadow curving the room's corners.

"Of course, tomorrow the most important parts of your wardrobe will be transferred here. I have enough space."

"Your priests' shirts are very like the officers' shirts of the Northern army, in which they also sleep."

"You have experience of that, naturally." He held out one full goblet to me.

"Yes. I was with the Northern army more than a year. Also the men sleep in their boots—even in billets, at least according to the ladies of your Capital who sued for various damages . . ." I didn't realize till later that I was avoiding an awkwardness.

"Something to eat, bread and cheese?"

"Please. I hear he's coming here?"

"Who?"

"Zerd—"

"Don't worry. He'll not get far with that army. Their regulars were a tiny nucleus before this giant campaign was recruited for—the scum of the Northern drinking-shops. Anyone with any money bought himself off—At a pinch even a war-office can be warred against, but not the little individual officials in it—" Kaselm munched placidly, his shadow jerking a parody of each mastication.

"He's held them so far," I said dubiously. "It wasn't a pretty journey, actually, Holy Kaselm."

"He's a good general, that's acknowledged through the known world. But he's not yet had one battle to try those raw recruits—and men can ford streams hand-in-hand even in the most exotic scenery, it doesn't stop them being raw till they've seen a bit of action—more than half his youthful raggle-taggle will break in battle, and unfortunately for him their first is going to be pretty important."

"I shouldn't think he'd be risking so much if that were so."

"No? He's little to lose, hasn't he? The whole idea was a suicide-jaunt from the first. The Dragon-General has seemed a threat under the Northern King's nose for some years—"

"Isn't it possible Zerd accepted the job with enough faith in
350

his own ability to pull it off, Atlan and all?"

"Anything's possible," the priest agreed, "but I should think he's found out his mistake in the last few months, bogged down by the ominous on every side, trapped, cut off behind our mountains."

"He's dangerous enough. I know he gathers in the tail-ends of every plan-structure before making his next move, he takes account of every aspect of living for his army from movement to movement, week to week—month to month they've survived far more than his King presumably expected. He's brilliant enough to be taking account of the greater plan, too. He's the calmest person in the world. *I* should be very surprised," I said, embarking on a cheese sandwich, "to find that he has ever considered the word failure."

"No matter how brilliant in himself, I don't think we need fear his advent. How could one man hold together such a deplorable force, very aware that they're ludicrously outnumbered in enemy territory—unless he's superhuman."

"He's ab-human. The Superlativity will surely declare open war on an ally whose great-grandmother was a crocodile —who—who can turn any enemies blue like himself, filling them with the poison which is his element but alien to his victims who die within a few days. He must be exterminated!"

The priest turned to stare at me.

"How do you know this?"

I whispered, "I must be one of the only three people in the world who knows this and still live."

"How does he inflict the poison?"

"A bite, a scratch, maybe at times without purpose, through carelessness—I couldn't be sure of the exact way."

"The Superlativity may be interested by this information," Kaselm said thoughtfully, snuffing the candle. I nodded sleepily. "Kill the Demon." I snuggled into my pillow.

What seemed the next instant the room was flooded with light. Bird song liquefied space. The priest· Kaselm was nowhere to be seen.

My sleep must have been immediate and profound—and long. The priest had gone to the Temple morning-meal, leaving me to rouse myself in time for the later breakfast of the Court. I yawned and stretched. I was already feeling better for my sanctuary. I wriggled out of bed and the priest's spare shirt, dressed in my own clothes, went to the doorway, started down the long, bare, fresh, clean corridor. I felt well and alive. It

351

occurred to me for the first time that the priest might have drugged my wine to ensure a profound sleep. The friendly sound of my footsteps kept up with me.

Out in the Temple grounds, where I'd never been before, I realized just how early it was though. I'd emerged from the wrong end of the corridor and had a mile, perhaps a little less, to traverse before I got back to Court. I didn't mind a bit. The grass was silver-gold with dew. Flower petals could just about be seen unfurling. The morning was swift with that kind of movement, but there was not another human being to be seen.

The resilient turf stretched up. I followed the incline beside a long white wall, formed of blocks decayed in places. There were not even any windows. I felt so healthy and happy, it was the last place in the world I expected to hear groans.

Muffled groans, as if subterranean, but with no attempt at concealment. They were reckless wild groans, the expression of despair, but the angry expression.

Such bad-tempered hopelessness from below ground—I knelt beside the wall. There was a crash as if something unwieldy but substantial had been thrown. My hand came to a rusty grating—the top segment of a barred window, just enough to admit air to an underground chamber—the rest of the window must face earth. I scrabbled a bit and pulled away enough weed to be able to peer through the grating. There was nothing, no darkness, nothing, a suffused colourless yet murky gloom.

I put my lips to the grating and called clearly but softly.

"Is anybody there?"

There was hardly an instant of breathless silence, then a rush and suddenly strong, pale fingers were round the bars before me, then fast groping savagely out between them. My face was touched before I backed with a gasp; the fingers followed but the hand-knuckles were unable to pass through.

I was afraid I had meddled with a shut-up madman, so I didn't say anything and was getting ready to up and run when a hoarse voice came from the invisible. "Who are you?"

"Who are you?" I countered.

"Who do you think?" The hoarseness stumbled on a laugh. The tone struck me as contemptuous.

"Listen," I said. "I'm no one. I don't belong here. I was passing and I heard you, that's all."

"What do you mean you don't belong here? Are you trespassing?"

352

"I've a right at least to be here, I've been with a priest. What were you throwing?"

"How—?" "When I heard you—'

"Dead rat. At least it was dead when it hit the wall, after I threw it." The fingers were gripping the bars again. "Listen, you sound very young—Why are you talking to me?"

"I don't know. Curiosity, at first, and now I just haven't left yet. Are you shut up down there or can you get out if you like?"

There was a burst of fierce laughter. He was laughing his head off. The fingers shook on the bars.

"You're a criminal? That's a Temple dungeon?"

"Sure, sure, very pretty, all correct."

"Is there anyone else with you?"

"No." He was relaxed again. He sounded uninterested. His fingers were long and the nails jet-black rimmed, the skin a pale tan under a lot of dirt. "Hey kid—boy or girl? Girl isn't it—that's nice. Can you get me something to eat? Something little, something fresh and nice—Y'know? Just shove it through—"

"Why not skin and eat your rat?"

*"No fooling—"* I was glad he couldn't get at me.

"I'm glad you can't get at me, with a violent temper like that."

I heard swearing behind me as I went to the nearest fruit tree. I returned with three ripes, which I pushed through to him. "Gods bless your dear little heart—"

"I only brought three because you can't have too many to hide, your gaoler would notice—Have you anything at all to hide things in, down there?"

"Filthy straw—"

"I'll bring more to eat tomorrow morning—How well do they feed you here?"

"Bowl of weevily gruel a day, big bowl, I wolf it down, maybe a hunk of meat with something wrong with it; there's a pitcher of water, always in the corner, always gets a green scum before they change it. I let the rats pee in it, leave it alone, unless I'm particularly thirsty."

He was eating the fruit now, the hands left the bars, I could hear him, also the spitting out of pips.

"I may be able to bring a flask of wine. Could you hide that amongst your straw?"

"Sure. Sure." There was a short pause while he gnawed thoughtfully at the fruit. "Why you doing this?"

353

"Just tell me why you were put in here."

"I'm Kond," he said, but hearing that didn't ring a bell, "second-in-command of Ael."

"Where's Ael?"

*"Where's Ael?* Look, lovely, you a moron or what? Ael, you know, Ael."

"Doesn't matter how clearly you hiss it, I don't know it."

*"Him.* Most dreaded bandit chief in the Empire, especially in these hills."

"I didn't even know there were hills near here." I was disillusioned; I had fondly believed I was doing good for a rebel of the old Religion, since he was stuck in the Temple dungeons. "Listen, whoever you are, I will be back tomorrow unless discovered—Is there anything else you want?"

"A knife."

The Court have taken it in good part that I am sleeping in the Corridors because of nightmares. Some of the ladies seem to envy me for being under Kaselm's protection, but when I seemed bewildered everyone believed at once in my innocence and there have even passed conniving glances—nobody means to enlighten me in case I am worried.

There was sympathy and well-wishing about my nightmares. My night-things and some of my clothes have been transferred to Kaselm's cell.

I saw Forialk at two of the meals. He was rather bandaged and has two black eyes and a split lip and looks very dashing. He would have spoken to me but there was too much of a crowd. I can't remember whether I saw Ecir.

At night there was a big send-off, I was escorted with streamers to the Temple, but managed to hide some things under my cloak.

In the candlelit cell I drained my goblet.

"You drug my wine, don't you, Kaselm?"

"I won't if you don't wish it."

"I've tried sleeping-draughts myself but they were never strong enough."

"I hope this will prove so tonight. You were far more tired last night."

"Kaselm—Tell me, who is Ael?"

"The bandit leader? Who told you about him?"

"I heard of him today in the Court."

"Oh, he's nothing but one of the thorns in the flesh of the law—His gang are impregnable in the hills, they roost in a net-

354

work of caves and swoop on travellers. Not even the best armed escorts can be certain of being much use—apart from the fact that many of them are secretly in Ael's pay. He doesn't scruple to rob or kill the most important personages—"

"What is he like?"

"A big, ugly tyrant, nearing forty in appearance but he's said to be in his late twenties, half his nose gone and his whole skin a patchwork of scars—"

"And his second-in-command? Haven't you got him here?" I held my breath, wondering whether the Court are supposed to know that.

"Yes, I believe we did catch him, several months ago. Of course Ael will have found someone else now, so he's no longer a valuable prisoner."

"Haven't the gang tried a rescue-swoop?"

"Why should they bother? They could never get far, whereas in their eyrie . . . Ael's surrounded by too many competent toughs to repine over their individual loss in fight or capture. No, our young man is safe with us, and when we need the dungeon for someone else we'll have him executed without trouble."

Once in the night I awoke and found myself shuddering in every limb. A sound of knocking seemed to converge upon my ears from every side. I pressed my hands to my eyes and moaned. In a swift movement the priest Kaselm had rolled over on his pallet, risen, and was crouched at my side. "All right, all right, little one." He lit a candle and held my hands till I stopped shuddering. He did not blow out the flame when at last I lay weakly back again.

In the morning the priest was gone and I was alone in the light—and song-flooded room. I dressed, hid the objects under my cloak, and went out into the sunlight.

I found the grating after a little difficulty. I hadn't properly memorized where it is, knelt to it and called softly.

"Kond."

There was a sound of movement.

"Here I am."

"Here is a flask of wine and some cold meat, as I promised . . ."

He groped and took them, breathing heavily. "I'm sure you'll get to heaven . . . "

"You can manage O.K.? You're standing with your arms raised?"

"I don't mind the strain, for this . . . " There was a puase. "Did you bring it?"

"You want to kill the jailer, don't you?"

"What else."

"Then you'd be out, killing anyone else who got in the way, and up to the hills again."

"Well?"

"I'm not eager to help you . . . "

"Can't you get it? Can't you try for tomorrow?"

"I may bring you food again, but I don't want to help a brigand to be at large again—"

He grasped the bars fiercely, if the bars had been a little less hard they would have winced, and I knew they were meant to be my throat. "Listen, what do you mean, what are you talking about? Of course you want to help me—"

"I don't, no."

"Damn your soul," he whispered after a while.

"I see how you want it."

"No, you don't. You're not going, are you? Look, there's no reason we can't work something out, I can give in a bit, don't leave me after we got friendly—" He was saying with frantic persuasiveness at trip-tongue speed when I whispered fiercely, *"Shut up."*

"Good morning, holy priest," I added.

"Good morning, my child. What are you doing here?"

I held up a ragged bunch I'd been pulling up absently while talking to the prisoner. "Picking flowers, holy priest."

"But they're weeds, child!"

"Oh, I think they're pretty, holy priest!" I looked at them with affection, holding back from their rank smell. I walked away with the old priest, chattering as disarmingly as possible.

This morning I did not go to the grating. I've had enough of helping people, it's time I learnt that lesson.

I stood in the front row of the spectators on the biggest ground floor balcony. I had a basket of roses to throw, but my hands were too listless. They all cheered so my head ached, the crowd along the route were so many (*so many*) stupid specks, beginning to churn into a vortex attacking my eyes. In other words I had a splitting headache, it was mainly the sense of injustice. All those people had been hanging round for hours in the sun-glare to ensure that nobody pinched their chance of a good view, yet they were awfully energetic. I'd only been out a few minutes because everyone knew I must be in front —already I wanted coolness and dark.

The procession was already approaching. The cheering was spreading towards us, a sure forerunner. Damn enthusiastic fools, they were not only treating him as the ally the Superlativity had declared he still definitely is, they were already taking him to their hearts because he is to be a novel treat, a handsome, famous, scale-skinned—

"Mainly your work, mine and yours,"—Kaselm had said last night. "I told my master the Superlativity of the Dragon-General's personal—er—well, powers. He seems to be convinced that the ally can only be a demon, perhaps equal to his godhead, and must be treated with discretion until it becomes clearer what plan of action should be employed."

My ear-drums throbbed angrily as the crowd below and the aristocrats with me cheered. They began to toss flowers. The sun whirled round and round in an unnecessary perhaps-would-be decorative maelstrom of curly fire, the only part one's eyes could bear.

Small black drums flanked the Northern army's horns, hideous as mastodons' squeals.

The crowd were delighted by the birds. They advanced eight abreast, claws sixteen abreast, on the petal-deep roadway. Their crests were up and they shied at the ceaseless fragrant shower. The crowd's cheering extinguished the riders' muttering but not the tightness of their mouths and the white knuckles of their rein-hands. I had a handful of roses but had thrown nothing. My pulses spun as I saw the red cloak, bright and immaculate, recently dry-cleaned, spread regally over the crupper of the high, black, thoroughbred bird. My pulses steadied to a staccato as I saw the black mane, held in a silver band studded with agate.

It was a thousand to one chance that he would look up then, this being the last and most important balcony above his route, but a fair-haired girl in the crowd had thrown a big pink-edged magnolia and he was busy catching it and bowing.

My mouth relaxed. The flowers slid between my fingers.

I'd never been in the main hall of the Temple before, but I wasn't getting much idea of it now either because it was all pitch dark. There were a lot of people standing round to every side of one, but they were not rustling or whispering much. I think a lot of it was awe. The only lit thing there was the

357

throne, an ancient boulder of jade, roughly shaped ages ago into a chair-shape and with a stiff net of wrought gold over it. Where the loops of gold crossed each other jewels had been set, some big, some tiny, and apparently scattered quite haphazardly, no pattern. It was cunningly lit by some hidden lamp or something, and it was what we were all looking at but it seemed a long way away even to me. I was again in the front row of the crowd owing to my divinity, which was the only clue we had in the dark of the hall's hugeness. The throne stayed empty a long time.

Then there was a spreading rustle of heads turning and one saw little lights advancing from a distance. Or rather, it looked like one little light jerking in a stately way towards us. This also lasted a long time. Then suddenly the little light reached the throne and was no more, and there instead was the Superlativity sitting in it, all bathed in the throne's glory and wearing a loose black robe which was supposed to symbolize simplicity but actually made him look pregnant. I was very impressed, even though Kaselm had already explained the lights to me the night before. Three attendants were with the Superlativity as he approached in darkness, one casting down little balls, the second lighting them by touching them with a stick which ignites at a touch, the third extinguishing them: so his progress through darkness was marked by spasmodic balls of fire.

We all laid our faces to the ground when we saw the Superlativity suddenly on the throne; and a lot of heavenly voices from some unseen gallery above us burst into a song of praise that the nation's god had deigned to appear in the flesh amongst us. He blessed us, and then benignly made us all get up because he said that though worship is necessary for us it means nothing to him. Then, over the heavenly choir which was badly organized and got too loud at times—making it difficult to hear him—he gave a long speech welcoming among us the leader of the men who will help us at last in the near future to break down the selfish horror with which the continent Atlan has for so long cut off herself and her resources from her sister continents, from her loving ready-with-forgiveness mother the World.

This went on for ages. Then all the lights came on with a blaze. Everyone blinked and rubbed their eyes for a moment and then saw the Northern General going up to the Superlativity. He made a speech, thanking the Superlativity and his people for their kindness and cordiality and saying how we were all together in this undertaking of (in effect) rescuing Atlan from herself, and he called forth beauteous slaves, mainly golden-skinned ones—they're always good for effect but becoming almost conventional—who laid their foreheads to the step of the throne and presented the Superlativity with presents. There were one or two awfully good presents—had Zerd had them all the time or how had he got hold of them?—mastodons' tusks hooped with gold, that sort of thing. The hooping was rather clumsy, perhaps home-made by the army, but it gave a barbaric sort of look, as if they were old and therefore just as valuable. But the balance of the presents were just fill-ups, rather poor stuff, hastily gathered together, hand-embroidered cloaks (probably done by Lara and her ladies) and uncut gems: just bulk, nothing exquisite. There were feathers, and a quartz drinking-trough which I'd seen hundreds of times before and never thought anything special, and as the *pièce de résistance* a young white bird was brought in. The Superlativity accepted these gifts graciously and with every sign of proper pleasure. I'm sure it wasn't tact, he always believes in what he's doing at the moment, he's a wonderful god really, intrinsically proper and respectable. It's what nations need. And then he blessed Zerd and with a wave of his hand included us in the blessing before the lights went out again and away went the little fire-balls. I was sure he must be awfully stiff, probably etched all over after sitting in that tracery-covered throne.

When the lights went on again we were all free to crowd around the presents and Zerd and his commanders and household, and touch and make cooing noises. The only presents I wanted to look at closely were some pterodactyls' eggs. I wasn't sure whether they were fake or not, but in any case . . . Everyone was thrilled by the white bird, the men asking his grooms questions and the ladies recoiling with screams every time he moved. He was quite good-tempered considering all the confusion, but stood on the eggs before I had a chance to get at them.

Lara was being made an awful fuss of by about a dozen nobles. I was contemptuous at first and then suddenly realized that there are a lot of factors in favour of her being the next Court meteor. Northern General's pretty little wife, and of course she is quite pretty, was wearing a pink dress over pink trousers banded in sequins; Forialk was one of those making most fuss of her which brought me comfort. The way he ignores me, never even looks at me let alone speaks even when

359

we're put together, it's most flattering. Then someone led me over to Zerd before I realized—

"General, one of our most adorable ladies, the Goddess Cija. You should have a lot in common with each other, I believe she was born somewhere north of our mountains, you were, weren't you, darling?"

The General did not bow for a perceptible while.

He stood looking at my face, seeming to search it. I was close enough to see the smoothly overlapping texture of his skin, simply the colour of a thunder-cloud against his red cloak and over his polished leather breastplate. I could smell his sweat, faint this afternoon, pungent. I believe he saw my nostrils widen.

"Goddess—"

He bowed.

I nodded coolly, then smiled as a gracious afterthought. "We really are glad to have you among us, General." The right brand of aristocratic-female mock-cordial cordiality. I was not in just any grand pretty dress—it was white lace, slim, long-sleeved. I was elegant and immaculate. I moved away amongst the crowd, no need to glide, no need to try for effect, I was an effect in myself, the best kind. Safe. But watch out for lonely walks, watch out for villainous-looking Northern sergeants, you know the formula, the most important factor there is, the key to the war, he must be pretty certain you haven't told it yet but you're dynamite, alas.

"You are pale."

"Yes, it was—it was—seeing him again today—" I shall not tell him Zerd wants to kill me, I might get protection, on the other hand they might find out I know the formula and I want to hold that as a trump-card.

"You are safe here."

"I know, Holy Kaselm."

"Just never let him bite you—" He smiled as he handed me the wine. "Do you know if anyone has ever survived that?"

"A friend of mine, owing to prompt and exhaustive care, but it may have been an accident that he was harmed, I can think of no reason—"

"The Superlativity is grateful to you for this knowledge concerning the General—he is now satisfied that the General is a demon as he himself is a god, and if he hadn't known that he would be at battle with him now, maybe unfortunately, instead

360

of welcoming him as an ally while he feels his way. So he thanks you—"

"I am very surprised I have not been condemned to execution because my father is a priest vowed to sacred celibacy—"

"Your father is not an ordinary priest." Kaselm trimmed the candle. "He and your mother both have divine blood on both sides—it is permissible, even high-minded—for a priest to bring into the world a *divine* child." He lay down, turned his head sideways on the pillow to smile at me. "That's a new rule: it hadn't been invented before, it hadn't been needed; you are unique."

Two smiles from the black-a-vised Kaselm in one evening.

Zerd's main army is cantoned outside the town, but with his household and commanders he is occupying a very large grand building on the road to the Court.

Lara is the new meteor.

The ladies are *very* sympathetic to me.
Life has become rather flatter.
Zerd is not often at Court.

It poured with rain today. Of course, Autumn is drawing nearer. In the open courtyards one couldn't tell which was fountains and which rain. In the distance there were red flashes.

"What are those red flashes—there, miles off through the rain?"

"The mountains must be erupting again."

It rained for hours. There was no boundary between day and evening, when evening came the sky was as grim as it had been all day. None of the servants had thought to turn off the fountains. A strong wind had been blowing for a couple of hours and there were pools everywhere. Coming down a staircase, Lara slipped in water and immediately there was a crowd of nobles about her. They began to carry her to the bottom. She ignores me, whether because she has recognized me and doesn't know what line to take or because of simple arrogance, I don't know. One's foot splashed at nearly every step on the marble. The songs played in the cushioned hall were nearly all about Lara. The others are about me, but I don't like out-of-date modern-culture anyway. It is the first time the Court has seemed dreary to me. At an impulse I wrapped my cloak about me and scurried out into the wet gloaming.

"Kond, it's me, are you awake?"

"Yes, nearly half-drowned."

"I was afraid that's how you'd be in this weather. I thought the earth wall before your window might have turned into slime and deluged your cell a bit—"

"Very kind of you to come and bother to see—" His dignified hostility was precarious, under it there was a terrific surprise that I'd come, and maybe twice as much gladness. He now proceeded with cunning tact to doff the defiance and gradually smarm me back into the right state of mind.

"Brought the knife this time, gorgeous?"

He added, "Why you laughing?"

"I'm sorry. I just realize why my attitude to you last time was wrong."

"Yeah, that's it," he said eagerly. "But I wouldn't hold it against you, you're a nice kid. How old are you?"

"Eighteen, I think, so I'm not so young. I know I sound it. I've brought you some meat and wine and fruit. I wish I could give you a blanket too but your jailer would notice."

"Look, darling. Why not the knife?"

I spoke in the same voice of reason. "You're a notorious brigand. You'll kill with the knife. You'll get out and back to your tribe and you'll kill and pillage. I'm not to know that the very first man you'd kill, the jailer, isn't a very nice good man and just the sort I'd like."

"He's a bastard."

"I'm not to know."

"I can tell you're a kind little girl, full of sweetness and all. You want to be kind to everyone. All right. You don't want me to be executed soon? I know it is soon. I don't know when, but I know it's soon. They're doing us systematic, bunch by bunch, and it's our turn soon, me and a couple of sneak-thiefs and the old priest across the passage—"

"Old priest? What's he like?"

"I been loosening the earth with me fingers, well the rain done that for good and all only it bakes up again, I been at the bars but a *knife*, for the love of—"

"What is the priest like?"

"Old, I dunno, wears priest-clothes—"

"Is he—is he—" How could I put it? "Anyway, does he belong to the old religion?"

"Wouldn't be in here unless."

"If I gave you the knife could you get him out too?"

362

"What is this?"

"I'm against executing priests—"

"Oh." He didn't let himself take offense. "All right, darling, you give me a knife and I'll do whatever you want."

"I want a guarantee."

"Ah, now you're being difficult." He sounded annoyed. "How can you expect all this nonsense, I'm in a difficult position enough. Don't you trust me?"

"No. And keep a civil tongue in your head, I needn't stay here any more kneeling in the dark on the drenched grass—"

"Of course you needn't. You've a lovely heart and I don't deserve the use of it. But then, did I ever say I did? Now you want to help the priest and I'll get him out sure if I kill the jailer. I've only to take his keys."

"I can trust you. I know you'll do no better with the life I'm giving you, but I hope you'll let him out too before you go. Please risk the extra minutes. Kond, I'll bring a knife tomorrow morning."

He muttered, "Thank you." He said quietly, "I hope you don't get a chill from being here."

"I'm sure I won't. Well—"

"If the jailer's here when you come tomorrow I'll put up my arm like I was stretching and flex my fingers. You whistle when you come. This mustn't go wrong."

"I can't whistle."

"What a kid. Well—well—I dunno. Can you sing?"

"I'll sing this marching song." I hummed the tune.

"Pretty, pretty. Tomorrow then."

I walked away humming it through the rain.

It was raining heavily the next morning. It is the first time I have ever wakened in the priest's cell and thought it not yet morning, so dark was the silver of the light. But I found the priest gone and I huddled myself into my cloak.

Out in the long cold corridor.

Out in the deafening, dreary tintinnabulation of the downpour.

My thin summer sandals were soon totally water-logged, there were squelchings between my toes and at each step the grass would let my soles go only with a sucking sound after an effort on my part. Up visible through the rain and seeming a separated phenomenon, clouds like juice-swelled plums. Foliage showered my shoulders. The marching-song caught like croup in my throat.

363

I knelt on the queasy ground by the grating.

"Kond! . . . Kond?"

Louder.

"Kond!"

I peered through the grating, but there was no hand to be seen no matter how pale in the gloom. There was no sound.

Is he asleep? Or perhaps it is a trap, perhaps they've found out and are waiting for me to declare myself?

I looked behind me, to either side. I started up and began to run, in bad slow-motion, for the grass wanted my feet and even the hems of my trousers and cloak were heavy with a rim of slow globules.

The thunder blockaded the clouds. The trees were obscene cataracts.

In spite of the rain, I saw them some way ahead of me. The slow procession, black-robes, no chanting, not even a little mumbling, silent, under the black canopy held over their holy heads making a sound like a big black drum as the raindrops bounced on it like so many humourless imps on a trampoline.

I darted up the incline, keeping among the trees. Now I was alongside the procession. The black-robes were mainly short, grizzled nonentities. I couldn't see Kaselm among them. The prisoners were flanked to either side, and were hard to get glimpses of. As far as I could see there were indeed four, walking separately with only their hands tied behind them, and most important, one *was* in the grey leather robe of the priests who refuse to accept the Superlativity as the national god. Slipping between the trees, I kept beside them, one freezing hand clutching the cloak in its cowled folds round my shoulders and head, the other hand now curling as if for dreamlike reassurance round the knife in the cloak's swinging inside-pocket.

The procession turned in to the trees and I was only just in time behind a great, fragrant, moss-slimed trunk.

Here there were drifts of blue bell-flowers between the roots. The black-robes were wet-ankle-deep. They all seemed to be hopping a little now.

A wind skirled and fleered out from behind the thunder as I followed, not a heavy wind but thin and keen, and the blue bells lashed at my legs in a purple frenzy.

Yes, here we are, a tree with a big out-sticking bough and they're stopping in front of it. The priests break formation and shuffle to each other to discuss proceedings, and the prisoners stand hands-tied and eye the bough and the bough faces back at them, ready with a cordial welcome. I can see the prisoners unobscured now, mainly their backs; I might be able to see their profiles if I sneak round among the trees, but on the other hand the priests might then spy me.

A priest in grey leather, his white hair plastered to his skull by the weight of rain he's been respectfully escorted through (only driblets reach us here, slipping and sliding and oddly spurting precariously through layers and levers of leaves); a thin, rat-bearded, middle-aged man with slumped shoulders under his rags; a young brown-haired man likewise huddled morosely in rags; another young tough with a blood-stained headband and a striped mantle, full of holes, its edging of tassels fluttering above the fluttering blue bells.

Through these now come a little coven of priests, hopping to keep their hems at least half as dry as possible, bearing a length of rope. It is a long coil and they are going to quarter it. One produces a pair of ivory-handled gold Temple scissors. The prisoners have turned a little to watch, I can see their faces as, silently and without expression, they watch what is to be their last scene—

It is, it is my priest! Anywhere I'd know that lined urchin's face!

This must be stopped, I can't see them hang him.

I dodged closer. He is separated from me by Tassel-fringe and the morose one, Tassel-fringe is the nearest to me and Rat-beard farthest away. Which is Kond? I begin to hum the marching-song, at first it is only a thread amongst the rain-noises, then it swells a little and I think the prisoners have heard it. The only black-robe who might hear is the one by them cutting the rope, I pray he's too busy. The prisoners are glancing round, anything is interesting to them when it is to be their last experience. Which is Kond? A burst of thunder drowns the song. The rain must have doubled its force, it teems white upon the priests who look up in alarm at the foliage and tut-tut. They move away and try to pull their tight necklines up about their ears, but there is nowhere for them to go. What a day for the execution to have been scheduled for. They look impatiently at their brother measuring the long rope for its next place of snipping. The prisoners cannot be more drenched than they are, they stand in their sodden rags, each hole a waterfall, flowers springing between their hairy toes, some of the least stale dirt sluicing off. The blood on Tassel-fringe's bandage is fresh, he must have fought them when they came for him this morning. The priest makes a sign with his scissors over each half-yard of rope before he measures it off, and before he

365

makes any cut. This must be a kind of ceremony, necessary to be done just before the execution. Our whole little world under the trees seems to be sternly crackling and beating: it is only the rain. I squelch even closer and begin to hum again as loudly as I can, which makes it nasal.

All the prisoners are listening.

I am thinking I'll bet on Tassel-fringe, his bandage makes him seem the most belligerent though his unshaven upper lip is slack, when the morose young man behind him turns round slowly, as though aimlessly to keep movement in his legs, facing in each direction for several moments. As his back comes to view, I notice his hands: wrists caught together in the brace behind him, his fingers flexing. He begins to whistle my tune.

I fumble in my pocket, bring out the knife, get a mobile-wristed grip on it and there it is quivering in the wet grass by his foot, rain already trickling down the hilt.

This is real slow-motion now. I watch every detail of every second so that it seems four minutes where it is half a minute. The prisoners are silent and still, none has yet even drawn a breath. Kond stoops by the knife; the others' eyes are on the snipping priest. But his head comes up; he has heard the little swish of the thrown knife. Tassel-fringe makes a pace towards him, his back now to me, the ball of his calf gleaming. The priest sees Kond: Kond draws his bound wrist across the blade stuck upright by its point in the grass, the priest gurgles and gestures. Tassel-fringe reaches him, glaring meaningly, but the priest will not look at him, he embarks on a better gurgle. There is a line of blood bright on Kond's arm, the blade wobbles and collapses but a strand of cord hangs loose. Kond strains his wrists apart, the cord taken by surprise gives a little and before it can tighten again one hand is through and in one movement is grasping the knife while the other hand shakes off the wide, now useless, bracelet of cord. Tassel-fringe leaps upon the priest who trembles and raises the scissors. He is thrown to the ground, under Tassel-fringe's full length, but has the ill-sense to screech. Kond bounds forward, at a slash severs Tassel-fringe's cords, and they both begin to throttle the poor old priest who drops the scissors and gasps. The other priests turn towards the screech. They see the heap on the ground and with expressions of horror hurry across. I curse Kond: my priest is still bound. I risk everything.

"Kond!" I cry. "Free the priest!"

Tassel-fringe has throttled the black-robe who lies still. Kond, knife in hand, turns crouching a little to face the others.

366

One of them has snatched up the scissors and without compunction is closing in ready to stab Kond in the stomach. Rat-beard begins to stamp and moan with shivering impatience. He tries to tug his wrists apart and chafes the flesh. My priest stands by as though watching a carnival-tournament, his head a little bowed, his eyes very bright over their large debauched-looking bags, no smile and no grimness on his compassionate mouth.

The black-robe with the scissors stabs. Kond catches his wrist with one hand, twists the knife forward and up, rips into the belly. First there is only the sound of tearing cloth, then a gushing of blood. The black-robe falls untidily to the grass, where the blood is soon diluted with rainwater. Kond stoops for the scissors, has to tug because they're caught in a loop of entrail, shoves them at Tassel-fringe who grabs them and shows his teeth. The black-robes stand at bay. Tassel-fringe and Kond go forward stooping. Tassel-fringe beats a black-robe over the head with the scissors, Kond thrusts down another who jabbers for mercy even while he's dying. They're cutting down potential pursuit before making their getaway, though I'm not sure it's necessary, and that's taking a tolerant view of it; it looks like plain viciousness, and it's sheer slaughter for there isn't a single weapon among all the black-robes. I've unleashed this pointless brutishness and my priest is still bound. Rat-beard is whimpering, not because of the slaughter around him but because he's afraid they're going to make off soon without their bound companions. So am I.

"Kond!—"

Kond leaps towards the priest, slashes apart his wrists. My priest, non-bewildered gravity, bows.

Tassel-fringe runs bent double among the trees, towards the open, back the way I usually take to the Temple wall. The priest picks up his skirts and follows, his old competent feet slapping down the grasping grass. Kond comes to the side, his hand is on me before I understand. "Let me look at you, my little sweetheart—" He pulls me round.

"Let me go, you fool, you must get away and I must too."

"Pretty," says Kond's familiar voice, his familiar hand under my chin, his unfamiliar face appraising mine. "Sure, and together, you're just the girl I always wanted in the hills. I'll thank you there."

"I'm not coming with you—" I chop his hand away with the edge of mine and am away, farther on among the trees. He had grasped my cloak, but torn only part of the edge. I know he

367

daren't detour from his direction to get me.

The rat-bearded man screams a curse and falls weeping to the grass, his bound hands thrashing.

I got back to Court and was greeted with amazement and alarm.

"I fell on my way back in the rain, the thunder frightened me and I ran too fast—"

"But part of your cloak is torn right off—"

I brushed them aside and ran up to my room.

I washed off the blood, Kond's hand had grasped me after reaching for the scissors in the pool of the murdered black-robe's blood.

Those ornate and valuable, not to mention sanctified Temple scissors must now be somewhere in the rocky hills of Ael's brigandry.

The news did not reach Court till the evening meal.

"This morning several prisoners about to be executed broke free and murdered nearly half the priests escorting them. All the prisoners except one escaped, including a priest of the old religion who is believed to have been a spy for Atlan. Every effort has been made to recapture him but he seems to have disappeared."

I received curious looks.

"Did you see any of this, Cija? You arrived so upset and dishevelled this morning—"

"I saw nothing. I heard screams, I was frightened but thought them part of the storm—"

"You are odd—"

Lara began to whisper behind her hand. A pretty scandal, the goddess Cija connected with some of the things she can tell them, and her word that of an honourable accepted ally.

To make worse matters which could hardly have been nastier in the first place, I have a perfectly horrid cold and am sneezing and sniffling all over the place. I wanted to stay in bed but that would have looked cowardly, so I have gone round inflicting germs on everyone who gives me sidelong glances—and they all do, for one reason or another.

Last night Kaselm asked me if I had seen any part of the escape. I said "No."

Tomorrow night I have to face an evening feast in honour of Zerd and his wife.

I am glad to be able to report that trouble is, however, start-

368

ing up again between the allies in the town, though they are so sweet to each other in higher places. You just can't keep it down for long. Down by the wharfs the Northern army have been unloading a lot of stores they've taken the opportunity to order. They got them all right, but their loading line was prevented from getting much done by a Southern horseman of high rank riding ceaselessly back and forth along the ramp and therefore through the line. The Northern sentry came up to the officer in charge. "This bastard's stopping all work, sir; shall I do him?" The officer rubbed a finger down the side of his nose. "Of course you mustn't *do* him. What are you talking of, corporal? By the way, I shall be looking in that direction over there for the next ten minutes." When the rider next passed a spear went through his cloak, half-hooking, half-pushing him right off his saddle into the mud. The officer said it was an unavoidable incident, the sentry was turning and his spear accidentally swung too far. No action was taken.

This story was told to the Court by the Northern officer in question. Everybody laughed pleasantly.

The only part of day I now look forward to is night when I take my drugged wine and sleep in Kaselm's cell, in which he leaves the candle burning all night for my sake. I don't even like the early morning walks, the half-hidden grating seems to shriek its emptiness. There is still no news as to whether the priest has been recaptured. Thank my Cousin. I had no idea my priest was working for Atlan.

I am quite sure I am the object of a Court scandal, especially the way Lara and her especial friends look at me and titter.

I still have my own friends, but they also would and do slander their own mothers for the sake of a little gossip, and I suppose I laid myself open to anything like this exciting them because of my impregnable virtue during my months here. It won't be long, in my opinion, before Lara takes to publicly calling me "Winegirl". Being a hostage to the Northern army had indescribably more cachet, though even that I tried to mention to as few people as possible. As I have still given no cause for scandal since coming here, I may in time live this down but at the moment it hasn't even reached its height.

The feast was quite interesting I suppose.

It was held on the Central Lawn because it was a fine night lit by stars and the distant misbehavings of the volcano, and everyone arrived in litters, and wearing shoes with such long tasselled points that it was difficult to walk even a few steps in them—it's a new fashion, signing that one belongs without doubt to the idle nobility.

I wore a dramatic velvet scabbard of a dress, black, making my skin glow white, with a cloud of white gossamer trailing from each wrist, and a haughty gold-encrusted head-dress adding several inches to my height, also gold-encrusted trousers. The effect of all this may have been vaguely spoilt by the fact that I kept sniffing and snuffling all the time and had to keep hunting down my neckline for the hanky which I'd put between my breasts for want of anything else, as my sleeves were too wide and I had no pocket.

In my opinion Lara's hat was a pointless idea, but lots of people cooed over it. It was a little gilded cage in which a turquoise and pink humming bird had barely room to stretch its wings. A rim all round the bottom of the cage protected the wearer from any droppings.

However, my cold seemed to have aroused sympathy or something, because undoubtedly I was the success of the evening, though not the unqualified success I have been at other times. However, the crowd round me was larger than hers. Even Forialk has got fed up with hanging round her, and brought me some wine.

"You may have noticed that I haven't spoken to you lately," he said in a low voice, which struck me as rather naïve so I didn't have the heart to retort that I hadn't been noticing him at all.

"I am glad to see your eyes better, my lord."

He was looking very eloquent, the arrows embroidered on his clothes all pointing to the centre of his anatomy, those on his jerkin pointing downwards, those on his tights upwards, those on his right side to the left, vice versa. All this embroidered clamour drew attention to the codpiece shaped and coiled like a beautiful huge rose.

"The points of your shoulders are stars to light us, Goddess," said someone beside me, it embarrassed me that it was Ecir with a frighteningly sincere poetic look, he hadn't noticed Forialk. In order to avoid a clash which might worsen my reputation I allowed myself to be drawn away to the buffet by an uninteresting elderly intellectual and later I was awfully sorry because neither of them got near me again all evening, not even separately.

To say I was the success of the evening, of course, is only counting the females. The real success of the evening was His

Mightiness the Dragon-General, for while the young nobles were divided between Lara and myself with me winning slightly, all the other women, young and old, flocked round him. He got a little drunk, whirled a delighted young lady of high degree round in his arms till her underskirts knocked down a small table, kissed various shoulders and necks (he prefers fleshy springy ones) and gave an exhibition of sword-twirling and thrusting; and it all only made him more swooned over than ever. His eyes glittered black all over the place. He was dressed mainly in uniform, probably because he hasn't much else, but the sides of his jerkin fell in tasselled points to either side of his codpiece to accentuate its size. I had the distinction of being the only woman he came up to, the whole evening he was submerged in females but they all swarmed up to him.

He came up, bowed, flashed a courteous grin meant to be a smile, offered his arm.

"Would you do me the honour of a few words, Goddess?"

I was able not only to refuse for the sake of my safety, but to do it with style, because of course a goddess is more important than a foreign general.

"Wait a moment, please; I just have to go and give someone something to take somewhere . . . " I drifted vaguely away, found my page playing with others under the buffet, and told him to run a message to Kaselm that I should be late. After that I sat in an arbour and listened to songs about myself. Having been undernourished for a while, I have rediscovered a taste for them.

I'm still not sure what happened, nor indeed how, but here am locked in my own room. I was talking in The Cloisters, and a number of priests came by, nobody ever takes much notice of them, and then Rat-beard was pushed forward by one of them, he said, "That's her," and the priests seized me by the shoulders and led me away and everybody stared like anything and called out questions and I just smiled in a bewildered way and opened my hands and shrugged my shoulders, and the priests brought me up to my room and wouldn't answer when I said things to them and they locked me in and went away—

I never before realized what an inconvenient room this would be to be locked in, there is indeed a balcony outside the long windows but it is terribly high up and there is no way of reaching any roof or any other balcony from it. I have been here several hours now, getting hungry, have rung repeatedly for my maid but she must have been ordered not to answer—

I have only just thought of writing in my Diary, but there is nothing to write except these few salient, deeply ominous facts—

I have been trying the chimney, it is far too narrow for me to get even my shoulders up.

I have been out on the balcony several times, but there is no way of getting away from it. Far below the grounds begin to haze as sunset approaches, they are empty, there is no one down there to whom I can signal, they are all in the banqueting hall now— Earlier there were people about, I waved my arms frantically and called but the distance is just too wide to carry sound, no one looked up except one large lady, too far away for me to recognize her, she waved back to me and went leisurely walking, obviously thinking I was just being friendly.

It is evening—the hangings are not drawn across the big windows through which pours golden light dimmed, as it were, and made dusty by the age of the evening. Indeed I have never known such a long evening. The raised designs on the rich ceiling throw straight blue shadows upon it and each other.

I count the geometrically placed knobs on the ceiling and join them with imaginary lines, which raises me to such a pitch of the sense of futility as I wait literally in a trap that my nerves are raw and my stomach seems to be whirling in extreme anger—

I feel very alone in the huge, desolate, empty room. The rafters above the grand ceiling clatter at the force of the wind upon the roof. I shudder at the lengthy eerie moaning of it, I wonder what I would do if at any moment the huge disc-shaped grey face of the wind appeared to me at a window. Terror uses me at the thought, which I cannot keep from my mind. I get up again from my chair and hysterically pace the room, flinching at the always rising heights of noise attained by the wind, every minute or two forcing myself to turn round to the windows to see if the face is there. My fingers clench so tightly into my hands that when I open them I find the palms swollen and disfigured with the deep indentations of my nails.

I heard Them coming long before they actually entered. The building was empty, this part of it, at this time, except for me and now them. Up the staircase, along the gallery in a bevy, their robes whispering friendly and a little ashamed of it. They unlocked the door in an ordinary, everyday way as if nothing were farther from their collective mind than matters of life and death—the ancient peevish lock snarled at the rapist key, unattractive ancients together, the hand of the procurer priest faltered with casual incompetence and had to try again, the handle turned, metal heavy with the opulent way it was wrought, had to be turned twice. It really seemed all like that to me and when they came in I was weak with the obscene suspense of a couple of seconds.

"Sit down, holy gentlemen," I said and flopped into a chair.

They did not sit. Clustered in a group facing me, accusing jawlines jutting so righteously at me they were nearly free of their saggy neck-cords.

"Goddess. The Superlativity is tremendously grieved that you have been keeping from him something you knew important to him."

I inclined my head. "And that something . . . ?"

"Why, Goddess, that you are a spy for Atlan."

The spokesman priest was a tall greyhead with an actor's hands. He must be enjoying himself. He was presenting to me this deadly grimness with an incongruous, cruel absurdity.

"I am in my turn grieved," I said, "that the Superlativity could think this of me. Perhaps he has been faithlessly counselled?" The priest ignored my last remark.

"Even goddesses can blaspheme, against higher gods. And blasphemy it was, triple blasphemy, Goddess. You offended the Superlativity as a host, as a god, and as the head of all Temple affairs—"

At this quibbling mention of the Temple I realized what this was likely to be all about.

"Rat-beard managed to gabble a betrayal before his own execution, revenging himself on me because he was the only prisoner unable to slaughter and escape—"

"The thief we would have hanged today, yes, he betrayed you if you call it that. But you underestimate the importance of his information to us. We were so pleased to get it we even let him go free—"

"To keep the gallows free for bigger game?"

"Crude, Goddess." He was pained. And the gazes around him were all on me, all avid. No sympathy among all those holy elderly gentlemen for the girl with her hands clammy and her feet trembling and her throat knotted at the effort of verbal defiance. "Have you any warrant for believing me an Atlantean spy simply because I rescued one of your prisoners who adheres to the old faith? He was my friend."

"Exactly. He is also a spy for the cause of Atlan."

"I swear to you, I am not."

"Come, come, Goddess, don't sound so heated. It is all one, spy or blasphemy, the penalty is the same. But that priest is dangerous loose. He seems to be one of those spies' top people. Where is he?"

"I don't know." I sneezed.

"And yet it was you who went to all the trouble of arranging his escape?—Thus *betraying*, since that is your own word, the debt of gratitude you owed the Superlativity, and blaspheming his divine will—"

"I do not know the present whereabouts of the priest," I said slowly and reasonably, "nor where he went after he had been—rescued. I didn't even see which way he went. For a moment or two I was—detained by one of the other prisoners. I apologize that they got away. It was unavoidable."

"I must warn you, Goddess, this ignorance is foolish. I said the penalties for spying and blasphemy are both the rope." And truly the dignified straining of his throat reminded me of cord. . . . "But unless you give the whereabouts of the spy-priest, you will be tortured."

"Listen," I said, each breath shallow and scorching, I was so afraid I wouldn't get the right number of words out in time, "I have not tried to deny my hand in his escape. I don't know where he went. I didn't know he was an Atlan-partisan. In earnest of my good faith I will tell you something which will convince you torture would be useless, and you will hang me without this fuss. I will give you the formula which unlocks the Atlan vacuum."

In hope, my lungs sore, I watched their faces. It did not matter at all to me that I was losing this war for the Northerners. Now the Southerners would be their masters, place their ray-spurred boots upon the neck of the little Northern army which had for so long staved off this hour, in another few weeks the Southern army would embark and the veil be torn, the ancient Peace destroyed . . .

"You cannot possibly mean this, Goddess."

"I do, I do. I overheard the General—He knows, he wanted me killed but I escaped. Escape, it was a thing I used always to be lucky about, only I always went to something worse —Please believe me. That's why I came here. And he knows I know and he's trying to get me alone but he didn't try frantically enough, did he? He knew I hadn't told your Superlativity yet and he thought there was some time, he knew I'd hold such a secret till I could use it to save myself from

374

something or push some great bargain—He didn't know I'd rescue an old priest who was my friend and be in the greatest danger right away—"

Their faces were all glowing with a triumph so strong they didn't fear for it, even at this early date. They didn't hold it in, their eyes gleamed, still no room for any thought of me as human and in need. It is the first time I have loathed the divinity in my blood. They know I am different from them and they don't care that the difference is only slight.

"You tell us this to save yourself torture?" said the spokesman. "And yet you withheld this—this *vital*—from the Superlativity when you first arrived here—and have known for so long now how greatly we desire this one piece of all-important knowledge—Really, Goddess, the extent of your loyalty to the South which has welcomed you is hardly—"

"And nor is my loyalty to the North," I gabbled. "I tell you, I heard the formula. And my loyalty is my own to place. I am *here* because of my loyalty to one of the only friends I've ever had, I helped to kill the other, and of course maybe I *would* have let this one die too if I'd known quite how I'd end up by helping him, and now my real loyalty is to myself and I want to be hanged not tortured—"

They waited courteously for me to finish all that, as if I were an eminent drunk at the maudlin stage.

And I told them the formula I overheard on that hot, stinking, noisy day in the shut-bed Smahil and I used to share.

They went away.

My trembling grew until I was relieved of my tension, and I thought of the little moment of pain. I felt my throat and it is so delicate, easy to break. I think of the green orchard where I shall hang, one of the brotherhood of the bees and the fragrances, until I am a sweet odour myself and I will fall and all my friends of the orchard will grow richer and riper because of me . . .

Quietly I wait for them to come back.

They were back in less than an hour, I'd laid down my pen and was waiting quietly like I last wrote, and they said, "We've checked that formula with our scientists. It was an impossible formula. You've tried to trick us." "You're bluffing." "We must remind you that insolence may be dearly paid for—Tell us the true formula or the priest's whereabouts." "I don't know either." "You have three hours. At the end of that time if you have told us what we want to know you will be hanged. If not, you will receive the traditional torture of a spy—" "But I don't *know* any other formula! I thought that was the right one! He wanted to kill me because I knew it—I don't understand!" "In any case, you're a spy. Tell us where the priest is—we shall come at the end of the three hours. If you do not tell us then you will immediately be flayed . . . slowly . . . upwards from the feet . . . you'll be able to watch, right till the last, the slow curling back of the peeling skin, the veins all laid bare, the curling . . . curling . . ." "You must be a frustrated poet."

They have left me alone.

Help me, God. God. God. God. God. God. God. God.

*(There follow four pages of God, scrawled each time very large with great intensity and with slow, slow, elaborate curlicues added afterwards. J.G.)*

When the door was next unlocked I was behind the wimpled-glass screen separating the fountain from the rest of the room. I had one tiny chance. And at least I had nothing to lose. No matter how I infuriated them, they couldn't take worse action than was already to be inflicted on me. I had filled my priceless big coral vase with water and threw it all over the black-robe who entered. I made a dash for the door but the black-robe caught me. "You're in a hurry," he said, and proceeded to brush the water off himself.

"May I borrow this?" He scrubbed his head briefly with my embroidered towel.

I had nothing to say after "Kaselm—" I was wondering whether it would be worse or better to be tortured by someone I knew well, at least whose face I knew well though I'd never be able to fathom his thoughts or feelings, I decided it didn't make any difference.

"I had no idea you'd get yourself into this," he said in a low but untroubled voice. "Why didn't you tell me? It's lucky I found out in time. Put on your cloak."

"You mean—You're going to—"

"If I can. Don't hush yourself. Keep talking as much as you like, though not loudly." We were now out of that gorgeous room which in one evening had become the most hateful of places, and we were walking down the stairs, he casually, myself trying but with melting knees, a lady and a priest in conversation. Oh, no one look closely. "Unluckily I found out only quarter of an hour ago that you were in such danger. If only I could have come during the feasting hours when the rest of the place is deserted—on the other hand we'll be less conspicuous."

"And there are few lights now because they embarrass the courting courtiers—"

"When I came in and found you in your fountain-room I thought you were emulating the last woman we tortured, who took care to bath beforehand—"

"I'm awfully sorry I soused you like that," I said with trembling contrition. This was no time to boast that I actually do bath generally once a week.

This heavy Diary which I'd surreptitiously put in my cloak-pocket banged against my knee.

A bull-necked priest was about to pass us on the staircase. He peered at me. "Hey, hey!" He grasped my arm and started to pull me. I whimpered. Kaselm's hands encircled his bull-neck from behind. "Keep walking up the stairs," he said in a grim whisper. "Don't turn round. As soon as you show signs of turning, you'll get a thrown knife between your shoulder-blades. Keep on up the stairs and turn along the passage at the top."

Kaselm released the bull-neck, who started resentfully quivering up the stairs. Kaselm pulled me into a dark corner and we watched for a few seconds, then he dragged me out and shoved me down the next flight. We were hidden from above.

"He'll raise the alarm," Kaselm said. "Run as though your Dragon-General were after you."

Down more flights, his hand hard on the small of my back. I had no thoughts, but to trust in his competence and strength. In the very back of my head was a doubt that he might not be trustworthy, but I had no option. The vague doubt sprang from the facts that I have rarely been able to trust anyone at all for more than a short while, and I've long suspected Kaselm of a deep game.

Down more flights, completely unlit. Now below courtyard level. I'd never been this low before, and expected that we'd soon strike the servers' quarters. But we continued down, his strong fingers now over mine in the blackness, and somehow I did not stumble.

"Do you really have a knife?" I dared to whisper hopefully when we reached a deserted, low-roofed, dim-lit corridor, and could hurry on the flat for a while.

"You think a High Priest would carry a knife?" he whispered reprovingly and pulled from under the side-loop of his robe a curved gold sheath which must usually hang hidden against his thigh.

"Will you suffer greatly for helping me?"

377

He laughed quietly, the sound resonant in the pit of his throat.

"I am the Superlativity's right ear, right eye, right arm. I have my finger in a thousand plots of my own and if any dare to accuse me weightily I have all the clever vermin of the wharfs at my back."

I remembered how I'd met him talking like an old friend to the captain of the boat I'd stowed away on. I'd wondered then about such things as smuggling, no more . . .

At the end of this corridor, down again. Damp blackness. And now we could hear some kind of commotion above us, but descending.

"Kaselm—They're coming!"

He pulled me right against a blank wall. His hand, still with mine in it, went over the wall surface which was very old and musty and scarred with cracks and split seams. A little trickle of mouldy mortar drifted down. I sneezed and began to sniffle. The priest's finger found one crack, which seemed to me indistinguishable from the rest of the network, and there was a grating noise right before us. I started and clung to him.

"In, child. Part of the wall has swung open. Get in."

I groped. Suddenly my hand went right through the wall. A damp, musty breeze breathed straight in my face. I tried to scramble through but my knee struck wall. My hands were already through and I was in a panic. Strong arms hoisted me up from behind. I dropped into a cold, stony dark. Landed on one knee and scraped my hand on rough stone paving. I heard him come through after me and then the harsh grating as the wall swung to shut out the growing noise of pursuit as righteous priests flurried down the wooden flights, clattering in their hurry against the treads and each other. We heard them go past on the other side of the wall.

Kaselm and I, hand in hand, started walking. I was sure the echoes from the stone enclosing us must be heard for hundreds of yards. The steady sounds of our steps hit the walls and roof more than the pavings. From the sounds I thought the roof must be vaulted.

Speaking of vermin, scuttlings now began across our path. I knew they must be rats and kept calm. But a whirr above my face, flapping a wind through my hair, made my hand twist in Kaselm's.

"Bats," he said. "It's not the last you'll meet now. They don't like to be disturbed but probably they won't attack. However,

378

the only sure thing to keep them off would be a fierce torch held high."

I murmured an acknowledgement of the information. Speaking frightened me. Kaselm's voice still reverberated.

Soon the whirring flapping above us became intense, multitudinous. The tip of a hooked leather wing lashed across my face. I heard the priest draw his knife from its sheath. He continuously whirled and flashed the knife above his head. There were occasional little grunts or moans from above us and the flapping diminished as far as we were concerned, though I could hear the rest of the vaulting thick with it. The flashing knife also gave a sort of intermittent gleam which was not much good to see by but was comforting down here. It reminded one that light did exist. Once, however, his arm tired and he stopped. Immediately the bats were at us again.

I offered to take a turn, but he pointed out that I was too short and would only succeed in cutting his eye open.

Presently there assailed our eyes what I thought a blaze of light. It was only the saffron of torches in iron wall-sockets, turning the stone walls umber. The presence of torches did not even mean someone had lit them recently, down here there was little to stop them slow-burning for days. There are no bats in the lit sections of these Vaults.

But I decided with wonder that there were inhabitants. Other passages divided off the main one. Kaselm always seemed to know which to take. His stride never faltered. We were no longer even in a hurry. It was as though now, down in these Vaults, Kaselm was in his kingdom—more primitively, in his element. I took my hand from his. I no longer needed help for haste in dark, and I rarely like being touched by people. It worries me.

There were almost definite signs of present habitation. Ragged but not mouldering curtains hung across rather smelly orifices in the walls, here and there a spear lay or leaned, not at all rusty, there were sometimes fountain-basins in the middle of a cross-space where several passages branched. The fountains were not springing but there were unrusty metal cups chained to them and puddles by them. Insects, centipedes and horned beetles, bustled in the upside-down forests of fungi on the ceilings.

"Do these fountains still work, Holy Kas—?"

He stepped to one, pressed the knob of a metal figure's navel and there were glug-glug sounds and then water gushed from one of her nipples and jetted from the other, and began plop-plopping and gurgling down the vortex of the basin-drain. There was a chugging of subterranean water-pipes, but no doubt about it, they were working. Kaselm filled the chained cup and offered it to me. I drank though it was quite dirty. It was extremely cold and had almost a dry taste.

At this moment I actually saw one of the inhabitants. He emerged from a side-passage and padded past us and disappeared into another. He gave a palm-up salute to Kaselm as he passed which Kaselm answered. He was dressed in a filthy leather tunic with a hood hanging at the back. He also wore wide, slit-sided, striped breeches with fringed bottoms, a floppy leather boot and one foot bare. His belt was stuck full of variously and murderously shaped weapons—knives, a chain with a spiked ball on one end, a saw-edged dagger. He was pale and had a lot of greasy hair of an indeterminate colour.

Kaselm and I moved on.

"Who lives in these labyrinths?" I said.

"Oh—various people who prefer it to any other life," he said.

Those I saw were all ruffianly and pale. Most ignored us, but some saluted Kaselm and he replied in kind. What were they? Gangs of smugglers? Wanted criminals who at some time or other had escaped Justice? Families who had been here since ancient centuries?

"Do the Court and Temple know of them?"

"They don't know the labyrinth exists. We're a long way underground here, you know."

At this moment my breath caught in my throat. A blackrobe was coming towards us. Kaselm advanced without surprise. Could he mean to betray me after all? Were the torture-chambers at least down here? As the figure passed I saw it was a girl, walking demurely, painted lids lowered, pink-nailed fingers catching up a trailing fold of black vestment.

There were several layers of labyrinth, for we passed stairs leading down and up. There were occasional gratings and ventilation-chutes. The temperature in the lit sections was tepid, even warm at times.

I saw none of the ruffians' women, unless they look exactly like the men, but in a hewed alcove we passed three children. They all had a lot of unkempt hair falling over their pale faces, and stopped their work to stare at us from violet-rimmed eyes hard with unafraid appraising suspicion. A boy about eleven was sharpening a blade, a fierce blonde girl of eight or nine feeding spoonfuls of chunky meat-gravy to a thin baby playing with a jewel-studded bracelet. An iron pot hung on a chain from the alcove roof, over a fire full of blue flames.

Later our feet splashed in pools of water but there were no fountains about. I kept quiet for a while, till I noticed a bunch of real sea-weed in one of these large puddles.

"Where does this water appear from, Kaselm?" Somehow I no longer thought to call him Holy.

He didn't bother to answer. He turned a corner and a sudden blast of air got me clutching my cloak to myself. At the same time I found myself up to my calves in water, fresh moving brine-water, a virile salt wind scudding it in long ripples hard against me—Kaselm's hand plucked me back. I stood behind him and sneezed as I looked up a slope and through a tunnel-arch of black green-slimed stone. All I could see was a pale sky, all movement, clouds scudding in it pursued by the wind as it pursued water. Because it was late evening the paleness of the sky had a violet tone richening its wild dreariness, but there must have been squally weather while we were traveling in the labyrinth—there was no gleam of setting sun nor rising star.

The tunnel slope before us was sliding with brine, collecting in the anciently-worn hollow at the bottom, but there was no other sign of life except that a gull could be seen wheeling mewing for an instant in the patch of sky. But I didn't miss the rails on the slope for crates.

"Has no visitor to the wharfs ever noticed this hole?"

"Maybe. But none can come down here to find out what goes on. Even a punitive force wouldn't dare it. It wouldn't matter if they did. The people here don't bother with passwords which can be betrayed even from day to day—they kill or capture and use anyone they don't know they can trust."

"Can I get away from this point—? A boat?"

"Where is your goal?"

"I've no idea," I said after a pause of amazement that I'd not considered this. "For one year after leaving my own country I had no goal but the Southern Capital. My months at the Court here I never thought of my future if I could help it—It was deliberately a state of being, an existence to relax, to slough off all the stresses of that former life which rose to screaming-point—I would never have gone except that now existence is again a threatened thing."

"You've no wish to stay here?"

"In the Labyrinth? My personal God tells me No."

381

"Have you any ambition?"

"No."

"Consider. You are a displaced person, wanted by the Temple as a spy"—and by the law as a murderess, I added silently—"and you have no friends, no family, no chosen home, no purpose—To go out, alone and small and as far as I can tell impetuously incompetent, and with a bad cold, into a dangerous alien land thirsty for your pain and blood—Just in order to find a roof and food, it isn't worth it."

"I want more than food and shelter from weather. I want freedom—and the knowledge that not only tomorrow, but the next day and the next will find me secure in the same place."

"You shudder at the thought of existence in these Vaults. They would provide shelter, food, drink, warmth—and complete safety under my guardianship."

"Among wild men and animals, crime and dirt?"

"Do you hope even to cross the harbour up there safely—To find at once the clean friendly home you seek in a land racked with war and a dozen internal strifes?"

"Frankly, Holy Kaselm, I don't want to be so near the Temple and the Court, to feel them pressing down upon me from above. I am eternally grateful for what you have done this evening. But you tell me your finger is in a thousand plots—and I know you are far too intelligent to worry about using me as a pawn in any of them."

Seeing that I realize him to be ruthless, he didn't try to press or reassure me, thus merely worrying me further. I am beginning to prize him properly only now.

"I'll find you a boatman who'll take you to some little secluded place of safety, far from here," he said. "Wrap your cloak closer. At least you'll be fed soon."

I followed him away, down another passage.

Presently a man emerged from a side-turning. He looked at me but saw Kaselm and saluted. "Wait, Guts," said Kaselm. "Your boat is leaving tonight? How soon?"

"The wind is blowing from the convenient fourth of the world, and the tide will be right in less'n an hour."

"Have you room for a passenger?"

Guts looked at me. "Her?—She'll fit in."

"We'll discuss terms and wherefores over a meal," said Kaselm, but it was quite settled. Guts now grunted and led us along farther till we came to a leather curtain which he lifted. Kaselm's arm round me guided me into a big, smoky, pungent, dark cavern, crimson and gold fires roaring gustily; and, sitting round eating and drinking with crude concentration which left little time for speech but wasn't exactly noiseless, a whole crowd of ruffians, their giant shadows dovetailing with the flames, Guts, Kaselm and I sat down in a group which made room for us. Someone handed Guts three sizzling chops which he evened between us. Various people saluted Kaselm. Almost at once I felt great warmth soothe the long anxiety of my very bones. I sneezed, yawned found in my eyes tears of weariness so intense it was voluptuous.

Kaselm supported my shoulders with one arm, set a goblet to my lips. The wine was very harsh, my head swam and my inside burned beautifully.

While I sleepily busied myself digging kidney out of my chop (and getting rather muzzy with wine as well as sleepiness) Kaselm and Guts had a long quiet conversation.

What seemed at the same time much later and far too soon, Kaselm was standing me up and laughing. "Ready, child?" I don't think he has ever called me Goddess. Anyway, I can't remember him ever calling me Goddess.

"Going now?" I said.

"The tide won't wait. Listen, Guts is taking you to his mother's village, three weeks down-river. You can trust him implicitly—he won't let a priest or lawman set an eye near you. Don't bother about giving him money. I've seen to it."

"I couldn't anyway, I have none now—Oh, thank you, Holy Kaselm."

We went with Guts to the tunnel-slope. The patch of sky was now murky black. "A good, starless night," Guts grunted. He whistled and we waited. Presently a rope slid down the chute and jerked. Guts tied one end to his belt, jerked, and was drawn climbing up.

"Your turn in a moment," Kaselm said. "Ready?" I nodded sickly.

The rope came bown. He tied it round me, then folded me in his arms. I remembered all the warnings at Court. Rocking me a little, he kissed me on the cheek. He jerked on the rope before I could say anything. I went up, dizzy, scraping an arm on the side. Guts and two other men seized me, steadied me on the wharf and untied the rope. Kaselm did not come. They hustled me up the gang-plank.

# CHAPTER EIGHT

## ESCAPE

The small ship swayed on the black currents. There were no stars, only wind and clouds in the sliding sky. The clouds were ghostly-looking, a slightly-luminous-middled black in blackness. I huddled in my cloak against the poop. The small crew took no notice of me. There were various stacks of crates about, some haphazardly "hidden", with more faith than anything else, behind sailcloth. It was none of my business. In my mother's country I would have hated and despised smugglers, but I don't care how the economic balance of this nation is mucked about with.

I was enclosed in my own thoughts and did not notice the commotion till its cause was far too near.

"As the wind is, we can bash right through their line." "And as the wind is, they'll be after us in no time." "Ah, we're a racier craft." "I'm not having her identified as a rogue ship, we'll stop and get through the usual. Like as not they'll take our word and not insist on opening 'em up. But keep your knives handy." The sailors' voices impinged. "Hey—wait—the girl!"

I started up and was just about blown for'ard, skimmed along the deck. "Guts, Captain, I mean—are those lawships out front?"

"Sure, we're all right with them. Routine check. But there's already a reward out for you. There's only a cubby-hole below. Can't even stow you lumpy and suspicious-looking under a bunk pallet, we kip on deck."

"How near are they?" I quavered, peering ahead. "Is that them?"

"Mp-hm."

I tugged off my sandals. "Goin' to swim for it?" they said, catching on fast. "And not a moment too soon. You a good swimmer, missy? Make for that bank over there. Work forward. We may be able to pick you up at the ruined warehouse, though there's no saying."

The muffled oars of the law, smugly and rather pathetically certain it was sneaking up on these experienced river-farers, were now sending wash against our bows and making occasional plop noises which I suppose it fondly imagined would be mistaken for fish rising.

Guts helped me off with my dress, helped drag off my trousers. In my little shift I put my hands together and dived off the bulwark. I made the water with as little sound, just about, as the oars of the law. This now cried "Halt!" in a loud voice. My heart froze so I didn't even notice the coldness of the new element. Guts' voice bawled back, "Waddya mean, Halt?" There was a clash of grappling hooks, canvas hauled down and my friends allowed themselves to be boarded. Something hit the water beside me. My sandals, straight down, knack-thrown. My dress, trousers and cloak in a bundle. They didn't want any trace of me left on board. A sudden sense of loss sent me for that bundle, entangling myself in the wash of the now floating vessels. I hit an oar and hoped like hell that no one was at the top of it. I got that bundle just as the cloth was begin to spread out under the surface of the water. This heavy Diary in the swinging purse-like pocket of the cloak, it acted like a plummet-stone.

Swimming with the Diary bundled in the cloak clasped to my breast was difficult. The water was cold and sent little electric shivers against my limbs. I struck out for the bank they'd indicated. This was very different from swimming in the tower-top pool where I learnt. This was the farthest bank, the nearest one was a mass of wharfs and movements and lights, this was a row of gardens and big private mansions and little quiet, dark, private, landing-stages. Not too soon, I began to smell the wafted fragrance over the pervasion of salt and river-weed which in the small rounded enclosure of my nostrils seemed to suggest a wideness of miles.

Two lights ribboned past—long flutter-gilled eels, lambent in their own phosphorescence.

For a moment my swimming hand was lit underwater—a strange, thin, pearl object, a confident clawing on the element, on life . . .

I began to recognize some of the fragrances. Magnolias—sweet magnolia, heady magnolia, scent tangible as the flower itself, reclining languorous on the black air.

I pulled myself on to the little wooden landing-stage, which immediately creaked. The water was heavy now that I was half out of it, and I was very chilly. I got off the landing-stage. I was now on a narrow white path, disappearing as a thin thread into fogs of shrubbery. Over the patter of my feet was the silly pitter-pitter of sea-drops from my sodden self, shift, and bundled cloak containing the Diary. I wanted to stop and see whether water had got into the bundle and harmed the Diary, though it would have been too dark to discover much; I wanted to stop and take off my horrible clammy shift, but I had now noticed lights advancing from the right and I hurried on through the gardens.

The shrubberies rustled, metal and marble statues gleamed out at me, the lights came nearer. Now more lights in front of me: but they are stationary. They are torches held by sentries in front of a great house. I pause, amazed, on the outskirts of the shrubbery. The sentries are indeed sentries, not sentinel servants, and are wearing Southern army uniform!

Of all the places to come to! I turn to dive back into the doubtful sanctuary of the shrubbery. But the other lights have come up on my right. They pass me at a distance of four or five yards. They are Northern soldiers, they are escorting the General himself home from a day at Court. He is not riding, but walking as though he were marching, as though he were one with his escort. His instincts are all soldier-instincts. Lara must have stayed later at Court, there are not even any girls with him. Eng walks beside him; they are both silent. Clor and Isad follow, talking.

They come to the marble staircase, each step a momentous scimitar-shaped sweep, on which Southern sentries stand. As the Northern soldiers approach, the sentries stiffen: they are longing at least to scowl, but they each raise their torches with a ceremonial-cry as the General passes them. He ignores them. except to salute their captain at whom he glances absent-mindedly.

Of course I understand now. I have come to the very mansion lent by the Temple-Court to the Northern General for his stay here—and as an additional mark of honour they provided him with a sentry-corps of their own soldiers. Is he exasperated, for they must spy on him and would probably try to keep him prisoner if the circumstances arose?—

He and his commanders disappeared into the great doorway.

Now comes the part which fills me with irrational shame, it's almost comic. Of all the ways to be discovered—I mean, there were about three hundred other likely ways for me to be discovered, if Fate insisted on it, but no, it has to be the classic way, the way heroines (and usually child-heroines, at that)

386

were always discovered in the books I was actually *allowed* to read in my own childhood.

I sneezed.

The nearest sentry heard at once. He came straight towards me leisurely, holding up his torch.

I tried to creep back among the rustling swaying shrubs, but I'd've done better to run madly and not bother about concealment. He saw my face anyway. That was that. He recognized me. He didn't yell out to his comrades; he wanted the reward all to himself.

He talked to me like a hunter to an animal trapped but edging away from him, like a soldier in a sacked town bothering to seduce a frightened girl he could rape.

"Come here, little coney, there's no safety behind you, only the sea's, there, now, now, don't dash like that, it won't do you no good, you're only entangling yourself in the foliages, you're getting yourself in a panic, you need to keep your pecker up for what's coming, you'll have a bit to face but remember while they skin you that you've won an honest sentry a fat purse of *lovely* metal—Ah, now, you're really getting excited—Here, just hold out your hand and I'll have you. No need to struggle any more for it ain't no use—"

His voice had belied the harshness of his grip when eventually he got me. He twisted the bundle from me, puckered his lips as we regarded each other.

"This your cloak? Best put it on, them legs are a bit bare, aren't they? Good thing your shift isn't a coupla inches shorter." He flipped at its hem with heavy fingers and laughed as I recoiled. He laughed again as he looked at my face, I hadn't taken my eyes off his, I suppose I looked mesmerized already as a skinned rabbit. "You don't want to interest my mates too much, do you now? Nor do I—they'll ask too many questions. Pull your hood over your sweet face, now." The rhythm of his conversation reminded me of Kond's which used to come up from the blank impersonal grating: I felt almost homesick, for those had been safer moments.

His comrades were calling. "Found what the noise was, Number 58?"

"Yeah, yeah, a trespasser, that's all." He pulled the Diary from me. "What's this?" He looked at it and said in wonder, "A book." He opened it but could make little of my mixture of shorthand and abbreviations. He probably found reading difficult at the best of times. "Well, I'm sure the Temple will find that interesting, too. A record of spying, I shouldn't won-

387

der." He put it in my pocket, pulled the hood over my eyes and propelled me forward again.

The Northern soldiers who'd been escorting the General were down the steps again by now, and just marching off to their barracks. Their leader saluted my captor, who saluted with his free arm. The Northern leader frowned; it was the wrong arm. "Meant no disrespect, sir," said my captor hurriedly hustling me to the other arm.

"What have you there?" said the Northern leader.

"A trespasser, sir, who I'm about to take to the Temple."

He had the right arm free now, saluted, and was about to hurry on but the leader stopped him by speaking.

"Has another sentry been detailed to take your place?"

"Well, sir, I was about to go off duty anyway and this is an emergency—"

"You all go off duty a few minutes too early and without bothering to report. Just because most of the day there's nobody to watch you all but the statues . . . I find this a very slack outpost of your army. Go back to your post for the necessary five minutes."

"Sergeant don't mind, sir—" said my captor almost bullyingly, very aware of his superior nationality and army.

"Are you slandering your officer?" said the Northern leader smoothly. "I am quite sure your sergeant minds. Leave the trespasser with me. I shall see he is taken, not to the Temple but to the General, whose grounds after all these are."

The sentry saw his reward slipping through his fingers. The look he gave the leader was murderous but brief, he hurried back to his place on the steps as the leader, without one single glance at me, ordered a soldier to take me to the General.

I was marched away again, not up the steps, but to a small doorway round the corner of the building. We were passed in. This soldier had used his sense: by hurrying up the servers' stairs, we were in time to meet the General as he emerged leisurely on the second landing of the winding grand staircase inside the house.

We approached, the soldier saluted.

The General stopped. He was alone, the commanders no longer with him, he looked as if were going to his chamber, continued taking off his jacket as he stood before us, his cloak was already over his arm.

"Caught a trespasser in the grounds, sir," said the soldier.

"A spy, hm?" said the General absent-mindedly.

I darted forward. The soldier was startled and reproachful,

I'd been a good prisoner till then, he pinioned my arms again but I had got the General's attention. "General," I said, "may I speak to you alone, only for a few minutes?"

"Ho, I don't advise that, sir," said the soldier. "Not but what it sounds like it's only a girl. But you never know with these assassins."

"Yes, very likely, but you may go," said the General. The soldier saluted and departed.

I fell forward into the arms. I was trembling horribly. "They want to flay me." My voice was small but hoarse: I thought, 'I sound hideous' but could not control it. "There's a reward—they're all after me." There was bile in my mouth. The checkered marble was spinning and rising.

"And you came to me?"

At the strange sound of his voice I looked up, my nausea arrested.

His eyes were on mine but somehow did not meet mine. He looked surprised, odd. "Why to me?" he said. His gaze shifted away.

I was so anxious to show that I wasn't an idiot, that he *could* help, to beg from him, that I forgot to say that in any case it was an accident that the house I'd come to was his.

"Zerd, I know there is complete hatred between us, but you are the only one who can save me. Kill me, but don't let them torture me. I am yours, I surrender completely, I am your prisoner but don't let me be theirs."

He had lifted me suddenly, one arm round my shoulders, the other under my knees. "Why are you wet through?"

He carried me up the farther stairs, kicked open a decorated door, laid me on something soft. I was warm. I was in a big room, a fire gigantic in the hearth and torches round the walls, I was on a great circular bed which was covered by a musky musty fur.

He took off my cloak, and held my arms, clasped together at the wrists in one of his hands. My teeth were chattering. He pulled my shift up over my head. "Did he fish you out of the harbour?" I had closed my eyes. My eyelids were almost unbearably irritated, as though it was grit and not tears sliding from beneath them and streaming down my face. I felt him lifting the fur in handfuls and rubbing my body with it. "Salt water, it'll be bad for the fur—" I think I jabbered. He lifted me again. I was aware of the sinews under the scales. He was tucking me into his bed, folding my arms like a baby's, smoothing the sheet. Was I asleep now? No, I couldn't be, because there was a thumping on the door. My heart? No, definitely on the door.

I opened my eyes. The General was flinging off his shirt, boots, belt. On his way to the door he dishevelled, with a thrust, the bed he'd just finished smoothing. He opened the door, scowling, doing up his belt again.

There was a force of Southern soldiers outside, greenjackets, not the sentries attached to this house. They fidgeted: the General didn't even say, "Well?"

"It's been reported to us, sir, by one of our—your—sentries, that the wanted girl is in hiding here. We have orders to search."

"Even in my bedchamber?"

They cleared their throats uncomfortably.

He stood aside, with an ironic gesture invited them blushing in. "The only girl here, gentlemen, is this one." They all looked at me in the dishevelled bed, at the General's scowling state of undress. "But by all means search. I mustn't keep you from carrying out your duty. Look under the carpet, the floorboards, even the mattress. No spy must be allowed to escape."

They searched very perfunctorily, their ears bright with embarrassment, keeping well away from me, poking tentative spears at hangings they took care not to tear. "Thank you, sir. That'll be all. Obviously no one in here. Sorry to have interrupted—disturbed you—Sir."

They all saluted while jostling each other out.

I was sitting in bed weeping.

He came and sat beside me, an arm round my shoulders. "I needn't have saved you, but I did."

"I *know* you needn't have." A ridiculous, almost delicious suspicion struck me, as it did once before at another terrible moment when he was taking me to execution and I had refused to sleep with him and it had turned out that he is sensitive about his skin. I think he is actually rather naïve: a soldier, a lecher, a powerful leader, each aspect simple, brilliant but unadulterated. All that complicates him is his unaffected cynicism, his knowledge of human nature, the way *nothing* in any way unreal can sway him.

"General, I apologize for this, it can throw suspicion on you."

"It has. But I'm glad you came."

Then I remembered that he's wanted to get me for ages because I know the secret of the formula.

I said, "If I were in my right mind I wouldn't tell you this,
390

but death will seem kind when it is not—*that* way of dying—and you may be vengeful, you may torture me, but I don't think it will be that way either." He was waiting, watching me with a sort of smile. I took a deep silent breath. "I told the Temple black-robes the formula."

His face went completely blank, the last thing I'd expected it to do. I went on, tripping a little over my own tongue, "They said they'd—flay me—if I didn't, so I did. They must have been determined to finish me off anyway because they came back and pretended it was the wrong one—Then Kaselm helped me escape but he gave the captain of the boat all that money to go to waste, because I had to get off and I swam here—Kaselm is too clever and powerful to suffer for helping me, he rules a whole kingdom underground—but I have brought trouble with me—And I have told the formula—You must know—I am sorry that I am a coward, and have made it impossible for you to destroy Atlan." I really was sorry, too. I felt utterly and completely maudlin, as though it wasn't enough to offer myself for execution in return for rescue from alien torture, I had to be enormously remorsefully overcome by my ruining all the plans I had always hated.

"You have thought, all these months, that you knew the formula? I can understand your believing it in the first shock, which I took advantage of, but that you never realized afterwards—You are really incredibly naïve." As I had just finished thinking that of him I was rather nettled.

He was drawing two fingers across his chin when I looked up at him again. "Wait a moment," he said. He got up and went out, bare-chested and barefoot. He was away half an hour, as it turned out. I was still awake but very drowsy when he came back. I was lying huddled in the bed, curled as though in a dark, wonderful, safe womb, luxuriating in safety as though I could quench thirst, feed hunger and ease pain with it.

He sat down almost on my feet and I twisted to regard him. I could feel the clearness of my own eyes. He gazed into them with all the darkness of his.

"Can you sleep?"

"I think I no longer need to. I would sooner you talked, General if you don't actually despise the idea. I take it I'm no longer facing imminent death?"

"You never faced it from me. Well—not since we reached Southernland." He said, "Floss-hair." Then he laughed. To a certain extent, his eyes were glittering and his voice vibrant. He

391

was near excitement—he was waiting for something I didn't know about and I was connected with a kind of expectation too. At the same time he was lazily amused about everything —whatever everything was.

He leaned back, stretched, the now dimming flames delirious on his calm, vibrant muscles. He has crazy elbows which go into sort of veined, mild whirlpools when he straightens his arms. His crocodile-strength is apparent in every part of his fabulous, almost mythical body.

"So," he remarked, "all Summer you've been the Court's rave under the impression that I was waiting to *get* you. Charming. You're such an extraordinary child that you're never pathetic. You were tremendously interesting to watch in your kitchen days—and your legs were always fascinatingly un-selfconscious—but though it was obvious that at times you had decided you were suffering, one never felt it was time to step in. And I always put it off for another day, like a wine which is all the better for the leaving, but rarely for more than a day at a time, because you were so invariably amusing in your certainty about your anonymity. And then suddenly you were no longer there. And on that very hot day at the beginning of Summer, you overheard that formula—did you seriously think about it and still think we would have gone round mentioning the all-important formula, so casually? The formula you cherished was that month's nickname for the real formula—a kind of doggerel for it, not even a key-word, nothing to do with the real signs of it. But I'm sorry it got you into trouble with your hosts the black-robes."

He paused, smiled, busy with his lazy amusement and something else again.

"Have you ever had the sudden lift when you realize you can actually respect someone? Even though you were hoping for the sake of your plans that they'd succumb?"

I couldn't understand him, he meant he'd respected me at least once (I wasn't being too optimistic), but considering I'd been matter-of-factly selfish, ever since he'd first noticed me . . .

"No, I could never have cared less if you told the Southerners that formula. The chase was solely for your benefit, to get you."

I lay, not moving, but the clearness of my eyes was beginning to sear me and was no longer serenity, and safety became heavier. Those amused powerful lies to stampede me into sleeping with him. Did he care quite a bit about actually possessing this personality of mine he's been studying, or not at all?

There was no more to be said.

He had just saved me from what was literally far worse than death. I could not, by any stretch of the imagination, hear myself saying to him, "It wasn't fair to get someone to sleep with you by pretending that the only alternative was immediate execution—and the only prospect execution anyway."

He is cruel, lazily amused by analysis.

He sat watching me as I felt myself let go, drift back into drowsiness, still without moving.

"I hoped you would say something, anything, Floss-hair. In fact, I never thought that you would say nothing. But then, you are a very sleepy little thing, aren't you, and have been through a lot today, and you don't really understand being wanted. I am sure you have decided, there is no more to be said. Yes, sleep if you can. We'll be away before the first cock shocks the town."

Away!

I woke as I was being lifted into the chariot. The air was outdoors air again, that was the first thing I noticed, chilly with that wind which skirls and fleers before the dawn, smelling of sea and magnolias—and birds. There was the busy sound of a large body of men and birds being as silent as possible without getting fussy over it.

I was wrapped in my cloak again. As I was handed into the chariot the Diary banged and half lurched out of my pocket.

I was already in the chariot and, momentarily, fully awake. Zerd had discovered *this book!* I sprang to intercept him with an anguished cry. He turned it over, amused, looked at the cover, said, "Well, well, No. 8. High Quality Paper Account-Book, eh?"

He tucked it back in my pocket.

"Where are we all going?" We were swinging into motion. Oh, *familiarity;* the sounds of men and birds on the march. We passed the dark gardens on one side, the white steps on the other, and on each step a Southern sentry lay dead.

"You have declared war by doing that."

"It was time."

Presently we were joined by other regiments. We must be complete now, a vast army, though small by Southern standards.

"We've been ready organized for some time now."

"This road isn't taking us through the Town. Are we going

393

to follow the river? Surely they'll find it easy to follow us?"

"It's quicker through the hills. It'll do them no good to follow us—they have a reasonably large force here but they won't want to have to face us in the hills, with us above them. I'm making towards the coast—they'll try to head me off and get me between here and the Capital where they've got the rest of their force. Well, they have a navy on the beaches but who knows, perhaps we can deal with that if we don't allow ourselves to be trapped between navy and army. Are you cold?"

"It is chilly . . . "

"It'll be chillier soon." He wrapped a fur rug round me, folding it under my chin. Then he set a leather bottle of wine to my lips, and then made me eat meat and two apples. It was a narrow, high-slung chariot, a racing chariot and very draughty, drawn by a brace of birds unusually trained as a team, but I think he would have preferred to ride and was grateful to him for staying with me.

"Is your wife the princess in another chariot?"

"No—My wife is no longer of use to me."

I shivered beside him.

"You're colder?"

"Depressed—" I didn't say horrified, and thought I was being tactful; then realized that Lara's disappearance was something I'd often willed.

"Depressed? Because my wife has been left behind at the Court? There's no need to be depressed, I should think she'll come to neither harm nor good." He started to pick his teeth with a dagger. The chariot jolted high and I hoped he'd cut his tongue. At once I cheered up. The wish showed me I was throwing off the old, muzzy weakness of irrational gratitude.

Then I realized he was looking at me. "When I said she was no longer of use to me—and she isn't, one doesn't need a decorative, high-born wife to be mistress of one's household and hostess at one's parties when the whole situation's about to dissolve with a burst into war—you thought I meant I'd got rid of her?"

I could only stare at him.

He said, watching me and the quirk at his mouth-corner deepening, "That chase when you thought you'd found out something I would kill you for knowing—You found out something of a similar danger—You saw a dying woman, blue with poison, and heard her blame me. You remembered the illness of your friend, the hostage Smahil, on the hot plains?"

Indeed, I had been picturing the pink princess Lara, blue as

Smahil and that discarded mistress had been.

"I saw no connection," I began to say, but it came out in a whisper. "You may have poisoned her—But the surgeon said Smahil's illness came from a bite, like a snake's—"

"Then let it rest," he said, continuing to pick his teeth. "No, I did not poison Smahil. But it is strange that you did not think so."

I realized that a real threat had passed over me. This only confirmed all that I've guessed. With a bite or scratch, accidental or vicious, he can loose his own deadly poison through the system of the other and higher form of human being.

The air became bright within itself. There were still cold stars in the cold sky. We were in the hills. All the trees were coniferous and the rocks were enamelled with lichens like those on the rocks I studied so often below the tower. The shadows were brooding black and spicy. There were all our numberless, rough, savage sounds to help wake the waking forest, up here—the Hai, Hai of men to animals, barks of birds glad or irritated to be on the march again, squeals of wheels, whip-cracks, hundreds of grunted conversations, beat of boots and sandals, etc., etc. We were moving fast—There was hardly a road, but the climb was easy, the rocks mainly huge and flat. We had hardly any baggage-train compared to former days. It was also rather astonishing how comparatively many men we had lost during the months of continuous brawling and rioting in the Capital.

I suppose I shall always think of the Northern army as "we". I've been part of them so often, and so many intense months at a time, through so many dangers, and I understand them so well. Nevertheless they are my hereditary enemies, and the enemies of that beautiful ultimate privacy, Atlan.

We passed waterfalls and could occasionally hear birdsong between all the rest of the row.

Half-way through the morning we were handed more meat, and soup. Zerd left me for a while and rode about seeing to an awful lot of things and visiting every part of the line. I seized the opportunity to scribble in this, though it came out rather jolted.

I was feeling very alive. Now it was warmer, but I realized for the first time that I was wearing nothing under the fur rug and my cloak but a little shift. Yet within the fur my thighs against each other were warm and smooth and reminded each other of their life.

Mid-evening we camped without tents. Neither are there any

winegirls, jugglers, dancers or musicians. Only Isad had killed a rodent that day, spearing it from his saddle, and he made a ghirza from half of a hard, hairy gourd with a long arm an strings of rodent-gut which he'd dried in a few hours.

Zerd, I (still rug-wrapped like a convalescent) and the commanders sat round a fragrant fire—the fuel was dried dung the men had been gathering—and Isad sang to his rather flat-toned ghirza, love songs which are the rage at the Court we've just left.

> The sickle of his smile
> Cut me to my middle—
> Made my heart lurch a mile—
> Explain me now that riddle.

Zerd watched me, I knew that he wanted the ceaseless love lyrics with their hypnotic tunes to beat ther way past what he thinks my unnatural frigidity—and as a matter of fact, when I looked at his dark face his white fierce smile in it did seem the shape of a sickle . . .

The dark spirit of his nearness flows to me, laps me and enfolds me, the tide of his wanting me and his consciousness of myself is strong enough to overflow his own body and lap me warm. With two fingers he touched the cut across my cheek, made by the batwing in the Vaults. He asked me what it was, his tingling breath not leaving it while I told him. He holds my bowl to my lips, his eyes waiting for mine to come up and meet his. Yes, he wants me. He should have taken me when I was confused with gratitude. Now that I am properly alive again, the very invigoration of his own presence is making me strong enough to ignore him.

I am a spectator to life—I always feel like an interloper, an impostor posing as a human being. I think that even had I not spent my formative years enclosed in the tower, I would always have felt like this. It is invigorating and exhilarating to be with someone like Zerd—someone who is very firmly rooted in life, someone to whom my whole inner mind, should he ever discover it, would seem abnormal—and who is, in spite of his liveness, someone who is aware of all the tricks human beings employ.

Zerd is human evil.

He is not ab-human, nor sub-human, nor even superhuman. Any strong intelligent man could equal his feats of strength and brain. His ruthlessness is the root of human selfishness. He is elemental man—his skin is the same sort of thing as the highly developed fangs of some primitive races, atavistic remnants of the earlier life of the world, signs which more civilized artificial man has long since thrown off.

I went to the chariot to sleep. He wanted me to stay with him under the trees. When I was in the chariot I had a nightmare. I woke and lay looking up. The whispers seemed too loud and well-formed to be wind in the foliage. Before dawn Zerd appeared, he said he'd seen I was awake and we could talk to pass the time. We did not talk much, I pretended to be sleepy and he stroked my hair and held me cradled against him, but as soon as he appeared the whispers had gone. His is so actual a nature that the unreal can't be sustained near him—he comes, haunts go.

With him I get the feeling I am safe from the rest of life—but am in peril from him. He is handsome, desired by every woman, feared by soldiers, popular with mankind. Continents do shake at his tread.

A chilly, grey-skied day—when the sky can be seen.

The forests are thicker and more like jungle, with fantastic undergrowth, difficult, ridged ground and conical boulders difficult to find a way between, stony ice-cold streams that have to be forded.

Zerd has given me a shirt of his, and trousers far too big, absurd and flapping, which I've had to tie at the ankles with odd bits of cord. He hooted with laughter at me and then after that whenever I caught him looking at me he gave me an oddly tender smile. That pleases me so much that I have to remind myself he is good at that sort of thing.

Every now and then we catch a glimpse of the great mountain of the Capital—it is vomiting violent fire.

Unforgivable pain. I opened my eyes. Night. Pain in my leg, exquisite pain which I've never suffered before.

I was lying awake under the thick trees some way from the camp-fire. In my sleep I had thrown off my rug and should have been chilly in the night air, but instead I thought my leg was burning. Had some unnatural spark from the fairly distant fire set me alight without anyone noticing?

I tried to move my leg. I couldn't.

There are two of the worst kinds of nightmare I've had in my real life—the monster you cannot kill, every time you think you've managed it he appears again, and now the limb with the awful heaviness you cannot control. I am rather proud of the fact that even at that moment I was actually managing to think this, though my head was muzzy as though pain were a drink of which I had had too much.

"Zerd," I whimpered, "Zerd." I clenched my teeth. I thought I was about to faint.

An arm groped to me from the darkness. "Floss-hair?"

"Zerd," I was hanging on to the name and it was difficult to remember other words to say. "I think my leg is on fire."

There was a spattering of sparks, a flare of flame, and he was holding a torch behind me. By its light we looked for my leg. I met only two narrow eyes, I believe they were reddish, and eyes were rather the last thing I'd expected. Before I did faint from the pain, I saw just enough more by the torchlight to show me a giant snake, very sinuously thick and with it coils stretched way out among the farther trees, lying there intently swallowing my leg, edging itself up by its teeth.

When I came to, I was in Zerd's arms. He was soothing, calming my shuddering. "Don't move, it'll hurt worse."

"Please, please get it off me."

"It has thousands of tiny teeth, sloping backwards like a shark's—your leg would be a pulp-covered bone if I pulled the snake off, even after killing it. But I'll kill it. Keep very still."

This (I had another thought) would teach me to sleep out of the range of the pickets. My leg was swallowed up to just below the knee. If the snake got to the top of my thigh its teeth wouldn't be strong enough to get farther, it would just lie there digesting my leg inside it, I wouldn't be free till my leg had rotted right off—

Zerd was now stooping with an axe. The snake was too busy eating me to notice. He brought the axe down on the snake about twelve inches below where he judged my foot to be. The snake, shocked, dug all its teeth in. I screamed. Two commanders and three sentries appeared all in a hurry. "Keep back," grunted Zerd. I presume they did, watching in horror, but I didn't look at them. Zerd was hacking at the snake which in its death agonies began a series of horrible jerks and kicks and thrashings which in their completely wild abandon were far more dangerous even than the deliberate squeezing-coils of such a snake would be when alive. The pain was terrible. I screamed again and again. I think I heard other people arriving and Isad sending them way again. Blood spurted everywhere.

It lay dead, still twitching like a death-convulsed eel, scores of times bigger than the ones I used to cut up at H.Q. Zerd slit it down the sides from its jaw hinges, eased off its teeth, extricated my leg. It would in every way be silly to try and describe the pain. Having lifted me into the chariot and ordered everyone to leave us alone, he soothed unguents on to my leg, finally bound it again and again.

"My trousers which were so loose on you before will have to be slit now to enclose this bandaging," he said matter-of-factly.

I was sobbing.

"Oh, thank you, thank you. No one has ever been so wonderful to me—You have saved my life so many times, and it was so horrible—Will you ever forgive me that I was going to kill you, or have you already forgiven me out of your generosity?" I have never been so completely sincere, like a child saved from a terrible nightmare by a nurse whom it knows it was unforgivable to the very day before, and knows its unworthiness—no, I have felt like this one other time since childhood, when I met the grey-robed priest in the merchant's house.

*"Were* you?"

"Going to kill you—Oh, not of course since I arrived in Southernland, it was all really too much for me right from the beginning but I was very grimly determined—"

"To assassinate me?"

The astonished laughter in his voice made me realize he didn't know, it was *new* to him.

"Didn't Ooldra tell you?"

"Why should she have?"

"When I was discovered in your room by Lara and I had to run—And it turned out Ooldra, whom I thought was helping me to kill you for my mother (didn't you know that was the only reason I was let out of the tower?)—Ooldra wanted to betray me, she was going to tell you I meant to kill you, and she had witnesses to prove it—So I had to escape, one of the very narrowest escapes I've ever had—" My leg, deadened by the unguents, throbbed as though it were leaping a yard at each throb. It was all too much for me. I remembered vividly that night which had been the cause of delivering me into the governor's hands—the horror of my lovely Ooldra's revealed hate for me and for my mother, her arranging for my death and Zerd's by getting me to kill Zerd and the informing on me—But I hadn't killed Zerd, so she'd had to content herself with gloating over my death only, and I'd had to get away—"Didn't Ooldra tell you, after all, that I'd been working

399

to assassinate you ever since you let me join your army as one of the hostages?"

"You have no idea how much this interests me," he said—unnecessarily, I should have thought. "So you were playing the mythical heroine, who lures her country's desecrator to bed so that she can stab him? Poor little innocent on the altar of your mother's hate and patriotism. But you played your part very well at times—It was easy to think you a high-born lightskirt like your companion hostages. How sad it was all wasted, and I was interested in you only when you showed that other side of your personality—what I've come to realize is the real side of it. I suppose I saw it only when your acting was wearing thin—I exasperated you often, didn't I, and you threw caution to the winds. *Very* reckless of you, and you new to life. I was the first man you ever saw."

I remembered Smahil and the Capital mentioning Ooldra's "disappearance". I pictured her, realizing I'd escaped, not bothering to tell me but abandoning me to the dangers of the South and embarking on her own journey back to my mother's land. "So Ooldra never told you?"

"She didn't get the chance. As soon as I found you missing she was killed for failing to keep you. After all, wasn't she supposed to be your nurse and companion?"

That took my breath away.

He'd searched for me that very night after I ran from him—I'd been nowhere to be found—Had he been enraged at Ooldra for failing to keep an eye on me? He had treated her, *Ooldra,* like the servant no one else had ever thought her, and had had her executed.

Ooldra was dead.

Ooldra is dead—So *that* is the haunt!

Ooldra's ghost, following me with its long hate, her whispers in my ears—

"Turns out an even better thing I had her executed, now that I know she was going to inform on your nefarious activities. If word of all that had reached my princess, you'd have been done for. But I never liked your Ooldra being around."

"She hated you."

"Years before, she'd thrown herself at my head and I'd—spurned her. Yes, that's the word, because the whole scene did become quite melodramatic. But I don't like cat-faced females." He started whistling.

"I didn't think she was sexy enough to throw herself at anyone," I said. "She was cold and high above the world—"

400

"Didn't you know she was your father's mistress?"

"Oh, yes, she told me on the last night but that still doesn't mean—"

"And they have several children, whose backs were branded before they were turned out on the world to high-born foster-parents who never quite realized how they got the children—"

I had never forgotten the tiny brand on my lover's back, I had known it so well.

Eng came to ask Zerd to confer round the camp-fire with the other commanders.

My loneliness gushed upon my being.

Now it is clear why I am so open to the haunt.

That time of magnetic flaming in the middle of the cold squalor, the obscenity of Terez, the violence, the bewildered near-hate, the yearning to all the delirious strength and tenderness in him—and he my father's son, my father the high priest's and Ooldra's—

Horror, corroding horror, revulsion from oneself and the beloved (if Smahil was "the beloved")—a weight of guilt whose possible weight was hitherto unguessed; and beneath it all a kind of pride, for it really is a wicked sin one has committed: incest, very obscure and sinful; not many people have done so. My leg throbs and the whispers crowd on me. "Zerd," I whimper, "Zerd." And horribly it is repeated, a repetition clogging the air so that he cannot hear the original. Small insidious whispers, clogging air, thicker—thicker . . . Nearer, nearer, from all sides, I couldn't hear any *human* speech though the camp-fire conference was so near—Then he came, and dawn.

The army moved on.

Shall I ever be happy again?

"Bandits on the Golds' left flank, sir," said the officer reporting.

We were driven there at once, for Zerd's bird was being groomed somewhere else.

I lay back in the fur, hardly watching anything we passed, too weak with different kinds of pain. I realized that Smahil is somewhere about in the 18th Foot. At the thought of meeting him any possible minute, by some accident, my stomach did not turn over as it should. But my knees went weak, and that made me feel rotten.

Presently we met the deputation of bandits.

They were a ragged, motley, dirty, picturesque group and they were fully confident in their own hard ruffian flamboyance even though they were meeting the military man most famed for brilliance in the known world.

They wore big coloured sashes and most of their clothes were striped, fringed and tasselled. (And stuck full of weapons.) They were in appalling condition (the weapons were the only thing they wore immaculate) but because the original material and design of the clothes had been impressive they didn't seem to realize they'd changed. Some were on foot, some astride muscular skewbald ponies with fierce eyes, showy but insufficient obviously unnecessary harness, and so short their riders' feet nearly dragged on the rocks to either side.

When they saw Zerd they all saluted without waiting to be informed it was him. You could tell they were proud to have recognized him. Their salute was a wild, syncopated arm movement, each man made it separately, they hadn't been trained as a unit.

"I greet you," said Zerd, getting out of the chariot.

Then there was a lot of talking I couldn't hear. Zerd sent someone for wine and the bandits politely drank a lot of it to show they didn't dislike it.

Finally Zerd came back. He ignored me and talked to Clor, Isad and Eng. Huddled near them, I made out that it is very tricky for an army to get anywhere near the Capital as the sentinel mountain and several others are *raining* fire nearly all the time, and so are quite a few mountains on the way to the coast. It is annoying of Southernland's mountains to all start their eruption-period now, but the bandits say everyone knows the great Southern magicians are working against him and the eruptions are the result. Zerd naturally laughs at that as he doesn't believe in magic, also he says it'll make it rather awkward for the even larger Southern army, and it will obviously be coming to guerrilla warfare and he thinks he can beat them at that. Well, the bandits say tactfully, it's well known your army isn't worthy of you, and raw troops have never before been known to be much good at guerrilla tactics. And they offered their own service. They said they are hereditary enemies of the Southern army and would ask nothing more than to have the satisfaction of hindering them.

"It's too easy," growled Clor. "They don't ask for medals, goods or women. It's a trap. They want to report our plans to the blasted South."

"They've invited myself and commanders to a feast in their stronghold, to discuss with their chief."

"Let's risk offending them by refusing," Clor urged

gloomily. "While they're getting us drunk their main force will fall on ours with the help of the Southerners who can't be far behind now."

But of course they went over to join the bandits.

One on a skewbald started forward and they all folllowed him. As he was about to climb the cliff-slope behind me he looked at me and called to the General.

"And your lady-wife, too!"

The General cocked an amused eybrow at me, remembering me, not aiming the amusement for me to share. "The lady is not my wife."

I expected the bandit to ride on past but for a couple of moments more he stared, which embarrassed me and I smiled at him and shifted in my furs to give an order to the chariot driver. I heard the bandit say in that ceremonious-naïve way they have, "She is your lady-mistress? You must bring her to honour our chief's trough." (As I later found, they have troughs instead of tables.) I turned and saw the bandit staring at the top of my cloak left revealed by the fur.

"She is incapacitated for the ride by a leg only just beginning to heal," Zerd said, not denying that I was his lady-mistress.

"I will esteem it an honour if you will let me drive her chariot," said this courteous and hospitable bandit. "It is a beautiful narrow chariot, and I can easily drive it here. I know these rocks and boulders as well as I know my girl-friend's bottom."

Zerd didn't bother to say more. The driver got off the chariot-perch on to which the bandit bounded, a foot-bandit took his vacated saddle, and we moved up the periolous joggy ascent, the Generals and commanders' marvellous birds making as light work of it as the skewbalds used all their lives to it, but making a lot of fuss and flapping their wings with that ugly tearing sound.

The bandit drove expertly but very carelessly, keeping the reins in one hand and turning round to show me something he'd been fishing for in his sash.

What he held was a piece of ragged cloth, exactly matching cloth and colour of my cloak.

"You reckernise this?" he said.

"You must be Kond." He looked rather different now. The young man who'd torn my cloak that slaughter-morning in the rain had been thinner and crazier-eyed, with dirt-thick hair plastered to his skull. He was still ragged and dirty, but dry, and with a different air, of dangerous well-fed flamboyance.

"Ha," he said, "little did I realize I was being succoured and rescued by the General's mistress. No wonder you wouldn't come to the hills with me, eh? And now here you are after all."

I was mildly amused by his conversation though I didn't bother to answer. I hardly felt nervous even about his driving. If at this reckless speed we overturned and I fell, helpless with my bandaged leg, and cracked my head on a rock, it would put an end to various things. For one thing, the cold. I wasn't in the state of mind to be exhilarated by the unnecessary cold. Not much farther up than the main army, but on rocky ridges bare to the winds except for stunted trees twisted almost parallel with the ground, the cold numbed my jaw but pained my leg and spiked my eyeballs. The bandits wore decrepit clothes but several layers of them, though far less than I'd've needed.

"I kept this bit o' stuff," he shouted, waving it at me as we lurched terribly, "In case you ever came, to prove to you it was still me."

"You thought I'd be gratified to find I'd saved such a handsome bandit?"

He laughed uproariously as if I'd said something very witty, and for the moment devoted his attention to tucking the piece back in his sash.

In spite of this driving, we were still wheels-down when we reached the great squat opening. The ponies were led away. I was helped out of the chariot. The new warmth was badly irritating my leg and I also had a fit of sneezing. I didn't notice many details till I was in the great Cavern.

Not tightly, respectfully, Kond carried me to a big carved chair with a pelt across it. Zerd and the commanders were being greeted by a horrible man. He was very big, with skin like leather, muscles like springs, and very cold, dark-blue eyes. He wore a black bearskin slung over one shoulder and belted with a wide studded weapon-band, over shaggy pony-skin trews. He was so scarred that at first his agate-studded dull-metal bracelet seemed just more scars, his skin was so coruscated. He had a clear pleasant voice, rather light. This was Ael, the bandit chief.

We all sat in front of an elaborately carved trough full of bubbling stew, and dipped in. I didn't eat much because I didn't like getting my fingers so messy. I'd been seated too far from Zerd and Ael to hear much unless I made an effort. I didn't bother. I watched night come on outside the cavern entrance. A woman brought us mulled wine and I asked if I could have milk instead. She nodded but didn't come back with it for me. There were dark openings round the rocky walls, they must lead to inner caves, and the roof was never more than seven feet high but in some places it got so low one would have to stoop. Under the low parts pallets had been set for sleeping. There were other troughs and groups in the cavern but the bandits didn't make too much noise—when they got noisy enough to disturb their chief's conversation with Zerd, Ael looked up and across at them and that was enough, except that once they were absorbed in the wrestling of two of their comrades and didn't see him and so fast one hardly realized what was happening he seized a spear from beside him and launched it at them. With powerful straight force it went through the fleshy part of a man's arm and he yelped and hurried to the women's end of the cavern. After that it was very quiet for a while, but Ael allowed a reasonable buzz of noise everywhere. Also, there were dogs tumbling and barking round the fires. I saw only one or two oldish children, I suppose the rest were down the women's end, where I couldn't make out much more than dark moving forms against the glow of cooking fires.

There were only stars to be watched outside now. Part of the time I watched Ael, though each second I was frightened he'd notice. But neither he nor Zerd looked my way at all. The bandit chief's deep blue eyes were colder and more analytic than I'd ever seen, even the pale eyes of the few sadists I've met.

"No wine for you?" asked Kond.

"Oh, hi. No, I asked a woman for milk instead and she promised to bring it but hasn't turned up since."

"Milk? Feel sick?"

"A little—and a headache," I said.

He got up and strolled purposefully away. When he came back he was accompanied by the sullen-eyed woman bearing a jug. She set this down before me and went away again. Of course, in addition to showing her she must obey, he would not have performed the feminine task of carrying it himself. I drank from the jug-lip. The milk was hot and had a thick surface of rather smoky cream.

"Thank you. Is it safe to leave your chief's conference to fetch milk for a girl?"

"I know all they're saying, though it'll take the evening. Besides, one must be polite to the guest-of-honour's mistress."

"Oh—Well, if you're depending on that—You'd better lay

405

off looking after my comfort, I'm not the General's mistress, only I was arrested by his Southern sentries the night he left, so he brought me with him."

"I'll still look after you," he said sweetly. "Didn't you cleverly save my life, and you only a baby and thinking me ungrateful at times, which I never was, but I just wanted to kill that bastard my jailer, and your sweet nature wouldn't allow it. It's a nature must be obvious to everyone, and I wouldn't believe the General hadn't taken advantage of you except I remembered your leg." He directed a sympathetic regard on it. "Drink up. How's your poor little head? By the way, what were you arrested for?"

"Trespassing."

He gave a hoot and a splutter of laughter, went "Haw-haw" and slapped his thigh. "Ah, you're a one, you are. You're good at being in the wrong place at the right time."

I remembered he'd thought I was a trespasser when I first discovered him in the Temple prison grounds.

Ael was honouring these guests to whom he was offering his martial support. Women now bore to us bowls of fresh-roast bear hams, a rare delicacy which impressed on us the valour and might of Ael's bandits. As a further gesture, he summoned a man whom he referred to as his taster, golden-skinned slave they'd captured once. I could guess from my knowledge of Zerd's casual everyday life that he thought a taster in a bandit tribe ridiculously ostentatious. "All the men dislike him because he's a yaller-skin and finicky at avoiding fights, but good with the women," said Ael, amused by his double mastery: his rough, tough men and his civilized slave. The taster gave a demure smile as he approached the ham; this was his moment. A piece of the toughest ham had been set aside for him (his function was merely nominal). Almost before his adam's apple had bobbed up again after he swallowed, he let out a screech and clasped his abdomen. He screeched again, fell to the rock floor, writhed, disturbing a few filthy goatskin rugs, and died with froth on his lips.

Ael gave a happy tenor giggle like a child's.

"I told you the men disliked him." He picked up a ham and started to eat it. Eng gave an involuntary movement. "Oh, no, they knew which he'd be given," Ael said. "There's no danger. It's a case of the poison *meant* for the taster."

The body was left before us till we'd finished eating and it was time for the entertainment. A comely girl came forward. She carried a shut basket and was accompanied by two fierce-

406

looking adolescent boys with primitive tambourines. She had red hair in two very long plaits which went down the neck of her tunic and appeared with her ankles from the other end. The boys sat cross-legged and started to sway their bodies and instruments; she stood, swaying in time, opened her basket and took out a thin green-and-yellow snake. Although snakes were something which still made me shiver, I was fascinated by the things she did with this one. Finally she encouraged it to crawl up one of her nostrils and reappear out of her mouth.

She was clapped and Zerd threw her a brooch, so then the commanders threw her things too. I wanted to give her something but was wearing no jewellery at all.

Now it was time to go. The men rose and clasped each other's arms. It was arranged that Zerd should travel on towards the coast, getting his army as best he could between the volcanoes, and the bandits would wait only for the Southern army, to harry it for all they were worth, and follow it hindering it from every direction and giving Zerd time to reach the coast and deal with the Southern navy there.

The whole point was that the bandits expect a jolly good whack in Atlan, which under no circumstances would they get from their own government. I shan't be able to help laughing if after all this trouble everyone breaks through into Atlan and finds it a miserable place with no resources or wealth.

I hadn't realized how warm and comfortable this one evening had made me until I realized it was time to return to the cold, painful, jogged travelling.

"You're going to have to travel at speed, General," said Kond.

"I think I can manage that," Zerd replied.

"What about this young lady?" said Kond. "I understand you brought her with you out of kindness. It won't half be a hard journey for such a young lady with such a sore leg."

Zerd looked suspiciously at Kond. Yet he couldn't deny it. "I don't deny it," he said impatiently.

"It'll have time to heal up proper if she stays the few days with us before we come on to join you," Kond said. "Where with you it may never heal, what a shame it would be and all, and complications might even get it."

"Cija?" Zerd said angrily, he knew what I'd reply. "Do you feel you need to stay?"

"It would be an unexpected delight," I said, "not to have to travel like this."

"It would be very kind," Zerd said, turning to Ael, "if you

407

would keep her till her leg is nearer healing? I shall emphasize that I want her returned to me. She's not for sale," he half-indicated Kond.

"She will be well treated," Ael assured him.

I was *furious* at being talked of as a slave. Nor for sale! He might be trying to keep me safe while I was left alone here, by making them think me his property, or more likely just meant to keep me for himself, but I am damned well not a slave, never have been, and never will be. There's no need never to accord me the respect he'd given his damn forest princess, whose blood was probably many times worse than mine.

The bandits and Northerner took ceremonial, cordial, temporary-leave of each other. Zerd came over to talk to me, which at least is an improvement, there was a time when he'd just have left without another look at me.

"You aren't nervous at staying?" he said. "No," I said, though I was a little.

"Probably you should be," he said, with a saturnine glance, but that was only to upset me. "Do you want me to leave anything with you?"

"The clothes I'm wearing, if you can spare them."

"I think so." He seemed at a loss, but didn't once mention my pain and hope it would be helped.

"Goodbye, Your Mightiness."

"We'll be meeting again in a couple of weeks, Floss-hair."

He and his commanders went out escorted by Ael and others.

I saw the wind meet their cloaks as they went out past the entrance and into the cold, roaring, icy-starred, black night. Kond was one of the escort.

While I waited for Ael and Kond to return and deal with me I just lay back in the big chair. The fires in the huge low cavern were now glowing to death. The dogs had stopped barking so much and were growling over bones and scratching for fleas. People were lying down on the pallets. I myself thought I already had some fleas. The smell of this place was pretty strong but it was rather comforting—I suppose if the temperature outside were less cold the smell inside would be actually horrid. But even all those fires only warm the place in bits—it is full of cold islands and draughts.

Finally I did ask a passing woman if there were any fountain-rooms. She stared resentfully and said I'd have to be satisfied with the communal pits above the ravine. "What if I want to wash?" I said. "Wash!" she repeated. "I've a bad leg,"

I said. "The ointments'll need washing off and renewing every so often. Don't you wash your men's wounds?" "I suppose you can have a bowl of boiled water every now and then," she said, in the same voice the other woman said I could have milk.

Later I heard, "She's fell asleep, poor little soul, don't it just show how she needs the rest."

"Kond . . . " I murmured.

"Kond's here," he said soapily, then I heard his chuckle. Obviously one of those people whose own behaviour-patterns strike them as very funny. "You'll have to sleep in my bed—there aren't any spares at the moment—but it's good and wide." Having blinked awake, the first thing my eyes met were two very cold eyes. I was looking past Kond, bending over me, to Ael who was leaning against his high-backed chair and regarding me for the first time. "You have no objection, chief, eh?" inquired Kond.

"It depends what you can trust her to tell the General. And you can't cut out her tongue, unless you can think of some reason to account for such an accident."

"Ah, then," said Kond. "I don't mean her no harm *to* cut her tongue out because of. There, baby, Kond will carry you safe to bed now. Tell the Dragon if you like, if he don't have an innocent mind enough to take it on the chin, well I can only say he won't win many battles if he don't never believe what he's told."

When he'd laid me on the pallet, lain down beside me without removing even his boots, and dragged the pelts and rugs up over us, he did start pulling me towards him but I acted sleepier even than I was. He threw a heavy arm over me and I was content for about ten minutes thinking he'd dozed, then he was caressing my breast in an almost unexceptional, friendly, courteous way. I started and said, "Oh, look, I thought you—" "All right, darling," he said good-naturedly, desisting. He tugged me closer, grunted a few times, burrowed his unshaven head on my shoulder and was soon snoring into my neck.

It was only one new set of snores added to a dozen others. We were surrounded on either side, to our feet and heads by other pallets with sleepers over which Kond, stooping because of the low roof, had stepped nimbly when bearing me here. I could smell the boots of the man sleeping behind us—if he thrust with them during some nightmare, my head might be done for. There was just enough firelight left to play over the roof and show me, as I lay on my back staring up, a very pornographic drawing (though not badly-done, and lively) recently made by passing a candle under the roof and letting the carbon line more blackly the stale-smoke-black rock. I continued, however, to stare straight up as, if I looked to either side, I was embarrassed by similar scenes on the pallets. I did not mean to shut my eyes till I was very tired, for fear of the whispers. My mind wandered back to Kaselm and his offer of safety in the Vaults which I'd rejected as a life of crime and dirt. And now . . . Oh, well, it was only for a few days and was better than hard, fast travelling among bitterly cold hills without a road and with a leg which gave me dizzy pains. Kaselm—during all my time of distrust (I'd become almost proud that I never trusted anyone) his "deep game" had been kindness. But *now* I was again alone, and ill too, which I'd never before been, it might interfere with my small but hitherto sufficient resourcefulness.

No whispers came. I don't suppose Ooldra could have borne it in that sort-of-hole crowded with tough humanity.

At once I knew it was all right, somehow, I wasn't frightened even when I was wakened by something heavy bounding on me and something hot, wet and harsh on my face. It was a dog, admittedly a puppy, but it wasn't going to be much good at hunting bears if it was always that friendly to strangers. I got my hands out from under the bedclothes and it and patted it awkwardly, and when if snuffled too much at me (perhaps, after all, it thought I was some kind of prey in a burrow) I hit it away so deliberately that it went. Just as well—its teeth were already well-developed.

It was morning, if I could trust the faint colourless light just percolating to here. I was still surrounded by snores. I'd wakened stiff and tried to shift but discovered I was pinned down. Besides Kond's head on my shoulder, there was his heavy arm across my ribcage and some time in the night he'd flung one leg over me as if he'd been dreaming of straddling a horse. Luckily it was my O.K. leg his was across.

I wondered how long ago dawn had been, and when the tribe woke. I hadn't been lying awake long when I heard a clatter and saw the sentries coming in from outside (of course didn't know then who they were). Because of the roof-dip where I was I could only see their legs.

A little later the whole cavern seemed to be waking up. Some had heard the sentries come in, they stirred, that woke others. Underneath all the roof-dips in the cavern, the island o pallets, people were waking, then rising. It didn't take them long to get up, they'd all slept fully clothed.

Kond gave a series of grunts, like those he'd gone to sleep with, and then nuzzled his head about on my neck. "Do you mind?" I said. "Your bristles aren't exactly soft."

"Urr . . . rr?"

He opened his eyes, looked blearily up at me from my shoulder, flashed a grin, brought up a hand and pulled my hair, suddenly caught me a hefty whack as he pushed out his elbows, he stretched and gaped a yawn.

"Well, how did you sleep, angel-face?"

"I now have my full quota of fleas."

"S'right, big, hairy fleas they are here. You'll be interested when you catches your first."

"Oh, I'm already fascinated, don't worry."

"Can you walk to breakfast?"

"I can limp if you help me and don't mind walking slowly."

"We better start now then, or everybody'll've wolfed our share."

He swung from under the covers, rose, held down a hand for me. I got up awkwardly, remembering at the last moment not to bang my head. Stooping, we made our way over the pallets, occasionally standing on bits of prone figures who soon let us know about it, till we could stand upright and saw bandits converging on the newly-filled troughs beside the new-lit fires. The women served, and would have their meal later on what the men left. A very few other women were eating with the men, but none of the older or very young ones.

Kond and I sat where we had last night. I was rather put-off to find the same kind of stew in the trough again.

"Where's Ael?"

"He's served in his own room."

"Room?"

"He has a private cave, one of the smaller ones off this."

"Do you have this stew for breakfast, midday and dinner?"

"Doncha like it then?"

"It's all right but don't you get bored with it?"

"Oh, you won't get bored with it," he cheerfully assured me, so for fear of sounding neurotic I didn't say I already was.

Now the men around the cavern were rising, wiping the backs of their arms across their mouths, taking spears from stacks and gathering together. Kond began the same procedure.

411

"Where are you going?" It hadn't occurred to me I might be left alone on my first day.

"Day's hunting—some hunting animals, some waiting above the pass for travellers."

I felt a stiffness of distaste. "And what shall I do?"

"I'll call a woman to see to you." He was already striding away.

"Make it a nice woman," I begged hastily catching at his sleeve. He turned to grin down at me. "What you want a nice one for? You're nervous, aincha?"

I tried to think of an answer and the pause was enough to make him grin more broadly than ever as he went away. He liked me being nervous of his everyday life.

In a few minutes he was back with a middle-aged woman handsome but incredibly weatherbeaten and pockmarked However, that didn't put off the bandits; I'd already noticed her at breakfast, how many men smacked her as she served them and teased her just in order to be able to crow in delight over her monosyllabic replies as if they were hard-won compliments. I'd have preferred someone much smaller and gentler but Kond was already saying, "Well, see you." About to dash away, he looked at the woman, winked at me, came back lifted me up by clasping me in both arms and kissed me on the mouth. Ael appeared and everyone left noisily.

The woman and I were left facing each other. I felt at disadvantage as I'd just flopped untidily into a chair again when Kond let me go.

"I understand you're going to help me. It's very kind of you," I said, trying the cavern approach though I knew perfectly well she had to obey Kond. "But before you bathe my leg hadn't you better get your breakfast?" The other women were getting theirs.

"I can fix myself up a tasty broth later," she said. "I'll do you now."

While she was unwinding my bandages and bathing the sticky painful mess underneath, she said, "I'm Golra."

"I'm Cija. Don't call me Mistress." She'd shown no signs of doing so, so perhaps that was rather hopeful of me. She just grunted and next time she spoke started right off calling me Lady. I felt she didn't want to accept my insincere, nervous alien intimacy.

It was a horrid day, full of the usual pain and a lot of dreary empty spaces. Before the noon-meal I managed to sleep a little. The whole day I hardly moved from the same chair. After I' been shown where they were, I had to drag myself to the communal pits above the ravine. They were pretty sickening but the beastly numbing cold kept down the smell and at least there are separate pits for the sexes. In the afternoon I noticed definitely how all the women ignored me except for a group who seemed actively to dislike me. What seemed a whole age after the morning, I was sewing some deer-hide I'd begged as something to do from Golra, the men walked in.

Immediately the cavern's atmosphere lit and became charged with life. The women patted their hair and ran to and fro very industriously, as if they hadn't been dawdling all day; the men threw down their spears, kicked their dogs, also any children who got in the way, and bawled for something to drink.

I found myself shrinking.

I've lived with an army, off and on, for two years—I've even masqueraded as a boy for months—but I can't lose a kind of shock at them, especially if there are a sudden lot of them. Two years ago I thought there was no such thing as a man, that they were extinct from a feminine planet. They are a bit overpowering in the mass, surely anyone would admit that.

Through all the hoarse din, Kond appeared at my side. A girl was hopping along beside him, trying to get wine safely into his mug as he walked, and when she'd succeeded he drank and hit out at her and she affectionately bit his arm and giggled and raced away.

"Have some," he said, sitting beside me.

I drank from his mug which he held to my lips. "Thanks. Did you have a good day?"

"The usual rodents—" he spat on the rugs—"No travellers, and not a sign of the Southern army. But they can't be even a day behind yours. Our scouts'll probably find them tonight."

He called for a girl who came and shaved him. That couldn't happen more than twice a week. He kept moving his head and talking about the hunting, but when she cut him he cursed and threatened that if it happened again she'd be done for. He asked if I'd had a good day and I nodded, but when the girl had gone and he was feeling his new chin, I said, "Golra's all right, but some of the women seem to dislike me. One of them is the woman you made give me milk last night, do you suppose she resented it?"

"Ho," he said deeply.

"Is she stirring them up?"

"No, they all disliked you before that."

413

"But—how?" I began, alarmed. "Because you're with 'em," he said. "I'm too tactful to tell you they think you are actually mine, but there it is. They're Dalig's women, and the women-friends of Dalig's women."

"Well, who's Dalig?"

I got Kond's scowl in all its unshaven grimness, unmasked by stubble.

"He's the dirty bastard who used to be under me—since I was away in that mucking priest-ridden prison he's become Ael's second-in-command."

"And everyone knows you hate each other?"

"One day soon it'll be him or me for good and all."

He brooded, pulling his lip.

"Point Dalig out to me," I invited, feeling as though I were humouring him.

He got behind my ear and directed my line of vision to a tall man, younger than I'd expected, wearing a leather jerkin on which bosses of metal had been sewn to serve as armour, but some of them were now hanging uselessly by threads, he had greasy hair to his shoulders, probably it had once been red, and at some time his nose had almost all been sheared off. Now there was a sort of nothing there, a white-scarred nothing, and his lips had had a few little rubies set in them.

"That makes it very rough when he kisses," growled Kond. "But they seem to bloody well like it enough."

"Have you fought yet?"

"Only once seriously—but they pulled us apart as I was about to do him."

"If you did, you'd be second-in-command again?"

"You said it." He kicked a passing dog. "Would I!"

After brooding some more, he suddenly turned round and said, "What's your name?"

"Cija."

"Cija—Funny I never knew it. I often wondered what it was, remembering you and the way you helped me and then yanked yourself away."

I started up, embarrassed (though he could have asked my name a whole day earlier if he'd really often wanted to know it still he had kept the bit of cloth and a man of this type and used to this life would be too much for me to handle unless he were kept at arm's length) and I forgot I'd a bad leg and he started up with his arm round me. "Want me to take you somewhere?"

414

"I'd forgotten my leg—I'd like to ask Golra if there's such a thing here as a hairbrush."

"I dunno, they may have one—You can borrow my comb."

Perhaps he was too naïve to know he'd worried me, perhaps he thought I wanted to make sure the General got me. Funny how people always think I'm his.

Kond's comb I received gingerly. It had been in one of his scabbards, with a saw-edged knife, and had dirt thick between the teeth. It was wooden and rather warped and the teeth so widely spaced quite big knots would go between them. Still, I couldn't get a cleaner one here—He pulled it out of my hand, roughly unwound my hair and started dragging the comb from root to end of each strand. This was a community so based on the system of woman's subservience that for him to do this publicly wasn't at all demanding, just showed he wanted to.

"Ow! Ow!" and *"Ow!"*

Behind me I heard him laughing into my hair, then he stuffed some into his mouth and said it tasted nice. His senseless crudity was getting on my nerves. "Let go, barbarian."

"Barbarian? What's that, eh?" I'd been ashamed of using such a corny, feminine, petulant word so I just growled, "Oh, never *mind*," and then saw Dalig coming over—He stood in front of us and threw back his head, his thumbs in his hip-belt, and laughed. I could see all the other faces in the cavern turning to watch with three little dark circles in each, two wide eyes and an expectant mouth.

"Kond the maidservant! None of the women can get the tangles out as well as Kond!" hooted the noseless bandit.

It was just a way of challenging, and Kond showed he appreciated that and wasn't going to waste time. He stood up, smashed his fist into Dalig's eye while he drew his knife with the other. Dalig got his leg behind the crook of Kond's and tried to crash him down but was pulled down with him and fell jarringly for a moment on the rock as Kond slipped from beneath him. Kond kicked him in the belly, which wasn't as effective as it sounds because of the metal-sewn jerkin, and then threw himself on him, trying to pin down his arms. Dalig got away and we all settled down to watch a good dirty fight.

I realized later than everyone else that it was matter-of-factly a fight to the death.

They both had knives out. Kond at one point managed to hold off Dalig's stab and at the same time get Dalig's weapon-belt unbuckled and sling it away, but at once he was off

415

balance and Dalig nearly got Kond's arm twisted up behind his
back—Kond swung over Dalig's shoulder, chopped with the
side of his hand hard on Dalig's adam's-apple—Dalig coughed
and got kicked, got his hand on Kond's knife-wrist, twisted
roared as he pulled him over (it was the first sound either had
made with their voices) and was tripped himself. They rolled
over top to toe, each gripping the other's knife-wrist with a
spectacular-tendoned arm, each trying to kick the other's head
in. As a fight there was not much future in this and the au
dience began to yell.

Somehow one of the rugs had got bundled in between them
and a flap of it caught at Kond's eye—Kond got his knife-wrist
free—so did Dalig, parried Kond's thrust, got his ankle
hooked round Kond's neck, lay heavily on him, jerked, slashed
at his throat. Blood appeared on Kond's shoulder, paused, then
poured out. Dalig slashed again, quickly, twice, and made a
welling cross-hatching on Kond's shoulder and neck but hadn'
got any vein. Scrabbling with their boots and legs, Kond
managed to tip Dalig off him and they were both on their feet

Then they started circling each other, stiff-legged, wary
armed, ready any instant to stab or dodge. Kond's arm and
side were red, gouts began to drip to the rugs and collect in th
rocky hollows. The dogs round the circle began to sniff and
pant and their masters held them back by their collars.

Now and then one would stab, and cut or be parried; soon
both were decorated with thin slashes oozing red bead-driblets
and part of Kond's tunic was in ribbons.

Presently each man's panting could be heard, loud an
uneven, and harsh as though it came from a throat of gravel.

Suddenly, just at that moment when everyone has been ex
pecting it just long enough for it to startle them when it does
happen, Kond's knife-hand flashed in low and up, under th
stiff hem of Dalig's jerkin. The decisive thrust had come an
gone just like that. Dalig must have been a very brave man.
expected him to scream but he only gave a sort of "Ug" an
his eyes glazed at the shock of the final *defeat*—Kond mean
to step away that instant, but one of the loose hanging bosse
on Dalig's jerkin had got itself wedged in an interstice c
Kond's tight, elaborate, metal bracelet. Staggering, lurching, h
eyes glazing, blood everywhere and the bones of his face stand
ing out like white stone, Dalig howled, brought his big-toothe
knife held in both hands down with all his force on Kond
head, and fell sprawled in blood. Kond was Kond, young an
new-shaven with two eyes and a firm mouth and unkemp

416

brown hair, and then his two eyes were sliding apart from each other and his head had been split right down.

There was an immediate high keening of women, Ael who had been watching everything without a change of his eyes motioned with his hand, he had survived so many similar battles but more scarred than not; and they came and folded the sprawled limbs and the women wept over them and they carried them away and the women followed . . .

I was sick again and again and a hard hand held my forehead, the scars against my brow increasing my grief and my nausea.

I saved him once and he came to that.

The Southern army was reported by scouts to be on its way through the pass. Things were organized and ready for this, only the women had to be bade farewell . . .

"This litte bitch won't half be an encumbrance, chief."

"She's to be delivered to the Dragon. But I think she's had a relapse, feverish—Someone take her direct to him."

I don't understand. How can the pain in my leg make my head, eyes and ears, and my arms and stomach sore and aching and dizzy?

"I'm all right."

"You'll be no good in guerrilla warfare—and if you stay here it'll mean bad blood with the Dragon. Better if you get to him dead than we say we kept you."

He spared two men to ride fast with me, and told them to feed me well and keep me warm, or run the risk of being executed if they delivered a corpse to the Northern Dragon. If they rode hard, allowing for the detour to avoid the Southerners, it would take little over a day and night to catch up with our army. I was wrapped in furs and finally Ael himself lifted me into a light wicker chariot which would go fast but jolt terribly. His eyes went over me as if checking on me, then rested briefly on mine. They held for a few moments, but without a hint of expression, then there was a "Hai, hai!" and we sprang forward. I wondered muzzily if he blamed me for the killing of both his commanders, but surely he is too intelligent not to know better. It was in the air, it would have happened any time.

I think I was delirious a lot of that journey. There were only stars and a wind, sleet in my face, thick whispering and more and more, then red flashes and when everything was clearer I realized that we had halted above a plain on which the delirium was actualized, there were black figures everywhere and behind that the mountain spurting flame and the river on the plain winding between the combatants, some splashing in the fords, and reflecting the eruption as though it were a stream of lava.

"Is this a battle between the Southerners and Northerners?" I asked.

They said, Yes, it was, but indeed I could see that for myself.

"But I thought we'd reach him before the Southerners would—"

"We was delayed a few hours by the sleet, it was so thick for so long—but this must be the Southern army that was in the Capital."

"You stay here," they said. "You'll be all right. They won't come up here—just stay put." They were itching to be in the battle, and they ran down the slope, becoming black silhouettes as they went distant from me in the warm air, then tinged with red reflection as they neared the river which in its turn reflected the towering eruption which seemed even nearer than it was. Now and then some black flakes would float towards us, but it was very occasional. I couldn't hear much of the rumble and thunder because of the din of the battle. One of my escort plunged into the ford at the hill's foot and at once became merged with the fighters there—the other caught a spear through chest and back almost before he'd got there, and staggered a few feet, then pitched on his face.

They'd left me with a leather bottle of gullet-warming, stomach-warming rum, bread and cheese, fresh fruit and rodent-steak which had been roasted that morning and was reasonably tender.

I made a good meal, to keep my mind off my position, but I found that the combination of food, warm air and urgent excitement had me feeling strong and well. I no longer felt a trace of sickness or delirium. I pushed back the furs and felt my leg. It ached but must be healing. It was suicide to stay stuck in a chariot, waiting—especially when one was perfectly strong—I got out and fell on the ground at once, I was weak from the days before.

I picked myself up, grazed in several places. My head went dizzy and there seemed confused black and yellow spots in my eyes—then I saw the fighting below me again, gritted my teeth and felt better than before.

418

Yes, I was really in an ideal position. This was what I'd wanted all along. Quite alone, free of captors and forcible escorts, and everyone too busy to take any notice of me.

I was light-headed, thought I was walking at one angle and found myself walking at another—lost balance several times, and bumped into boulders I thought I'd avoid by many inches—but my mental confidence made up for that and slowly I made my way round the hill above the battle at which I hardly looked, till at last I'd skirted it, I couldn't see it at all round the hills' bend, and if I climbed down now and trekked in a straight line towards the volcano, I'd miss the battle altogether.

I sat on a flat stone, cushy with pink moss, or maybe it was just glowing pink in this light, and said to myself, "But *why* do I want to get to the volcano?"

"That's a good question, Cija."

There was a long, smug pause.

"Then answer it."

"Oh. Well, because the city's behind it, beside it actually from where I am, and I can search through the city for my grey priest."

"Is he there?"

"I don't know where else he'd be. He must have taken refuge there with those underground movements we're always hearing about—and at least it would be terrible not even to *try* to find him. He's the only person who'll know how to deal with Ooldra, if anyone knows he knows. Don't you realize, Cija, I must get rid of these whispers or I'll have them all my life."

I'd sobered by the time, at red twilight, I reached the city and found the masses of frightened evacuees milling out.

Some of the roads were clogged with wagons; others were deserted. I learnt that the streets nearest the mountain were paved with red-hot lava, but the outer parts of the city were safe and most people were staying there, except for the many families who'd left in case the eruption became even more violent and engulfed the city. The eruption had lasted a long while and almost everybody thought it was giving signs of cooling down.

But also there were looting deserters and wounded of both armies—panic had spread among the citizens. Families who would have stayed were leaving because their neighbours were gone and they felt insecure.

As I penetrated the city, often having to try several roads

before I could find one where I wouldn't be trampled by the streams of traffic in the opposite direction, I found chaos, all trades and normal life at a standstill.

Animals were wandering about, abandoned by their owners, already fierce with starvation. They fought and snarled on window-sills, roofs and cobbles. A small, fluffy cat, a domestic pet, was standing guard before a heap of rubbish. I approached. The cat's belly went down, its head up, and it screamed a threat.

I decided that the first place to try to get a lead on the priest—I knew by now it was pretty impossible, but here I was—was the merchant's house where I first met my priest. Someone there might have an idea where I could go for news of where to look.

I thought I'd remember well enough how to get there, but when I reached the alley I was impeded by a flux of people all surging the other way—I managed to get against the wall and work myself along. The dusk was heavy with floating flakes and there was a red glare over people's faces. Everyone was grimy and paid no attention to anyone but themselves. I was limping but my leg hurt only when it was jogged.

I reached the merchant's house. The door was wide open. I ran up the shallow steps, through the passage, into the inner room. There was no one there, only a disorder of clothes and objects as if the family had left hurriedly. The knocker shaped like a little man warming his hands had been wrenched off the door but they had forgotten it after all, it lay on the floor in the folds of a child's dress. To make sure, I ran down into the cellar and then through every room in the house; but it was empty of life, except for the scuffling of an indignant rat across the floor as I entered the bedroom it had thought safe at last.

I limped out again and forced my way into the alley.

I caught at people's sleeves, aprons, trying to ask them if they knew where the merchant had gone, but they paid no notice to me. Then I was nearly squashed against the wall as a family passed with a heavily laden donkey and a young goat which made a pathetic row, its udder was huge with long-overdue milk. I caught at a fat woman who looked mother-ly—"Please, could you just tell me if you know where the peat merchant went?" but she jostled me heavily aside.

I saw it was useless. Dejected, I stood watching them all pass with their single-minded faces and bundles of gear. Families with wailing children, a keen-eyed pedlar in grey rags, a band of gutter women clutching belongings but obviously more interested in breaking into the various deserted inns about, singing raucously. This was getting worse. I decided I'd better try once more while there was still a chance of asking families who'd lived locally and would know the answer.

"Does anyone know where the peat merchant who used to live here has gone?"

My voice was nearly lost and might as well have been completely drowned—and then the pedlar turned round, and said, "Sorry, I'm a stranger here myself."

"Oh, what a *useless*—" I could have hit the man for turning round and raising my hopes for that.

He forced his way back to my side. "Why do you want to know?"

"Oh, I might as well tell you—" I thought that as he was a pedlar he might not be fond enough of the law to tell on me —"A priest, one of the old régime, those who wear grey leather, he used to come here—"

"You just came back to the city? I hate to tell you, but he's probably been dead months, they've been killing them off—"

"No, I happen to know he was alive early last week at least—" I remembered his deep-sea eyes and his everything-face and how his presence cleansed and undemandingly made one not only whole but wholesome. Unconsciously I used his own phrasing. "But where he is now I dare say they know only in the Land Beyond the Rain-gusts."

His eyes narrowed.

"Why do you want to find him again?"

And then I was alert too, bravo, Cija the beautiful spy. "I'm sorry, I'd prefer not to tell you till you tell me why you want to know why—"

"Mine was a normal query from a friendly pedlar," he said. "But you seem to be hiding a guilty secret."

I looked at him in alarm. He half-smiled.

"He described you to me—I couldn't mistake you," said this pedlar, his accent losing its roughness. "You're even wearing the same cloak he described you as wearing the day you engineered the escape."

"He glimpsed me then?" I cried eagerly. "And he knows *he* was the prisoner for whose sake it was done—he heard me call to Kond to release him—Did he also recognize me—Did he say he'd seen me before, as a page?"

"A page?" The pedlar, quizzical, pushed back his hood a little to scratch his head of thick, long, pallid-gold hair. "Well, everything's possible—And all that old man knows, they maybe realize in the Land Beyond the—"

"You've seen him recently? Where is he?"

"There is an inn with a big, brass sign in the 8th Winding Street from the 7th Bridge—Wait, if I can find some charcoal I'll sketch you a map—"

"It's all right, I know this city very well. Thank you—Thank you very much—" We parted very briskly in our opposite directions.

Now as I pushed my way on into the city I found that many houses were on fire. At first I thought this due to eruption-sparks. Then I saw how much looting was going on—soldiers in Northern as many as Southern uniforms, deserters, or wounded, but not too badly for this sport, many of them drunk, too, roaring and firing empty houses they'd emptied and, if they were Northern, also firing inhabited houses to frighten out the occupants. One thing interrupted all this jollity: if Southern and Northern met looting the same house, they dropped all their plunder and at once set on each other. There were camp-women too—looting a confused city was better than watching their men in battle. Going into houses in bands they were efficiently rapacious. When they were with soldiers they confined themselves more to receiving and sorting the stuff.

In the courtyard of a burning house, which a throng of nuts in blackened Northern uniforms were busy ransacking, a few women sat among piles of cloth, food, furniture and jewellery, sorting it into baskets and laundry-bins and shoe-boxes and in fact any old thing. Needless to say, I was hurrying all I could, limping so fast it was a dragging hop. Each time I passed one nasty place I came to another but something about one of these women caught me and made me look again.

She was sitting, greedily stuffing cheap gauds into a biscuit-box. She wore patched dilapidated clothes. A man's sweat-rag had been holding up her hair but slipped and the long, black hair was all round her shoulders. Her face was smoke-streaked, her glorious bones showing more sharply than before, but it was easy to recognize the Beauty—except that at first I hadn't thought to connect her with this avid slattern.

Well, of course, all this time men were shouting out at me, or catching at me; I was seized and kissed a couple of times and once chased; which was awkward with my leg, but he was

422

drunk and fell down before I did.

With all this I was as dirty and dilapidated as everyone else. I was also limping more joggily, you can't keep up limping speed for long.

To avoid a group of Southerners roaring along ahead, I turned up a roofed alley. It was very dark and when I cannoned into something I was horribly shaken.

"Oi-oi," said a man's voice echoing in the tunnel. "Look where yer going, mate."

I tried to go on, but found my wrists gripped. I twisted and stopped short, he was really holding hard.

"What do you think you're doing?"

"It's an old trick, mate. Bash into someone in a dark alley, pick each other up apologetic, and off you go with my pocketful." He started to frisk me, patting my pockets which were as barren as a great-grandmother, then his hand went into my shirt. "Well," he said. "This is more interesting than a couple of jewelled goblets, isn't it?" His other hand crawled up my neck, the underside of my chin, pinching the flesh there a little, and up over my mouth and nostrils. His hand smelt of metal and dirt and blood and warmth. It explored further. "You have nice hair, too."

"Please let me go," I said calmly. "I'm in a hurry to get somewhere. It's important to me—I'm not bluffing."

"I like to be asked so nice. But you'll need company in this area."

"Don't change your direction for me." "I weren't going nowhere special."

We emerged into the red glare. Immediately we turned to assess each other, and grinned as we caught the other's eyes. He was a big man, quite young, with a short, shapeless beard of coarse, black hair. I'd a right to resent his suspicion of me—he had a sack over his shoulder and it was full of loot.

"Well, where are you going?" he said.

"The 8th Winding Street from the 7th Bridge." I didn't mention the inn in case I wanted to get rid of him later. "Thank you for your company," I said circumspectly.

He was useful, for no one at all any longer annoyed me with him there beside me, and he didn't ask all the questions I'd expected either.

But we soon passed a tavern and he said, Would I like a drink? When I said, "No" he said, Well, he would and I might as well have one with him as wait thirsty.

"But I told you, I'm in a hurry. Please come on—Or if you're dying of thirst, I'll go on alone. Thanks for coming this far."

He gave me an amused look and came, but I could tell he was getting sullen underneath. He was thinking what was there in this for him after all, and he'd also come far enough with me and scared off enough trouble for him to think I owed him something. I decided I'd like to get rid of him soon, or else talk him into genuine friendliness, but with the city and men in this mood I wasn't hopeful.

"Do you know who's winning on the plain?" I said.

"Blasted Northerners," he growled. "But if our lot can hang on long enough there'll be reinforcements coming up, whole new army from the Temple-Town."

"I hope Ael and his hoodlums have done their work well," I thought.

"How did you get your leg in that state?" he said. I said it had been mauled while I was in the hills, and he said I was lucky I had him with me.

"Any of these scoundrels could have made quick work of you by now," he said virtuously. "Well, here we are already at the 8th Winder. Which house do you want?"

"It's all right, thanks, I can find it myself."

"I get it. Well, we'll part here then. Give us a good-bye kiss." I didn't want him to get nasty about being dismissed so I stood on tiptoe and put only one arm round his neck. Before I knew what was happening he'd taken the opportunity to grab me. He hauled me over the ruins of a broken gate and into a fitfully red and black courtyard.

"Please—please—"

"Ah, now it won't take long. Not a virgin, are you?"

I was furious at the way I'd let myself be tricked, but I had to admit it didn't seem the end of the world. It was anger and fear more than horror that made me fight—a good thing because I think horror is physically weakening unless one is lucky enough to go actually a bit mad with it.

"Please—" I kept saying, but he took no notice. I hooked an arm over his shoulder and got one of the goblets in his sack and tried to stun him with it, but he seized it from me and laid the sack aside. He was trying to pin me down and though he was strong I wriggled too much, though it was only this way and that, I couldn't get free.

"You're only delaying yourself," he remarked through teeth clamped into a grin in his beard. "Come on now, what's so unfriendly about you? Anyone would think I was doing you a bad turn instead of having saved you a lot of bother." His hand came past my face and I bit it as hard as I could—he grunted and tried to shake me off, but I hung on. Finally he hit me with the flat of his hand across the side of my head—not hard, but enough so my head swam and my teeth unclenched. He took his hand away, streaming red-hot blood, and we continued the fight. "Think of your sack," I said. "If anyone came in now it'd be theirs for the taking—" "This is a chance I'd sooner not miss," he said, which I suppose I should have taken as a compliment, only I knew I was streaked with grime and tattered.

At last he got me hands-fast. I couldn't kick because of my leg. He lay on top of me and kissed me thoroughly. The maddening thing was that I found my body warm and expectant and it believed it right to be held curved close with his. My humiliation was sharp, only in my head. Damn it, you can't really call it a rape, can you, when you're enjoying it?

He was very competent though rather heavy and I didn't have any more chance to fight. I shivered under him but when I said, "please" I think we both knew it meant the opposite from before. I was crying and then felt drowsy. He was considerate enough and also by then perhaps fond enough of me to hold me in his arms for a while and as I looked up I realized that the very same flame-glows were skedaddling about among the black shadows of this high-fenced courtyard, and we had indeed lost very little time.

"Let me up," I said. "I have to get on."

He rose with me, half-supporting me, and we neither of us bothered to look at each other. I wanted to get away as quickly as possible and he knew that and had had what he'd wanted, but as I stumbled out over the gate-wreckage he came up beside me and said, "Here," thrusting something at me.

I hit furiously away, he knew damned well I wasn't a whore.

"No, take it," he said roughly. "You may need it the way you're going round in this city, you're asking for bother." And he made off, striding briskly.

What he'd left for me was a little statue, transparent crystal, not very valuable at all, though its long semi-circular eyes were a massed iridescence of tiny points of crystal and jewels. It was heavy, and what made me keep it was the least valuable-looking thing about it—perfect and unwithered in the vacuum of the statue's inside was a real flower, not artificial, but a kind I'd never seen before. It had a lot of curved, folded petals like glossy but very soft silk, shading from completely pure white

425

to drowningly deep blue, flat violet leaves, and a central petal folded right over and so fine it was like a bubble with purple veins in it. I couldn't imagine where he'd got this statuette, possibly some temple. I wrapped it with the Diary in my cloak, in the inside top pocket he'd never reached, and I hurried on up the glaring cacophonous street.

I came to the inn. It had not been deserted. In fact it was crowded to overflowing. I went in and sat down.

I looked round and wondered who to approach. The tapsters were all busy and would it be stupid to trust them?

There was talk of the eruption, the battle and the dangerous streets. Everyone knew it was the end of an era for the Capital. Presently a big man walked in from outside. He had only red wounds where his eyes had been and he was beserk angry with the world about it. He lurched straight to the long bar-counter and with his hand oblivious of cuts swept all the glass tumblers and metal tankards off it to the floor. One of the customers put a hand on his shoulder and he bellowed and turned on him. A free-for-all started, I'll never know how they do, people are just eager and being the very first is the only thing they don't like but if someone else will begin they're fine. The tapsters waded in, clonking everyone on the head with brooms and shoving them outside where the fight continued.

Someone came up to me. "Out of here, girlie."

"I was doing no harm—and I want to talk to the inn-master."

"You all do. No, we've had enough."

He hustled me to the door and felt the bulges in my cloak. "Ho, what have we here?"

"Nothing of yours."

"We have to make sure—" He gaped at the statuette. Then I was very glad I hadn't cringed and sworn innocence, which is always a temptation when one's been pushed around as much as I have. He at once leapt to the right conclusion (though actually the wrong one) and respectfully asked me to sit down again.

"I'm sorry, please forgive me, it's so easy to suspect the wrong people nowadays. Boss! There's a lady to see you."

A burly man with a nice tough face appeared. The tapster said, "She brought this, wanted to see you."

The inn-master took it reverently and smiled at me. "Thank you. We were sure it was lost forever, it was nowhere to be found. It seemed too much to hope that one of us had got hold of it, but here we are after all. This is marvellous. I see you've a bad leg. We'll boil some new bandages for it while you feed."

"Is the priest here?"

"Which, love?"

"The old one—the one with a face like—"

He smiled at my inability to describe him and went away. Later he came back. "He's in the cellar. Jeel, light her down."

Jeel the tapster's candle threw huge descending shadows. The walls were dripping with slime when we'd gone down three twisting flights. I waited, desperately weary, while Jeel moved a chest and levered up the trapdoor it'd stood on. The perpendicular rusty iron ladder which led down inside the trapdoor was nasty work what with my leg, and Jeel unable to help much because of the candle, which wasn't very happy anyway in the damp, musty air, not that *we* loved it. Also the ladder swung a bit, it wasn't fixed at the bottom; I suppose this was so if anyone unwelcome climbed down it they could be given a violent series of swings from the top till they fell off.

At the bottom. Now we walked along a slimy stone passage, opened a well-oiled door and suddenly the air was better and it was warmer. My priest was sitting at a table with a good meal. There was a fire and ventilation from a revolving wall-screw, obviously the end of an air-well.

The priest didn't say anything, just grinned at me and that meant welcome and recognition of all that had previously passed between us.

"When you and the young lady's finished, the Boss says he thinks it a good idea if you come up," said Jeel. "It wouldn't be very gay if you was stuck down here if any earthquakes started. And there's such confusion up top, you're as likely to be killed without any malice at all, they've no time to recognize you if you're in disguise, which you are."

"Earthquakes!" I said. "It's only an eruption."

"Well, I don't know about the city," said Jeel, "But earthquakes on the plains are giving the armies bother, that's the latest. You can't very well fight a battle when the battlefield's splitting up under your feet and besides, dividing all the companies." He left.

"Feed, child," said the priest. I watched him as I obeyed. He was making a hearty meal, using both hands, and was wearing black and grey rags like any layman. "I have to thank you for many things," he said.

"Not so many—I came to ask a favour—"

It's a small hope, I said to myself, but while he listened I told

427

him all about Ooldra—my sin with her son, my brother Smahil, the whispers, the lot. "Is there anything can be done?"

"It seems she hated you so much, and was with you so long, that she stays now she is dead, bound by a link of malignant concentration. And you were laid open—It is more terrible that he is her son than your father's. But you have many things to expiate and nullify. Apparently your birth was in every way very inauspicious. Evil and good are balancing each other on a hair-fine quivering equilibrium; if one gets too great, it will over-balance the other. You have to fight harder than most people. But I dedicate you to absolving your birth prophecy in a bigger way than revenge on Zerd for little ravages. Do you accept this?"

"What must I do?"

"Warn Atlan. So far all attempts have failed—but a small, lone girl may have a better chance of slipping through the coast-watch, and you already seem to be good at survival. Can you swim?"

"Quite well."

"I will give you your instructions later," he said calmly. "Now put out all the candles but one. And stay close to me and quite quiet." His voice became very gentle, as if he were about to weep over something. "Close your eyes."

Immediately I was in blackness, no light of candle or fire seemed to penetrate my lids. For a while I heard him breathing steadily but as if under strain—then that sound went. Suddenly I was afraid in emptiness, I wanted to open my eyes to see if he were still there but they were not mine to open, they were heavy and cold as all my muscles.

Then, after dark emptiness in which I had forgotten movement, I did feel something stirring. And it was in me, but not mine. Some coldness was moving in me. At first it was vaguely pleasant, this stirring, and I was in the darkness which I realized was myself, or at least my consciousness, and it was vast, though I couldn't feel all of it at the same time.

Now the movement which was not me was a fast turmoil, it was beginning to thrash wildly, sending waves of me against myself. I tried to cry out but my mouth was too far away. Then I realized that its agony was far, far worse than mine, that it was being torn out of me.

I could hear the priest's voice from far away and above, but each word was not a sound, it was a weight. They were falling like sledge-hammers and the thing in me was squirming wildly to avoid them.

428

"Ooldra—" said the priest in conclusion. She knew she had been recognized to her central essence. The other words had been each commanding and terrible, and besides all together had formed a pattern from which there was only one way out. She gave a cry, half a scream, and it was the most passionate, desolate sound I've ever heard. It was not a sound from a human throat, it was stripped of all memory of humanity. It was harsh with despair, but despair still passionate, as it faced into the total loss. The chill that ran up my spine I welcomed: it told me I was still in the world.

I saw the flames and felt my body.

"I love you, Highest God," I said aloud from the love that was in me, that had grown from that endless glimpse of the agony of evil.

"And the agony of evil," said the priest, "is the light of the Highest God seen by those that have rejected him though he is in their selves. He is still in their self, but they are too shrivelled to bear it."

It seemed a long time later, after we had rested, that we took the one candle and were climbing up the way I had come. I was remembering my own little God, my Cousin in Divinity, as I clung to the swaying ladder, and thanking him for making it that statuette the man had given me instead of anything else in his sack. I was thinking of all sorts of little things—a twisted nail in the wall, the slanting candle flame, a strand of hair in my eyes—Just as I had when I was riding in the carriage with my mother and Ooldra, going to do away with our enemy.

As they bathed my leg in the inn's back-room, the huge thought lulled me. Just like that he had said, "Warn Atlan" —and that was why I had been spared through so much.

Should I ever see inside of that last memory of the World as it was created, that last stronghold of Divine peace, which had sealed itself anciently and remained sealed while the rest of the World multiplied in mortal turmoil, each petty nastiness contributing to the high mass-meaning evil?—

The battle was over.

Yes, the Southern reinforcements had arrived from the Temple-Town, but they were like a stag with a puma on its back, the brigands in small bands from first to last had not let up worrying and decimating them, and hardly one had been caught in return. The battlefield had heaved and cracked: nearly whole platoons had disappeared at a time, according to the survivors. These were swarming into the city. In every door-way, on every pavement and in the gutters they were resting, tending each others' wounds, looting, and continuing the battle without any organization. The surviving officers were faced with a superhuman task in gathering them together let alone controlling them, and many officers, particularly Southerners who had not so much to lose, were shrugging their shoulders and letting go.

My priest and I bade the inn farewell and thanks, were given knives and hurried out into the chaos with our cloak-hoods well down over our faces. The air was very hot now.

We steadily made towards the plain, which with luck we could cross—We'd then be safely on our way to the coast.

"If we can always keep a little ahead of the war—" I said hopefully.

"This World is doomed to war," he said cheerfully, slapping out sparks which had caught his cloak. "It will end in war, having been in war ever since the gods were tempted by the sight of the daughters of men, and fell." I had always thought that a good thing!—but remain deeply fond of my Cousin, especially now I know he's a real World-god and by his nature implicated right up to the nose in the affairs of this World and no other.

The priest hadn't yet told me what to do to get from the coast actually *into* Atlan—he said he'd tell me when we were out of the city. It was urgent that no one have the slightest chance of over-hearing. At last, Atlan to be entered—Certainly the end of an era.

The priest said. "The Earth-Serpent has entered the lists: in Heaven's timeless War with Hell, the Earth gods, those who loved men and fell and became one with this World, and are drunk with the dark Earth, and yet though they fell from Heaven are not Evil, for Earth has its own rightness as it has its own centre of gravity—those gods were not till now in the War, but they are in essence war-gods—and their strong blind-sighted offspring the Serpent will bring earth-war to the Land Beyond the Rain-gusts, and pierce its Heavenliness with the powerful scales of his own mortality, and thenceforth the earth will be all of Earth."

Presently we came to a square where Northerners were lying in untidy rows. Their wounds were being tended by over-worked surgeons who seemed to have lost most of their instruments and anaesthetics—beside them dog-tired officers, still in blood-caked uniforms, held candles and tried not to drop tallow on the patients whose wounds were being dug at with penknives sterilized by being passed through candle-flame.

Suddenly we were startled by a sort of hoarse choking cry behind us over the steady groans and moans.

"Cija!"

I turned. An officer, nearly unrecognizable under blood and weariness and dirt and smoke-black, leapt towards me and suddenly I was clasped tight to him, my nose squashed on buttons.

"Cija!"

"Smahil, please, Smahil—" I disengaged myself with a strength of revulsion.

"Gods, I haven't seen you since the day we left here a season ago—have you been here all the time? What's happened? Your leg—Tell me everything—Have you been all right all this time? Why couldn't you join me?"

"I didn't want to, Smahil."

Something in my tone stopped him and made him look at me. There was a pause, then he said, "You bitch" softly.

"Ah, no, Smahil—Listen—Smahil—"

I had forgotten the priest who stood waiting while I told Smahil all I'd discovered.

"You see now? We're brother and sister—"

"So what? It only makes it more interesting."

His tone and manner were off-hand, his eyes glittering in his pale face. I could tell I'd made him furiously angry about something.

"So you want to get back to your demon lover and you're seizing any excuse to leave the only person who's ever been any good for you—Bravo, it's even a virtuous excuse and you've always been hot on virtue—"

"You know there's nothing between him and me—"

"So I'm your moony Ooldra's son, so the High Priest's my father, so O.K. this is a shock to me, I always knew I was a foster-child but this is a shock to me—and all you can do is leave me. You hate me because we've made love, you never want to touch me again, it's all over your face and the way you're acting—"

Yes, I did hate him then. All right. No, I disliked him—but I wanted to tell him how he's always *owned* me, how at times he drove me frantic with that, and most important how although even the haunt of his mother was at last dead (though he wouldn't understand that) and so we were out of danger if we did continue in our sin, I was starting on a high mission and had to leave him—But he gave me no chance to say all this.

431

"By everything in you, Cija, I hope one day, one day but it will only be after many more years, you'll realize how immature you are. You've never even loved, have you? Have you? Your torrid emotional life has been confined to a bird and a little serving-girl—and a girlish fascination for the big, bad General."

"I love him," I said in a low, vehement voice, indicating the priest who was wandering from us, moving his feet in a little sort of tap-dance, tactfully paying no more attention to us, but looking at the wounded for whom only surgery could do anything.

"That elderly labourer? I suppose you think he looks fatherly. I've never seen such a lecherous, sly face—"

"It's wonderful, a *total* face—"

"See that shack, planks slanted against the wall over there? You'll find an orderly boiling soup in there. I'll be with you soon."

"No, Smahil—"

About to walk away, he turned back, his brows down, whole face edgy.

Our eyes met. He caught me to him. "We'll discuss it tonight—little sister. Go on, and don't worry. Don't worry. I've always known what's best for you—I'll look after you. Off you go."

"Smahil," I was desperately worried, but for a moment wanted to touch my finger to his scar, then drew back for it was newly opened, "I'm not staying with you. I'm going with my friend there—"

"Oh, are you?" His eyes glittered, but with even more impatience than anger. "That's soon put a stop to." He strode to the priest, who was stooping over a casualty, ran his sword through him and without waiting to watch him collapse said to me. "Get some soup inside you till I come," and walked away to continue with his duty.

I ran to the priest, crouched by him, lifted his head from the chest of the wounded man who moaned faintly for water.

My priest was quite dead. His face was still his in every way except that the twinkle in his eye had already become opaque.

So who now would show me the way to Atlan?

But I had pledged myself to that, and soon I was on the outskirts of the plain. Emerging from the crowded city, my heart and eyes numb, I met the shambles of the plain and realized only then that I had seen nothing as I traversed the streets.

The plain looked like the heaving chest of a prone giant, but this was not because the earthquake was still continuing. The ground at the edges of the great brand-new gaping fissures was still trembling, and every now and then a clod would drop thundering to the bottom—otherwise the movement came from thousands of crawling or upright men and animals, helping each other out of the fissures, giving a shifting appearance to the edges of the several immense mounds which hadn't existed last time I was here.

The row was terrible, screams of wounded men, and frightened animals which careered around increasing the numbers of the wounded, and the cries of those caught in the cracks.

Large black sky-birds were already wheeling above it all, uttering harsh cries, and increasingly landing on mounds and settling down to gorge.

Enormous grave-pits were being dug, and corpses tipped in: other units were building pyres of corpses and firing them, which smelt horrible.

I noted an odd disturbance and went nearer. Then I saw that some people were watching, some feebly dragging themselves out of the area of a fight between two great birds, riderless, the elaborate harness awry on their bodies like a signature of man's attempt to subjugate such elemental force: it was not the birds but the harness which looked ridiculous.

They had obviously met after the excitement of the battle and something had slashed them mutually into one of those characteristic rages. Unlike fights between other species of bird, there would have been very little ogling or fighting shy; they would have darted right in at each other with immediate savagery. Horrid murder-eager barks, thick blood and big, curved feathers hit the air.

I don't think I was watching so much as I stood in that thin ring of spectators, I was waiting. I had known it would be, even before I recognized the one-eyed, black bird—the other was a speckled grey with half its crest torn off—and I stood there, wind in my hair and clothes, various aspects of the death-smell everywhere, the blood coursing through my veins while I stood—For yes, all comes to that blood, to me; I had been given the statuette by what seemed the luckiest coincidence, and now that I was about to start on a journey it was

433

really about time I sank my fear of the bird—and here it was. It would be very useful, when it had done with this fight.

The rapid wings rasped, the feathers came, the hooked beaks thrust in and tore out after a brief stay, the spurs were in danger of becoming locked but they were intelligent fighters. I was annoyed at the thought that they would tear each other to pieces. But Ums was not badly damaged, and the grey already becoming exhausted. He had been pierced in many places; and with a guttural squeak he sank to the ground, a heap of blood and feathers. Ums in a sort of dainty paroxysm did a little dance on him, occasionally bending to sink his beak in him, and then gradually quietened and presently stood still, staring with his one eye out over the battlefield.

So I began to walk to him.

A Southern N.C.O. caught at me. "No, miss—not over there. Just because he's stopped a moment, don't mean he's not still dangerous. If you're looking for someone—"

"No. It's all right. He's my bird."

"Oh? I seem to remember there was our commander Iro riding him—No sign of him now—But even if you haven't made a mistake, miss, don't think he can be approached now. He won't know you, and if he did it wouldn't make no difference," he said ominously.

The bird stood like an arch-beaked, two-legged, black monolith, giant against the wheeling, croaking, red sky, the horizon low, flat and distant between his legs.

I continued to approach him. At first I had a low feeling of loss—Oh, yes—Lel—Iro dead—But really, Lel had long since ceased to be any of my business. And there'll always be someone to succeed Iro. I continued to approach. The blind eye was grey, the staring eye red with the frozen triumph of the animal, where a human would be merely exhausted. When they had given him to me, before each new meeting was a little more and a little more a giving of myself to him, they'd told me he'd lost that eye in a fight over a female. Well, that female was long since forgotten, and now I am approaching him to take up again that fierce loneliness between us.

He sensed the approach—the eye in a swift bird-movement cocked my way; for a moment I felt pain, I felt that he is far too elementally an earth creature to have been sent to me to help Atlan, leave him alone, go on your way, stop taking every coincidence as a personal tribute—

He stared and then stalked towards me. It was different from the mad, rushing scamper he's always used before. His eyes

434

glowed into mine. He uttered a series of short, quick, staccato barks. Then he thrust his head under my arm and crooned and crooned and crooned.

The Southern N.C.O. looked at me in amazement and awe.

I had hardly to twitch the reins before, with that complete almost pre-understanding which has always existed between us, he had turned in the direction I wanted.

He picked his way, claws spread, over the mangled dead, separate arms and ears, horses' nostrils, smeared together, the flotsam of every battlefield.

Behind us the funeral fires churned up russet-purple into the sky.

# CHAPTER NINE

## THE POSSESSION

As we left the environs of the City behind us and came among the high, harsh, black pines, I think we were pursued by animals like big pumas. It was strange. They were never near enough for me to know what exactly they were, and whether they were after us or busy with each other. I thought even that it might be one swift one, as we didn't see more than one at a time, but it would have to be in such different places so quickly. I don't know if Ums noticed, he didn't turn, only his crest was laid back. Then in a burst of eruption-light I saw three big pumas bounding at us. In some lights they seemed silver, in some glaring golden. I was not sure if they were really white like mine in the mountains. Later we went among many trees, and didn't see them again.

We slept against each other, way past where the town gathers in the hoop of the lazy, slavering moors. On the long journey from here to the coast, there would be no more civilization. I did not know what I could do when we reached the coast; meanwhile it was enough to get there. The night was full of sounds of wilderness. The wind screamed through the stark, purple grasses. Ums was very warm. We had eaten a good meal, I'd cooked the lizard, nearly three feet long, which he'd killed. I'd had to stamp out the embers, the wind would have carried them everywhere in an instant like dangerous seeds. It had been hard work keeping the fire from blowing out or getting too big. We had fallen back easily into the old way of his taking half the raw meat of his kill, letting me take the rest for my cooking. Actually I always take less than half, as he needs more, though like all magnificent fighting animals he is lean and can exist on a minimum.

Somehow I'd thought I'd never have another nightmare after Ooldra's exorcism. Yet there was a sense of warning which made me sulky.

I suddenly started awake; the warning receded and there was

only stillness flowing into and into and into the bowl of the night, and the thin, high kreeep-kreeep, kreeep-kreeep of the crickets was the pattern on the side of the bowl.

Dawn is falling into the night.

I close my eyes and hear the sough of the wind across the plains. The soughing of the wind lives here. A man could be born and live and die here, and every minute of his life hear the regular beat, the distant roar, the showowowoow of the wind.

There are not and will be no farms, cottages, huts, bridges.

The plain stretches to every side, bright gold, trees ignoring their shadows, taut menace behind every line of tall grass, tiny animals and large insects before our feet, somewhere over there the sea, there mountains (always mountains) with their blue, white, grey, mauve and purple shades suggesting valleys of firs and high, stark slopes with scree and caves and huge, warm, unfriendly, shaggy bears.

The early morning sky was a kind of yellow. And the sun, like a white hole in the yellow, pouring out light . . .

I remembered the Superlativity teaches that the sun is the glory of thousands of pure souls all shining together.

I knew that speed was necessary, and once we found the river all we'd have to do would be to follow it South and East—So I was glad when we came upon a sort of network of shallow streams running all together over a vast expanse of pebbles, each pebble glinting whether or not under water, the water blue and clean, white skull here and there, where some animal had breathed its last by the water—there were no other kinds of bones, they must all have been carted away by scavengers for their marrow.

We went all together towards the river—Ums and I, the little streams plinking busily, the many small, shrill, blue birds overhead. I halted Ums with my knees. By our path a lone blue rock rose higher than my head; a spring gushed from it in a great hurry to join the others. It was little, and I waited a long time till the thin trickle would cup fully to the brink of my hands. I drank, then waited another while for full hands, then bent forward over Ums' head and got him to drink. He slurped sideways to avoid cutting me, but it was not enough and we got acrid milk from spurge plants later.

Ums objected to the little blue birds. They twittered and swooped in patterns low above our heads. I was enjoying this

437

till he rose up, stretching his neck so I had to cling, and gave as long a hoarsebellow as he could sustain. They fled for a little way, then they were back again and beneath us the streams in the same joyous haste.

The pebbles and streams became a river over the bank of a rise. We rose too; we had come out of a dip in the plain, and the sky and river were turbulent with dark grey and dark white, and the wind meets us like a curling, turning, curling, spurling sea-edge all waves and patterns and he breasts it and its blast strikes us and does not slay and the wind parts and runs past us like a river.

My hair and clothes follow the backwards rider's-lean of my body. My Cousin! What it is to ride one with a creature whose each savage stride is part of a rhythm like the swiftened, terrible rhythm of the mountains growing.

The wind's force against my breast, against us, is so great that at first I am lost in wind, my six senses aware only of wind, then the force of our motion into it is more highly active.

And the rhythm continues with each savage stride.

Later the wilderness became less sullen. Armadillos scurried in the scrubby undergrowth. Over there long ripple after long ripple makes it seem as if the tall, saffron grasslands are gliding towards us, but it is only wind scudding the thousands of feathery grass-heads against the flanks of the herds grazing in it. There are boar, grunting, hacking, turning bloodshot practically useless eyes here and there; the wind is ours inasmuch as it does not tell their disgusting nostrils of us. There, majestic as unhurried swimmers, dark and shambling on the horizon, mammoth: the leader's tusks are growing at such a back-curve that in a few more years they will have got to his own eyes—perhaps he will have been able to keep their points at bay by filing them on bark. There are lumbering, trundling, giant ground sloth, desiccating foliage.

These great bulks, in their own element, would have crushed me with terror before even noticing me, had I been alone. Now I was a lord of the wilderness, for I rode one of their lords, one of the swiftest, fiercest and strongest, and he was my loyal companion. he would let nothing happen to me.

Several times we saved time by crossing loops of the river, now broad and swift and shining, blue enclosed between its high, rocky, flowering banks. Ums trod daintily down these, in places nearly perpendicular, then stepped without stride-change into the swift blue where it gurgled at the bank-foot. Often, still without altering rhythm, I would find him swimming under me; a broad spearhead wake following us across the noisy, glittering, blue and white currents. Once there came a disturbance: I thought we were approaching one of those periodic whirlypools which had suddenly appeared before us; but it was approaching us, and presently the head slid up out at us. It came at us, longer than Ums' own, and grinning with ruthless conceit. I thought, "What can be done? Ums is not in his element, smaller than this thing, and hampered by me."

This was a river-snake, an amphibian with a long, glaucous body merging into tail (competently thrashing water) and covered, I now saw, with a starring of yellow warts. These constellations nestled in the wrinkles of a skin which must be far too thick even for Ums' beak to pierce easily—and the beak it would have to be, for his claws were underwater. He continued to swim towards the reptile which continued to bear down on us. It took no notice of me, except that there may have been slight amusement and contempt in the huge, gold-speckled, oval eyes fixed on Ums. Here was a creature which allowed men to ride it! Its long snout writhed, revealing diseased gums edged with bone, a single, circular tooth. A sort of ululating shriek of anticipated triumph echoed over the river; Ums made no sound but continued straight at the onslaught, lifted and thrust his neck, sank his beak between those two eyes which went glassy amazed and offended—there was a blood-spout—Ums uttered several barks, started a wide detour just in time to avoid even the first of the convulsions as the tail was so far away it took a few minutes for the news it was dying to reach it, and we elegantly climbed up the farther bank, leaving behind us the now purple river.

When we reached bushes half hidden under wild vines, it was high time I dismounted. My leg was stiff of course, also sore, but obviously on the mend and all the better for being forgotten a while. I ate a great deal—found gold sloes near, also huckleberries which I was hungry enough to eat though it's a nuisance, continual seed-spitting. It wasn't really a filling meal, still less for Ums, but we also found a nest deserted among reeds—four largish oval eggs, three to him and one to me (a little raw egg goes a long way for me) which we pierced and sucked.

After all this, and running water too, I lay down under a fragrant vine-tangle in which gauzy insects skittered round—of course I never tether him.

439

I wrote quite a while in this book and was astonished when a chilly feeling made me look up and out and I saw how low the sun was in the sky. I leapt up, clutching Diary and pencil dangling on its tape (nearly frayed through in places now) and looked for Ums. He was in sight—actually I shouldn't think he'd ever let me out of his sight, which is both possessive and protective, especially in a place like this—and though I didn't like to call and attract I don't know what monster's attention, he soon looked up, saw me standing watching him, and came at once. He extended to me a claw with a rather mangled lizard, but I showed him it was to be his own and he swallowed it and I mounted.

Dusk fell around us like the drifting settling of unnumbered tiny mauve motes.

I'm such a fine heroine, so fit to save almost-lost causes. Never underestimate the army.

Soon, in the dusk, I came upon a Southern encampment, just settling down for the night and all heads turning startled as I, equally startled, spurred Ums right through them, spattering the sparks of the fire they were just in the process of lighting.

Well, I thought as we settled back into a steady canter, that's done it. How often does a girl on a Northern bird ride through their camp and on? But I was on them so suddenly in this dark, wooded country, I didn't have enough warning to skirt such a sizeable camp. There's no sound of pursuit. They must have decided to let me go—I'm only one, and not even a soldier. That'll teach me to think myself so far ahead that I can afford to relax. Of course, they must know more about this terrain than I can—which river-loops to miss, for instance. I had a head-start when I set off but I might well have ruined everything.

Later still I was hunched in thought on Ums lolloping along under a starry sky, when I became aware that his crest was rising and he was giving slow throat-snarls. Almost at once I heard a whirr, felt something yank me off the saddle. I cried out. The lasso dragged me on the ground, though one foot (luckily the good one) was still entangled in the stirrup and Ums was rearing and would soon be charging in the opposite direction.

Then four men on ponies approached from the dark trees, zig-zagged towards him so he didn't know where to charge, and though he was soon fighting hard they managed to get my foot from the stirrup incidentally to muzzling him. By the rope on the muzzle they dragged him to a nearby tree to which they tethered him. He went on barking and striking muzzle and claws into the tough bark, making short dashes as far as he could.

I was picked up and immediately swung at my dark companions. But with a low guffaw someone caught my arm and held it away.

"What is this?" I said. "Can't a traveller go a few miles even in the wilderness, without interference?"

"Bring a brand over and let's see what we've got," said someone. "Sounds like a youngster or a girl."

A brand was brought, which told me there must be a fire well hidden behind the trees. It was thrust nearly in my face. I winced and blinked. The glare lit not only my face but theirs—

"Bandits!" I said. "What *is* this?"

"By the Dugs of my Mother, if it's not that whey-faced ladygirl, the one the Northern General left with us and Kond got killed with," said a jovial man with lank plaits.

"What're you doing here, love?"

"We thought you was a lone Southerner, that's why we treated you this way. Sorry. Your leg all right?"

"Perhaps she is working for them. Why else should she be riding round here?"

"Use your nut. To join the Dragon when he arrives."

"A right devil of a bird she got hold of, didn't she?"

I said, "The Dragon? Is he coming?"

"Be there tomorrow morning, I should think, yes. Didn't you know, then? There's a Southern camp, maybe you sniffed them, over the rise, they want to reach the coast and warn their navy to be ready before the main Southern and Northern forces have time to get there—half the navy's supposed to be in the middle of careening right now, which'll be a right old hitch for them—they don't know we've been trailing them all day. We're gonna fall on them tonight when they're snoring their sweet dreams."

"Well," I said reluctantly, "they no longer think they're quite alone. They saw me—" I didn't say I'd galloped right among them.

"Ah, don't worry, it's a nuisance but don't think you've bitched it all. Just, it'll mean a fight sooner and not so easy. Though actually I'd've thought they'd be after you before now. They're a slow lot. Or perhaps they thought you was coming to join a camp they'd not guessed of—so maybe they've got scouts out now, sniffing for us."

"I've brought a lot of trouble—" I said feebly.

441

"Don't mean a thing to us, darling. Near half of us were against falling on them asleep, but howled down by the rest. In a case like so, the chief lets the vote decide it, d'y'see. Now we've won after all—makes a better fight if they're all awake. I'll just tell all our lot to be ready—they don't need it. We're always ready enough for anything." The man with plaits made off behind the trees.

I turned to another bandit, whose gold ear-rings in the shape of nude couples cast a glimmer on his face.

"Do you mind giving me back my bird?" I said humbly. "I'm on a private mission—got to get somewhere in a hurry—'

"Private mission in *this* kind o' land, eh? Oh, well, maybe you know what you think you're talking about. But how you can ride that demon at the best of times I dunno. And now you're here you may as well get a bite—we'll attend to your demon, too, if you like—and then watch the fight or make off again, whichever you like. If you leave us now you may only ride straight into the arms of their scouts."

He led me down a dip, behind the screen of trees, and I was in a hollow lit by several fires whose argent wood-smoke was lost long before it could top the surrounding foliage. There was not much noise, but nobody was falling over himself to keep silent. My teeth watered as I was sat down and given a hunk of roast festooned with strip-sliced onions. A few hungry curious hyaenas stared with pale eyes from among the boles at the top of the further slope—Ael and his new second-in-command were holding a conversation with each other as they urinated against a tree-trunk over there, and the man with plaits waited civilly till they had finished and turned to him, rebuckling their belts.

I supposed their attention was being drawn, among other things, to me but I was too busy eating to watch.

"Not having milk?"

I turned round and there they were watching me, but not grinning or looking pleasant.

I didn't know what on earth to say so I shrugged and went on eating, getting rather smeared with fatty gravy.

They lowered themselves on to the long flattened grass, which served as a thick straw mat, the second-in-command to my left and Ael to my right.

Ael reached a brawny scar-patterned arm ended by a dagger, sliced off a roast-hunk, and bent to gnaw it. "You've come a little late," he said, not looking at me. "The Dragon's already asked for you—I said I sent her on to you, with two of my men. Their bodies were found on the battlefield, and the chariot she should have been in was discovered empty on the hillside with the remains of a hefty meal beside it, he told me. This is a great pity, I said politely. But the Dragon said, She can't be dead. Who would have kidnapped her, I said reasonably, and yet not yet contacted you for the ransom. We decided perhaps they, or she, or both, were killed just before they could. He was angry and distrait. His two brows became one bar, and that black. But I said my rascals must have died defending you, and because we need each other he took that, and there was no schism because of the betrayed trust." He wiped his mouth along the harsh back of his arm. "He will not think to find you with us any more," he said.

"So you aren't keeping me here to give to him, since he doesn't expect it? I can journey on after this—this kind hospitality?" I said gladly.

"Bustling little bitch," said the Second without any particular malice.

"To go where, in this wilderness?" said Ael, his composed voice and look quite opposite to the sudden action of his body as he hurled a bone across the glade and hit a hyaenodon which yowled affrontedly and limped away whining. Ael giggled a little.

I was trying to think quickly of an answer which would acquit me of trying to get to the coast to warn the Southern army, when there was a complete unexpected burst of howls out of the darkness and the Southerners who had found our position and crept up were upon us. They must have dealt with the sentry.

In a flash I was alone at the cooking-fire, staring bemused at hunks of deserted roast. Every bandit had seized his saw-edged knife and chopper-ended spear, and sprung forming an instantaneous mêlée. The glade suddenly rang with the clash and gurgling shouts. The hyaenas stared in amazement from the distance to which they'd retreated, but presently ran down and began tugging away the meat farthest from the fight. The foliage swayed and disturbed birds, but I couldn't hear their rustling above the din.

I got up, stuffing meat and onions into my hood and getting a long-lidded pitcher of rum hooked by its handle through my belt. I hurried over to Ums and untethered him. (He'd already been unmuzzled to be fed.) I mounted.

About to ride him up the bank, I paused.

The fighting bands were about the same size. The bandits

443

fought like devils, it was their trade, unmindful of themselves as long as they could hew down the opponent in as short a time as it could all be over. But many of the Southerners were mounted, and though ever ready with their arms the bandits had not had time to unhobble their ponies.

I spurred Ums back to the scene.

I had only a knife, given me at the priest's inn, but this I brought slicing down on any Southern anatomy I could see. All my usual hesitancy and squeamishness was submerged by my long hate for the uncleanness of the Southern civilization. I sliced for the child-wives buried alive, for the artificial vegetables, for the gentle priests murdered. I had no time to be appalled by the butchery I was causing—I was dodging the next stroke and causing more. Ums needed no second bidding. He was the reason I could venture thus and stay protected by his height and ferocity. He reared and clawed and butted with that horrible hook on the end of his beak. He clawed down only those whom I chose. The bandits redoubled their battle-exultant yells. I had never been in any battle. The lid of the pitcher at my side broke open and swung clattering on its hinge while the rum gushed out over the Southerners on foot. Ums pulled down a horse, a stallion whose eyes and nostrils flared vermilion as he side-feinted to get Ums' throat with his noble big yellow teeth, but the beak was too quick, it ripped into his lung and he rolled over on his rider.

My first battle was over. Remaining Southerners skulked their awkwardly large camp. Bandits jeered after them.

Over, the slashing maiming, the orgasmic slaying, the throbbing, reasonless, dark life in the womb of an earth-goddess. I looked at my hands and wrists and they were bloody, the hilt of my knife slimy and its blade disgusting.

Between my legs the bird quivered and barked. This it had helped me to. Could I be cleansed?

Ael walked to my side. He stood there, his head not much below the level of mine. He took a knife, of which nervelessly my fingers let him relieve me, wiped it methodically with the tall grass near, handed it back to me. His deep blue eyes did not move from mine.

"Never leave a blade to rust," he said in his light high voice.

"You think I deserve killer's lessons?"

"You are new to me," he said. "I've not known a woman slay so well, and yet you're a woman."

I looked the few inches through the muzzy dusk to the depths of his eyes.

444

"You are kind to notice me at last," I said. I felt a triple uncleanness, gentle and languid and welcoming, Ums' and my own and his, yet everything was really the same.

"You're a child," Ael mused. "I wondered why Zerd valued you. Yet you've much to learn. I will teach you. You've found yourself freedom, a fine mount, and done much on your own. You hate the military and government of this country as much as we do. Do you hate the Northern military too? No one shall give you back. Among us you are safe, with the lawlessness we maintain strictly. Postpone whatever reason it is you want to reach the coast. We'll get there. I'll teach you the two arts—love, and war." The bandit chief reached up his coruscated arm for me to take and so dismount.

I kneed Ums, who at once lolloped into motion, up over the rim and on into the night.

Two days later we reached the coast. The river became more impetuous as I became more cautious—then the surge and boom and surge was clearly heard, resolved from the low sibilant pounding it had lately been in my ears—then finally I saw a horizon of shimmering flatness. Blue, grey, silver—a cloud of spume, battering the rocks between which our foaming river thrust itself. I was seeing again the sea. I have not seen the sea since my childhood.

For years, and years (seventeen years) I watched the sea in its numberless moods. I watched it blue and flat; I watched it mauve and crawling, slightly wrinkled, like an ancient crocodile; I watched it crawl away and leave a wavy-ribbed stretch of purple ooze, dotted, pitted with debris unidentifiable through distance; I watched its smile lilt glittering under the glittering sun; I watched it, a robust sighing wraith, under a mezzanine sky of wheeling, mewing, sun-touched birds, under rose or green or crimson or gold sunset, under twilight, under eclipsing dusk, under black night and night drowning stars in the intent mirror-eye of its darling; I watched it huge and gusty, white and blue, uproarious with winds; I watched it foaming on beaches overhung by trees, beaches which climbed swiftly to become mountainous slopes; occasionally I saw tiny figures race along the white shores, or into the sucking, swift blue laced with white aureoles and high-flung, quivering mists of foam—they dragged in wriggling-silver-glinting-heavy nets, but I could not see more than their tininess, and I thought them females. I was not so placed that it was possible for me to see any harbour, any boats, or ships of trade. The city's bay was behind the nearest mountain. I watched the sea grey, shiny under drizzle; grey, churning under heavy rain; I watched it black, rising and howling, its foam rearing high and whirling its funnels, lashed by storms. But always I was high above it, safe, untouched, its virile smell, the details of its action far below me and totally inaccessible.

Since then I had met the harbour-mouth of a great river, crowded with shipping and lined by wharfs, but now I had come upon the ground-floor of the shore; I looked cautiously round, but could see no coastguard, let alone sign that I had come anywhere near the careening navy. I left Ums and advanced between the rocks; there were stiff star-shaped flowers on them. A sort of tortoise-spider, big and red and as though covered with shell, scuttled away sideways. I passed the rocks, taking off my sandals because of all the little green rock-pools, in which I glimpsed lovely moving things, or perhaps they were just still and water-swayed, and presently fine gritty sand spurted between my toes. I kicked away a tangling ribbon of rubbery green, then the sand was sticky and crumbly, and then recurring flat wavelets hissed up and away and up and licked my toes.

I had reached this—this great new experience, and I had no idea what to do.

My brother had killed my priest before I could be told what must be done—And all I know is that Atlan must be warned that the world is after her like a pack of belling, baying, tongue-lolling hounds, and that her vacuum is no longer of use.

I didn't dare light a fire and despaired of finding any real vegetation—but Ums displayed unexpected resourcefulness. From what instinct or sense I know not, he waded out into the waves till they reached his breast, and stared intently into them with his one eye, beak poised ready. Suddenly it flashed down—and came up with a furious, desperate, silver fish, fat and jumping galvanically except in the middle where it was pinioned. Ums laid it on the sand and skewered it before it could leap away.

I chopped off its head, which was staring with a reproachful and hardly yet glassy eye, and its green, strong, frilly tail, and removed its spine, etc., while Ums fished for more.

I didn't really fancy raw fish. But fresh water was near to hand of course (the river) and luckily several of the fish turned out to be carrying roe.

I crouched, picking at raw fish with scale-silvered fingers, while Ums, having already golloped his, stood with wide-spread legs, menacing profile lifted in each direction for an indefinite period of time, changing with a short jerky bird-movement, a giant black silhouette between me and that close primeval sea, which divided us from that continent which has lain apart from the world since the gods fell.

Cold winds were beginning to flow in and across the shore. I shivered bitterly, rinsed my fingers and mouth and looked round for somewhere to sleep.

The sand was too flat. It was cold, also anything could find us there unprotected. Scouts from the Southern Advance maybe, or their navy which couldn't be far distant from here. A rock pool seemed the only likely shelter. But over there was a cliff, its sides argent with guano, already tinged with richness as the sun began to set. There were no sea-birds on its summit now, it couldn't be the reason, but it looked friendly, easy to scale, though very little vegetation and that scrubby. Surely there'd be a cave-niche of some kind where we could huddle. I led Ums to the cliff and we started to climb. It was easy, but we found nothing and I was beginning to despair when, nearly at the top, a flight of sunset-coloured butterflies fluttered out, disturbed by our approach, and we saw they'd come from a small murky opening between bastions of honey rock.

I wondered if we could get in there. I found that I could, and that it was big enough inside, though only just, for both of us. But how could I get Ums through the opening? He stood on the ledge outside, looking through at me; then extended his head on its neck, then his breast—he was now in a straight line, and his legs came through fairly easily. He looked smug and nuzzled my shoulder, thereby nicking my already travel-worn cloak. How we were to get away quickly if we had to I didn't know, but never mind, eh? Here we were and we settled down to sleep in the cramped gloom, I with my head twisted uncomfortably but eagerly so I could watch the sunset.

"Gosh!" I said. Ums, realizing from my tone that I'd not seen danger, did not raise his gaze.

From this height, though blurred by the sunset, there was visible a mass, curvilinear, of uncertain colour, not very high but of endless length, beaming dazzling upon the horizon as though the sun itself were burning forth from it as it sank lower into its heart.

I don't know what woke me. There seemed no sound above that of the sea—even the winds had cessated. There was a sharp awareness in the air—or a communication from the air to me of the sense of becoming aware. Ums, unusual in a highly alert brute of prey, was still asleep. I was reminded of the night last autumn when I woke and found a huge shining puma, and Ums still asleep . . .

I looked out of the opening and saw a brilliant star, then another and another. They were tiny and cold, but once your eyes were used to picking them out you realized they were everywhere. The sea heaved under them. I could no longer see that miraculous distant coastline, unless it were that faint radiance far out, as it were a diffusion of starlight hemming the waves. I looked down below me—and saw dim figures walking towards the shore.

They made no sound on the sand, they carried no light.

Were they Southern scouts? Naval? Or bandits?

But yes, they had a light with them. Or rather—always just behind one of them. They were all men, about a dozen, all barefoot as far as I could see, and the leader left a golden aureole on the sand after each footstep. This glow lingered, too faint to do more than throw shadows on the ankle-bones of those following, until the leader took his next step. This obviously could not be an artificial light—for one thing it served no purpose down there, not even lighting the way; for another, it could not be a signal, and was rather dangerous than otherwise, as these days in these parts any light shown by a small party is unwise; also, it seemed too soft to be artificial. Yet a man whose bare feet were attended by haloes was surely too good to be true.

I watched them, my breath bated. I could make out that they were walking gravely but without signs of search or flight, straight towards the shore, not in single file nor two by two but in an orderly way not at all straggling, their heads uncovered. There was nothing remarkable about their clothes, which were townsmen's plain tunics and leggings, except for the leader whom I realized with a sort of calm shock was wearing rags. I half expected them to walk straight on into the sea, but just before the spurling of the first froth-creamed wavelets, glistering their points licking on the sand, the company stopped and seated themselves cross-legged in a circle.

I was agog to see what would happen next, though surely they'd do no more than talk a while at least, and I couldn't hope to hear, but now behind me Ums stirred and coughed.

I don't think they heard, but *he* was awake. He thrust his

yawning head past me, grew still as he saw men below. "Quiet, Ums," I muttered. "They're too many for us." Really I only wanted to be able to go on watching them, but instinctively placatory I thought of the reason most likely to appeal to him. But he had stiffened, apparently, with malevolence. Throwing his usual creature-of-the-wild-sense to the chill winds, he scrambled out with surprising speed, and started down the slope barking.

The men rose and faced him. They seemed full of consternation. They made no move to find weapons; it was as though here, on the edge of things, they had expected no trouble, certainly not a furious Northern bird with which they could not speak.

I raced down after the creature.

"Ums! Ums!" Finally I called to the men. "Scatter! He's not bluffing!"

They scattered, still gazing with fascination at his rapid approach, except the leader who stood there still. As Ums rushed to him, and I too raced nearer, we saw his keen grey eyes glittering with a starlight of their own, a movement lambent. Ums did not falter, but rushed right up to him, then stopped with his beak within a few inches of the man's chest.

"Pedlar!" I said.

This seemingly scornful greeting brought home to me that I did not know his name, but that I ought perhaps to have said "Lord!"

However, he didn't seem to mind. Ignoring Ums, who still stood as though transfixed, he put his hands behind his back and strolled over to me. He looked quizzical.

"The little girl of the City riot! You've come a long way. Is your leg better? Did you find the priest?"

"Perfectly better, thank you. I took the bandages off finally yesterday."

I stood and looked at him. His thick strands of pallid-gold hair stirred in the breeze. His rags, also, stirred, showing the hard honey muscles. Who was this man who had travelled the ways of the South disguised as a pedlar, while I myself was making my immense but rambling Journey? The others were coming back. They regarded us and Ums with curiosity. "What is she?" asked a slender boy with a toss of sun-fire hair.

"A friend of the old grey priest's," said the pedlar.

"He sent me to warn Atlan," I said. I could tell these people were his real companions, that there was no need to be silent
449

before them. "So of course I came to the coast, but as far as I know nothing else is possible now—he was killed before he could instruct me."

They grew very grave and drew closer together round me, though not one uttered any exclamation.

"Who was the murderer?"

"My brother, " I said and there was a silence. They studied me—I felt it was consideringly. Did they think me unfit, unbalanced, or outright one of an enemy syndicate?

"He did not realize what he did," I said in a low voice.

"Of what do you intend to warn Atlan?"

I hesitated. At first I thought he was being sardonic because of my unworthiness.

"Of the coming invasion—behind her centuries-old silence she can have no inkling that at last the outside world has forged its spearhead. She may even have forgotten any other methods of defence."

"You think she needs to be notified to prepare?"

"Of course—"

"Have you all been busy evolving new lungs?" asked the boy.

"More or less. The Northerners have discovered a way to air-flood even such a huge vacuum."

The pedlar stood by, the wild breezes caressing him. The boy stared. He was only about thirteen, straight and tall but still with young, sloped shoulders and a hollow at the top of the back of his neck. To him, and I think some of the others too, my statement was news. But it was typical of them that there were no moans nor even exclamations.

"The Northerners are those led by the one called the Dragon, aren't they?" said the boy.

"Yes," I said, which couldn't reassure him.

"Does your brother know you've come here?" asked another.

"He has no idea," I muttered.

"Sit down," the pedlar ordered. I did and so did everyone else.

"Have you any food?" I couldn't stop myself asking eagerly. "And can you release my bird now—he'll do no harm."

"Are you sure?" asked the pedlar, smiling grimly at me, but before I could work out how seriously he meant it and how to answer he'd sort of carelessly snapped his fingers in Ums' face and Ums gave a long shiver. He turned his burning eye for a long time on the pedlar, then to me. This decided him. Moving as if each great muscle were throwing off the recent bewildering indignity, he came to me and stood just behind me. Then he began a series of grunts and snarling coughs.

I was glad the pedlar didn't start to speak through this, get fed up, and petrify him again. He started to gather large shells—there were so many he hardly had to move, though I'd noticed very few before—and he fished about in each with his dagger, and without fail each yielded a whelk or an oyster or something. Another volunteered to fish, catching them in his hands, chilly work at the best of times. I thought of offering Ums' services but didn't know how he'd behave. However, the fisher seemed to have as good luck as the pedlar. The others sat around talking in low voices, then fell to on the meal. It was raw though, because of course sending fire-smoke up in the sky was out of the question.

The pedlar sat friendly beside me, but I was rather afraid of him.

Also, I noticed that my arms as I ate were rather grubby, with a sort of mottled grey effect which I myself thought quite attractive, but which he probably wouldn't. I haven't washed properly for ages, since the night I escaped from Court with Kaselm, but I could imagine the pedlar thinking *"Ho.* She had plenty of opportunity to wash in rivers and things on the way here, even if she was in a hurry. Ho." Or words to that effect.

"If," he said after a while, "you ever got there, how would you set about warning their leaders?"

"I'd have to find the nearest city, of course. After that it'd be easy."

"You have infinite resource, obviously."

"I have led a very unusual life, full of desperate ventures," I said expansively. "I've had to accomplish a lot and generally I've succeeded in—well, in muddling through," I amended more honestly.

He gave a laugh, a sort of brief peal, a definite Ha ha! "You've come from what? Apparently you're completely alone, no family, no guardians? And where have you aimed your life—before you were directed into the Atlan adventure?"

"I think," I said slowly, "I wanted always to come to Atlan. The first time I heard the word I felt a singing, here, for which the voice that spoke it couldn't have been responsible—Did you know that she can be seen from this coast, if you get high up, say on that cliff? I never thought of that possibility, that though she's outside the world she's visible, rather like that prehistoric phenomenon the moon—I couldn't see much, it

451

was sunset, but she is long and low and blazing—"

"I know," he said and put a hard honey-colour arm round my shoulders. "And I see that we really shall have to take you there."

"T-take me—there—?"

"Surely such an ingenious lady has guessed that we belong there?"

"I didn't realize properly—"

I paused, then suddenly bombarded him with questions—no doubts. "How did you get out? Were you born this side? Have you any means of repulsing an army?"

"We have our method of getting In and Out. We have an army of our own—but it's not huge and has had no practice. Every man in it is, of course, an Atlantean—and courage and intelligence so universal must help an army tremendously. But we have seen no action whatsoever—our fathers, our fathers' fathers' fathers have seen none—And every one of us has a rooted repugnance for blood-spurting."

"But have you no advanced weapons?"

"Advanced weapons?"

"You are so highly developed that you could devise your vacuum—Have you no chemicals, like the Southerners, who can throw into the air a gas which immediately ignites as of itself, and just—just burns up everything near?"

I realized that everyone else had stopped talking. They were simply all staring at me. The boy regarded me without fear, but with terror and distaste. His eyes were gold, even in the night.

"The future Emperor of Atlan," said the pedlar, indicating him. "I am His Momentity's regent until he reaches puberty."

I regarded the future Emperor almost with irritation. "His Momentity must forgive my nasty story. Some might regard swift fire as better than the forms of poison they release in a mist of disease. But of course these are expensive, elaborate weapons—they've been reserving them all as a special gift for you, because they were so sure your scientists would have provided you with even more elaborate ones."

"We have no scientists."

How could I believe this? Yet after the first impact, it did fit with my long idea of Atlan as an earthly paradise.

"But the whole world regards Atlan as synonymous for the most advanced possible warfare!"

This they took differently. Some felt distaste, the pedlar-regent looked amused but of course it was an old story to him, the boy-emperor looked almost flattered for a moment. "Then

452

perhaps they'll handle us carefully!" he suggested.

"Yes," I agreed. "With more care and more cruelty." "And the Dragon, too, is on our track," he said.

My fingers curled in to my palms. I found them sticky. I shivered, but was only mildly shocked to find my fear voluptuous.

Now they talked. I found out my pedlar, The High Regent himself of Atlan, is named Juzd and had spent the last half-year in Southernland. What he'd found about the world's designs on his own continent had got the Atlantean leaders extremely worried. (I thought that was putting it mildly, myself.) But now he was due to return, and these lords had come to the mainland to meet him and escort him back. It was typical of their innate trust and innocence, undisturbed for centuries, that even the Emperor had been allowed to come. But what Juzd had told them of the latest developments had divided them a little. The majority were inclined to think they should take a sortie and go and deal with some of these small bands of enemies wandering towards them.

I said, "May I say I happen to know that's an excellent idea? You have no weapons but your trick of freezing anybody by looking into their eyes should come in most useful."

"No weapons?" they said. If they weren't Atlanteans I'd have said they scoffed. They drew from the folds of their tunics and cloaks short spears tipped with the vital parts of stingrays which were dead but still electrically charged, also small shields composed of the whole shells of turtles. I felt a fool. As I've learnt, as soon as one realizes the innocence of Atlanteans, one must be careful not to think of them as children.

"Beloved," said Juzd to me, "you are little and tired. Lie down to sleep. Tomorrow we shall show you the way to Atlan and you will go there with your bird, which we will allow to enter to be with you. You have no need to warn anyone of anything any more now, but you will be happy in safety."

Atlan at last! Offered to me. "But don't you need my help for battle?" I said. "There are few of you, you need every one you can get, even against small parties for they are used to battle, and my bird too is fine for—"

"We don't need you," Juzd said. I don't know why I believed him. "And you need at last a refuge. How often have you rested in safety in the last few years?"

I was waked before dawn. We gathered the usual food, and sat cross-legged on the sand to eat it. Juzd and I sat together.

I looked at these men who were embarking on a warlike adventure. None of them seemed excited or pleased (though calm and fearless) not even the boy. As future Emperor, he was surely to have gone to safety with me, but he had insisted on staying. This, however, wasn't from a desire to make his first kill and become a man, but because he must be actively present when his land was threatened. Anyway, I was amazed when they gave in to him. They didn't seem to realize they might lose him. Smahil would have said, Perhaps they didn't much care.

I thought of how I feel about battles and bloodshed. It sickens me, to be sure, but that is a mixture of conscience and reaction; I'm always as eager as anything beforehand except when I'm afraid for myself or friends. Normal natural cruelty doesn't horrify me in the least, I'm quite at home with it, though then again I'm different from the Atlanteans in the opposite way: I'm more inclined to squeamishness and resentment.

"Have you, who seem to know so much, ever met the Dragon?" Juzd asked. I said circumspectly. "As a matter of fact, yes, once or twice," and he said he hadn't got that far and what was he like?

I said, "At any rate, in spite of his brilliance and ruthlessness, he is more human than the Southern government. That's strange, actually, as only his father (who was a great General himself) was what we call human. He seems to have been a more haughty and aristocratic leader than his son, who stoops to various tricks to gain quite petty ends incidental to his campaigns—from marrying anyone susceptible enough not to recognize his greed for advancement, to telling quite silly lies."

"That is what comes of a union with a lower species," Juzd observed. "His mother was one of those big bluish females from the North, I've heard."

"And I bet, though he took after her, he was always pretty arrogant with her," I said. Suddenly I imagined Zerd as a horrible little scaly boy, and I didn't know whether to laugh or what. Then I thought of him, at the Court of his father's king, daring everyone to snigger at him because of his skin, the nobles, the ladies, lady-maidens, and his own brothers and sisters who even if illegitimate must all have been better-born.

"When higher mates with lower," Juzd said slowly, "there is always a fall. The lower is never raised to the higher's level, but pulls down. Just as when the gods saw the fascination of Earth and mated with Earth's daughters, just as when man commits sodomy." He looked at me till I wondered if he thought my relationship with Ums, gift from Zerd, too intense. I felt like saying, Oh we're just good friends.

But I know that even to be with Ums is bad for me.

If ones loves everything, saving only war and cruelty and inside-out mockeries of realities, one is right from heaven's point of view; love everything, as I incline to do, having come from the tower where I had nothing to love except the sky—love *everything* (but it must be *love*) and one is *right* for the spinning, dark, self-sufficient Earth. Those are the thoughts the bird-demon infused me with.

Juzd looked at me with all the grey keenness of his eyes: he seemed to know what I was thinking.

He said, "There are Three Deeps passing through this World (though their Beginnings and Endings are in other Places). They are Hell, Earth and Heaven. And as we also pass through the world, we pass through them. At first they seem to intermingle; but at last there come lives when our sensitivities are sharpened and the Three Deeps hit us separately. And then every man must choose: whether he belongs to Good, Evil or the Earth."

"I choose the Earth," I said.

He smiled, but already sadly. "Think well, Beloved; for remember that in The End the Earth, the hot mystic One Element, will also have to choose to whom its mysticism is directed. There can be Three for a while, but then there must be One. It is dangerous to serve Earth, though good for a while, for at The End all your service to Earth may be taken by Hell."

"Can't you see Earth serving Heaven?"

He shrugged.

"Or Heaven and Hell serving Earth?"

"In the End, that would be blasphemy, Beloved," he said.

Soon it was high time for me to get going and leave them grimly but calmly to it. Juzd asked if I can swim—said he hadn't asked before as the priest'd hardly have sent me if I couldn't, but might as well make sure. And could Ums? I said, "Certainly."

I said good-bye to them all and mounted Ums. I was so happy to be going to Atlan, but I did have qualms at leaving Juzd. Dawn was coming up. We must be there by full light. I turned and watched the dull thud and roar of the surf and waves on the shining grey beach. Each wave was decapitated by the back-curling spray of the wave before it. Ums plunged in.

When I next looked back the shore was a thin line, even the cliff.

I was drenched. Ums had nothing to carry but the saddle, myself, the Diary and a bag of provisions, but I insisted he stop once or twice on the rocks if only for me to wring the sea out of my clothes. A haze soon rose on the spurling vision-line, a gold-green haze this time, but it would take ages to reach her.

There was no danger of missing the important rock. It was the last, before us a vast empty expanse, and it jutting up shiny dark in its strange convolutions continually washed over by the waves.

We landed, slipping a little, for the waves were strong and there was not much of a ledge. I dismounted and led Ums to the leeward side of the main jut. It was—Well, I wanted to cry at the things I think about him sometimes, he followed me without question, when I rode him straight out and out into the sea he made no demur at all.

As I regarded the side of the jut I felt misgiving, though. The door was certainly well hid. I would have sworn it was solid rock. But I lifted aside a strand of seaweed and finally found the knob; it was even better disguised than I'd been told, as some little creature had hooked its shell on it. It clung there while I twisted the knob and lo and behold there was a harsh rasp and a cavity appeared dark green. Not without timidity Ums and I scrambled through—and stopped half-way. There was nothing there, beyond a short down-slope of hollowed rock—nothing but green sea, with fish passing. Where was the tunnel I'd been promised? Had it been demolished since they'd traversed it? Ums whickered and tried to nudge me out.

But I noticed there was no water at all on the floor of the short downward rock tunnel which faded directly into the sea which reached above its roof. I went down in, ready to run as soon as I met water—I came to the end of the rock and stepped right into the sea, above me and to every side. I stood breathing and dry, yet when I looked down I nearly screamed. Passing just beneath my feet, in the endless depth was a huge white shark, twisting, belly and corpse-mouth up. Then at last I realized that I was in a transparent under-sea tunnel—walls, roof and floor transparent. I went back up and led Ums firmly in; I showed him how I could walk safe in the sea, and coaxed him, and he came shivering with his eye a fixed glare. I shut the door after us as I had been told. We were alone, in a submerged green existence.

I led him slowly. Though I knew that if there were a breach anywhere in the tunnel it would be full of water, I had a horrid feeling each time I put a foot down. I don't know why the air was so good, as there could be no ventilation, but though it wasn't exactly fresh it wasn't at all unpleasant. Also I realized how thick the glass must be (if it were glass) to with-stand—well, centuries of sword-fish, giant squid, sharks sharpening their teeth, and congers bashing themselves against it every now and then, though I suppose most of the local fish knew by now to swim above or under it. Yet it was as clear as though it were a fraction of an inch thin, there was no distortion.

When he was more confident, I mounted him. I've no idea how many miles we travelled under the sea, but he galloped as only a powerful bird can.

We were a long way under. Up above the day must be getting strong, but the green down here became only a little more translucent.

Funnily enough, though the undersea journey must have taken a whole day and night and near all the next day too, it didn't seem too long. It was such a new experience. The food held out, for we stinted ourselves. There were oysters, crab, fish of various kinds—but though it was well packed it wasn't very enjoyable, as it was all raw. There were two leather bottles of fresh water. I had to drink from the bottles' lips, and Ums had to plunge his beak in and slurp.

Every so often in the side of the tunnel was an ordinary-looking latrine, which must however have flushed into the sea by a series of air-locks or something. They were screened off on three sides from the rest of the tunnel, but on the other side fish could look in all they liked. I couldn't help feeling silly. Ums couldn't use these, and I felt guilty, but presumed Juzd had known what he was doing when he let him come, and perhaps the tunnel was cleaned sometimes. When the green grew very dark, and I felt very tired, I judged it was night. I simply lay on the hard transparent floor, Ums roosting beside me, and I went to sleep in the middle of a large school of silver fish.

Parts of the tunnel were obscured on the outside with anemones suckered to it or with growths of coral through which tiny fish loitered. In places, we travelled under a roof of ribbon-like weeds, blue and green and rosy, whose streamers fluttered.

We witnessed innumerable pursuits, some of which ended in

disaster. Once a gigantic octopus rushed eagerly at us, poor thing, and wouldn't give up for ages, swimming alongside and launching dashing attacks, immense oval eyes going cross-eyed over his or her horrid orange beak, arms waving galvanically in all directions and occasionally getting a grip round some of the tunnel. He or she must have been awfully puzzled. Ums, who had by now quite got the hang of the situation, was amused and raised his head and nodded it in a jeering triumphant way. Finally the octopus, from sheer frustration, loosed a cloud of murky ink stuff and made off.

Later a school of big fish like dolphins went past high up, playing with each other delightfully and not at all ponderously in spite of their size. Several of them had protuberances from their bellies which I couldn't understand. Then I saw they were embryos, already partly emerged, tail first, so that in the few weeks before birth they could learn to swim.

Even when huge active creatures passed, I couldn't hear sound of the water, and if it hadn't been for Ums I should have got a feeling of deafness. We were by now going fast, lost in contemplation of this all-enveloping subterranean world through which we tore, though we might have been ghosts for all the difficulty we suffered. My legs got tired, especially the convalescent one, but I am used to long treks and Ums is so powerful it's practically impossible to tire him.

The tunnel passed into a wider tunnel outside a vast subterranean cavern. It rapidly became dark, a murky gloom—a real gloom, with a quality of melancholia more than claustrophobia. For the first few yards I could see spires of rock in the weirdest shapes, surrealistic under and behind the water, fish passing amongst them like jewels in a moving pattern, shapes like butterflies, fins flowing, till one could not tell which were fins and which plants—but in the dark we walked onwards, only our brains ordering us to trust. Presently pale eyes began to appear, to watch us, to flash or drift past or zip towards us—I could have sworn they were right in the tunnel with us, separated from us only by darkness.

The slope upwards was so imperceptible I never knew when it began. But when we got out of the cavern, the light was an incredibly purer green, like the liquid skin of baby apples, and it couldn't have been just the sudden contrast that made it seem so.

The floating jewels about us now had all an upward curve, fish and plants and the intermediates somewhere or other between the two, all streaming up or with fins or crests or ribbons pointing or swaying up, as though the creatures of this level were here because they wanted to get even higher. A shoal of tiny fish, each no bigger than a glinting, but nearly transparent pink fingernail, but each with a long dorsal fin and tail like a length of net, passed up in a cloud to every side of us, above and below, and must have taken about five minutes to get left behind even though we were moving through all the time.

The element became a visual carillon of sliding flakes of liquid crystal—here was every shade and tone of blue, light violet, green—as we went higher and higher so some of the blues became silvery, the greens nearly cream. Yellow beams began to pour down, sharp or diffused—the ascent was steeper, yet we were almost running.

Without warning I was dazzled. We rose into a light at first shockingly brilliant, then realized it was simply the light of day above the sea. Instantly I looked eagerly ahead. There it was—before me a great swelling cliff-line, mounting in mighty undulations to the sky, hiding the interior of the island continent. It was clothed with trees diversely the shape of fountains, and all gave a rich gleaming, glowing effect, as though each seventh or eighth leaf must be a brighter emerald, silver or gold than all the other normal leaves. These glowing foliages moved a little, back and forth and almost all together, as though there were a small but strong wind up here, and streaks of burnished colour which must be birds darted among them. I wished I could hear the wind and birds and waves —suddenly the silence seemed terrible, which had not crushed me all those hours in the sea. Yes, a wind—for I looked about me and the waves on the surface of the sea were choppy, blowing inshore alongside me with all their white manes tossing and spurling; sleek silver flanks dived and looped amongst them: dolphins, whose undersides I had been watching from below a few minutes before.

Directly ahead, at the beach, I could not look. It sparkled and shot rays of light as though chunks of meteor recently fallen from the sun lay on it.

A bare raft of black rock thrust out from the hillside. The tunnel, in which we felt baked as the day beat on the glass-substance, curved round and went right under the rock before plunging again under the surface. The rock's tepid shadow fell over us—but there was no one on it. I realized it must have been a look-out post, where the tunnel rose bearing its helplessly revealed occupants for inspection, but so long had the safety of the Atlanteans lasted, they no longer manned this post.

A few more furlongs under water—and a blank door lay before us. With sudden panic I caught at the handle but it opened at once. There was no lock I could see. The door was low, Ums had to bend his head. We emerged on to a beach, difficult and uneven, blinding to look at. It was covered with huge reflecting crystals: so intense that rainbows shimmered over some of them. So, unobserved, we entered Atlan.

Ums made no sound, but he was quivering at this emergence. Before starting inland, I stood and looked back. Only sea. I advanced to the edge, the waves licked my toes. I leaned forward—and fell at once. I gasped but no air reached my lungs. I should have heard my own crow for breath, but it hardly reached me. Ums seized my cloak in his beak and pulled me on to the crystals again before the cloth ripped.

So the dolphins out there were playing a game of catch-as-catch-can with danger: there was no air above the surface for them to breathe.

No wonder there were no sea-birds above the waves. I didn't know how high the vacuum extended, but even so there was a risk of plunging heavily, unsupported by atmosphere, for any unwary bird. Atlan to herself—her own species, insulated, no migrations to and from the shores of the world.

But as I learnt later, on other parts of the coast the atmosphere starts a little further back for the convenience of fishermen.

So we rose and went inland, treading carefully over the rocking crystals, avoiding their sharp points and corners, their lights playing on our faces.

There was no hurry, nor even a goal. This was the final leisure—for I had to warn no one. I had no one to meet.

We started up the hillside. The trees were rarely thick enough to impede the light. Where they were, shadow lay like fragrant turquoise velvet on the turf. I could see the birds properly and Ums snorted angrily at them—though they took no notice of us. They flew low and had wonderful long crests and tails. Now I could hear them properly too, but was surprised. They gave shrill squawks, and seemed very busy about nothing. They reminded me in shape but not in fragile colour and dignity, of the vast shoal of tiny fish we had passed.

460

Presently flowering trees began to intersperse the others —gradually the others gave way altogether, and everywhere one looked there were masses of blossom. I caught a glimpse of the first living creature, other than birds, that I'd seen in Atlan: two very long eyes glowing out at me, they were large liquid eyes like a gazelle's but almost alarmingly unnatural in their length, they curved right round the sides of the ears. No, the face did not emerge, it was in fact retreating (though without apparent fear) but it was striped in grey and black and took time to be realized. The swish-therefore-flash of her golden mane and tail showed her to me just as she retreated right amongst the flowering trees. A thin, striped mare—a tiny, ungainly, striped, gold-tailed creature moved with her, tottering on its new legs, without removing its head from under her belly.

We came under the edge of the trees, and looked out over a wide blue meadow which ran downhill to another belt of trees, dark trees this time, though only their tops showed. The sun was lower—we had already been in Atlan several hours. We had seen insects, glinting and hairy, but nothing further. We had eaten the last of our food in the tunnel—but what was there to eat here? Nevertheless, I was not hungry.

As we went out into the meadow—it was so steep we needed to brace ourselves not to run downhill—I saw it was completely ankle-deep with blue flowers of a type unknown to me, yet strangely familiar. They were many thousands like the one I had found in the statuette given me by that ruffian—it must have lain in its own tiny vacuum to be a sacred memory for the exiled colonists, unwithered since before the Great Sealing so many centuries ago . . .

Now I could smell them and no longer behind crystal, they were fresh and fragrant, and soft on my legs . . .

Ums' droppings reeked among the flowers. Some were crushed irreparably. Suddenly I was guilty, I was ashamed. I felt an alien bringing crudity: I had no right to pretend I took joy in the ways of Atlan for I was bringing this into her. Yet what had I done really? Surely there was slaughter and excretion here—there were animals.

Many meadows, hillsides, cliffs, woods, later it was twilight, though not chilly. The sky was violet as those flower-petals: graded from blue to purple, and a colourless light lingered on the edge of navy clouds.

A waterfall fell from a great height, a cliff in a wood. The torrent did not sparkle much in this light. It gurgled, gushed, plashed, sent up a fume, at its foot and all down its length, over rocks and boulders of pure crystal. Lichens and moss lay atop some of them—a rich shadow lay on the boulders beneath those with the mat of plant-life. There were orchids in the waterfall, flowers such as I had seen in the jungle-forests of the Dragon's March (strange how I used now the name the Southerners had given him)—The twilight advanced, deepened, intensified over this wild richness which gave me a sense of—well, yes, of such a richness of wilderness that though it would not be unwholesome it might prove perilous.

Here now there was a tangling of great leaves and blossoms, less than half-seen in the twilight but their smells heavy. They made sounds of movement too, though I could feel no wind. But it was as though they were fringed and tasselled and swaying. My bird began to grunt, he made a hack with his beak at anything that impeded him no matter how little. Occasionally great trees, spread-foliaged like pyramids, loomed before us; they seemed dead black, as though no light at all could strike response from them. Yet this was no thick forest. There was no undergrowth, only grass and clumps of ferns. Here and there we were open to the sky that glimmered violet upon us; white flowers resting on the surf were like reflected stars.

Occasionally we saw the starlight of cool blue and white water, or heard its skinkling on stones. Also, under the sky, I could see that the air was stencilled by streams of moths and winged beetles and flies—each stream was making in the same direction, ours but more to the right. They must be what made the noise against the leaves. Also there was a buzzing from the flies.

Now winding to us, faint echoing as though separated from us by so many trees, so much wood-life, all of which was absorbing its share, came a melody, a kind of potent wailing, as if from some kind of pipe.

I caught my breath. Ums tossed his head, he coughed, if he had not been a bird he would have slavered. The roots of my hair felt like quick-silver. I ran forward—now we were going in the same direction as the insect-patterns, but when I had turned I didn't know. The turf tingled when my feet touched it, or perhaps vice versa. The pipe soared louder, then made a sort of low ululating noise.

Good heavens, I thought, how can one instrument make sounds like that? Then I realized they were other sounds —grouped around the pipe, probably in motion—there were squeaks, twitterings, chirruping and yapping. Then abruptly a bellow rose above the rest; it grew and reverberated from a roar to a yawl and sank away in something like a sob. The realization that it had in its own way accompanied the rise and wail of the pipe did nothing to soothe the prickle of my scalp. What were we advancing to? I hastened on—I couldn't turn back, yet I went on with a pulsing eagerness, a kind of loving terror.

We were there. Through the blonde low-hanging foliage animals played with an incessant delicacy. Their hooves, their claws, their paws, huge or tiny—the touch of each was delicate on the glowing sward. A delightful urgency was in the air. Continuous movement, the joyous playing, the swaying unmathematical lines, they mingled, dancing and chasing in and out of the groves of trees, gambolling, they obeyed the leaping ululation. Our friends the winged insects flittered and zoomed above our heads. A lion roared on his hind-legs, roared to the pipe, passed a stag, weaved among a line of swans, his eyes and mane fire-amber. There was a goat, just an ordinary-looking brown and white goat with a goat-smell, who moved zigzag through a crowd of animals like ant-eaters which looped about his thin, cleft hooves. So they danced seemingly without knowledge that they would be enemies, hereditary enemies again when this night was over; that instead of partners in an enchanted dance, they would be hunters and hunted. The earth seemed suddenly to glow with an intensity which melted its visual solidity. I could see under it little lizards with scales like lit emeralds and rubies and amethysts, spread claws, flicker of vermilion tongue, a dart to here and a stare from oblong eyes and another dart to there. There were worms, naked and pale as pink silk, beetles, baby spiders hardly visible and swarming blue blotched, hairy spiders, labyrinths of grass- and flower-roots.

No animal seemed to notice me. If they saw me, I was just another of the creatures all around them with whom they did not habitually mingle.

Where the music throbbed most, the dancing was deepest. But I caught glimpses, rarely, of the piper beween their movement. His pipe was long and twined with green; insects were clustered, quivering on it. He was seated on a knoll and naked, his smooth, yellowish skin reflecting no light from stars nor glowing earth, umber nipples hardly rising or falling on the wide chest, but his cheeks ballooned a bit, so making his narrow, dreaming, black eyes seen more slanting. He had straight, black hair to his waist. I think his eyebrows continued out each in an arc beyond the sides of his head, as though they were the antennae of a moth.

Hung about his shoulders, like a shepherd, he carried a little gazelle-thing with spots and smudgy horns.

Ums beside me edged forward. His splayed talons gripped nervily on the turf and threw black shadows on the glittering insects and lizards beneath.

I saw at what his one eye was glaring. A female bird, a little smaller than himself, white with an uneven edging of grey-blue on her wings. She had bluish eyes and a bluish crest, half raised in ecstasy. Her crest and spurs were smaller, her tail shorter than his.

She'd not yet noticed him.

He left me, moved forward to her. He seemed so black in that tender pulsing, rainbow radiance. The eager strength in him was not going to be controlled. I realized, though merely with surprise, that he did not regard her as a specially enchanting creature, worthy to be a me of his own kind—she was female. He was going to take her.

She saw him. She came towards him, her silvery-rose claws—she was altogether a fairy-tale bird—gripping the turf. She was about to pass him, with a sort of impersonal lovingness, to change her dance to pass him as he had (she believed) specially come to pass her. Her steps, like those of all the other animals, were timed to the pipe which only excited Ums. He moved forward without grace, or with the grace only of power, not to pass but to meet. She found her way blocked, accepted this as part of it all and side-stepped to loop round him. He emitted a hoarse, impatient, brief protest, and again barred her way. His crest rose jerkily, disturbed a heavy red cluster of berries big as grapes and a cloud of humming gnats rose unsettled from it. She stared with wonder, the beginning of alarm, at his head.

Ums' wings lifted, shut down, lifted. The rasp hit the music as the warbling bellows of the larger animals had not. The animals near turned and regarded him as though he had made an unpleasant noise in church. The female passaged away again, as though nervous to dissociate herself as soon as possible from this intruder.

Ums followed, before her at every turn, he had no intention of letting her get away and his wings fell and rasped up more rapidly. His bird-of-prey red eye gleamed. It was like a hot coal. A topaz-striped tiger, horribly long and lean, pacing near with a flock of stately-happy flamingoes all together, turned and stiffened and began to lash his tail from side to side.

The female, still in time to the music, tried to escape behind the goat. She was nervous but calm. Ums followed. The goat, following the condemnatory dislike which was spreading among the animals—heads everywhere were turning—butted and bleated, no more than a hint to "get away". Ums, hot coal still fixed glowering on the female, lifted a foot and raked his claws down the side of the goat's head, at the same time shoving him away.

Blood dripped steaming; where it fell, the turf dimmed and then became opaque.

The female at last faced him again. He thrust his neck over hers, a rough fore-play, a way of getting control. He moved behind her and she turned awkwardly, brought her lovely wing up and flapped it in his face, a warning. At this insult, this added playing-coy after all the rest, he let out a harsh, deep squawk of fury, seized the wing in his beak and dragged her over to the side of the dance. She went perforce, uttering bewildered pain-moans, white and blue feathers drifting everywhere. Ums clawed aside a peacock in the way; other feathers were added to the drift.

The dance had all but stopped. They were animals again; Ums' squawk was answered by the challenges of lion, tiger, a big bull with a yellow arc of horns, the shrill belligerent cries of foxes and rodents. The smell of the blood had broken the pipe-spell. There was tail-lashing, uncertain growls which would soon be certain, but no longer singing. Eyes fixed glaring on Ums who pushed the female behind him and stood poised ready with eager arrogance. Eyes from the peacock's tail lay staring on the grass.

A cold little wind rustled. I realized the pipe had stopped. I glanced round, saw in the night on the knoll the man standing naked, the pipe dangling in one hand, the other up caressing the little whimpering gazelle about his shoulders. His narrow eyes were not clearly to be seen, it was all much darker without the earth-light, but I think they were watchful on the ring round Ums—then he turned full to me. I met his gaze with curiosity and a readiness, he the shepherd of his creatures and I of mine which were having an argument as creatures will. My look was turned back into me. His was of disgust, complete. Then, as though he dismissed me, he was gone.

A dark blue bird with red crest up, and plumage edged with red, left the ring of animals and approached my black bird. The other animals, I thought, would leave it at that, their bird spokesman for all their wrath, single combat, diatryma v. diatryma.

The few circled each other for a few tense-wary moments, but Ums was a born fighter even among such a savage race as his own—he belonged to that separate species Fighter just as Ael did, and the sergeant with pale eyes, and Zerd who had given me this one—and he soon put an end to the ogling, darted in and sank his hooked beak in the other's neck. The blue bird was not a Fighter. He squealed with pain and defiance, and lashed out but missed. He had courage. But Ums was still unscathed when the blue's blood spurted out. Every dark nostril widened, there was a low growl, swish-swash as the lion's tail beat in the grass and up like a stiff springy rope on his own flanks.

The blue got up a foot.

Gods, I thought, don't let Ums lose his other eye.

The blue had had his say, for incompetent it was proving. This was to be no single combat, Ums was no honourable foe, he was an intruder. The tiger sprang almost before the lion did. Their teeth and claws dug in simultaneously. Ums was brought to his knees, to his belly, leg twisted. Low growls thrummed the air. More animals joined, ignoring the blue bird which staggered to the female. They watched a moment, then went away into the trees. The smaller creatures scampered away too—some turned in the wood and looked back at Ums being eaten alive.

But nothing, even with Ums' powerful heart, could have survived long under that onslaught of beasts. As I drew my knife, which I did almost immediately for though I knew it was useless and death, I could not leave him who had taken me through so much, I realized there was no need; there was no longer quivering, tossing of the Fighter dying fighting under the rending suffocation. The beasts fed gurgling and tearing. A grey wolf lifted his wolf-head to the stars and howled. A little marsupial, with rat-teeth and running on hind-legs, darted in and came back with a curved black wing like a shield, which often it had been to me, or like an exotic lady's-fan except that it gouted crimson at the stump. In a deep smear on the turf all patterned with the prints of hooves and claws and pads and paws, a single stirrup lay. The rowelled spur, which I'd so rarely used, glinted. My instep ached as it remembered how often it had fitted over that metal bar, now lying loose, its frayed strap no longer proud and taut.

I stumbled on among the trees. I looked up. In the starlight rain slanted like ghirza strings across the hills. I didn't know where I was going, only to get away as far as I could from the scene of Ums' death, which seemed the ultimate in the deaths of my companions, for really he had been the nearest to me, it was almost the death of part of myself, and I was newly *alone*.

Suddenly the sky itself became a waterfall, like the one I had seen earlier only greatly more vast. Thunder followed lightning. The trees wailed.

I did not call myself fanciful when it seemed to me the wind pursued me. I *was* a new germ introduced into Atlan. I had brought with me the air and thoughts of my world, without wishing ill I was ill.

My Atlan hated me.

The dark was complete, every now and then huge clouds made their sluggish way between Atlan and the stars. Or perhaps they were moving at a great rate: their size made them take so long to pass.

A hard wind rose straight before my feet, lifting my cloak. I paused. I could only just see, narrowing my eyes, the sheer precipice over which my toes thrust unsupported.

I drew back with a cry the wind hurled deafening in my own ears, and ran on to the left, and back into the wood.

I passed the wood, and came on to the loneliest hill-top I've ever known. Black wind rushed past me and on over the valley. Queer things turned as they too rushed past, leered at me and were gone before I properly saw them.

The beat of hooves galloping, galloping across the valley.

I myself came down on to the hard road. It wound away, spasmodically lightning-lit, and amongst the gallop of the horses I could hear the strain of axles, the creak of wood, the crack of whips. Chariots! I must crouch hidden to watch them pass—for in Atlan all were enemies to me who had given Atlan such love.

First riders dashed past on the dark-shine of the road, their flaxen hair free, for though they had pulled their cloak-hoods up over their heads, their speed had tugged them off again. Those were Atlanteans, and here were the chariots they escorted. There were no torches, but by star-gleam and lightning-flash I saw the fair men standing in the first chariots. My pedlar, Juzd the regent! But I hesitated to run forward. Dark men in the next chariots that streamed in hurtling line up the road. And one, standing mighty behind his driver, his face hidden behind the bronze helm that made the eyes narrow and the nose thin and straight, in the fitful light of the gleam of a gold pelt over his wide shoulders—

I dashed out on the road even as the high-hub wheels blurred roaring past, the spray they made drenching me as much as the rain did.

"Wait! Stay!"

The wind tossed and tumbled my voice as though it were a plaything, a despised plaything.

A rider pulled his horse up plunging behind me. A hoof, fetlock hair swirling, just shaved my sodden hood. A voice cursed.

As more chariots passed, I could see now they were drawn by birds. I doubled over and retched.

"Well, who are you, what is it?" said the voice, still cursing.

"You are no Atlantean," I babbled at once.

"Big surprise, eh? Yes, we've got through at last, us from the other side, and your regent with us, we're making for the capital by his invitation. You shut us out but you're glad enough to welcome us at need. Out of the way. Questions later. The whole continent can ask its questions later."

"Is that your General, in the gold sheepskin?"

"One thing I'll say, you've sharp eyes to know it's sheepskin. Yes, he's all in style to ride into the Great City. A new Emperor must impress his people."

"Emperor!"

The man chuckled. He held down a hand, I could locate it by the gleam of the finger-nails. "Up you come. You sound comely enough. I'll see what Atlan maid is like—and be the first of us to ride with one into our new H.Q.! It'll make up quite a bit for entering this Atlan on a dark, rainy night—for all we can see of her we might still be the other side of the ocean. I'll explain all on the way."

I rode pillion, my arms gripped round his back, as we hastened on.

"Well, tell me it all."

"What's your name?"

I wished he would cut the courting and get on with the story. "That shall be the price of your tale." He growled good-humouredly that we of Atlan set a high value on ourselves. "Don't think just because you've been sealed away from us we'll think you rare. There'll be more than enough of you even for our needs for a while, till the rest of our army is shipped over and yours taught how to work with it. Or perhaps it'll take even longer—our Blue-Scales'n all may decide to keep the air-lessness as they call it intact, and we'll all come over through that there tunnel. I'd give a lot to see our sergeant-major think-ing a shark was coming at him!"

"But how did this start? The Dragon to be *emperor*—What did he do to Juzd?"

"Ah, you've been hearing narky tales about him, even away here? You're bemused. He wouldn't hurt a *fly*. Have no fear, he's not to lay Atlan to the sword. This is to be *our* land, and we'll treat it well. No, it's the Southerners, and the Northerners too, the Northerners that sent us on what they thought would be a wild-goose chase and the death of us all and our gallant Blue-loins, too, it's all them that think it safe to be our enemies we're going to show—"

"But *how*—"

"It's a long story and I'll tell it when we're snug out of this pesky downpour. But the end was, after fighting the Southern-ers in the middle of their own earthquake, we was all split up regiment from regiment, and no time to re-form. Ah, they seized their chance. Their reinforcements, that wasn't split up at all, hunted us to the coast. They hoped to crush us atwixt them and their navy. But we went willing, too. Lads, says our Blue-Nose, we'll hope for a trick or two on them yet, I know more'n they think, he says. For by ill management their navy was more than half careening when we gets to the coast, where they're having a right good time with fires and drink and noise, and we marches raggle-taggle up to them and says Very retir-ing types, these navy types, eh—for one minute they're so noisy it's ironic to say that, the next they're running for their lives. Retiring as fast as they can. So we all holler with laughter and lay into them. Then up comes this fair gentleman and his little band. You are killing our enemies, they say, as if we done it all just for them. Well, the leader hangs back a bit, but the rest are right eager and they all go in a huddle with our Blue-Chin. He tells them what danger they're in, how the Southern-ers and the Northern King and now the priest Kaselm at the head of as deadly an army of wharf-rats and hole-dwellers as ever was, are all coming against their precious Atlan, and how each of them, the lot of them knows the secret that'll fill the airlessness—which, as I understand, is a lie, none of the South-erners knowing a mite of the secret—but how us lot have nobly—well, valiantly and gallantly—been holding them off and how they all hate us, ah, even the Northern King that sent us to get rid of us first on the Southerners before he sent his favourites for the Atlan pickings. (Didn't trust our Blue-Shins, he didn't, though he might have a go for the throne one of these days. And now he's higher than him!) Ah, said these fair gentlemen, you're a great General, you save us. My army's scattered, says our merry Blue-Thighs, and me with no base to gather the lads to and from. Use Atlan, they says, it's clear times have changed and our secret is threatened on all sides, and by all accounts you're a brilliant General and can lead your army and ours and set all to rout. Ah, says our Blue Blood, but I'm to be of high rank. And their Emperor hisself, stuck gaping at him since he first sets eyes on him, as clear a case of what they call hero-worship as ever I'll see, says, You're the New Man, you're the New World. You are my Emperor!"

Weak, I shuddered.

"So you see how you must welcome us," said my host. "There'll be no ravaging here, no screaming bonfires, no little girls tossed on spears spitted through their nicest parts—But justice, sweet, clear'n impartial."

His stupendous stupid Momentity the boy with the sunfire head, the noble, innocent Atlan counsellors—they rode on gladly before us. The land, older and wiser than its inhabitants, shuddered and wailed and rumbled in great relief and great wrath at our passing.

We camped for the last hours of the night in a very damp dell at the foot of a hill on the far side of that valley. Every man had his own pack of food, most of it furnished, like the horses, by the Atlanteans as soon as they got through the tunnel—wherever the cache was I'd missed it—and my—host, captor, whatever he was—shared dried peas and meat with me, and then expected to roll me up with him in his blanket. "No." I said firmly. "Atlan girls aren't like that. Why, I've not even seen you, and you've not seen me."

"You sound sweet enough," he said nicely.

Oh, this was so much the last kind of familiar dialogue I'd expected in Atlan! "Well, I've not formed that opinion of you," I said. I was going to refuse. I had business of my own. I didn't feel guilty over taking his food: he'd get plenty when he was the guest-conqueror in the Great City. But it seemed Atlan was no longer Atlan before I'd spent even a day there.

"Come and feel me," he said persuasively. "Beyond a bit of stubble, you'll find me fine. I'm twenty-nine, brown eyes, five foot ten—"

"Oh, you're spoiling all the mystery," I said. I got up and wandered, ignoring his calls. Used to the lay-out of camps, I guessed where the General would be and presently found out I was right. Nobody took any notice of a cloaked figure wandering in the dark rains, Atlan's weeping sky. I saw him. He was talking with Juzd. I waited till Juzd left. I didn't want Juzd to see me again so soon, crawling *to* the Dragon.

He sprawled back against the bank, where a little overhang made the rain sputter on to his boots, leaving his head to dry from the journey.

I went softly up to him. Through the drum and patter I said, "Zerd."

He leapt to his feet (nearly banging his head) sprang at me and seized my wrist. He said, "You!"

I was pleased.

"Yes, it's me—Emperor."

"Juzd said a girl—You—What are you doing here? How do you know to call me that?"

"Oh," I said lightly. "I fell in with a man of your escort when your chariot passed me on the road, and he told me everything. Now I suggest you bring me in out of the rain."

"I always said you'd make the best spy I ever—" He yanked me under the overhang. I sat down composedly, glad he couldn't see the smirk of delight I couldn't get off my mouth. He hunkered on his heels, staring full at my all-but-invisible profile.

"How long have you been here?"

"One day. I was just in time to see the old, real Atlan before you take over and turn her into a second North kingdom. Are you glad to see me?"

He started to grab, then let me go. He said uncertainly, "You've changed. I always knew you would, yet now it's—You've disconcerted me, Cija." He was almost asking for sympathy. I held in my giggles: I knew they might go on and on. The hysteria was bubbling feverish in me. "You're mine at last?"

"I'm yours at last."

He took a deep breath. Still he did not grab. "You've made me wait long enough," he grumbled. "What made you come to your senses?"

"It happened an hour ago. And I didn't decide. It happened. Even in Atlan, you pursue me. Or rather," I said modestly, "you come. It's no good holding it off. I think I must belong to you."

471

"So you're a fatalist . . . This Atlan, from what you say you don't approve of my being given it? Mind you, it was a gift, I didn't take it."

"I'm sure that wouldn't matter to you except when you're trying to impress someone like me. And *she*, not *it*."

"Uh?"

"Atlan, she not—"

"You don't approve?"

I said slowly, "You are a brilliant General, a meteor who will stay up, but ever moving, ever blazing. Your blaze is power; but you yourself are power-lust. I see you, old, then dead, never leaving the world, still at the head of a train of regiments whose marching feet and axles lift the earth and fill men's hearts with dread, and you at the head, grinning death's head, lusting after power, marching after it."

He peered at me for a few moments.

Then he said, "Yes. You are right."

And the half-smile did not quite reach his dark eyes.

"Nevertheless," he said, "you'll benefit as my Empress. You'll see. We'll have—"

"Empress?" I sort of squeaked rather without dignity.

All at once he was the one to take command of the situation as it dangled. With a hint of the old amusement in his voice he said, "So you haven't come to me because of my new preferment? You meant to be my loving, loyal slave-girl? But surely you realized no one else would be my Empress?"

"You have two wives at least that I know of," I said primly, an effort in itself as my heart was going like mad. It wasn't that I was so bowled over at the thought of being an empress, not even a princess or queen but an empress, and of Atlan—Well, it wasn't *all* that—but mainly because I was to be his wife, the first one he had ever married without the ulterior motive of rising in the world.

He yawned loudly. "Them? What, one princess in the Southern Court and the other in the Northern, both soon to be conquered by me? When one is an Emperor one can start over again as far as wives are concerned."

I didn't really take to the sound of that plural. "You really think I'm worthy of this honour?"

The sarcasm went right over his head. "If," he said seriously "it had ever occurred to me (which of course it never did) to wish for some particular kind of a girl, you are what I would have wished for."

"You'll look after me? And be with me? And not put me

472

aside when someone greater comes by? But then, I suppose no one can be much higher than Empress of Atlan and Southernland and the Northkingdom."

"And you can't have forgotten you're a Goddess, too? I'll even have the gold-coin-floor of the Northern King transferred here for you."

"Smahil said it must be mythical. He said gold is so soft they'd lose their imprint as soon as they were walked on and might as well not have been coins in the first place."

He laughed. "That up-and-coming young officer was far too smart. Gold coins are invariably made with an alloy that hardens them. Look—hail coming down outside." He reached out into the shimmer and clatter, said, "Open your mouth." I thought of the wrath, the heart of Atlan pouring out its icy lament, its last passionate protest, but I let him feed me hailstones. It was good to be foolish with him, to forget the passion he had aroused for he would lift me high above it. Presently he said softly, "Would you mind if I held you?"

So I discovered that Zerd's neck is eight kisses long.

He has won. It is all over, all defence, all despair, the purpose and the fighting done with. And I am held in the arms of the death's head, close to it, separated from its corruptness only by his body's and young soul's own ignorance of the corruptness time will break him to, separated from the corruption of earthly war itself only by time and his present ignorance and glory, the blaze of his beauty and arrogance and his body's no-knowledge and I love him.

# EPILOGUE

Well, here I am on the last pages, and I will have to go quickly. I am very nicely settled with everything I can ask for, gold floor and all, in the Palace of the great City built into the mountain (all the terraced streets and main buildings and open places make use of the natural bridges and caves, to say nothing of all the stalagmites and stalactites, and it is a white and blue-veined mountain) on the innermost island of all the concentric circles of land separated by narrow circles of sea which make up Atlan.

The courtyard of the Palace is a glass floor over a deep, green lake. When their masters are late in coming, or when an octopus passes underneath and disturb them, the horses will strike with their diamond hooves on the courtyard. Their hooves are shod with crescents all of whole diamond—and when they snort and paw the ground the diamonds cut and groove the thick glass. It has been happening for years, the glass is grooved all over, and that is why nobody slips on it.

Yes, all the other lands we have known are subservient to us, and after the most elementary of campaigns. The Northern King's final humiliation is among the keenest of my husband's triumphs.

I insisted on accompanying him, as I've put up with so much while a hostage that campaigning seems nothing with the comforts of an empress, and we had some wonderful times together, though it all went so easily that we could hardly have been said to have had any adventures. I think the most memorable incident was seeing a scarecrow by the wayside dressed in the Superlativity's robes.

It was a shock when my mother came bustling to me. I'd almost forgotten her. "Clever girl, to get him. You're not going to kill him though." "I wouldn't dream of it." "Good girl. I offer him my country—I presume he'll let me stay to rule as regent—on condition he deals with the High Priest. Your father is getting too much for me." That old quarrel, that old striving for that little mastery, had been going on all the time! It was like the unending struggle we are told souls suffer in hell, trying over and over to get the drink which is always removed at the last instant and then with toil nearly gained again.

So at long last my little birth-land is famous and important, the base from which an eye is kept on Northkingdom.

And my birth-prophecy, about which all that fuss was made —I have helped to bring my country under stranger-rule— though, heaven knows, in a very quibbling way, one could say only by being married to the stranger.

I took the opportunity to visit my tower. The nurses were gone; in the old book-room, my books, which nobody ever knew I read and so learnt about men and women even while I believed men had vanished from the face of the earth— mouldy, my favourite pages stuck together with green spots; my Passage had fallen into rubble without my loving use and seemed far smaller than I remembered. I went to the end of it where I had seen the first man I ever saw, and stared out at the mountains again. In all my life mountains have been big. And these, which I watched all my childhood, seemed to symbolize the states of my freedom. The first, conical, terrible, the opening of my cage for my task; the second, about to lurch forward, Southernland; the third, insubstantial shapes and shades shifting, Atlan, the unknown goal.

When we settled home again here I was still telling myself I was terribly happy sometime before I became aware that Zerd was hardly ever with me any more, and that to let "I am ever so full of joy" become a habit is as dulling as to let misery become a habit.

His desire for me is more spasmodic, but still as intense. I try to forget that too may not last. His desire is of course very satisfying, I mean for me. It satisfies me to be wanted, but I want more from him than this want of his which is a selfishness, the branch of his power-lust which includes me. Well, he has me now. And, yes, he is now frequently unfaithful. There is a girl with pale gold hair—she has held out nearly a year. He is beginning to love her, she has provided him with the time.

Before I knew that the Southern way of making food chemical has been adopted in Atlan, it was too far gone to be stopped. I did try, but was looked upon as a crank. They said, "Yes, yes," politely, but it was useless. It would have been just the same if I had kept quiet, except that my stock with my sub-

475

jects went down a little. I pleaded with Zerd and he laughed.

The Atlanteans are wild about all the new things we are showing them. They are intermarrying with us enthusiastically. Eagerly they helped, for industry, to silt up the plain where the animals danced to the pipe. The Northerners, lords every one of them, each with a household of idolizing Atlanteans, have no need to work and so they spend their time hunting the unicorns which they discovered are fine to eat. They will soon be extinct.

I am Empress in Atlan. Two white pangolins play at my feet, a white peacock drifts across my lawn, a white unicorn waits in my stable. He has no name. I have never been able to name any other mount. The little girl who had adventures is over and done with; no mature balanced woman has been able to take her place. I am an observer, there is nothing active about me. I am neutral, perhaps negative.

I have reached the end of this book.

My nurse Glurbia's account-book is quite filled, with minute, cramped writing, even the margins have been used up. Now I shall start another diary—for I *must* always have such a private degree of my identity—but it will never be the same as this one.

However, the inmost kernel of my soul I *must* retain. All the rest of me belongs to him, my beloved, to him.

And he loves me sometimes.

# BIBLIOGRAPHY

It may seem pretentious to include a bibliography for a book which in the main is an adventure-story, but its almost every detail has some basis in prehistory. This is a list of the books which helped most.

*The Book of Genesis*
*The Riddle of Prehistoric Britain* by Comyns Beaumont.
*Prehistoric Animals* by Dr. Joseph Augusta & Zdenek Burian
*Moons, Myths and Man* by H .S. Bellamy
*Built Before the Flood: the Problem of the Tiahuanaco Ruins*
         by H. S. Bellamy
*Peru* by G. H. S. Bushnell
*A Guide to Earth History* by Richard Carrington
*Gateway to Remembrance* by Phyllis Cradock
*The Eternal Echo* by Phyllis Cradock
*The Lost Continent of Mu* by James Churchward
*The Immense Journey* by Dr. Loren Eiseley
*The White Goddess* by Robert Graves
*The Secret of the West* by Dmitri Merezhkovsky
*Myths of Pre-Columbian America* by Donald A. Mackenzie
*The Celts* by T. G. E. Powell
*History of the Conquest of Mexico* by William H. Prescott
*The Story of Atlantis and the Lost Lemuria* by W. Scott-Elliot
*Celtic Myth and Legend* by Charles Squires
*Secret Cities of Old South America* by Harold T. Wilkins
*Mysteries of Ancient South America* by Harold T. Wilkins

# THE CITY

Before the dawn of history, Cija, the young estranged wife of the Emperor Zerd, is sold as a slave. She finds herself in a nightmare country ruled by hooded priests, where the heads of blasphemers are exposed on pikes and children are fed to the alligators of an evil Witch.

She escapes, only to be captured and fattened as food for the children of a tribe of primitive ape-men, one of whom takes her as his own. . . .

"A fecund and fantastic imagination in full spate."
(Times Literary Supplement)

"A glut of frightful and exotic ingredients reeled off with considerable style."
(Christopher Wordsworth, *The Guardian*)

". . . A mixture of Rider Haggard, Mervyn Peake and William Golding." (New Statesman)

(64-450, 75¢)